Be Prepared

Be Prepared

The Complete Financial,
Legal, and Practical Guide
for Living with a
Life-Challenging Condition

David S. Landay

St. Martin's Press

New York

Although I am an attorney and have spent a number of years counseling people with life-challenging conditions, as well as working to help provide for their financial comfort, nothing in this book is meant as a substitute for legal and/or other professional advice. It is prudent to consult an attorney, financial planner, or tax adviser before making decisions based on the information in these pages. This book will attempt to enhance your discussions with these professionals by detailing the issues to be considered.
Every effort has been made to ensure that the information in this book is accurate and up-to-date. However, constantly changing laws and procedures are subject to evolving interpretations. They should be verified prior to taking any action.

BE PREPARED. Copyright © 1998 by David S. Landay. All rights reserved. Printed in the United States of America. No part of this book may be used or reproduced in any manner whatsoever without written permission except in the case of brief quotations embodied in critical articles or reviews. For information, address St. Martin's Press, 175 Fifth Avenue, New York, N.Y. 10010.

Design by Susan Hood

Library of Congress Cataloging-in-Publication Data

Landay, David S.
    Be prepared : The Complete Financial, Legal, and Practical Guide for Living with a Life-Challenging Condition   / David S. Landay.
        p.   cm.
    Includes bibliographical references and index.
    ISBN 0-312-18048-9
    1. Finance, Personal. 2. Estate planning. 3. Insurance, Long-term care. 4. Sick—Family relationship. 5. Aged—Long-term care—Finance. I. Title.
HG173.L36   1998
332.024'02—dc21   97-37936
                                                                          CIP

First Edition: October 1998
10 9 8 7 6 5 4 3 2 1

In memory of
David E. Hankermeyer

Contents

Chapter 12: Retirement Planning   127

Chapter 13: Investments   135

Part V: New Uses of Assets   231

Chapter 19: Life Insurance, a Liquid Asset   233

Chapter 34: Funeral Arrangements   365

Part VIII: Your Team and Other Matters   373

Chapter 35: Support Groups   375

Chapter 36: Your Support Team   378

Contents

Acknowledgments

Although my name appears as author, *Be Prepared* is the result of the same kind of team effort I espouse in the text. Seldom were more than two of us together, in person or on the telephone, but the input and cross-pollination was an effort of an incredibly gifted and caring team. I was lucky to be the captain.

Be Prepared would not exist were it not for the enthusiasm, support, and gentle guidance of my editor, Bob Weil. The excitement of the St. Martin's family has been gratifying, especially Steve Boldt, John Karle, Becky Koh, Andrew Miller, John Murphy, and Sally Richardson.

The first-rate research team, Miriam Gladden, Andrea Ovanesian, and Thomas White, was put together by Elizabeth Humphreys, Esq., and was led by Jim Williams, Esq., who also acted as sounding board, editor, and adviser.

Everyone at National Viator Representatives, Inc. (NVR) pitched in to help at one point or another, including Cory Crayn, Rob Green, Keith Limitone, George Martino, Lenore Raeger, Douglas Ramirez, and David Wilson.

I was lucky to have the following team of professionals who so willingly gave of their time gratis to share their knowledge with you—in interviews, review of drafts, sharing thoughts, or all of the above. In alphabetical order, they are Diane Blum, C.S.W., Donna Brown, Kimberly Calder, M.P.S., Jacques Chambers, Jerry Chasen, Esq., John Cutler, Esq., Kenneth Doka, Ph.D., Richard Feldman, Esq., Carl Galli, Charles Garfield, Ph.D., Audrey Gartner, Eli Goldbaum, Rhonda Villard Growney, C.L.U., C.F.P., Leslie Jameson, Ph.D., Ronnie Kasowitz, Barry Katz, C.P.A., Don Kaufman, Donald Lefari, Esq., Arthur Leonard, Esq., Thomas P. McCormack, Bernie McKinnon, Lee Miller, Thomas Moorhead, Esq., Michael Naimy, Jon Nathanson, Helene Novin, Neil Novin, M.D., Robert Prull, Capt. Jerry Rosanbalm, Richard Scolaro, Esq., Debbie Shulman, Ph.D., Corinne Smith, Ph.D., Bob Stella, Janet Stokes, Kathy Strickland, Sam Wasserman, Julia Wellin, M.D., and Catherine Nellis White.

My support team consisted of my close friends across the country who provided encouragement, listened to my moaning when the work and deadlines seemed overwhelming, and provided suggestions from their own expertise. My sister Ellen Novin's loving support has always been important in my life. My friend Erma Bombeck gave me inspiration and encouragement. Barry Shulman, Esq., not only provided daily friendship, advice, and encouragement, but also access to the expertise of his law firm, Scolaro, Shulman, Cohen, Lawler and Burstein, P.C. Sheila Zubrod was instrumental in expanding my thoughts and shared her creativity. Paul Rice graciously and lovingly bore the brunt of my obsession with this work.

Andrea DiLascia Busk, Esq., overcame her own pain to share experiences and help edit this work.

Which brings me to Jeffrey Barnes, Esq. Jeffrey worked with me for the past few years helping to conceptualize, narrow the massive amount of information and scope of this book, and act as my conscience, editor, and sounding board.

Last, but not least, are the many people living with a life-challenging condition who shared their stories and another group (many of whom Cancer Care, Inc. kindly assisted me in locating) who took the time to read a draft of the text from a reader's point of view. For the sake of their privacy they all live in this book under assumed names.

Words fail to express the deep appreciation I have for each of you. Thank you.

Introduction

It seems as if most of my life has been spent preparing for writing this book.

My father was a healer at heart. Although he was forced to abandon his premed studies after my grandfather's early death, he and my mother found an outlet for their shared desire to take care of people through their insurance business. Anticipating continuing the family business, I majored in insurance at the Wharton School of Finance and Commerce and went on to Harvard Law School.

I learned immediately after graduating law school that my father had lung cancer and wasn't expected to live more than a year. In those days, people whispered that he had "c" or "the big C." He had spent his life helping other people, but given the times, he didn't wish to go public about his condition. We found little practical information available, particularly about dealing with the side effects of his surgery and treatments. We seemed to be living in a vacuum—isolated from the world we'd known and not able to access other people with cancer. If there were any mechanisms for support, we didn't find them, and therapy was only for the mentally ill, not for people who were having a difficult time coping. At the same time, we held out an "everything's okay" face to friends and colleagues. Although home care was much less expensive than hospitalization, the health insurance company wouldn't agree to it since it wasn't provided for in the policy. Worst of all, in his final days his discomfort was unnecessarily prolonged by the health care system.

As a caretaker for a loved one with leukemia a few years later, I was again faced with the reality that, while there was more practical information available, we still had to navigate a vast expanse of uncharted territory. Since in those days doctors were still treated as dictators, we had to push to obtain information on alternative therapies and their potential consequences. With no guidelines, facing decisions about disability and when and how to tell his employer was agonizing for all of us.

I had practiced law, run a life insurance company, and was producing a show on Broadway when the AIDS crisis hit. The theater community and my friends were devastated by the disease. It made us all want to do something. In addition to caring for friends one-on-one, I became a founder of Broadway Cares, the theatrical community's response to the disease.

My life partner's bout with the disease was even more challenging. Choices for treatment were limited, and the messages as to which of those to use were mixed. The condition was still new and the potential life span was uncertain. We had to fight the insurance company when it refused to pay for an expensive treatment it called "experimental." Home care had become prevalent and sophisticated in our area, and daily nurse's visits replaced much of the need for hospitalization.

By then, the late 1980s, many books and avenues were available for emotional support, and Guardian Organizations were offering some practical advice, but there was still no easy road map to help guide us over the rough practical terrain of living with a life-challenging condition. In an effort to realize some lifelong dreams, we complicated matters by purchasing a new home, a "fixer-upper." The purchase was possible because, as a lawyer, I knew that the lending banks could not refuse a mortgage based on the fact that part of the income that justified the mortgage came from a disability policy rather than a traditional job. We also took an extensive trip around the world. Even though we had both traveled a lot, we still had to think through the practical aspects of the trip very, very carefully.

After my partner's death, I decided to use my education and experiences full-time to help people with life-challenging conditions. Because of my background in insurance and law, I was drawn to a new industry that was helping people sell their life insurance policies for cash, a percentage of the death benefit of their policy that would otherwise have gone to a loved one. This new industry, the viatical settlement industry, gave people with life-challenging conditions access to funds many of them desperately needed. They also required representation in the process. I started

National Viator Representatives, Inc. (NVR), in response to that need.

In addition to helping people sell a policy, we provided information and advice—including when not to sell a policy. Our clients were from all across the country, living with all kinds of life-challenging conditions with all kinds of problems. Much of what you read in the following pages is a result of our years at NVR searching for answers. As part of my research, I attended a course taught by David Peterson, a financial planner with a life-challenging condition who had developed certain strategies for people like himself. David's passion was a significant influence in inspiring me to write this book.

Through all my experiences, I have come to realize that many concerns, questions, and answers are basic to all life-challenging conditions. I have also learned that the conditions people call "terminal" are not always 100 percent terminal. There are many survivors. What is "terminal" today may be cured or transformed into a treatable condition tomorrow. Consequently, I have chosen to use the words *life-challenging condition* to describe the diagnoses that are at the heart of this book.

While it is clear that knowledge truly is power, even with all the available information there is still no single source that provides a comprehensive overview, much less a guide, to living with a life-challenging condition. *Be Prepared* is my attempt to provide such a source.

The information and tips contained in this text are the result of over three years of research and thirty years of personal experience, as well as extensive discussions with health-care and other professionals, caregivers, and people living with different life-challenging conditions. There is no magic—although, as you will see, in many areas the conventional wisdom no longer applies.

Be Prepared is the book I wish my father, my friends, and I had. I hope it helps you.

Special Features of Be Prepared

Summary. The contents of *Be Prepared* are summarized in chapter 1 to provide an overview of the subjects discussed in this book, including legal protections of which you may not be aware.

❖ Many of the concepts in this book appear to fly against conventional wisdom or instinct. To help you focus on these areas, they are noted in chapter 1 (the summary) with the symbol ❖. I call them *CASH* for *conventional advice switched on its head*. These suggestions are among the most important aspects of the book.

Using this book. You can access the information contained in *Be Prepared*
- by reading straight through the text, from beginning to end.
- by means of the table of contents.
- by reading the summary contained in chapter 1.
- by means of the subject index.

No matter which route you take, at least read chapter 1 in its entirety.

The information in this book is intended to provide a sufficient basis for you to make informed decisions. If the information is more than you want, you can read just the beginning of each section to get the general idea—or ask a friend or family member to read the section for you. In some instances, no matter how much information is provided, getting further assistance or information from an expert is strongly advised.

It is important to filter the information and principles in this book through your own emotional and psychological makeup and quality-of-life choices.

Chapter introductions. If you are turning right to a subject in which you are interested, please glance at the introductory material in the pertinent chapter. The introductory material is often helpful in understanding information presented later in the chapter.

Tips. You'll find simple, practical tips throughout the book that result from years of my personal experience and research. Tips are intended to make your life and various choices easier.

Guardian Organization = GuardianOrg. I refer to an organization that serves, advocates for, and/or does research on specific conditions as a **Guardian Organization,** which in shorthand becomes **GuardianOrg.** The choice of the word *guardian* is a not very subtle tribute to the people who choose to live their lives in the nonprofit arena. My hat is off to them, one and all.

Bold type and definitions. Words that may be unfamiliar to you are printed in bold the first time they appear in the text. Definitions of all such words follow within the same paragraph in which the word is used.

↑↑↑. Certain facts may apply to more than one section in a chapter. Rather than repeat this information, the ↑↑↑ symbol alerts you to also read the previous information in the chapter for a more complete understanding of the subject.

Time. Every step on the road to financial health takes time. For example, credit is important. Applying for a credit card should not take long, but if you first have to clear your credit record, it can take months or even years. When time is a critical element, it is included in the text.

Pronouns. With the hope of making the text as accessible as possible, the use of masculine and feminine pronouns alternates by chapter. Male won the toss to be the pronoun in the first chapter.

You and your economic unit. For the sake of expediency, the text often refers to "you." If you are part of an economic unit, whether wife/husband or significant other, tailor the advice to your situation.

Friends and family. If your decisions will affect others who are close to you, it may be useful to involve them in the process described in this book. If your assets are intertwined, it may be necessary.

As you make your decisions, bear in mind that if the exercises described in the text indicate an ultimate financial shortfall, including people close to you in the process may include them in assisting to find the solution. At the least, they will be aware of the problem.

Worksheets. You will find worksheets throughout the text to assist you.

Toll-free telephone numbers (and other phone numbers). Wherever possible, when an organization is mentioned, current contact information is provided, including a toll-free number. Each number has been verified from New York City. If the number does not work from your area, call directory information at 800–555–1212. If that doesn't work, try the local directory for the area in which the organization is located. If all else fails, feel free to contact the author and I will give you whatever information I have.

Resources. So as not to disrupt the flow, resources in addition to those mentioned in the text are included at the end of the book under the heading "Resources."

People identified in this book. Throughout the text, I often illustrate a point or idea with a personal example. In every instance names and other details have been changed to protect confidentiality, and in some examples composites of various experiences have been drawn to better illustrate a subject.

Part I

> > > > > > > > > > > > > >

A Summary

Chapter 1

In a Nutshell

Stanley T. was an executive at a publishing company when he was diagnosed with leukemia. He had excellent health coverage through work, but was concerned about what would happen if he let them know about his diagnosis. He wondered what his rights would be if the chemotherapy interfered with his work.

Linda L. was just three weeks past her breast cancer operation when she decided to examine her job and financial affairs. She took the job ten years ago because "it was the first one that came along." Is this what she wanted to do with the rest of her life? What would happen if the cancer reappeared? How would she cope financially? And what would happen to her children if she died?

Neil S. knew there were times when AIDS affected his brain and his thought processes. How could he be sure that his treatment wishes were carried out, and was it too late to write a will?

Introduction to Chapter One

There is no beginning, middle, or end to successfully living with a life-challenging condition. Being diagnosed with a life-challenging condition affects all aspects of your life.

This book provides the tools to help you successfully enter and navigate the maze of issues raised by your condition, so you don't have to waste precious time taking wrong turns and going up blind alleys. How you use the tools is up to you. There is no right or wrong way to use them, only the way that suits you.

This chapter provides a condensed version of the material that will be presented in much greater detail in the succeeding chapters. As you read these pages, don't be daunted by the number of concepts and facts packed tightly together. Take your time. Stop and digest the ideas presented. Take several days to read this chapter if necessary, noting subjects of particular interest to read more about in the text.

Once a year, or more often if there are any changes in your health or financial condition, revisit this text. Like your health, the other aspects of your financial, legal, and personal life also need periodic checkups.

The Groundwork

The key to living successfully with a life-challenging condition is to strike the critical balance between expecting the best and preparing for the worst. Embracing these two complementary points of view is the first step in facing an uncertain future.

Expect the best. This empowering positive attitude provides a framework for getting the most out of each day. According to the most successful survivors, expecting the best means

- learning to "live with" your condition instead of possibly "dying of" it.
- recognizing that no shame is attached to any health or financial condition and no blame.
- accepting responsibility for making the final decisions about your health care and treatment. After all, it's your life that's at stake.
- realizing that you can't go it alone and that you don't have to. Friends, family, and professional advisers, including your physicians, are part of a care team that you captain.
- balancing the emotional, legal, and financial pros and cons when thinking about who, what, when, and how to inform about your condition.
- understanding that bouts of depression, fear, or anxiety are normal and also that you, the people close to you, and your caregivers have options for coping with them.
- appreciating the importance of living in the moment.
- remembering how precious each moment of daily life is—a concept I refer to as Life Units—and reexamining your priorities to reflect that value.
- taking time to relax, every day.
- realizing it is never too late to change your attitude.

Prepare for the worst. This separates an informed positive attitude from simple blind hope. It re-quires an honesty that will enable you to prepare for the worst in order to maintain the kind of health care and environment that will encourage you to expect the best. At first, this kind of preparation may sound impossible. I assure you it is not. In fact, you have already started to make progress by picking up this book.

Every day you live past a diagnosis makes you a survivor. Traditional and alternative health professionals already have a vast arsenal of drugs and treatments available—and medical advances are being made almost daily. Still, it is possible that you may be unable to earn an income by working, you may need care, you may become incapacitated—unable to manage the tasks of daily living much less your financial affairs—and you may die.

If you plan ahead, you will be able to take maximum advantage of the many alternatives available to keep your life manageable. You will also realize that lifetime goals you may have previously abandoned may still be within your grasp.

Be Prepared

Access to the medical system. I suggest entering the maze by examining the most important asset you have, whether on your own or through a spouse or significant other—your health insurance coverage. It provides access to medical care without draining all your assets or even bankrupting you. If you don't have it, you should do everything you can to get it.

To provide a map that can be used regardless of your situation, *Be Prepared* focuses first on income, then expenses, then new uses of assets that will affect both, and finally on other important subjects that will impact you. Health coverage is summarized below. However, when you finish reading this chapter, I suggest you immediately skip to the health coverage discussion in chapters 14 and 15.

Your finances. The next step is to look at the reality of your health condition and what statistics indicate may occur. Don't focus on it as if this is what will happen to you: this kind of information is statistical, and statistics are based on large numbers of people rather than the individual, history rather than today, and do not take into account continuing medical advances.

With this information you can prepare for the possible financial effects of your condition, since finances are key to continuing your lifestyle and realizing your professional and personal dreams.

Start by putting together snapshots of where you are today, beginning with what you own (net worth) and your income and expenses (cash flow). To complete the picture, project what your finances would be like if you became disabled, and on the other hand, what you will need to obtain your goals. If you are married or in a stable relationship, create these pictures for the two of you.

If necessary at this point, just make a guesstimate of the numbers, and only examine the parts of your finances that most concern you. When you have the time, you can use the worksheets in chapter 4 to refine the numbers.

Please don't focus on a shortfall. The remaining parts of the text provide the steps to take, including ideas for increasing your income, minimizing your cash outlay, and obtaining new sources of cash.

Take a few minutes to request information about employment and Social Security benefits to which you may be entitled, as well as your insurance and credit information on file at central bureaus. It will be important to you, and requesting it now will avoid frustrating delays when you can least afford them. The contact information is in chapter 3.

Journal and Letter of Instructions. You should consider a few other steps at this point. Again, they don't need to be done right now. However, as you will see, the results will be helpful in many different contexts. Perhaps a friend or family member could do one or all of these chores for you.

First, start keeping a daily journal that describes your symptoms, if any, and how they affect you and your work. Include positive and negative drug and treatment reactions. Be specific. If you don't keep the journal daily, at least note significant changes.

It would also be beneficial to create a Letter of Instructions—a brief outline of the steps necessary to maintain your personal and business affairs. Include as much detail as you can, from paying important bills to plumbing and other home-repair contact people. This list will help keep you organized, ensure important coverages don't lapse, and save you time in the future by providing a map for others to follow in case you travel or become incapacitated.

This is also a good time to be sure your filing systems and valuable documents are in order.

Legal protections. ❖ Federal and state laws prohibit discrimination against you due to your health condition. The protections start from the moment you inquire about a job and continue through your working days. Employment protections even extend to your leaving a job on disability. Under the federal program COBRA, and similar state programs, if you have health insurance through work, you are permitted to continue your health coverage and to take other advantageous steps after you leave. You're even protected if you take a new job as long as there is not too large a gap between the termination of your old health coverage and the start of your new job and coverage.

Employment. For many of us, our job is our primary source of income. ❖ If you work, use the worksheet starting on page 33 to calculate all the time and expenses that relate to your job (including all the time and money you spend socially that is work-related as well as diversions you need to help you cope with the stress). The odds are you're going to be surprised by the result, what I refer to as True Net Pay. Rather than accepting the status quo, now is the time to work to increase your True Net Pay and/or reduce the hours devoted to work so you'll have them to pursue whatever you find fulfilling in life. Perhaps there is someone at work you can tell about your condition who can help maximize your income. If you are up to it, this may be a time to change jobs—or even careers. Of course, you should think carefully about all the pros and cons before leaving your current job and taking a new one. Keeping your health insurance has to be a major consideration as are any other benefits a new employer may offer. ❖ Whether you leave your job for another one or go onto disability, set a wish list of what you want from your current employer, prioritize your wishes, and negotiate for them.

If you are currently unable to work, there may be government programs to pay the costs of retraining to help you return to your old job or to start a new one.

Private and government disability income. In the event you need to stop work because of your condition ("disability"), there are three potential sources of income: private disability income insurance, state disability insurance programs, and Social Security.

Private disability income insurance replaces part of the monthly work income that may be lost. If you don't already have disability income insurance, it is unlikely that you will be able to obtain it now on your own, but you may still obtain this coverage as a member of a group, such as through an employer. Employers might also provide short-term income as part of a salary-continuation program.

As of this writing, California, Hawaii, New Jersey, New York, Rhode Island, and Puerto Rico have state-mandated short-term disability insurance programs.

Social Security provides two income replacement programs if you become disabled. Disability for purposes of these laws basically means you are unable to work in any occupation for which you are suited.

Social Security Disability Insurance (SSD) entitles you to government benefits regardless of the amount of your assets or other income because you paid "premiums" for the coverage in the form of Social Security (FICA) taxes. These taxes must have been paid for a minimum number of calendar quarters for you to qualify for benefits that, in limited circumstances, also cover spouses and children. Benefit payments are not paid until the seventh month after the onset of disability.

Supplemental Security Income (SSI) is intended to provide income replacement and medical care to disabled people with limited income and assets. Certain assets and income are disregarded in determining eligibility. You can collect SSI even if you never paid into Social Security through FICA taxes so long as you are a U.S. citizen or fall into one of several exempt "alien" categories. SSI payments begin immediately upon disability. A person who has a "presumptive disability" doesn't even have to wait for the application to be processed to obtain the first check. Dependent children may also be covered under SSI.

Preparing for the possibility of not being able to work. ❖ Disability does not generally happen overnight. When you stop working usually involves a degree of choice. Starting preparations now ensures your control over the situation if and when it arises. For instance, in your journal, document as they occur developments that may interfere with your ability to do your job. Ask your health professional to enter the notes in your medical file. Also keep a record of positive formal and informal evaluations of your performance. Review your coverages and increase your benefits to the maximum possible. Also, continue or increase contributions to your retirement plans and reduce debt—particularly debt that doesn't have credit life insurance. Look for a mentor at work with whom you can talk and who can help you maximize your benefits, line up your physician's support, and start thinking about what you will do while you're on disability. Since a disabling condition can be emotional as well as physical (or a combination of the two), you can also consider working with a mental health provider who can help define disability when the reality is still questionable.

The timing of when to go on disability involves your health and finances—not morality.

Once you decide to go on disability, understanding how the system works will help you get it right the first time. Only about one-third of SSD applicants are found eligible on submission of their first application. Provide as much of the requested documentation as possible. Complete the forms with a view to satisfying the examiners. If you have to appeal your claim through the Social Security appeals process, using an attorney is strongly recommended.

You will not receive SSD payments until the seventh month after the onset of disability, so start saving money to provide for that period.

While on disability. It is important to continue to keep health, disability, and life insurance policies in force by paying premiums promptly. If investigators check on whether you are still disabled, be guarded but honest with your responses.

❖ When you become well enough to return to work, take the opportunity to determine what kind of work you want to do with a view to maximizing your True Net Pay and fulfillment. Returning to work will affect benefits such as health insurance and Medicare.

Private disability income policies and Social Security encourage returning to work, even on a trial basis, by making sure your coverage either continues or is immediately reinstated if you stop work again. Programs are available to help you learn new skills or bring old ones up to required current levels. If you're looking for a new job, list your résumé in terms of job experience rather than chronologically—and keep in mind your protections under the Americans with Disabilities Act. Be sure to let

Social Security know about any of your work activities.

Retirement planning. ❖ As long as you have a taxable income, it is advisable to continue to invest in retirement accounts. Unless you are at an end stage, you should also continue to plan for retirement. Set goals and look at retirement benefits to which you may be entitled under Social Security and employer-sponsored retirement plans. Consider individual retirement plans.

Just in Case Fund. It is also advisable to do your best to create a "just in case" fund to cover unexpected contingencies, and a cure fund to cover costs of the cure that will hopefully be developed for your condition.

Investments. ❖ For the most part, your investment strategy should be keyed to your projected longevity on a statistical basis. Keep in mind that statistics relate to a large group of people, are historical instead of current, and do not predict an outcome for any particular individual. In setting your strategy, assess the pros and cons of seeking professional advice versus investing on your own.

Factors to consider in making investments are liquidity, risk, return, fees, taxes, and administration.

If your current condition could mean years of health during which continued gainful activity is possible, begin an investment strategy focused on growth—with built-in liquidity—as soon as possible. Your investment plan should be somewhat less risky than that of the average person who does not have a life-challenging condition—and your plan should avoid complicated investments because you need to be able to change strategies quickly.

With a statistical life expectancy of more than two years, but less than five, I recommend a strategy that combines income with growth in a relationship that depends on your particular needs—preferably with no investment that cannot readily be sold.

With a statistical life expectancy of less than two years, your strategy should recognize that the difference between income and principal is not as important as maximizing your available cash.

Health insurance. Income is only one part of the equation for achieving financial security. The other equally important part is expense. You can minimize expense by spending less and having insurance pay as many bills as possible.

Whether a traditional indemnity-type plan or a managed care plan, *health coverage is your most important asset.*

Understand the terms of your coverage and how to make the system work for you. What is and what is not covered? Under what circumstances do you need prior approval for a given procedure or emergency room visit? How do you file claims? What do you do with rejections? How do you file appeals?

If you have a managed care plan, it is important to evaluate the quality of its specialists in your condition. ❖ Ideally your plan will permit unlimited access to your specialist or allow you to designate him as your primary care physician. With a managed care plan it is also important to understand the potential treatments for your condition, so that you have an objective standard against which to measure your care. With this information you can be sure you are not being steered toward the least expensive care at the cost of your health.

❖ If you don't have health coverage, it is still possible to get it! For instance, if you are still able to work, you can change jobs or go to work if you haven't been working. All large corporations offer health coverage. No matter what kind of work you do, some large corporation can probably use your services. The federal government provides excellent benefits and so do most state and local governments. Your state may also mandate that you be provided access to private health coverage. Perhaps you qualify for a professional or other as-

sociation that offers health coverage to members. If you are single, you may even consider marrying.

If you are no longer able to work and don't have Medicare or it hasn't started yet, you may qualify for Medicaid. If you have too many assets to qualify for Medicaid, there are ways to qualify for coverage immediately except for nursing home benefits, which require a waiting period. Although many people assume only doctors in poor neighborhoods will accept Medicaid, many doctors connected with teaching, research, and university hospitals will as well. Read chapter 14, sections 2 and 3, for the factors useful in evaluating health coverage.

Medicare and Medicaid. If you qualify, Medicare coverage automatically starts twenty-nine months after leaving work on disability. If you are over age sixty-five, you can purchase Medicare.

Medicare consists of two parts, Part A and Part B. Part A is basic hospital insurance including inpatient hospital care, some skilled-nursing-facility care, limited home care, and hospice care. Since you paid for Part A through your FICA taxes, there is no further cost to you. Part B is medical insurance. It covers doctors, outpatient hospital services, and some medical supplies and equipment. While you automatically receive Part B coverage, you must pay for it through a deduction from your SSD.

If you qualify for SSI, Medicaid coverage is generally available *immediately* upon becoming disabled.

It is possible to receive both Medicaid and Medicare. If you qualify for both, do it! Medicare will pay medical bills up to whatever its rules allow, and Medicaid pays the rest. You avoid having to pay deductibles and copayments that would otherwise be due under Medicare. Also, Medicaid pays for some things Medicare doesn't cover at all, such as prescription drugs. Medicaid will even pay for the Medicare Part B premium. These are complicated areas and should not be considered without expert advice.

It is also possible, and beneficial if you can do it, to obtain both Medicare and private health insurance, such as through an employer. There are also state and local programs to provide health services to people of limited means.

If all else fails, under the federal Hill-Burton program, hospitals that accepted federal money to help in construction, renovation, or expansion must provide a set amount of free or low-cost care each year. If Hill-Burton care is not available, there may be other free programs in the facility or in your state or local community.

Long-term care. At some point you may need care at home, in an assisted-living facility, or in a nursing home. Each alternative should be carefully evaluated. Long-term-care insurance is worthwhile if you can get it. Coverage under Medicare for long-term care is limited. ❖ Medicaid covers more long-term care than Medicare. While your instinct is probably more focused on creating and keeping assets, this may be the time to spend, give away, or change the nature of your assets to qualify for Medicaid. If you are considering this possibility, read chapter 15 before you take any action. If all else fails and you need assistance at home, consider turning your residence into an assisted-living home (see chapter 22, section 2.6) or seek assistance provided in your community.

Property and casualty insurance. In general, your remaining insurance needs are the same as those of a person with no health concerns. However, it is even more important to be sure you have appropriate insurance coverage because an unreimbursed loss could jeopardize your lifestyle or health care. Likewise, you should take the time to find the least expensive coverage. Ask about available discounts and learn how to maximize your reimbursement in the event of a loss. It is particularly important to have coverage for people who

may come to your premises to assist you, such as home-care assistants.

Financial management. We've all heard it before, but creating a budget helps you focus on whether an expense is core, discretionary, or unnecessary, with a view to finding acceptable ways to save money. It is worth the time and effort to create a budget and stick to it, although strict compliance with a budget is not as important as keeping reasonably on target. If you fall off the budget for a while, get back on. Keep in mind, No Shame and No Blame.

If you come up short, see if you can reduce your debt by using your assets to obtain cash, increasing your True Net Pay, or moving to less expensive quarters. When looking at your debt, set priorities, then work with your creditors to decrease debts and/or to create a realistic repayment plan. Professional help is available to deal with creditors. If necessary, bankruptcy wipes the slate clean of all debt except such debts as taxes and child support.

❖ While standard advice is to work to increase the amount you save, depending on your circumstances, it may be appropriate to consider the reverse—a negative savings rate that reduces your capital but permits a continuation of a reasonable lifestyle and health care.

Grace periods and time limits. Most health, life, and disability insurance policies contain a grace period that permits payment of the premium within a number of days after the due date (e.g., fifteen to thirty-one days). There are similar grace periods for paying rent or mortgages. Public and private benefit programs have dates by which actions must be taken in order to secure or preserve the benefits. Don't rely on the insurance company or anyone else to remind you of due dates. Keep track of them yourself or have a trusted friend or family member do it for you. Coverages or benefits are too important to risk missing a deadline. If it appears that you won't be able to meet a deadline, call before a default occurs or a deadline passes. Mentioning your diagnosis may help. If money is tight, consider the new uses of your assets described below. Remember, some of your coverage and benefits may be irreplaceable.

Tax. Every reasonable attempt should be made to minimize your taxes. Medical expenses can be deducted from your income for tax purposes if they exceed 7.5 percent of your Adjusted Gross Income.

Most deductible medical expenses are obvious, but some aren't. For example, transportation to and from your physician is a deductible expense, as is the cost of changing your home to accommodate any physical needs to the extent it does not increase the value of your property. A wig for hair falling out due to chemotherapy is generally not deductible, but when it is prescribed by your physician as a prosthesis, it should be.

Flexible savings accounts and medical savings accounts should also be considered. Try to manipulate your income and expenses to your best advantage. It helps if your accountant is experienced in working for people with a life-challenging condition.

New uses of life insurance. ❖ For insureds with a life-challenging condition, three mechanisms can turn most life insurance policies into liquid assets: (1) loans from the life insurance company or from lenders using the life insurance policy as collateral; (2) accelerated benefits where the life insurance company permits an advance on the death benefit for the policyholder; and (3) a sale of a policy for cash equivalent to a percentage of the face value, known as a viatical settlement. None of these methods should be used without first balancing your needs against those of your beneficiaries, as well as exploring the other available alternatives and their consequences.

If you are considering leaving a job that includes group life insurance, convert the life insurance to an individual policy that you can use as a liquid asset if and when needed.

❖ You can still obtain life insurance and should purchase as much as you can afford! (See chapter 19, section 5.)

New uses of retirement plans. ❖ As a general matter, if you become disabled, you can access money in your retirement accounts without penalty as a loan and often as a withdrawal. This option should not be exercised without careful thought—money in retirement accounts is protected from creditors. Even the IRS can't go after this money for back taxes. You may also need the money for retirement.

New uses of credit. Credit helps preserve cash, which is particularly important to you. Credit can also be used to purchase additional life insurance. Credit life insurance pays off insured debts if you die. You can even use credit to obtain cash to purchase life insurance, which you may use to increase the value of your estate or sell. Credit disability insurance makes minimum payments on your credit card debt if you become disabled. ❖ If your life expectancy is under two years, pay only the monthly minimums. Instead of using cash to pay off the balance, save or invest it.

Credit can also be manipulated near the end of life to increase the money in your estate.

If you don't have credit, consider creating a credit history by obtaining a secured credit card, opening a charge account with a local store that reports credit transactions, or taking a small loan from a commercial lender.

Do whatever you need to do to keep a good credit record, including doing your best to pay your bills on time.

New uses of real property. I do not recommend that anyone with a life-challenging condition purchase a home unless there are overriding emotional reasons and/or a specific financial strategy (such as increasing the value of your estate by obtaining a credit life insurance policy to cover the mortgage debt or to avoid creditors).

❖ A home can provide cash through a loan secured by the house (either as a mortgage, a loan against your equity, or a reverse mortgage if you are old enough). Other methods of obtaining money from your home include a sale leaseback arrangement, a life estate, or even renting it in whole or in part.

New uses of other assets. ❖ Personal assets, from stocks and bonds to art, antiques, or jewelry, can be turned into cash by securing a loan from a commercial lender, family, or friends. With certain valuable personal items, an auction house may provide the loan if you agree to a later sale. As a last resort, pawn shops can provide short-term money, although with a high interest rate. At worst, you can consider selling these assets.

Physicians. ❖ The traditional doctor/patient relationship should change from "unquestioned dictator/powerless victim" to that of "medical adviser/ultimate decision maker."

It is important to choose your doctor with care. Find one who works for and with you in an atmosphere of open communication. Prepare for your visits with your doctor in order to maximize your time together. Take your journal with you. Ask for a second opinion when you feel you want one, even if the news is good. If you're not satisfied, change doctors.

If you want to consider alternative-care practitioners, do so cautiously.

Medical records. The records kept by your doctor, group, or clinic are important. Check them periodically to be sure they are completely accurate. A misstatement in your records can cost you money when reviewed by Social Security or your employer.

Taking care of your physical health. It is important for you to decide how much you want to

know about your health, medicines, and treatments. An incredible number of sources are available today to provide information about these subjects, including your physician, periodicals, research services, and the Internet. I recommend learning everything you can about each of these subjects, but what's important is to maintain your comfort level. Of course, when you evaluate information, be sure to consider the source for self-interest, bias, and reliability.

Drugs. Be informed before you decide to take a recommended drug. Never take over-the-counter drugs without consulting your health adviser first, as there may be a dangerous interaction.

If you are not satisfied with the current drugs on the market, you may want to consider experimental drugs that are produced by reputable manufacturers who are conducting controlled studies known as clinical trials. While there must be some indication that the drugs will work before trials begin, there is no guarantee of the effect. Be sure to read an "informed consent" document before agreeing to enter a trial.

Alternative medicine and treatments include any medical practice or intervention that lacks sufficient governmentally recognized proof of safety and/or effectiveness against a specific disease or condition. If you want to use them, research the advantages and disadvantages. Also be aware that with natural substances such as herbs, there is no standardization. Use unproved medical treatments only with extreme caution.

Rather than going to the most convenient pharmacy for your prescriptions, choose your pharmacist and pharmacy carefully. Consider using a mail order pharmacy. Your pharmacist can act as an important source of information and a line of defense against adverse drug interactions. If you have a complex pill-taking regimen, compliance aids are available.

If you cannot afford the medications you need, they may be available free of charge from the companies that make them or other sources.

Treatments. If you are considering undergoing any treatment such as surgery, radiation, or chemotherapy, consent only after considering the advantages and the risks, and take all the appropriate measures necessary to assist in a successful outcome. Edit the wording on the consent document so it reflects only matters with which you agree.

It is your right to refuse any and all treatment!

Nutrition and exercise. Good nutrition (including safe food handling) and exercise are important complements to your medical treatments. Free information is available that is specific to most life-challenging conditions.

Choosing where you live and where you will be treated. ❖ In general, as a person diagnosed with a life-challenging condition, you cannot be discriminated against if you attempt to purchase or rent an apartment or house. With a rental, you may even be entitled to reasonable modifications to accommodate your condition.

In determining the best place to live, think through the possible course of your condition. With all the services available in the home today, perhaps you can stay in your home, with or without modifications. If it is likely that you will need an assisted-living facility, a nursing home, or a hospital, evaluate those facilities now, while you are feeling healthy, and find one that works for you. If you're not up to it, ask a trusted family member or friend to do it for you. In addition to the appearance of each place, it is important to research the quality of care.

If you do go into a hospital, think of it as another member of your care team. Take the initiative in monitoring your care or ask a friend or loved one to do it for you. Personalize your room. An inexpensive answering machine will help make your hospital stay easier—informing friends of your condition without disturbing your rest or convalescence. A phone tree is another alternative for keeping everyone up-to-date and creates a ready-made support group for friends and loved ones.

Checking your hospital bill carefully after you leave a hospital is one of the easy ways to save money.

Hospice. At some point, you may want to shift the focus from fighting your condition to maximizing comfort and managing pain. Hospice care is a multidisciplinary approach to fill this need and is available at home, in assisted-living facilities, nursing homes, and hospitals. If money is a problem, hospice care can be provided free.

Bodily changes. While the old adage "The better you look, the better you feel" still holds true, you are much more than how you look. Still, if you do make an attempt to keep up your looks, you will feel better. There are wigs for baldness, and cosmetics that don't even look like makeup. Clothes can be temporarily altered in case of large weight losses. Prostheses are also available if necessary.

Advance directives. Because any of us can become incapacitated, leaving us unable to make our own decisions or to care for ourselves, all of us should consider executing legal documents to express our desires in that event. If we don't, next of kin will make the decisions for us. It is possible a court will appoint a stranger to make the decision. Among the directives to consider are:

- **Medical power of attorney:** Used for health matters only. If you become unable to communicate, it gives the person you choose the power to make decisions about your medical care.
- **Living will:** Describes your desires with respect to life-sustaining medical treatment and procedures in the event of incapacitation.
- **Do-not-resuscitate orders:** Prohibits revival of near-death patients when the heart stops beating or the lungs stop breathing.
- **Durable power of attorney:** Appoints an agent to take care of all your personal and financial affairs (generally excluding health decisions).
- **Pre-need decisions about children:** To assure that minor children will be taken care of, arrangements can be made with a pre-need desig-

nation of a guardian, an adoptive family, or foster care.

These documents must always be executed in accordance with laws of the state in which you reside. They should also comply with the laws of every other state in which you spend a lot of time.

Providing for the passage of your assets to your heirs. Every adult, regardless of health or age, should have an up-to-date, legally binding will. A will must include who will receive your assets, what they will receive, when they will receive them, and how the distribution will be administered. If your will is written after your diagnosis, it is especially important that it be as challenge-proof as possible.

Wills are not the only method of passing assets to heirs. Other avenues to explore include registration of the title of the asset, trusts (including the use of a revocable living trust), and making gifts while alive. Steps should also be taken to minimize estate taxes.

To avoid fights and unrealistic expectations, think about discussing your will with your heirs.

Funeral arrangements. While we do not like to think about death, much less our own funeral, given the rip-offs in the funeral industry, it is helpful to think about these matters ahead of time, including the arrangements, prepayment, disposition of the body, and the final resting place.

People in grief are vulnerable to pressure tactics and likely to spend much more money than necessary. The Federal Trade Commission requires many disclosures and prohibits some gross practices, but usually funeral arrangements are made in an atmosphere of heightened emotion when time is limited.

Keep in mind that funeral arrangements are basically for the benefit of surviving loved ones. Even if you execute a document donating organs for transplant, consent of your surviving spouse or heirs is likely to be required. It is helpful to discuss these matters with your heirs.

If you don't want to consider this subject, at least inform the people who would have to make the arrangements about the existence of this book.

Support groups. Support groups provide local access to practical information for coping with your condition as well as understanding and companionship. There is evidence that participating in a support group improves your physical and emotional health. Support groups can be accessed in person, over the telephone, or even over the Internet.

Your team. Your support team of friends and professionals will be important to you. Choose each member carefully to match their talents to your needs. This involves thinking through whom you will need on your team at any given time, narrowing down the field of potential people ahead of time, interviewing them, and actively considering how to maximize their contribution. Team members to consider, in addition to your physician, are lawyer, home-care team, pharmacist, financial planner, accountant, claims assistant, dentist, social worker, insurance broker, support group, stockbroker, nutritionist, and spiritual adviser. A mental health provider can help you through any rough times and can be useful if you want to be deemed to be "disabled." Your family and friends are part of your team, so don't be afraid to ask them for help. Chances are they will be delighted.

Travel. ❖ There are ways to travel safely and comfortably (even in developing countries), unless your doctor recommends against it because of a specific condition. All that is required is careful planning—in choosing the destination, making the arrangements, packing, and taking precautions en route, such as watching what you eat and drink. If your immune system is compromised, you can easily check on the water in all potential locales in which you may be traveling or carry your own. This applies to any water you swallow, whether in the shower, the swimming pool, or when brushing your teeth.

Be sure to check your health coverage before

you travel—and don't purchase travel insurance without considering what coverages you do and do not already have. It's a good idea for everyone to travel with a copy of a living will "just in case."

Other matters to consider.

- **Public accommodations:** The legal protections of the Americans with Disabilities Act protect against discrimination due to your health condition by health care providers, hospitals, places of lodging, restaurants, stores, and any place of public gathering. Reasonable accommodation must even be made for your needs.
- **Sex:** Your physical condition, drugs, or even your emotional state can cause changes in sexual performance. A change may be alleviated by altering the treatment. Discuss this with your physician.
- **In your wallet:** Carry a summary of your medical history, including your diagnosis and current medications. If you have insurance, include your insurer and policy number. If you have any advance directives, mention them, as well as contact information.
- **Medical identification:** Medical ID can save precious time in the event of an emergency and prevent adverse drug reactions.
- **Misrepresentations:** ❖ Many people who have been diagnosed with a life-challenging condition feel that they can get away with lying when completing applications and the like. My experience has been that this is a major mistake.
- **Pets:** Pets can benefit you emotionally and even physically. Their excretions should be treated with care if your immune system is compromised.
- **Transportation:** If needed, free or low-cost transportation is usually available to get you to and from physicians and/or treatment centers.
- **Meals:** Meals can usually be delivered to you at home if necessary.
- **Documentation:** When applying for, or working with, public or private benefits, a few helpful hints are:

- Retain a copy of all forms you complete.
- Note the date you submit each form.
- Obtain a receipt for each form delivered in person.
- When you mail forms, send them certified mail and retain the receipt in your file.
- When you receive mail, note and abide by any time limits stated in the notice.
- Note the date, name, title, and phone number of each person with whom you speak or visit. Summarize each conversation.
- Create at least one file for each benefit to which you may be entitled so all the information will be stored together.
- Be proactive and follow up. If you don't receive satisfaction, speak with a supervisor. If all else fails, consider appealing.

Primary sources. When determining your rights and benefits, always obtain information from the proper source or a reliable expert. Because many employers undervalue employee-benefits expertise, seek benefits advice and information only from a supervisor. Be sure to obtain written copies of all advice, opinions, and relevant contracts. By familiarizing yourself with the information in these chapters you will know the right questions to ask and when to seek second opinions.

Note. When speaking with insurance company or government representatives, try to keep your emotions under control. The key is to use emotion when it will seem to benefit you. Sometimes being emotional helps. Being too emotional may give the other person an excuse not to deal with you, or your request. If you need to vent your emotions, do it in your support group or with friends and family.

In sum. Completing the circle, it is worth repeating the two critical keys to successfully living with a life-challenging condition. Expect the best. Stay positive and empower yourself. Prepare for the worst, enabling you to access the health care you need and keep the lifestyle you've earned.

Part II

The Building Blocks for Successfully Living with a Life-Challenging Condition

Chapter 2

The Keys to Success

I believe it is the quality of life, not the quantity, that is the most important. . . . There is no right way or wrong way to deal with a condition. The
difference is between dying of a condition, and living with it. . . . I've used
each stage as a challenge to grow.

—Anthony T.

Self-pity never accomplished anything constructive. Self-determination is
the key that opens the right doors.

—Kathy S.

This chapter focuses on expecting the best.

Section 1. Keeping Positive

More and more studies confirm the importance of
the mind/body connection to your health and
your immune system. The concept of "living with"
something, instead of "dying of" it, leads to a happier life that in turn tends to be healthier and
longer.

Negative emotions such as depression keep you
from taking care of yourself, your health, and your
financial needs. It is understandable that you will
have your ups and downs, but keep in mind that
the glass is always half-empty *and* half-full. You
have the power to choose how to perceive it.

George Solomon, M.D., a leader in the field of
psycho-neuro-immunology (the scientific term for
the mind/body connection), advises that it is never
too late to change your attitude. As Andrea B. put
it, "We can't change the facts. But we can change
the way we relate to them." A positive attitude
makes each day more enjoyable—and there's no
downside.

Don't be afraid of call on friends, family, members
of support groups, and even professionals, if necessary, to help keep you positive. They are likely to be
more than willing. There are also innumerable
books that your physician, GuardianOrg, support
group, mental health professional, or spiritual adviser can recommend. A book that was particularly
influential in my thinking is *Love, Medicine, and Mir-
acles* by Bernie Siegel, M.D.

Section 2. It's Your Health and Your Life

As you read through the text and apply the information gathered here, remember that

- we are talking about *your* financial and emotional health.
- you have more at stake than anyone else. Consequently, you have to be the decision maker.
- there is no right way or wrong way. After you have the facts, trust your intuition as you make your own decision.

Section 3. The Team Approach

Whether you like it or not, you cannot go it alone. You will need to at least consult your current medical specialist. The odds are that at some time you will even require several physicians in different specialties.

I encourage you to consider all the assistance that is available. Think about which advisers you may need, and put together a team that fits your needs and finances. You are the captain. No matter how educated or high-powered any particular member may be, they are your advisers, not the decision makers. Encourage them to speak with each other and to act as a real team to advise you on how to achieve your goals, including the best financial, physical, and emotional health possible.

Empowerment may be a new role for you, and it may even provoke anxiety—but it is critical to your well-being.

Section 4. Now Is "When"

This is the time to consider those things you've always wanted to do "when"—when you have enough money; when you retire; when you get to that certain place in life. You will soon have a fix on what you can afford and what you can expect financially. Within that structure, balance your responsibilities to your loved ones and decide how you want to live your life.

Kathleen R. used her diagnosis as a spur to stop working in publishing and finally start the bookstore she'd always wanted to run in the town where she lives.

Michael M. sold one of his life insurance policies to finance a trip around the world he'd always wanted to take.

A client, Herb S., and his wife thought their differences had become irreconcilable and were discussing divorce after twenty-seven years when he was diagnosed with lung cancer. His illness reminded them of what they loved about each other. Their differences faded into the livable background.

Section 5. Coping

From coping with a diagnosis to handling treatment, to dealing with long-term emotional and financial concerns, people dealing with a life-challenging condition often face stressful situations. Some of the most common stressors are changes in self-image, practical problems such as medical bills and job issues, relationships with family, friends, and coworkers, uncertainty about the future, fears about the return of a condition, and death.

The following tips come from the National Cancer Institute, based on the experiences of survivors in the American Cancer Society's I Can Cope program. They apply to all life-challenging conditions.

- Be kind to yourself. Instead of telling yourself you can't do something you *should* do, focus on what you can do and what you want to do. Instead of telling yourself you look awful, think of ways to make the most of your best features.
- Don't be afraid to say no. Polite but firm refusals help you stay in control of your life.

- Talk about your concerns with others or with a support group. It's the best way to release them.
- Learn to pace yourself. Stop before you get tired.
- Give in sometimes. Not every argument is worth winning.
- Take time for activities you enjoy, whether it's a hobby, a club, or a special project.
- Take one thing at a time. If you're feeling overwhelmed, divide your list into manageable parts.
- Set priorities. Don't try to be Superman or Superwoman. (Ask for help when you need it.)
- Solve problems like an expert. First, identify the problem and write it down, so it's clear in your mind. Second, list your options, including the pros and cons of each. Third, choose a plan. Fourth, list the steps necessary to accomplish it. Then give yourself a deadline and act. Sometimes just having a plan can reduce the stress of the problem.
- Get enough sleep.
- Focus on the positive. If you have a setback, think about all of the good things you've done.
- Eat properly.
- Get enough exercise, if you are able. It's a great way to get rid of tension and aggression in a positive way. (Even if you are bedridden, you can do isometric exercises by tightening and releasing the muscle groups you can move.)
- Help others. Reaching out to someone else can reduce the stress caused by brooding.
- Laugh at least once a day.

Section 6. Options for Getting Emotional Support

There are many options for obtaining emotional support.

Call a telephone hot line in your community for your particular condition. Your GuardianOrg may have a hot line or can steer you in the right direc-

tion. Or look in the yellow pages under "social service organizations." Ask the hot line to match you with someone with a history similar to yours. He or she can give you practical advice and emotional support over the telephone. Family members can also be linked to "veteran" family members who've coped with similar issues.

Talk to your friends and family. Help them understand how they can help you. Talk about your needs for support. Don't let the conversation always center on your condition.

Join a support group. Emotional support is one among many reasons to join such a group (see chapter 35).

Get counseling and practical help. A social worker who specializes in working with people with your condition may be able to help. You can find social work services through your GuardianOrg or your local hospital. If your needs are beyond the abilities of a social worker, consult a nurse therapist, psychologist, or psychiatrist. Talk about how to handle your fears and concerns and ask questions. Talk with your spiritual adviser.

If your spouse or family needs assistance in sorting out issues your condition has raised, consult a licensed family therapist, psychologist, or psychiatrist.

Support yourself. Draw on your own strength. Read about how others cope. Ask at your local bookstore for accounts by other survivors. Be your own advocate. Ask for what you need from your doctor, hospital, family, friends, and coworkers. Stand up for your rights with health insurers, health maintenance organizations, and employers.

Section 7. Worrying

World-class worrying can accompany a diagnosis of a serious condition. Worrying about the worst

19

possible outcome of a test or what will happen tomorrow is common—but useless.

Susan R. was concerned about the results of a CAT scan and feared that she might need another round of chemotherapy. A meditation teacher suggested that she play out the outcome of whatever she was afraid of and figure out how she would handle it. He suggested that she could then put the fear away. Once Susan realized that she could handle what she feared and knew what she would do, she could let the worry go.

Instead of worrying, "be prepared." It's more productive and ultimately more rewarding.

Section 8. No Shame, No Blame

Working with money often brings a lot of emotional issues to the surface. This is normal. Jessie V. still gets depressed when she thinks of the bad investment she made in her friend's "can't lose" business idea. Don't get mired in "If only I had . . ." or "If only I hadn't . . ." The objective is to move forward and do your best. Doing your best is all that is asked of you. Shame and blame will only interfere with your ability to achieve financial and emotional well-being.

Section 9. Relaxation

Relaxation has been found to slow the heart rate, soothe the digestive system, ease muscle tension, diminish anxiety, and reduce pain. There are many relaxation techniques from which to choose: from engaging in pleasurable activities to meditation and other Eastern practices. The list is too long to include here, but it is crucial to recognize the importance of relaxation. If you're tense, seek out the method that seems right for you to help you relax. Your physician may have suggestions, or your friends and certainly members of your support group or GuardianOrg.

Section 10. Volunteer

Many people have found hope and healing through helping others. Helping others can also make you feel stronger and more in control. Studies show that volunteering helps promote health and longevity. How and what kind of time and energy to volunteer is a purely personal choice.

Think about helping other people with your condition who may not be as healthy as you are. You may want to offer your services to a telephone hot line, support group, or a special patient-to-patient program. Your social worker or local GuardianOrg may be able to put you in touch with survivors who could use your help.

If you volunteer for a GuardianOrg associated with your condition, you will also have support, a place where you can speak freely, and an important source of information.

Tip. If you volunteer for your GuardianOrg, particularly if you are in a position of authority such as on the board of directors, be sure the organization has liability insurance that covers you. If there is no coverage, check with your insurance broker to determine your risks and coverage.

While all the private insurance coverages and governmental programs I have seen permit volunteer activities (including working at an organization without pay), check your own policy and/or government program "just in case." While Rob W. was on disability, he ended up with volunteer speaking engagements all over the country plus hours and hours each day of giving people advice on the telephone. He worked as many hours and with as rigorous a schedule as when he worked for pay. Still, he was considered legally disabled.

Section 11. Charity

Why give. Aside from the moral benefit associated with giving to others, giving to charity can be directly beneficial to you. Your GuardianOrg can be critical not only to your physical well-being, but also to your emotional and financial well-being. In this imperfect world, just as a squeaky wheel gets more attention from a physician, a donor tends to receive more consideration from a charity or hospital. When Marni was admitted to Mt. Sinai Hospital, her insurance coverage was for a semiprivate room, but the hospital moved her to the executive suite, which happened to be vacant at the time. Marni had been an active volunteer on the development committee for two years before her hospitalization.

Look before you leap. Make sure you know the exact charity to which you want to donate: many sound alike. Request written information on the group's finances. The less they spend on administrative overhead and fund-raising, the more they have to put toward worthwhile programs. The better charities spend an average of only 23 percent of their budget on overhead and fund-raising. If the charity only passes money through to other charities, overhead should be much less.

Tax exempt. Make sure the group is tax-exempt as a charity or contributions may not be tax-deductible. There may even be something fishy about the organization. You can confirm an organization's status by asking for a copy of its IRS tax-status-determination letter or by contacting your state charity registration office or the IRS.

Tip. One way to give gifts to your friends, and still benefit a charity, is to give gifts of items sold by a charity or for which a charity receives part of the proceeds. Some charities have their own catalog. There are also catalogs that include items benefiting a range of charities concerned with a given condition. (See the resources section under "Gifts.")

Stretching your dollars. A gift to an organization that does effective advocacy work to increase governmental spending for research and/or services can mean many times that amount in research and/or services about your condition. Also, many employers have matching-grant programs that double the amount of your contributions.

Section 12. Whom and When to Inform

Keeping secrets of any kind can be stressful and exhausting. Nevertheless, depending on your condition or the other people involved, there may be overriding reasons not to inform coworkers or superiors about your condition. There may be certain friends and even family members who don't "need to know" right now. If you decide to tell, who, when, and how should be carefully thought through. The following discussion provides issues to consider in both the work and personal setting.

General considerations.
- *There is nothing about any health condition to keep secret or be ashamed about.*
- Since it is difficult to remember whom we tell what, and even more difficult to guess who may have told whom, it is better to tell everyone you care about and who cares about you—*unless there are overriding reasons not to inform them.*

When to inform others. For all settings, here are some general guidelines:
- Educate yourself about your condition before any discussion, so you can answer questions and anticipate others' reactions.
- Timing is everything. Don't even try to inform other people when you are in the midst of a trauma that requires all your emotional and/or physical strength. Traumatic occasions include the time immediately after diagnosis or a dramatic change in condition. In fact, those are not good times to make any major decisions.
- Consider the risks and benefits of informing others.

- Ask yourself whether the person under consideration really needs to know.
- In a personal situation, and even in some work situations, consider whether this is a good time in the other person's life to hear this information.

Why tell. Carefully consider why you want to tell someone and whose interests are best served by telling. Ask yourself:

- What will be gained if they react positively, and what will be lost if they react negatively?
- Has the person already figured out your condition, but is waiting for you to tell?
- Will they learn about it from someone else, possibly with the wrong facts?

Tip. You will never know how people will react. Keep in mind when you tell, "No shame. No blame."

How to tell others. Once you've decided to tell someone else, how you do it can be important. Think about it carefully before proceeding. Your way of relating to people and your history with each person are important factors to consider. Are you more comfortable

- talking in person where nonverbal communication can be important and the two of you can take whatever time is necessary?
- on the telephone, which is more impersonal but an easier way for some people to share personal feelings?
- writing a letter where the recipient has time to digest the news alone?
- having someone else tell them so you don't have to deal with the possibly negative reaction, or even the possible level of sympathy?
- talking to the person in a public place, or in front of a third person, so as to possibly temper their reaction?

What to disclose to others. You also have to decide how much you want to disclose to people.

- Before you begin a conversation, decide how much you want to disclose, yet be ready to be flexible depending on the conversation.
- Prepare your answers, particularly to questions you may think of as sensitive.
- If you are uncomfortable with a question, communicate that and feel free not to answer it.

Whom to Inform

Family and friends. For each individual, weigh the cost in stress to you of not telling against the possible emotional and even financial support you may gain or lose by telling that person about your condition. Sally Fisher, author of *Life Mastery,* suggests telling now the people you think of as your friends. It will avoid the unnecessary pain that comes with finding out when you're not well that some "friends" are only fair-weather friends.

If you don't want the news to spread, think about whether the person you are considering telling can be trusted not to tell anyone else.

Consider telling people in clusters. When one person knows, the rest of a group probably knows.

It may be worthwhile to know how to access a support system for the person you are telling. Most GuardianOrgs have hot lines to answer questions and support groups for family members. Your spiritual adviser may also be a good source of information and emotional support.

If you are a parent. Consider how telling other parents or a school might affect your child. Planning for the custody or guardianship needs of your child (see chapter 32) might also influence whom you tell and when. See the next section concerning communicating with your child.

Neighbors. Be careful whom you tell in your neighborhood. There is no right and wrong, but you probably already know what particular neighbors think about particular health conditions. Keep in mind that telling neighbors may impact on your children.

Tip. Some conditions, such as HIV disease, currently come with a lot of baggage. If this applies to you, perhaps there are some people you should never tell.

Be especially careful about telling people at work. It's up to you whether or not to disclose your diagnosis to your coworkers and your employer. Read chapter 6 for a discussion of this issue.

Your professionals. Under the Americans with Disabilities Act, the professionals who take care of you cannot discriminate against you based on your health condition.

Caretakers may need to be informed in order to better address your needs and/or to take necessary precautions against contagion. If there is any possibility of spreading an infection, you owe it to the persons who work for you to inform them. If they do become infected, you have less chance of financial liability if you've disclosed your status.

Be aware that all professionals with whom you discuss your condition should keep it confidential. There may even be state laws protecting your medical information against disclosure by any of your team members. Note: *Confidential* is not the same as **privileged.** All your discussions with your doctor, lawyer, and clergyperson are privileged in addition to being confidential. When information is privileged, the professional with the information cannot be required to disclose it, even in a court of law. Discussions with your accountant and financial planner are confidential, not privileged.

Sex partners. Telling a person with whom you are about to have sex can be embarrassing. If your condition is not contagious, the choice is yours alone. However, if your condition could be contagious, you are setting yourself up for a liability problem, in addition to a possible criminal act, by not informing the person. Consider the psychological and physical risks to you and your partner. If you have a contagious disease, and if you choose not to notify past sex partners about your condi-

tion, there are departments within your state department of health that will notify them for you. If you wish, these departments can usually be approached anonymously.

Section 13. Children

When a condition strikes a family, it is likely that children of all ages will sense a change no matter how you try to hide it. Trying to protect them will only allow them to imagine that things are even worse than the real situation, and to possibly blame themselves. It will also prevent you from helping them to understand and eventually accept what is happening.

It is important not only to communicate with your children, but to listen to them to make sure they understand what is happening.

Talk with the child in a language and in a manner that the child can understand, taking into account the child's age and individual characteristics. Consider using drawings or dolls to clarify what you're communicating. If there is an ongoing treatment, make sure the child understands the nature of the treatment and what it is hoped will be accomplished. Ask a child to explain back to you what you said so you can be sure he or she understands.

Before you tell a child

• prepare yourself for the child's reaction with a bit of self-exploration. How have personal separations and losses affected your thinking and behavior? Did you have a distinctive pattern such as disbelief, protest, disorientation, withdrawal, sadness, acceptance, or reattachment to remaining persons? Knowing how you reacted can help you anticipate possible reactions from your child and also give you the patience and understanding to deal with the child's reaction.
• anticipate that each child will react according to her own personality.
• keep in mind that a young child's capacity to

understand far exceeds her capacity to verbalize.

- be truthful.
- choose your words with care. Consider practicing what you want to tell your child.

If you need assistance telling your children, consult the appropriate members of your team or *How to Help Children Through a Parent's Serious Illness* (see the resources section).

Be sure the children understand

- that they had nothing to do with the cause of the condition.
- that they are still loved and will be cared for.
- that despite possible shifts in attention, the children's needs will still be addressed.
- if the condition is contagious, there is no risk to them.
- the reality of the situation, in terms they can understand.

Tip. Look for ways to involve your children in taking care of your condition, such as asking them to run errands for you.

Adult children. Informing older children about your condition may bring up issues of role reversal as well as mortality. It may also bring up unresolved issues that suddenly take on more urgency.

Section 14. Privacy

In our modern world, it is unlikely that your health condition will be totally confidential. *If pri-*vacy is a concern to you, you should be aware of the potential sources of a breach in confidentiality.

Potential privacy problems may arise when people unwittingly put information about their medical profiles into the public domain. Purchasing medical supplies with a credit card, using a toll-free number to learn about new drug treatments, and even going on the Internet to get information about illnesses and therapies can result in having your name put on a variety of lists for product pitches.

Sometimes there are data leaks to employers or even the general public about personal medical information. While balancing patients' right to access with adequate privacy is becoming a hot topic, to date no federal law offers universal protection of the privacy of medical records. State laws vary.

As discussed in more detail in chapter 3, when you apply for life, health, or disability insurance, your health information may be shared with other companies by the Medical Information Bureau.

There are some basic consumer tactics that you can take to limit circulation of your personal information. The first is to be skeptical about signing whatever your health-care provider puts under your nose. Negotiate to disclose only what is absolutely necessary for the specific purpose. When you sign an insurance form, try to narrow its scope if possible, rather than endorse wholesale transfer to the carrier of your entire chart. Cross out permission to give the information to any person, group, or agency that does not have a need to know. Some insurance companies may reject release forms that have been rewritten. Make the changes you desire, and discuss it with them later.

Chapter 3

Gathering the Information You'll Need

If you plan for the best case and the worst case happens, you are in bad shape. But if you plan for the worst and you end up with the best, then you are only slightly inconvenienced.

—David Petersen, founder, Affording Care

This chapter starts you on the path to understanding where you would be financially if you didn't make any of the changes discussed in this book. It's necessary to understand that reality before looking at the alternatives available to make it better.

Spending a little time now to obtain and check the information described in this chapter it will save you a great deal of stress and time in the future.

Tip. Making requests for information is standard and provides no clue about your health condition.

This chapter refers to "you," but also applies to your spouse or significant other where relevant.

Section 1. Employment Benefits

Employer. Your employment benefits will be described in a document generally titled something like "Summary Plan Description." This document summarizes your health, life, and disability insurance plans as well as your pension plan. If you don't have this kind of description of your benefits, ask your employer or union, or both if appropriate, for a copy. You are entitled to this information from your employer under federal law, as well as various state laws, and you don't have to give a reason for why you want it. If you have a retirement plan, ask how much your interest is worth. If you haven't received reports lately that tell you about the finances of the plan, this would be a good time to obtain them as well.

Short-term disability benefits. Find out if your state law entitles you to any short-term disability benefits. Your state Labor or Insurance Department (see resources section) are good sources of information about the terms of the benefit including what it covers, how much it pays, and for how long.

Section 2. Other Insurance Coverage

Assemble copies, or at least summaries, of all your other personal insurance policies, including all life, health, hospital, disability, and long-term-care policies. Also, pull together all the policies that cover your property or liability, such as homeowners and/or fire and liability, automobile, excess liability, umbrella, and workers' compensation coverage if you have in-home employees. Don't worry about any business coverages. This book only deals with your personal situation, not any business you may own.

If you know you have a policy but can't locate it, you can obtain copies from your broker or directly from the carrier if it is a company that writes coverage directly to the public. While waiting for the actual policies, your broker can supply a summary of your coverages (usually called a "schedule of insurance"). If you deal with companies that do not use brokers, you can get the basic information on the phone while waiting for copies of the policies. Most companies have toll-free numbers for their customers.

Tip. If you do not have any of the listed coverages, please review chapter 16 to determine what coverage you should obtain as soon as possible.

Section 3. Social Security Information

To find out how much disability, retirement, and survivor benefits you're entitled to under the federal Social Security system, simply call the Social Security Administration (SSA) at 800-772-1213 and use the automated system, or visit your local SSA office to request the form known as "Personal Earnings and Benefits Estimate Statement" (form SSA-7004). The amount of your benefits depends on your contributions to the system throughout your working life. The form shows your earnings record, the taxes you have paid to the Social Security system, and the amount of benefits that you or your eligible survivor(s) would receive if you retire, die, or become disabled in the current year. Once you have sent in the completed form, it

will take three to four weeks to obtain the information.

Tip. An immediate means of accessing these amounts is through the Internet at www.ssa.gov. After you complete a form on-line requesting the information, SSA will E-mail you a personal code (as a security precaution). You then have to return to the Social Security site, complete the form again, and submit the activation code. Earnings histories are not available at this site, so you will still have to obtain this information, as noted above, to confirm its accuracy.

When you receive the statement, check the numbers to see if they are approximately what you recollect and review the rest of the statement for accuracy. Even a minor error can complicate collection of benefits. It can take a long time, and a lot of work on your part, to correct the record. Do it now while you're feeling up to it. You won't want unnecessary delays when you are ready to apply for the benefits.

Usually errors are noticeable, such as having no entry where you know income should be. If it is wrong, call SSA to have the record corrected. If the error is a misspelled name or an incorrect address, you may be able to resolve the matter over the telephone. If the wages in the report are incorrect, you may need to submit copies of your W-2s and tax returns to get the record corrected. If you don't have your old W-2s, you should be able to obtain confirmation of the correct facts from the pertinent employer.

Tip. It's helpful to review your Social Security statement every few years to make sure it continues to be accurate. According to a study by the General Accounting Office, earnings records are incorrect for one in ten people. I suggest also doing it within a year after changing jobs or if the continued existence of your employer seems shaky.

Section 4. Your Health

Switching conventional advice, your physical health rather than your age, marital status, or dependents becomes the most important part of your planning foundation. Two facts are important to learn: longevity *on a statistical basis* and anticipated costs.

"On a statistical basis." Your longevity is the number of years you would live if you were a statistic, instead of the unique person you are. By definition, statistics only tell what happens to a large group of people at a similar point with a similar condition. It does not, I repeat, does not predict your personal outcome. I've had friends with a diagnosis that indicated they had a year to live, and they are still alive today, almost seven years later. You should treat this number as no more than what *might* happen. According to the doctors who study the mind/body connection, if you mistakenly focus on it as a reality, it may become a self-fulfilling prophecy.

Tip. If research into this area is a problem for you, ask a family member or friend to do it for you.

Costs. The second fact we need is the "average" cost timetable for treating conditions like yours, so you will know how much to prepare for, and when. For example, with cancer, the cost curve is generally like a barbell: costs are heavy just after diagnosis, then somewhat low until the end of life, when they tend to increase again. With HIV/AIDS, there is a high annual expense for drugs, which may be followed by heavy medical and hospital expenses toward the end of life. Alzheimer's is characterized by a lot of expense for custodial care. Diabetes has a wedge-shaped pattern: the direct medical expenses keep increasing until the end stage.

Your health care provider should be able to describe your statistical longevity and possibly the average cost of treatment. If not, contact your GuardianOrg.

Journal. It is helpful to keep a daily journal describing your symptoms and how they affect your activities, including work. The journal will help provide your physician with a complete picture of your health and the effect of various treatments; evidence necessary to leave work on disability if you have a choice as to the timing; and, if you receive disability income of any type, will help provide evidence of continuing disability if you are questioned. The journal should include physical and emotional reactions, and both positive and negative reactions to drugs. The descriptions should be specific rather than general. For example, if pain is involved, see the descriptions in chapter 24, section 5.

Section 5. Your Credit Status

Credit is an important source of cash when you need it, whether for medical bills, travel, or other expenses. If you don't have credit accounts now because of a prior impaired credit history, skip this section and refer to chapter 21 for some advice on how to get credit.

Whenever you apply for credit or use your credit accounts, creditors forward information about you to credit bureaus. Because lenders make the decision to extend credit based on the information in the bureaus, and because errors are common, you will want to make sure that this information is correct. In a 1991 survey, *Consumer Reports* found that of 161 credit reports it examined, 48 percent contained errors; 19 percent of them contained errors serious enough to affect employment, credit, or insurance.

You have the right to correct any information in your file that is not accurate and current.

Step 1. Get a copy of your credit report. To review your records, request a copy of your report.

There are hundreds of local and regional credit bureaus, but the most important ones are the three national credit information bureaus:

Experian
P.O. Box 2350
Chatsworth, CA 91313-2350
800-682-7654

Equifax
Wildwood Plaza, P.O. Box 740241
Atlanta, GA 30374-0241
800-685-1111

Trans Union
P.O. Box 390
Springfield, PA 19064-0390
800-916-8800

A credit reporting agency can charge $8 for a copy of your report. I suggest you order all three. If you only order one, I recommend that you obtain the report from Experian (formerly TRW). You are entitled by federal law to a *free* report if a company has taken adverse action against you based on the credit report *and you request the report within sixty days of receiving the notice of action.* The action against you can include such acts as denying you credit, rental of an apartment, or the opening of a telephone account. The letter you receive notifying you of a denial is required to specify the name and contact information of the bureau from which it obtained your credit report.

You are also entitled to one free report a year if you can prove that you are unemployed and looking for a job, plan to look for a job within sixty days, are on welfare, or that your report is inaccurate because of fraud. Entitlement to other free reports varies from state to state.

When requesting your report, include your name, addresses for the last five years, date of birth, social security number, and telephone number. Also, include any other names by which you have been known, such as maiden names or previous married names. In case there is a problem or no response, use certified mail, return receipt requested, and pay for the report with a check or money order. Keep track of the date that you make your request. If you do not hear from the bureau within thirty days, send another request with a copy of the first request.

Step 2. Review your credit report. When you receive your report, review it carefully.

The following checklist is a guide for reviewing your credit report. The report may include coded information. If it does, it should come with a key that explains the codes. Feel free to contact the credit bureau and request an explanation for any information you do not understand. Check the following information:

- Your name and Social Security number. It is possible that your report includes information about someone else who has a similar name or Social Security number.
- Make sure the report accurately reflects whether the account is single or joint with someone else.
- Account number.
- Is an account still listed as open, even though you closed it years ago?
- Type of account—is the type of account accurately reflected as installment, revolving, or some other kind?
- Is the outstanding balance on the account correct?
- Highest credit—this is the credit limit on the account or the highest amount you have ever charged.
- Status of account. This can be a difficult section to review. This section relates to your payment history on the account. Credit bureaus use codes to indicate the number of times you paid the account on time, or the times that you paid 30, 60, 90, or 120 days late.
- Late-payment history. This is a summary of your total late-payment history.
- Comments. Both you and your creditors may supply comments to the credit report. If there are any, are they accurate?

- If any suits, judgments, tax liens, or similar items are listed, are they still outstanding? If so, are the facts correct? These facts are important for your future credit.
- Are there any other claims against you listed on the report? Are they accurate? If so, consider clearing them up. At least provide the information necessary to defend against the claim to the person or people who would handle your affairs if you become incapacitated or die, "just in case."
- Is there any other inaccurate information in the report?

Step 3. If there is an error—fix the report. If you find an error on your report, contact both the credit bureau *and* the creditor.

The letter to the credit bureau should identify who you are, your reason for writing, what is wrong with the report, why it is wrong (including any story and proof), why it won't happen again (e.g., it was an aberration), and what you want them to do. Include a request for confirmation that the action you require was completed, thank them for their consideration, and sign the letter. Correspondence should be sent by certified mail, return receipt requested, and should include copies (not originals) of documents that support your position.

Once the credit bureau receives your letter disputing information in the report, the bureau must investigate the items in question, usually within thirty days, unless they consider your dispute frivolous. The investigation consists of the bureau contacting the creditor and forwarding all relevant data you provide about the dispute. After the creditor receives notice of a dispute from the consumer reporting agency, it must investigate, review all relevant facts you have provided, and report the results to the consumer reporting agency. If the creditor finds the disputed information to be inaccurate, it must notify all nationwide consumer reporting agencies so that they can correct this information in your file. When the investigation is complete, the consumer reporting agency must give you the written results and a free copy of your report if the dispute results in a change. If the creditor says the information is correct, you will receive notice from the bureau advising you that the information has been checked and is accurate.

If a creditor fails to respond to an investigation, the law requires that the disputed item in the report be removed until it is verified by the creditor.

Finally, if you still believe that the information provided by a creditor is not accurate, and the creditor won't change it, you may exercise your legal right to have a hundred-word statement included in your file to explain your side of the story.

Tip. At your request, the credit reporting agency must send a notice of correction to anyone who received your report in the past six months.

Step 4. If there is an error—follow up. If you find an error in your report, chances are it is included in other reports maintained by the other credit bureaus. If you haven't already done so, I suggest you request reports from the other credit bureaus as well.

Tip. Once all the errors in a report are supposedly fixed, request your credit report again to be sure the errors were really taken care of.

Step 5. Periodic reviews. Consider requesting your credit report annually to insure its continued accuracy.

Tip. At minimum, order an updated credit report before applying for any credit. It's better to head off problems before they occur.

Credit fix-it services. There are services that guarantee to fix your credit, for a fee. They are a waste of money, since it is so easy to insure by yourself that the information in your file is accurate and current. Neither you nor anyone else can legally delete accurate, yet negative, information from your report, so don't waste your time and money on services that claim this is possible.

Section 6. Life, Health, and Disability Insurance Information: The Medical Information Bureau

The Medical Information Bureau (MIB) is a non-profit association that was created by and for insurance companies to protect against fraud by sharing information among member companies. When life, health, or disability insurance is applied for, the applicant is usually asked to sign an authorization granting the insurance company broad access to medical information concerning the applicant (including information from your doctor or hospital). This information, together with the results of the company's investigations, such as the results of a physical exam, are submitted to the MIB. The MIB has records on approximately 13 million people.

As you will see in chapters 14 and 19, in spite of your condition, you can still apply for health and life insurance coverages. If you do, the insurance company will probably request that the MIB provide it with any information it has concerning you. The insurance company compares the information provided by you with the information in the MIB. If the two are not consistent, the insurer will seek clarification from you or other sources. Thus, it is in your interest to insure that MIB information concerning you is accurate. If you have not applied for health, life, or disability insurance in the last seven years, MIB should no longer have any information concerning you, as information is only kept for seven years.

There are two other activities of the MIB of which you should be aware:

• The MIB will tell member companies about claims filed against disability policies for the purpose of "coordinating benefits" between dif-

ferent policies. The MIB does not, however, receive information based on claims you make against any health or life insurance policies.

• The MIB maintains an Insurance Activity Index: a report by each member company of all applications for the purchase of life insurance. The file is kept for two years so a company can check to see whether you have applied for other life insurance in that period. If you apply for several policies within a short time, the activity may cause a company to question why you need so much insurance and/or question your health.

To obtain a copy of your record. Contact MIB at 617-426-3660 and ask that it send you the form necessary to obtain a copy of your MIB record. You can also mail a request for the form to MIB, P.O. Box 105, Essex Station, Boston, MA 02112.

In most cases, you will be charged $8 for your record. The record is free if within thirty days prior to your request, your application for life, health, or disability insurance was declined and the insurance company that declined the application provided you with notice that MIB was an information source. To qualify for the free report, you will have to provide with your request a copy of the notice denying coverage.

Correcting information at the MIB. If you find incorrect information in your record, you can request a reinvestigation by the insurer that provided the wrong information. You should also send a statement from your physician setting forth the correct information. If the MIB agrees, that's the end of the story. If they continue to list the inaccurate information, you have the right to have a statement included in your file.

If you find information that was correct but was inappropriately reported to the MIB as a result of claims made on your health insurance coverage instead of as a result of applying for insurance, you can request that the information be removed from your record.

Section 7. Your Financial Information

It will also be helpful to pull together

• statements for all your bank accounts, including canceled checks, as well as your credit-card and investment statements for the last twelve months. Don't worry if one or a few are missing: this information is used just to obtain your general financial picture. If your spending patterns don't fluctuate greatly from month to month, you can reduce your data-gathering to one six-month period or to every other or even every third month for the past year. Be sure to include once-a-year items such as a major vacation or annual and semiannual bills.

• a list of all your stocks and bonds and other income-producing items.

• a list of your debts and other obligations.

• tax returns for the last three years.

• expectations of future income or loss that are out of the ordinary for you.

• any other information concerning your finances you may have on hand.

• a copy of your last will and testament.

Chapter 4

Assessing Your Situation

David B. worked for seven years as a collection manager for a garment manufacturing company. After he took a look at how much he spent on his job,
including gas, oil, repairs on the car, lunches, keeping his business shirts and
suits clean and pressed, and, as he said, "a little here and a little there," he
found he could stay at home, work part-time near where he lived, and save
money even though he only made half of what he had been making.

David took two of the concepts described in this chapter, True Net Pay and Life Units, and applied them to his own situation.

To prepare for the worst, it is important to examine your own situation honestly. At the same time, the sooner you identify and plan for your goals, the better the chances are that you will be able to take the necessary steps to meet them.

This chapter starts with the place where you probably spend most of your waking hours, your work. If you're like the vast majority people who have done this exercise, you're in for a surprise.

If you don't work, at least read section 1.2 before skipping to section 2.

Section 1. Your Employment

1.1 True Net Pay

Evaluating your net pay. Regardless of whether you work for others or are self-employed, if I asked you how much you earn per hour, you would probably either tell me the dollar amount if you work on a straight hourly basis or your weekly or monthly pay divided by what you think of as

your workweek, usually between thirty-five and forty hours. However, this equation only begins to tell the story. Many incidental costs, both in money and time, are connected with any job.

To determine your **True Net Pay,** the amount you actually earn per hour before tax, complete the worksheet on pages 33–35 (if you do not have actual amounts, use estimates). The odds are, you're in for a surprise.

1.2 Life Units

The term **Life Units** reflects the amount of hours of our lives we spend to do something. If your True Net Pay is $10 an hour and you want to purchase a shirt that costs $40, it will require trading four hours of your Life Units to purchase that shirt. That's 4 hours out of the 8,760 hours in a year, which really equates to 4,380 useful hours when you realize approximately 50 percent of our hours are devoted to necessary body maintenance, i.e., sleeping, eating, eliminating, washing, groom-ing, and exercising. If you have a life expectancy of twenty years, that's 87,600 useful hours; thirty years is 131,400 useful hours.

> >

True Net Pay Worksheet

	Number of Hours (per week)	Amount of Money (annual divided by 52)
What you earn on a gross basis	—	$
Health insurance (company contribution)	—	
Cost of other employer-provided insurance	—	
Employer's pension contribution	—	
Employer's 401(k) contribution	—	
Vacations and paid leave*	—	
Performance incentives**	—	
Extras***	—	
Total of Above *Line 1*	—	$
The average number of hours you work at the job each week *Line 2*		—
Your commute, door-to-door (include time for traffic jams or late and/or broken-down trains)		
Other travel and/or transportation costs that are not reimbursed and the time involved		
The time and money you spend reading periodicals or taking courses or whatever you do to keep current for your job		
The time and money you spend socializing for work (socializing you wouldn't do if you didn't have this job)		
The amount of time each day you need to decompress after coming home from work		—
The average amount of time you spend working in the early morning, at night, and/or on weekends		—
Other time relating to your work		—
Work-related entertainment that is reimbursed		—
Work-related entertainment that is not reimbursed		
Breakfasts, lunches, snacks, and dinners: the extra amount you have to pay because your purchases are incurred at the more expensive places at or near work. Don't forget to include the extra	—	

Continued on next page

True Net Worth Worksheet *(cont'd)*

	Number of Hours (per week)	Amount of Money (annual divided by 52)
expense for the convenience dinners you purchase that are more expensive than those you could make if you had more time.	—	
Clothes and other items you wouldn't purchase if it weren't for the job—clothes you don't wear in your time off or on vacations (include the time you spent shopping as well as the expense of the clothes)		
Cleaning your work clothes		
Items relating to your personal appearance or grooming that you incur because of the job		
Entertainment you probably wouldn't need were it not for the stress of your job		
Vacations and expensive toys necessitated by the stress of this job		
Extra expense you incur for exercise near the office		
Child care		
House and clothing cleaning that you would do yourself if you didn't have this job		
Repairs you don't need others to do, but don't have the time for		
Job-related illness		
Other:		
Other:		
Other:		
Total *Line 3*	**(A)**	**(B)$**
Hours you thought you worked (line 2)		—
Plus the additional hours you do work (line 3A)		—
Total hours really worked per week (lines 2 plus 3A) *Line 4*		—
Gross pay per week (line 1)	—	

Continued on next page

True Net Worth Worksheet (*cont'd*)

		Number of Hours (per week)	Amount of Money (annual divided by 52)
Less the additional costs (line 3B)		—	
Net pay (line 1 less line 3B)	*Line 5*	—	
True Net Pay per Hour (line 5 divided by line 4)		—	$

*To determine your annual paid vacation, multiply your weekly salary by the number of weeks of vacation you have. Determine your paid leave by dividing your annual salary by 365. Multiply the result by the number of days you receive paid leave for holidays and personal days. Divide the total of annual vacation and leave by 52 to determine the amount per week.

**Include such dollar amounts as bonuses, the value of stock the company gives you, and the value of any stock option you may have (the difference between the price you pay and the market value).
***For example, the value of company-paid dues or a lease on a company car, tax advice, and professional dues.

Life Units are precious. They are limited and cannot be replaced. Healthy people tend to think of hours on this planet as infinite. However, this is not true of anyone who has realized at some point that he or she may have a life-challenging condition. Even if your condition is in remission or is entirely gone, you will never again view time in the same way. Whether life continues for a day or forty years, time will always be more precious.

1.3 Fulfillment

Now that you have an idea of your True Net Pay, and the real amount of hours you devote to your job, let's focus on a more subjective ideal—fulfillment. Remember, the happier and more positive you are, the healthier and longer your life is likely to be.

If you feel fulfilled in your work, or even content, then skip this section. If you want more out of work, read on.

Assessing fulfillment. If the world is truly your oyster, and you could do anything you want, is your current job what you would do?

If the answer doesn't immediately spring to mind, a few questions may help guide you in deciding what fulfillment means for you, and how much you find in your job. As you answer these questions, be aware, and let go, of the strong pull in our society to define ourselves by our jobs. We've come to identify ourselves and our self-worth with our jobs to the degree that we don't say, "I *do* carpentry or law." We say, "I *am* a carpenter or I am a lawyer." Ask yourself:

• Would you do your job if you didn't have to work for a living? If not, what would you want to do if you didn't have to earn money?
• What did you want to be when you grew up?
• What have you done in your life that makes you proud?
• If you knew you were going to die within a year, how would you spend that time?

1.4 Two People in a Single Economic Unit

If you and a spouse or life partner form a single economic unit, consider looking at True Net Pay and fulfillment for each of you. Most families with two incomes spend large amounts of money on items that are needed because both people are working. For instance, if only one person were working there would be little need for child care, convenience foods, restaurants, and housecleaning. If both people are fulfilled in their jobs and there is a net income from both jobs, then the exercise may be unnecessary. But if one of the people is less than satisfied at his or her job, the value of the income of the less fulfilled partner may not be worth the lack of fulfillment.

If you do the calculation, subtract from the income of the less fulfilled partner the cost of all the convenience items. If you combine taxes, figure the tax on the income of the less fulfilled partner by calculating the taxes on the two incomes together, then the taxes on the fulfilled partner's income alone. Subtract the difference from the less fulfilled person's income. Again, you will probably be surprised at the results. However, before eliminating the less fulfilled person's job, make sure you consider the value of that person's health and other benefits.

Section 2. A Financial Snapshot: Today

This section shows you how to put the information you've just gathered into the picture you'll need to assess your situation. You don't have to wait until the information comes back from the credit bureau, SSA, or even the MIB. You'll only need the information described in chapter 3, section 7, "Your Financial Information."

For purposes of this chapter, the reference is to "your" finances. If you are part of a couple, and you combine your income and/or expenses, the numbers you insert in the various worksheets should reflect that. Likewise, your goals should reflect your goals together.

When amounts of money are discussed, you only need a ballpark estimate—not the exact dollar amounts. Round off the numbers to the nearest

$100 or $500 or whatever works for you. If you can't find a number readily, let's say within five minutes, then estimate it using your best guess. Please don't make any major financial decisions until you replace the estimated numbers with more accurate ones. When you eventually locate the accurate information, you can return to the form and update it.

As you put these numbers together, remember, no shame and no blame. This is not the time to kick yourself for the investment that did not do well or the investment you didn't make that made your least favorite person rich.

You may want to make copies of the forms so that you can reassess your situation in the future.

Tip. Don't worry if your numbers indicate a shortfall. We will focus on appropriate treatments for your situation in later chapters.

2.1 Net Worth

The first goal is to determine your **net worth:** how much you are worth today after all the things you own and all the amounts you owe are taken into account. Finding this number is really no more difficult than completing a credit card application.

If you have completed a Net Worth statement recently, pull it out and skip the rest of this section. If not, the form starting on page 38 will provide an easy mechanism for determining your Net Worth.

There are a few instructions you should be aware of:

• Use only the first three columns for now.
• When you insert numbers that are for items other than cash or cash equivalents (such as stocks and bonds or certificates of deposit and anything else that can quickly be converted to cash), estimate what you would get if you sold them today—not what you would like to obtain or what you paid or a fictitious insurance value.
• Include the full value of each item in what you own, without deducting any debt or mortgage

you owe with respect to that asset. You will be asked to list the mortgage or debt due under the heading of "what you owe."

• When you list what you owe, include what you owe today, not what you may owe at some future time.

• Keep things simple by using the balances from your last statements instead of trying to add on any new purchases or subtracting any payments from the last statement.

• For future reference, retain a brief description of where or how you obtained your values.

Tip. There are probably as many different worksheets for determining Net Worth as there are books and computer programs on the subject. If you are more comfortable with another worksheet, please use that one. A word of caution: If you use another worksheet or software program, look for a hidden agenda. Many programs are reasonably priced and provide much useful information, but they basically exist to help promote the company's financial products. You can judge a software program by the following criteria: First and foremost, it should be easy to use. Second, it should be flexible, allowing you to try a number of "what-if" scenarios, and even to change the program's assumptions. Third, it should be informative, explaining the concepts. There is no single answer—so if the program says there is, pass it by.

2.2 Cash Flow

Now that you know your net worth, the next step is to determine your **cash flow**—what and how much money comes in and where it goes.

Adapt the Cash Flow worksheet starting on page 41 as necessary to reflect your particular situation. The goal is to include all your regular and unusual income and expense.

Before you start. Some guidelines are:
• Please make several photocopies of this worksheet. You'll use one now, and you may wish to use other copies to periodically check where

you are in the future. Keep at least one blank copy for use with the discussion in chapter 17.

• Cash expenditures will probably be hard to reconstruct, but you can come up with a pretty good estimate if you think about a typical week and how often you buy things for cash. For example, if you eat lunch at work five days a week and that's $7 a shot, that's $140 a month. An alternative is to keep track of your spending for a week, or even just one typical weekday and one typical weekend day, and estimate your weekly spending based on those days.

• It will help to pull out a current pay stub, which shows your income for the year to date as well as all deductions, and last year's W-2 or pay summary, showing income and withholdings.

• For now, we are interested only in the columns headed "Per Month" and "Per Year." The rest of the worksheet will become relevant later.

Tip. To take control of your financial situation, you need to know how much money you spend daily and on what. In a notebook or a budget workbook (available from any stationery store), track all your expenses, in detail, for the next three months to find out where your money really goes. Categorize your spending narrowly. For example, say "movies" or "theater" instead of "entertainment." Write down every penny you spend. Don't forget to include the cash you get from the ATM. An easy method is to keep the cash withdrawal slip in your wallet and note on it your expenditures every time you pull out your wallet to get cash. Don't try to do anything about your spending pattern: the key is to first get a handle on it.

Section 3. A Financial Snapshot: If You Become Disabled

Now that you know where you are today, let's take a look at what would happen in a reasonable period of time, say two years, in the event that your condition leads to a disability likely to last more

﹥﹥

Net Worth Worksheet

	You	Your Significant Other	Together	
	(1)	(2)	(3)	(4)
What You Own (assets)				
Immediately Usable Assets				
Bank accounts (checking and savings)				
Money market accounts				
Cash value of life insurance				
Amount obtainable on sale of life insurance policy*				
Stocks				
Bonds				
Publicly traded partnerships/units				
Mutual funds				
Annuities: current value				
Precious metals				
Easily salable personal property such as jewelry, silver, and cars				
Trust funds				
Restricted Assets				
CDs				
Pensions (at present lump-sum value)**				
IRAs and Keogh accounts				
Employee savings plans				
Stock options				
Assets That Would Take Time to Sell				
Net interest in a business				
Your home(s)***				
Commercial real estate				

Continued on next page

Net Worth Worksheet *(cont'd)*

	You (1)	Your Significant Other (2)	Together (3)	(4)
Art/antiques				
Other valuable personal property such as furs, boats, tools, coins				
Private limited partnerships				
Other investments				
Personal property****				
Money due you (loans)				
Other assets				
Total: What You Own *Line 1*				

What You Owe

Charge accounts				
Credit card(s) debt*****				
Current bills******				
Mortgage, the amount you owe on your residence******				
Mortgage, the amount you owe on commercial property*******				
Cars: amount you still owe*******				
Education loans*******				
Life insurance policy loans*******				
Tax arrears				
Projected income tax due				
Local and property taxes due				
Other debts				
Projected capital gains taxes on sale of assets				
Total: What You Owe *Line 2*				

Continued on next page

Net Worth Worksheet *(cont'd)*

	You	Your Significant Other	Together	
	(1)	(2)	(3)	(4)
What You Own (line 1)				
What You Owe (line 2)				
Net Worth (line 1 – line 2)				

*As you will read in chapter 19, if your condition has a life expectancy on a statistical basis of five years or less, you will be able to access money from your life insurance. Include a ballpark estimate of what you would receive if you sold all insurance covering your life. For current purposes, assume you would receive an amount equal to 80 percent of the death benefit with a one-year life expectancy on a statistical basis, 60 percent with two years, and 40 percent with three years and more.

**Only include the vested portion, the amount you're entitled to no matter what happens. If this is a lump sum, include the lump sum. If the plan is a defined contribution plan, include the amount to which the contributions have grown. If the plan is a defined benefit plan, ask the plan administrator for the current value of the projected stream of income. This is a common request for financial planning purposes and will not indicate any health condition.

***For your home, use a value that's an average of recent sale prices of similar homes in your neighborhood. Check your newspaper real estate section or contact a real estate broker for a valuation.

****Include collectibles, household items, clothes, and anything you could sell at a yard or estate sale, at the price you would expect to receive. Many people use 10 percent of the value of their home as an estimate.

*****If you consistently pay off all credit card debt, these numbers should be zero. The numbers will appear on your cash flow statement. If you carry a balance, list the balance.

******Only list an amount that you carry as a balance from month to month. Current balances will be included on your cash flow statement. Include such bills as utilities, rent, mortgage payments (but not the outstanding debt), life as well as property and casualty insurance premiums, and monthly auto installments rather than the full amount owed on the car.

*******Outstanding balance of principal: the total amount you owe if you paid off the debt today.

than twelve months. The underlying assumption is that for the next two years you have income and expense that are the same as you now have, and that you then become disabled. Hopefully, you will not become disabled—but you don't want to be caught short if it happens. Again, if this exercise comes up with a shortfall, don't worry. That is what this book will help you through.

3.1 Net Worth in Two Years

Use column (4) on the Net Worth worksheet starting on page 38 to reflect an assumed date to go on disability (e.g., two years).

•**Net money:** Look at the Net Discretionary Money you just calculated and estimate how much of that you will be able to save each year until then. Add that amount to an account you're likely to put the money in. For example, if you normally put any net income remaining after expense in your savings account, include it there.

•**Mutual funds and other investments:** Change the amount to reflect what you conservatively estimate the value will be. The goal here is to try to find out what reality, rather than your dream, would be like. An average increase over the past five years may be a good guide to the future, unless those years have been exceptionally good or not so good.

•**Retirement plans:** Include the amount of money you would be able to access at or before the time you become disabled.

˃ ˃

Cash Flow Worksheet

	You		Your Significant Other		
	Per Month	Per Year	Per Month	Per Year	
	(1)	(2)	(3)	(4)	(5)
What You Take In (income)					
Salary with bonuses					
Self-employment income					
Interest					
Dividends					
Capital gains					
Rents and royalties (net)					
Social Security					
Pension income					
Other income					
Total Income *Line 1*					
What You Spend (expense)					
For the roof over your head:					
Rent/mortgage/fee*					
Utility payments**					
Maintenance					
Property taxes					
Cable TV/satellite					
Telephone					
Repairs					
To get around:					
Car payments					
Car maintenance/repairs					
Gas and oil					

Continued on next page

Cash Flow Worksheet *(cont'd)*

	You		Your Significant Other		
	Per Month	Per Year	Per Month	Per Year	
	(1)	(2)	(3)	(4)	(5)
Tolls and parking					
Bus/subway/railroad					
Commuting expenses***					
Debt repayment:					
Loan payments					
Debt on credit card****					
Insurance premiums:					
Life insurance					
Health insurance					
Disability insurance					
Long-term care					
Car insurance					
Residence insurance					
Credit life insurance					
Liability insurance					
Other insurance					
Income taxes					
Employment taxes					
Professional expenses (associations, classes, etc.)					
Clothing and accessories					
Maintenance and cleaning of clothing and accessories					
Food:					
Market					
Restaurants/takeout					
Other					

Continued on next page

Cash Flow Worksheet *(cont'd)*

	You		Your Significant Other		
	Per Month	Per Year	Per Month	Per Year	
	(1)	(2)	(3)	(4)	(5)
Medical expenses:*****					
Physicians and hospitals					
Dental/vision					
Therapy					
Drugs					
Travel for medical					
Other					
Educational expenses					
Fun:					
Vacation					
Entertainment					
Gifts					
Pets					
Hobbies					
Books and magazines					
Other					
Children:					
School/child care					
Baby-sitters					
Tuition					
Vacation/camp					
Clothes					
Allowance					
Child support					
Other					
Alimony					

Continued on next page

Cash Flow Worksheet (*cont'd*)

	You		Your Significant Other		
	Per Month	Per Year	Per Month	Per Year	
	(1)	(2)	(3)	(4)	(5)
Charitable contributions					
Exercise (gyms, equipment)					
Personal items (haircuts, makeup, other)					
Accountant					
Attorney					
Financial adviser					
Other professionals					
Retirement plan contributions					
"Just in Case" fund (see section 4)					
Other payments******					
Total of What You Spend *Line 2*					
Total income per year (line 1)					
Total of what you spend (line 2)					
Discretionary Money (line 1 – line 2) *Line 3*					
Savings/investments *Line 4*					
Net Discretionary Money (line 3 – line 4)*******					

*Use the amount of your rent or the amount of your monthly mortgage payment if you own your residence, plus cost of monthly maintenance if where you live is a co-op or a condominium.

**Include cost of gas, oil, electricity, water, and/or sewer.

***Include all costs. For example, if you drive to a commuter station, include expense of using your vehicle to and from the train, parking at the train, the cost of the train, and conveyance from the train to your office. If you drive, don't forget the use of your car and commuting fees or tolls. An easy estimate for use of your car is 31 cents per mile.

****Only include debt that you did not record on your Net Worth statement.

*****Do not include medical expenses that are reimbursed by insurance or government programs.

******Retain with this worksheet a list of the payments in this category, with description and amount, so you will be able to recall the makeup of this item later.

*******As you review this number, bear in mind that the calculation already includes such "discretionary" items as fun, baby-sitters, and personal items.

- **Life insurance:** Increase the amount obtainable on a sale to reflect decreased life expectancy due to the passage of years, even though new drugs or treatments may occur to change this projection.
- **Other assets:** Add in other assets you may gain access to, such as money in a trust fund that you gain control over during this time.

3.2 Cash Flow on Disability

Using column (5) of the Cash Flow worksheet, label it "Disability" and create a projection of what would happen if you become disabled. Start with the numbers you've already filled in and make the following adjustments, using realistic instead of optimistic projections:

What you take in (income).
- **Salary:** Include the amount of net income you would continue to receive under any long-term formal or informal plan your employer uses. There is no reason to include a short-term disability plan since, by definition, it is only short-term and won't give you a true picture of what it will be like to be on long-term disability.
- **Bonuses:** Include them if any can reasonably be anticipated.
- **Self-employment income:** Include any self-employment income you can reasonably foresee even if you are disabled.
- **Interest, dividends, and capital gains:** Adjust these numbers to reflect any principal or savings you may have to take out to live on.
- **Social Security:** If you already have the response from SSA, use the numbers they note as a ballpark. If you don't have their form yet and have worked at least forty calendar quarters in the past ten years, then approximate a number based on the following: The average award is between $700 and $800 a month. The current maximum award is approximately $1,200 a month. Awards are even less if you worked less than the required quarters. Note: If you will re-

ceive disability from your employer, check to see if the amount includes or is in addition to any payments you may be entitled to receive from SSA. If it includes Social Security, then note Social Security income at zero since it will already be included in your income from your employer.
- **Pension income:** What you can expect to receive per month on disability.
- **Other income:** Include any money you will receive from private disability policies as well as any money you may receive from an association, union, or religious organization to which you belong. If the policy requires a deduction for Social Security payments, put the gross income here, and put zero in the Social Security space. Also, include all income you can expect from any other source (e.g., perhaps acknowledging the contribution you made to their lives, your children have agreed to give you a monthly income).

What you spend (expense).
Medical expense: Since the assumption is that your condition creates an expense during the next two years, estimate the amount of medical expense that will not be reimbursable from your insurance company, employer, or government program. The simplest projection may be to use the numbers you obtained as part of the "average" cost curve with respect to your condition (see chapter 3, section 4), less the amount you will be reimbursed. If you want to try to get a more accurate grasp of your own situation, use the following calculations instead, less the amount of any reimbursement.
Physician expense: Include attending physician and any specialists.
Medical travel: Include the cost of going to and from the doctor or the hospital and parking. This may not seem like a lot of money, but Connie T. took approximately three hundred trips to the doctor in a year.
Medical supplies: Not generally covered by insurance since they are not prescription items.

Psychotherapy: Even if it is covered, coverage is usually for a limited number of visits and the amount of overall coverage may be limited as well.

Home care: Most insurance coverages limit the number of visits. Most companies will waive the limit if they think the only alternative is expensive hospitalization, but don't count on it.

Prescription drugs: Medicare does not cover any prescription drugs out of the hospital, unless you have MediGap plan "J." Many other plans have drug caps of limited amounts, such as $500 per year.

Private hospital room differential: If you want to use a single room in a hospital instead of a double, you have to pay the difference. This can be at least several hundred dollars a day. Generally, hospitals only move patients to single rooms at no additional cost when the patient is deemed to be contagious.

Medical insurance premiums: Once an employee shifts to disability, she has to pay the full cost of the premiums that before were often paid in full or in part by the employer. Generally, for the first eighteen months of disability, premiums may not exceed 102 percent of what the employer continues to pay for the coverage. For months nineteen to twenty-eight, the premiums can escalate to 150 percent of the premiums the employer pays. If a right to convert to individual coverage exists, approximate the premiums for the individual coverage or use the figure charged for premiums during disability.

Deductibles: Include the amount that may be payable with respect to health insurance.

Coinsurance or copayments: All types of health insurance require that you pay some part of your medical expense. This is called coinsurance in indemnity-type plans, or a copayment in managed-care plans. Copayments of $15 or $20 may not seem like a lot, but they can add up to $500 or $600 per year. Sometimes they are capped. Often, they are not.

Usual, customary, and reasonable: If you have indemnity health coverage, there may be amounts payable in excess of "usual, customary, and reasonable" charges.

Alternative therapies: These therapies, such as Eastern medicine and disciplines, are not generally covered by health plans, although some plans may cover them.

Experimental treatments: Any new drugs that are not yet approved by the federal Food and Drug Administration are "experimental" and not reimbursed without a struggle, if at all. Sometimes even new uses of approved drugs are considered experimental.

Clinical trials: If you participate in a study of an experimental drug (see chapter 25, section 8), you may incur expenses that are not reimbursed, such as travel and outside tests.

- **Clothing:** Reduce the expense to the cost of the clothes you will need if you're not working.

- **Food:** You will no longer need expensive meals at work and may have time to cook more. On the other hand, you may plan to eat a special diet that costs more money.

- **In general:** As you look at the rest of the items, remember that you are no longer working. Perhaps that means less in child care, or maybe it means more because of your disability. You may not need vacations anymore or you may want to take the vacations you've been postponing. Whatever your situation, think about how it could reasonably be expected to change and insert the number that results. The rule of thumb for a person on retirement without additional medical bills is that expenses are 70 to 80 percent of preretirement expenses.

As you prepare your worksheet, also include items that apply to everyone, regardless of health history, such as:

- **Inflation:** Adjust all numbers for reasonably anticipated inflation.

- **Residence, including mortgage or rent, utility payments, maintenance of residence, property taxes:** Adjust to reflect a possible change in where you live, which may be required by your condition. Even if there is no change, factor in the increases you can expect, such as in property taxes or in rent/maintenance.

• **Taxes:** Estimate to reflect what they would be with your new income. If there is a net change from your current income, call the IRS for a free estimate of the tax rate at the different net income at 800-829-1040.

Section 4. A Financial Snapshot: Your Goals

You've just worked through a forecast to obtain an idea of what would happen if you have to stop work and go on disability in the future. It's worth taking a few minutes to do another forecast, except this one is at the opposite extreme: What are your goals, and from today's vantage point, if you remain healthy, how close are you to realizing those goals? For example, do you want to pay college tuition for a child? Have funds for your retirement? For another purpose?

A general rule of thumb to determine how much you will need if you retire is to multiply your annual expenses by 0.7 if you have children living at home, or 0.6 if your children have left home.

A "just in case" fund. One of the goals you should consider is setting aside liquid assets to serve as

• **a contingency fund,** which should be large enough for you to weather unexpected decreases in your income.
• **an emergency fund,** to weather unforeseeable emergencies.
• **a cure fund,** to cover the purchase of the cure that will hopefully be developed for your condition, as well as the expense of revamping your life at that point.

Tip. While the following section describes the preferred amount to retain as your Just in Case

Fund, the practical goal is to do whatever you can. Just do your best. Create and add to the fund at whatever level you can. Doing anything is better than doing nothing at all. Don't make yourself nuts.

Ideally, the Just in Case Fund should equal your anticipated fixed and variable expenses for twelve months. At the least, the fund should equal an amount for your Cure Fund, which considering the current cost of new drugs and treatments should be between $15,000 and $20,000, plus an Emergency Fund equal to a multiple of your income. If you work for the government, the Emergency Fund should be at least three months of income; if you are self-employed, if your income fluctuates, your work is seasonal, or if you rely on commissions, your job or income may be more at risk, and six months would be more reasonable. If you work for a private employer with a steady income, the fund should be approximately four and a half months. If your income greatly exceeds your expenses, your fund should be at least the equivalent of the above number of months' worth of fixed and variable expenses.

If you are part of a two-income unit, consider the likelihood that you will both lose your jobs at the same time. The likelihood may be high if you both work for the same employer. At the other extreme, it would be very unlikely if you work in fields that are affected differently by the same economic conditions. For example, if one of you works as a bankruptcy attorney and the other sells luxury items, a downturn in the economy would affect each of your incomes differently. If the likelihood is low that you will both lose your jobs, then a Contingency Fund equal to three months' expenses plus $20,000 for a Cure Fund would be reasonable.

You can make do with less cash if you have credit available or if there are assets you can easily borrow against, such as a retirement plan at work.

It is preferable that these funds be retained in a low-risk liquid asset (see chapter 13).

Tip. To work up to the necessary funds, think of payments into your Just in Case Fund as a priority debt that has to be paid every week. Make payments convenient: consider asking your employer to deposit a portion of your paycheck into a savings/investment account, or ask your bank to make automatic transfers. Start off easily, at perhaps 5 percent of your income, and work up to your optimal savings rate. *The amount you start with is less important than getting started.* The habit of saving is what becomes critical. Keeping a chart of your progress may help you reach your goals.

Prioritize goals. Once you have identified your goals, unless you have a large amount of resources, you need to quantify and prioritize them. The worksheet below will assist you in setting your priorities. Fill in a number between 1 and 10, 10 being something that is of most importance to you.

Prioritize Your Goals Worksheet

Goal	Short-Term To 1 Year	Medium-Term 1–5 Years	Long-Term 5 Years Plus
Just in Case Fund			
Buy a residence			
Make home improvements			
Buy_____			
Buy_____			
Buy_____			
Reduce debt			
Take a vacation to_____			
Take a vacation to_____			
Have money to retire			
Have children			
Provide disability income			
Start a business			
Retire early			
Other:			
Other:			
Other:			

Once you have prioritized your goals, you need to turn them into dollar amounts so you can determine how much money you will need, and when you will need it. For example, if you want to purchase a house, you need to estimate how much it will cost, how much you will need as a down payment, and when. From there, you can estimate how much you have to save and over what time.

Photocopy the Net Worth and Cash Flow worksheets and add columns to suit your needs, or use those worksheets as a model and create your own.

From today's vantage point, project your net worth and net income at the various stages that are most important to you (such as when the children are in college or upon retirement), inserting the numbers that seem reasonably appropriate. The idea is to determine how your financial picture will look at each stage if you stay on your current course, and to determine whether there could be a shortfall. As before, don't worry about shortfalls. This book will help you overcome them to accomplish your needs and desires.

Chapter 5

Keeping Your Financial Information Organized

Disorder is our worst enemy.
—Hesiod, 800 B.C.

Your valuable papers should be systematically filed and stored to protect them, prevent confusion, delay, and loss of money, and to smooth the way for whoever may need access in case of your incapacity, travel, or demise. A List of Instructions should also be created.

Section 1. Where to Store or File Your Papers

Column (1) in the worksheet beginning on page 52 indicates the "best" place to keep each of your valuable documents. It would be worthwhile to note in column (2) where they are actually located. Update the chart as you make changes.

Safe-deposit box. Safe-deposit boxes are sealed by the bank in most states as soon as they receive word that the boxholder is deceased. Generally the box is not opened again until a representative of the local taxing authority is present. Do not use your safe-deposit box as the place to keep

- cash, since it indicates evasion of income tax.
- your original will, cemetery deeds, or burial in-

structions since they should be immediately accessible.
- unregistered property belonging to someone else. It will be presumed to be yours. Proof to the contrary may be difficult.

If you want to avoid a sealing upon death, consider using a box that is registered in a corporate name. Generally, safe-deposit boxes registered in a corporate name are not sealed upon the death of a principal.

Tip. Be sure that a trusted family member or friend is a cosignator or deputy, which permits them access to the box so that papers can be removed when needed, especially if you become incapacitated. At least be sure someone knows where your safe-deposit box is, as well as the location of the key.

Section 2. A Filing System

It is a good idea to keep your financial information in a simple filing system. What system you use doesn't matter so long as

- you use it.
- you use it the same way all the time.
- you can get your hands on any major piece of paper relating to your financial situation in ten minutes—except of course for the contents of your safe-deposit box.
- it includes a place for current bills as received, as well as a place for reminders about ongoing obligations for which you do not receive a bill (such as a personal debt that you repay monthly).
- it is easy for others to understand in the event they need to get to your papers. If you have a question as to whether your system fits this goal, ask a friend to review the system to see if he or she understands it.

When you complete your tax return, move your papers from your daily system to your tax file.

The "shoe box" method of filing. One simple filing system is the "shoe box" method, which involves five separate boxes (or files):

Box #1: This box is just for your current bills. As you pay these bills, move them to Box #2. Box #1 should include a day-of-the-month expandable file (or thirty-one file folders). As you receive each bill, place it in the folder whose number corresponds to the date that is five business days *prior* to the date the bill is due or the date on which you consistently pay the bill. For example, a bill due on the first may be filed for the twenty-third. For each fixed or monthly bill, such as mortgages and rent, place a note card in the appropriate day indicating the information about that bill. If the bill is not paid monthly, note on the card for which months it is paid.

Box #2: Paid bills and financial obligations, including general bills and invoices, credit card statements and receipts.

Box #3: All bank accounts, including statements and canceled checks.

Box #4: Medical expenses and reimbursements.

Box #5: All records or documents concerning government-sponsored programs that relate to you. Keep separate files in this box for each program. Keep copies of all application forms, supporting documents, memos of conversations, including with whom you had the conversations and the date, award letters, and all correspondence. *Never give any government agency the original without keeping a copy in this file.*

Tip. Consider attaching to your filing system a summary of how it works in case someone else has to use your system for you.

Section 3. List of Instructions

Now that you have a focus on what is necessary to keep your financial life in order, it's time to spend a few minutes and write a **List of Instructions,** summarizing it all. The list will be the final step in providing you with a financial overview. Since we all face the possibility of being unable or unavailable to manage our affairs, whether due to mild depression, extended travel, or incapacity, it also provides guidance to whoever may need to take over.

The form of the List of Instructions is not important. It should be comprehensive and easy to amend as the facts change. It should be filed in a safe place, with a copy to the person who will need to implement it if necessary. Please do not confuse this list with a will or any of the advance directives such as a living will described in chapter 32, which have formal requirements dictated by various state statutes.

What to include. The List of Instructions should include everything necessary to enable another person to step in and manage your affairs. For example, in addition to information about your filing system, the list should include, in no particular order:

- **Your hiding places:** Where you hide cash or other items.

> >

Document Storage

Items	Where Each Item Is Stored
(1)	(2)
Safe-Deposit Box	
Government bonds and other investments	
Certificates	
Property deeds, titles, and bills of sale	
Household inventories	
Photos of household items	
Military service records	
Birth certificate	
Marriage certificate	
Citizenship papers	
Divorce papers	
Adoption papers	
Baptismal records	
Death certificates	
Important contracts	
Patents and copyrights	
Automobile title or bill of sale	
Notes due you	
A list of where your important papers are	
A Fireproof Box or Filing Cabinet That Is Accessible (e.g., in your home)	
Income tax returns*	
Important canceled checks	
All bank accounts including checking, savings, certificates of deposit, and money market funds**	
Stocks, bonds, and brokerage account statements**	
Canceled checks**	

Continued on next page

Document Storage *(cont'd)*

Items	Where Each Item Is Stored
(1)	**(2)**
Sales slips**	
Records of loans or other debts with schedule of payments	
A list of the location of each of your important papers	
Business records	
Employment record	
Education record	
Passport	
Copies of all insurance policies	
Health records and information concerning your health insurance***	
Copy of your will	
Copy of your living will	
Copy of durable power of attorney	
Copy of health care proxy	
Cemetery deed	

File in a Safe Place (which can be in your fireproof box or filing cabinet if there is room)

Instruction books and guarantees for appliances and other household items	
Employee benefits booklets	
A photocopy of your medical identification card in case you misplace the original or a representative needs to access the information	
A contact list of all your team members	
Location of original of your living will****	
Location of original of your durable power of attorney****	
Location of original of your health-care power of attorney****	

Continued on next page

Document Storage *(cont'd)*

Items	Where Each Item Is Stored
(1)	(2)
Location of original of your will****	
List of assets including location and identification numbers	
Funeral plans, including final requests	
List of Instructions*****	

In Your Wallet

Identification card	
Driver's license	
Auto insurance card (with a duplicate in the car in case you let other people drive it)	
Health insurance card (listing company, policy number, and telephone number)	
Contacts to notify in case of an emergency	
Blood type	
Card showing if you are diabetic, epileptic, or allergic to certain drugs	
History of your medical condition and what drugs or treatments you are taking	

With Your Attorney

Will (the original)******	
All documentation proving mental competency at time of executing your will	
Information needed to administer your assets if you become incapacitated or die****	
Durable power of attorney	
Designation of guardian with phone number and address	
Trust documents	

Continued on next page

Document Storage (*cont'd*)

Items	Where Each Item Is Stored
(1)	(2)
A list of locations of all safe-deposit boxes and location of other important documents****	
Location of your hidden safe, if any****	
With Your Attending Physician and Your Specialist Living will	
Copy of your health-care power of attorney	
Do not resuscitate order	
With Your Pharmacist Copy of your health-care power of attorney	

*For at least the last three years, with appropriate backup for each year filed by year including stocks, bonds, and brokerage account statements. If you own real property, keep all returns and backup from the first date that either the purchase or improvements to the property are included in your tax return. You will need proof of cost ("basis") in the event of a sale or other transfer.

**Each year when you prepare your taxes, move these documents from their daily place to permanent storage. Since these documents all relate to your tax return, they should be filed together. Eliminate documents that are no longer necessary.

***Be sure to at least include the name of your insurance company, policy number, a list of what procedures and treatments must be approved beforehand, and the telephone number.

****If you complete the List of Instructions suggested in section 3, you will not need to also include this information in this chart.

*****This list is described in section 3.

******If the attorney will not hold your will, give it to the person named as personal representative/executor to place in his or her safe-deposit box.

- **Safe-deposit box:** Location and the name of any other person who also has access to it.
- **Locked places/keys:** Location of your various locked places and keys, as well as the names of other people who have copies of your keys or know your combinations, such as
  - a safe-deposit box (and the location of a second key, if any).
  - post office box.
  - a grandfather clock with a key.
  - combination lock and/or safe (with location and combination).
- access card/code.
- mini/public storage.
- home-alarm service codes and passwords.
- **House/apartment:** To whom rent, maintenance, and/or mortgage payments are payable, listing amounts and due dates; where the home circuit breaker and water-shutoff valve are located; what you do to maintain the house and when you do it; contact information for the plumber, furnace person, gardener, electrician, and painter whom you have used before or whom you would call; how and when to service the swimming pool and

smoke alarms; pest control; burglar alarm codes and service company; and apartment house superintendent.

- **Other real property:** Where the property is located; if owned with another person, identity of the co-owner and contact information.
- **Securities:** Where your stocks, bonds, and other securities are maintained, with contact people and phone numbers.
- **Bank accounts:** Where your bank accounts are located, the account numbers, and names of any other people who have authority to access those accounts.
- **Social Security number.**
- **List of credit cards:** Include issuer, account number, and date of expiration, as well as the names of all other people who have duplicate copies of the cards and/or are authorized to use each account.
- **Health, life, disability, long-term-care, and property and casualty insurance:** Include the type of policy, the name of the insurance company, policy number, when premiums are due, in what amount, and mailing address to which they are to be sent. It may also be appropriate to include grace periods, if any. Also include telephone number of the broker, if any. If you don't use a broker, include the phone number of the insurance company policyholder service department and of the claims department.
- **Personal property:** Where you keep your list and photos or videotape of personal property as well as location of the receipts (and cost and/or value of each item); where the negatives of the photographs are filed.
- **Title:** Where titles are kept for all registered property, such as motorboats and automobiles.
- **Computer:** Your passwords at home and at work, as well as the files in which pertinent information is located and passwords for those files if any.
- **Car:** Identify the car or cars; maintenance schedule; garage or mechanic to which you take it for maintenance; location of snow or regular

tires; insurance broker and/or insurance company; location of proof of insurance; whom to call in event of a claim.

- **Children:** Names and ages, where they are living if not with you, guardian, school name, location, and contact person; where to locate records concerning the child's history; any pertinent facts that would be useful.
- **Family:** Other close relatives and people you think of as family.
- **Pets:** Name and breed; age; contact information for the veterinarian; what shots the animal(s) have received and when (this could be critical in an emergency). If you don't know the shots, at least list the contact information for the person who would know.
- **Sources of current income:** Royalties; rental income; dividends; interest payments; annuities; worker's compensation; child support; trust income; and any other source.
- **Taxes:** Federal, state, and local tax due dates as well as amounts, if known, and where to send. The list should also include whom to call if a tax bill is not received. Include a date by which your tax situation for the year should be examined so decisions can be made to minimize taxes, such as to consider selling appropriate stocks and/or bonds before year end to offset taxable gains. This should generally be done by December 1 at the latest, so there is plenty of time for an assessment and to take appropriate actions.
- **Employer:** Contact person at your employer and direct telephone number, if any.
- **Team members:** Include your physicians as well as all members of your professional team described in chapter 36.
- **Medical history:** Identify the location of your records. It would also be helpful to let either the physician or facility that has these records know that the named person has authority to access and/or copy those records, as well as to write a simple letter giving the named person that authority. For safety, in case it is required later on, your signature on that letter should be notarized.

- **Personal information:** Include or indicate where to find personal data; employment history; education; military record; past residences and dates at each; marriage information; significant relationships; former significant relationship(s); other personal information.
- **Debts:** How to determine your debts or where to find a list of them.
- **People to notify:** A list of people to notify if you are incapacitated and/or die. It is a good idea to also include a list of people not to contact, if applicable.
- **Location of important papers relating to your estate:** List who has your living will, health care power of attorney, durable power of attorney, will, and any other advance directives described in chapter 32 as well as their names and contact information for the named agents.
- **Location of each of your other important papers:** Include personal documents such as birth certificate, passport, license, marriage/divorce papers, immigration/naturalization papers; educational, professional, employment, religious, ceremonial, military, and other personal documents.
- **Estate information:** Contact information for personal representative/executor(s). Since this List of Instructions will probably be more read-ily available than your will, it would be helpful to include a copy of your funeral and burial wishes in this document if you have them (see chapter 34). If this is the only place you state your funeral wishes, be sure to sign and date the list so your heirs know the document really reflects your wishes. There will be even less question if you have a witness or notary sign as well.

Tip. Once you have compiled all this information, it would be helpful to create a chart with a timeline showing what has to be paid by what date, as well as what has to be done in each area of your life. Please don't forget to include a date by which to assess your taxable income for the year and to take any tax-saving actions. A timeline may seem like overkill, but it's easy to create now, while you have the information at hand. It will save you time and anxiety and be a major help to anyone who may have to take over if you become incapacitated.

A Break

Whether you've gone through the process described in this chapter or just read it over, it's time to take a break and remind yourself of your goals. Keep them in mind as you read on.

Part III

›››››››››››››

Income

Chapter 6

Legal Protections—Employment

Debbie S. had been an office manager for a good-size medical practice for eighteen years when she was diagnosed with colon cancer. At first, her employers told her they would do anything they could to help her. Six months later she found one of her employers asking what she would do when she was on disability. Over the next few months there were more hints that led her to believe they didn't want her at the practice anymore. She was then terminated with the explanation that decreasing profits were the cause.

Debbie's story is not unusual.

Federal, state, and local disability laws offer protections to employees and families facing life-challenging conditions. The laws address all aspects of employment, from preemployment through termination of work and job changes. The laws also protect against discrimination in housing, public accommodations, communications, transportation, and construction. This chapter focuses on employment.

In general, you are considered to be "disabled" for purposes of coverage under the Americans with Disabilities Act of 1990 (ADA) and other disability discrimination laws simply because of a diagnosis of a life-challenging condition. The underlying assumption about disability in these laws is that you should not be discriminated against merely because of a diagnosis. When it comes to work, the law assumes a worker *can, and should be allowed to,* work despite the disability.

You are protected only if the employer or other party is informed about, or has reason to believe, you have been diagnosed with a life-challenging condition. The employer and other covered person must maintain strict confidentiality about your condition.

The term *disability* for purposes of the ADA and other discrimination laws is not the same as the term *disability* for purposes of assessing eligibility for Social Security Disability benefits or disability insurance where, as you will see in later chapters, a condition that prevents a person from working is required.

Note. These laws are fairly new and their meaning is still being developed in the courts. This chapter is intended to provide a general overview of how these laws apply so as to assist you in reaching informed decisions. Readers who encounter problems in the areas discussed are urged to seek legal counsel on how the law applies to individual situations.

Section 1. Employment

Under the ADA and the Federal Rehabilitation Act, a covered employer (see section 1.1 below) may not discriminate against a *qualified individual* with a *disability* because of the disability. The meaning of this prohibition will be discussed at length throughout this section. Areas protected under the law include preemployment inquiries, reasonable accommodation, leaves of absence, telling and confidentiality, and access to benefits.

Note: The ADA and the Federal Rehabilitation Act differ only as to which employers are covered under each act. Otherwise the requirements and interpretations are substantially similar. For purposes of this discussion, both acts will be referred to as the ADA, except as to the questions of covered employers.

While these laws do not apply to all employment situations, it is important to understand the scope of their protection because state and local disability discrimination laws may apply when the ADA does not, and many of them rely on the ADA as a source for interpretation.

1.1 Covered Employers

- Employers with fifteen or more employees are covered by the ADA.
- State and local governments must also comply with ADA requirements.
- Employees of the U.S. government, or a corporation wholly owned by the government of the United States, are covered by the Federal Rehabilitation Act instead of the ADA. The military, however, does not have to obey either the ADA or the Federal Rehabilitation Act, except with respect to civilians.
- Employers with fewer than fifteen workers are covered by state or local laws. Contact your state or local "equal employment opportunity" or "human rights" office. Check the state and local government section of your telephone book. The Equal Employment Opportunity Commission Public Information system can help you locate the correct agency (800-669-4000). For additional advice, contact your GuardianOrg.
- Organizations exempt from taxation under 501c

of the Internal Revenue Code are not covered under the ADA. These organizations include charitable organizations that fit within 501c(3), "bona fide private membership clubs," and labor or fraternal organizations.

1.2 Disability for Purposes of the Americans with Disabilities Act

Disability for purposes of ADA means

- a physical or mental impairment that substantially limits one or more major life activities; or even
- the perception of disability—which can come from the current perception of an impairment as well as a history of impairment. For purposes of the law, the mere diagnosis of a life-challenging condition such as HIV/AIDS and cancer can create the perception of "having an impairment." In addition to those currently battling an illness, the ADA also protects survivors from future discrimination based on past illness.

As this book was going to press, the meaning of the term *disability* as it applies to symptom-free people diagnosed with a life-challenging condition was under consideration by the U.S. Supreme Court. As a practical matter, for most people in this category the need for an accommodation does not arise. If you are asymptomatic and develop a problem at work related to your condition, consult your GuardianOrg or an attorney for advice tailored to your needs.

1.3 Hiring and Rehiring

Voluntary information. A preemployment interview is not a confessional—you do not have to volunteer any information about your health. The only information that is relevant relates to your ability to perform the essential duties of the job you seek.

Questions from employers—before an offer is made. Before the ADA, prospective employers often requested medical information from the applicant at the same time as other information. Those rejected had no way of knowing if a medical condition was the reason for not being hired. The ADA was designed to isolate the employer's consideration of health information, enabling applicants to assess whether the employer unlawfully discriminated against them based on disability.

Under the ADA, the only questions a prospective employer may ask you *during the preemployment process* relate to your ability to perform the essential duties of the job under discussion. Prospective employers may not ask any questions that tend to elicit medical information or require medical examinations until after a provisional offer of employment has been made. Thus, at this interview stage, it is illegal to ask you or your previous employer questions related to your health, including what prescriptions or over-the-counter drugs you take or even whether you've missed work in your previous job due to illness.

If your disability is somehow apparent, even if the employer has reason to believe that the disability may interfere with or prevent the performance of job-related duties, the employer may not ask about the existence, nature, or severity of the disability. On the other hand, the employer is allowed to ask specific questions about your ability to perform the essential duties of the job. For example, an employer may ask an applicant with one leg who is seeking employment as a home washing-machine repair person how she would be able to transport herself and her tools down basement steps. It would not be appropriate for the employer to ask how the applicant lost her leg, because the loss of the leg may indicate some underlying impairment that may be a disability under the ADA. It is also inappropriate to ask an applicant with a known disability how she would accomplish a task not related to her disability, unless the inquiry is made of all applicants.

Employers may not refuse to hire you now because they fear you will become too ill to work in the future. The only relevant consideration is how well you can perform now. They also cannot take into account possible higher medical insurance costs, workers' compensation costs, or absenteeism.

Employers may discriminate against people who pose a direct threat—a significant risk of substantial harm—to the health or safety of themselves or others, as long as that risk cannot be eliminated or reduced below the level of a "direct threat" through reasonable accommodation. An employer may not just assume that a threat exists: there must be objective, medically supportable proof.

Tip. If you want to know more about the questions an employer can ask you, contact the EEOC at 800-669-3302 or 202-663-4900.

For tips on what to say and what not to say during a job interview, see chapter 7, section 4.3.

Questions from employers—after an offer is made. *After* a conditional offer of employment is made, the employer may request medical information and require medical examinations, *but only*
- *if such information is asked of all applicants, and*
- *if there is a legitimate business reason for asking.*

If information about a disability is revealed during this process, and the applicant is not offered the position because of the disability, the employer must be able to demonstrate that the exclusion is (1) job-related, (2) consistent with business necessity, and (3) that no reasonable accommodation was possible. (See the next section for a discussion of "reasonable accommodation.")

Reemployment inquiries. Your employer is allowed to seek information about your health when you return to work after a disability leave. Again, the scope of the inquiry is limited to your ability to perform the duties of the job, nothing more.

1.4 Reasonable Accommodation: When a Disability Interferes with Work

Once an offer has been made, as well as during the entire period of employment, the ADA protects workers with disabilities (under the law, such a person is known as "a qualified person") who can perform the *essential functions* of the job they have or seek with or without *reasonable accommodation*. There is no requirement to be able to perform the job perfectly, only that you are qualified for it and that you can perform the essential functions.

Essential functions. Essential functions refer to those tasks that are absolutely necessary to the successful performance of the job. To determine the essential functions of a job, consider three factors:

- Performance of the task is the reason the position exists.
- A limited number of employees are available to perform the task.
- The task may require highly specialized expertise, limiting hiring to persons with those skills or training.

For example, the essential functions of a secretary are to answer the phone, to take messages, to work on a computer or a typewriter, to handle people, and to organize schedules and paperwork. The ability to walk is an incidental or marginal job function, not an essential one.

Reasonable accommodation. With many illnesses, there will be a disability-based limitation that will require some kind of an accommodation. The law requires that employers provide "reasonable accommodations" for employees with disabilities who can perform the essential functions of the job. An employer may do more than required by the ADA, but may not do less.

The law only comes into play when an employer is aware of a disability and an employee seeks reasonable accommodation. *In other words, you are not protected unless the employer is aware of your condition.* This means that if the lack of an accommodation is affecting your job performance, but you do not request accommodation from your employer, you would not be protected by the ADA if you are discharged for poor performance.

Under the ADA, "reasonable accommodation" may include

- making existing employee facilities readily accessible to, and usable by, individuals with disabilities.
- job restructuring; part-time or modified work schedules; reassignment to a vacant position; acquisition or modification of equipment or devices; appropriate adjustment or modification of examinations, training materials, or policies; providing readers or interpreters.
- something as simple as permitting an employee to telecommute (work at home with a telephone and perhaps a computer).

Any accommodation will be an inconvenience to the employer. That doesn't matter. The employer must provide accommodation so long as it does not result in an "undue hardship" to the employer. *Undue hardship* is a relative term and must be examined in each instance. *Undue hardship* means an action requiring significant difficulty or expense when considered in light of various factors, including but not limited to

- the nature and cost of the accommodation.
- the overall financial resources of the employer.
- the number of persons employed.
- the effect on the employer's finances or resources or other impact of the accommodation.

A company like General Motors will clearly be required to do more to accommodate its employees than a small law firm.

Examples of reasonable accommodation.

- Kathy B. is a schoolteacher who experienced problems with memory, coordination, concentration, and balance as a result of an automobile accident. A school district could reasonably accommodate Kathy by providing her with a teaching assistant.

- Rhona L., a chemist with severe depression, had limited ability to deal with the public. However, only about 5 percent of her job involved communication with the public. Her employer reasonably accommodated Rhona's condition by changing the job and allowing her to communicate by mail, or if telephone contact was required, providing someone to talk for her.
- An employer with many offices and locations might be required to consider transferring a worker to a location where better medical treatment would be available if a similar position is open there.
- Jim W. worked as a night-shift data-entry operator, but could no longer work at night because it made his clinical depression worse. Since no accommodation could be made in his current position, his employer could reasonably be required to accommodate him by transferring Jim to a day-shift data-entry operator position if one was available, or even a *different* day-shift position for which he qualified if no daytime data-entry operator positions were available. This does not mean that Jim's employer is required to bump workers from other positions or that the employer must create a new position.
- *An employer is not obligated to provide the accommodation that the employee desires. The employer is only required to provide some reasonable accommodation.* Thus, a hospital was not required to offer a transfer to Peter N., a probationary hemodialysis nurse who was having difficulty mastering the tasks of his job because of his disability, where instead the hospital offered Alan additional training. While transfer may have been a reasonable accommodation, so was the additional training, and the employer could exercise its discretion in offering its preferred accommodation.
- Requiring a small law firm on the fourth floor of a walk-up building to put in an elevator is an undue hardship.

Tip. Be aware that if the accommodation involves doing less work, your employer may pay you less. However, your insurance benefits may not be decreased.

If you requested a reasonable accommodation such as recovery time after a chemotherapy treatment and it was rejected, don't just take the time off and call in sick. Write a letter to human resources as well as to the appropriate person in the chain of command, such as the president of the company. Explain that you requested the day off, which should have been granted under the Americans with Disabilities Act (or other appropriate law), and that you would appreciate reconsideration.

Tip. Where there may be a reaction that will prevent your working for the next day or two, schedule chemotherapy and other treatments for after work on Fridays or before holidays.

Getting a reasonable accommodation at work. You need to make an honest personal assessment of what workplace accommodation you require to enable you to continue working. Talk to your physician(s) for advice about the limitations imposed by your illness. This is an assessment that you will have to revisit if your health changes.

Negotiating a reasonable accommodation from your employer involves balancing your needs against the financial resources of the employer. As you undertake the negotiation, think of your relationship with your employer as a cooperative problem-solving relationship rather than an adversarial one.

Tip. Start the negotiation by jointly reviewing your job description and the essential functions of the job. Identify and evaluate potential accommodations. Look for the accommodation that works best for you without "undue hardship" on the employer.

If you are aware of others in your workplace who have required and received accommodation, you might want to try to learn from their experience. You might also want to ask for advice from the Job Accommodation Network (JAN). JAN provides free information about job accommodation and the employability of people with disabilities. With a call to 800-526-7234 (8 A.M. to 8 P.M. ET, M–Th, and 8 A.M. to 5 P.M. on Fridays), a professional consultant will ask a few simple questions about the requirements of the job, you, and the work environment. Based on the information you provide, JAN will recommend accommodations for your situation.

Where appropriate, JAN will provide the names and phone numbers of employers or workers who have made similar accommodations and provide other information, such as training programs, job descriptions, funding resources, and tax incentives.

1.5 Confidentiality and Disclosure

Whether or not to disclose your diagnosis to your employer and your coworkers is up to you. Legally

- you are not required to reveal any information about your health status to your employer unless there is a legitimate business reason.
- you can't be discriminated against because of your disability. However, the law only comes into play when your employer is aware of your disability. The only way you can prove that the employer had such an awareness is if you can document that you informed your employer. When asking your employer for a reasonable accommodation, it isn't sufficient to say, "I have a disability covered by the ADA that causes problems at work." The employer has the right to medical documentation of your disability and the limitations resulting from that disability.

The only exception to the rule that you don't have to disclose your health status is if the disease is somehow relevant to the performance of the essential duties of the job. For example, a court has held that a hospital could require, as part of its infection-control practices, that an HIV-infected worker disclose his HIV status. Discharge for failure to do so is viewed as a discharge for failure to comply with an employer policy, rather than discharge because of a disability.

In addition to obtaining a "reasonable accommodation," disclosing your condition may elicit social support, care, and generosity from your coworkers, as well as information from others who have been in a similar situation. Disclosure, particularly if it is in writing, may even prompt your employer to find out what his/her legal rights and/or obligations are. It also lets your employer know that you know your rights and won't accept any less.

On the other hand, a lot of people view the situation as Michael N. does: "If you don't have to tell, don't tell the employer until you're ready to jump off the boat into disability." Not only do you avoid any questions about matters such as pay raises, you may also avoid subtle (or not so subtle) changes in work relationships. While not telling may be the most protective strategy to maximize your income, there is the price in stress of keeping this major personal event secret.

Tip. It is helpful to do a Life Units analysis here. Disclosing your condition and getting accommodation will mean making your job more doable—less time-consuming or tiring—resulting in an increase in Life Units available for anything else you want to do. Figure out if telling will cause you more or less stress. Will it have other consequences? The bottom line is, if you want or need some accommodation at work, some disclosure of health information will be required.

What you disclose to your employer is confidential. Any medical information that you provide to your employer *must* be maintained on separate forms and in separate medical files and must be treated as a confidential medical record. The only exceptions to the requirement for confidentiality are that

- the employer may provide relevant information to supervisors and managers regarding necessary restrictions on your work duties and necessary accommodations.
- supervisory and safety personnel may be provided with relevant information for emergency situations.
- government officials investigating compliance with the ADA must be provided with relevant information on request.

Whom you tell will vary depending on where you work. In a large employment setting, consider telling someone in the human resources department rather than your immediate supervisor. The larger the company the more likely that someone in human resources will have the knowledge, training, and/or experience with the law and company policies to secure the accommodation you need, and to keep the information confidential as required by law.

Tip. The reality of most employment settings is that nothing is confidential. However, it is some consolation to know that the law provides a remedy if you are harmed through your employer's disclosure of information.

Prepare what you will say. Before you talk to your employer, play out the discussions in your head and prepare yourself for all conceivable reactions to the news. Decide whom you will tell and decide whether you want any others present. You may even choose to have someone else tell your employer, such as a union representative or someone in personnel. Decide up front how much you wish to tell, but be flexible so that you can be prepared for any conversation. Carefully prepare so that you do not disclose more than you had planned.

When to tell your employer. Consider the timing of your disclosure. You may not have any choice if you need some accommodation immediately. However, if there is no immediate need to disclose, consider not disclosing at all or timing your disclosure so that it comes at the best time for you—not during a crisis and not before a raise or bonus is due. After disclosure, you should be prepared for the possibility of a job and salary freeze.

Tip. If timing when you tell is important to you, and you have health insurance coverage through your employer, consider whether the claims you make under the plan will result in a disclosure before you are ready. Under the law of most states, information relating to your health is confidential. The insurance company is not supposed to inform your employer about your health. However, a friendly relationship between the benefits person in your company and the contact person in the health care company can lead to gossip. Under an indemnity policy, you can choose to pay the costs yourself until either you are ready to tell or the dollar amounts become so large that you are willing to take the risk.

What you disclose to coworkers is *not* confidential under the ADA. Before proceeding, carefully evaluate your motives for telling a particular person and the benefits of such disclosure. It is also important to recognize that there may be some people you should never tell.

Keep in mind that with respect to accommodation, coworkers may wonder why your schedule has suddenly become flexible, or why you have received some other accommodation. This can lead to negative attention as opposed to the support that you *might* get if your coworkers were aware that your schedule has been modified because of your life-challenging condition. Consider discussing with your employer the possibility of providing coworkers with information about your illness. In fact, employer education of the workforce can be a part of the accommodation necessary for you to be able to do your job.

Reactions can change over time. Keep in mind that reactions may change as information is processed and others see the extent to which your condition does or does not affect your performance. An initial negative reaction may change to a positive one. On the other hand, when they first learn of your condition, many employers will tell you they will do anything they can to help you, but they may have second and third thoughts as they live with the situation.

1.6 Protecting the Family and Friends of a Disabled Person from Discrimination at Work

Sometimes workers will be subjected to discrimination at work because a family member or someone with whom they are known to have a relationship or association suffers from a disability—even if the cause of the disability is not contagious. Such discrimination can be caused by a variety of motivations including ignorance, prejudice, or a fear that the disability will increase the costs of family health benefits coverage for everyone. In addition to prohibiting disability-based employment discrimination, the ADA also prohibits excluding or otherwise denying equal jobs or benefits to a qualified individual because the person is known to have a relationship or association with an individual who has a disability.

1.7 Advancement Issues and Bonuses

An employer is prohibited from limiting your duties based on a belief it is best for you or based on a presumption of your abilities. As in other areas, the law requires that an individualized assessment be made as to the employee's ability to advance.

Your employer is also prohibited from demoting you, denying you pay raises, or limiting your bonuses based on your condition.

Tip. Obtain copies (or at least make journal entries as they occur) of positive job actions such as a performance evaluation. They can help prove you were qualified for the job in the event you are later discriminated against.

1.8 If You Are Discriminated Against

Discrimination can be difficult to prove. Discrimination is generally not like a car crash: it doesn't usually happen all of a sudden. It's seldom as overt as an employer telling you your salary is being cut or your raise is not being given or you are being terminated because of your condition. A discriminatory employer is more likely to blame your job performance or economic conditions for a decision to demote or terminate you.

As soon as you believe you may be subject to discrimination:

1. Immediately start keeping a journal of the events that appear to be discriminatory. Update the journal daily, at night rather than at work so people don't see what you are doing. Include dates, a description of what happened, and list the names and addresses of all participants and witnesses, if there are any. Preferably, the journal should be handwritten so it shows it hasn't been altered. Don't "fix it up" later, that hurts the value of the journal. Be sure to include positive performance comments or evaluations that may help to prove you were qualified for the job.

2. You don't want to say something that could jeopardize your legal rights. Consult a lawyer familiar with employment discrimination. The lawyer will also know the statutory deadlines you have to keep in mind, some of which can be very short.

3. With the advice of a lawyer, try to resolve the matter with your employer.
- Use your employer's policies and procedures for resolving employment issues.
- Perhaps one of your support team members can help negotiate a reasonable accommodation.
- Enlist the cooperation of coworkers—they may need similar help one day.

• Consider requesting that your employer use a third-party mediator.

4. Get help from federal, state, or local agencies that safeguard the rights of people with disabilities, including the federal Equal Employment Opportunity Commission.

Tip. If you believe you have a claim against your employer and leave your job for whatever reason, signing a release to the employer will prevent you from doing anything about that claim.

Before you can sue. If your state does not have antidiscrimination laws, you must file a complaint with the EEOC within 180 days after the alleged discriminatory act. If your state has an antidiscrimination regulation, you must file a complaint with that agency first. You can file a complaint on your own, but I suggest seeking legal advice first.

Also, think about

• what you want to achieve in a lawsuit. Do you want your job back? Money? A change in the employer's policies to benefit other workers? Something else?

• the advantages and disadvantages of a suit. Is what you want to achieve worth the stress and the alienation of your employer and/or possibly your friends at work?

Damages under the ADA. If you win a claim for violation of the ADA, you win

• your costs.

• damages to the extent that you were not able to mitigate (reduce) them. For example, if you're fired, you have to look for another job, even one that may pay less. Keep a log of what you did to mitigate your damages. A journal of your subsequent job search would include want ads, phone calls, interviews and results—with names and dates.

Your damages may include

• back pay (what you would have received).

• benefits.

• front pay (wages you'll lose because you can't

get another job, or compensation if you do get one for less money).

• compensatory damages to make up for any other damages you may have incurred.

• injunctive relief such as reinstatement.

• punitive damages up to $300,000 to punish the employer and deter it from future illegal discrimination.

• attorney fees.

Collecting disability benefits while pursuing a suit under the ADA. In several court cases, workers who were discharged because of their disabilities have filed suit against their employers, alleging disability discrimination, and in the meantime have sought disability benefits under Social Security. There is a conflict between alleging discrimination that indicates you are able to continue to work while at the same time requesting benefits under Social Security, for which you have to state you are disabled and cannot work.

Some courts have recognized that workers may be "disabled" for benefits purposes, but could work if reasonable accommodation were provided. Other courts have held that seeking disability benefits is inconsistent with seeking protection under the ADA. Officials of the Equal Employment Opportunity Commission and Social Security are attempting to resolve this matter as this book is being written. If this matter is of concern to you, ask your GuardianOrg or an attorney for the latest information.

Federal Rehabilitation Act. If your employer receives federal funds, you should file the complaint with the federal agency that provides the funds to your employer. Remedies are the same as under the ADA, except there are no punitive damage awards.

Tip. Consider filing a complaint with each relevant enforcement agency. You can put a complaint on hold or drop it after you see which agency is responding best.

Section 2. Leaves of Absence: Family and Medical Leave Act and the ADA

If you need to take a leave of absence because a serious health condition prevents you from performing one or more of the essential functions of your job, you may want to consider whether you are entitled to a leave under the Family and Medical Leave Act (FMLA) before you request a leave as part of a reasonable accommodation under the ADA. A leave of absence is also available under the FMLA to care for your spouse, child, or parent with a serious health condition.

2.1 Leaves of Absence Under the FMLA

Eligibility. To be eligible for a leave under the FMLA

- you must work for an employer covered by the law. All state and local government employers are covered by the FMLA, but the law only covers private employers with fifty or more employees who work within a seventy-five mile radius of your job site.
- you must have been employed by the employer for at least twelve months and accumulated 1,250 hours of service with the covered employer for the twelve-month period prior to the leave.
- you must provide a reason for the leave that is covered under the law.
- you must earn less than the employees in your company's top 10 percent salary range of employees within a seventy-five-mile radius of your job site.

Tip. If you are not covered under the FMLA, check to determine if your state has comparable provisions under which you may be covered.

Amount of leave of absence. An employee entitled to FMLA leave may take up to twelve weeks of leave in a twelve-month period. An employer can choose to count accrued paid benefits such as vacation, sick leave, and personal leave days as part of the leave or add them to the leave, depending on the company's policy. For example, if an employee already took two weeks' vacation, there might only be ten weeks of protected job leave left.

Special rules apply to employees of "local educational agencies," including elementary and secondary schools, but excluding colleges, universities, trade schools, and preschools.

Continuity of leave of absence. If the leave is for an employee's own condition, the leave does not have to be continuous. It can be broken up over the year, and only the time actually taken counts.

Continuation of health coverage during leave of absence. Employers are not required to pay an employee while on leave. However, a major protection in the law is that the employer *must* maintain the employee's existing level of coverage in a group health plan, including a continuation of the pattern of paying premiums. Thus, if an employer pays part or all of an employee's premiums, it must continue to do so while the employee is on leave.

If the employee pays for part of the health benefit, the employer's obligation to continue health benefits in force ends if

- the employee doesn't make premium payments when due (including the grace period, if any);
- the employee quits or doesn't return to work; or
- the employee has used all the time permitted under the act.

In these instances, the employee should look at the discussion about COBRA to determine if there is a right to continue coverage under that act (see section 4 of this chapter).

Employment after leave of absence. Another good feature of the law requires the employer to reemploy the employee in the same or a similar position at the end of a leave. If the employee is no longer able to perform an essential function of the job at the end of the leave, reinstatement is not required. If the inability to perform the essential function is due to a disability covered by the ADA, the ADA's reasonable accommodation requirements come into play as outlined below.

Notice of leave of absence. If leave is requested, the employer must be given at least thirty days' notice unless the situation was not "foreseeable," in which case notice must be given as soon as practicable.

Proof of medical condition. If leave is requested, the employer may request, and the employee must provide, proof about the physical condition of the employee or the person to be cared for.

Complaints. If you believe your rights under the FMLA have been violated, you may file a complaint with the Employment Standards Administration, Wage and Hour Division, of the U.S. Department of Labor.

2.2 Leaves of Absence Under the ADA

If your employer is covered by the ADA, leave may be available as a reasonable accommodation, so long as leave does not cause the employer undue hardship. The undue hardship concept also governs the available length of ADA leave. During an ADA leave, the employer only has to maintain benefits coverage for an employee if it maintains coverage for other employees on similar leave. At the end of an ADA leave, the employee is entitled to reinstatement unless the employer can establish that keeping the position open is an undue hardship. The employer must then consider placing the employee in available equivalent positions. If none exist, then the employee must be considered for positions at a lower level. The duty to accommodate ends after that.

Tip. The requirements of the FMLA and ADA are only minimum requirements and, as you have seen, only govern in certain instances. It is worthwhile to check your employer's policies: they may go well beyond the legal minimum. Even if they don't, you may be able to negotiate better for yourself.

2.3 Combining Your Rights to a Leave of Absence Under the ADA and the FMLA

Leaves of absence for yourself.
• If you work for an employer subject to the FMLA and you meet the leave eligibility requirements, you are *entitled to* a leave upon request to your employer. If, however, your employer is not covered by the FMLA, but is subject to the ADA, you can *request* a leave as a reasonable accommodation, so long as the condition for which you seek leave is a disability under the ADA. Your employer, however, is not required to provide the leave, if such leave poses undue hardship or if some other reasonable accommodation is available and the employer offers it.
• If you take a leave under the FMLA and still require more time off after twelve weeks, you may request that your employer consider leave as a possible ADA reasonable accommodation. The condition for which you seek leave must be a disability under the ADA, and the undue-hardship analysis comes into play.
• If, during a twelve-month period, you have taken a leave as an ADA reasonable accommodation, you would only be able to take an FMLA leave during that same period to the extent that the prior leave did not exhaust the twelve-week FMLA maximum.

Leaves of absence to care for others. While a worker may be entitled to a leave under the FMLA to care for an ill child, spouse, or parent, such leave is not available as a reasonable accommodation under the ADA. Reasonable accommodation only applies to a *worker's disability-related limitations*.

2.4 The FMLA and "Nontraditional" Family Relationships

The FMLA only allows a leave to care for a husband, wife, father, mother, or child. If you need to take a leave to care for someone who does not fit into one of the FMLA "family" categories, consider requesting such a leave from your employer, pointing out that the relationship you have with the ill person is similar to one of the FMLA categories. Unmarried heterosexual or same-sex couples in such a situation should determine whether local law or employer internal policy prohibits discrimination based on marital status or sexual orientation. If such a prohibition exists, you could suggest to your employer that failure to provide leave violates it because leave is conditioned on being married. You might want to discuss this issue with a lawyer should you wish to pursue it.

2.5 Unprotected Leave

Even if your employer is not covered by the FMLA, you may request that you be provided with an unpaid leave to care for a loved one. For many employers, providing unpaid leave is preferable to losing an experienced worker. In addition, while they are not required to do so, many employers allow workers to use their own sick-leave time to care for an ill family member.

Section 3. Benefit Protections While You Are Employed

When an employer becomes concerned about increasing insurance costs associated with employee illnesses, it may attempt to take steps to limit costs. An employer's ability to do so may be limited by the Employee Retirement Income Security Act (ERISA), by the ADA, and by the Health Insurance Portability and Accountability Act of 1996 (HIPAA).

3.1 ERISA

ERISA prohibits an employer from discharging or discriminating against a worker for exercising rights under an employee benefit plan. That means that you cannot be fired or otherwise discriminated against because you are using the employer's health plan.

3.2 ADA

Under the ADA, it is unlawful for an employer to discriminate on the basis of a disability with respect to the benefits it provides to its employees. This ADA prohibition does not affect preexisting-conditions clauses in health insurance policies offered to employees unless a preexisting-conditions clause can be shown to be a cover for discrimination. To illustrate, a preexisting-conditions clause that limits coverage only for a discrete group of related disabilities such as hemophilia or leukemia is an unlawful disability-based distinction, unless the employer can show that the exclusion is not discrimination.

Similarly, caps on the dollar amount of coverage are lawful so long as they do not discriminate based on a particular disability. For example, an insurance plan that caps benefits for all physical conditions except AIDS at $500,000, yet provides a $50,000 cap for AIDS, would be an unlawful disability-based distinction unless the employer was able to prove that it was not a subterfuge for discrimination. But an employer's plan does not violate the ADA, for example, if it provides a lower level of benefits for the treatment of mental/nervous conditions than it does for physical conditions, or if it limits coverage on medical procedures that are *not* exclusively, or nearly exclusively, used for the treatment of a particular disability.

Section 4. Benefit Protections After Leaving Your Job: COBRA

There are several ways to continue coverage after terminating employment. The most commonly used method is **COBRA,** the federal Consolidated Omnibus Budget Reconciliation Act, under which certain former employees and their beneficiaries continue health insurance coverage under the prior employer's group plan for up to eighteen months. If you become "disabled" during the first sixty days of your COBRA coverage, COBRA can continue coverage for an additional eleven months to a total of twenty-nine months. The continuation period was set in a 1989 modification to COBRA known as OBRA so people would continue to be covered by health insurance until Medicare starts, which is twenty-nine months after leaving work for disability (a five-month waiting period, plus twenty-four months of Social Security Disability benefits). If COBRA does not apply, state laws generally provide the same coverage. It is also usually possible to continue coverage to some extent by the terms of the employer's plan, such as by means of conversion to individual coverage.

Employers covered by COBRA. The law generally covers group health plans (including self-insured plans) maintained by employers with more than twenty employees during at least 50 percent of the prior year. The law applies to private employers and to state and local governments. It does not apply to the federal government and certain church-related organizations. Many states have similar laws that apply to employers with fewer than twenty employees. If you work for an employer with fewer than twenty employees, contact your state Department of Insurance for more details (see the resources section). Some employers not required by state or federal requirements to offer continuation coverage do so anyway, and some employer plans offer continuation for more than eighteen months.

Coverage that is continued. Health, dental, and vision benefits continue under COBRA. Life and disability benefits do not. The health coverage to be continued is required to be the same as offered to the employer's other similarly situated employees covered under the plan for whom a qualifying event has not occurred. This can be a double-edged sword. If the group coverage for current employees is expanded, so is the continued coverage. On the other hand, if the insurance is eliminated or the company goes out of business, the right to continue the coverage is lost.

When former employees are entitled to seek continued coverage. Under COBRA, former employees may continue health coverage if it would otherwise be lost due to a **qualifying event.** Qualifying events include

• voluntary or involuntary termination of employment, including termination due to disability—so long as the termination was not due to "gross misconduct."

• reduction in the number of hours of employment.

• for people over age sixty-five, Chapter 11 bankruptcy filing by the employer.

The COBRA disability continuation. The COBRA disability continuation is not automatic. It must be applied for. To qualify for the continuation

• you must apply for and receive an award of Social Security Disability Insurance benefits (see chapter 8, section 8.1) prior to the end of the eighteen-month COBRA period. Even if you are not eligible for this government benefit, Social Security will still review the claim for continuation purposes, although you may need to see a supervisor.

• the date of disability onset as determined by Social Security and stated in the Notice of Award Letter must be before or within sixty days after the date your COBRA coverage started.

• a copy of the Notice of Award Letter *must* be

sent to the COBRA administrator (usually whoever collects the premiums) within sixty days of receiving the Award letter.

An employee's spouse or dependent—continued coverage. An employee's spouse or dependent may continue coverage subsequent to "qualifying events," which would otherwise result in termination of coverage, including

- termination of the covered employee's employment for any reason other than "gross misconduct."
- reduction in the hours worked by the covered employee.
- covered employees becoming entitled to Medicare.
- divorce or legal separation from the covered employee.
- death of the covered employee.
- in the case of a "dependent child," loss of dependent child status under the plan rules.

Length of time you or your beneficiaries are covered. As you will see in the chart below, the period varies depending upon the qualifying event under which the employee or the employee's beneficiary became entitled to seek continuation coverage.

COBRA coverage may be retained even after you obtain new group medical insurance to the extent the new employer's health plan limits coverage with respect to preexisting conditions.

Tip. Consider asking your employer to continue you as part of the group indefinitely. Your employer may agree and may even agree to continue to pay your premiums. There seems to be little, if anything, to lose by asking. To be sure this doesn't become a problem for the employer (and your coverage), the employer should inform the insurance company of the arrangement.

Notice requirements. Notice requirements are triggered when a qualifying event occurs.

- Your employer is legally required to provide you written notice of your COBRA rights within fourteen days of leaving the job.
- Employees must notify plan administrators within sixty days of a qualifying event or the date you were notified of your rights, whichever is later.
- If a qualifying event affects a qualified beneficiary, the employee must notify the plan administrator within sixty days after the qualifying event. The employer then has fourteen days to notify the beneficiary of the right to continue

COBRA Coverage

Qualifying Event	Beneficiary	Coverage
Termination or reduced hours	Employee, spouse, dependent child	18 months
Employee leaves work and is "disabled" for purposes of Social Security	Employee	18 months plus 11-month continuation = 29 months total
Employee entitled to Medicare and there is a divorce, legal separation, or death	Spouse, dependent child	36 months
Loss of dependent child status	Dependent child	36 months

coverage. The beneficiary has to notify the administrator if the beneficiary wants to continue coverage within an additional sixty days of the date notice is sent, or sixty days of the event, whichever is later.

If you qualify as disabled under Social Security, and you plan to exercise your right to the additional eleven months of coverage, you must notify your employer or the plan administrator during the initial eighteen-month period *and* within sixty days of the Social Security Administration (SSA) determination of disability. The notification must state that you have been determined to be disabled by the SSA and request continuation of your health coverage for the entire twenty-nine-month period.

Tip. The notice to your employer should state the date on which the SSA determined you were disabled and that you plan to exercise your right to any continuation of coverage authorized under applicable law. Send the notice in such a manner that you receive a receipt proving the notice was received. Keep a copy of the receipt and a copy of your notice with your important papers.

Tip. If you do not receive COBRA notification, contact your employer's personnel office or plan administrator and request a COBRA election form. A check payable to your employer for an estimated monthly premium should be enclosed with the letter. Send the letter in a manner that provides a receipt showing it was received.

Payment for the continued coverage. In most cases, the employee or other beneficiary pays the cost of premiums. The employer can voluntarily agree to pay for continued coverage. The premium charged to an employee cannot exceed 102 percent of the cost to the plan for "similarly situated individuals who have not incurred a qualifying event." There is usually a thirty-day grace period after the due date to pay premiums, but it is best not to take advantage of the grace period because if the premium is late, the coverage can be can-

celed and will probably not be reinstated. If you cannot afford the premiums, there may be a local program to pay for them. Ask your GuardianOrg.

During the additional eleven months permitted for employees who leave work for disability, the premium may be increased to a maximum of 150 percent. Since this "disability" is determined by the Social Security Administration, be careful when you complete your Social Security application (see chapter 10).

Note: You (and your beneficiaries) have forty-five days after the initial COBRA election to make the required premium payment. The payment should be for the full premium retroactive to the start date.

Termination of COBRA. Cobra ends if
- premiums are not paid as due, or within the thirty-day grace period.
- you become eligible for coverage under another group policy (such as with a new employer)—even if the coverage is not as good as the coverage that is terminating. As an exception, under HIPAA, if the new coverage has a preexisting-condition exclusion that applies to you, the COBRA coverage continues until the preexisting-condition exclusion expires or the end of the COBRA continuation period, whichever is earlier.
- the employer stops offering group health insurance to current employees or goes out of business.
- you qualify for Medicare coverage. If this is the reason for termination, and you anticipate substantial unreimbursed costs under Medicare, consider converting your COBRA coverage to an individual policy or a Medicare HMO.

Section 5. Protecting Your Benefits After Leaving Your Job: Other Rights

5.1 Conversion

If you do not have a legal right to continue your health coverage and have no other method of obtaining health insurance (see chapter 14), look at your group coverage to determine if it contains a right to convert it into individual coverage without evidence of insurability. If it does, the individual coverage is usually expensive and is seldom as good as the coverage from which you are converting, but it is better than nothing. Generally, the conversion must be applied for within thirty-one days of coverage termination.

It is preferable to have both conversion coverage and a disability extension of benefits (see section 5.3 below) simultaneously. The disability extension pays for medical conditions that caused the disability, while the conversion coverage pays for claims not related to the disability. The conversion policy becomes your primary coverage when the disability extension expires.

When plans are converted, employees are usually offered several plan options. It is preferable to choose the option with the best benefits, even though it is probably also the most expensive.

5.2 Changes in the Benefit Plan While You Are Exercising Continuation Rights

Many workers continue to be covered by a former employer's plan after they are no longer employed. If an employer changes plans while a former employee is exercising continuation rights, the former employee will be covered under the new plan like the rest of the group. Sometimes an employer attempts to make a disability-based change (either by changing plans or within a plan), which could violate the ADA. At least one court has held that because someone exercising continuation rights is no longer an employee, he cannot rely on the ADA to challenge such a change since the ADA only protects employees. This decision is not consistent with other civil rights laws, which have been interpreted to protect former employees. If you have a problem like this, you should consult your GuardianOrg or an attorney familiar with employee benefit and disability law.

5.3 Disability Extension

Under your plan or state law, if you are disabled at the time your group insurance ends, no matter what the reason for the termination of coverage, your health insurance coverage generally continues as an "extension" (usually for one year). Coverage is typically limited to medical expenses directly related to the disabling condition. The disabling condition is the underlying condition, not a resulting condition. For example, if PCP resulting from HIV/AIDS is the immediate cause of disability, health matters relating to the underlying HIV/AIDS would be covered, not just PCP. On the other hand, if you developed medical problems not relating to HIV/AIDS, they would not be covered.

There is no charge for coverage during the extension.

While the extension can start anytime after your group insurance ends (not just when you leave your job), it can be particularly useful if you obtain new health insurance that has a preexisting-condition exclusion, such as with an employer not covered under HIPAA. The new policy would probably exclude a preexisting condition for up to a year, but you would be covered for the condition during that year by the extension of your previous coverage.

Disability extensions are different from COBRA. COBRA must be elected prior to exercising a disability extension. However, disability extensions may be available after COBRA terminates.

The disability extension should be requested in writing from your employer or plan administrator. Since the extended coverage is only for medical expenses caused by the disability, the physician should describe the exact cause of the disability as broadly as possible. All disability-related conditions should be included in the diagnosis.

Tip. If you have to convert your coverage, you may want to exercise your right to a disability extension at the same time. *It does not cost anything to extend coverage in this manner,* and any expenses paid by the insurance carrier under the extension are not applied against any maximum payment that may be included in the converted policy.

Section 6. Health Insurance Protection: HIPAA

The Health Insurance Portability and Accountability Act of 1996 (HIPAA)—also known as the Kassebaum-Kennedy Act—helps prevent job-lock for people with life-challenging conditions by limiting the use of preexisting-condition limitations in employer plans. The law does not force any employer to provide group health coverage—it only provides what happens if an employer does offer such coverage.

Coverage in a new job. Under HIPAA, no employer group health policy for two or more employees can refuse an otherwise eligible person health coverage *if all* of the following factors are satisfied:

- You have at least eighteen months of "creditable coverage" and not more than sixty-three days have elapsed between the end of that coverage and commencement of the new coverage. **Creditable coverage** means health insurance of just about any kind, including group or individual, COBRA, Medicare, and Medicaid, provided there is no gap in coverage that lasts more than sixty-three days between the end of the last coverage and enrollment in the new plan. To assist in proving coverage, the law requires employers to provide departing employees, in writing, the number of months covered under the plan.
- The most recent part of the creditable coverage was under a group health plan of an employer, the government, or a church plan.
- Your last coverage was not terminated due to nonpayment of premiums or fraud.
- You are not currently eligible for group coverage, Medicare, or Medicaid and you do not have any other health insurance in place.

- If you had a chance to continue your former coverage under COBRA or a similar state plan, you selected the coverage, and it is exhausted.

If you qualify under this law, you are also guaranteed the right to renew the coverage. The insurance company can ask health questions, but the information can only be used for rating purposes. The new plan must apply the time you were covered under your prior plan toward the new plan's preexisting-conditions waiting period. The sixty-three days measured for purposes of prior lapses does not count any probationary period at the new employer.

The law also provides additional protections:

- Your health status and medical condition cannot be considered in determining initial or continued eligibility for health coverage.
- A "health status–related factor" cannot be used to charge one employee higher premiums than other employees.
- The amount or nature of benefits may only be limited or restricted if it applies to all "similarly situated individuals." For example, a cap on coverage would affect people with a health condition more than the average worker, but it is permissible if it does not discriminate.
- For employees who sign up at the commencement of a new job, the period of a preexisting-condition exclusion cannot be greater than twelve months from the commencement of employment. This limitation ties in with the twelve months' extension that most people have when they leave previous employment (see section 5.3 above). This preexisting-condition exclusion period can be extended to eighteen months if the employee signs up for the plan after commencement of the new job, so don't wait.
- The length of the exclusionary period is reduced by the length of previous creditable coverage. To illustrate, if Kristy had health coverage for six months with her previous employer, and only thirty days lapsed between her old and new jobs, and her new employer's plan has a twelve-month exclusion period for coverage of

preexisting conditions, Kristy's preexisting condition would be covered under the new plan starting six months after she starts the new job. If she had coverage in her old job for at least twelve months, there would be no preexisting-condition exclusion at all!

If HIPAA does not provide the protection you need, check to see if there is a similar law in your state.

Preexisting conditions. HIPAA limits "preexisting conditions" to conditions that required "medical advice, diagnosis, care or treatment . . . recommended or received" within the six months prior to the new employment. If treatment for your condition was not recommended or received within that time (no matter the extent of treatment prior to that time), an exclusion cannot be imposed by the new employer.

Enrollment periods. The law also provides for special enrollment periods for employees with health conditions who did not sign up for the coverage on commencement of the new job.

Self-employment/New employer without coverage. If you leave an employer with a group health plan and become self-employed or go to an employer that does not offer health insurance, in addition to your rights under COBRA, if there was prior coverage for at least eighteen months and you obtain the new coverage within sixty-three days after termination of coverage, you will be able to obtain coverage from any company writing individual health insurance in your state with no preexisting condition exclusion. The law requires the insurance companies to offer at least two of their most popular plans based on premium volume. The law does not set any rate limits on this coverage.

Tip: If you are going from group to individual coverage, anticipate the end of coverage and start applying for the individual insurance prior to the end of COBRA or the state continuation if the group you are leaving is not COBRA eligible. It often takes more than sixty-two days to identify the company and the plan you want and to have the policy issued.

Chapter 7

Employment

Michael R. worked as an accountant, but he loved to garden. When he was diagnosed with an early stage of prostate cancer, a small ad caught his eye for a local corporation that had a campus-type building and was looking for a "groundskeeper." He got the job, which had terrific health and other benefits, and the chance to use his landscaping talents every day. The thought that he could actually earn a living doing something he loved had never occurred to him before.

This chapter guides you through a reconsideration of your job—from making your current job work better for you to the possibility of looking for a new one. If you are currently looking for a new job, skip to section 4.

Section 1. Reconsidering What You Do for a Living

1.1 Make Your Job Work Better for You

Benefits of staying in your current job. Staying with your current employer has the advantage of keeping your current benefits, with the probability that any exclusions in health coverage for conditions that existed before the coverage went into effect (**preexisting-condition exclusions**) are not relevant or have already been satisfied. You may also have built up goodwill and made friends with coworkers. Assuming your health insurance and other benefits are adequate, before you look for a new job, consider trying to make your current job

work better for you. There are a couple of ways to approach this.

Job accommodation. Chapter 6, section 1.4, examined the concept of "reasonable accommodation" under the Americans with Disabilities Act (ADA). If that law applies to your employment situation and you are unable to perform the duties of your job the way you have been, but you could still do the job if you received an accommodation from your employer, you could think of this as an opportunity to seek some modification that will increase your job fulfillment and/or True Net Pay (see chapter 4, section 1.1). In pursuing an accommodation, you must disclose to your employer information about your health that necessitates that accommodation.

Or consider another approach—you may choose to seek changes in your duties without disclosing anything about your condition to your employer. If you take this tack, however, you are no longer protected by law and you will have to rely solely on your negotiating skills.

With these guiding principles in mind, consider:

- Is there some other way to do the same work at the same or increased True Net Pay and still have more time to enjoy your nonwork hours? For instance, there may be an office closer to your residence. Or maybe you can work freelance and still keep your benefits. Consider working different hours, such as part-time a few hours a day or a few full-time days per week or even full-time for a number of months per year and taking off the remaining months. These sorts of accommodations are common in the ADA context. If, however, you choose not to disclose health information, perhaps you can barter or offer your employer something for this kind of change.

- Is there work that is different from what you are now doing that would either increase your fulfillment or your True Net Pay or both? Although not required by the ADA, many employers are willing to consider changes in job assignments for current employees because they would rather work with a known employee than hire someone new.

- If there is no acceptable ADA accommodation or you choose not to seek one, could you at least receive a raise if you requested one with a persuasive argument?

- If your employer can afford it, consider requesting a continuation of your salary while you work "on loan" to a nonprofit organization that can gratefully use your expertise. Many large corporations do this as a means of keeping employees engaged while polishing the corporate image. Working on loan provides you with the opportunity to obtain more fulfillment while continuing to receive your salary and benefits. Consider working for a GuardianOrg relevant to your condition.

Do not be afraid to manipulate the meeting to take care of your needs. If the meeting goes in a direction other than the one you hope for, rather than let it end on a negative conclusion, ask for time to consider what has been discussed and set a date for another meeting. This will give you a chance to consider alternative arguments and/or approaches.

A few words of caution.

- In some circumstances even hinting to your employer that you are unhappy with your current position may jeopardize raises or advances. If you are going to have the discussion, perhaps you should wait until after decisions about raises and/or advances have been made.

- If you work for a boss or company that discriminates in spite of the law against people with conditions such as yours, think carefully about disclosing health information.

When you're part of a couple. When determining your own ideal with respect to your employer, if you are married or living with someone, consider alternatives that might work for both of you. For example, Kate and Ron B. both worked full-time when he was diagnosed with cancer. They realized that since Kate's income was larger than Ron's, if he shifted to part-time work, they would be able to increase their total True Net Pay because Ron would be home in time to take care of their children. In addition, it gave a better quality of life to both Ron and their kids. For Ron, this meant losing his health coverage, but it was acceptable because he was fully covered under Kate's health coverage and their relationship was solid.

Performance review. Your annual or semiannual performance review may be another opportunity to improve pay or fulfillment. As a general matter, always prepare for performance reviews. Don't assume your manager is aware of everything you've done. Preparation should include a review of your accomplishments and abilities (from your company's point of view), as well as additional educational courses you may have completed or experience you have gained. Also think about how you could do your job differently. This may also be the time to let your employer know about your condition.

1.2 Is Now a Good Time to Change Jobs?

You are not locked in. If you can't get what you need from your current employer, changing jobs may be the answer. Your diagnosis alone should not prevent you from looking for a more fulfilling job. Everyone has things they can and cannot do. You are no different. As you read in chapter 6, there are laws to protect you in your search for a new job.

Before you start down the path of exploring other job or career opportunities, keep in mind the pitfalls that you have to avoid and the stress you are likely to incur when thinking about, and actually, changing jobs. Also, be aware that while the "grass is always greener," few of us are lucky enough to find a job that truly maximizes fulfillment and True Net Pay.

Benefits. If your current benefits are not good enough, it may be worthwhile to look for a new job, even with a lower salary, just to obtain appropriate benefits—especially good health coverage.

Time off. If you need time to explore other job possibilities, review your employer's guidelines to determine whether you would be entitled to time off, with or without pay, without disclosing the reason. If your condition is active, you may be eligible for leave under the Family and Medical Leave Act or the Americans with Disabilities Act. Even if you are not entitled to leave by employer policy or by law, your employer may voluntarily give you a leave if you ask for it. *Before requesting any type of leave, make sure that your benefits continue, and find out for how long.*

Retraining. Consider going back to school or entering a training program if that would lead to your ideal job. Other factors in your life may dictate against it, but your diagnosis as such should not be one of them.

Section 2. Leaving Voluntarily

2.1 Considerations Before Leaving Your Current Job

Now that I've encouraged you to be open to changing jobs, please don't resign before considering the following:

- The risks associated with exchanging the known for the unknown.
- Loss of goodwill and possibly the friends you've made in your current job.
- The economy.
- The new job may not work out.
- True Net Pay is difficult to calculate until you actually start the new job. Talking with other people who do a similar job may give you an idea, but you won't really know until you start.
- **Benefits—insurance evaluation:** *Before you leave a job with insurance benefits, make certain that the new position provides comparable or better health, disability, and life insurance coverage* (unless you can obtain these coverages on your own or have sufficient coverage through your spouse or significant other). There are guides for evaluating health and disability coverages in chapters 14 and 8 respectively. Chapter 19 discusses the important features of life insurance policies. Also, look at when the various coverages start for you as a new employee. For example, some companies have disability-income insurance that is only available to employees who have been in the company for a minimum time, such as five years.
- **Gaps in coverage:** Avoid gaps in health coverage. If the health coverage at the new job does not start immediately, exercise your COBRA rights (see chapter 6, section 4) to extend your current health benefits to take up the slack. If there are exclusions in your new employer's coverage (such as for preexisting conditions on health policies), it is important to determine

how that meshes with the coverage you are leaving. Usually an extension of your current policy will cover you through the period of the new preexisting-condition exclusion. In addition to HIPAA on the federal level (see chapter 6, section 6), various states are beginning to enact laws that prohibit exclusion of preexisting conditions if the gap between new and old coverage does not exceed a limited period, such as sixty days.

- **Your current life insurance:** In most group life insurance policies you have a right to convert to an individual policy when you leave the company or retire. If this is the case, you should look closely at the option since, as you will see in chapter 19, you should keep and obtain all the life insurance you can. It is a new liquid asset for you.
- **The effect on your retirement plan:** Unless you're vested and have an unqualified right to the funds in the plan, you may lose any money your employer contributed to your account. If vesting is imminent, it may be in your best interest to wait until vesting occurs before you give notice. With a 401(k) and 403(b) plan, no matter why you're leaving, you're entitled to any money you paid into the plan. Before you decide to make a move, check the details of your current employer's pension plan. Find out whether you are permitted to transfer funds to either an individual plan of your own or to a new employer's plan without incurring a tax. If you will incur a tax, it is important to know the amount and when it is payable. This is a complex area, and no transfer should be made, even if it appears to be tax-free, without first consulting an expert.

Tip. Roll over the cash into your new employer's plan or into a tax-deferred individual retirement account (IRA). If you're not permitted to enroll in the new plan right away, invest the funds in a so-called conduit IRA, an account you can open at your bank to hold your money until you're eligible to roll it into the new plan.

2.2 Negotiate Before You Leave Your Job

If you've decided to leave your job, don't just walk out. Even though you are leaving voluntarily, you should negotiate to obtain as generous a severance package as you can. This really is doable.

Do your homework.
- Look carefully at your employer's benefit plan and see which of the benefits you are entitled to.
- Know what others of your level, tenure, and experience have received, in terms of severance money, benefits continuations, outplacement services, and other benefits.
- Read the summary to find out if you can convert your group life insurance policy to an individual policy. The odds are you can. The only question is whether it is for the full amount of the coverage or a reduced amount. If the plan summary doesn't tell you, your human-resource contact should be able to.

Set a game plan.
- If you're not going directly to a new job
  - *you need to take health coverage with you.*
  - you should bargain for whatever may assist you in finding the job you want, such as outplacement services that will help you assess who you are, what you want, and how to get it. Many companies, of all sizes, provide some level of outplacement. Outplacement firms provide valuable information and training in all aspects of a job search.
  - you may need a loan of your office or computer or other equipment until you find a new job. An empty office with a computer and a phone, or at least voice-mail service, can be helpful, so that prospective employers won't know you're out of a job.
  - ask yourself what other low-cost assistance

the company could lend or give you that would help you find a new job, such as a laptop computer, a company car, or a pager.

- ask your current employer to hire you as a freelancer, perhaps even to finish a project you've been working on or maybe to get a new one started.
- If you have unused vacation or personal or sick days, ask for the cash to compensate. If you usually receive an annual bonus, try not to forfeit the whole amount. Request at least a pro rata portion of your bonus.
- If you have options to purchase the company's stock, the odds are you have to exercise the right before you leave the company, or within a short time after leaving. Compare the price of the company's stock against the price in your options. If the market price is less than your option price, consider arguing that the money your options were supposed to provide doesn't exist, so you should receive a larger severance package.

Last, but not least.
- Prioritize your desires. Once you know what you want, make every effort to negotiate for it *while* you're still working.
- This doesn't necessarily mean hiring a lawyer. You'll probably be better off doing it yourself, since you can more easily work on your employer's sense of fair play or, as a last resort, guilt. Keep in mind that the higher up you are in the company structure, the less likely the company will want to come off looking mean or cheap. It may still be a good idea to have a lawyer or financial planner to advise you about your rights in preparation for these discussions.
- Do not take the first offer you are given, and don't sign anything until you've had time to read it over and think about it. A request for twenty-four hours to think about it, even if they've given you everything you want, is understandable.
- Your employer doesn't have to know you are

headed toward another job, but it could be helpful to let the employer know that you have been diagnosed, and with what. "I don't want to talk about it, but I thought you should know . . ." is an appropriate lead-in that will arouse sympathy without exaggerating the seriousness of your condition. Nevertheless, think carefully about using this tactic if you're seeking work in the same industry. Word does get around.

- Most employers prefer to avoid lawsuits. If your employer has not been reasonable, you can use this as leverage in negotiating your severance package.
- Don't let your employer play the "this is our standard policy" card. There is no rule that can't be broken or at least stretched. Grumbling often leads to a better deal. And definitely do not hesitate to play on your employer's guilt. This may be the time to bring up your accomplishments at the company and/or sacrifices you've made for the company.

Tip. If you're near retirement age, but not "disabled" as defined by your employer's benefit plans, you can ask your employer to add a few years of service to your employment record so you will qualify for an early pension.

Tip. Before you go, build your reference file by asking for references from your boss or other company executives, colleagues, or clients. Similarly, if your firm lets employees photocopy their employee files, photocopy above-average performance reviews.

Exit interview. If your company requires in-depth exit interviews, accommodate the request to keep your relationship. It is always helpful to keep good relationships with ex-employers and not burn any bridges unnecessarily. Remember that the interview is for the employer's benefit. Assume that nothing you say will be kept in confidence, including any steam you let off.

Section 3. If You're Fired

No discussion about jobs would be complete without addressing the possibility that you may be fired.

If it is because of your condition, refer to the discussion about the ADA to determine your rights. If, however, it had nothing to do with your condition, then you are in the same position as anyone else whose job is terminated. If you believe you have redress of any kind, speak with a local attorney.

Review the discussion in chapter 6, section 4, about COBRA and similar state laws. Together they assure you the right to continue your health insurance.

Section 4. Looking for a New Job

4.1 Identify Your Ideal Job

Time is short. Look for the job that will be most fulfilling and will pay you an adequate True Net Pay. As critical as fulfillment is, you must also be sure you already have or can obtain adequate health insurance through the new job. I cannot repeat too often how critical good health insurance is to you.

Tip. The Internet is an excellent supplement to traditional job-finding resources. In addition to listing job openings, many companies have chat rooms for their employees. It may be worthwhile accessing a chat room to find out what they think of working for the employer.

If you can't identify your ideal job. Here are several time-proven methods of helping determine your ideal job.
- Richard Nelson Bolles—author of the classic text in the field, *What Color Is Your Parachute?*—suggests that as an aid to finding out what you want to do, spend as much time as necessary writing an article entitled "Before I Die, I Want to . . ."

You may find that it is practically impossible to keep the focus only on your career and that some dreams creep in concerning leisure or learning or other non-job-related experiences. Include them and be as specific as possible. According to career-change experts, the more you tap into your dreams, the more you increase your chances of finding the right job.
- An alternative approach, expanded in *Do What You Love, the Money Will Follow* by Marsha Sinetar, is to think about what you enjoy doing, with the idea that it will most likely take you to your real skills and what you do well . . . and thus, a job.
- Consider seeking professional help through aptitude and skills testing. Look in your yellow pages under "career and vocational counseling." The oldest and one of the leading firms is Johnson O'Connor Research Foundation, with offices throughout the country (800-452-1539).

If your ideal job doesn't exist, consider creating it. Try it with an existing employer or start your own business.

4.2 Considerations Before Taking a New Job

Before you take any steps toward moving to a new job, be sure to consider:

- **The details of the new employer's benefit package.** Evaluate health coverage according to the charts in chapter 14, sections 2 and 3.2, and disability income coverage according to the chart in chapter 8, section 1. You may be lucky enough to find an employer that considers their benefit package such a selling point that they will open up the subject in a job interview and possibly give you an employee handbook to look over. However, if details of the prospective benefit package are not volunteered, consider the following means of obtaining the information without tipping your hand:
  - Have a financial planner or other adviser call

the company identifying himself as a planner or attorney who cannot disclose the name of his client.

- Obtain a copy of the plan from a current employee who is a friend.
- Between the time of receiving the job offer and accepting it, tell the new employer that your financial planner insists on seeing the plan. For positions below the executive level where use of a financial planner is not the usual practice, you can change "planner" to someone with whom we can all relate, such as "my obnoxious brother-in-law, who happens to be a financial planner . . ."

- **Don't discriminate against yourself.** Take an honest look at your current skills and capabilities. Then only apply for jobs you know you can do. Don't try to do more than you are able to handle—or settle for less (unless, of course, the point for you is you *want* to handle less).
- **Your field.** Consider whether you want to remain in the general field in which you have been working, or whether this is the time to change.
- **The way in which you work.** Don't be bound to the concept of a full-time job or even going to an office.
- **Relocating.** Maybe this is the time to move to the place where you've "always wanted to live." If you are considering relocating to seek or accept a job, determine what it will cost to live in the new location before you make the move. You may find that an apparent increase in salary really results in a decrease in your standard of living. If you need help in crunching the numbers, there are companies that will help such as Right Choice, Inc., 151 Woodland Meade, Suite 4, South Hamilton, MA 01982 (800-872-2294). You can access the classified ads of major newspaper dailies through the Internet. For smaller papers, AdOne Classified Network links the electronic classified sections of community newspapers across the country (see www.adone.com). Also, check out the Monster Board at www.mon-

ster.com, a free Web-based career search site. It has more than fifty thousand job postings in different locations.

- **Volunteering.** If wages and benefits are not an issue right now, consider working as a volunteer or as an intern.
- **Working more than one job.** You may even want to do two jobs, one for yourself and one for an employer while your own idea is getting off the ground.
- **Large corporations and the government.** Both large corporations and the government offer a sufficient variety of jobs to make it possible to find fulfillment. They also tend to offer a wide range of benefits, usually without an exclusion for preexisting health conditions. In fact, a new job with the federal government includes the right to sign up for life insurance with no questions asked in an amount equal to a multiple of your salary, as well as health coverage.
- **Independent contractors.** Try to get hired at a full-time job for the minimum period of time that makes you eligible for your state's various programs. For example, in New York, if you work as an employee for just eight weeks, you are eligible for New York's short-term disability coverage. Even though the maximum benefit is only $170 a week for six months, that means over $4,000 to you.

4.3 Tips for a Job Interview

Don'ts.
- Don't volunteer health information if no one asks. You have no legal responsibility to mention your health history unless it directly relates to the job you seek.
- Don't lie about your medical history if an employer or an application asks you directly. Lying could be grounds for dismissal, regardless of the subject matter.

Dos.
- **In case you are asked an impermissible question about your health,** it is a good idea to be

prepared with your answer. Be confident and avoid sounding defensive.

- I suggest starting the answer with something like, "You and I both know you can't ask me that question, but I'll answer it anyway."
- Answer truthfully.
- Stress your current abilities to do the job.
- As an alternative to answering the question directly, the National Coalition for Cancer Survivorship has prepared this response: "I currently have no medical condition that would interfere with my ability to perform the duties of the job for which I am applying."
- In case you do discuss the specifics of your condition, have with you a letter from your doctor (on office or hospital stationery) that explains your health situation for employers. The letter should include a description of your physical ability to perform the type of work you are seeking. If you are in good health now, the doctor should verify your good health in the letter. The doctor also may include statements about the documented work ability of survivors of your condition nationwide. Even if you decide that you do not want to share this information with an employer, knowing that you have it when you need it can provide peace of mind in a job search. Caution: ask your doctor not to include this letter in your file in case you later want to sell any life insurance coverage while working.
- Be sure to make notes after you leave the interview and keep them in case you need to file an ADA claim.
- Consider working with a job counselor, who can help you prepare fully for your job search and interview.
- Organize your résumé to your best advantage. For example, a chronological résumé may raise questions if treatment or recovery interrupted your career. To avoid highlighting those gaps, you might organize your résumé by skills or achievements instead of by dates of employment.

- If you're over fifty, play down your age when preparing your résumé by not including your birth date or the year you graduated. Only list the last fifteen or twenty years of experience. Emphasize your up-to-date skills such as with computers.

Think about.

- If you are angry or depressed, work through those feelings before you start dealing with other people who may be in a position to hire you. Otherwise, that anger may hamper your efforts. Try doing mock job interviews with a friend so that you can practice what to say and what not to say.
- How you would respond to being asked, "Tell me about yourself"? Create an answer, then videotape yourself saying it. The answer should convey solid confidence, knowledge of your skills, experience, and what you want to contribute to an organization. Critique the tape with a friend. Remember, enthusiasm and a positive mental attitude are contagious and appealing.

Talking salary with a new employer. Try not to specify a figure. Get the other person to mention one first. If the employer asks, evade the question with a statement such as, "The salary in my last job is not relevant because the job I did there was very different from what I'll be doing for you." Instead, ask for the company's salary range. If there is none for your position, ask for the salary range of workers who would be reporting to you. And be sure to ask for a performance and salary review in six months.

Kathy Strickland, an internationally renowned outplacement expert, suggests, "If they ask how much you made in your last job more than twice or seem annoyed, then answer. Do not lie." Ms. Strickland also suggests that before the interview, in order to be comfortable with talking about money, practice saying the amount you earned in front of a mirror or on a videotape. "Money is the most sacred topic in our society, even more than sex. We give ourselves away through cues other than the words we say, such as stammering. Talking about salary is a difficult thing for any of us to do."

Salary includes benefits. When considering whether a salary offer is fair, be sure to add in the value of the benefits. Asking about the "value" (i.e., amount of money you would have to pay to get the same benefits) may be a way of introducing the subject of the benefits and details.

Tip. In your new job, sign up for the maximum benefits for which you are eligible. If you do not sign up within the time specified for new employees, a physical will probably be required before you can obtain the coverage.

Chapter 8

Disability Income Replacement— Private and Government Programs

> I never really paid attention to what would happen to my income if I got sick. I'm glad those guys in Washington did. It's the first time I remember feeling grateful to politicians.
>
> —Alberto V.

Perhaps your condition or the treatment of your condition is interfering with your ability to do your job. Or maybe you and your doctor(s) believe that stopping work is medically necessary, either permanently or temporarily.

The discussion in chapter 6 covered a temporary disability leave from work. This chapter focuses on **permanent** disability, which, for purposes of this discussion, is a disability that is expected to last more than six or twelve months, or until death. The discussion includes private income replacement as well as government programs such as Social Security Disability and Supplemental Security Income.

You may think the section on private disability income coverage only applies to you if you have the coverage. It is indeed unlikely that anyone with a diagnosis of a life-challenging condition would be able to qualify for individual disability insurance. However, you may still be able to obtain disability coverage from sources that do not require medical exams, tests, or questionnaires, such as individual nonmedically underwritten insurance, credit disability insurance, or group disability insurance. You may also be able to find

disability insurance coverage that excludes your current condition but covers any other disabling event.

Tip. When thinking about your cash flow, keep in mind that all disability payments, government and private, are paid at the end of a period, never at the beginning.

Section 1. Private Insurance: Individual Disability Income Insurance

Disability insurance is "lost-income insurance." It provides you and your family with monthly benefits to replace all or part of the work income that may be lost due to illness or injury. *Disability insurance provides coverage that is usually equal to a percentage of your base salary. Typically, it does not cover lost income from commissions, bonuses, or retirement fund contributions.* Benefits are paid regardless of your assets, your non-work-related income, or your spouse's income. Disability income policies can be purchased on an individual or a group basis, such as through an employer, a union, or an association.

Evaluating a disability income policy. The chart beginning on page 90 reviews the basic features of this type of coverage and provides a standard of evaluation. Features that need to be explained are described on the pages immediately following the chart. The chart can be used to evaluate both individual and group disability coverages. The columns headed "Plan A" and "Plan B" are for you to complete for any coverages you may be considering obtaining. If you are comparing more than two plans, you have my permission to photocopy the chart.

Qualifying definition of *disability*. The first consideration to review with respect to any disability income policy is, what is the qualifying definition of *disability*? There are two general types of qualifying conditions:

• a disability that prevents you from performing *your own occupation*.
• a disability that prevents you from performing *any occupation for which you are qualified*.

Some policies combine the two. For example, the policy could provide that it will pay if you are unable to do *your* job for a given period of years, and then benefits only continue if you are unable to do *any* job.

The best is "own occupation" coverage because it is easier to qualify for benefits, even though your premiums will be higher. The only question in case of disability is whether you can perform the work you do, not any other kind of work. For example, with "own occupation" coverage, Philip T. received disability income when a spinal injury prevented him from continuing to perform neurosurgery. If he had had "any occupation" coverage, he would not have collected under his policy since he could still act as a general practitioner.

Extent of disability. Does the coverage include total and/or partial disability? In many policies,

certain pre-specified conditions are considered total disability, such as loss of sight, speech, hearing, or use of limbs. Loss of a body part that is not a complete bar to working (e.g., the loss of one arm) is a **partial disability.** Some policies do not cover partial disability at all, while others require a period of total disability before partial disability is recognized.

Extent of benefits. Benefits can either be full or residual. **Full benefits** are provided only if disability results in full loss of your income, whereas **residual benefits** are provided if the disability results in partial loss of income. For example, if you lose one-third of your income, you receive one-third of the benefit. This kind of clause would also pay a salesperson who goes back to work but loses money in the beginning because of the time off. She would receive a continuing but reduced income, until she makes up the slack. The policy describes the dollar amount of benefits in each instance.

Rehabilitation benefit. A provision that pays to rehabilitate you.

Illness and injury coverage. "Illness" covers disability due to any cause, including illness, while "injury" only covers if the disability is due to injury.

Amount and duration of coverage. All individual policies pay a predetermined amount tied to the amount of your income from work at the time you purchase the policy, generally as a percentage of that income, such as 60 percent. The policy will also set forth the period during which you are eligible to receive disability benefits, such as, until you recover or die, until retirement age (sixty-five), or for another predetermined period.

Integration-of-benefits provision. There are three different integration-of-benefits provisions to consider. The first is the "offset" provision generally

▸ ▸

Disability Income Insurance

	Range (from worst \ best)	Plan A	Plan B
Definition of disability	requires unable to perform any occupation \ unable to perform any occupation for which reasonably suited by education, training, and experience \ unable to perform own occupation		
Pays for partial disability such as loss of a limb	no \ yes, following total disability \ yes		
Residual benefits	no \ yes		
Rehabilitation program	no \ yes		
Insured condition	injury only \ sickness and injury		
Mental/nervous disabilities	excluded \ included with limitations \ no limitations		
As a percentage of income	less than 50% \ 50–60% \ over 60%		
Maximum benefits period	1–2 years \ 5–10 years \ lifetime to a maximum of age 65		
Integration of benefits	yes, with individual and family SSD, workers' compensation, and other insurance and other benefits \ yes, but only with SSD benefits \ none		
Premium disability waiver	no \ yes		
Elimination period	12 months \ 6 months \ 1–3 months		
Cost of living increase during benefit period	no \ 4% per year \ tied to a consumer price index		
Renewable	not guaranteed \ guaranteed		
Cancelable	yes \ no		
Option to purchase additional insurance with no evidence of insurability	no \ yes, but only to a certain age, such as 40 \ yes		

Continued on next page

Disability Income Insurance *(cont'd)*

	Range (from worst \ best)	Plan A	Plan B
Rating of insurance company	C or lower \ B+, B- \ A+ or A		
Contestable	standard is 2 years		
Exception to limit on contestable for fraud	yes \ no exclusion		
Amount of premium	—		
Preexisting-condition exclusion	requires 12 months without treatment before condition is covered \ all preexisting conditions excluded for 6 to 12 months \ none		
Confinement	requires confinement (at home, nursing home, or hospital) \ no requirement		
Step-rate premium that increases periodically	no \ yes		

found in group policies (not generally in individual policies), which provides that any other income benefits to which you are entitled (most notably Social Security Disability payments) are deducted from the amount the insurance company pays. The second type of integration provision is usually found in individual policies. It provides a maximum percentage of income that can be replaced by disability coverage when you add together all private disability coverages, including group coverages. The maximum is usually 80 percent. The third type pays a predetermined amount without considering any other policies you have.

Tip. If you are self-employed or work for an employer that does not provide disability coverage, to get the most coverage possible, purchase individual coverage first. When the individual insurer asks if you have other disability coverage, you can then honestly say no, and you will be able to purchase coverage in whatever maximum the com-

pany allows based on your income. You can then acquire coverage for a total of more than the individual insurance company would allow if you then purchase group insurance such as through a professional association.

Waiver of premium. This provision waives your obligation to pay premiums in the event of your disability. Without such a waiver, your obligation to pay premiums continues during disability.

Tip. If your policy contains a waiver-of-premium clause and you become disabled, until the insurance company confirms the waiver in writing, continue to pay the premiums on time and write on the check, "Contested premium, should be on waiver."

Waiting or elimination period. Also known as a **time deductible,** this is the period between the onset of your disability and the receipt of benefits.

This period can range from thirty days to one year. To collect disability benefits, you must demonstrate that you have a disability that prevents you from working longer than this waiting period. Under group coverage, the length of the waiting period may relate to your employer's sick leave and other short-term disability policies. Generally, policies with shorter waiting periods will have higher premiums.

Tip. Do your best to accumulate money in the Just in Case Fund (chapter 4, section 4) to cover the waiting or elimination period.

Tip. If you're lucky enough to have both employer and individual disability coverage, and if your employer coverage provides benefits during the early months of your disability, consider increasing the waiting period under your individual policy so as to lower your premiums.

COLA provision. A **COLA** provision is an elective provision that adjusts your disability benefits for cost-of-living inflation, without which the buying power of your monthly benefits would deteriorate over the long term.

"Noncancelable" and "guaranteed renewable" provisions. As their names imply, these provisions mean that the coverage cannot be canceled by the insurance carrier, and that it must be renewed from year to year regardless of your health *so long as* you pay your premiums on time. These provisions also generally ensure that the insurance company cannot increase your premiums unless premiums are changed for an entire class of policyholders of which you are part.

Tip. Don't rely on the insurance company to remind you of a renewal date. Make a note in your calendar each year, or even better, find out if your premiums can automatically be deducted from your bank account. It is not uncommon for an insurer to "forget" to send a bill, particularly if the policyholder has submitted significant claims.

"Guarantee of insurability" provision. This elective provision allows you to purchase additional coverage at any time, regardless of your health.

Insurance company ratings and insurance agent licensing. Be careful to choose an insurance company that will be around to pay your benefits. Five agencies rate insurance companies: Standard & Poors, Moody's, A. M. Best, Duff & Phelps, and Weiss. Each uses a roughly equivalent rating system (highest ratings with each company are AAA, A++, and A+, respectively). For disability insurance, select an insurance company that has consistently received top ratings from at least two of the ratings agencies.

Incontestable. Generally disability policies become incontestable two years after the issue date. Some policies provide that the right to contest coverage continues indefinitely for fraud. The insurance company is primarily concerned with your health and your income when you apply for coverage.

Premiums. Your premiums will depend on the basic provisions of the policy you choose, any special riders you elect, your occupation, your health, your age, and sometimes your gender.

Applying for disability income insurance. When you apply for private disability insurance, you will have to fill out an application disclosing any "preexisting medical conditions" you may have. Never lie on your application. The insurer will take your premiums, but when you file a claim, it will check your medical history with your physicians, prior insurers, and the Medical Information Bureau (MIB). Any mistakes, omissions, or misstatements on your application that initially go undetected will, once discovered, probably result in denial of your benefit claims and/or the cancellation of your policy.

Tip. If you have a life-challenging condition and have been asymptomatic, you may be able to obtain disability coverage by answering questions on an application positively and truthfully—provided the carrier does not request a physical exam. In some states, the insurance carrier can argue when a claim is submitted that you are not covered because it only covers disabling conditions that did not exist at the time the policy was issued (i.e., the carrier admits the policy is valid, but still wiggles out of payment).

If you think there is a chance of qualifying for a disability income policy, submit a trial application that is informally reviewed by the agent/broker with the company underwriters to see whether a policy might be issued. Also review the discussion about the Medical Information Bureau in chapter 3, section 6. Make sure the information contained in your file is accurate, since inaccurate information may affect your ability to get coverage.

Tax on individual disability income policies. Disability benefits received under individual policies are tax-free if you pay the premiums with after-tax dollars.

Section 2. Group Disability Income Insurance

Group long-term disability coverage can be obtained through your employer, professional association, or possibly through a union. Even if you have disability coverage through employment, it is also worthwhile to examine any other group coverage available through professional associations that you already belong to or that you may be able to join. If you are self-employed, you may be able to obtain group disability coverage through trade associations, small-business organizations, or your local chamber of commerce.

Premiums for employer coverage are typically "level premiums" (premiums remain the same for the duration of coverage), whereas premiums for association coverage are typically "step-rate premi-

ums" (premiums increase as the insured grows older). If you are considering association coverage, make sure your policy contains a protective provision that guarantees that the insurer cannot discontinue or modify any individual's policy without making the same changes to all policies in the group.

The standard provisions of group disability income coverage and individual disability income coverage are the same. See the chart in section 1 of this chapter and the discussion that accompanies it. Unlike individual policies, the benefits in group policies are tied to your income at the onset of disability.

You should consider several benefits and drawbacks to group coverage when comparing the different types of disability coverage available to you.
Benefits:
- Group coverage is easier to obtain than other types of coverage—typically you qualify without proof of your medical condition (**insurability**).
- Group disability coverage is less expensive than individual disability coverage.
- Group disability benefits may be tax-free. See the discussion below.

Drawbacks:
- Group coverage is not "portable"—if you change jobs or terminate your association membership, you lose your disability benefits regardless of the premiums that have been paid in. There is no right to convert to individual coverage.
- Group coverage generally does not start as soon as a person starts working in the new job. The waiting period until coverage commences can be as limited as six months or in some cases as long as five years.
- Group coverage is typically less comprehensive than individual coverage.
- Group coverage is typically reduced by any benefits paid under workers' compensation or Social Security. Group coverage may also have a maximum monthly limit of perhaps $3,000.

Tip. If you are considering leaving your job and disability is a real possibility in the future, consider staying with your job for the disability income if the coverage is reasonable.

If you believe you may be terminated from your job and could possibly satisfy the definition of disability in the policy, consider going on disability right away.

Tax on group disability policies. Disability income is taxable if payments are made directly by the employer or *if payments are attributable to employer contributions to a funded plan.* Income benefits are not taxable if the employee pays the premiums with after-tax dollars.

Tip. If your employer has been paying the premiums for your disability coverage, while you are still working, consider asking whether your employer will allow you to reimburse the premium payments at least for the policy year in which you go on disability, and preferably for the two years prior to that as well. While there have been no cases on point, this should allow you to receive disability payment income-tax-free. The suggestion to go back two years instead of one is from a benefits tax expert who suggests that the additional period is more likely to provide the desired tax result. Do not attempt to do this without consulting with a tax adviser prior to speaking with your employer.

Tip. If you are still working, consider asking your employer to change procedures to reflect the idea that the employer paid each employee an additional amount equal to the premium and the employee paid the premium himself or herself. The employer would have to start withholding taxes to reflect the additional income. The other employees will probably grumble at the withholding, but they should be placated when they realize the much greater net amount they would receive if they became disabled.

Tax withholding. Federal income tax withholding is required on employer-paid disability benefits. Disability payments attributable to employer contributions are considered taxable income to the employee subject to Social Security tax for a limited period at the beginning of disability, generally six months. After that they are not considered wages subject to Social Security tax.

If the benefits are paid by a third party such as an insurance company, the employee may elect withholding.

Section 3. Other Types of Group Disability Coverage

3.1 Group Short-Term Disability Coverage

In contrast to group long-term disability coverage, group short-term coverage provides lower benefits, over a shorter period (up to fifty-two weeks), and with a shorter waiting period (up to two weeks). Tax treatment is the same for both types of coverage.

3.2 Employer Salary-Continuation Plans (Sick Pay/Leave)

Employers may provide employees with short-term disability benefits through **salary-continuation plans,** also known as **sick pay** or **sick leave.** Salary-continuation plans provide employees with their full salary at the onset of their disability, typically for a period of several weeks depending on their length of service. Generally, employees are not eligible for salary-continuation benefits if they are eligible for workers' compensation.

Tip. Be aware that taking sick pay may adversely affect your other disability benefits (for example, by increasing the effective waiting period before you can begin to collect other group disability benefits) since the waiting period for disability is often tied to how long you are out of work due to that disability, *not* due to sick leave.

Tax. Salary-continuation benefits are treated as wages and therefore are subject to income tax.

3.3 Workers' Compensation

Workers' compensation is an employer-sponsored program, mandated by state and federal laws, that provides employees with limited coverage for *work-related* disabilities. It does not cover disability due to illness, unless the illness is work related.

Workers' compensation covers lost income, medical expenses, rehabilitation services, and survivor benefits for total/partial and permanent/temporary occupational disabilities. Disability benefits vary widely from state to state, with maximum benefits up to 66⅔ percent of gross wages for a maximum of up to ten years. Employers may cover their workers' compensation exposure either through private insurance or competitive state funds.

Tax. Disability benefits received under workers' compensation are exempt from income tax.

3.4 Group Life Insurance

Group life insurance policies may provide the following disability benefits if the feature is built in to the specific policy:

- **Waiver of premium:** The obligation to pay policy premiums is waived in the event of your disability, although your coverage continues.
- **Accelerated death benefits:** Permits you to receive a portion of the death benefit prior to death (discussed in detail in chapter 19, section 2).
- **Chronic or terminal illness benefit:** In the event you are disabled, you receive monthly payments over a fixed period based on the face value of your policy.

3.5 Group Individual Retirement Plans

Although retirement plans are traditionally designed to provide a retirement income, many contain special provisions that permit you to tap your retirement funds as a source of disability income. For example:

- Under most employer retirement plans, your retirement account becomes fully vested (inclusive of any employer contributions) in the event of your disability. Because contributions cease during disability, your future retirement income could be significantly reduced. However, some disability policies provide "retirement funding benefits" that replace these contributions during disability.
- Some employer pension plans may permit early retirement or may permit pension credits to accumulate during disability.
- Withdrawals from qualified retirement plans, although subject to income tax, are exempt from the 10 percent tax penalty for preretirement withdrawals in the event of disability.
- Even if you are not disabled, withdrawals from retirement plans made to fund medical expenses that exceed 7.5 percent of your adjusted gross income are also exempt from the 10 percent tax penalty for early withdrawals.
- Disability benefits received under a qualified retirement plan that also serves as a health or accident plan may be exempt from income tax.

Depending on the type of retirement plan you have, other special provisions may apply that allow the conversion of your retirement funds to disability income. Check the specific provisions of your plan, along with current IRS guidelines.

Tip. Unless you need to access your retirement funds immediately, roll them over to an IRA and wait to take distributions until you are unemployed and therefore in a lower tax bracket.

Section 4. Individual Retirement Account (IRA)

Just as with group retirement plans, many IRAs contain special provisions that permit you to tap into your retirement funds as a source of disability income (see section 3.5 above). The tax treatment for withdrawals from or disability benefits received under an IRA is the same as described for group retirement plans.

As with group plans, check to see if there are other special provisions that may permit the conversion of your retirement funds to disability income. Be careful to coordinate any distributions from your retirement account with your Social Security benefits.

See chapter 12 for more on retirement funds.

Section 5. Credit Disability Insurance

Typically sold by credit card companies, credit disability insurance either pays off your credit card debt directly or pays you a monthly income in the event of disability. Although this type of insurance is expensive, it can usually be obtained without a medical evaluation and is, therefore, a worthwhile option for those who anticipate a disability in the future. It should be noted that if you do go on disability and make a claim under a credit disability insurance policy, your doctor may be contacted by the insurance company each month to confirm your continuing disability. You should at least warn the doctor to expect these requests. The doctor may be able to stop constant questioning by giving you a permanent disability opinion for the insurance carrier. See chapter 21 for more information on credit disability insurance.

Tip. Getting credit disability insurance is quite simple. Often there is a box on your credit card statement that you can check to begin coverage.

You can also call the customer service number for your existing credit accounts and find out how to obtain disability coverage.

Section 6. Individual Life Insurance

Individual life insurance policies may provide the following disability benefits:

- **Waiver of premium:** The obligation to pay policy premiums is waived in the event of your disability, although coverage continues.
- **Accelerated death benefits:** This option, which can be sold as an integral part of your policy or is sometimes added as a rider at a cost or for free, permits you to draw on the face value of your life insurance policy during the final months of your terminal illness. See chapter 19, section 2, for more information.
- **Critical illness policy:** In lieu of a traditional insurance policy with accelerated death benefits, this type of policy pays a lump sum upon diagnosis of certain predefined "critical illnesses." Don't expect to obtain this kind of coverage to insure a condition you already have.
- **Chronic illness policy:** Provides income per month in the event of chronic illness, which can include life-challenging conditions. The benefit is a percentage of the death benefit, and benefits paid are deducted from the death benefit.

For more on life insurance, see chapter 19.

Section 7. Coverage for Self-Employed Professionals and Small-Business Owners

7.1 Disability Income Policies

If you are a self-employed professional or small-business owner, you will need more disability coverage than the average person because you will need to cover business as well as personal expenses. Disability can be covered by the traditional group and individual disability income policies we have been discussing, through various business-type coverages, or some combination of both.

Disability income policies that require no medical underwriting (i.e., have no medical questions) can provide personal coverage for small-business owners and their employees (minimum of three to five people needed in order to qualify).

To enhance the basic coverage offered, small group policies may also provide upgrade options that employees can purchase at their own cost. When reviewing these policies, particular attention should be paid to the definitions of disability, which are often limited.

Talk with your tax adviser about the possibility of avoiding income tax on benefits by either not deducting the premiums or asking employees to pay the premiums, which the employer can reimburse through year-end bonuses.

Tip. It may be worthwhile for a small-business owner to pay the premiums to cover the entire group if it means the owner who has a preexisting condition can obtain coverage that would otherwise be unobtainable.

Tip. An employee/owner who cannot obtain disability income coverage for her group may be able to obtain the coverage by transferring employment of all employees including herself to a leasing company with disability income benefits. These companies "lease" employees to other businesses. For example, a doctor makes an arrangement with a leasing company whereby the leasing company employs the staff, but they work in the doctor's office, under the doctor's control. The doctor pays a monthly check to the leasing company that covers salaries, taxes, and benefits, as well as a fee for the leasing company.

7.2 Other Coverages to Consider

Business overhead insurance. In the event of the business owner's disability, fixed monthly pay-ments are made to the company to cover overhead and other continuing business expenses for a limited time until the company can be reorganized or sold. This type of coverage is expensive and limited in duration because you can decide whether to return to the job or take another action with the business. This coverage may be difficult to purchase by a business owner with a preexisting medical condition.

Business recovery insurance. Provides benefits to the owner once she returns to work full-time and while she is reestablishing a customer base.

Key-person insurance. Protects a business against loss of income resulting from the ability of a key employee.

Disability buyout policy. For jointly owned businesses, this type of coverage provides funds to buy out a disabled partner's share of the business.

Taxes. As noted above, disability benefits may be subject to federal and state income tax, although many states exempt these benefits from taxation. Any benefits that are subject to income tax are also subject to Social Security tax.

Section 8. Federal Disability Programs

Social Security Disability Insurance (SSD) and Supplemental Security Income (SSI) are both federal programs that provide income to people who become disabled. Both programs are administered by the Social Security Administration (SSA).

SSD is much like private disability insurance: you are entitled to the benefits because you paid "premiums" for them in the form of Social Security taxes. Instead of a private insurance carrier, the benefits are paid by the government. Entitlement to SSI is means based and is intended to provide income replacement and medical care to the disabled poor. Both programs are based on the same definition of disability.

8.1 Social Security Disability Insurance (SSD)

Eligibility. To be eligible for SSD, you must
• meet the SSA's definition of *disability,* and
• you must be "fully insured."
Undocumented residents may be eligible for SSD, but Social Security will not pay benefits until they legalize their residence in this country or until they return to their country of origin.

Disability. Generally speaking, **disability** under SSD means an inability to engage in *any* substantial gainful activity (not just your own job) by reason of a medically determinable physical or mental impairment or a combination of the two that is expected to result in death or that has lasted or can be expected to last for a continuous period of not less than twelve months. For purposes of SSD, you are not considered to be engaged in "substantial" work if you are earning less than $500 a month after allowable deductions.

Fully insured. In most cases, to be "fully insured" for purposes of SSD, you must have worked in **covered employment** for a minimum number of quarters (three-month periods). The number depends on your age at the time you become disabled. The minimum number required is six out of the last thirteen quarters prior to your disability if you are under the age of twenty-four, and the most is twenty out of the last forty quarters (which is the equivalent of at least five of the past ten years). There is "covered employment" when Social Security contributions are deducted from earnings or are made by separate payment if self-employed.

Benefits. Benefits continue for the duration of your disability, but do not begin until the sixth full month after the "onset" of disability—in other words, there is a five-month waiting period. The

date of the onset of your disability is important for various purposes, such as determining the time during which notification must be given to extend COBRA coverage (chapter 6, section 4), as well as the time until Medicare kicks in. Chances are the onset date of your disability predates your application for SSD payments and the five-month waiting period. In that case, benefits can be paid retroactively for up to twelve months.

Monthly benefit rates depend upon your past earnings and family status. The average monthly benefit in 1997 for a single person was $720. For a person with a wife and child it was approximately $1,200. Benefits are larger if you are married. Benefits are paid regardless of your assets or your spouse's income. After twenty-four months of receipt of SSD, recipients automatically become entitled to Medicare benefits. Medicare benefits are discussed in detail in chapter 15. *If you have not already done so, you need to contact SSA to make sure that the information that they have about your earnings over the years is correct. See chapter 3 for further discussion of that process.*

SSI and SSD—Qualifying for both. When you apply for SSD, you also apply for SSI, unless you tell SSA you do not want to apply for SSI.

Presumptive disability. During the five-month waiting period, you may be considered to be **presumptively disabled** by the SSA if you meet poverty-level income and asset requirements and are deemed disabled. This permits you to receive temporary cash payments until the waiting period is over. Medicaid, and in many cases food stamps, are offered when there is a presumption of disability. State disability programs may also provide payments during this period.

The receipt of other types of disability benefits, including those from private disability policies, does not affect SSD payments.

Tip. It is better to go on disability at the end of the month instead of the beginning since the month in which you apply does not count toward the five-month waiting period. Keep in mind that you will not receive your first SSD check until month seven.

You can arrange direct deposit of Social Security benefits into your bank account. This can save you Life Units and ensure safety. Contact SSA for information

Benefits to children and spouses. Monthly disability benefits can be paid to a disabled worker's unmarried children under age eighteen (or nineteen if full-time high school or elementary school students); to unmarried children age eighteen or older who were severely disabled before age twenty-two and continue to be disabled; to a wife or husband age sixty-two or older; and to a wife under age sixty-two who is caring for the worker's child who is under age sixteen or disabled and receiving benefits based on the disabled worker's earnings.

Tax. Benefits are not taxable (on both federal and state levels) until you receive or earn a certain amount of other taxable income in the tax year. The approximate calculation is: if half your annual SSD benefits plus your other taxable income (including interest on municipal bonds) equals $25,000 or more ($32,000 for married couples filing joint tax returns), then half of your annual SSD benefit is taxed at the same rate as your other income. If half your benefits, plus your other taxable income, equals $34,000 or more ($44,000 for married couples), then 85 percent of the SSD is taxable. This formula also applies to disability benefits for railroad employees.

Lump-sum benefit payments (for instance, a large settlement from SSA) can be included in your current tax year's income or, if the payment covers past years, can be distributed over those past tax years. The taxpayer has the choice of whatever works best. If you have questions about taxes, call the IRS or your tax adviser, not SSA. SSA employees are only allowed to discuss taxes in a general way.

8.2 Supplemental Security Income (SSI)

SSI is a "means-based entitlement" for disabled people with limited assets and income.

Eligibility. *There is no requirement of minimum payments into the system* nor is it necessary that you stop working if your income is under $500 a month. In addition to the requirement that a recipient be disabled, aged, or blind within the meaning of the Social Security law, SSI recipients must have limited income (it cannot exceed the amount of the SSI benefit plus $20) and few resources.

Help from friends or family such as free rent may be included in your income.

To determine whether income is sufficiently limited ("net countable income") SSA "disregards" (deducts)

- $20 of any income per month; then
- if you are working, $65 and one-half of the remainder of any earned monthly income.
- If you work, medical expenses paid from your own money to directly support your work attempt. For example, if your condition requires that you take a taxi to work instead of public transport, the cost is deducted before determining net countable income.
- If you are a student and under age twenty-two, another $400 a month is disregarded.
- If you are blind, work-related expenses of any kind not already disregarded are disregarded.

The net effect of the disregards is that a working person can earn a bit more than twice the required level and still qualify.

When a husband and wife share a common household, a spouse's income and assets are deemed to belong to the applicant spouse. This is the case even if they prove they are not sharing income and assets. If a household is not shared, only actually proven transferred income or assets are counted.

In determining eligibility, **exempt** assets are disregarded. Exempt assets include a vehicle of any value (if used to go to medical care at least four times a year or to work), business equity and equipment worth under $6,000, reasonable household goods, and your lived-in-home no matter how valuable. The only residences that qualify are those occupied by applicants, their spouses, or their minor or disabled children. Second houses are not included as exempt assets. Also exempted are a separate bank account of up to $1,500 for "burial" and $2,000 cash or cash equivalent for individuals and $3,000 for married people living with their spouses.

Generally, the program does not care if an applicant sells assets for less than fair market value or even gives them away in order to qualify for SSI.

Aged and disabled legal aliens in the United States as of August 22, 1996, are eligible for SSI. With a few exceptions, most legal aliens who enter the country after that date are no longer eligible for SSI unless and until they become citizens. Illegal aliens are not eligible for SSI.

To determine the eligibility requirements in your state. Contact SSI at 800-772-1213.

Benefits. The amount of the benefit from the program is determined by the amount by which your income is below the standard. For example, if the standard is $500 per month and your income is $400 per month, SSI will pay $100 per month. In 1997, the SSI standard for one person living alone was $484 monthly. Some states raise the standard and pay the difference between the amount and their own standard. For example, in 1997, the standard was $570 in New York and $640 in California.

In addition to a minimal monthly income, recipients of SSI are automatically entitled to Medicaid in most (but not all) states and food stamps (although they'll also have to visit the welfare office to complete processing). Medicaid is discussed in detail in chapter 15.

Dependent children may also qualify for assistance from government programs administered by each state.

Many states provide a "home and community based waiver" program that provides a supplemental income to recipients living in assisted-care facilities. Some states extend the program to people living at home who need assistance (see chapter 15, section 2).

SSI applicants are eligible to receive payment the first day of the month after either the month in which they apply, or the month they become eligible if eligibility is withheld pending a spenddown of assets. SSI checks are issued on the first of each month for that month.

Applicants with a severe enough condition may be eligible for **presumptive disability** under SSI. Presumptive allows for immediate access to SSI benefits while your application is being processed. Social Security can make presumptive payments for up to six months while your claim is being processed, or while you wait for SSD payments to begin.

If you have a presumptive disability, in many Social Security offices an emergency advance payment can be made the day of application. The applicant must present a case of dire need, which usually means that health, nutrition, or home is endangered because the applicant does not have any income. The advance check will be deducted in six payments from the subsequent monthly "presumptive" checks. If you receive presumptive payments, but your claim is ultimately denied, you will not have to pay back the money.

Tax. SSI income is never taxed by the federal or the state governments, regardless of any other income earned or received during the past year.

8.3 Veterans' Pensions

Veterans who have served for at least ninety days on active duty, including at least one day during "wartime" (even if they never entered the war zone), can receive what the government calls "pensions" for disabilities if both income and assets are below certain levels. The "pensions" are actually payments to bring the recipient's income up to the level of $700 per month for single veterans. This amount increases for each additional dependent and for out-of-pocket medical costs. Pensions are also increased for housebound veterans or those who need "aid and attendance"—a broad term for almost anyone with limited mobility. The VA rules for disability are somewhat more liberal than those of SSA. Surviving spouses and certain grown children of wartime veterans can also collect pensions if they are poor enough. For information, contact VA Benefits Information at 800-827-1000.

Section 9. State Coverage

9.1 Disability Insurance

California, Hawaii, New Jersey, New York, Rhode Island, and Puerto Rico have state-mandated short-term disability insurance programs (known as SDI), which were designed to bridge the gap from the time a person can no longer work until SSD starts. Under these programs, workers suffering from a non-work-related disability collect weekly benefits for differing periods of time set by the state (up to six months in New York or eighteen months in California). You should check the eligibility requirements in your state. Generally, these programs are based on having worked for a minimum number of weeks for an employer covered by the system. The part of SDI attributable to the employee's contribution prior to disability is not taxable.

Self-employed people can generally elect to be covered under SDI as a bridge between work and SSD, or for short periods of illness.

SSA sometimes reduces the amount SSD pays if you are also collecting SDI. This occurs if the two awards equal more than 80 percent of your former average monthly wage. When SDI ends, take the Notice of Exhaustion of Benefits to SSA to get your SSD award increased to its full amount. Get a signed receipt from SSA.

It is possible to collect SDI and SSI together if the SDI income is under the monthly SSI payment level. SSI adds $20 extra per month to its regular payment if an individual is also collecting disability benefits from either SDI or SSD.

If as an SDI recipient you are eligible for SSI when your state disability runs out, you can file your SSI application before your SDI expires. You will have to wait to show SSA the Notice of Exhaustion of Benefits before SSI can start paying, but the processing will be complete.

9.2 Workers' Compensation

Workers' compensation (mandated by or written through a state fund) provides benefits to people who suffer on-the-job injuries or disabling conditions caused by work, rather than a health condition. Once a workers' compensation claim is filed, a claim for federal or state disability coverage is usually precluded.

9.3 Unemployment Insurance

Unemployment insurance is a benefit program for people who have recently lost their jobs, are not disabled, and are actively seeking employment. It may be advantageous to collect unemployment and then switch to SDI if you need income for longer than SDI will cover you but you are not medically eligible for Social Security. However, unemployment proceeds are subject to tax, and you would not be able to claim disability benefits such as a disability waiver of premiums on your life insurance policy.

Chapter 9

Preparing for the Possibility of Not Being Able to Work

The people who get on in this world are the people who get up and look for the circumstances they want and, if they can't find them, make them.

—George Bernard Shaw

Thinking about being disabled and no longer able to work at some distant time is not easy—especially when you're feeling healthy. But, any life-challenging condition can lead to this kind of situation, and it is best to be prepared "just in case."

Section 1. Preparing to Go on Disability—Long-Range Planning

There is no better time than the present to start making long-range preparations for the possibility of disability.

Budget. In chapter 4, you looked at what your financial life could be like if you became disabled. If it appears that you won't have enough money to meet your goals, look at chapter 17, to start working on ways to decrease your expenses. For instance, if you're going to need to downsize your living arrangements, this is the time to start thinking about what you would do and where you would do it.

Documenting your "disability." The earlier you begin documenting changes in your health, ability to work, and daily functioning, the easier it will be for others to agree you are "disabled" if you ever want them to. Keep a daily journal that includes

• information concerning all physical symptoms, major and minor, as they occur—particularly pain, loss of appetite, and energy level. Note how any symptoms interfere with your ability to function, particularly at work. Social Security asks that you describe the type of pain (aching, burning, cramping, crushing, stabbing, stinging, throbbing, or other), how long the pain lasts, and how often it occurs.

• information about medications (what you take, in what dosage, when you started taking it).

• doctor's visits, hospital stays, and emergency care visits.

• mental and emotional symptoms.

Tip. If you expect that you will need the help of a therapist to be considered disabled, you need to start seeing the therapist for an appropriate time before. It is unlikely that you will be able to see a psychiatrist and have yourself declared disabled the following week.

Your physician. Ask to read the doctor's notes in your chart to be sure all the information is accurate. Provide any additional relevant information that may be useful to have included in your chart. Include specifics indicating how your condition affects your ability to work and other activities. (See chapter 24, section 4.)

Check the records periodically, say once every six months, to be sure the records continue to be accurate.

Your benefits. Now is the time to review your insurance coverages and government entitlements, as well as any benefits to which you will be entitled at work. It is also the time to obtain replacement for your income in case you become disabled (see the discussion in chapter 8). Obtain life and health coverages, if you don't already have them, and increase all the benefits you do have to the maximum.

- One method of accomplishing these goals is to find out what jobs in your company have the best benefit plans and to try to move to one of those jobs.
- Another method is to examine the corporate benefit plans and figure out what you can do to maximize the coverage you can take with you. For example, a married employee may have a more lucrative benefit package. If so, consider getting married. The plans I've seen only speak of marital status, not whether the couple lives together. Caution: if this is an option for you, consult an attorney with respect to rights and obligations that accompany marriage.
- If your corporate benefit plan has disability coverage, and you see how it can be improved to give an added benefit to employees the company cares about (of course, including you), speak with your employer about changing it. Changes in a plan can occur on the annual renewal date. Stay aware of the renewal date so you can present your ideas to the employer well before that time.

- Add credit disability insurance to your credit cards. It generally has to be in force six months to a year to eliminate the preexisting-condition exclusion.
- If you have your own company, review the information in chapter 8. You can expect that group disability policies for small groups will always have a preexisting-condition exclusion, but that's why you're planning ahead.
- If you locate a possible source for individual disability income coverage, be sure to complete the application truthfully. You can probably find a broker who will be glad to write the policy and make the commission. However, be aware that most disability carriers do their primary underwriting when they receive a claim, not on receipt of the application, and the more they are likely to have to pay out, the more they examine the claim.
- **SSI and Medicaid eligibility:** It is possible to transfer assets or set up trusts to qualify for SSI and Medicaid, even Medicaid long-term care. Advance planning is required. See chapter 15, section 2.3.

Estate planning issues. Any time is a good time to get your affairs in order. See chapter 33.

At work.
- Identify a person or several people who are in a position to make things happen at your employer's in case you need some special consideration. For example, a supervisor may be in a position to request, and get, an exception for you from various company policies, or to let you keep company assets like your laptop computer. It would also be helpful to find a person (possibly the same one) to give you inside information and advice; someone who can strategize with you. This person can be critical to achieving what you want while you continue to work, and especially when you go on disability.
- Sock as much as you can into your retirement

plan, especially if the contributions are matched by your employer. Tax on these contributions will be postponed to a time when your tax bracket will be lower, and there will be no penalty for withdrawal. Money in a retirement plan is also exempt from creditors' claims.

- Speak with people at your job who are on disability, or who have been on disability before, to learn about the practical aspects of being on disability with your employer and in your state.
- Review all plans as discussed under "Your benefits" immediately above and do whatever you can to maximize your benefits.

Tip. If you need information about your employer's benefit plans, the entry-level people in human resources are not the most reliable source of information. If your question is detailed, or individual to you, ask for the opinion of a supervisor. Get any opinion in writing.

Debt.

- Do what you can to reduce your noninsured debt to minimize expenses if you become disabled.
- If you have unmanageable debt, find out if, in your state, your creditors can force you to sell your life insurance policy in a viatical settlement transaction or accelerate the death benefit from the life insurance company (see chapter 19). If you will probably qualify for a means-based entitlement, find out if your state agency will require acceleration or a sale. If either of these situations permit access to your life insurance coverage, talk to a lawyer about transferring ownership now to a trusted friend or relative so the coverage won't belong to you anymore. *Trusted* is the operative word, since that person will now be the actual owner, able to do with the coverage whatever he or she wants. There may be a gift tax to consider.
- If you can't pay your creditors their full due, find out whether in your state your disability income is exempt from creditor claims. If it is not

exempt, find out if bankruptcy would eliminate your debt but permit you to keep your disability income.

Your emotional well-being.

- Start thinking about what you will do if you go on disability. If you would be anything short of bedridden, you will have the time and ability to accomplish many things you've always wanted to do, or new things such as working as a volunteer.
- Have a conversation with people who are on or have been on disability about how they learned to cope—particularly people who share your condition. Learn from their experiences. It helps me to make notes of multiple conversations so information doesn't blend together.
- Start the dialogue with your support team (family, friends, therapist, support group, spiritual adviser, and/or GuardianOrg) about the kind of emotional support you will need or can obtain for yourself during the transition.

Section 2. Preparing to Go on Disability—Short-Range Planning

If you are no longer as able to do your job as you once were, you should look objectively at whether any reasonable accommodations (see chapter 6, section 1.4) would permit you to perform the essential functions of your job or if you are qualified for any other jobs that you could still perform. If not, the question becomes whether your condition would qualify you as "disabled."

Keep in mind that for purposes of employer leave policies, private disability insurance policies, and Social Security benefits, *disability* is a term of art, and it may have different meanings depending upon the particular context. Read each policy or government summary carefully and understand their terms *before* you act so you can be prepared to present your case in light of the relevant criteria.

If your situation isn't clear, speak with your

GuardianOrg or social worker who has had experience in this area. They can give you an idea whether people with a situation similar to yours qualify or not. It would also be helpful to obtain a copy of SSA's write-up about impairments necessary to qualify for disability with your particular life-challenging condition. Don't rely on these guidelines as definitive. You may still qualify for disability if an unlisted impairment or a combination of impairments is at least as severe as those described in the guidelines.

Morality. In general, the decision whether or not to go on disability should be about your health and your finances. It should not be a moral dilemma. There are no moral issues around disability. If you become disabled, you are entitled to stop work and to receive the monetary benefits for which you've been paying.

Emotions. Ideally, you should be prepared for the emotions that will come up during the transition, but they should not be an overriding factor in the equation of whether, or when, to go on disability.

Timing. You can go on disability too soon, too late, or right on time. Earlier is probably better than later, because it gives you the advantage of being able to plan in advance—an advantage that you lose if you wait until you become so ill that the time and choices available to you are severely limited.

Tip. Always be aware that *from the point of view of employers, insurers, and the Social Security Administration (SSA), disability is not something that you choose. You either are or you are not disabled. Therefore, when dealing with employers, the SSA, and insurers, do not (and because it is so important, I repeat), do not discuss disability as if it were a choice.*

At work.
- Talk with the person in the company you've already chosen to help you in the process (see sec-

tion 1). When you tell them you plan to go on disability, be prepared if they ask, "What can we do here at work to help you?"
- Ideally you want your full salary to continue as long as possible—or at least until long-term disability income or Social Security starts. You would also like the company to pay for your continuing medical insurance premiums.
- An increase in salary will provide you greater disability income and money in your retirement account, so it would be "nice" if a friendly employer would increase your salary for as long as you're on the payroll. If the employer doesn't agree to the raise, merely requesting it may make your employer more willing to give you other assistance.
- If there are no disability income benefits, perhaps you can negotiate a continuation of salary. Jeff B. worked as an assistant to the head of a small but successful company that did not have disability coverage for employees. He convinced his boss, the president of the company, that it was the boss's responsibility to have obtained this coverage. The boss agreed to continue 60 percent of his salary (the amount that would normally be payable under a group disability plan) for life.
- Be prepared to initiate the disability leave process at a moment's notice. This is particularly important if there is a possibility of being "downsized." Have readily available an undated letter informing your employer you are going on disability. If you are called into a meeting at work where there's even the slightest possibility that downsizing or your being laid off for any other reason could be discussed, have the letter in your pocket. Hand it to your employer before the employer has a chance to let you know you're being laid off. Once you're laid off, there is no option under your employer's benefit plans to claim that you left work due to disability.
- Determine whether you are entitled to a leave under the Family and Medical Leave Act and/or whether you are entitled to leave or accommo-

dation at work under the Americans with Disabilities Act or state or local disability law. If both the FMLA and the ADA apply, what is the better option for you right now? (See chapter 6, section 2.3.) If there is no duty to provide a "reasonable accommodation" or leave, can you negotiate a leave or some other accommodation with your employer?

• Consider the timing of the leave. If you take the leave now, will you lose any year-end or other bonuses or an impending pay raise?

• Consider going straight from full-time employment to total disability in order to maximize disability benefits. If you begin to work part-time and receive a part-time salary, disability coverage may be based on the part-time salary, rather than your higher full-time salary. This may not be an issue if you continue to receive full-time wages while on a reduced schedule. However, you should also look at whether part-time work would disqualify you from total disability status, which it would under some disability policies.

Your insurance coverages.
• Review the disability insurance discussion in chapter 8, section 1, and determine what disability benefits you will be entitled to, when they will begin, and how long they will last.

• Determine what health insurance coverage will be in effect while on disability leave.
  • Will you be covered under your employer's plan?
  • State or federal law may require that you be allowed to continue coverage by paying premiums yourself. The law may also include a maximum you can be charged for the coverage (see chapter 6, section 4).
  • If you're not covered, can you get coverage under a spouse's policy?
  • If you are disabled within the meaning of the Social Security law and have few assets, other than the house you live in and a car to go to the doctor, which are excluded from consideration

(see chapter 8, section 8.2), it may be worth spending what you have left to qualify for SSI, and thus Medicaid. If this is a possibility, be sure to read chapter 15, section 2.3, before acting. Medicaid, not SSI, cares whether you give disqualifying assets away. Keep in mind that if you are eligible for SSD, Medicare coverge does not begin until twenty-four months after first receipt of SSD benefits.

• Will you be able to return to your present job at the end of the leave? Does the ADA or the FMLA apply? If neither law applies, can you negotiate with your employer on this point?

• If you are considering short-term disability leave (and therefore, are not eligible for SSD or SSI), but lack available coverage privately or through work, and are not eligible for state or federal coverage, consider unemployment benefits. Your employer would have to cooperate by laying you off and not contesting your eligibility for benefits. Be aware that in seeking benefits you have to declare that you are "ready, willing, and able" to work. This is contrary to eligibility for disability benefits, in which you have to declare you are disabled and therefore not able to work. Also, keep in mind that with unemployment the COBRA continuation of your health insurance is only eighteen months. You would not qualify for the continuation beyond eighteen months, which may leave a dangerous gap in coverage until you are eligible for Medicare to start.

• Look at your insurance benefits and determine the deadlines by which you have to access any and all benefits you can take with you. Don't rely on your employer or the insurance company to notify you of these rights or deadlines. For example, if you won't have to pay premiums for your life insurance policy because of a provision permitting a waiver of premiums due to disability, what is the period after the onset of disability during which you have to request the waiver? If the policy is to be converted, during what time frame do you have to initiate the conversion? As a reminder, since you can probably sell your policy, it is generally worthwhile to convert and pay the higher individual premiums until you negotiate a sale rather than letting the coverage lapse.

Tip. If you do have a premium waiver included in your disability policy, continue to pay the premiums and do not assume they are waived until you receive a written notice to that effect from the company.

Physician. Tell your primary physician that you are considering going onto disability and find out his opinion. It is not wise to apply for disability and then find out your doctor will not support your application or, even worse, may even say you are able to work. Consider discussing such questions as:

- Does he think you will fit within the SSA definition of disability in the foreseeable future?
- Does he think leave is medically necessary at this time?
- How much choice do you have medically speaking?
- How long a leave is necessary?
- Could a change in your job duties or work accomplish comparable health results?

If the doctor agrees that you qualify for SSA disability, this may be a good time to request the letter discussed in chapter 10, section 4.3.

If your doctor does not support your decision to pursue disability leave, you will have to decide what's more important, your doctor or the leave. Whether you are applying for disability benefits from a private insurance carrier, SSA, or another governmental body, you will need evidence of disability from a physician. Carefully evaluate your physician's opinion in this regard. Get a second opinion if necessary.

Mental and/or emotional.

- Disability can be caused, in whole or in part, by a mental or emotional condition. If you are already seeing a mental health provider, ask that person if your condition would help in a determination of disability.
- If you are considering working with a mental health provider, remember that for purposes of determining whether a person is disabled under Social Security and insurance standards, therapists in order of preference are
  (1) a psychiatrist, an M.D. with a specialty in mental health. Note that only a psychiatrist can prescribe medications such as Prozac or other mood-enhancing drugs.
  (2) a psychologist with a Ph.D.
  (3) a psychologist with a master's degree.
  (4) a social worker or similar person—the greater the educational background, the better.

If you need help determining whether you may qualify as "disabled." Seek out an experienced social worker or attorney. Since "disability" can be such a gray area, the more experience the person has with the definition of disability, the more likely that you will obtain the information you need.

Tip. As much as you may need the immediate income, plan as if you will not go on sick pay but will go directly onto disability. COBRA coverages plus the disability extension extend your group health coverage for twenty-nine months until the start of Medicare. If you start disability with sick pay, there can be a gap in health coverage equal to the period you are on sick pay. Also, lesser payments for sick pay may become the base for disability income payments instead of your full salary.

Chapter 10

Applying for Social Security: The Process

> Desire to have things done quickly prevents their being done thoroughly.
> —Confucius

Only about one-third of applicants for Social Security Disability income are found eligible on first submission of their application. This chapter provides the necessary background to increase your chances of doing it right the first time.

Keep in mind that from the point of view of employers, insurers, and SSA, *disability is not something that you choose to do.* You either are or are not disabled (i.e., unable to do any kind of work for which you are suited for at least a year or until death). *Do not discuss disability as if it were a choice.*

The following discussion is specifically about filing a Social Security Disability claim. However, the process is the same for each situation in which you have to prove disability. If you are filing a claim for any other reason, the procedure is much simpler.

Section 1. Before You Begin

Determining whether you are disabled under the Social Security law starts with a determination of whether you are insured or have recently worked.

Those determinations are straightforward matters of mathematics. However, whether you are sufficiently disabled within the meaning of the law is subject to interpretation.

Unless it is obvious that you are disabled, you should seek advice and assistance from your GuardianOrg or an attorney before you seek Social Security benefits. Your GuardianOrg may have advice tailored to your situation based on information about others with your illness who have sought Social Security in your area. The rules and regulations are national, but each office has its own way of doing things. Your GuardianOrg can probably provide a referral to a benefits specialist or lawyer who can provide assistance should you need it.

Section 2. A Case Study

Experience has shown that it is not just the reality of your condition that determines whether you are approved for disability, but how third parties such as the personnel at SSA interpret the facts. For example, on Lewis L.'s disability report he stated he had AIDS. He described his job as physically taxing. He stated that he was in charge of the local office for his national firm where he supervised forty employees and was responsible for locating and keeping clients. He stated that he had to work long hours, six days a week, and had to be on his feet most of the time. In answer to every question, he repeated his responsibilities and that the illness caused "fevers, fatigue, body aches, and fungal infections" that made it "impossible to work." He indicated that he was already approved for disability by the firm's group disability carrier.

Lewis noted that his doctor suggested he reduce stress and "take care of my health." He mentioned that he does "shopping . . . on days I have the strength to do so [and] items are delivered to reduce stress. My wife, who works, cleans. I do some when I have the energy." Answering questions about hobbies he stated, "I paint at home and take walks when I have the energy." Elsewhere he stated, "I have frequent visits from friends and relatives when I am feeling able." No supporting documentation was requested, and none was attached.

Lewis sounds like a person who is "disabled," but the SSA didn't agree. From their point of view, the answers were too generalized. They could have applied to many people with the condition who continue to work.

An attorney specializing in helping people with life-challenging conditions rewrote Lewis's "Request for Reconsideration." He was more specific and tied the conditions to the requirements of the job that Lewis could no longer fulfill. The new form stated that since Lewis had filed his claim, "his symptoms have continued or intensified. Fatigue restricts him to bed an average of one day per week on which days he often cannot maintain basic personal grooming. On other days he requires frequent rest and naps. Severe diarrhea 2 to 3 days per week, regular chronic gastric bloating and pain, and occasional constipation greatly impair his ability to function; sporadic sleep at night further reduces his energy, as do 2–3 day bouts of

low-grade fever (100–100.5 degrees), accompanied by night sweats every other week. Furthermore, fungal infections in his feet and pain in his left quadriceps make standing or walking for prolonged periods impossible. . . . The severe diarrhea and gastric pain he experienced at the time of his claim continues to circumscribe the amount of time he can be away from home. The pain in his feet and left leg continue to make standing or walking for prolonged periods impossible. Certainly, standing or walking for even two hours out of the day is beyond his capacity. . . . He can do basic food shopping on days he feels well. . . . Aside from making his bed, his wife performs all other household tasks. . . ."

The request for reconsideration was accompanied by a letter signed by Lewis's wife repeating this information and stating specifics of more things Lewis could not do in his personal and social life. It was stated that Lewis's social life was practically nonexistent due to his condition. This time around, Lewis received his SSD.

Learn from the case study. While describing your symptoms, state them *graphically and in detail* so any reader can understand why you are unable to work due to your medical or emotional condition. Although it is not generally the case with SSA personnel, assume for purposes of completing the forms that the reviewer is biased against awarding a disability. State your case as strongly as possible, but don't be overly optimistic or unrealistic about your work or personal care abilities. Don't leave out any details, no matter how embarrassing you may find them to be, or how distasteful you think the reviewer will find the subject.

Tip. As Lewis found out the hard way when the SSA called to check on some of his answers, it's a good idea during the time SSA is considering your request to keep a set of your papers near your phone in case SSA calls. Be sure to repeat the key phrases that indicate why you can't work. Don't volunteer additional information. And don't talk as if you have a choice about going on disability. When in doubt, hire a professional to help, or at least contact the social workers at your GuardianOrg.

Section 3. Preparing the Paperwork

Keeping Lewis's experience in mind, take the following steps in preparation for filing your claim:

• Obtain the appropriate procedure and forms from the Social Security Administration (SSA).
• Identify someone experienced with your type of illness and with your local Social Security office to provide you with advice and assistance should you need it. It is best to find someone who has worked with several others with your condition who have successfully obtained benefits.
• Decide what date you will use in answer to the SSA question "When did your condition finally make you stop working?" The date is critical for the commencement of SSI, the waiting period for SSD, Medicaid and Medicare, and even the continuation of your health insurance under your COBRA coverage. *Keep in mind that SSD waiting periods start on the first day of a month, so unless you apply on the first day of a month, the five-month waiting period will not start running until the first day of the succeeding month.*

Since Social Security will pay SSD retroactively for a maximum of twelve months, you can *and should* backdate the onset of disability as far into the past as your medical records will substantiate. Onset dates can be backdated to cover periods when you collected unemployment, state disability income, when you were not working, or even over periods (generally up to three months) when you were working, as long as you were out sick more than you were at work.

You can also backdate disability over what Social Security calls "closed" periods of disability. For example, if you left work for a year because of a condition, then returned to work for two months, then left permanently, SSA may accept that year as a "closed" period of disability and set the onset date at the start of that year.

• Be sure your journal is up-to-date (chapter 9, section 1), and that it includes how your condition affects your job performance. This record can be important, particularly if your claim is denied and you have to appeal. Social Security will ask for a copy of the journal if you have one.
• When you apply for SSD, SSA will automatically request information to determine your eligibility for SSI. This is done so that you will receive the benefit (as well as Medicaid coverage) as soon as you are determined eligible. If it is clear to you that you are not eligible for SSI based on your assets and/or income, you can inform the Social Security claim representative that you are not interested in pursuing SSI. If you are pursuing SSI, see below for additional information you will need to gather.
• As illustrated in the case study above, one of the main areas about which SSA requests information concerns how your illness interferes with your ability to work. Thus, in your application, keeping in mind Lewis's experience, describe the duties of your job and focus on the specifics of how your illness makes it impossible for you to do your job rather than how your job is interfering with your health.
  • To help identify your symptoms, think about your worst days.
  • To help you focus on how your health has interfered with your job, compare how you do your job now to how you did it two years ago or even one year ago. Also look at how your job duties may have changed since the earlier date.
  • Social Security will ask for information about changes in your ability to function in everyday life including personal care, cooking, housekeeping, bill paying, ability to do

errands, recreational activity, physical mobility, and ability to use transportation. As you did with your job, focus on the specifics of how your illness interferes with these activities. Compare today to two years ago and think of your worst days.

- It would be helpful to obtain letters from friends, family, neighbors, and/or former employers about your functional limitations. They should include how your symptoms keep you from performing normal daily activities, including household chores, your normal social functioning, or contribute to loss of memory or concentration.
- Begin assembling the information described in section 4.3 below.

Tip. Always use your own words when completing SSA forms. Analysts are suspicious of canned answers.

Qualifying for SSI. If you may qualify for SSI, in addition to the above information, you will also need to assemble information relating to your income and resources including bank records, tax records, W-2s, insurance policies, car registration, and if you are married, information about your spouse's income and resources

You will also be asked about your living arrangements since you must be paying your "fair share" of rent, food, and utilities. If you rent a room, a letter from your landlord should be sufficient. If you have one, make a copy of your lease or proof of ownership such as evidence of a mortgage. If someone gives you money for your expenses, or if you are living rent-free, a reasonable amount may de deducted from your benefit. However, if someone loans you money for rent and the like, it will not count against you (although you may be asked for signed loan statements indicating you must pay back the money). Government and nonprofit assistance for rent or food are not counted against you.

It is also a good idea to research the criteria in your state for qualifying for SSI. If you are over the income or asset limit by even a small amount, you will probably be disqualified. It's better to know the criteria up front and plan accordingly.

Presumptive disability for SSI. If you fit the criteria for "presumptive" disability, you may be awarded SSI immediately. SSA publishes guides written for laymen defining presumptive disability for several conditions, as well as a guide geared toward medical professionals known as "Disability Evaluation Under Social Security." SSA uses these guides to determine "presumptive" disability benefits. If you do not fit the presumptive description, you may still qualify if an impairment or a combination of impairments is at least as severe as those described. If it is finally determined that you are not disabled, you will not be required to refund the payments.

You can still receive SSD even if your disability does not qualify under the criteria of a presumptive disability.

Section 4. Starting the Process

File your request for Social Security benefits at any SSA office in the country immediately upon becoming disabled and leaving work. When deciding which filing office to use, consider

- convenience, since the process will probably take several months and you may want to stop in the office as necessary.
- if it is not clear that you are disabled, whether the office handles situations similar to yours and does so favorably.

4.1 In-Person or Telephone Interview

The request for benefits starts by making an appointment with SSA by calling 800-772-1212, 7 A.M. to 7 P.M., M–F. Social Security will send you forms to be completed prior to your appointment if you don't already have them.

You can choose a telephone interview (so you can do everything by telephone and mail) or an in-person interview at a local SSA office. Doing the interview in person means that you will not have to send vital documents through the mail. It also means that if you make a mistake, you have a person sitting in front of you who can help correct it. If you schedule a telephone interview, you can provide the information from the comfort of your home, but then you don't have the option of correcting mailed-in mistakes, which become part of your permanent record. Many advocates advise that it's best to do the interview

- in person;
- in the middle of the week; and
- in the middle of the month.

If you are eligible for a determination of "presumptive disability" under SSI or an SSI emergency payment, do an in-person interview. Be sure to request those benefits during your interview rather than relying on the SSA employee to bring them up. If the claims representative does not file for presumptive, and if the claim leaves the office and goes to a disability analyst, then the Social Security office may have to defer to the analyst for a presumptive decision, which adds weeks to the process.

Ask for a "receipt of claim" when you initially submit your papers. This is proof that you applied.

Tip. Always be prepared for a long wait at the Social Security office.

4.2 A Representative

If you cannot physically go to the SSA office or do not want to, you can ask a friend or family member to handle your Social Security business for you. All they need is your written consent on the SSA form used for appointment of a representa-

tive. If the person is also to receive benefits for you, the person must register with SSA and be qualified as a representative payee. A person with your power of attorney does not automatically qualify as a representative payee.

4.3 Documentation

Whether you apply over the telephone or in person at your local SSA office, there will not be a review until all the required documentation is supplied to SSA. Since the burden is on you to prove your disability, it is important to compile the information described below to the best of your ability.

If you're missing documentation, ask your SSA representative whether that, in and of itself, is enough to disqualify you from a disability determination. If it is, then fill in the gap before turning in your application (unless you believe you can qualify for SSI, in which case you want to turn in your application as soon as possible because SSI awards never predate the date of the application, while SSD dates back to the beginning of the disability).

Tip. The key to a successful SSD/SSI claim is well-documented, carefully written forms and attachments, all of which together show how and in exactly what way a claimant's condition and symptoms prevent ongoing, sustained work.

Social Security Disability Insurance. The following documentation will be required to process your claim for SSD. If you haven't already done so, obtain form 7004 from SSA and be sure to check it for accuracy (see chapter 3, section 3).

Medical.
- Letter from your doctor setting forth the following information:
  - Detailed diagnosis and prognosis—details are important; make sure all of your symptoms are included (such as weight loss, fatigue,

headaches, and depression as well as major infections or diseases).

- Results of supporting medical tests including biopsies, X rays, and the like.
- A description, preferably based on the information you have been providing, that states specifically how your condition affects your ability to work and engage in other activities.
- A statement that you will be unable to work for at least a year due to your illness.

Tip. If your doctor is not familiar with SSA requirements, ask SSA for a copy of its current publication describing the information needed from your physician, which you can give to your doctor. Check the letter against these criteria. If the letter is not adequate, don't hesitate to speak with the doctor and point out the areas that need improvement. Let her know that you recognize the difference between her real optimism about your condition and your needs for Social Security purposes.

- Copies of medical records relating to your disability. Don't rely on SSA to obtain this information. Overworked SSA employees can take an endless amount of time to obtain information from overworked staffers in your doctor's office, clinic, or hospital. For absolute safety, don't rely on the mails: pick up your medical records by hand. Be sure to mention, and secure, records and reports about current or past physical or mental conditions that could possibly relate to the condition that prompts your disability.
- Copies of medical records relating to any other ongoing or past condition, physical or psychological, that affects your ability to function.

Work related.
- Letter from your employer setting forth when you stopped being a productive employee (even though the employer may have left you on the payroll for other reasons, such as compassion). This date should coincide with your doctor's statement relating to the onset of the disability.

- A summary of where you worked in the past fifteen years and the kind of work you did.
- All pay stubs from the current year (to prove your earnings to date for the current year).
- W-2 statements (or if you were self-employed, your federal tax return for the last two years).

Other.
- Your journal.
- Birth certificate (original or state-certified copy only). If you can't find it, contact the hospital in which you were born. If that doesn't work, try the city government or as a last resort the state's department of health.
- Green card, passport, immigration/naturalization papers.
- Copy of driver's license or other identification with picture.
- A copy of your Social Security card or at least your Social Security number.
- Documentation relating to any other government programs for which you may be receiving benefits.

Supplemental Security Income. If you are applying for SSI, prepare all of the documentation requested for SSD. In addition, compile the documentation described on page 111, under the heading "Qualifying for SSI."

Section 5. Determination of Disability

Once SSA determines your file is complete and that you satisfy the credit and work criteria, your file is then sent to a state agency known as Disability Determination Services (DDS), which is responsible for the initial disability determination. The determination is made by a two-person team consisting of a medical or psychological consultant and a disability examiner.

If DDS determines that you are disabled for purposes of Social Security, SSA then looks to see if you are otherwise eligible for SSI and/or SSD. If they agree, and you are eligible for SSI, your monthly benefits and Medicaid coverage will start immediately, with the first check covering funds back to the date of the application. You will also be eligible to apply for food stamps. At the end of the sixth full month from the date determined to be the onset of your disability (i.e., in month seven), an SSD payment will be made to you for the sixth month only. Keep in mind that with SSD, there is no payment for the waiting period of the first five full months after the onset of disability and that checks are then written at the end of a month in which you are disabled—not the beginning.

Tip. When you file your claim, Tom McCormack, author of *The AIDS Benefits Handbook,* suggests, "Ask the SSA claims representative for the name, address, and telephone number of the DDS worker or branch to which the claim will be sent for review. . . . After a decent interval, call the DDS worker or branch and inquire what additional information, records, files, or statements you might submit to assist in processing your case."

Tom also advises, *"Never* mail *your only copy* of any document, report, or form and *always* [if possible] hand-deliver submissions to SSA or the DDS."

Tip. During the period from submission of your disability claim until it is approved, medical files from new doctor's visits should be sent as they occur to SSA or the DDS analyst as the case may be.

If you are sent to "consultative" exams, ask the analyst if reports from your own doctor would be satisfactory instead.

If your health insurance is still on a COBRA eighteen-month continuation, remember to send a copy of your Award letter to your COBRA administrator within sixty days of receiving it to qualify for the eleven-month continuation.

Tip. If you're not satisfied with the way that Social Security is handling your situation, call one of the following: your state or local office on aging; the National Committee to Preserve Social Security and Medicare (800-966-1935), an advocacy group; or the office of your U.S. senator or representative. Every member of Congress has a caseworker whose sole job is to help constituents who are having problems with Social Security or other federal programs.

Section 6. If Social Security Denies Your Claim

If SSA denies your application, you have the right to appeal the decision. While the appeal is ongoing, which can take from several months to a year, there is no automatic right to Medicaid or any other benefits that would accompany a finding of disability. Even worse, any presumptive benefits you may have been receiving would stop.

It is preferable to appeal rather than withdraw your application and start again. While any eventual award of SSD will date back to the commencement of the disability, whether the award is through an appeal or a new application, an award of SSI can only refer to the date of the filing of the application.

If your application is turned down, ask SSA for the current form that describes the appeal process as well as the dates by which appeals must be filed. In general, appeal rights must be exercised within sixty days of any adverse decision. Follow the dates precisely or you may inadvertently lose the right to appeal and will have to start all over again. The appeal process consists of four stages of review.

1. Reconsideration: A DDS reconsideration of disability determination is made by a different team in the DDS from the one that handled the case originally. DDS agencies seldom reverse themselves, but you should still treat this appeal seriously and request a reconsideration as soon as your application is turned down. The DDS reconsideration becomes part of the record that is passed on to the next appeal level.

2. Administrative hearing: The next level of appeal is a hearing before an administrative law judge who works in the SSA's Office of Hearings and Appeals. Practically speaking, this is the most important level of appeal. The judge acts as a judge, jury, and in a sense, the lawyer for the SSA, since it is the judge who will ask the questions (in addition to your own lawyer, if you have one). If you have not done so before, consider submitting affidavits from professionals, friends, and neighbors about your disability. Also, consider hiring an attorney to help you. You have a right to review and copy the SSA file prior to the hearing. Consider submitting a prehearing memorandum outlining the evidence and identifying the issues for the hearing.

3. Appeals council: Makes a decision based on the record, with no oral argument. Appeals are not usually successful at this level.

4. Federal court: The judges do not revisit the question of whether you are disabled, but only question whether the SSA followed its own rules and gave you appropriate "due process," or whether there are any constitutional issues. This venue is of little value because of the limited nature of the review.

Under the Privacy Act, you may ask to see all the evidence used to evaluate your application for disability benefits.

Tip. During the appeal process, make sure your medical records are continually updated and that any changes in your condition, including new facts, are brought to the attention of the appealing body.

Tip. If, as part of the appeal process, you are required to submit to an examination by a consulting physician, review your notes and/or medical file so you will be able to discuss all your symptoms.

Section 7. Hiring an Attorney

If you follow the suggestions contained in this book, you should not need the help of a lawyer to file for Social Security benefits. However, it is a good idea to have an expert at your GuardianOrg, your social worker, or other knowledgeable person at least review your application before submitting it.

If you don't have an attorney by the time you have to appeal, you should consider hiring one to help with the process. Aside from reducing the stress of the situation by having an experienced representative working on your case, you will receive help in framing your case in a way that enhances your chance for success. Firms that specialize in these matters work for a percentage of the amount you receive from SSA for retroactive benefits—from the date you are determined to have been disabled to the date of the determination. The standard fee is 25 percent of the amount awarded you. A representative cannot charge a fee without first getting written approval from SSA.

If your GuardianOrg, your friends, support group, local bar association, and/or legal aid program cannot recommend an attorney, contact the National Organization of Social Security Claimants' Representatives at 800-431-2804 for suggestions. See chapter 36, section 3, for how to choose an attorney.

Chapter 11

On Disability

You can't live tomorrow before it gets here. If you get a good day, take it and run. It's called survival.

—Erma Bombeck

People on disability are quite diverse. They include those who need time off to overcome a particular crisis, those at the end stage of illness unlikely to recover, and everyone in between. Regardless of how or why someone comes to be on it, disability, like any other life change, often involves the loss of a sense of identity, bringing up a range of emotions that can include depression, fear, anxiety, uselessness, and rage. On the other hand, it can bring a newfound sense of freedom, which may or may not last.

Section 1. What to Anticipate

1.1 The Emotional Experience

There is no right or wrong experience and no right or wrong way to handle what you experience while on disability. Treat being on disability as another stage of life to be explored. Maximize your fulfillment and enjoy each day. Be gentle on yourself.

Experience has shown that, while on disability, it is easy to get stuck in a negative emotion such as depression. It is also easy to move from being a proactive person, directed and fulfilled, to a reactive person waiting for life's next blow. This seems to be especially true if a person is in the mode of "I am dying of . . ." rather than "I am living with . . ." As Lynn L. said, "We cannot change the facts, but we can change how we relate to them."

We are all dying. The question is what we do with each day we have here on earth. Each day can be a new opportunity. This is difficult to remember some days—even some weeks. But it is true.

Michael Naimy, an expert in helping people with life-challenging conditions reenter the workplace, observes, "Those that really enjoy the best level of mental health are people who, at some point after dealing with all the emotional pieces of going on disability, begin to become proactive again. It becomes a question of personal focus, or mission or vision, if you will. It doesn't have to be work related. The range of choices is almost endless: from volunteering to getting an education to working on the self, working part-time at a job, or working on the spiritual side . . . anything that takes the mind away from the negative feelings of being on disability and creates some type of positive experience."

If you find yourself stuck in depression or some other negative emotion, access a support group or a therapist, or contact your GuardianOrg for assistance or recommendations.

1.2 Checking on Whether You Are Still Disabled

As a general matter, once a person qualifies for SSD because of a life-challenging condition, SSA does little checking to determine whether the person continues to be disabled. Depending on the determination, there is no reevaluation until three, five, or seven years from the award of the disability status, unless SSA receives information that the person may have returned to work or appears to have improved, in which case a review will then occur.

While you can expect that insurance companies will do an investigation before deciding to commence disability income payments, once the payments are flowing, there is generally little checking on whether the recipient continues to be disabled. So long as their requirements are met (such as annual reports from a physician that the disability continues), insurance carriers generally continue to pay benefits until informed that a beneficiary is no longer disabled or is deceased. If the disability is due to a mental condition, the company will likely start questioning after a year or two whether the disability continues. Some insurance companies may be more aggressive in their review of any continued disability.

Tip. Some employers are beginning to conduct their own investigations to limit their disability income insurance costs. If you're covered through a group plan, it's worth checking on your employer's procedures in this regard.

Contact by an investigator. If you should be contacted by an investigator for the SSA or an insurance carrier that is paying you a disability income or even a former employer, keep these guidelines in mind:

- The general rule is "Cooperate—within reason." It is easy (particularly for an insurance company) to stop payment of your checks if you don't cooperate. You would then have to prove you're due the money. While you do have to cooperate, you don't have to "roll over."

- If an investigator calls you, tell him that you would be happy to respond to any inquiries he has, but that you will have to call him back to verify that he actually works for the insurer or SSA. Once you have established that he is legitimate, decide whether you want to talk with him at that moment. It may be better to schedule the conversation for another time when a family member, friend, or someone else can be there listening on an extension or perhaps when you are feeling better.

- If an investigator shows up at your doorstep with credentials but without an appointment, first verify who he is. Explain that you would be happy to meet with him but that now is not a good time—you're not feeling up to it or you have a doctor's appointment. Do not say you have a tennis date or some other physically active event. Set up an appointment for when it is convenient for you and whomever else you wish to be present. If you would feel more comfortable in another location, such as at the benefits department of your GuardianOrg, set the meeting for there.

- When you do speak with him, get the investigator's name, telephone number, and record the time, date, and place of interview. Answer questions, but don't volunteer any information. It's preferable for you to have a family member or a friend present as a witness.

- The investigator will ask questions about your activities to ascertain whether you are in fact disabled. Answer truthfully, but you can qualify all answers by saying, "When I feel up to it, I . . ." Always keep in mind that your answers should indicate how your disability continues to interfere with your ability to work. Make notes of the questions you are asked and of your responses. Keep this record with your copy of your disability policy or other relevant file.

- Volunteer the symptoms you've been experiencing, particularly ones that would keep you from doing the essential functions of your former job and any other jobs you might be required to accept under the insurance policy or program.
- If any questions make you feel uncomfortable, ask what relevance the question has to your claim. If you continue to feel uncomfortable in spite of the answer, ask that the question be put in writing, along with a written explanation for the reason that the question is being asked. Tell him that you will respond in writing. If you prefer to stop the interview, fatigue is a reasonable excuse.
- If the interview is in person, do not go overboard and try to look "disabled." At the same time, there is no need to try to look your best for any meeting either. Look how you always do.
- If it makes you too uncomfortable to meet the investigator, tell him that you will answer questions over the telephone or provide written responses.
- If you are doing volunteer work and that comes up in a review, communicate that *you* set the hours and the pace of the work. You want to distinguish your volunteer experience from work for a wage. If applicable, explain how your bad days or the side effects of your medications or treatment schedules etc.—which are unpredictable—interfere with a regular schedule. From the insurer's perspective, if you can show up on schedule and do regular tasks, you can do work for wages.

Tip. It would be helpful to look at your policy or the government guidelines as the case may be to determine the kind of jobs you must not be able to perform due to your disability. Provide your investigator with a list of your physical, mental, and emotional symptoms and show how each would impact the essential functions of each possible job. Attach a list of people who would be willing to write a letter about your inability to do these functions.

1.3 If Payments Stop or May Stop

If your insurer informs you it is going to stop or actually stops payments, for assistance contact an expert in helping people defend disability benefits, such as your lawyer, GuardianOrg, or in the case of a private carrier, your insurance broker. If you feel comfortable representing yourself in this matter, speak with the supervisor. If you get no satisfaction, try the president of the company. If you have a good relationship with your former employer and the benefit is through the employer's plan, consider whether the employer could use its clout with the insurer to help you. If all else fails, contact your state Insurance Department (see the resources section).

If SSA informs you it is going to stop your payments, consider appealing (see chapter 10, section 6). Also see section 3 below.

Section 2. Tips for People on Disability Leave

- **Paying your premiums:** *Make sure that you continue to pay the premiums on your health and life insurance coverage, as well as your disability coverage, on time.* If you cannot afford to keep up with the health insurance premiums, contact your GuardianOrg for advice on any state-funded programs that may be available to help you maintain coverage. If you believe you qualify for a premium waiver due to disability, do not stop paying premiums until you receive a notice in writing from the insurance carrier that premiums are waived.
- **Health and life insurance:** If you need it, remember you can still obtain health insurance, life insurance, and even credit life insurance. It is advisable to have both Medicare and private health insurance.

• **Journal:** As you did when you were preparing to go on disability, continue to keep a journal of your condition, focusing on daily experience of symptoms, pain, etc. Include emotional and mental symptoms such as problems with concentration or memory. The journal not only helps you in the event of a review by your insurer, but also helps you communicate with your physician.

• **Your physician:** Remind your doctor that he may be contacted by the insurer periodically to verify ongoing disability. Tell him that you appreciate his optimistic support in your visits, but that when it comes to dealing with insurers or the SSA, to please focus on how ongoing symptoms and treatment establish continued disability. You are not asking him to lie, but rather to be truthful without optimism about the ongoing nature of your illness.

Take your journal to your physician and ask that the symptoms be included in your medical record. The more often debilitating symptoms are repeated, the more likely your disability income will not be disturbed.

If a form is to be completed, make a special appointment with your physician to emphasize the need for getting it right.

• **Former job:** You may want to stay in touch with people at your former job. They can be a good source of information on benefit issues and other problems. And who knows, you may even want to go back to work one day.

• **Relationships:** Being on disability can be a good time to work on your relationships—to let go of those that don't matter to you, and to strengthen those that do. This is also a good time to let go of whatever else you are hanging on to in your life that is no longer important to you so you can spend your Life Units on what is.

• **Fulfillment:** Reread the advice starting in chapter 4, section 1.3, about how to determine what is fulfilling to you at any given time.

• **Income replacement:** Speak with social workers or other knowledgeable people at your Guard-

ianOrg to find out about any local income-replacement programs for which you may be eligible.

• **Discounts:** Many discounts and free admissions are available to people with a "disability." This is particularly true for entertainment and transportation, including subways and buses. Explore these programs with your social worker or your GuardianOrg. It couldn't hurt to check with GuardianOrgs that represent other conditions to see if they know of any discounts or free admissions to which you may be entitled.

• **Volunteering:** Working for a charity without pay is not overriding evidence that you are no longer "disabled." A volunteer does not have the same obligation to show up every day and is not subject to the stress and demands of doing a good job. If your volunteer work begins to be full-time over an extended period, especially if it involves a lot of stressful travel, check with your attorney to determine how it could impact your benefits, or whether you should make some minor changes that would bring you safely within the definition of "disabled."

• **Work:** If you're up to it, think about at least working part-time. Work will increase your spendable income and help you stay focused. Before you consider working part-time or returning to work full-time, be sure to read the next section to help determine the effect of any work on your benefits.

Section 3. Returning to Work: Part-Time or Full-Time

3.1 What Work to Return To

When considering returning to work after being on disability, your first instinct may be to return to the work you did before the onset of the disability. While this may be a perfectly fine idea, revisit the discussion in chapter 4, section 1, about True Net Pay and fulfillment. Perhaps another employer, or maybe even another occupation, would provide more of both—and maybe even provide health insurance if you don't have it.

Returning to your former employer. If your decision is to return to your previous employer, take a new look at the benefits package to see if there have been any changes to the plan. Find out the details of the current plan and how it applies to you. For example, are you subject to any waiting period normally imposed on a new hire? Is there a preexisting exclusion that would now be applied to you? If you had a group life insurance policy from work that you converted and then sold, do you qualify for life insurance again?

You may also want to consider updating your skills before returning to work.

If you are considering a new employer.
- Take a hard look at your particular skills to determine if they satisfy what the new job requires, and whether they are up-to-date. For example, if you have computer skills, do you know the newest workplace programs? If you lack skills, you should acquire them before you apply. Ask your GuardianOrg about state and local rehabilitation programs, and other places to learn or update your skills.
- Identify current references to provide to the prospective employer.
- Look for an employer that will provide a maximization of fulfillment and True Net Pay (see the discussion in chapter 4, section 1.1).
- Consider a job requiring computer skills. Demand is high, the job is indoors and not physically demanding, and you can often find flexible hours if needed. It may even be possible to find work you can do at home.

Read chapter 14, sections 2 and 3.2, about assessing a new employer's benefits.

3.2 Preparation

Is additional training or education needed? Particularly if you are considering going back to work full-time, determine whether additional training will be necessary to reenter the workforce. Contact your state office that provides assistance to people with disabilities or your GuardianOrg to learn about governmental programs that will pay for educational fees and retraining expenses of people on disability. There are even programs where people on welfare can put money aside tax-free to start a business while continuing to receive benefits. As you will see below, the federal government encourages people to return to work by allowing test work and retraining.

Another alternative, particularly helpful if your job is professional and you have not worked for several years, is to update your skills by working as an apprentice or intern. Or take a refresher or new course.

Additional work experience. It is helpful to create a current work history, but do not be overly concerned about gaps in your résumé. Many totally healthy people have them.

Look at what you've done since your last job and think about how to put the most constructive spin on it. For example, if you have been doing volunteer work, you can describe it and explain how what you did can help with the new job. Or consider volunteering in a capacity that will teach you or hone the skills necessary for the type of job you want. At the least, it will show you are interested enough to do something to qualify you for the new job.

If you have done something entrepreneurial, you can say you wanted to give self-employment a try, but it didn't work out.

Consider going to work for a temporary employment agency, particularly if you can't on a permanent basis find the kind of work you want to do. Temporary employment does not usually entail a job interview or the need for a résumé. It also gives you an idea whether you really are ready to return to work and how much time you'll need to take care of your health. Later, when you have to explain the gap since your last job, you can tailor the explanation to fit your situation; e.g., that you wanted to change your job and have been doing "temp work" to hone your skills and "test the waters."

Tip. People who have done temp work report that success depends on a positive attitude. You have to be ready, able, and enthusiastic to work whenever you are called. The more times you say you are not available to work, the less likely you will be called. If it happens too often with one temp agency, look for another where you'll have a clean slate.

Résumé. Consider writing your résumé in terms of types of experience, rather than dates. Include any life experiences that will benefit the company hiring you. For instance, a seat you held on the school board or church committee signals experience in making decisions and teamwork.

At worst, you can always explain the gap in your résumé by saying, "I had to attend to a personal or family matter," or "I needed time off to deal with an illness in the family."

Interview. Reread chapter 7 about tips for a job interview. Decide how much, if anything, you want to disclose about your condition. As you saw in chapter 6 in the discussion on the Americans with Disabilities Act, an employer cannot ask about your current or past health condition. You may choose to disclose your status, even at the first interview, especially if you know you need an accommodation of some kind to do the job. But if you don't have to disclose it, put yourself in the employer's position: if you had two applicants for a job, and they were equally qualified, would you choose the person with the health history or the one without it?

Be prepared to address the issue of what you have been doing by rehearsing your response before a job interview. Even if an employer asks for more information, you are not required to give it. If you don't want to respond to a follow-up question, rehearse the answer to this type of question as well.

Do not lie. It is likely to come back to haunt you.

3.3 Your Private Disability Income Insurance

Most disability policies provide an incentive to return to work. Some insurance policies may provide "transition or recovery benefits" while you return to work, and some may offer a "recurrent disability provision" without a second waiting or elimination period. Some insurance policies subsidize "rehabilitation training," to develop up-to-date skills for rejoining the workforce. If it's not written into your policy, contact your insurance company to find out what may be applicable.

Tip. Some policies have a six-month return-to-work provision under which you can go back to work, and if during a six-month period you become disabled again, the disability income resumes immediately. If you are seriously considering returning to work and have a policy like this

• read your policy carefully and speak with the insurance company about how the provision works. Request the response in writing.

• have an attorney or qualified benefits person contact the insurer to see if the trial period can be extended. For example, if the period is six months, ask that it be extended to eighteen months. It's in the company's interest to have you go back to work and get off disability, so they may go along. The downside to the request is the company may try to argue you are no longer disabled even if you don't go back to work, which is why I suggest you have an attorney or qualified benefits person do this negotiation for you.

3.4 Your Health Insurance

How your returning to work affects your health insurance coverage depends on the type of coverage you have.

COBRA/OBRA. Returning to work will not affect coverage under the *extension* of a prior employer's coverage. If you receive health insurance at the new job, COBRA terminates when the new coverage covers your preexisting condition.

Voluntary employer continuation. If your health coverage is incidental to disability payments that stop when you start the new job, you can extend it under COBRA.

Individual health insurance. Not affected by returning to work.

3.5 Your Life Insurance

Your life insurance coverage should not be affected except to the extent that it is being continued without cost under a waiver-of-premium benefit that will cease. You will have to start paying the premiums.

If your insurance is part of a group life policy, returning to work will probably terminate the coverage, but you can (and should) generally covert the group life coverage to an individual policy.

3.6 Effect of Earning Wages on SSD and SSI

Earnings from employment will affect your receipt of SSD and SSI benefits. If you are considering a return to wage work, you should consult a social worker familiar with Social Security for advice about how receiving wages will affect your eligibility for benefits. The following discussion provides the background information you need for an informed discussion.

3.7 Medicare

If your SSD is discontinued, you must take immediate active steps to keep your Medicare. *Even if you have another health coverage by that time, it is suggested that you keep Medicare.*

If you have both Medicare and private health insurance:

• You'll reduce or possibly eliminate all fees, deductibles, and copayments.

• You will reduce your overall medical bills to the more economical Medicare rate schedule rather than the higher rate schedule used by private insurance, which should decrease any part of the bills you pay.

• Medicare has generous hospital coverage including psychiatric and substance-abuse care, virtually unlimited medically necessary home health visits, and unlimited outpatient psychiatric care without the severe limitations imposed by most employer plans. Medicare also covers inpatient hospice care, which many health plans don't cover at all.

• Medicare pays 80 percent of all medical supplies such as wheelchairs or oxygen, compared to sharp limits in many employer plans.

• You are always at risk of losing a job and its health insurance coverage, but Medicare continues as long as you have your health condition whether you have a job or not.

• If you are a federal employee, many of the federal employee plans "reward" you for signing up for Medicare by waiving deductibles and copayments.

If your SSD is discontinued for any reason, when you receive the last SSD check, visit your SSA office and tell your representative you want to continue your Medicare and request the paperwork. You then start paying for Parts A and B directly since A is no longer free, and there is no SSD payment from which to deduct the premium for Part B.

3.8 SSA Incentives to Return to Work

Social Security has a number of incentives to make it possible for you to test your ability to work without losing your rights to cash benefits and Medicare or Medicaid.

SSD. Incentives include:

1. Trial work program and extended period of eligibility: *For a cumulative period of any nine* *months in any consecutive five-year period, there are no limits on the amount of money you can earn in what SSA refers to as "substantial gainful activity" while you continue to receive full SSD benefits.*

- Each month in which earnings are more than $200 (or more than forty hours of work in a month for the self-employed) is counted as a month of the trial work period.
- Any month in which you receive more than $500 in unemployment insurance is also counted as a trial work month.

After nine months of substantial gainful activity, cash benefits continue for three *more* months, which serves as extra money to help you return to the workforce. Even after that, there is an "extended period of eligibility," which is a thirty-six-month period during which cash benefits can be reinstated without a new application, disability determination, or waiting period. If you become ill and cannot work, all you have to do is call the Social Security office, let them know you are no longer working, and ask that the check be sent out for that month. There is no paperwork and you don't have to qualify again. In addition, you can attempt to go back to work under these programs and stop as often as necessary.

People who work freelance have been known to bill every second or third month as if the work is only performed in each of the reported months. The idea has been to postpone the cutoff period for up to eighteen months if you are paid every other month, or twenty-seven months if paid every three months. This is a technical violation of the rules, which consider not just what the recipient is paid, but also what should have been recompensed daily, which is then added up for the calendar month in question. The question to SSA is not when the check arrives, but how many days and at what rate the person is being paid "in truth."

People have also been known to try to avoid the restrictions on earned income by incorporating and leaving the profit in the corporation. If SSA learns of this arrangement, it will look through to the substance of the situation.

2. Excess compensation/busywork: For a variety of reasons, some employers create work that is not necessary to the function of the business or pay people with a disability more than their work is worth. This kind of "busywork" is called "subsidized employment" by SSA. Pay that exceeds the actual value of the services performed is not counted to determine "substantial gainful activities," so it does not affect eligibility for SSD.

Tip. If your employer knows about your disability and is sympathetic to your situation, you may consider enlisting his assistance by asking him to write a letter to SSA stating that you are being paid more than your services are worth (e.g., you need more time off, more supervision, or work more slowly than your coworkers). Be cautious: focusing your employer's attention on the fact you may be receiving a "subsidy" may prompt a reconsideration of the situation. Of course, the statements must be true, and the person who writes the letter must be prepared to testify to the facts to SSA.

3. Impairment-related work expenses: You may be able to offset expenditures against your monthly earnings. Such expenditures must satisfy the following tests:

- They are required to make it possible for you to work, even if those items and/or services are needed for activities other than work.
- You paid for them.
- You are not being reimbursed.

For example, the cost of drugs and treatments necessary to control a disabling condition so you can work are deductible, as are expenses for a wheelchair or special transportation. Drugs used only for minor physical problems are not.

4. Medicare coverage: You are entitled to continue both Part A and Part B Medicare coverage during the trial work period, plus a three-month grace period and a thirty-six-month "extended period of eligibility" (i.e., a total of thirty-nine months beyond the trial work period). When SSD checks stop, be sure to send a check to SSA for the

Medicare Part B premium since you will no longer be getting the SSD check from which it is normally deducted. After the thirty-six-month extended period, you can continue to stay on Part A, but you have to pay a premium for it.

If you haven't yet qualified for Medicare at the time you start working on the trial work period, the months in the trial work period, the grace period, and then the extended period can be counted toward the required two-year Medicare waiting period.

As long as you continue to have the condition that originally qualified you for SSD, even if that lasts throughout a long lifetime, eligibility for Medicare continues—no matter how much money you earn or for how long you've returned to work.

Tip. If you obtain health insurance from an employer, keep your Medicare as well. Having both coverages is advantageous with a serious condition. (See section 3.7.)

5. Vocational rehabilitation program: For people who improve medically and are therefore no longer "disabled," benefits continue if the person participates in an approved program that is likely to enable the person to work permanently.

6. Blind people: There are special rules for people who are blind. You don't have to be totally sightless to be "blind" for SSA purposes. People with corrected vision worse than 20/200 qualify, as do people with certain conditions that affect eyesight.

7. Under twenty-two years of age: There are also special rules for people under twenty-two years of age who are attending school or a vocational course for at least eight hours a week.

For further information about these programs: Contact SSA at 800-722-1213 or visit your local SSA office and request a copy of *Red Book on Work Incentives* (publication no. 64-030).

SSI. While people on SSI are also encouraged to return to work, the programs are not as generous as with SSD, since SSI is a welfare program. For instance, SSI does not have a trial work period. SSI features to note include:

1. Plan for Achieving Self-Support (PASS): PASS is an SSI program that allows recipients to set aside income or resources for a specified period for achieving future self-support. For example, a person could set aside funds for training or for starting a business. It's even possible to save all your income in a PASS account, which would mean your "countable" income for SSI purposes could be reduced to zero, so you would qualify for a full SSI payment while saving money! There is no limit on the amount of money that can be saved in a PASS account.

To obtain PASS

- your plan must appear to be reasonable and achievable within four years.
- your plan must be endorsed in writing by a public or private social service, vocational rehabilitation or disability group or agency.
- you must place the income and/or assets being set aside in a separate bank account that must not be touched and that SSA will monitor.

If you violate any PASS rules, you can lose all your SSI benefits.

Tom McCormack, author of *The AIDS Benefits Handbook,* notes you can turn a PASS account into cash to supplement SSI payments by using the bank account to collateralize a secured credit card (see chapter 21, section 4.2). You can live on credit card charges or cash advances while keeping the account open to satisfy PASS. To keep this solution viable, you must meet minimum monthly payments to the credit card firm, which should be easy because each deposit into the account allows you to increase your credit limit by at least the amount of the deposit, and perhaps more. Adding credit and disability insurance to the account is an added bonus, but Mr. McCormack advises against claiming disability or unemployment while you expect to continue using the card, the PASS, or the secured account because your card will be canceled for future charges and your account balance may be debited by the credit card company's insurer. That could well mean a loss of your Medicaid and other benefits.

Note: The artificially reduced PASS income, rather than your actual income, is what other assistance programs such as public housing and food stamps must count by law, so in addition to saving money, PASS may result in an increase in other benefits. There are other state assistance programs for which the states are also permitted (not required) to use the PASS income.

2. Impairment-related work expenses: As with SSD, these expenditures may be offset against your monthly earnings (see above).

3. Excess compensation/busywork: Unlike with SSD, this type of income does affect eligibility for SSI (see above).

4. Continuation of Medicaid eligibility: Medicaid may continue for SSI recipients who are disabled or blind and earn over the SSI limits if they cannot afford similar medical care and depend on Medicaid in order to work.

5. Students with disabilities: Tuition, books, and other expenses related to getting an education may not be counted as income for recipients who go to school or are in a training program.

SSI counts all earnings except for $85 a month and one-half of the remainder of your earnings before comparing your income to the maximum allowed.

Ask for advice on how your monthly earnings will affect your SSI payments and Medicaid coverage. There is a program under which you can work and still qualify for Medicaid coverage if

- you still have the condition for which you qualified as "disabled";
- you meet all the SSI requirements except for the amount of your earnings;

- you need the Medicaid in order to work; *and*
- you get advance approval from SSA.

You can keep your Medicaid up to a maximum income that varies depending on the state in which you reside (between $20,000 and $30,000 a year).

If you are receiving food stamps or other public assistance, ask your social worker how working will affect those benefits.

For further information about working while on SSI: Call SSA at 800-772-1213 or visit your local office and ask for a copy of *Working While Disabled: A Guide to Plans for Achieving Self-Support While Receiving Supplemental Security Income* (publication no. 05-11017).

3.9 Inform SSA About Work

Let SSA know when you are considering going to work, and when you actually work, even if you only work for one month. The IRS reports all earnings to the SSA, so SSA will ultimately find out. Even income "off the books" or that you earn under a friend's Social Security number and name could be traced if it goes through any bank account or supports a lifestyle that could not be accomplished on your reported income.

The notification should preferably be in writing, when you start or end a job or when there are changes that affect your earnings. Keep a copy of the notification. If you do the notification in person or on the phone, always note the name of the person to whom you report your work activities and the date you make the report, in case you need proof at a later time.

If you don't report your activities to SSA and you are caught, according to one seasoned SSA representative, "you not only get the book thrown at you, but you have an agency that no longer trusts you, and that's not good." A former SSA employee relates that past practice has been that if a person receives SSD beyond when he should, SSA only requests a return of the overpayment, without interest or penalty. If no response is received from SSA calls and letters, the practice has been for SSA to turn the matter over to the Internal Revenue Service for collection of the overpayment. As a practical matter, this has only meant collection of the overpayment from people with assets.

As noted in section 3.7, if your SSD is discontinued, take the necessary steps to continue your Medicare.

3.10 State Programs

Various state and local programs provide grants for tuition and possibly for ancillary expenses for retraining and educational programs. While "disabled," Ralph T. learned to do graphic illustrations on a computer at a school of his choice. Tuition and expenses were paid by the state. Contact your GuardianOrg or the state office for people with disabilities for more information.

Chapter 12

Retirement Planning

> The thing I should wish to obtain from money would be leisure with security.
>
> —Bertrand Russell

This chapter discusses retirement planning issues that are important to people with health concerns. If you have one, you should understand certain essential features about your employer-sponsored **retirement plan,** not only so you can understand your benefits and rights under the plan, but also so you can compare your employer's plans to other retirement plans for which you may be eligible. A retirement plan (also known as a **pension plan**) is a separate entity into which money is placed to be invested until withdrawal upon becoming disabled, reaching a certain age, retiring, or other specific events.

Section 1. Why Plan for Retirement?

Although you are confronted with a life-challenging condition, you should still plan for your retirement and put as much money into pension plans as you can spare because

- you can deduct the contribution to the plan from your current higher tax bracket, postpon-

ing the tax until you are in a lower bracket due to disability, decreased income, or retirement.
- if you become disabled, you can access the funds in the retirement account without the penalty that usually accompanies early withdrawal of these funds.
- retirement assets can serve as a contingency fund that can be converted to current income as needed.
- retirement assets can serve as a legacy to your heirs.
- your condition may go into remission, you may outlive your diagnosis into retirement, or you could be cured.
- retirement assets are protected from creditors.

As you will see, retirement planning is complicated. Before you start a new retirement plan, withdraw funds from an existing plan, or even transfer funds from one plan to another, consult an expert. Mistakes in this area can be expensive.

127

Section 2. How Much to Save for Retirement

While the following discussion describes the ideal amount of money in the ideal retirement plan, the key is to make "what is" better, not to get aggravated over what "is not."

As a general rule, you will need 80 percent of current expense, adjusted for inflation, to maintain your lifestyle during retirement—assuming there is appropriate health insurance coverage.

To give you an idea of how much you will need to save for retirement, complete the worksheet below.

Section 3. Types of Investments

Maximize tax-deferment. Investments outside of retirement accounts and investments in retirement accounts should be part of an overall strategy. How-ever, a distinction between investments within retirement plans as compared to investments outside of retirement plans is that maximizing the tax-deferred treatment of these moneys in the plans becomes the primary investment objective that drives the other two objectives of maximizing income and growth.

Investments placed in retirement plans have certain tax benefits that are not available to other types of investments:

- Your investments, known as contributions, are tax deductible up to certain limits for pretax savings.
- If you invest through an employer retirement plan, your pretax contributions may be eligible for matching employer contributions—which essentially means you receive "free money" to invest for retirement.
- The earnings on your contributions (yield, also known as your investment and capital appreciation, the amount by which the value of your asset increases) are tax-deferred until distribu-

› ›

Retirement Worksheet

Current monthly expenses (including cost of health insurance, deductibles, copays, and uninsured expenses) $_____		
multiplied x .80 = Line 1		$
Less monthly Social Security income		
Less monthly retirement plan income		
Less other sources of monthly income		
Total of deductions Line 2		$
Total = surplus/shortfall (line 1–line 2)		$

tion—which means your contributions will benefit from faster compounded growth.

• Tax-deferred compounded growth also makes after-tax contributions worthwhile given a long enough time horizon.

These tax benefits will not only help you to save and invest for retirement, they also reduce your current tax bill.

Term. As a general matter, investments made in retirement plans generally have a longer term than other investments. Normally funds in a retirement plan cannot be accessed until age 59½ without incurring income tax and penalties. However, as you will see, under certain circumstances—such as permanent disability—you can access your retirement funds before you retire, sometimes with reduced tax consequences so your investments can be shorter term than the norm for retirement plans.

Section 4. Overview of Retirement Plans

If you already have a retirement plan and are making your maximum contribution, then skip to section 8. If you don't have a retirement plan or aren't sure you're maximizing the amount you can place into it—read on.

Types of plans. There are three general types of retirement plans:

• Social Security, sponsored by the federal government.
• an employer retirement plan.
• an individual retirement plan.

You may be eligible for more than one type of retirement plan, so make sure you prioritize your contributions to plans that maximize tax deductions, tax deferral, or liquidity, in the following order:

1. Employer-sponsored plans that provide matching contributions.

2. Any plans to which you can make pretax contributions.
3. After reaching your limit for pretax contributions, any plans to which you can make after-tax contributions.
4. Other retirement vehicles that provide options for tapping your retirement funds prior to retirement.

Establishing a retirement plan. You can establish a retirement account through the same channels as other types of investments, either on your own or in conjunction with a financial/investment adviser. These channels are your employer, financial/investment adviser, banks, savings and loan associations, credit unions, mutual fund companies, brokerage firms, and insurance companies.

Section 5. Government-Sponsored Retirement Plan—Social Security Retirement Benefits

Overview. Social Security provides American citizens and their families with four types of benefits: disability benefits, retirement benefits, survivor benefits, and Medicare benefits. Social Security retirement benefits are not intended to provide for all your retirement income needs—but rather to provide a subsistence level of income for basic necessities, just as Medicare covers basic medical coverage.

Who is eligible and when. Eligibility for Social Security retirement benefits requires

• work in *covered employment* for a minimum number of quarters. To be fully insured, you must have forty quarters of coverage (a total of ten years in covered work). Once the forty quarters are acquired, you are fully insured for life, even if you spend no further time in covered employment or covered self-employment.
• attaining age sixty-five, sixty-six, or sixty-seven depending on your date of birth, although you

may elect to receive reduced benefits at age sixty-two, or slightly increased benefits at age seventy.

If you qualify for Social Security retirement benefits, then your family (i.e., spouse, ex-spouse, and certain dependents) also qualifies to receive "family benefits" while you collect retirement benefits and "survivor benefits" after you die.

Unlike other types of retirement plans, your Social Security retirement benefits are not based dollar-for-dollar on the amount you pay into the system. You may receive more or less than you pay in, depending on eligibility requirements. (If you haven't requested an estimate of your Social Security retirement benefits from SSA, see chapter 3, section 3.)

Claims. See chapter 10 if you are filing because of disability. For any other reason, contact SSA for the forms and procedures.

Living abroad. If you are a U.S. citizen, you can travel or live abroad in most countries without affecting your eligibility for Social Security retirement benefits (unless you also work abroad).

Tax. See chapter 8, section 8.1, with respect to tax on SSD.

SSI. Note that if you don't qualify for Social Security, or if your Social Security benefits are low, you may be eligible for Supplemental Security Income (SSI). There are strict income eligibility guidelines for SSI. See chapter 8, section 8.2, for a further discussion of SSI.

Section 6. Employer-Sponsored Plans

Employers are not required to have pension plans. If one exists, there is no requirement that it apply to all employees. However, if you are part of a plan through your employer, or if you are considering a new job, the essential features to focus on are:

- **Qualified versus unqualified plans: Qualified plans** qualify for tax-deductible, tax-deferred status by complying with certain IRS regulations. Examples of qualified plans include 401(k)s, IRAs, and Keoghs. **Unqualified plans** do not comply with IRS guidelines and therefore do not qualify for tax-deductible and/or tax-deferred status. An example of an unqualified plan is a deferred annuity (which is tax-deferred but not tax deductible).

- **Defined benefit versus defined contribution plans:** The traditional employer-sponsored pension plan used to be a **defined benefit plan.** Upon retirement, participants in the plan receive a predetermined amount of monthly benefit based on their salary and length of employment. The contribution may vary to assure there will be enough assets in the plan to pay the benefits, but the benefits do not change. Today, employers are emphasizing **defined contribution plans** (also known as **retirement savings plans**). They require a defined contribution each year (which could be a fixed dollar amount or one determined by a formula). The amount received on retirement fluctuates according to the amount in the plan.

- **Contribution limits:** Your annual pretax contributions are limited, based on how many and which retirement plans you participate in. The maximum contribution (combination of employee and employer amounts) cannot exceed 25 percent of your salary or $30,000, whichever is less.

- **Investment options:** When evaluating different retirement plans, find out what investment options are offered under the plan, whether you may transfer your retirement assets among different investment options, and whether transfers are subject to certain fees (e.g., commissions or penalties). Generally, individual-sponsored plans provide broader and more flexible investment options than employer-sponsored plans.

- **Eligibility to participate in a plan:** You must be in a covered category of employee. Generally, you must also be at least twenty-one and have completed one year of full-time service (more than one thousand hours of work) to be eligible for an employer-sponsored plan. Part-time or seasonal employees may also be eligible depending on the terms of the plan.
- **"Accrued benefits" under a plan:** Benefits, options, and rights may accrue differently depending on your years of service from the date you become a plan participant.
- **Hours:** Your plan may reduce your benefits if the number of hours you work is reduced. Check your plan if you are considering reducing your work hours.
- **Your rights under the plan:** Look at your right to borrow, make withdrawals and/or transfers from the account, early-retirement benefits, optional forms of benefit payments, and similar matters, all of which differ according to the particular plan. It is particularly important for you to identify and understand the disability provisions of your retirement plan—for example, the definition of disability, termination of contributions, vesting under disability, accessing your retirement funds if disabled, and exemption from tax or tax penalties. Many retirement plans provide that you are fully vested upon disability and may withdraw the funds in your retirement account with reduced tax consequences (such as no 10 percent premature-withdrawal penalty tax).
- **Your "vested benefits" under the plan:** Vesting refers to the number of years of service you must complete before you can claim nonforfeitable rights to your accrued benefits. Employer vesting schedules typically range from five to seven years. Your "individual benefits statement," available from your plan administrator, will describe your total accrued and vested benefits. *Your own contributions and their earnings are always 100 percent vested.*
- **The payout options for receiving your benefits:** Generally, retirement benefits may be received as a lump sum or in periodic payments.
- **Assessing your plan's performance:** You are entitled to receive an annual statement of your benefits as well as a "summary annual report," which gives you general information regarding the plan's status, including whether it is adequately funded.
- **Federal protection of retirement benefits:** To protect employee pensions from a private employer's potential financial deterioration, vested benefits in *defined benefit* pension plans are insured by the Pension Benefit Guarantee Corporation (PBGC), which guarantees employee pension benefits up to certain limits.
- **The plan's disclosure requirements:** Either automatically or upon request, the plan administrator is required under ERISA to provide you with certain disclosure documents: the Plan document and a Summary Plan Description, your Individual Benefits Statement, Summary Annual Reports, IRS form 5500, Summary of Material Modification, Notice of Plan Funding, and PBGC guarantees, if applicable. If you have difficulty obtaining copies of these documents from your employer or plan administrator, contact the Pension and Welfare Benefits Administration of the U.S. Labor Department at 202-219-8776.

For information about an employer or potential employer's plan, ask the employer or plan administrator for a copy of the Plan document, a Summary Plan Description, and the latest annual report. As a participant, you are entitled to receive copies of these documents within thirty days of your written request (although you may be required to pay reasonable costs). If you have questions, consult a pension specialist or financial adviser. If necessary, your attorney or accountant can recommend pension specialists.

Tip. To help understand the language in pension plans, request a copy of "What You Should Know About the Pension Law," Consumer Information Center, P.O. Box 100, Pueblo, CO 81002. The cost is $.50.

Section 7. Individual-Sponsored Plans

Retirement plans you can start on your own are:

Individual retirement account (IRA).
- Generally, if you are not an active participant in another qualified plan and you meet certain income limits, you can make an individual tax-deductible contribution up to $2,000 to an IRA. Investment gains accumulate tax free and are subject to tax only when withdrawn after you reach age 59½. Earlier withdrawals are generally subject to a 10 percent penalty.
- There are special rules for married couples.
- **SEP (IRA):** Intended for individuals with supplemental self-employment income (i.e., "moonlighters") as well as for small companies and their employees. Maximum pretax contribution is 15 percent of gross income up to $22,500.
- **SIMPLE (IRA):** For individuals with supplemental self-employed income as well as for any company with fewer than one hundred employees. Maximum pretax contribution can be 100 percent of gross income up to $6,000, plus 3 percent of earnings.
- **Roth (IRA):** Contributions to the account are not deductible. Earnings compound tax free and are taxable only in a nonqualified distribution. Tax-free "qualified distributions" include those made

because the taxpayer is disabled, a first-time home buyer, over age 59½, or upon death. No payment can be qualified until five tax years after the taxpayer first contributes to the Roth IRA. The maximum contribution permitted is $2,000 per year minus the taxpayer's deductible IRA contributions. The $2,000 limit is phased out as adjusted gross income increases above $95,000 for single taxpayers and $150,000 for a married couple filing jointly.

Keogh plans.
- A retirement plan for self-employed individuals and their employees, or for individuals with supplemental self-employment income.
- There are three types of Keogh plans—profit sharing, money purchase pension, or a combination of profit sharing/money purchase pension.
- Depending on the type of Keogh plan, the maximum pretax contribution is 13.04 to 20 percent of gross income or $30,000, whichever is lower.

Tip. If an IRA or Keogh plan is funded with borrowed money, your interest payments as well as your pretax contributions will be tax deductible.

Deferred annuity. Although not a formal retirement "plan," deferred annuities issued by insurance companies have traditionally been used as retirement investments. Unlike retirement plans, contributions are made after tax, therefore there is no limit on contribution amounts. While contributions are not tax deductible, they still benefit from tax-deferred compounded growth. A deferred annuity may be a worthwhile retirement investment for an investor who has already made the maximum annual pretax contributions and would like to make additional tax-deferred investments (provided the investor is in a high enough tax bracket to benefit). *An annuity may not be a suitable* *investment for an investor with a shortened life expectancy, given the long-term investment required (typically ten years) to realize returns and amortize fairly high costs. Instead, after-tax contributions to an IRA may be more worthwhile.*

Section 8. Ten Commonsense Tips for Retirement Planning Success

1. Investment and retirement planning are not separate activities. The essential distinction is between investments you make inside or outside of tax-sheltered retirement vehicles. Both types of investments should support a common investment strategy and result from careful financial planning.

2. Be proactive in your retirement planning, since self-reliance is by far the most dependable retirement income source. Although it's a long shot, certain sources may not be available when you need them (e.g., Social Security may no longer exist by the time you retire; your employer retirement plan may not be sufficient; spousal retirement benefits may no longer be available if you divorce).

3. As with any investment portfolio, make sure the funds you allocate, both within and among various retirement plans, are appropriately diversified.

4. Be careful which investments you make through retirement vehicles, because not all types of investments are appropriate for tax-deferred retirement vehicles:

- Do not place tax-exempt investments (i.e., tax-exempt bonds or money market funds) inside tax-deferred retirement vehicles. They would lose their tax-exempt status upon distribution, when they will be subject to income tax.
- Do not place tax-sheltered annuities inside retirement vehicles. The only benefit to placing a tax-deferred investment inside a tax-deferred retirement vehicle is for the annuity salesperson, who receives a commission.

- Do not roll over your employer stock to an IRA, because all IRA distributions are taxed as ordinary income even if derived from capital gains. Bear in mind that for equity held outside of retirement vehicles, capital gains are taxed at the capital gains rate—whereas for equity held inside retirement vehicles, capital gains are taxed at typically higher income tax rates. Ultimately, the decision to place certain investments inside retirement vehicles will depend, in part, on whether you have a long enough investment horizon so that the benefit of tax-deferred compounded growth outweighs the drawback of taxing capital gains at income tax rates.

5. Receive your next raise, bonus, or unused vacation pay "tax-free" by funneling it into your employer retirement plan.

- As a pretax contribution to an employer retirement plan, your compensation is not only "tax free" (i.e., the contribution is tax deductible), but also benefits from tax-deferred compounded growth.
- Your contribution may also qualify for an employer matching contribution (in essence meaning you receive "double compensation" tax free).

6. When you roll over or transfer funds among retirement accounts, *never* take direct possession of the funds or you may be subject to 20 percent withholding, additional income tax, and a 10 percent tax penalty for early withdrawal.

7. Consider consolidating your various retirement accounts to simplify investment management, eliminate duplicate fees, and reduce administrative burdens, or shift funds between retirement accounts to optimize your investment strategy. Don't take these steps without considering the special rules for trustee-to-trustee transfers or IRA/Keogh rollovers.

8. Select trustees that charge low, flat fees.

Tip: Even if your retirement accounts are "self-managed," they will still be placed with a trustee that may charge any of three types of fees—establishment fee, annual fee, and/or transaction fee. Depending on the complexity of your retirement accounts, try to avoid trustees that charge fees as a percentage of your account or per transaction.

9. Maintain accurate documentation on your retirement accounts. Keep your own copy, review it at least annually, and update it as necessary.

10. Designate your intended heirs as beneficiaries on your retirement account registration forms rather than in your will to avoid probate.

Tip. Financial and investment planning does not end when you retire. Periodic checkups are too important to ignore.

Chapter 13

Investments

'Tis money that begets money.
—Thomas Fuller, M.D.,
1732

This chapter offers investment suggestions tailored to the needs of an investor living with a life-challenging condition.

The chapter discusses the development of an overall investment strategy, then describes the various investment criteria the strategy uses, and finally covers available investments in terms of these criteria.

If you haven't already done so, this is a good time to complete the Net Worth worksheet in chapter 4 so that you have an overview of your financial situation. You may also want to consider whether to involve your spouse, your significant other, and/or heirs in the decisions. In addition to considering investment strategies, you should also consider what will be left for your heirs.

are based on the laws of large numbers and averages. Statistics, by their nature, reflect past, not future, events. Doctors can be wrong, even in the category of six months or less. Having been given a life expectancy of a few months two years ago, Sean S. is still alive.

Throughout this chapter, the discussion focuses on three different life expectancies. The time frames, and the abbreviations that will be used to identify them throughout the rest of the chapter, are

- life expectancy (LE) more than five years (LE>5);
- LE between two and five years (2<LE<5); and
- LE less than two years (LE<2).

Section 1. How Much Time?

Your investment strategy depends on life expectancy. The information described in chapter 3, section 4, should give you a sense of your life expectancy on a statistical basis.

Please keep in mind that statistical projections

Section 2. Personal Planning

The strategy (LE<2) (2<LE<5) (LE>5). There are certain financial goals to aim for regardless of life expectancy. These were already covered in chapter 4, but are summarized here because of their importance:

- Identify, quantify, and prioritize your financial goals.
- Develop an action plan while keeping in mind that meeting the costs associated with your illness is another goal you need to include in your overall plan. Some resources currently earmarked for growth (or some other financial goal) may have to be shifted to provide for your health needs.
- Monitor results. Strive for the following:
  - disciplined, consistent implementation.
  - accurate measurement through monthly and yearly income statements.
  - periodic reevaluation and revision.

Section 3. Professional Advice

In considering whether to consult a financial adviser, it may help to do a quick cost/benefit assessment of the alternatives.

For the investor employing an "income strategy," using a professional adviser may be unnecessary since the majority of investments will be in simple cash equivalents such as money market accounts. Your banker or accountant should be able to point you to the available alternatives. However, for more complex "growth strategy" investments (such as mutual funds), as well as for overall financial and investment planning purposes, using a professional adviser may be worthwhile. The chart on the following page lists the possible costs and benefits of each method.

How to select professional advisers. See chapter 36, section 7.

Section 4. Develop Your Investment Strategy

Once you have identified and prioritized your financial goals, the next thing to do is to adopt an investment strategy and stick to it.

As will be described in detail in section 5, an investment strategy is made up of **investment criteria**—the things you need to think about when evaluating whether a particular investment is appropriate for your needs. All investment vehicles must be evaluated with your statistical life expectancy in mind.

In planning your investment strategy, review chapters 19 through 23, which concern new uses of existing assets. In the circumstances noted, these assets can be converted into cash when needed.

Tip. Reevaluate your investment plan if your health changes significantly.

The investment strategies I suggest during each of the three periods under consideration are:

Less than two years (LE<2). Maximize available cash in case you need it. Adopt an **income strategy** (cash return on your investment such as dividends or interest) that maximizes **liquidity** (the ability to turn an asset into cash) and minimizes risk. If you need to access principal to meet your current needs, take this into account when projecting future income. If the return on an investment stays the same, but the amount of the investment decreases, the income earned on the investment will also decrease. When you consider liquid assets, don't forget the assets described in chapters 19 to 23.

If you have the resources, you may decide to simultaneously pursue a **growth strategy,** which increases the dollar value of assets. A growth strategy is based on traditional long-term financial planning to meet goals such as increasing wealth, putting children through college, and estate planning.

More than two years less than five years (2<LE<5). Some combination of income and growth strategies is appropriate. The extent to which you need to access principal to meet cur-

﹥ ﹥

	Do It Yourself	Financial Adviser
Control over financial and investment planning	total	as much or as little as you want
Fees and costs	minimal: can use inexpensive trader	costs to trade securities vary from 0.75 to 2.5 percent; management fees range from 1 to 3 percent*
Satisfaction/fulfillment	is enjoyable for some people	less stress
Life Units	can be extensive	very few
Risk of loss	can be great due to inexperience or lack of immediate knowledge	can obtain sound financial and investment planning from an expert who works at making investment decisions full-time
"Value added" services	none	generally includes portfolio management, administration, and research

*When considering a professional adviser, your net rate of return is more important than payments to the adviser incurred to obtain that return.

rent needs has to be taken into account in assessing potential return. *It is important for investors in this category not to adopt a strategy that is too focused on the short term.* You need to be prepared for the possibility that you may live longer than your current life expectancy. For you, the assets described in chapters 19 through 23 serve as supplemental investments that are available for unusual needs.

More than five years (LE>5). For those people diagnosed with a condition that could mean years of health and gainful activity, it is essential to begin an investment strategy focused on growth—with built-in liquidity—as soon as possible. Your investment plan should be somewhat less risky than that of the average person who has no health con-

cerns—and your plan should avoid complicated investments because you need to be able to change strategies quickly. If you have to access principal when you are not earning income, keep in mind that your potential to realize interest income decreases. The assets described in chapters 19 through 23 provide supplemental investments, some of which are available for emergencies.

Section 5. Investment Criteria

To reach the optimal balance of income and growth, the most important investment criteria to consider are **liquidity, risk, return, fees, taxes, and administration.** *No investment should be eval-*

uated on the basis of any single criterion, but rather on how well the composite of relevant criteria support your overall investment strategy.

5.1 Liquidity

The relative liquidity of an asset is determined by its degree of **marketability** and **flexibility**. Highly liquid assets can be readily purchased or sold (marketability factors) and readily modified (flexibility factors). For example, an investment in a mutual fund would be liquid if you could sell your shares at any time you wish with no charge or penalty. The investment is highly marketable and flexible because you can increase or decrease the investment at will. On the other hand, if there is a charge for the sale, or if you are limited to investing or selling at certain times, the investment is not so liquid.

LE<2. For an investor using an income strategy, maximizing liquidity is the most important investment criterion. Ranking liquidity as the most important criterion has a direct influence on other investment criteria. For example, highly liquid investments will also be associated with lower risk, less emphasis on the need for diversification, and lower returns.

2<LE<5, LE>5. Liquidity is an important concern for anyone with a life-challenging condition, since you will always want to have access to cash for the needs associated with your condition. The longer the time that you have to work with, the less weight to be given to liquidity as compared to other considerations.

5.2 Risk

Risk refers to the possibility that your investment may decrease in value and is measured by the volatility of total returns on your investment.

Different investment classes (e.g., cash equivalents, fixed income, equity) are associated with different types and degrees of risk. Different types

of risk to consider are issuer-default risk (also known as credit risk), market risk (also known as beta or diversifiable risk), interest-rate risk, and inflation risk.

Keep in mind that while some investments may be liquid, you may not get what you paid for them if you have to sell them at the wrong time. Stocks are liquid, but the price you can get when you have to sell might be lower than what you paid. This illustrates market risk. Treasury bills too are liquid, but if you have to sell before maturity, there is the risk that interest rates will be higher (inflation risk) than when you purchased yours, which would mean you would receive less cash on a sale.

For an investor with a shortened life expectancy (LE<2), interest-rate and inflation risk are less of a concern due to the shortened investment horizon. Inflation risk and interest-rate risk take on greater significance the longer the investment horizon (2<LE<5) (LE>5).

Risk can be minimized in various ways. Allocation, diversification, and dollar cost averaging all need to be considered when making investment decisions.

- **Allocation** is the minimizing of risk by investing across different investment classes (e.g., cash equivalents, fixed income, equity), or more simply stated, "not putting all of your eggs in one basket."
- **Diversification** is close to allocation, except with the more specific goal of selecting a portfolio of assets whose values tend to move in different directions. The objective of diversification is to minimize risk by allocating your total portfolio of investments across different assets that tend to perform differently at any one time. The principle of diversification applies both to different investment classes (e.g., fixed income versus equity), as well as to different assets within the same class (e.g., blue-chip versus small-chip equity). One common method of diversification is to invest in mutual funds or index funds rather than individual securities.

• **Dollar cost averaging** is investing equal amounts periodically—each month or each quarter for example—instead of investing a lump sum at one time. Dollar cost averaging spreads your investment across time, which minimizes the risk of adverse swings in the value of your investment. Using this strategy, your monthly investment purchases more shares when prices are low and fewer shares when prices are high. Adopting this strategy helps you to establish investing as a priority.

LE<2. For the investor applying an income strategy, minimizing risk is a primary investment criteria. The basic risk principles of allocation, diversification, and dollar cost averaging are less meaningful for the investor using an income strategy because the majority of this investor's portfolio will be in low-risk, highly liquid "cash equivalent" investments. However, as the primary investment criteria for an income strategy are satisfied, and there are additional funds to pursue a complementary growth strategy, these risk principles become fundamental.

2<LE<5, LE>5. People with a longer statistical life expectancy have a higher tolerance for risk: the more time you have, the higher the tolerance. Remember that time and risk are relative: a person at age thirty-two without a life-challenging condition could afford an investment in a friend's "wild scheme," but not the same person at age sixty-eight, unless he has plenty of other assets. Allocation, diversification, and dollar cost averaging become more important the longer the time with which you are working.

5.3 Return

Return is the earnings you receive on your investment. Usually, return relates to the risk of a particular investment.

An investment's **total return** consists of two components—**yield** (interest and/or dividend in-

come) plus **capital appreciation** (increase in the value of your investment). Depending on the type of investment you make, your return will consist of one or both of these components. When considering return, also consider the type of interest rate (fixed or variable) and the payout method offered (period or at maturity).

The term *return* is used with different meanings. When comparing returns, make sure you are comparing apples and apples. Although the following uses are standard in the securities industry, confirm the meaning of each term whenever it is used:

• **Real return** is equal to the quoted return less inflation.
• **True return** is equal to the quoted return less inflation *and* less fees.
• **Average return** is equal to total annual returns divided by the total number of years during which you own the investment.
• **After-tax return** is equal to your return after taxes are subtracted.
• **Equivalent taxable yield** compares a tax-free yield to one that is taxable. Equivalent taxable yield is yield subject to tax, before deducting the tax. The idea is to figure out what investment has a greater yield, taxable or tax free. To make the comparison, start with the sum of your federal and state tax rate. Determine the tax on the taxable investment. Subtract the tax from the return on the investment and compare the result to a tax-free investment. Notice that if your tax rate is low (say for example while you are on disability), your yield on the taxable investment increases.

LE<2. For the investor applying an income strategy, return is not an important investment criteria, since the emphasis is on maximizing liquidity and minimizing risk.

2<LE<5, LE>5. The longer the time you have to work with, the greater your tolerance for risk, and thus the greater the opportunity to benefit from potential higher returns. Remember, however, that as compared to the average investor, you want to pursue a less risky strategy.

5.4 Fees

An investor with a shortened life expectancy has a shorter investment horizon not only for realizing returns, but also for amortizing fees and other related costs. Fees, therefore, are also an important investment criteria.

There are several types of investment fees including

- management fees for asset-management services.
- transaction fees such as sales commissions and trading charges.
- "hidden" fees such as charges for withdrawals, transfers, or redemptions.

Your investments may be subject to any or all of these fees, depending on the type of investments you make (e.g., simple cash equivalents as compared to more complex mutual funds), and the investment method you use, such as do-it-yourself instead of using a financial adviser.

Investment fees and related costs can take a large bite out of your annual returns. As with any new investment you make, some basic research and comparison shopping will save you money. Review prospectus documents carefully to determine fees. If your investments are made through a financial adviser, ask how their fees are determined (the more fees are tied to performance the better). Are there lower fees for different amounts of investment? Don't be afraid to bargain for discounted fees, particularly if you're investing a significant amount of money through one adviser.

5.5 Taxes

Taxes are another important investment criterion, particularly for the investor whose primary con-

cern is liquidity, simply because any tax due at the end of the year will be a drain on precious cash flow. Keep in mind that taxes vary depending on your tax bracket. While no investment should be made based solely on the criterion of tax (or any other single criterion), investments should be made with due consideration given to avoiding or deferring tax (for both you and your heirs).

Generic types of investment tax to consider.
- Tax on interest/dividend income and tax on capital gains.
- Local, state, federal, and property tax.
- Estate tax.
- Alternative minimum tax.

Tip.
- Keep in mind that your tax rate will change with your income.
- Consider whether return on a particular investment will change your tax bracket, making it less valuable.
- Try to maximize pretax contributions to retirement plans. Income will eventually be taxed, but not until the years when your income will probably be less (during disability or retirement).
- Try to sell investments that will produce a loss this year (claim tax deductions for investment losses while your earnings are high) while buying investments that will produce a gain next year (defer capital gains tax until your earnings may be lower).
- Pay careful attention to tax deadlines.
- Depending on your overall investment strategy, try to invest in tax-exempt or tax-deferred investment vehicles. Before you invest to receive nontaxable income, be sure you understand the value to you. A higher return that is subject to tax may be better for you than a smaller tax-free return. To compare the two, take your tax rate (both state and federal) and tax the taxable investment. Then, compare the after-tax return to

the tax-free investment. If your Adjusted Gross Income is over $117,950, then the amount of your itemized deductions and personal exemptions are subject to reduction because of your high earnings. Thus your calculation should also include the benefit nontaxable income has on the retention of itemized deductions and exemptions. If numbers are not your strength, your accountant or financial adviser can help compare returns for you.

Income-tax and estate-tax planning. If taxes are an issue for you because of the size of your income or estate, consult a professional tax adviser for assistance in planning a strategy that maximizes your net return.

5.6 Administration

The administrative burdens associated with a particular investment are also important to consider.

- What is the minimum administrative effort that a certain investment vehicle will require of you?
- Do the investment's benefits outweigh its administrative costs and use of your Life Units? To illustrate, take a second to contemplate the administrative burdens associated with three investments of differing complexity—CDs, mutual funds, and real estate.
- Do comparable investment vehicles offer any options for reducing administrative burdens? Following are examples of available options for reducing fund transfers and paperwork:
  - automatic deductions from your payroll for retirement plan contributions.
  - automatic deductions from your bank account for mutual fund contributions.
  - automatic credits to your bank account for interest and dividend payments.
  - telephone redemption of shares.
  - interest and dividend reinvestment plans.
  - dollar-cost-averaging planning.

Section 6. Investment Vehicles

Now that we've covered the basic investment decision criteria, we can focus on various types of investment vehicles available. There are three generic types of investments: cash equivalents, fixed-income, and equity investments. As the name indicates, **cash equivalents** generally refers to investments that are less than one year in maturity and can readily be converted to cash. **Fixed-income** investments are those in which the return to the investor is set in the investment documents. They may or may not be readily salable. The most common fixed-income investment is a bond. **Equity investments** are ownership interests, the value of which varies with the value of the company in which you invest. The most common equity investment is common stock. Real estate is another common example.

Because cash equivalents are a basic part of every investment strategy, they are discussed in detail below. Likewise, mutual funds are discussed because they are a popular means of purchasing investments. Annuities are also investment vehicles that warrant mention.

6.1 Cash Equivalents

LE<2. Highly recommended for the investor with a shortened life expectancy. Cash equivalents meet the essential criteria of maximizing liquidity and reducing risk.

2<LE<5. Recommended for the investor with a two-to-five-year life expectancy. It is important that you maintain liquidity but also plan for the possibility that you will live longer than expected. You need to constantly strive for a comfortable balance of income and growth.

LE>5. Recommended as part of an overall strategy that combines concerns about accessibility to cash with concerns about growth.

The chart starting on page 143 compares features of the various cash equivalents. The interest paid on each account will vary over time, so it is advisable to periodically compare rates offered by competitors.

6.2 Mutual Funds

Mutual funds are investment vehicles that permit the investor to diversify a limited investment. Each fund has its own investment guidelines and priorities. Mutual funds may be composed of bonds, stocks, or money market funds, or any combination of the three types of investments. Do not confuse mutual funds with bank money market deposit accounts, which are FDIC guaranteed.

LE<2. Not recommended unless part of a growth strategy after income-strategy funds are in place.

2<LE<5. Recommended. Should be considered in achieving desired balance between income and growth strategies.

LE>5. Recommended.

Types of mutual funds.

1. **Closed-end versus open-end funds:** Closed-end funds represent a fixed portfolio of investments and a fixed number of shares issued, whereas open-ended funds represent a flexible capital structure and have no limitation on the number of shares issued. The price for open-end fund shares is based on the most recently computed net asset value (NAV) of the fund. The price of shares for closed-end funds is determined by the supply and demand for the shares on the market and is not tied to the share's NAV. When the market price exceeds a share's NAV, it sells at a premium; when the market price is less than the NAV, it sells at a discount.

2. **Single-family and supermarket funds:** Several funds in one portfolio account.

3. **No-load versus load funds:** No-load funds do not charge commissions (loads) but may still charge fees and other associated costs. Load funds

charge front-end commissions (a commission payable upon purchase) and/or back-end commissions (a commission upon redemption).

Tip. There are mutual funds that waive the commission charges in the event of disability even if you are disabled when you purchase the investment. If you are going to invest in a mutual fund, this feature can mean a substantial savings to you.

When considering a mutual fund, look at:

- **Denominations:** Typical minimum investment is $1,000.
- **Sales channels:** Mutual funds may be purchased directly from mutual fund companies or through banks, brokers, financial advisers.
- **Risk:** Depends on the underlying securities in the fund.
- **Return:** Depends on the underlying securities in the fund. Take note whether reinvested dividends are subject to tax.
- **Term:** The term of a mutual fund depends on the underlying securities in the fund. For example, money market funds are short-term maturity, but typically more than one year.
- **Fees:** *Review each prospectus carefully.* Expect to incur one or more of the following expenses:
  - Commissions, "loads," or other transaction fees.
  - Annual management and administration fees (typically 1–2 percent of your portfolio value).
  - Advisory fee (typically 1 percent).
  - You can avoid certain fees by purchasing directly from mutual fund companies.
  - If you use a broker, ask what amount of initial investment might qualify for a break on commission points. Also, ask yourself whether you receive above-average returns plus value-added services that justify the fees you are paying.

Tax. Mutual funds are required to make annual distributions to investors on at least 90 percent of the interest, dividends, and capital gains on the underlying investments in the funds. Distributions

> >

Cash Equivalents (1 of 2)

Feature	Savings Accounts	Money Market Deposit Accounts	Money Market Mutual Funds*
Maturity	open-ended	open-ended	securities in these funds usually have an average maturity of 30–90 days
Minimum	usually none	minimum varies	varies by fund
Sales channels	banks, savings and loan associations, credit unions	banks	contact the fund directly
Liquidity	high	high	high; some funds permit transfers among funds in the same family
Risk	almost none—FDIC guaranty to $100,000	almost none—FDIC guaranty to $100,000	low, but no FDIC guaranty
Return	low, variable	low, variable, higher than on savings accounts**	low to moderate, variable rate, generally greater than on money market accounts
Fees	usually none	only if below a minimum balance	varies depending on services offered
Taxes	interest subject to tax	interest subject to tax	depends on whether underlying securities are taxable or exempt
Estate planning	no probate with co-owner or payable on death or Totten trust	no probate with co-owner or payable on death registration	no probate with co-owner or payable on death registration
Administration	none	low	low

*__Money market mutual funds__ invest in short-term interest-bearing securities such as commercial paper, jumbo CDs, and U.S. treasury bills.

**Note that a "guaranteed" rate does not necessarily mean a fixed rate.

⟩ ⟩

Cash Equivalents (2 of 2)

Feature	Certificates of Deposit (CDs)	U.S. Savings Bonds Series EE and Series HH*	U.S. Treasury Bills
Maturity	3 months to 3 years	HH: 10-year maturity EE: 30-year maturity	3-, 6-, and 12-month maturities; can be less
Minimum	varies	$100 to $1,000 minimum face value; maximum annual purchase limit per person: $30,000	$10,000
Sales channels	banks, savings and loan associations, credit unions, brokers	employers, banks, savings and loan associations, issuing financial institutions, or directly from the Federal Reserve; series EE bonds are often available through payroll-deduction programs	banks, brokerage firms, telephone purchase directly from Federal Reserve branches—e.g., in NY call 212-720-5965
Liquidity	high**	high, but 6-month minimum holding period	moderate
Risk	almost zero	almost zero (backed by U.S. government)	almost zero (backed by U.S. government)
Return	low, fixed and variable rates, higher than savings or money market deposit accounts	low, variable rate ***	moderate; if T-bill is purchased after offering return varies based on differential between discount price at which bond is purchased and maturity value
Fees	low, early-withdrawal penalty, other fees if linked to other types of accounts	none if purchased from government; otherwise varies	if purchased from government: none to $100,000, over $100,000 is $25 fee; if purchased from private sources, fees vary
Taxes	interest subject to income tax	both EE and HH subject to federal tax, but exempt from local and state taxes****	subject to federal tax, but exempt from local and state taxes

Continued on next page

Cash Equivalents (2 of 2) (*cont'd*)

Feature	Certificates of Deposit (CDs)	U.S. Savings Bonds Series EE and Series HH*	U.S. Treasury Bills
Estate planning	no probate with co-owner or payable on death registration	no probate with co-owner or payable on death registration	can be used as a "flower bond" (see chapter 33, section 4.6); no probate if registered with co-owner or "in trust for"
Administration	low, monitor maturity dates for rollover purposes	low	low

*Series HH bonds may only be purchased in exchange for series EE bonds of $500 minimum face value.

**If you need cash prior to maturity of your CDs, you can use the CDs as collateral for a loan from your bank or credit union—however, make sure to compare the interest charged on the loan (expense) as compared to the interest received on your CDs (income).

***Variable rate (if purchased after May 1995) based on average market yield pegged to U.S. treasuries adjusted twice per annum (May and November). Series HH pays interest semiannually, which can be credited electronically to your bank account. Series EE pays interest only at redemp-tion. For current U.S. savings bond rate information call 800-487-2663. For redemption dates, interest rates, and current redemption values for all your existing savings bond holdings, for a small fee contact the Savings Bond Informer at 800-927-1901, 9–5 ET, M–F, or at www.bondin-former.com.

****Note the tax-deferral status of EE bonds since interest is paid out only at redemption. Since you can put off paying taxes on these bonds, you benefit from the tax-deferred compounding of interest. As an alternative, you can claim interest earned on the bonds each year.

are declared as of an "ex-dividend date" before the end of each calendar year and are subject to income tax or capital gains tax.

6.3 Tips Regarding Mutual Fund Taxes and Fees

There are several important tax consequences to bear in mind when selling or purchasing mutual fund shares:

• Avoid paying income tax on someone else's gain. Time the purchase of your mutual fund shares by purchasing after a dividend date to avoid a gains tax on the newly purchased shares without having realized any capital appreciation.

• Avoid double taxation of capital gains. When you sell your mutual fund shares (at a profit), you will be subject to capital gains tax. Make sure to account for any prior capital distributions (as cash or shares) made by the fund on which you have already paid capital gains tax—otherwise you will pay capital gains tax twice.

• One of the major disadvantages of mutual fund investments are the associated tax consequences—specifically the lack of control investors have over the timing of distributions. This problem is compounded by the fact that most mutual funds are managed without specific consideration given to taxes, and mutual funds and their managers are judged on pretax performance. There are two possibilities to alleviate this problem: (1) make mutual fund investments inside tax-deferred retirement vehicles or (2) invest in recently established "tax-managed" mutual funds.

Tip. Consider a mutual fund withdrawal program. Sam W. invested $10,000 in a mutual fund for his aunt Sandra. He advised the fund that he wanted a $100 monthly capital gain. Sandra gets that amount every month. It's possible that the fund could perform at better than twelve percent, providing a capital appreciation as well as the monthly return.

6.4 Annuities

An annuity is a contract between you and an insurance company, where you invest a premium in exchange for a series of future payments (annuity) over your lifetime or a fixed number of years. An annuity differs from a life insurance policy in that it insures you against the financial risks associated with outliving your life expectancy, whereas life insurance insures your beneficiaries against the financial risks associated with an early demise. Typically, the insurance company deposits these premiums in a portfolio of securities until the time when those assets must be converted into annuity payments. Annuities can have either a fixed or variable return.

LE<2, 2<LE>5. Not recommended.

LE>5. Only recommended under limited circumstances for those doing retirement planning. Annuities and retirement plans both serve as tax-deferred investment vehicles for retirement. Most retirement plans are limited by a maximum or pretax contributions, whereas annuities do not face this limitation. An annuity may be worthwhile for an investor who has already made the maximum pretax contributions to retirement plans and would like to make additional tax-deferred invest-

ments for retirement (provided the investor is in a high enough tax bracket to benefit from doing so).

Characteristics of annuities.
- **Types of annuities:**
  - **Immediate annuities:** You begin receiving money immediately after paying a premium.
  - **Deferred annuities:** You begin receiving payments no earlier than one year after you pay the premium. There are three types of deferred-payment annuities: fixed rate, variable rate, and indexed. With a **fixed rate** annuity, both interest and principal are guaranteed. With a **variable rate** annuity, neither interest nor principal is guaranteed. The rate varies according to the value of stocks and bonds the insurance company purchases. There are two types of variable rate annuities: single-premium payment and payment of premiums over time. With an **indexed** annuity, neither interest nor principal are guaranteed. The rate varies according to a specified index that varies from company to company. Note that while a "minimum interest rate" may be offered, that does not mean the rate is guaranteed, and there are often hidden caps on returns to policyholders. Also note that both variable rate and indexed annuities are considered "securities" and are thereby regulated by the SEC.
- **Term:** Can be for a fixed period of time or a variable time.
- **Sales channels:** Insurance companies, banks, S&Ls, third-party sales agents.
- **Liquidity:**
  - Vesting schedules may be ten years or longer.
  - Early withdrawals made before age 59½ are subject to both a contractual penalty and a 10 percent tax penalty.
  - There can be waivers and surrender clauses for terminal illness. Some companies offer an annuity with a **terminal illness waiver** or **terminal illness free surrender clause**—

meaning that upon diagnosis of a so-called terminal illness, the insured can withdraw 100 percent of the account value of the annuity without penalty. To be eligible for the waiver, the insured must have a life expectancy of twelve months or less.

- **Risk:** Consider both the quality of investment portfolio underlying the insurance company's annuity obligations and the solvency of the insurance company.
- **Return:** Compare rates of return on comparable investments—e.g., fixed rate annuity versus CDs, variable rate annuity versus mutual funds, and index annuity versus stock index fund.
- **Fees:** Depending on the type of annuity you select, fees may include any of the following:
  - annual contract charge.
  - investment management fee.
  - commissions.
  - front and/or back-end fees.
  - surrender charges.
- **Taxes:** Applicable tax issues include
  - tax deferral of investment income.
  - capital gains taxed at income tax rate (versus lower capital gains rate).
  - 10 percent tax penalty for early withdrawals before age 59½.

Section 7. An Example

To illustrate how the strategies described in this chapter may be applied, following is an example of an investment strategy that could be recommended to a person with a two-year life expectancy who does not have securities expertise.

- Put six months of living expense into a money market fund. The money would be available daily, yield more than a bank savings account, and maintain a net asset value of $1 per share on your deposit. The investment is liquid; di-

verse; highest current rate of return among the cash equivalent investments; fees are calculated before determining rate of return; no administration. Income is subject to tax as available.

- Put six months of living expenses in short-term bond funds. These funds have average maturities of three years or less. The investment is liquid; diverse; has an even higher rate of return than a money market fund; money can be accessed when it will probably be needed, but not immediately; fees are calculated before determining rate of return; no administration; income is subject to tax, but not before it is, or can be, received.
- If there is still money left over, put it in a no-load mutual fund with government or corporate bonds—preferably one that waives all fees in the event of disability. The investment is low risk; flexible; has a good rate of return for low risk; lowest fees; tax to be considered in choosing the fund; cash available, if necessary, though there may be a loss due to timing.

Section 8. Ten Commonsense Tips for Investment Success

1. Investment is simply a means to an end, therefore the measure of your investment "success" will be how well your investments enable you to realize *your* goals.

2. Shop around—for investments and advisers. Evaluate your investment options relative to each. Remember that your "true" rate of return is equal to the nominal rate minus inflation minus fees and costs. Make sure any verbal claims or promises are confirmed in writing.

3. Stay informed—even if you use advisers. Always do some basic research yourself. Do not invest in something with which you are not familiar or otherwise comfortable. If necessary, "sleep on it" until you have more information to make a better decision. When evaluating prospective investments, bear in mind that historical performance is *not a guarantee* of future performance.

4. Be aware that investment vehicles purchased through a bank are not necessarily guaranteed or FDIC insured like bank deposits (e.g., mutual funds purchased through a bank).

5. Be careful not to purchase tax-exempt or tax-favored investments (e.g., U.S. savings bonds) for vehicles with tax deferment such as 401(k) plans. Otherwise, tax-exempt or tax-favored investments will be treated as if they are tax-deferred investments and will be subject to tax upon distribution.

6. Pay attention to the timing of the purchase of your investments. Unless you are a professional investor, the market-timing approach (i.e., anticipating the best time to purchase an investment) is not a good one. For investors with at least a one-year investment horizon, the *dollar cost averaging* approach is recommended.

7. Be careful not to redeem an investment before a payout date, otherwise you could lose accrued interest or dividends. For example, redeeming a savings bond one day early could result in a loss of six months' interest.

8. Make investing a priority by treating it like the purchase of a monthly necessity.

9. Periodically review your investment strategy, financial requirements, and personal goals to ensure they are still synchronized.

10. Do not allow emotional attachments to influence your investment decisions. Don't invest based on hot tips, rumor, or gut feelings.

And finally. Don't worry about how your investments are doing every day. This book is being written at a time when a bull market has been roaring ahead for ten years. The nightly news programs feature the market daily. It's easy to think, "If only I had put everything in stocks . . ." But some night the news is going to talk about how the bear market may have taken over, or has taken over, or the story could be about how the company you speculated in was hit with a huge liability suit such as the asbestos industry went through. You may not have the time to make your capital over again. It's one of those times when an old adage truly works:

➤ ➤

It really is better to be safe than sorry.

➤ ➤

Protection Against Increased Expenses

Chapter 14

Health Insurance Coverage

When Paul R. had a small surgical procedure at his doctor's office, he was amazed at the $2,500 bill. Since the procedure ultimately resulted in a diagnosis of stomach cancer, it was only the beginning of the surprises.

Unless you are very, very wealthy, medical insurance is your most important asset. This chapter provides an overview of private individual and group health insurance coverage and tips for maximizing their use. If you do not currently have health insurance, ideas are included to help you obtain it.

Section 1. Private Health Insurance—Overview: From Indemnity to Managed Care

Until recently, the average person with health insurance—whether through an employer's plan, a separate group policy, or through an individual policy—had **indemnity coverage.** Indemnity insurance permits patients to manage their own care with the freedom to select doctors, hospitals, and treatments. Increasingly, employers and insurers are moving toward so-called **managed care** plans under which the insurance company "manages" your care by selecting the physicians you can choose and overseeing treatment options. With managed care plans your freedom of choice is limited.

Managed care plans evolved in response to the following perceived problems with indemnity plans, among others:

• The plans were too costly, with no incentive to keep costs down.
• The plans led to the oversupply of specialists and the undersupply of general practitioners.
• The plans raised concern about the quality of unmonitored care.
• The plans failed to emphasize staying healthy and early preventive care.

Unfortunately the managed care trend—while attempting to address all these very real problems at the same time—has resulted in a system that can more precisely be called "managed cost."

If you don't have coverage now, knowing what to expect out of both systems will help you obtain the best coverage you can. If you do have one of these coverages, you may want to focus only on the applicable section.

Section 2. Indemnity Health Insurance: An Overview

Evaluating coverage provided by indemnity plans. Under indemnity coverage, the patient receives a service provided by a doctor or hospital. The patient either pays the bill and then obtains reimbursement from the insurer or the bill is submitted directly to the insurer for payment. Reimbursement depends upon the following factors, which are described in greater detail below: whether the service is covered by the plan; the deductible; coinsurance; whether the fees are reasonable and customary; and lifetime benefit limits.

Covered services. Your policy will describe the services that are covered under the plan.
- **Medically necessary:** Health coverage is generally limited to treatments that are medically necessary. Preventive care is usually not covered.
- **Reasonable and necessary fees:** Insurers have schedules of fees for covered services that are intended to reflect their reasonable costs. The insured is not prevented from incurring a higher bill for the service, but the insurance company will not pay above the maximum for the particular visit, treatment, or procedure. To illustrate, if the "reasonable and necessary" fee for Paul's procedure was only $2,000 instead of the $2,500 he was billed, then $2,000 instead of $2,500 becomes the starting place for the calculation.
- **Deductibles:** A deductible is the amount of covered medical expenses that the insured must pay for *each year* before any benefits are paid by the insurance company. The idea of the deductible is to eliminate the claims that the insured can absorb without much pain. To illustrate, the starting point for Paul's procedure for reimbursement purposes was $2,000. If he had a $500 deductible, the insurance carrier would ask for proof of how much Paul had paid in medical bills since the beginning of the policy

year. If it was less than $500, the difference between that amount and $500 would be deducted before determining how much the carrier would pay toward the bill. Paul had previously spent $200. So the company would pay $2,000 less $300 (the $500 deductible less $200 he had paid) or $1,700.
- **Coinsurance:** Coinsurance discourages overuse of the medical system by requiring the insured to pay part of his medical expenses. Indemnity policies generally cover only a percentage of the covered costs incurred, typically 80 percent. To illustrate, let's take the above example one step further: say that Paul's policy also had an 80 percent coinsurance provision. The company would only pay 80 percent of the $1,700 or $1,360.
- **Lifetime limits:** Typically policies have limits on benefits to be paid by the insurance company during the insured's lifetime of between $250,000 and $1 million.

With these general concepts in mind, the chart starting on page 154 is a guide to evaluating coverage under a particular plan. It lists various features typically available under indemnity plans. You need to look at your condition (as well as the health of your family if covered) to determine which features may be more important to you.

Columns headed "Plan A" and "Plan B" are provided for your use to help you understand what coverage you have or to compare two coverages.

The amount of the deductible, coinsurance factor, and maximum an insured pays per year are directly related to the amount of the premium.

Tip. Compare premiums at the various alternative limits. It may pay you to take a higher deductible for a lower premium and keep the difference in an interest-bearing bank account. If you are not a person who saves money, it may be better to pay a higher premium for a lower deductible so you won't have the stress of needing to find cash to pay the deductible when you are not feeling well.

A rule of thumb to consider is not to spend $1 unless you expect to receive at least $3 in benefits.

Tip. As you evaluate the various alternatives, consider whether the features of a particular plan will address the projected statistical progression of your condition and which plan will work out best for you economically. Contact your GuardianOrg for information on the statistical progress of your condition and the potential health care costs to anticipate.

Tip. Indemnity plans send the insured an **Explanation of Benefits** (EOB) that explains why they paid what they paid (or didn't). It usually also includes a phone number for questions about payments.

Section 3. Managed Care Health Insurance ↑↑↑

3.1 An Overview

In general. Under managed care plans, a single company pays for *and* also provides health services. The company collects premiums and then pays the providers directly.

The primary care physician becomes a **gatekeeper** to the health system. In addition to taking care of your general health, she either opens the gate, referring you to specialists or other treatments, or not. The gatekeeper must follow guidelines that are established by the particular managed care organization (MCO) with respect to treatments, access to specialists, prescription drugs, and procedures and must seek approval for any deviations. Referrals are only to specialists who have also signed up with the MCO. Specialists must also follow guidelines and seek approvals. If you are not referred to the specialist or if the specialist is not in the plan, the MCO will generally not pay.

The facilities in which treatments take place, in-

cluding hospitals, also must be part of or at least approved by the MCO.

Since it is all part of one system, there are *no* bills or maximums for the insured to be concerned about. Bills go from the doctor or facility directly to the insurance carrier. There is generally no deductible, and coinsurance is replaced with a **copay.** A copay is generally a small dollar amount, such as $15, that the insured pays for each access of the system, whether it is for a visit to the doctor's office or a $1,000 MRI procedure.

Most managed care plans do not impose any waiting periods for preexisting-conditions.

Unlike indemnity policies, managed care plans generally cover preventive care, such as an annual physical examination. The downside is that "managed care" often becomes "managed costs," and you lose some freedom to determine your medical destiny.

Another concept that is introduced in managed care policies is **capitation.** Capitation is used as a means of reimbursing physicians with an eye to controlling costs. Under capitation the insurance carrier "capitates," puts a cap on, what it pays the physician per patient. If, for example, the company pays the doctor $2,000 per year per patient and the doctor sees the patient only one time, she makes money on the patient. However, if she sees the patient once a week, she makes less money.

Tip. *If the doctor makes less because you require more attention, that does not necessarily mean you will receive less care. It only means that you should be aware of potential hidden financial forces that may affect the amount of time a physician spends with you on your health care.*

Types of managed care organizations. There are several types of managed care plans. In this book, they are referred to generically as MCOs. The types of MCO plans from the least to the most restrictive are:

• **Preferred-provider organization (PPO):** A preferred-provider organization may be a true MCO if it assumes the insurance function, or it

> >

Indemnity Health Insurance

Feature	Range (from poorest to best)	Plan A	Plan B
General Features			
Lifetime maximum	<$500,000 \ Unlimited*		
Deductible per year	>$1,000 \ <$30		
Coinsurance (paid by insured)	50% \ 20% \ 0%		
Coinsurance limit (maximum coinsurance insured pays per year)	$10,000 \ $5,000 \ $0		
Basis of deductible and coinsurance	a period such as per year\ per illness or injury		
Preexisting-condition exclusion	12 months \ 6 months \ none**		
Renewals	not guaranteed \ guaranteed with conditions \ unconditional renewal guaranteed		
Hospitalization			
Basis on which to reimburse costs	dollar limit per day \ payment of "usual, customary, and reasonable"*** \ payment of all expenses		
Emergency room coverage	pre-authorization required \ full coverage		
Preadmission authorization	authorization required or face a penalty \ no penalty		
Days of hospital coverage per year	<30 \ 365		
Psychotherapy			
Inpatient	not covered \ limited \ unlimited coverage		
Outpatient	not covered \ covered for a maximum number of visits for a specific dollar amount \ unlimited coverage		

Continued on next page

Indemnity Health Insurance *(cont'd)*

Feature	Range (from poorest to best)	Plan A	Plan B
Home Care			
Services reimbursed	skilled care only \ skilled care and custodial care only \ skilled care, custodial care, and homemaker services****		
Home care provider	must be certified \ must be registered \ no restrictions		
Hospice care	not covered \ covered for limited duration, such as 6 months \ unlimited duration		
Doctors and Treatments			
Basis on which to reimburse treatments and doctor visits	scheduled amount per activity \ schedule using standardized amounts such as Medicare schedule \ "usual, customary, and reasonable" charges		
Requirement for second opinion	yes for surgery \ yes for any elective procedures \ no requirement but will pay for it if insured so elects		
Organ transplants	not covered \ limited to a dollar amount\ unlimited		
Experimental organ transplants	not covered \ limited to a specific dollar amount \ covered if the center has transplant expertise		
Cosmetic surgery	not covered at all \ limited coverage \ covered		
Drug/alcohol treatment	not covered \ detoxification plus rehabilitation		
Preventive treatments	not covered \ specific treatment covered such as mammography, annual medical examinations		
Percentage of usual charges used as a basis for determining "reasonable"*****	60% \ 75% \ 90%		

Continued on next page

Indemnity Health Insurance (*cont'd*)

Feature	Range (from poorest to best)	Plan A	Plan B
Drugs			
Prescription	not covered \ covered with deductible and /or coinsurance \ limited amount of copayment per prescription by insured and remainder covered		
Experimental	FDA-approved drugs and usage only \ off-label use of FDA-approved drugs \ recommended as a treatment		
Travel			
Travel	no coverage \ USA only \ entire world		
Travel for procedures	not covered \ covered		
Medicare			
Relationship to Medicare	Medicare pays all \ pays the difference between Medicare payments and specified rates \ pays everything Medicare does not pay		
The Insurance Company			
Rating by the rating services	C or even lower \ B \ A or A plus		

*The symbol < means "less than." The symbol > means "more than."

**You may not be subject to the exclusion under federal or state law if you had previous health coverage. If you are subject to it, there may be a limit on the length of time for preexisting conditions to a period before coverage commences and/or limit how long the exclusion may continue (see chapter 6, section 6).

***"Usual" is when the health insurance company limits reimbursement to what this particular provider usually charges for its service. "Customary" is what other providers in the same region charge. "Reasonable" is "usual" or "customary," whichever is less. Some companies use "customary" alone.

****Skilled care covers a person who only does things nurses can do, such as give shots or take vital signs. Custodial care covers people who take you to the bathroom, get you dressed and bathed. Homemaker services covers people who cook and clean. The insurance companies are particularly concerned about homemaker services because abuse of the coverage is so easy.

*****Indicates the charges by a given percentage of local doctors that determine what is "reasonable" in a given area. For instance, if in Cleveland 60 percent of the doctors charge $100 or less for a procedure, 75 percent charge $125 or less, and 90 percent charge $150 or less, the percentage used determines the basis amount for the insurance company.

may be simply a group of doctors and/or hospitals with no gatekeeper that have negotiated discounted rates, either capitated or fee for service, to care for a group of people. These doctors and hospitals care for other patients as well. Members can choose services inside or outside the network just as in an indemnity plan, but the cost of services provided by professionals in the network is discounted.

- **Point of service plan (POS):** Under this system, members have a managed care plan that provides access to any doctors or services within the network. In addition, members can choose to go outside the system to see a physician or for a treatment without a referral. However, the member must pay for a larger portion of such services outside the network (such as an 80 percent coinsurance amount instead of a small copay dollar amount). Claims forms are used for nonnetwork services.
- **Individual practice associations (IPA):** Members must use doctors and hospitals in the network of affiliated individual practices.
- **Health maintenance organization (HMO):** Members can only use the doctors on staff at the HMO and the hospitals contracting with the HMO.

3.2 Evaluating Managed Care Plans

Several problems have emerged for patients as a result of managed care's attempts to manage costs. Because the financial success of the system is based on limiting use of services, there is a built-in incentive to limit patient care. This incentive plays out in different ways depending on the structure of the managed care plan. For example, many MCOs pressure doctors not to recommend costly or promising treatments whether they are covered by the plan or not. Also, MCO policies theoretically pay for out-of-network benefits if in-network specialists document that you require special out-of-network care. However, as a practical matter, in-network doctors may feel pressured not to recommend out-of-network care, or the MCO may not approve it. Examine your plan to know what to look for when managing your care under the plan. Talk with other people in the plan with your condition to learn from their experiences.

The place to start your evaluation is with the gatekeeper, since the gatekeeper is so important to your health. The remaining questions may seem daunting, but the more you know about your coverage, the more likely you'll be able to make the system work for you. The rule "Before you invest, investigate" applies as much to managed care plans as it does to investments.

The MCO gatekeeper. Gatekeepers (generally referred to as the primary care physician or **PCP**) can create difficulties for people with a life-challenging condition in several ways:

- Generally the gatekeeper is not a specialist. Since your condition probably requires the attention of a specialist, you would normally have to go to the gatekeeper for permission each time you want to see the specialist. Not only is it a nuisance for you that consumes Life Units, the gatekeeper probably has a financial incentive not to refer you to the specialist.
- Because the gatekeeper is usually a general practitioner, she may lack the experience to detect symptoms or subtle changes that may raise a red flag to the specialist. In general, the earlier a condition is noted, the more likely the treatment will be effective.

Some plans have acknowledged the problem for people with a life-challenging condition by providing that the specialist may also be the primary care physician. Others provide a system of easy access to the specialist by such means as allowing unlimited visits to the specialist once an initial referral is made by the primary care physician, or allowing a fixed number of visits to a specialist before another visit to the primary care physician is required to authorize more specialist visits.

Tip. If your plan does not contain either one of these solutions, ask your specialist to recommend a primary care physician from those available in your plan.

Coverage. The chart on page 159 can assist you in evaluating your plan or different MCO plans you may be considering. The first column lists some of the basic features common to managed care plans. Also consider:

- Interview the doctor who will be your gatekeeper, and the specialist you will use if different from the gatekeeper. Ask the questions suggested in chapter 24, section 1.4.
- Does the plan provide a consumer advocate, an ombudsman, or a consumer advisory board? If so, how are those people selected?
- Is the MCO "federally qualified"? If it is, one-third of the members of the MCO's board of directors must be consumer members with no financial relationship with the MCO.
- Does the MCO have a case-manager system for people with a chronic problem? A case manager can go to bat for you and knows how to work the system. Sometimes a case manager can even get you discounts on equipment.

Tip. If you have a choice, select a plan

- with many members who have the same condition you have. The more such members the MCO has, the more experienced and competent it is likely to be in addressing your needs.
- that has qualified specialists and treatment facilities for your condition. If you have a condition such as cancer that has different types, look for specialists in your type. (If you have a strong relationship with a particular doctor, choose a plan that she is in.)
- that provides easy access to those specialists.
- that monitors and coordinates all aspects of your health. This may be more difficult with a network of independent physicians. The plan may even have a "disease management" program for your condition. If it doesn't, look for a case manager or ombudsman who may be responsible for assisting people with chronic conditions and can go to bat for you.

- that is associated with hospitals that are the best in your area in the specialty you need.
- with the least restrictive options that you can afford. Plans that reimburse you (in whole or in part) for services outside the system assure you access to the specialists and treatments you choose. Generally, the fewer restrictions the higher the cost of the plan.
- with no gag rules.

Tip. Through the National Committee for Quality Assurance (NCQA), a coalition of MCOs and employers, managed care plans can pay to be evaluated. You can obtain a copy of these evaluations for free. Call 800-839-6487 or access them on the Internet at www.ncqa.org. It is also expected that the American Association of Retired Persons (AARP) will be evaluating plans by the time this book is published. AARP can be reached at 202-434-2277. Also, during 1997, new rules were adopted requiring Medicare HMOs to furnish information, at least some of which will be published at www.hcfa.gov. An MCO that has been disciplined for failing to provide medically necessary services or for other infractions is listed in the Cumulative Sanctions report at www.dhhs.gov/progorg/oig.

Section 4. Maximizing Use of Health Insurance (Indemnity and MCO)

In general, whether your coverage is indemnity or managed care.

- Any benefits booklet you receive is merely a summary of the plan's coverage. You are entitled to, and should obtain, a copy of the complete contract. Obtaining the copy now will allow you to find out exactly what your coverage includes and what you have to do to obtain services under the plan. It will also save time when it could be critical—such as if you need to appeal a decision, at which time you should attach a copy of the pertinent plan provisions.

> >

Managed Care Organization Benefits

Feature	Plan A	Plan B	Plan C
Preexisting conditions			
Covered? Yes/No			
If not, waiting period:			
Cost per year	$	$	$
Physician's office visits			
In network:			
Copay	$	$	$
Out-of-network:			
Deductible:	$	$	$
Coinsurance	%	%	%
Maximum you pay:	$	$	$
Physician services (such as consultation, diagnosis, and treatment by a specialist)			
In network:			
Copay	$	$	$
Out of network:			
Deductible:	$	$	$
Coinsurance	%	%	%
Maximum you pay:	$	$	$
Basis for payment:			
Other features:			
Outpatient diagnostic tests (e.g., X rays, lab work)			
In network:			
Copay	$	$	$
Out of network:			
Deductible:	$	$	$

Continued on next page

Managed Care Organization Benefits (*cont'd*)

Feature	Plan A	Plan B	Plan C
Coinsurance	%	%	%
Maximum you pay:	$	$	$
Other features:			

Inpatient hospital care (room, board, surgery, anesthesia, etc.)

In network:

	Plan A	Plan B	Plan C
Copay	$	$	$

Out of network:

	Plan A	Plan B	Plan C
Deductible:	$	$	$
Coinsurance:	%	%	%
Maximum you pay:	$	$	$
Maximum number of covered days:			

Maternity care (mother and newborn)

In network:

	Plan A	Plan B	Plan C
Copay	$	$	$

Out of network:

	Plan A	Plan B	Plan C
Deductible:	$	$	$
Coinsurance	%	%	%
Maximum you pay:	$	$	$

Emergency room care

In network:

	Plan A	Plan B	Plan C
Copay	$	$	$
Waived if admitted? Yes/No			

Out of network:

	Plan A	Plan B	Plan C
Deductible:	$	$	$
Coinsurance	%	%	%

Continued on next page

Managed Care Organization Benefits (*cont'd*)

Feature	Plan A	Plan B	Plan C
Pre-authorization required? Yes\No			
Mental health			
In network:			
Inpatient:			
Copay	$	$	$
Maximum number of days per year:			
Outpatient:			
Copay	$	$	$
Maximum number of visits per year:			
Out of network:			
Inpatient:			
Deductible:	$	$	$
Coinsurance	%	%	%
Maximum number of days:			
Outpatient:			
Deductible:	$	$	$
Coinsurance	%	%	%
Maximum number of days:			
Approvals required for tests? Yes/No			
If so, describe:			

Continued on next page

Managed Care Organization Benefits (*cont'd*)

Feature	Plan A	Plan B	Plan C
Preventive medicine			
Annual physical: Yes/No			
Other:			
Prescription drugs			
Copay	$	$	$
Deductible:	$	$	$
Annual cap, if any:	$	$	$
Coinsurance:			
Generic:	%	%	%
Brand:	%	%	%
Does MCO specify pharmacy Yes/No			
Other features:			
Student coverage			
Covered? Yes/No			
If so, to age:			
Specialist			
Primary care physician:			
Can a specialist be your primary physician? Yes/No			
If no, number of visits permitted with referral:			

Continued on next page

Managed Care Organization Benefits (*cont'd*)

Feature	Plan A	Plan B	Plan C
Specialists: How would you rate their quality? (from 1 to 10, 10 being the best)			
Average delay to see a specialist (in days)			
Second opinion			
Is it permitted in plan? Yes/No			
Is it permitted out of plan? Yes/No			
What restrictions?			
Use of nurse / nurse practitioner instead of doctor Yes/No			
If yes, describe services:			
Any "gag" restrictions on doctors?* Yes/No			
Hospital quality (from 1 to 10, 10 being the best)			
Home care Professional:			
Number of days:			
Dollar limit:	$	$	$
Personal care:			
Included? Yes/No			
Number of days:			
Dollar limit:	$	$	$

Continued on next page

Managed Care Organization Benefits (*cont'd*)

Feature	Plan A	Plan B	Plan C
Nursing home			
Included? Yes/No			
Maximum number of days:			
Limit:	$	$	$
The MCO company			
For profit or not for profit:			
Travel away from home			
Covered? Yes / No			
If yes, how?			
Appeals procedures			
Do they exist? Yes/No			
Does the plan provide for outside review? Yes/No			
Word-of-mouth rating of this company/plan (from 1 to 10, 10 being the best)			

* "Gag" restrictions prevent doctors from discussing procedures and/or treatments beyond those in the MCO guidelines.

Start by reading the "definitions" section first. An insurance policy is a contract, and the terms will be defined according to general usage, unless specifically defined in the policy. It may take several readings before the terms of the policy become clear. If you still have questions, ask for assistance from your employer or broker, social worker or GuardianOrg. Asking your employer for assistance in interpreting the provisions will not by itself alert your employer to your condition. Remember, you do not have to disclose your condition to your employer even if she asks.

• If you are told that something is covered, but you don't see it in the policy or the insurer's literature, ask for confirmation in writing. If you don't receive written confirmation, don't believe it.

• If your policy contains a provision waiving premium payments in the event of disability, check to determine when the insurance company must be notified of the onset of disability for you to be eligible for the waiver. If you do not act within the period mentioned, you may have to continue to pay premiums.

• Your state may require that health insurance policies include certain stated coverage as a matter of right regardless of whether it is spelled out in your policy. Contact your state department of insurance to find out what the law requires. Telephone numbers are included in the resources section.

• Find out as much as you can about the treatment of your illness. See chapter 25, section 3, for how to obtain this information.

• Share the information about maximizing the use of your coverage with others who may be in need of it. In addition to making you feel good, this makes you part of an information network that could provide you with helpful tips as well.

• If you need a letter or report from a physician and don't have time for delay, write what you want the physician to say. Then deliver it to the doctor (even via fax or E-mail) and ask the doctor to copy it onto her stationery and return it to you.

• Try to establish a friendly relationship with a person at the insurance carrier. Relationships can help speed up matters and are a good basis for getting rules bent.

• Be aware that insurance companies are beginning to distinguish between treatments that are "experimental" (e.g., Phase 1 or 2 of a clinical trial) and those that are "investigational" (e.g., Phase 3) (see chapter 25, section 8.1 for a description of the various phases in clinical trials). The further along in the approval process, the more likely the treatment you want will be covered (see also section 6 below).

• Do not be afraid to be the proverbial "squeaky wheel." If you have a group plan through your employer, ask your employer to help. The employer can threaten to cancel the contract with the MCO. (The employer may also offer to pay for treatments the plan refuses).

Don't be afraid to use the insurance company's appeals process if necessary. Another alternative is to speak with your state's insurance department. A phone call to your insurance carrier from this regulatory agency on an informal basis often works wonders in getting instant results. If all else fails, get legal assistance.

Tip. Keep your insurance carrier's name and phone number and your ID number in your wallet in case you need authorization for emergency services or to enter a hospital.

If you have managed care coverage. Especially with managed care, it is important to be proactive. Managed care can be managed by the MCO, the doctor, the employer, or you, the person receiving the care. Think of yourself as a consumer as well as a patient. You are purchasing a product or service—not receiving a benefit. In addition to the above advice:

• It cannot be repeated often enough: choose a primary care physician who is also your specialist if possible. If you can't do that, see the above alternatives. If you are not already a patient of that person, be sure the doctor is not overloaded and is able to see you as a new patient.

• Due to capitation, many doctors limit the amount of minutes they spend with each patient. If your doctor doesn't take the time to do a thorough job or answer your questions, complain. For advice on maximizing the use of the time with your doctor, see chapter 24, section 4. If necessary, change doctors.

• MCOs have treatment guides for illnesses that cover procedures the plan believes are appropriate for different conditions. In theory, a guide is supposed to improve health coverage by assuring that all physicians in the plan practice what the carrier considers to be the most up-to-date and appropriate medicine. However, all too often the guides become rigid, and physicians are not allowed to treat people beyond limits prescribed by the guide. Having a copy of this guide helps you to compare what the MCO thinks that your treatment should be against what you think your treatment should be. Guides are hard to obtain, but worth the effort. The best place to start is with your primary care physician, or ask your specialist to obtain the information from your primary care physician.

Many physicians will not be forthcoming with these guides for a variety of reasons. Perhaps someone else covered by your plan, or your GuardianOrg, will be able to secure this information for you.

• If your employer changes carriers during treatment, you will likely want the physician who started the process to finish it. Ask your new gatekeeper to recommend that your treatment be continued by your current physician. If necessary, ask for a referral to a sympathetic in-network specialist, then ask that person to recommend that your current physician is the best person to finish the job. If possible, the doctor should also state that staying with your current physician will be the least costly alternative. If necessary, ask your current physician to speak with the MCO.

• If you want a second (or a third) opinion, push for it. If you can afford it, it's better to go outside the plan to a physician who is likely to be more objective than in-network physicians and may have a different idea of the preferred treatment for your condition. Reports from these doctors may be important to your demand that the plan cover costly or experimental treatments.

• **Out of network:**

  • If you want to go out of the plan for a specific reason, find out how much it will cost and whether any portion of that money will be covered by the plan. Don't assume without checking that any costs are covered. For example, if you want to use a nonnetwork surgeon and are willing to pay his bill, don't assume that hospitalization is covered even though the hospital is one that the plan uses.

  • Suggest to a doctor within the network who is willing to work with you that care for your condition be handled by a physician outside the MCO. Once a course of action is agreed upon, the doctor within the network could prescribe any recommended drugs and treatments. Consequently, all treatments and drugs, to the extent possible, would be done

inside the system. If your current network doctor won't go along with this suggestion, look for other doctors in the MCO who will. Any agreeable doctor within the MCO will do since the expertise for your condition will be supplied by the outside specialist.

• If you receive reimbursement when you access services out of the network, find out whether the plan will reimburse you based on the out-of-network physician's bill or a standard such as what is "usual, customary, and reasonable." If the plan uses the latter type of standard, you will have to pay any difference unless you can convince the plan to the contrary.

• Learn about the procedure for grievances (general complaints) and appeals (requests for reconsideration of requested services and/or treatments you have been denied).

Tip. With an MCO, whenever you feel it is necessary, remind anyone who is making decisions about your treatment that your right to good health care comes before their drive to cut costs.

An excellent guide on how to use an MCO is *The HMO Health Care Companion, a Consumer's Guide to Managed-Care Networks* by Alan G. Raymond, HarperPerennial, 1994.

Tip. Since health coverage is so important, if you own your own small business and can't get health or other coverages such as disability, consider selling your business to a company that will give you the benefits you need—and hopefully eliminate some harmful stress.

Section 5. Claims (Indemnity and MCO)

Paperwork. With indemnity coverage, and some MCO coverages (when accessing a doctor or treatments outside the plan is permitted and will be reimbursed), your expenses will not be paid or reimbursed unless you file a claim with the insurance company in the time prescribed in your policy *and* in the form required by the carrier (usually on forms the carrier will supply you). With most MCO coverages, when you use the plan's services, you do not need to file claims as the system does the paperwork for you. If you have a question, rather than guess and have the claim eventually rejected, call the carrier's claims department and ask for guidance.

Tip. Make copies of all your bills. Keep your originals for follow-up unless your carrier is one of the few that insists on originals. If it does, make a good copy for your file.

Submit claims in the proper order. The patient's insurance is always primary. The spouse's coverage is secondary. As between Medicare and private coverage, see chapter 15, section 1.

Tip. If your policy has more than one coinsurance rate, calculate how much you will receive if you submit the bills in different orders, such as the bill with the highest coinsurance first and then vice versa. Keep in mind differing deductibles as well when you do this calculation.

How to submit claims. The safest way to submit claims is to use certified mail, return receipt requested. Signature by the receiving party proves the insurance company received the claim. If you insert the postal receipt number in the letter and keep a copy of the letter, you will also have proof of what was received as well as when it was received.

Records. Keep careful records of your health care expenses. Without them you may not collect the maximum benefits to which you are entitled.

Keep the records in a systematic order. Without a system, your finances can become a jumble quite quickly, and probably at a time when you are not feeling well. Furthermore, depending on your pol-

icy, you may have to advance payments to the doctor or facility. This can add up to a lot of money, and you want to be sure to be reimbursed as quickly as possible.

An easy, efficient system for keeping track of claims. Bill C. set up three separate folders. In the first folder he placed all his bills. Since his health policy required that bills be submitted within thirty days of being incurred, he marked his calendar to check this file every two weeks. At that time he submitted all new claims with a cover letter that gave a brief description of what was enclosed. He then placed a copy of the cover letter and the appropriate bills in a second file, which was marked "Claims Submitted, but Not Paid." As soon as he received reimbursement or was notified the bill was paid, he moved the notification, his letter, and the (now paid) bills to a third file: "Claims Submitted and Paid." If any other correspondence was received, or telephone conversations occurred concerning any specific bill, that correspondence or notes about those conversations were clipped to the appropriate bill. Whenever Bill checked the file with bills waiting to be submitted, he also checked file two to see if more than twenty days had passed without notice of payment or reimbursement with respect to the bills already submitted. He made sure the system would be continued if he traveled or became incapacitated by putting a note on top of file one describing his system.

If you have access to a computer, you can keep these records on a spread sheet that would show the bill, submission date and amount, as well as the reimbursement date and amount.

Claims personnel who work for the insurance carrier. Try to develop a friendly relationship with the claims manager or any other claims personnel with whom you work at the insurance carrier. It helps if you direct your inquiries and submissions to the same person every time. While each company has its own rules, a company is made up of human beings, and rules can often be bent if the people in charge want to bend them. Mary F. and her claims manager became so friendly that the manager suggested Mary explore treatments that were more expensive for the carrier but would help resolve a problem for which Mary's prior treatment had been ineffective.

Tip. Keep a record of all conversations with the insurance carrier, including the date, the time, the person or people with whom you spoke, their direct telephone number if they have one, and the substance of the conversation. If the advice you're given goes beyond something the person will do right away, ask for confirmation in writing. If the discussion is about medical matters, note the medical expertise of the staff member involved.

Go for the maximum. When it comes to filing claims with the insurance carrier, file claims for everything that relates to your health to ensure that you receive maximum reimbursements. It's your job, not the carrier's, to maximize your benefit. Let them deny the claim if it's not covered.

Assistance. If you need assistance in filing and following up on claims, find out if your GuardianOrg can help. In addition, there are independent claims representatives who will pursue claims for you for a fee. If your GuardianOrg or doctor doesn't provide a local referral, contact the National Association of Claims Assistance Professionals, Inc. (NACAP), 5329 S. Main Street, Ste. 102, Downers Grove, IL 60515-4845 (800-660-0665). These representatives can also help evaluate current or proposed policies or plans. Check the representative's experience: even if your state requires licensing, the requirements are minimal.

Section 6. Appeals If Your Claim Is Rejected

If your claim is rejected. First look at why. If something is missing from your claims form or incorrectly stated, correct it and resubmit the claim.

If everything was in order, look at whether you believe your claim is justified. If it is, continue on. *Above all, be persistent.*

Writing. If the carrier did not put the denial in writing, ask for a letter detailing the reasons why your claim was denied. If it is your doctor who turned down your request, obtain the letter from her. The facts will help in evaluating what you need to do to win your appeal.

Keep a written log of all conversations relevant to your claim, including the information described in the tip on this page.

Usual, reasonable, and customary. If the insurance company refuses to pay more than what it considers "usual, reasonable, and customary" (a standard applied in many indemnity policies), it will be up to you to prove that your doctor's charge meets the standard. Ask your doctor to write a letter documenting and justifying the charge. Also call specialists in the same geographic area in which you live and ask what they charge for the same procedure. Try to find at least ten specialists. Identify the procedure with the procedure code number that was on your doctor's bill.

Experimental treatments. Health insurance does not generally pay for experimental treatments. In some states, as long as the drug or treatment is approved for one use, insurers must pay for so-called **off-label** uses (uses other than the one for which the drug or treatment was approved). Perhaps you can obtain the drug and/or treatment free, or at little cost, by joining a clinical trial (see chapter 25, section 8).

If the carrier does not want to pay for the treatment and/or drugs you want, argue that the treatment is within a generally accepted standard of care for your condition and that it is medically necessary. In addition to asking your doctor for an opinion letter that fits the insurance contract language with supporting documentation such as peer-review study reports, obtain support letters from other specialists in the field performing the same procedure for the stated condition and from national patient-support organizations stating their experience with the acceptance of, and reimbursement for, this procedure. At the least, you should argue that the therapy is the best available for obtaining benefits that will save the insurer money down the line.

Tip. For a free evaluation of the suitability of an experimental treatment by a panel of experts, call the Medical Care Volunteer Ombudsman Program at 301-652-1818.

Cosmetic. If the insurance company claims that a procedure or device is not covered because it is for purposes of appearance rather than medically necessary, e.g., a wig, ask your doctor to write a letter explaining why it is necessary for your physical and/or mental health. The bill you receive should reflect medical necessity as well. For example, if the subject is a wig, ask the wig maker to bill you for a "prosthesis" rather than a "wig."

Find advocates. If the carrier rejects your requests, look for financial clout and relationships to apply pressure. If your coverage is through your employer, ask your plan benefits manager for assistance immediately upon notification of a claim denial. The employer has more clout than most individuals. The larger the employer, the greater the clout. Also, go back to your doctor and ask her to go to bat for you.

Erma B. had three minor outpatient procedures performed in a plastic surgeon's office. Each time she asked the doctor's nurse if she needed her MCO card. Each time she was told no. The fourth visit was a much more extensive procedure. When the doctor's office asked for authorization from the MCO, it incidentally requested coverage of the prior three visits. The MCO turned down coverage for the first three visits solely because they had not been pre-authorized. Repeated calls by the patient and the primary care physician did no good. Finally the doctor's office manager reminded an offi-

cer of the insurance company she knew that the doctor had been a member of the MCO for five years and would leave if this was not corrected. The MCO relented.

If neither the doctor's nor the employer's prodding help, ask for a second opinion from an outside source and have that doctor explain his or her reasoning in writing. While this is the recommended route, if paying for the opinion is a concern, you can usually obtain a second opinion that your plan will pay for if you use a network doctor. You can obtain free information to help bolster your case from your GuardianOrg.

Follow the grievance or appeal process. Pay strict attention to all deadlines. Send copies of all correspondence to your doctor. If you're not getting what you want, write a letter to your insurance carrier's administrative review board. The letter should
- state that you are enclosing
  - a copy of your medical report prepared by (name of doctor) on (date).
  - a statement of the treatment or payment for which you asked.
  - a copy of the denial letter.
- include a restatement of the reason or reasons for the denial as contained in the letter.
- state that you want to appeal the denial of the request for (treatment or payment) and describe what you are requesting that was denied.
- describe the part of the plan (whether in your employer's summary plan description or the summary the insurance company gave you) that covers the matter in question.
- include a copy of all the letters and reports you have gathered supporting your position.
- request that if they deny the appeal, they specify which of your medical records are in their possession as well as all other information that relates to the matter. Then ask the company to tell you, in writing, what portion of the records and the section of the plan description are being used to deny your request. This information

will be useful if you have to proceed to a court action. Also ask for the names of the people who made the decision to deny your claim.

• Give them a reasonable deadline by which to respond to you, such as fourteen business days.

You may also consider including a suggestion that if they deny your request, you would like the matter given an external (out of the plan) review. This request may prod them to see the matter differently, even if the plan does not include provision for an external review.

Tip. The hint (not the threat) of publicity may cause an MCO to move toward your point of view. Most companies do not want the publicity, or a lawsuit, about lack of adequate medical care. Be cautious with your hint—threats usually cause people to stiffen their position.

Regulators. If you're not satisfied with the answer you receive or the speed at which your insurance company is answering you, call your state insurance commissioner and department of health. Be prepared with records of all letters written, calls made, and decisions reached so you can provide a complete picture to the regulators. The prospect of a state regulator being involved may even spur the MCO to resolve the matter in your favor.

As a last resort, you can go to court.

If you lose your appeal for reimbursement. If you have medical expenses that are not reimbursed by your insurance even after exhausting the appeals process, do not just throw the bills away. You may be able to deduct them from your income taxes. See chapter 18, section 3.5. This information is also important if there is an annual maximum on the amount you are required to pay out of pocket.

Section 7. Keeping Health Coverage

Once you have coverage, keeping it in force is critical. As you will see below, you can still obtain health coverage if you lose your current coverage, but the new coverage may be subject to a new preexisting-conditions exclusion or other limitations.

Pay premiums on time. While every policy I've seen contains a grace period after the due date in which premiums can be paid without the coverage lapsing, it is better to pay premiums on time. If the insurance carrier is looking to cancel your coverage, you give it an acceptable excuse if your payments are received even one day late. Even if the insurer agrees to continue coverage, it can do so by "reinstating" the policy instead of just continuing it, which would mean that any exclusionary periods could start again from the date of the reinstatement.

Tip. If your budget can handle it, and if the insurance company will allow it, consider paying premiums annually or biannually. The fewer times you make payments, the less likely you will slip up. At least, note the monthly due dates on your calendar in case you don't receive a premium notice from the carrier or in case someone takes over your affairs for you. Your bank may be able to set up direct payments from your bank account. If you need help paying premiums, government money may be available since it is generally less expensive for the government to pay premiums than to pay for your actual health care costs.

Watch the period in which to exercise rights. If you have coverage through your employer and you leave work, be sure to exercise your COBRA or other right to continue coverage within the time allotted in your plan—usually within thirty days after termination.

If you leave work to go on disability. If you leave work to go on disability, read the discussions in chapter 6 about your right to continue your coverage under COBRA and similar laws as well as the right to extend coverage.

Notice of termination. If you receive a notice of termination of coverage from your insurance company, generally accompanied by a check representing a refund of premiums, *do not cash the check!* Find out what is going on from your broker or employer. If you are not satisfied with the answer, contact your attorney.

Section 8. Obtaining Health Coverage

If you are currently diagnosed with a life-challenging condition and do not have health insurance, the best way to obtain it is to go to work for an employer that offers health insurance—the better the coverage the better off you are. In fact, good health coverage may even be more important to you than the salary—particularly if it is also accompanied by disability coverage and/or life insurance.

Many plans, especially those of large employers, may not have a preexisting-conditions exclusion. Or you may have rights under HIPAA as described in chapter 6, section 6.

If a new employer's plan is not the answer, consider the following options:

• Contact your state's insurance department to find out if your state requires that insurance companies provide an annual "open-enrollment period" during which people with preexisting conditions can obtain coverage. (See the resources section for a listing of the insurance departments.) If your state doesn't have the requirement, consider moving to one that does. It cannot be emphasized too often how important health insurance is to your physical and financial health.

• Check with the "Blue" health insurance company in your state (e.g., Blue Cross and Blue Shield) to find out if they have an open-enrollment period.

• Watch for companies that are new to your area or that make an attempt to gain market share since they often have an open-enrollment period.

• Check to find out if, in your state, MCOs can deny you coverage or impose a preexisting-conditions exclusion. If they can't, refer to the MCO evaluation chart starting on page 159 to assist in deciding which one to join.

• Perhaps you are a member of or can join a professional or membership association, a union, a fraternal organization, or other group, through which you can purchase group coverage. The more experience and/or training required to become a member of the association, the more likely it will offer health coverage to members and the less restrictive entry requirements will be for any health plan it offers.

• Some twenty-five states have "high risk" insurance pools for people who cannot obtain conventional coverage. Contact your state insurance department for more information including whether there is a waiting list for enrollment. These coverages usually have high premiums even though the states generally subsidize a lot of the cost. They also have limitations on coverage and possibly even periods of preexisting-conditions exclusions—but they are better than nothing.

• Some states have programs for working individuals or small businesses for which you may qualify. If this is of interest, contact your state insurance department. It may even be the extra boost you need to consider starting your own small business if that has been part of your dream.

• Consider dependent coverage under a spouse's plan. To cover a spouse, all that is needed is a marriage certificate: the two of you do not need to live together. There may be an additional premium to pay, but this is insignificant compared to the benefit. There may not even be an increase in premium if the spouse already has children. If you ultimately divorce, you may be eligible for coverage for thirty-six months as a divorced dependent. (Note: Your spouse may even have spousal life insurance with no medical questions asked.)

- Consider moving to a country that provides medical care, such as Canada or the United Kingdom.
- Veterans with incomes below about $22,000 a year receive care at Veterans Administration hospitals at no cost. Veterans with incomes above about $22,000 a year, regardless of preexisting conditions, can get medical care on a space-available basis at VA hospitals. A veteran need not have been in combat. For nonindigents the charges are reasonable, such as only $2 per prescription. Veterans should contact the Veterans Administration information line at 800-827-1000 to learn more about available health coverages.
- A government program may be available. Review the discussion of Medicare and Medicaid to see if you satisfy or could satisfy eligibility requirements. A government program might also pay for the drugs you need, such as the Ryan White program for people with HIV/AIDS.

Tip. Before signing a health insurance application, be sure any preexisting conditions are listed if requested, and that all information is correct. False information or misrepresentation of health conditions on your application may result in the denial of benefits or cancellation of your coverage at the time you need it most.

Tip. If you are replacing an existing policy with a new one, do not cancel your current policy until you are sure you have been approved by the new company and your coverage is in effect. If there is a preexisting-condition exclusion period in the new policy, maintain your current coverage simultaneously until that period expires.

Section 9. Legal Protections

Federal and state laws do *not* require that an employer carry health insurance for its employees, or, if it does so, whether and to what extent the employee contributes to the premium payments.

The following laws relate to health coverage:

Health Insurance Portability and Accountability Act of 1996 (HIPAA): In general, under HIPAA no employer with two or more employees who offers group health insurance can refuse health coverage to anyone who recently had health coverage. See chapter 6, section 6.

Americans with Disabilities Act (ADA): The federal ADA prohibits discrimination in employee benefit plans. See chapter 6, section 1.

COBRA and other continuations of health care: Under federal and many state laws, you are entitled to continue health coverage provided by an employer after you leave work. See chapter 6 for details.

State laws: As with any insurance coverage, state laws govern health insurance. If you have questions about the laws in your state, contact your state insurance commission (see resources section).

Section 10. Hospital Indemnity (Income) Coverage

Hospital indemnity insurance pays a predetermined amount of money each day you are hospitalized, regardless of the cost of hospitalization or the reason. There is usually a six- to twelve-month elimination period, and it is generally sold with no health questions. Even though the benefit is relatively low per day—such as $100 to $200—payments can quickly add up. For example, if a chemotherapy treatment requires hospitalization overnight, that is two days in the hospital. If treatments are three times a month, the policy provides income of $600 per month. You can use the money for any purpose you choose.

While this coverage is not recommended for the average healthy person because of its expense, it is valuable for someone who anticipates the possibility of hospitalization due to an existing health condition.

Hospital indemnity coverage can often be obtained from your credit card company, as well as your insurance broker. AARP sells hospital indemnity policies to anyone fifty years of age or older, with only a three-month waiting period for pre-existing conditions (telephone 800-523-5800). The AARP policy also has additional benefits for a ninety-day period after a hospitalization.

Tip. If you are likely to require hospitalization, consider stockpiling a multiple number of these policies so the money you receive each day you are in the hospital really adds up. Sally F. received a total of $350 a day for each day she was in the hospital—over and above all expenses, which were covered by her medical coverage.

Tax considerations. According to IRS rulings, premiums for a policy providing guaranteed weekly benefits without regard to hospital or medical costs are not deductible. Any proceeds received are *not* treated as taxable income.

Section 11. Covering the Cost of Long-Term Care

As the name indicates, long-term-care insurance policies cover the cost of long-term care.

If you already have an affordable long-term-care policy of value, continue paying the premiums. If you don't have this coverage and have been diagnosed with a life-challenging condition, you may be able to obtain it through a new employer. Otherwise it will be difficult to obtain—particularly if you are likely to need the care. Long-term-care policies require medical exams. It is possible to obtain this coverage with an exclusion for your current condition, but I would not recommend it.

For those who don't have these policies, when it comes to anticipating paying for long-term care

• review your existing medical insurance coverage to see what part of long-term care would be covered.

• review your retirement investing to maximize the amount of money available to cover these costs.

• think about new uses of existing assets (chapters 19–23).

• consider the long-range planning necessary to become eligible for Medicaid long-term care (see chapter 15, section 2.3).

Evaluating long-term-care policies. Under the typical policy, benefits begin sixty days after a doctor certifies that the policyholder has lost the ability to do one or more of the following functions themselves: bathing, dressing, eating, moving without falling, moving from bed to a chair, and getting to the toilet. For an additional premium, the waiting period can be reduced.

The standard policy covers home care and care in a nursing home. At-home services are usually required to be provided through a home-care agency and can be limited to between four and six hours of care per day. Some policies provide direct cash payments for home care, which could allow for the hiring of a companion rather than using a home-care agency.

These policies cover the long term. Better policies have an inflation rider that increases coverage by at least 5 percent per year, and benefits should last at least three years. Preferably there should be a waiver of premium upon entering a facility. Good policies have provisions for respite care (to provide for breaks for family care providers) and adult day care. A policy should be cancelable only for failure to pay premiums. Carefully review the policy to identify exclusions.

Tax. Reimbursement payments received under a long-term-care insurance contract are excluded from income. On per diem contracts, payments up to $175 per day ($63,875 annually) are tax-exempt.

Amounts received from accelerated benefits of life insurance polices can be considered long-term-care benefits. Those are tax free if the benefits are paid to a person considered to be *chronically ill* and are paid under a contract provision interpreted as qualified long-term-care insurance.

Section 12. Excess Major Medical Policies

Excess major medical policies, also known as catastrophic major medical policies, provide coverage of medical expenses to the outer limits. They are relatively inexpensive to obtain, but have a high deductible, which can range from $5,000 to $50,000. They serve as a safety net over any health coverage limits.

These policies are difficult to find and may contain a waiting period for preexisting conditions of as much as two years. If an individual policy is not available, this coverage may be available through a fraternal or professional association.

Chapter 15

Medicare, Medicaid, and Other Government Programs

The one advantage of being broke is I can let Uncle Sam cover my medical expenses. Nobody cared when I was making my $25,000 a year.

—Jerry R.

While we do not have health care for everyone, you may be eligible for one of the health coverage programs provided by our federal and state governments. Medicare and Medicaid are the largest and best-known programs. There are similar programs for government employees and veterans, and other state programs.

Section 1. Medicare

Medicare is a federal health insurance program. Medicare premiums are paid by the taxes on your salary or on self-employment income. Like any health insurance plan, your other income is not relevant (i.e., Medicare is not "means based"). Unlike most private health plans, Medicare does not have a lifetime maximum.

1.1 Eligibility

Medicare is not available merely because you paid premiums (taxes). To be eligible to receive Medicare benefits

- *taxes (premiums) must be paid for a minimum number of quarters*—the same number of quarters as are necessary to qualify for Social Security Disability Insurance (see chapter 8, section 8.1)—and
- *you must have been receiving SSD for twenty-four months because you are disabled* or
- *you are age sixty-five or older and receiving Social Security retirement benefits* or
- you are blind and a Social Security recipient or
- you suffer from kidney failure and are a Social Security recipient or
- you are at least twenty-two years of age, your disability started before age eighteen, and you have a disabled, elderly, or dead parent who receives or would have qualified for SSD or
- you are a widow or widower at least fifty years of age, without enough quarters to qualify for SSD on your own, who was married for a minimum of ten years to a deceased worker who would have qualified for SSD.

Applicants for benefits who are over sixty-five years of age may purchase Medicare coverage if they do not have sufficient quarters to qualify for Social Security benefits.

Eligibility for Medicare can continue for a lifetime, no matter how much you earn or for how long you've returned to work, provided you continue to have the condition that acted as the entry point for Medicare eligibility.

1.2 Benefits

Medicare is divided into two parts, Part A and Part B.

Part A is hospital insurance. In general, it covers inpatient hospital care, skilled nursing facilities, physician-prescribed home health visits by nurses, or physical and occupational therapists working for a licensed agency. Part A even covers hospice care. The insured must pay varying deductibles and coinsurance amounts.

Part A is paid for through your payroll taxes, so you don't have to keep paying for it when you start receiving benefits.

Part B is medical insurance. In general, Part B pays for visits to physicians, outpatient hospital services, and some medical supplies and equipment. If you want Part B, you must pay for it, even after you start receiving benefits.

Medicare Part A. Coverage is described in the chart on page 177.

Medicare Part B—medical insurance. Once you pay a deductible of $100 per calendar year, Medicare Part B pays 80 percent of the cost of approved services including

- physician's and surgeon's services, whether furnished in a hospital, clinic, office, home, or elsewhere.
- emergency room.
- outpatient hospital diagnostic services.
- diagnostic tests including X rays.
- outpatient physical therapy and speech-language pathology services furnished by participating hospitals, skilled nursing facilities,

home health agencies, and therapy clinics, or by other companies that contract with and are supervised by participating entities.

- outpatient physical therapy and occupational therapy services furnished by a licensed, independently practicing physical or occupational therapist in the therapist's office or in the patient's home (not to exceed $900 in a calendar year).
- prosthetic devices including breast prostheses and surgical brassieres.
- home dialysis supplies and equipment.
- chiropractor's treatments.
- podiatrist's services.
- certain ambulance services.
- oral cancer drugs if they are the same chemical entity as those drugs administered intravenously and certain other cancer drugs.
- outpatient psychiatric services, but the copayment is 50 percent rather than 20 percent and there is a yearly limit of $1,000.
- home health care visits, which you would expect to find in Part B, are covered by Part A.

Medicare Part B does not cover

- outpatient drugs. It will, however, cover many outpatient infusion drugs and IV nutritional supplements when administered by licensed home health personnel. It may also cover some oral drugs that are the equivalent of infusion therapies.
- dental or eye care.
- hearing aids.
- routine physical examinations.

Physicians' bills. How much the doctor may charge Medicare, and how much he can also charge you, and whether payments for your deductible and copayments go to the doctor or to Medicare are determined by whether the doctor is a "participating" or a "nonparticipating" doctor.

A **participating doctor** accepts the Medicare approved rate as full payment for all services he provides to patients with Medicare, including you. The doctor submits the bill directly to Medicare.

Medicare Part A—Hospital Insurance

Period	Medicare Pays*	You Pay*
Inpatient Hospital Services		
first 60 days	all but $760 deductible	deductible of $760**
61 to 90 days	all but $190 per day	$190 per day
91 to 150 days	all but $368 per day	$368 per day
beyond 150 days	nothing	all costs
Posthospital Skilled Nursing Facility Care*		
first 20 days	all costs	nothing
21 to 100 days	all but $92 per day	$92 per day
beyond 100 days	nothing	all costs
Medically Necessary Home Health Care**		
unlimited	all costs except $100 on Part B series and 20% of medical equipment	nothing on Part A services, $100 on Part B services, and 20% copayment on medical equipment

Hospice Care for Terminally Ill

Medicare pays all costs associated with hospice care for those beneficiaries certified by their physicians to be terminally ill. Coverage extends for two periods of ninety days and for another period of thirty days. In addition, more coverage may be available beyond 210 days (90 + 90 + 30) upon recertification that the recipient is terminally ill.

*Annually.

You pay the deductible for hospital care for each **benefit period. A benefit period for these purposes starts when you are admitted to the hospital and ends after you have been out of the hospital (or the skilled facility you went to after leaving the hospital) for sixty days. If you are readmitted to the hospital after the sixty days, while you have to pay the deductible again, you also have another sixty days with no copayment.

***Medicare covers care in skilled nursing facilities only after a stay in the hospital for the same condition of three days or longer. You must enter the nursing home within thirty days after leaving the hospital. Medicare does not cover **custodial care** in a nursing home or in a custodial or residential care facility. Custodial care is the kind of care that a layperson can perform without special training or experience. Coverage includes bed and board, nursing care by registered nurses, medical care by residents and interns, and physical therapy.

****While no hospitalization is required, to be covered
- the patient doesn't need to be bedridden but must be homebound—confined to home except to go out with assistance for medical treatment.
- your condition must need care or therapy to prevent deterioration.
- you must need skilled services such as nursing care, physical or speech therapy.
- the service provider must be certified by Medicare.

Home health care benefits are limited to a maximum of thirty-five hours a week. The covered hours can be a combination of home health aide and skilled services if it is under a home health plan set up by your doctor and there are at least intermittent skilled services that may be no more than five days a week, but may be as infrequently as once in sixty days. Up to seven days and fifty-six hours can be covered if the services are for a predictable period of up to twenty-one days. Incidental household chores performed by a home health aide are permitted. Billing should be direct to Medicare.

Medicare pays the bill in full. Medicare then bills you for any deductible and copayment that you may owe.

A **nonparticipating doctor** may charge more than Medicare allows, but only to a maximum of 115% of the Medicare-approved rate. A nonparticipating doctor sends the bill directly to you. You have to pay it and then seek reimbursement from Medicare. Medicare will only reimburse you for the share Medicare is to pay. You will be out of pocket for any deductible and copayment *plus* the extra percentage over the Medicare-approved rate. For example, if the doctor usually charges $150 for a particular service, and Medicare only pays $90 for that service, the maximum the doctor may charge is $103.50 (115 percent of $90). You will be required to pay the deductible of $18 (20 percent of $90), plus the difference between $90 and $103.50 or $13.50—for a total of $31.50 ($18 + $13.50). In some states, the permissible extra charge is less than 15 percent. Doctors can be fined for charging more than these limits. Some surgeries are exempt from the limit.

If your doctor is nonparticipating, but accepts assignment for services rendered to you, the procedure and rules apply as if he were a participating doctor.

Tip. If your doctor does not accept assignment, to avoid paying the doctor more than is allowable, send the bill on to Medicare, but do not pay the doctor until you receive money and an Explanation of Benefits from Medicare or your insurance company if you have health insurance in addition to Medicare.

Voluntary waiver. Under a law passed in 1997, a doctor may ask a patient to voluntarily waive Medicare. If the patient agrees, the doctor can charge any rate that is negotiated between the doctor and the patient. To assure that doctors do not take unfair advantage of patients, if the doctor negotiates a higher fee for even a single service to a single patient, the law requires that the doctor dis-

continue receiving Medicare reimbursement for any service to all patients for a period of two years.

Outpatient services. Under Part B, outpatient services at a hospital are not subject to any Medicare-approved rate. You may be required to pay 20 percent of an outrageous sum. It is advisable to determine the cost before agreeing to outpatient procedures.

Tip. To determine whether you are being billed correctly when you receive Medicare treatments, keep a record of all your medical visits and any procedures that were done. This will also provide a record in case you have to appeal for more money due you. Of course, review every bill for errors.

Tip. Medicare provides to all Medicare recipients a directory of participating doctors. Even if your doctor is not a participating doctor, he might accept assignment of Medicare for the services rendered to you if you ask.

If you also have private insurance. There are no limits on the amount of fees your doctor can bill your private insurance company. Whether, and how much, the insurance company will or will not pay is addressed in section 1.5 below.

If you have a complaint about charges, call the Department of Health and Human Services hot line at 800-447-8477.

Travel. Generally, Medicare does not pay for care outside of the United States. However,

- if you live in the United States and need medical care and a Canadian or Mexican hospital where you could get treatment is much closer than the nearest U.S. hospital, you can go to a hospital in Mexico or Canada.
- if you are traveling in Canada or coming from Alaska to one of the other states, you can receive emergency care at a Canadian hospital.

Veterans. Veterans can get both Medicare and veterans' benefits. Medicare will not pay for services veterans receive from VA facilities except for certain emergency hospital services or if the VA pays for VA-authorized services received in a non-VA hospital or from a non-VA physician.

Appeals. Medicare has an administrative appeals system if a claim is inappropriately denied. If you go to a participating doctor or to a nonparticipating doctor who accepts assignment, the doctor will handle the appeal. Otherwise, Medicare's notice of denial should include instructions on how to ask for a review. If you're dissatisfied with the results of the review, and the amount in dispute is at least $100, you can request a hearing before a Medicare insurance-carrier hearing office. If you are still dissatisfied with the outcome after the hearing, and the amount in dispute is at least $500, you can request a hearing before an administrative law judge.

If you are a member of Medicare+Choice (see below), the information you receive from the company should also include details of the appeals process.

Note: If you are in the hospital and a decision would force you to leave, whether you are in Medicare or Medicare+Choice, you may be entitled to an expedited review.

Abuses. The Department of Health and Human Services runs the Inspector General Hotline (800-772-1213) to answer complaints concerning fraud, overcharging, or other abuses relating to Medicare or Medicaid.

1.3 MediGap

The coinsurance payments (your 20 percent share), prescription costs, and other costs not covered by Medicare can become quite expensive for people with a serious condition. Insurance policies known as MediGap policies cover these gaps. MediGap policies come in ten standardized categories, which are titled A through J. "A" MediGap policies have the least coverage, and "J" MediGap policies have the most, *including* limited prescription drugs.

If you are younger than sixty-five. In most states, insurers are not required to, and do not, provide MediGap policies to Medicare recipients under the age of sixty-five who qualify for Medicare because of a disability. A few states require a limited MediGap open-enrollment period for Medicare beneficiaries under sixty-five, and a few states offer MediGap through their health insurance pool. It's worth a call to your state's Department of Insurance to find out about the availability of MediGap policies to disabled Medicare recipients under age sixty-five. Also ask about state-sponsored health insurance. Some, but not all, of these plans are open to disabled Medicare patients.

Tip. Some employers will continue to provide some kind of medical benefit even after a disabled employee qualifies for Medicare. Check your benefits.

If you are sixty-five or older. For a period of six months from the date you are first enrolled in Medicare Part B and are age sixty-five or older, you have the *right* to purchase MediGap insurance. You cannot be turned down or charged higher premiums because of your health if you purchase a policy during this period.

If you have Medicare Part B but are not yet sixty-five, your six-month MediGap open-enrollment period begins when you turn sixty-five. A pre-existing-condition exclusion is permitted for up to six months. If, during open enrollment, you change coverage from private insurance to MediGap with no gap, the prior coverage counts against the six-month MediGap exclusion.

If you need assistance in finding or deciphering MediGap policies, contact your local Social Security office or call the Medicare hot line at 800-638-6833.

1.4 Medicare+Choice

Medicare+Choice provides another alternative for eliminating the deductible, copayment, and other gaps in Medicare—and possibly even for increasing coverage.

Medicare+Choice provides private-sector alternatives to traditional Medicare. Since it is part of the Medicare system, the eligibility requirements are the same.

Medicare+Choice plans must cover people with a disability the same as people who qualify because of age (with the exception that they do not have to accept kidney patients or people already in hospice care). They are permitted to limit coverage to a **low option plan,** a plan that must at least equal Medicare benefits without deductibles or copayments. Emergency services must be available twenty-four hours a day.

An amount equal to the Medicare Part A premium is paid by Medicare to the Medicare+Choice company. Participants in Medicare+Choice continue to pay an amount equal to Part B premiums. The private insurance companies offering Medicare+Choice coverage can charge premiums in excess of the Part A and Part B premiums, but cannot charge a higher fee or impose a different preexisting-condition clause or waiting period solely due to a disability.

You can terminate your participation in a Medicare+Choice plan and return to traditional Medicare at any time effective the first day of the month after the month in which you notify Medicare+Choice of your intent to leave.

Medicare+Choice includes all the types of managed care organizations described in chapter 14, section 3.1, medical savings accounts (MSA) described in chapter 18, section 2.4, and traditional indemnity-type health insurance policies described in chapter 14, section 2.

Managed care. Managed care companies are required to offer a benefit package that includes what Medicare itself would cover. **In addition, plans *can* (but don't have to) *offer***

- coverage of all or almost all of the Medicare deductibles and coinsurance situations that would otherwise be covered by MediGap.
- services that aren't even usually found in MediGap coverages, such as outpatient prescription drugs; preventive dental; hearing and eye tests; durable medical equipment; hospital, home-health, skilled-nursing, and hospice days over the Medicare limits. They can also offer heavily discounted dental and vision services. Read plan materials carefully to be sure you understand these "extras" and any limitations on them.

While it would appear on the surface that a Medicare+Choice managed care plan that eliminates deductibles and extends coverage to such items as prescriptions would always be better than traditional Medicare, consider the issues discussed in chapter 14, section 3, relating to managed care coverage in general. Also look at whether there are any annual or lifetime limits in the plan.

In addition to the quality and accessibility of the specialists in your condition, look at whether the MCO is a **risk contract** or **cost contract,** which refers to how the government pays the plan. The type of contract determines how, what, and where your plan covers.

- Under a risk contract, the MCO is paid a fixed fee from Medicare for all care provided. The MCO promises to provide all medically necessary covered services for the capitated amount Medicare pays. If you go outside the plan for any services, you have to pay for those services yourself.
- Under a cost contract, the MCO is paid according to what the plan spends on each patient. Thus, there is no incentive to provide you with inadequate care. If you go outside the plan, Medicare covers services you receive that are covered by Medicare, subject to the regular copayments and deductibles.

Where charged, the extra premiums for these packages have generally been low (e.g., $35 per month), with small copayments subject to a yearly maximum.

Tip. If you travel, request a "guest membership" to a Medicare MCO in the area to which you are traveling for the maximum period you expect to be in the area.

Participants in Medicare MCOs have specific rights of appeal. You can request an "expedited" review. If you ask for a review by a "peer review organization" (PRO) as soon as your coverage is denied, you are entitled to stay in the hospital at no charge until a decision is made. If the review is conducted internally by the MCO, you can also stay in the hospital during a review, but you may have to pay for the extra days if you lose.

Medical Savings Account (MSA). Under the MSA alternative, each year the government will pay into your account an actuarially determined amount equal to what SSA would have spent on you during the year. You are expected to purchase private medical coverage and pay from your own funds for any medical expenses up to the deductible. After that, the insurance coverage would take over. To illustrate, if SSA gives you $5,000 for your medical savings account, you buy a policy for a premium of $2,000 to cover all medical expenses in excess of $10,000. You then spend the next $3,000 from the account for medical expenses, then the next $7,000 in expenses from your personal funds. Any medical bills in excess of $10,000 would be covered by the insurance company.

Unlike a traditional MSA, (see chapter 18, section 2.4), any money in the MSA not spent by the end of the year can be withdrawn for your own use tax free. If you die and there is money left in the MSA or that originated in the MSA, it is also free of estate taxes.

Indemnity coverages. Since as of this writing the law is still new (it was passed in 1997), it is uncertain what the requirements will be with respect to indemnity-type companies. The only certainties are that they will have to accept both aged and disabled Medicare patients regardless of preexisting conditions and must offer, at a minimum, the basic Medicare benefits package.

Information. If you want information on Medicare+Choice plans in your area, contact your local Social Security office. The Office of Managed Care of the Health Care Financing Administration publishes "The Medicare Managed Care Directory" free. Call 800-638-6833.

1.5 The Relationship Between Medicare and Private Health Insurance

Medicare permits you to obtain additional private health insurance. If you have Medicare and can obtain additional health insurance through an employer or otherwise, you will reduce or eliminate your deductibles and copayments. *If you can obtain both coverages, I urge you to do it.*

Tip. If Medicare is your primary coverage and you have additional private health insurance, you may have access to experts in your condition unwilling to treat Medicare-only patients due to the plan's reimbursement rates.

Tip. You can probably convert continued group coverage to an individual policy. If the policy the carrier offers on conversions is too limited, look at purchasing health coverage on your own. If the new carrier won't let you have two private coverages, in month twenty-eight from the date you went on disability, don't pay the premium for your private coverage on time. Your private coverage stops if not paid on the due date and does not start again until the premium is paid within the grace period. You can now correctly state to the new carrier that you do not have insurance since the private insurance does not exist and Medicare hasn't started. Reinstate your former coverage before the end of the grace period.

Billing. Medicare has specific rules for whether it or private coverage is the primary payer with respect to all services and treatments. Medicare is secondary for

- disabled people with group coverage through their current employment or a health plan based on current employment of a family member if the employer employs one hundred or more people, or, if fewer than one hundred employees, is part of a multi-employer plan in which at least one employer has one hundred or more employees.
- people age sixty-five or over with coverage through employment or spouse's employment for employers with twenty or more employees.
- eighteen months for people with permanent kidney failure and with group health coverage himself or herself or through a family member.
- people with work-related illness or injury or if no-fault insurance or liability insurance is available to cover.

As a practical matter, this means that if your doctor, hospital, or other service provider does not take an assignment of Medicare, you must send the bill you receive to the primary provider first. If the primary provider is Medicare, you send the bill to the **Medicare carrier** (the company hired by Medicare to process claims) on the Medicare claim form that the local Medicare carrier uses; the carrier then sends you an **explanation of benefits** form (EOB). Then, you take that form and mail it to your secondary carrier. If your private coverage is primary, the process works in reverse—send the bill to the private carrier first. If you're lucky, an electronic database connection between the two companies will eliminate the paperwork for you once the bill is submitted to the primary carrier. Be sure to show your Medicare and other health in-surance cards to your doctor's office staff and tell them which is primary and which is secondary.

1.6 How to Apply for Medicare

You are *automatically* enrolled for Medicare after receiving SSD for twenty-four months. You will receive a notice in approximately month twenty-eight informing you that Medicare is in place for you, including A and B coverage. The notice also informs you how much will be deducted from your SSD payments for B coverage. It is then up to you to elect to refuse B coverage if you so desire.

If you choose to refuse Part B coverage, you must notify the SSA in writing. The letter should include your Social Security number, state that you are eligible for Medicare, and that you do not want Part B coverage.

Tip. An election with respect to B coverage is not permanent. You can discontinue it whenever you want. You can recommence B coverage every year (at a much higher than normal rate), but only if you so elect between January 1 and March 31. Even then coverage does not start until July 1 of the year you enroll. There are special enrollment periods for Part B coverage if you qualify for Medicare for reasons other than disability. It is always essential to take B coverage.

Others who may be eligible for Medicare should apply at their local Social Security office.

1.7 If You Need Assistance to Pay for Medicare Part B Payments, Fees, and Deductibles

Three federal programs assist low-income Medicare recipients pay Medicare premiums and/or deductibles and copayments: **Qualified Medicare Beneficiary (QMB), Specified Low-Income Medicare Beneficiary (SLIMB),** and **Qualified Working Disabled Individual (QWDI).**

For each of the programs, "net countable income" and assets cannot exceed a defined level, which is different for individuals, married people, and people with children. These programs determine net countable income in the same manner as for eligibility for SSI (see chapter 8, section 8.2). *Keep in mind that this means you can earn (from a job) slightly more than twice the limit and still be eligible.*

In calculating income for eligibility purposes, total SSD payments are included before deduction for the Medicare Part B premium. In late 1997, the net countable monthly income eligibility levels for a family of one are QMB, $658; SLIMB, $888; and QWDI, $1,315.

Under SLIMB, Medicare premiums are paid for the recipient (deductibles and copayments are the recipient's responsibility). As a bonus, the monthly deduction for Medicare Part B, currently $43.80 per month, is restored to the recipient's SSD check.

Under QMB, if the Medicare beneficiary's countable income is less than $658 per month, the Medicare premiums, the hospital admission deductible, and the copayment for doctor visits are paid for by the state. Eligible individuals receive full coverage for just about all medical care except prescriptions, dental, and nursing home care. These excepted items are covered by state Medicaid. Most states do not, however, cover adult dental care in their Medicaid programs, even though New York does. If you don't qualify for state Medicaid, see chapter 25, section 6.8, for advice on obtaining free medicines.

Under QWDI, only Medicare Part A premiums are paid.

If you are already receiving SSI, apply for these programs at your Social Security office. Otherwise apply through your local welfare office. For more information about these programs contact the Medicare hot line at 800-638-6833 or the Social Security Administration at 800-772-1213.

Additional information. If you have questions about Medicare, call the Medicare hot line at 800-638-6833, the Health Care Financing Administra-

tion at 202-690-6726, the Medicare Rights Center hot line at 800-333-4114 or 212-869-3850, or your local department of aging. You can also obtain a free copy of *Your Medicare Handbook* by writing the Health Care Financing Administration, Office of Beneficiary Relations N-1005, 7500 Security Boulevard, Baltimore, MD 21244-1850.

There are also state programs to pay Medicare premiums, coinsurance, and deductibles.

Section 2. Medicaid

2.1 Eligibility

Medicaid is a "means-based" benefit program that is paid for by the federal government but administrated by the states. Medicaid, which is known in California as MediCal, pays the medical bills for people with a low income and few assets provided they fit within one of six categories:

- disabled.
- blind.
- people under the age of twenty-one.
- pregnant women.
- members of families containing one or more children under age eighteen deprived of two fully functioning parents in the home due to absence, death, medical incapacity, or recent loss of a job (Aid to Families with Dependent Children or AFDC families). This category presents a second opportunity for qualification for Medicaid since the disability test for an "incapacitated parent" is far more liberal than the SSA standards for disability.
- people over age sixty-five.

Aged and disabled legal aliens in the United States as of August 22, 1996, are eligible for Medicaid. Most such legal aliens entering the country after that date are no longer eligible for Medicaid unless and until they become citizens. Illegal aliens are not eligible for Medicaid.

Most larger industrial states have their own programs, which they also call Medicaid, for poor people who do not fit in the six categories. Since the rules vary so much from state to state, check the specifics of your state. The following general description of Medicaid is meant to provide an overview only.

Basically, to be eligible for Medicaid, your income and assets must be less than the SSI or AFDC levels in your state. The asset tests are the same as those used for SSI and the Medicare means-based programs (see chapter 8, section 8.2). The deductions are also the same—except that with Medicaid, in all but thirteen states, you can also deduct a "spend down."

Tip. If you leave work due to disability and you have no health coverage, you immediately qualify for Medicaid if you qualify for SSI. This coverage can continue through the five-month waiting period for SSD. Since most SSD payments will be above the SSI income level, you would lose Medicaid coverage when SSD starts unless your SSD level is below the SSI level or you qualify through "spend down" provisions as described below.

Spend down. When income is too high to meet Medicaid eligibility requirements, the program allows income to be reduced by a **spend down** equal to the amount of medical bills that are *incurred* during the subject period. It is not necessary that the bills be paid—just that they be incurred. This generally includes premiums for Medicare and private health insurance. To illustrate, if the eligibility income level is $500 and you make $700, but you incur medical bills in the month for $200, your countable income becomes $500 ($700 less $200 in medical bills incurred) so you are eligible for Medicaid during that period.

Spend down provisions only apply to excess income, not to excess assets.

Generally, SSI and Medicaid do not care if an applicant sells assets for less than fair market value or even gives them away in order to qualify, except with respect to long-term care (see section 2.3).

Living benefits. If you obtain an accelerated benefit from the life insurance company or sell your policy in a viatical settlement, once you receive the money, you flunk the income test. You also fail the asset test—until you no longer have the money.

Getting your Medicaid card. In most states ("1634 states"), SSI recipients automatically receive Medicaid cards. In other states ("Title XVI states"), SSI recipients have to prove SSI eligibility to the state welfare office to qualify. In a third set of states ("209(b) states"), recipients must apply separately for Medicaid at the welfare office because Medicaid rules are stricter than SSI rules—although as a general matter most SSI recipients will qualify for Medicaid as well.

Spouses. When one member of a married couple moves to a nursing home and applies for Medicaid, there are protections for the other spouse's assets known as the **community spouse resource allowance (CSRA),** which vary from state to state. The spouse not in the home can usually also retain his or her income. There is also an allowance for the remaining spouse and a family income allowance for minor children.

2.2 Benefits

In addition to providing what could be thought of as traditional health coverage, Medicaid tends to become the payer of last resort for long-term care. Each state has its own program, which is subject to federal minimums. In just about all states, Medicaid covers

- physician services
- prescription drugs (subject, in some states, to limits per month).
- laboratory and X-ray services.
- medically necessary transportation to and from medical care (including ambulances and sometimes handicapped vans and taxis).
- care by a psychiatrist. Some states also cover psychologists and psychiatric social workers.

- clinic care.
- home care by professionals such as registered nurses and physical therapists. In some states, Medicaid also covers physician-ordered part-time skilled nursing, and homemaker services provided by certified home-health agencies—particularly if it would keep the applicant from having to enter a nursing home or a hospital. Likewise, personal care services may be covered if they are incidental to medical care. In all states except the District of Columbia, Medicaid will cover a personal care aide if ordered by a hospital under a "waiver" program. Some waiver programs even cover respite care. These waiver programs usually require the person be as impaired as someone who would otherwise be in a nursing home.
- assisted-living care if you qualify for a home and a community-based waiver of service (see page 188) if the facility is licensed by the state. This program may even cover case management, which is not ordinarily covered by Medicaid.
- hospital care, both inpatient and outpatient.
- nursing homes.
- hospice care (in about half of the states).
- family-planning services and supplies.
- at least basic dental care for children. A few states also cover adult dental care.

Medicaid payments are made according to a schedule of fees that varies state by state. The amount of payments is low compared to market prices and is generally even low compared to payments made by Medicare. The payments are made directly to the provider. The federal law allows requirement of a nominal copayment, which is not defined but is usually $.50 or $1 per office or clinic visit, per lab test, per prescription, and per other medical service or item. Federal law also provides that no provider can withhold an item or service if a Medicaid recipient cannot afford the copayment.

Participating physicians. In general, medical care providers do not have to participate in Medicaid. Many prefer not to because of the low Medicaid fee schedules and the requirement that the provider accept the Medicaid rates as full payment. As a general matter, the result is that doctors in poor neighborhoods accept Medicaid while most of those in middle-class and upper-class neighborhoods don't. Your GuardianOrg or your social worker may have a list of participating providers.

Tip. An exception to the general rule is that doctors who are involved in a clinical practice associated with a teaching, research, or large public hospital are effectively required to participate in Medicaid. Their patients receive the latest medical care. The doctors are paid the difference between what they receive from Medicaid and their normal fees through subsidized endowments, charities, and the like.

Managed care. With a law passed in 1997, the states have the right to require that Medicaid patients enroll in managed care organizations. See chapter 14, section 3.2, for factors to consider if you have a choice as to which managed care organization to use.

Payment of Medicare and private health care premiums. Since states have realized that it is less expensive to pay premiums for health coverage than to pay the actual medical expenses for poverty-level residents, all states pay for Medicare premiums, coinsurance and deductibles for Medicare beneficiaries, and premiums for private health insurance policies for Medicare eligible people. All states can, and a few states do, pay COBRA health insurance premiums for those with low incomes and assets even if they are not eligible under the state's regular Medicaid rules for other Medicaid benefits.

If you qualify for both Medicare and Medicaid. It is possible to be on both Medicare and Medicaid—for instance, when a person receives SSD but the amount of the monthly payment is below the SSI level. (When a person accesses both programs it is called **Medi-Medi.**) In that case, Medicare first pays medical bills up to whatever its rules allow, then Medicaid pays the rest. Health coverage becomes complete since prescription drugs are covered under Medicaid, and you won't have to pay the deductibles and copayments that you would otherwise face without Medicaid. Your health care providers are also happy because they and hospitals are covered by the better rates paid by Medicare, which makes them more likely to accept you as a patient and devote adequate time to your care. Also, when you are on Medi-Medi, Medicaid will start paying the Medicare Part B premium for you so your SSD check will increase by the amount of the Part B premium.

2.3 Impoverishing Yourself to Qualify for Long-Term Care

Long-term care, which includes nursing homes, hospice care, and home health care, can be expensive. To avoid having people qualify for this expensive care by giving away their assets to loved ones, there is a **look-back period**—the responsible agency "looks back" to determine if any transfers for less than fair market value were made by the applicant during a specified period. The states do not have to include this look-back period, but if they do, a period of thirty-six months is mandated. The look-back period is extended to sixty months if the transfer was to a trust.

Transfers of assets *to* spouses do not count as transfers at all but are considered assets of the applicant. (Neither do transfers to blind or disabled children.) Transfers *by* the spouse of a person who receives or applies for Medicaid during the look-back period can disqualify the applicant.

Although state regulations vary, transfers without full value within the three-year period *may* be permitted depending on the purpose for which the transfers are made, and when. Matters are often decided case by case, and you will have to prove the transfer was not made to qualify you for Medicaid. For example, it is likely that if your father needs a $20,000 heart operation, you will not be penalized for giving him the money.

Any assets transferred in the look-back period trigger a **penalty period**. This penalizes applicants to the extent that the transferred money could have been used for long-term care:

- Determine how much money was transferred without fair value during the look-back period.
- Determine how much supervised care costs per month in the applicant's area.
- Divide the amount that was transferred by the monthly cost of supervised care.
- The result is the number of months Medicaid will not pay for nursing home care, starting with the first day of the month succeeding the month in which you gave away assets.

For example, in the Syracuse, New York, area, nursing home care is assumed to cost $5,000 a month. If the applicant transferred $50,000 for no consideration to a son three months before applying for long-term care, then $50,000 divided by $5,000 equals ten months. The applicant would have to absorb the cost of a nursing home for ten months. Medicaid would start covering the costs of the nursing home in the eleventh month.

If the transfer is made *during the look-back period,* there is no limit on the term of the penalty period. In the above example, if the applicant transferred $300,000, the penalty would continue for sixty months. Thus, if the penalty would be more than thirty-six months, it is preferable to make the transfer and wait more than thirty-six months before applying for Medicaid.

Note: There are no federal prohibitions against transferring assets before applying for non-nursing-home Medicaid benefits. However, your state may impose such restrictions.

In response to abuses, Congress made it a criminal offense for professionals to give advice about divesting assets to qualify for Medicaid during the look-back period or during the penalty period. Advice given before the look-back is not a criminal offense, and neither is advice during the look-back or penalty period *if* the applicant does not actually apply for Medicaid coverage of long-term care until after the penalty period. The practical effect of this provision has been to make advisers more cautious about their advice. All of which leads me to state:

The following discussion is for information purposes only and is not to be considered advice or assistance with respect to disposing of assets to qualify for Medicaid long-term-care nursing home benefits.

People faced with the exorbitant costs associated with long-term care have become eligible for Medicaid by shielding assets to some extent or by transferring assets.

Conversion. The simplest method to qualify for Medicaid has been to shift assets into excluded categories (e.g., a home). For example, Sebastian L. could not obtain private health insurance but needed recurring expensive treatment for his kidney disease. He used his $100,000 nest egg for the purchase of a house. He rented a room to a friend, who pays for the expenses of the house instead of paying rent.

Divestiture. Another method used is divestiture (giving assets away). The common method of divestiture is to follow the "rule of half"—the applicant transfers one-half of his assets and keeps the other half. The rule of half is not arbitrarily set at 50 percent. Since there will be a penalty for the money given away, enough money is retained for the applicant to pay for the necessary care during the penalty period, while maximizing the amount that is given away. For example, a person with $100,000 gives $50,000 to a child and keeps the other $50,000, which is then used to pay for nursing home care. In the example we've been using in which nursing home care costs $5,000 a month, the $50,000 that is given away equals ten months in a local nursing home. In the eleventh month, the

person applies for Medicaid. The second $50,000 is no problem because it was transferred for value—for the services of the nursing home.

To exemplify the problem advisers are having today: If the applicant applies for Medicaid in month nine, there is no effect on the applicant. There will still be no Medicaid coverage until month eleven. Nevertheless, if, during the penalty period, an adviser advises an applicant to do this, the adviser could be deemed to have broken the law.

Supplemental needs trusts (also known as special needs trusts). Under federal law and under many state laws it is possible for a friend or relative to establish a "supplemental needs trust" for a disabled person under age sixty-five to provide for needs supplemental to what Medicaid and SSI pay for—such as vacations, special educational and recreational programs, special equipment, or modifications to the home to accommodate a disability. The assets remaining in the trust upon the death of the beneficiary can be distributed according to the desires of the creator of the trust. Your GuardianOrg or state or local bar association can probably provide a referral to an attorney specializing in this area of law.

In some states, these trusts can be established with a disabled person's own funds, which both reduces assets so as to become eligible for Medicaid and provides for additional needs. Generally, any assets remaining in this sort of trust after the death of the beneficiary are available to the state to recover the cost of care provided to the disabled beneficiary.

Keep in mind the practical difficulties of distinguishing between luxuries and necessities. For example, rent, food, and medical bills are necessities. For additional information, look at *Third Party and Self-Created Trusts: A Lawyer's Comprehensive Reference* by Clifton B. Kruse Jr. (Chicago: American Bar Association, 1995).

Annuities. Another method that has been used to avoid the asset test is to purchase a single-premium annuity, which changes an asset into a stream of income. For example, if you go into a nursing home, you can assign the income to the home, then reclaim the remaining income when you leave the home. This usually works best for people with a longer life expectancy.

Liens. For people over age sixty-five, Medicaid can eventually seek to recover money from the estate of deceased recipients, or even place a lien on real property owned by the recipient for money spent by Medicaid on long-term care. If a home is inhabited by legally married spouses or minor or "disabled" adult children, Medicaid does not place a lien on the premises to try to recover money spent on long-term care for a deceased recipient or recipients no longer living on the premises unless fraud was involved. Generally, there can also be no recovery if title to the asset is transferred. For people under age sixty-five, liens and recoveries from estates are generally not permitted unless there has been fraud.

Tip. If transferring or spending your assets to qualify for Medicaid seems appealing, be aware that

- Medicaid does not cover a number of tests and procedures, and, since payments are limited, may not provide access to the best care.
- when you give away assets, you actually do impoverish yourself and no longer have any control over the assets. For money, you must rely solely on the discretion of the person to whom your assets have been transferred. Your assets will also be subject to that person's legal and financial problems.
- the Unified Gift-Estate tax may apply (see chapter 33, section 4).
- you should consult a qualified attorney who is a specialist in this area. While being careful to comply with the new law, attorneys still give advice. To locate an attorney, contact your local bar association. The National Academy of Elder Law Attorneys, 1604 N. Country Club Road,

Tucson, AZ 85716-3102 (520-881-4005) can provide a list of its members for $25.

Waiver services. If home attendant care is the issue, and it is not covered under Medicaid in your state, it may be covered as part of home- and community-based "waiver services." This vague term permits less expensive home care (not normally covered) if it allows the person to stay at home rather than "risk institutionalization." The word *institutionalization* was apparently meant as expensive nursing home care, but it has generally been interpreted to also include hospitalization. States can even set broader eligibility requirements for people who fit this category. For instance, in waiver situations, doctors can be paid more than the regular Medicaid payments to be sure the person gets treated outside the institutional setting.

Tip. If you need long-term care and can't arrange it, get admitted to a hospital. You won't be discharged until an arrangement for your care is in place. It may not be what you want, but it's likely to be better than not getting the care you need. If not, you can always leave.

2.4 Appeals

You are entitled to a hearing if your application for Medicaid is denied or if your Medicaid benefits are terminated, suspended, or reduced. The written notice you will receive of cessation or reduction of your benefits will not only inform you about the action to take place, the reason and the date it will happen, it will also provide information about an appeal. The notice will describe the action you must take to continue your benefits pending a hearing. If you need to appeal, seek the assistance of an attorney with experience in Medicaid cases.

   More information. If you have additional questions about Medicaid, call the Medicaid hot line (800-541-2381) or directory assistance in your state and ask for Medicaid's telephone number or call your local department of aging.

Section 3. Hill-Burton—Free Hospital and Health Facility Care

In exchange for Hill-Burton program grants and loans to hospitals and other health facilities for construction, renovation, and expansion, the facility must give free or reduced-fee medical care to people with low incomes who are not completely covered by private health insurance, Medicare, or Medicaid. The amount of care a facility must provide is set (and audited) each year.

Hill-Burton does not consider assets. It covers inpatient hospital bills, but not doctors' bills. It is possible to apply after you leave a hospital for the Hill-Burton program to pay for your stay, but it is better to do it before entering. To locate a facility in your area that participates in this program, call the Hill-Burton hot line at 800-638-0742.

Tip. When calling a facility to determine whether it will admit you for little or no cost, ask for the "Hill-Burton coordinator" or a financial counselor. Even if the facility has used its Hill-Burton requirements for a year, it may have other programs to provide free or less expensive care.

Section 4. Veterans' Benefits

The Department of Veterans Affairs administers various health programs and needs-based income programs for veterans of the Air Force, Army, Coast Guard, Marines, Navy, the Environmental Services Administration, the National Oceanic and Atmospheric Administration, the World War II merchant marine, Army Air Corps Flying Services, Philippine guerrilla units, and commissioned officers of the Public Health Service. If you served in any of these organizations, contact the Veterans Administration at 800-827-1000 to find out about eligibility for health, income, and burial benefits. Generally, all veterans with honorable or general discharges who have at least 180 days of active duty can receive care at VA medical centers—even if they are not disabled under VA or Social Security rules and whether or not they served in a war zone or during "wartime." If income exceeds a prescribed level, a copayment is charged.

Tip. Be aware that if your illness is not service based, when you go for care, people with service-based problems are taken care of ahead of you.

Tip. VA care can provide prescription coverage for many severely ill and disabled veterans for whom such coverage is not generally available (even if they have SSD and Medicare). VA clinics and hospitals charge only $2 per prescription, and small copayments—even for high-income veterans.

Section 5. State and Local Programs

Many other benefit programs administered by states and localities provide for housing, medications, and other medical costs. To find out about these programs and whether you are eligible, you should speak with a social worker at the welfare office, county or city aging agency (even if you're not elderly), county or city housing department, and legal aid agencies. Also speak with your GuardianOrg as well as other people with your condition.

Tip. If you are told that no programs apply to you, seek a second opinion from another expert. Alan E. was told by a case manager that no local programs would benefit him, although he could (and eventually did) qualify for a local housing program.

Chapter 16

Property and Casualty Insurance

Accidents will occur in the best regulated families.
—Charles Dickens

Property insurance covers the risk of loss to property and its consequences (e.g., fire damage to a house and alternative living arrangements while the house is being repaired). **Casualty** insurance protects against liability to third persons. These coverages are particularly important to you now because the last thing you need is a major financial loss that could be avoided with a minimal cash outlay.

The discussion about each policy is not as detailed as the health insurance section since most of these coverages are standardized and free information is easily available from any insurance broker or insurance company that deals directly with the public (a "direct writing company"). I do point out the types of insurance every prudent person should carry, areas that may be of particular interest because of your health condition, and tips on saving money.

If you have your own business, be sure you work with a reputable broker to determine what insurance is appropriate to protect your business assets.

Section 1. General Considerations When Purchasing Property and Casualty Insurance

Brokers. You can purchase property and casualty insurance either through a broker who works on your behalf (even though she is paid a commission by the insurance carrier), or directly with an insurance company known as a "direct writing carrier."

Having grown up in a family in the insurance business, I am biased in favor of the broker system, which provides advice about types and amounts of coverage, compares and evaluates different insurance companies, and advocates on your behalf in the event of a claim. Nevertheless, there are perfectly good direct writing companies and the decision is yours as to which route to take.

No matter what your ultimate choice is, after you've read the basics described in this chapter, it is worth meeting with a qualified property and casualty insurance broker to discuss your needs and determine appropriate coverages for you, pricing, and information about the claims service of recommended companies. Your meeting with the broker does not cost money, and the expenditure of the few Life Units it takes for a meeting is a good investment. (See chapter 36, section 6, for advice on picking a broker.)

Before you consider which insurance you need and in what amount. You will need an inventory of your assets and copies of your current coverages (if any). The inventory list should include

- a description of the general items (e.g., sofas, chairs).
- description of specific valuable items.
- date of purchase (approximate if you do not have the exact date).
- whether the item was purchased new or used.
- purchase price.
- an approximation of what the item would cost to replace today.
- serial numbers, if any.
- which assets are used for business.

This may seem like a lot of work, but this inventory will be important in the event of a loss. It helps to also have a videotape or photos of the items, as well as the purchase receipts (or at least as many as you can find). Keep this information in your safe-deposit box or a locked fireproof file, preferably away from the insured premises. From now on, also be sure to keep copies of all purchase receipts in the same safe place.

Tip. Review your assets each year when your coverage is renewed to update asset values, add new assets to your list, and subtract any assets that have been disposed of since the beginning of the last policy period. The insurance company won't refund premiums for property you insure but no longer own.

Shop around. Most people do not shop around when they purchase property and casualty insurance. Once you determine the coverages you need,

and in what amounts, compare prices and quality of claims service among various insurance companies. Speak with your friends and associates about the claims experiences they have had or know about with respect to any company you are considering.

Tip. Every few years, at renewal time, obtain price comparisons again. Ask your broker to do it for you, or do it on your own if you use a direct writing company.

Complete file. Make notes of what you are told by the insurance agent or the company concerning the coverage you purchase. Keep the notes together with any promotional material you are given or shown when you buy the policy.

Section 2. Losses

To do immediately in the event of a loss. Photograph or videotape your loss, especially if you have personal injuries. Visuals are much more impressive than descriptions. If the damage is so severe that you must make immediate repairs, take photos, then make only temporary repairs until you contact the insurance company.

Before you contact the company. Review your policy and the notes you have with it before you speak with a company representative. If you aren't prepared, you may say something that the company may use to deny or limit the claim. If you have a broker, speak with the broker and let the broker make the initial call to the insurance company. In addition to checking the coverage, read the section concerning duties you have after a loss occurs.

Time limits. Be sure to follow the time limits if any, described in the policy for filing a claim. The company may accept the claim after that date, but do not take the chance.

The process. Once the company receives a claim, either one of its employees or an **adjuster** will contact you to begin negotiations as to whether the loss is covered and if so, in what amount. An adjuster is a claims expert who is experienced in negotiating the amount of a loss.

To maximize the amount of money you receive in the event of a loss.

- If you work with a broker, at each step along the way don't make a move or speak with the company or the company's adjuster without first speaking with your broker. The broker will be a major source of information and advice and may even do the negotiating for you.
- Videotape or take pictures of the damage before you clean up or start any work. If items have been totally destroyed, pull out any inventory or other proof of what you owned and its cost or value.
- Don't throw away any damaged property until after the adjuster has seen it.
- If the loss is due to a burglary or vandalism, the insurance company will want a copy of the police report.
- When you file a claim, take a fair position. The insurance company will tend to be reasonable if it thinks you are as well. Write your claim to fit the wording in your policy. If your loss is to your house, get a repair estimate from a local contractor as soon as possible so that you'll have a cost guideline when the adjuster arrives.
- If you vastly underestimate your loss up front, and that number is passed on to the insurance company, you will face an uphill battle in seeking reimbursement for your full loss.
- If the loss is large enough (for instance, in excess of $10,000), consider hiring your own **public adjuster** or an attorney to negotiate for you. For a negotiable fee, which is usually 10 percent of the amount the insured receives, the adjuster reviews the insurance contract to make sure no aspect of coverage is overlooked; will do most of the paperwork; works with engineers, apprais-

ers, and contractors to prepare estimates that reflect the cost of repairs or replacement; and negotiates with the insurer on your behalf, making sure the technical requirements are met. If the technical requirements are not met, courts have ruled that some claims are not permissible.

Before hiring a public adjuster: Negotiate fees; find out what services will be included and whether there are extra costs; find out whether she is licensed; and ask for and contact references to find out the services the adjuster performed, the timeliness of the services and the repairs, the nature of the settlement, and whether the person would use the adjuster again.

To locate a public adjuster: Ask your insurance broker if she knows of one or ask friends and neighbors. Adjusters are known to swarm to areas that suffer natural or other disasters, but that does not speak to the quality of their work.

- If you're being treated unfairly by the insurance company, before you sue, contact your state insurance department.

Section 3. The Coverages

The idea behind property and casualty insurance is to spread the risk of losses that may be too large for an individual to bear among people with similar risks. Insurance should not be used for small claims. Many insurance companies will not renew coverage for an insured who files several small claims, or the rates may increase.

Tip. Save money on your premiums by raising the deductible to between $500 and $1,000 or, depending on your economic circumstances, even higher. Compare the premiums at each different deductible level.

Tip. A canceled check is not proof that a policy exists. Do not assume coverage exists until you obtain a copy of the policy or at least written confirmation from the insurance company that the coverage exists and that the policy will follow.

3.1 Homeowners Insurance

General description. The homeowners policy is a complete package of property and liability insurance designed to cover the average residential and personal exposures of most individuals and families. It protects your home and your belongings against loss, and you from liability for injuries to others and liability for damages to the property of others. Home-based businesses may be included on a limited basis. There are various types of homeowner policies, but together they cover homeowners, condominium and cooperative owners, and tenants.

Coverage. You can purchase homeowners policies that cover specified risks such as fire, lightning, and similar risks. You can also purchase homeowners policies that are **all risk** coverages. They cover all risk of loss including the ones you would normally consider, except those that are specifically excluded because they are uninsurable or would normally be covered by other insurance policies such as automobile insurance.

In general terms, the policies cover the dwelling and other structures, unscheduled personal property that is anywhere in the world, personal property usually located at a residence of an insured other than the residence described in the policy, and loss of use, including additional living expenses. *The policies also cover the insured's personal liability, medical payments, and damage to property of others, which can be critical to you if health care professionals or friends come to visit.* Homeowners insurance does not cover the insured or members of the insured's household who are hurt on the property since those expenses are typically covered by a health insurance policy. The value of the land is never covered since it is not subject to an insurable loss.

Tip. Purchase the broadest coverage you can. It makes it less likely for a claim to be denied on grounds of noncoverage.

Defining the value of what is covered. Dwelling coverage can (and should) be written on a **replacement cost basis,** which means you receive money to replace the damaged or destroyed structure without deduction for depreciation. **Actual cash value coverage** normally only pays for the replacement cost of the property at the time of a loss minus the amount the property has physically depreciated since it was built or was purchased. Property depreciates even though its market value may be rising.

Coinsurance. Coinsurance in property insurance is different from coinsurance in the health field. In property insurance, coinsurance recognizes that most losses are not total, and that insureds can save money by only covering their real risk, rather than the full value of the structure. To provide sufficient premiums to pay losses (and make a profit), the insurance companies generally require that the insured carry at least 80 percent of the replacement cost. If the insured meets the requirement, any losses to the building will be paid to the full extent of the coverage. If the insured carries less than the 80 percent, then in the event of a loss to the building, the insurance company would pay only a part of the loss—i.e., the insured "coinsures" and has to pay for the rest of the loss.

To determine value. To determine replacement value, ask your insurance company to inspect your home and give you an evaluation. If it won't, your broker has a replacement-cost guide. If your home was custom-built, obtain an independent appraisal. Every year determine the current replacement value of your house and compare it with your insurance coverage. To assess the continuing valuation of your home, determine the square footage of your house and see what comparable houses in your area have recently cost to build.

Tip. Eighty percent coverage pays 100 percent of a small loss, but not all of the loss if the whole house burns down. Purchase 100 percent of replacement cost. The extra cost in premiums is worth the peace of mind.

Increases in value. In most states, you can purchase an **inflation guard endorsement,** which automatically increases the coverage limits periodically to keep pace with rising real estate values and construction costs. While it is worthwhile to have this endorsement, it is still important to periodically review the value of your property. Your policy limits should also be increased whenever you make substantial improvements.

Tip. If inflation is rapid in your area, ask for an endorsement that increases protection quarterly.

Other matters to consider.
- Standard replacement cost coverage doesn't cover the cost of meeting new building codes. This is a particular concern if you own an older home. A **code and contention** endorsement covers the extra costs, which can be substantial.
- To protect against changes in the zoning law, make sure your policy states that you can build your exact house, no matter what the cost, even on a different lot if you are not allowed to rebuild on your own lot due to zoning changes.
- If you live in an area prone to fierce fires or earthquakes, such as California, be sure to cover your foundation. While arguably the foundation shouldn't burn, it could be destroyed by one of these disasters.

Credit card. Homeowners policies generally cover up to $500 in unauthorized credit card purchases.

Restrictions. There are some common restrictions in homeowners policies of which you should be aware:
- In general, liability coverage is not provided for areas where there are separate coverages, such as automobile, workers' compensation, or flood.
- If you take a boarder, there is no coverage for

loss to the boarder's property, unless the boarder is related to you.
- Business pursuits in your home are not generally covered, so liability is not covered for business visitors, nor is a computer or computer discs if they're used primarily for business.
- Bodily injury or property damage that is expected or intended by the insured is of course not covered.
- Items that can be specifically insured under separate policies such as jewelry, furs, securities, stamp collections, artwork, watercraft, money, firearms, and flatware are covered for a low limit or not at all. Full coverage can be added to the policy by listing (**scheduling**) the items at an agreed value.

Co-op and condominium. If you live in a condominium or cooperative, the association generally pays for the insurance protection on the building as well as liability protection if anyone is injured in the common areas (e.g., hallways). You are still responsible for the interior of your apartment, the contents, and your own liability. These risks can also be covered under a homeowners policy.

The risk that you will be assessed to help pay for damages to the building not covered under the building's coverage (for example due to a large deductible) can also be covered by adding "assessment coverage" to your policy. The cost for this coverage is minimal, and at least one company includes it at no charge. It is worthwhile to obtain a copy of the condo association's policy and tailor your coverage to fit.

Tip. Many people with a challenging condition rely on residence employees to help with home upkeep and personal care. They can be covered under your homeowners policy.

To reduce the cost of your homeowners insurance.
- Ask for quotes from at least three insurance companies at the beginning and upon renewal.

• You can usually receive discounts of 5 percent to 15 percent of your premium if
  • you buy your home and auto policies (and possibly other policies) from the same insurer.
  • you stay with an insurer for several years.
  • you install antitheft and/or fire alarm devices.
  • you are a member of a Neighborhood Watch program.
  • you install a residential fire sprinkler.
  • in cold climates, you install a monitoring system that transmits an alarm to a central station when temperatures inside the home drop below freezing (this will generally qualify you for a 2 percent homeowners credit).
  • you are retired (retired homeowners are more likely to be home to spot fires or discourage burglaries).
  • you live in an area with a high level of protection, such as a gated community.
• Discounts are great, but always look at the bottom line. Some companies with high discounts start with high premiums.
• Consider raising your deductible. For example, if you increase your deductible from $500 to $1,000, you may save 10 percent of your homeowners premium to a maximum of $250.
• Ask what other discounts are available, such as for retirees or people who have taken classes in home safety or for improvements such as fire-retardant shingles.
• Don't insure the land.
• Find out if you are eligible for any group coverages, such as through an alumni association, employer, or business association.
• Consider purchasing your insurance from a company that pays dividends and has a long history of paying them.
• More and more employers are offering group home and auto insurance. Discounts of up to 10 percent off going rates are typical. However, do not automatically assume that the group rate is the cheapest. Ten percent off a high premium

may still be higher than the least expensive coverage you can get on your own.

3.2. Personal Articles Floaters: Jewelry and Fine Arts Coverage

A personal article **floater** (policy) is a specialized form of insurance that can be used to cover personal property on an itemized and scheduled basis. The floater contains an itemized schedule listing insurable property such as jewelry, furs, cameras, musical instruments, silverware, golf equipment, fine arts, stamps, and coins. For each article covered, an appraisal is needed. This type of policy provides "all risk" coverage for direct physical loss. Uninsurable property includes accounts, bills, currency, deeds, evidences of debt, money, and securities.

Tip. If you do not wear your valuable gems or look at your valuable collections often, put them in your safe-deposit box at your bank and ask your insurance agent for "valuable article coverage for in-vault jewelry." Losses from a vault are difficult, but not impossible. Banks are generally not liable for loss unless they have been found to be negligent in some way. Check your contract. Always retain proof outside the box of what you store in your safe-deposit box "just in case."

Adding a "floater" to your homeowners policy to protect these items may cost between $1.90 and $4.00 per $100 of value, while vault coverage can be $.30 per $100, plus a small amount for the few days a year when you take the jewels out of the safe. A few banks offer their own safe-deposit coverage, which is generally cheaper than a homeowners policy.

3.3 Fire Insurance (aka Dwelling Insurance)

The names **dwelling insurance** or **fire insurance** are used interchangeably and refer to the same type of policy. The basic fire insurance policy protects against losses in your home in the event of fire or lightning. Fire insurance does not protect you against other losses such as theft or personal liability for injuries to others on the premises. However, separate theft coverage forms and a personal liability supplement may be attached to fire insurance. Generally, you will need to purchase both fire and liability insurance to adequately protect yourself.

3.4 Rental Insurance

Damage to premises that makes them totally or partially unfit for occupancy means the tenant may have to pay rent for an uninhabitable space and the owner may lose rent income. Although basic fire insurance will pay for direct damage to the building or contents, it will not cover loss of rents or rental value. Rent insurance is used to protect the owner or tenant of a building after a fire and can be attached to standard fire policies.

This insurance is advisable for landlords. A tenant should check the lease before deciding if this coverage is needed.

Rental insurance is not to be confused with coverage against "additional living expense" described in the homeowners policy.

3.5 Liability Insurance

Generally, liability insurance covers your liability for bodily injury and property damage occurring to others, except as a result of business activities or while driving your car, watercraft, or piloting an aircraft.

Tip. Especially considering that a number of people may be coming onto your premises if you become sick or disabled, it is critical to have liability coverage if you do not have homeowners coverage.

3.6 Why Purchase Fire and Liability Policies Separately Rather Than a Homeowners Policy?

• If you do not need the full package of homeowners coverage, you may save some expense. For example, if you own two homes, you can extend the homeowners coverage on the first home to cover liability risks for additional premises, in which case you would only need fire insurance for the second property.

• The eligibility rules for fire and homeowners policies are different. A fire policy may be easier to get. Homeowners policies can have more stringent underwriting procedures due to age or condition of the house or neighborhood.

• It may be less expensive to purchase the coverages separately, even compared to a stripped-down homeowners policy. However, this may be a false savings if a homeowners policy would cover risks not included in either a fire or a liability policy.

3.7 Excess Liability and Umbrella Coverage

These policies are designed to increase the limits of your basic liability policy. An excess liability policy does so without broadening the coverage of specified underlying insurance coverage. Umbrella policies not only increase the limits, they also expand the personal coverage beyond policies such as the typical homeowners policies. They are worth the minimal premiums if your assets are near or in excess of the liability limits of your homeowners, personal liability, and/or auto liability policies.

3.8 Automobile Insurance

If you own or lease a car, automobile insurance is an absolute must. It covers loss to the vehicle as well as any liability as the result of an accident. The amount and type of liability coverage may even be mandated by state law.

Automobile insurance—liability coverage. The coverage most critical to avoid total financial ruin is liability coverage. There are two types of automobile liability coverage. The most important is **bodily-injury liability,** which pays for the other person's medical treatments, rehabilitation, and other loss if you are found to be at fault in an automobile accident. The second type is **property-damage liability,** which is coverage against damage to property caused by your auto when the driver is at fault.

Tip. In most states, the minimum requirements do not come close to covering the potential losses for which you should be covered. You will find that the cost is minimal to increase the limits above the basic coverages.

The other components of automobile insurance to consider are **collision** and **comprehensive** insurance. Collision insurance covers you when there is an accident, no matter who is at fault. Comprehensive pays after a theft or for the repair of damage caused by other events such as fire, flood, or windstorm. Both pay for repair or replacement of your car, and both come with deductibles.

Tip. If your car is more than five years old *and* has lost most of its value, consider dropping the collision coverage. The cost of insurance could exceed the value of the car. Don't drop collision coverage if your car retains its value.

Recommended auto coverage. The larger the deductible, the lower the insurance premium. Generally, deductibles are recommended in the $250 to $500 range, but I recommend considering deductibles of between $500 and $1,000. I also recommend:

- **Bodily-injury liability:** The minimum required by your state law if you have few assets and a low-paying job. If you have more assets to protect and/or a higher income, consider a minimum of $100,000 per person and $300,000 per

accident *plus* umbrella coverage as noted above, taking your limit to at least $1 million.
- **Property-damage liability:** Minimum of $50,000 due to the high cost of today's cars.

Note: Automobile contract coverages usually read as a series of three numbers, called **split limits,** e.g., $50,000/100,000/50,000. In this example, the first $50,000 is the maximum for bodily injuries to any one person in an accident; $100,000 is the maximum for all bodily injuries, no matter how many people are hurt in the accident; and the last $50,000 is the limit payable for damage to someone else's property.

Tip. As described above, inexpensive umbrella policies are available to extend the liability coverage of your auto insurance and should definitely be considered.

Price. Price comparisons for auto insurance between companies are published by the insurance departments of many states. Even if your state doesn't publish a list, it is worth checking to see what complaints have been filed against the company you use or any companies you are considering using.

Some companies offer new clients with a good driving record a standard rate that may be reduced to a preferred rate after you have been with the company several years. Other companies offer the preferred rate from the beginning. Even if you are able to find a price that is better than the one you are currently paying, you should hesitate before leaping to a new company because insurers often reward their longtime customers with discounts and accident-forgiveness-type programs.

Automobile insurance—miscellaneous coverages. Additional coverages to consider are:
- **Medical payments coverage:** Regardless of fault, covers your household members and passengers who may have insufficient health insurance. It also covers household members injured by a motor vehicle when they are pedestrians and provides for funeral expenses when necessary. This cover-

age is not important if you have good health coverage for you and your family. If you take this coverage, $5,000 is an acceptable maximum.

- **Personal injury protection:** Like medical payments coverage, but broader. It covers your household members and pays regardless of who is at fault in an accident. It also includes some lost wages and the costs of assistance in the home. This coverage is required in some **no-fault** states. (In no-fault states, you are only allowed to sue if the accident involves damages beyond a certain dollar amount or serious injury or death.) Only buy the minimum if you have adequate health, disability, and life coverages.
- **Uninsured and underinsured motorist coverage:** Covers your household against medical and similar costs resulting from an auto accident caused by an uninsured or underinsured motorist or by a hit-and-run driver. I recommend at least $100,000 per person and $300,000 per accident.
- **Glass breakage:** Covers when your cracked or broken glass needs replacement. This coverage is worthwhile if the cost is small enough.
- **Rental insurance:** Covers the cost of renting a car while your car is being fixed after an accident. This is worth purchasing if your car is your only means of transportation and your garage won't loan you a car while they work on yours.
- **Towing:** Covers the cost of towing your car after an accident or if the car breaks down. You can usually do better by joining an auto club that offers this service as well as additional perks.
- **Uninsured-motorist property damage:** Covers damage to your property by someone without insurance, or not enough insurance to pay the costs. If you have collision coverage, this coverage is unnecessary. If you don't, it is worth considering.

Tip. Before choosing medical-payments or no-fault protection, check with your state's insurance department for details of no-fault coverage in your state.

Tip. If you are purchasing coverage from a company because you have learned to associate its name with less expensive coverage, be sure you are dealing with that company and not a subsidiary with a similar name that insures higher-risk drivers in exchange for higher premiums.

Automobile insurance—assigned-risk or high-risk pools. Assigned-risk pools are state-sponsored pools that provide a means of obtaining coverage if you have trouble finding automobile insurance because you recently had more than one accident or moving violation. Rates for pool members are high. As soon as your record improves, start shopping for private carriers. The law of your state may even mandate that after a given period without accidents or violations, the private carriers must reconsider you.

Automobile insurance—money-saving tips.
- **Quotes:** Get quotes from at least three different companies to compare prices and services.
- **Discounts:** Check to see if you qualify for any of the following discounts (which are not offered in all states or by all insurance companies): more than one vehicle; multiple coverage with the same insurance carrier; good-driver record; mature-driver discount for drivers between fifty and sixty-five; restricted-mileage discount for those who drive less than a certain number of miles each year, such as 7,500; and passive-restraints, antitheft-devices, and antilock-brakes discounts. If your car isn't equipped with these last safety devices, compare the price of installing them against the discount you could obtain. Of course, do not pay so much attention to discounts that you overlook the bottom-line cost.
- **If you have moving-violation points:** Check to see if taking a defensive-driving course will entitle you to a discount.
- **If you have children under twenty-five:** Name them on your coverage as drivers of your least expensive car. It is cheaper to keep children on your policy than to insure them through the assigned-risk pools. The car the teenager drives

must be in your name to be covered under your policy. Discounts may be available for driver-education courses and/or a good academic record. The National Safety Council at 800-621-6244 will let you know if a driver's education course is offered near you. Another discount would apply if the child without a car is enrolled in a school more than one hundred miles away.

- **Young singles under thirty:** Married males under thirty pay the same rates as older drivers.
- **If you are fifty or over:** A driver's education course may entitle you to a discount.
- **If you commute:** If you merely drive to public transportation or are part of a car pool, you may be entitled to a discount.
- **If you are told you have to go into an assigned-risk pool:** Check with other brokers or insurance companies to see if their underwriting standards are different.
- **Limited damage reports:** Think twice before reporting limited-damage accidents and/or accidents that do not involve other people. One at-fault accident can result in several years of substantial surcharges, and more than one can mean nonrenewal of the coverage. If another person is involved in the accident, even though there do not appear to be any personal injuries such as in a fender bender, beware of surprises later. You can drop a note to the insurance company letting them know about the accident, that no one was hurt and no claim is expected. If a claim occurs later, you're covered. If not, it shouldn't count against you.
- **If you have an accident:** Don't repair the damage without prior approval of the insurance company.
- **Deductible:** Consider increasing your deductible.
- **Changes in status:** If there are any changes in your status that might reduce premiums, report them. For example, if you start carpooling or install an alarm system.
- **Good Drivers:** A good driving record lowers your insurance rates.

Tip. If you are in the market for auto insurance, first contact Comprehensive Loss Underwriting Exchange (C.L.U.E.). C.L.U.E. is a new national database with up to five years' worth of claims history that many insurers check to help determine whether to insure an applicant, and if so, at what premium. Check to see if it has a record on you, and if so, whether it is correct. Call 800-456-6004 with your driver's license number, date of birth, Social Security number, and if you already have auto insurance, the name of the carrier and the policy number. If there has been an adverse action within the last thirty days, the report is free. Otherwise the cost is under $10.

Also contact *Consumer Reports* auto insurance price service (800-807-8050, M–F, 8 A.M. to 11 P.M. ET; Sa, 9 A.M. to 8 P.M. ET). For residents of an ever-growing number of states, for a small fee the service searches a database to create a personal report listing up to twenty-five of the lowest-price policies.

If you are considering purchasing a car. Check the rates that apply to it *before* buying. Some types of cars carry much higher premiums than others. You can find out about the safety of a car by writing to the Insurance Institute for Highway Safety, 1005 N. Glebe Road, Ste. 800, Arlington, VA 22201, and ask for the Highway Loss Data Chart.

3.9 Insurance When You Rent a Car

Car rental companies have always charged for coverage for collision. However, recently a number of them also started charging for liability coverage, shifting the responsibility for this coverage to the renter.

Collision. Before you rent a car, check to see if you are covered for collision under any of your credit cards (and if so, use that card) or under your own automobile insurance policy. Don't assume just because you have collision coverage that it covers rentals, particularly if you are renting the car for business travel. If you have coverage under a credit card coverage as well as under your auto policy, the credit card coverage becomes "secondary coverage." This means that the auto policy pays first, so the credit card company only pays for the deductible. If you have credit card coverage, and not auto, the credit card is primary.

If you will be using the car for business, check to see if your employer insures the trip.

If you have no coverage, or if your policy covers you but you wouldn't file a claim under it, then consider purchasing collision insurance for business uses.

Liability. Check to see whether your policy covers liability if you rent a car, particularly if you are renting the car for business travel.

Tip. When you rent a car, be sure you are covered for both collision and liability coverage somewhere: your credit card, your own automobile policy, or the rental company's coverage. If the limits at the rental company are low, ask to increase them. If you rent cars often, consider either a policy known as a nonowner liability policy or an endorsement to your homeowners policy.

3.10 Workers' Compensation Insurance

If you employ others, and that includes people hired to assist your daily living or to provide nursing care, or even a cleaning person, you need to protect yourself from the possibility that they will be hurt in work-related injuries. Workers' compensation is a **no-fault insurance** policy that provides comprehensive benefits regardless of who or what caused the injury. This coverage is probably mandated by your state law, and the penalties can be quite heavy if you are supposed to have it but don't.

Tip. Just because the people who help you are employed by someone else, such as a home care company, you are not necessarily off the hook. Some states make it your responsibility to find out whether every person who works for you is covered, and to carry your own workers' compensation insurance if she is not. Ask for proof of this kind of coverage from everyone who works for or helps you at home. If you go to an assisted nursing home or a hospital, the employees are the responsibility of the facility, not yours.

Tip. If you are injured at work, you may be able to use workers' compensation to take care of your health condition (in addition to your work-related injury) if you don't have health coverage. In many states, workers' compensation laws allow the employee to choose the medical care provider, so you can choose a specialist in your condition and see the doctor for both your condition and the injury while your doctor is being paid by the workers' compensation coverage.

3.11 Travel Insurance

See chapter 37, section 4, if you are planning to travel.

3.12 Other Property and Casualty Coverages

Accidental-death insurance and flight insurance. The chances of dying in a plane crash or even accidentally are extraordinarily slim, which is why these coverages can be purchased cheaply. No medical questions are asked. I don't recommend this coverage, but if you've got the extra money and feel skittish when flying, go for it.

Cancer insurance and other similar policies. These policies pay a fixed amount per day if you are diagnosed with the disease specified in the policy. If you already have the disease, you cannot obtain the coverage. If you know you are predisposed to a certain ailment, it may be worthwhile to obtain this insurance, but otherwise not.

Child support insurance. Covers child support payments if the supporting spouse is thrown out of work. This is expensive insurance and provides limited coverage, since it doesn't cover if a spouse becomes sick or quits a job. Anyone under twenty-five or over fifty-five is not eligible. Coverage generally only pays for four months. It is not recommended.

Consumer credit insurance. Consumer credit insurance covers your mortgage balance, car loan, or credit card balance. *Take all you can get.*

Contact lens insurance. If you wear contact lenses, your eye service center probably offered you a service agreement that includes insurance to protect against the loss of your lenses. If your health insurance covers vision care, the cost of servicing and replacing contact lenses is already covered. If not, look at the coverage closely to see if it is worthwhile for you. Generally it is not.

Directors' and officers' liability (D&O). This policy covers against liability if you serve as a director or officer of an entity, including a nonprofit organization such as your GuardianOrg. D&O policies cover any **wrongful act,** which is generally defined as a breach of duty, neglect, error, misstatement, misleading statement, or omission. Since the courts are showing a greater tendency to hold directors and officers liable, and the impact could be devastating on you, if you are already on a board or if you are invited to serve on one, inquire into what protection you are afforded by the organization. Generally, the organization, rather than you, pays for the coverage.

Earthquake and flood insurance. These coverages generally only cover the dwelling, and not the contents or the outbuildings, although contents can be covered. If you have a mortgage, and if you are in an area where either risk is real, you should obtain this coverage even if your lending organization doesn't require it. If the premium you're quoted is too high for you, ask what it would be with a higher deductible.

Tip If you're not sure if you live in a flood zone, call the zoning department of your local or county government. Even if you're in a moderate to minimal risk area, you should consider flood insurance. About 30 percent of claims come from outside the high risk areas. Likewise, if you're not sure if you live near a major fault, call your state's department of geology or look at the National Earthquake Information Center's Web site at www.neic.cr.usgs.gov.

Pet insurance. Covers veterinary medical treatment and/or hospitalization for injury and illness to pets (not the pet's life). There is a limitation on the amount of coverage per injury or illness (generally between $1,000 and $2,500), and a deductible for each pet. Pet policies generally exclude preexisting illnesses and conditions, hereditary and congenital conditions, routine checkups, grooming and vaccinations, preventable diseases in animals that have not been vaccinated, and those conditions resulting from lack of vaccination. The policies do not cover animals over a given age, such as ten years old.

Tip. Certain breeds are prone to illnesses and it may be advisable to purchase pet insurance for them. Otherwise these policies are not recommended. Premiums and deductibles are high, and there are too many exclusions.

Chapter 17

Financial Management

Just about the time you think you can make both ends meet, somebody goes and moves the ends.

—Richard F.

This chapter discusses a variety of means available to help manage your finances.

Section 1. Money Management

1.1 Smart Spending

- *Think in terms of how many Life Units every purchase you consider will require.* If you don't think about Life Units, think of what the item would cost in pretax dollars. A good rule of thumb you can use is to multiply the purchase price by 1.65 to get your before-tax cost.
- If you have a life expectancy of two years or less, or if you have little money, make as many of your purchases as you can on credit or time payments (so you save your cash) with credit life insurance if possible (so the debt will be paid off at death).
- No matter what your life expectancy, if you can't get credit life insurance, it is better to save the money for the item you want to purchase and then pay for it in full. You exchange the instant gratification of buying on credit for the major savings of interest and other costs over time—

plus you have the cash available in the meantime in case you need it for your health.
- Use checks or credit cards wherever possible instead of cash to keep track of how your money is being spent. All other things being equal, the best credit cards to use are those with credit life insurance and credit disability insurance, or at least credit life. Leave the credit cards that have a higher rate of interest at home.
- Think about spending guards that work for you. For example, set a limit for the number of times per week you go to the ATM. When shopping, before you start, set a limit on what you are going to spend for the items you need. Or only take enough cash to pay for what you need and leave all the credit cards home.
- If you're saving money to purchase something, put a picture or drawing of it in a place you see every day, such as in your checkbook or with your ATM card. It will help you pass up impulse purchases in favor of accumulating the money you need to purchase the goal item. Tom M. kept a photo of the Eiffel Tower inside his closet door as inspiration to save for his eventual trip to Paris.

• Whenever you spend any money, make a conscious decision about whether the value of what you are getting is worth the loss of dollars needed to achieve your financial goals.

Consolidate debt. Consolidate debt by moving as much debt as you can to the credit account with the least amount of interest. Another alternative to consider is a **consolidation loan.** A consolidation loan is a single loan for the purpose of paying off all your debts. The payments on the new loan, because they are stretched out over a longer repayment period, should be lower than the total of all the old payments. A consolidation loan only works if you then balance your spending and income. If the consolidation loan is a home equity loan, the interest payments will be tax deductible. However, remember, with a home equity loan, if you don't meet payments, you may lose your home.

Retain your credit cards even after a consolidation loan but don't use them unless you have a short life expectancy with credit disability and/or life insurance for the card. You want to retain as much credit as possible "just in case."

Medical devices. Although you may be able to rent what you need, it is worthwhile to compare the cost of a rental against a purchase if you believe you will need the device for an extended time. Your GuardianOrg or social worker should be able to point you to the places with the best price if you have to purchase a device—or maybe even to a free source.

1.2 If Your Expenses Exceed Your Income

• **Reduce debt:** If you have outstanding debt, consider approaching your creditors informally about reducing your debt and creating a payment schedule that will work for you. This idea is described more fully in the next section.

• **Life insurance:** You can sell a life insurance policy in a viatical settlement to raise money to pay off debt and reduce the stress of constantly dealing with creditors. See chapter 19.

• **Tenant:** See the discussion in chapter 22, section 2.6, with respect to renting out real property to a tenant, turning your residence into an assisted-living home, or taking in Section 8 boarders. If you live in a spacious apartment, the discussion may also apply to you. Focus on extra "space" rather than an extra "room," because rooms can be created relatively inexpensively by renting portable walls without damaging or altering the structure.

• **Move:** Consider moving in with a friend or family member or renting a cheaper space for yourself. Don't give up your current space immediately—perhaps you can rent it or sublease it to increase income.

• **Your job:** Using the methods described in chapter 4, section 1.1, reevaluate your True Net Pay. What can you do to increase the net, either by reducing your expenses or changing the way you work?

• **Non-income-producing assets:** Consider selling assets that produce no or little income. See chapter 23.

• **Retirement plans:** Look at chapter 20. Your retirement plan can be used as a source of cash for daily living.

• **Reverse mortgage:** If you are over age sixty-two and there is equity in your house, you may be eligible for a reverse mortgage. See chapter 22, section 2.5.

• **Home equity conversion:** Consider taking a loan against your residence, either by borrowing the maximum amount or taking a line of credit secured by the house so you can borrow as you need funds. If your budget is tight, it may be preferable to avoid a loan with variable rates so you don't have to worry about interest rate increases. For other means of accessing money from your residence, while remaining in it, see chapter 22, section 2.

Tip. Never borrow an amount that results in more payments than you can safely afford. If you cannot make payments on time, you could lose the asset, which could very well be your home.

1.3 A Budget

Creating a budget may be painful, but it can be critical to achieving financial health. If your finances are already in good shape, it will help you decrease your expenses so you can increase the amount you invest to meet your goals. Think of the painful parts of the process, including any emotions that come up, as medicine: they may not taste good going down, but . . .

The starting point. A budget is an itemized summary of probable expenditures and income for a given period. If you didn't pull together your income and expenses when you read chapter 4, section 2.2, now is the time to do it. Don't worry about honing the numbers to pennies. Your objective is the middle ground between not having any idea where your money goes and knowing about every single penny.

Types of expenses. The next step is to distinguish between core, discretionary, and unnecessary expenses.
- **Core** expenses are essential, such as food, rest, and medical care.
- **Discretionary** expenses are generally nonessential. For example, at times entertainment would be considered discretionary, but at other times, due to stress or desire, some form of entertainment becomes a core expense.
- **Unnecessary** expenses are those you really never need to incur. If you're having trouble identifying those expenses, pretend you are looking at a friend's list of expenses—it may give you a more objective view. Or better yet, have a close friend or family member look at your list and give you his opinion. When you look at your entertainment expense, consider

whether it can be reduced—but do not eliminate it entirely. No play not only makes Jack a dull boy and Jill a dull girl, according to the doctors who study the mind-body connection, it is also not good for your health.

Involve all members of your economic unit in the decision as to what is core, discretionary, and unnecessary. A budget doesn't work unless all the members of your household are involved. A spouse's overspending can cancel out your savings. If you have children, make them part of the budget process. It's good for them to learn how to spend money wisely, and where better to learn it than at home? Setting the example for them may also help keep you on track. And everyone always has ideas on how *other* family members may reduce spending.

Tips for creating a budget.
- There is no required form to follow. Depending on your personality, make the budget as general or as detailed as you prefer. If you need a form, your local stationery or computer store will have many inexpensive suggestions.
- The savings part of your plan should come first, not the spending part. It may make living tighter than you would want, but it is advisable to be prepared with a Just in Case Fund for emergencies that could arise with your condition (see chapter 4, section 4).
- Don't break your budget into categories that are too small. For example, auto maintenance, gasoline, tolls, and subway fare can all be grouped as transportation. Too many categories only adds complication. When you refine your budget later, you can add more categories if you find it helpful.
- The plan should be flexible. Include a little extra money to spend as you like.
- Consider the ideas that come to you about your income and expenses as you read through this text. Work those changes into your budget.
- Create a weekly or monthly budget. I recom-

mend a weekly budget because no matter what happens, you start fresh again the next week. If you're comfortable with larger blocks of time, then you may prefer monthly.

- Think about items that are not paid weekly or monthly. Divide the cost of those items by fifty-two for the number of weeks or twelve for the number of months in a year and add that portion to your weekly or monthly expense.
- Just as with food diets, cutting back usually works better than cutting out since it is easier to sustain over time.
- If your spending exceeds your income, cut everywhere you can. If you can't find a logical place to cut, consider cutting all expenditures by the same percentage. This probably won't be feasible, but it will likely highlight areas that can be cut.
- Consider building in a weekly bonus for yourself as a reward for every week that you keep track of expenses (hopefully the bonus is something free, or something relatively inexpensive such as a compact disc or breakfast out). Even if your bonus equals what you would otherwise save the first few weeks, it will start you on the road to smart spending.

Tip. You can safely eliminate all "unnecessary" expenses. If that still leaves you with a shortfall, or not enough money to meet your goals, look at what "discretionary" expenses you can live without, or perhaps postpone. Review all "core" expenses again and see if any of them can be moved to "discretionary."

1.4 Living with Your Budget

The best budget is worthless unless you keep track of expenditures accurately, which you need to do in any event for tax time. A small pocket notebook is probably the easiest method—but you can just as easily keep track on your laptop or day planner. The place, or the style, isn't important.

Make a commitment to try your plan for a period of time that feels comfortable for you. Think seriously about that period and then stick to it. After the trial period, reassess your plan to see how it can be modified to fit your current daily needs while still giving you breathing space for tomorrow. The minimum trial period can be anywhere from several weeks to several months. I suggest three months (a fiscal quarter) for the best perspective.

Tip. Don't become discouraged if it takes time to actually change your behavior to meet your new budget, or if you fall off the budget any particular day or week. It takes time to adjust to the change emotionally. Take things gradually. The financial columnist Jane Bryant Quinn uses the rule of thumb that it takes one week for every year of your life to adjust spending patterns. The longer you have been doing something, the harder it is to change. If you bear this in mind, you are less likely to get discouraged and drop your plan entirely. Remember: No shame, no blame.

If at the end of a period you find you have more money left over than you anticipated, use a small part of it, say 10 percent, to treat yourself to a "luxury." Save the rest. Invariably, unanticipated expenses will eventually come up.

Monitoring. Compare your actual expenses to your budget at least once a month for the first six months, and once a quarter after that. This allows you to make adjustments proactively rather than reactively. Spend less where you can and allow more money for some things if you must. When new things come up, change the plan again. Keep adjusting it until it works for you.

Tip. While it would be helpful if you can stick to your budget, remember that it is only a road map, and you need to be flexible for the unanticipated events.

Section 2. Credit Management: Dealing with Creditors

If, in spite of your planning and money-saving efforts, you are having problems with creditors, don't panic. There are ways to deal with the situation.

Tip. *It is never a good idea to just ignore creditors.* Always respond to a letter and telephone inquiries, noting the date and the name of the person with whom you speak and the substance of the conversation. Store these notes with your bills so you can find them when necessary.

2.1 Set Your Priorities

Before you contact any creditor, or if you already have. Before you go any further, consider the following:

- The first step in dealing with creditors is to get a handle on how much you owe and how much you are able to pay. You will need copies of all your bills, and you'll need to know your monthly income and expenses.
- Prioritize your debts according to importance.
- Decide which bills you are going to pay in full and which you are going to try to reduce. To help make these decisions, determine which of your debts if unpaid will have the worst consequences for you and your economic unit. To me, this means your highest priority should be medical insurance and medical bills followed by "core" expenses: housing, utilities, and food. Include your automobile if you must have it for work or travel to medical appointments. These high-priority bills must either be paid or the monthly installments reduced by agreement with creditors to make them manageable.
- Examine the consequences of not paying a bill in order to help prioritize it. You could lose your entire purchase if the creditor holds the title to the property as security, such as with a home

mortgage or car loan. Secured creditors must be treated more carefully than creditors with no specific security for their debt.

- Next, look at how much debt has been paid to a creditor and how much remains. If you only have a few payments to go, it may be a good idea to finish them. With only a few payments left you may also find the creditor willing to grant a hardship exception based on your financial straits and health condition that would eliminate part of the remaining debt or lower monthly payments.
- Check the interest rate you are paying on each outstanding bill. Pay the bills with higher rates of interest first (unless they are covered by credit disability and/or life insurance).

As you prioritize your debts, consider the following.

House: Now is not the time to have to deal with repossession or eviction. Make every effort to make these payments. Recalling that you cannot be discriminated against because of your health condition, can you refinance the mortgage? Can you get a home equity line of credit? A reverse mortgage, since the lenders only look to the value of the house instead of your ability to repay? Can you use any of the techniques described in chapter 22? The interest on the home equity line is tax deductible, and you can use the money you save in taxes to pay off other debt.

Ask if you can pay interest only for three to six months and then resume your full payments, which include principal as well.

Tip. If your problems making mortgage payments are likely to continue, speak with a legal aid attorney who specializes in housing issues. Part of their practice is mortgage relief for people in dire circumstances.

Medical bills: Your physician and your hospital will probably be willing to work out a modified payment schedule. Try to stick to whatever agreement is reached with your health care providers as these relationships are important to you.

Utilities: You do not want the gas, electric, or telephone turned off. Utilities are generally quite good about arranging modified payment schedules for a short time. There may also be a plan for paying the bill or decreasing or eliminating it because of your condition. Check with your GuardianOrg, social worker, and/or the utility. If all else fails, there may be an extended-payment plan.

Car loans: How important is your car to you? If it is for recreational purposes only, maybe you should sell it. If it is essential for work or for getting to doctors' appointments, then this is a "core" expense. Look at whether the loan can be refinanced to make the payments smaller. Could you sell the car and get a less expensive model or lease? Like other creditors, your lender will probably be willing to agree to a short-term reduction of payments.

Child support: It is important to make child support payments. States have become aggressively involved in the effort to collect delinquent support payments. If you have a good relationship with a former spouse, it may be possible to work out a temporary arrangement. Like any negotiated agreement, it should be put in writing. If your financial situation has significantly and permanently changed because of your illness, the current support agreement may have to be revisited. If so, consult an attorney.

Bank credit cards: These are the folks who communicate most aggressively with the credit bureaus. Try to make at least the minimum payments. Bank credit cards often have the most room within which to negotiate. They would rather have you pay something than have you go bankrupt. If you have credit disability and/or life insurance on a particular account, just pay the minimum payments and let the insurance take care of the rest.

American Express and Diners card: Stop using, but *do not* cancel, these cards. Bills have to be paid in full each month. If you have an outstanding balance, contact American Express and Diners and

arrange a payment schedule. A valuable piece of advice from *Bottom Line Personal* is to put these cards in ice in your freezer. You'll be able to defrost them if there is an emergency, but you won't be able to get to them day to day.

Store credit cards: Generally these balances are lower, but the interest rates tend to be high. Pay the minimum.

Taxes: Without a doubt, the IRS is the most aggressive of the legally sanctioned bill collectors. If you owe taxes, negotiate a payment plan you can live with and stick to it. If it appears that you have to modify the plan, contact the IRS immediately. Never ignore the IRS. They can do such things as attach your bank accounts to get your attention.

Student loans: If you are on or facing disability, contact the lender to find out whether you are eligible for cancellation or deferral.

Note: Social Security Payments. SSD and SSI benefits cannot be attached by a creditor, including the IRS.

2.2 Create a Payment Plan

Now that you have your debts prioritized, come up with a realistic payment plan you can live with. This can include a reduced lump-sum payment, payment of the full or a reduced amount over time, or a combination of a lump-sum and a continuing payment. Dealing with your creditors will only work if you are realistic about your ability and commitment to pay.

Keep in mind that creditors don't want to hound anyone, much less commence litigation. They will often take a payment of less than the full amount in satisfaction of the debt if they think it will cost them money to collect the debt, or that they might not get anything at all. At the very least, a savvy creditor, including credit card companies, should be satisfied with payment of an amount equal to the debt reduced by the amount it would cost them to collect it upon default. For instance, if you owe $1,000 and offer to pay $750 now, the odds are a creditor will accept the offer.

The loss is probably less than it would cost to sue you, get a judgment, and then collect the money. This is always a point of negotiation for unsecured creditors, who prefer payment of part of a debt to nothing at all.

It is in your creditors' interest to help you figure out a way of paying because if you declare bankruptcy, they may get little or nothing of what they are owed.

2.3 Put the Plan in Action

Get in touch with each creditor, preferably before skipping a payment. Negotiate with your creditors to design a realistic payment schedule. If you explain your physical situation, most creditors will accommodate you, especially if you have paid your bills on time in the past. As a last resort, a nonthreatening mention that you are considering going into bankruptcy may help convince your creditor(s) to reduce the debt and/or work out a repayment schedule.

If you have several creditors, start your negotiations with the one most likely to agree to your plan. You can then use that agreement in discussions with other creditors to show that your plan is not only reasonable, but already accepted by another creditor or creditors.

Whatever agreement you reach with your creditors, send a confirmation letter by certified mail, return receipt requested, describing the details of the agreement. Retain a copy for your records. Stick to the agreement, always informing your creditor if a problem arises.

Tip. If you do make an arrangement with creditors, be sure to abide by the agreement. If you don't, you'll lose all credibility and may arouse the creditor to pursue you diligently for the full debt plus interest and possibly the costs of collection. If you are unable to make a payment, let your creditor know *before* the payment is due. Creditors are much more willing to be cooperative when they feel as if they are being treated with respect than when an agreement is broken by a skipped payment with no warning.

Tip. If you are on permanent disability with a fixed income and few or limited assets, it may be no more than a matter of informing the creditor of your ability to pay. Chances are they may write off your debt.

Tax. If a creditor forgives a debt, the amount you don't have to pay is considered income to you. You don't have to report the "income" if you cancel the debt in bankruptcy or because the time limit to sue to collect the debt expired or the amount forgiven is for late fees, interest, or amounts other than the principal. If your tax bill will be too high, you may be better off filing for bankruptcy to discharge the debt.

2.4 Available Assistance

If you need assistance coming up with a plan or otherwise handling financial problems, you can speak with your attorney, GuardianOrg, local welfare agency, or your legal aid society. You can obtain the address of your nearest credit counseling agency from the National Foundation for Consumer Credit, Federal Bar Building West, 1818 H Street NW, Washington, DC 20005. These nonprofit agencies provide free assistance to help you assess your financial situation, come up with a plan, and negotiate with creditors.

A national source of advice is Consumer Credit Counseling Services (CCCS) at 800-388-2227. This organization is supported by banks and other creditors. For little cost or for free, depending on the office, it provides advice and assistance to consumers with debt problems. However, before you decide to work with CCCS or companies like it, you should be aware that

• these companies are generally paid a fee by your creditors for working out a plan. This fee often equals 11 percent of the amount you actually pay to each creditor under the plan. Of course, this does not necessarily affect the validity of their advice.

- while the services can help you to negotiate with creditors to reach a payment plan, you do not have the same protections as you would under bankruptcy. Do not expect that these services will advise you when it may be in your interest to declare bankruptcy rather than enter into an informal plan with creditors. Explore bankruptcy with an unbiased counselor.
- if these companies do work out a plan for you with your creditors and administer it, the arrangement will show up on your credit report. If you enter into a plan on your own with creditors, it will not show up in your credit report.

2.5 A Word About Creditor Harassment

If your credit problems have progressed to the point where your file has been referred to a collection agency, under the federal Fair Debt Collection Practices Act, collection agencies are *not* allowed to

- call your office *if* you let creditors know your employer prohibits you from receiving such communication.
- call your home before 8 A.M. or after 9 P.M.
- address you in an abusive manner.
- call others in an effort to collect your debt.

Should you encounter any of these tactics, make notes and tell the agency to stop harassing you and advise them that you are reporting their activities to the Federal Trade Commission, the state attorney general's office, and/or the Better Business Bureau.

If continual notices from a collection agency are creating stress for you, you can notify a creditor or debt collector in writing that you either refuse to pay a debt or that you wish them to cease further communication with you. After such notification, the creditor *may* still pursue legal remedies, but *may not* pursue any other contact with you, unless and until it proceeds with a legal remedy such as a lawsuit to obtain a judgment. If the creditor per-

sists, and some actually do, keep detailed records of what happened and when, including a copy of the letter or the name of the person involved, so you can report the information to the appropriate governmental authority.

Tip. Be realistic. Do not waste the money that you have. If, after reading the above, it does not appear likely that you will be able to get out of your current financial situation, as a last resort, consider bankruptcy.

Section 3. Debt Management: Bankruptcy

If your debt far outweighs your projected income and assets, you may want to consider bankruptcy. Bankruptcy is a federal court proceeding designed to give people who are overwhelmed with debt a "second chance"—an opportunity to start over by eliminating some or all of their debt.

The two common types of personal bankruptcy are referred to by the chapter numbers of the U.S. Bankruptcy Code—Chapter 7 and Chapter 13.

Caution: Before, during, or even within six months after discharge of a bankruptcy, if you are considering selling or obtaining a loan or a living benefit from your life insurance, speak with your attorney to determine whether your creditors will have a right to the proceeds.

3.1 Chapter 7

Chapter 7, often called liquidation, allows the person who owes money (the "debtor") to keep certain property (**exempt property**—described below) despite the bankruptcy. All other property is converted into cash and divided among creditors. Once this is completed, creditors can no longer obtain further payment from you regardless of how much or how little they receive on their debt.

Only debts that exist at the time of filing are discharged. Debts incurred *after* the date of filing bankruptcy are *not* discharged.

Exempt property. A determination of what property is exempt from the reach of your creditors depends upon the state in which you live. In some states, you can choose between the property that is exempt under state *or* federal law. In other states, you have to use the state exemptions. State exemptions generally follow the federal law. The difference is the amount that is excluded. For example, in Florida, a debtor's home is exempt under most circumstances no matter what the value, which explains why people sometimes move to Florida and purchase the most expensive home they can prior to declaring bankruptcy. In New York, the exclusion for a home is only up to $20,000.

Exempt property under federal law includes (these amounts are doubled if a married couple files jointly)

- disability, illness, or unemployment benefits.
- home equity of $15,000.
- automobile worth no more than $2,400.
- $8,000 in household items (usually determined at garage-sale prices).
- $800 in personal property—or if the home equity exemption is not fully used, an additional $7,500.
- alimony and support.
- implements, tools, and professional books of trade.
- personal-injury proceeds up to $15,000.
- your right to receive Social Security, veteran's benefits, public assistance, and pension benefits.
- retirement plans.
- "health aids," such as wheelchairs, may be exempt.
- life insurance policies. While the cash value or equity in a life insurance policy is considered an asset that creditors can reach in a bankruptcy action, the remainder of the policy—the true insurance portion—is not subject to their claims.

Creditors cannot force a debtor to viaticate (sell) a life insurance policy or to take a loan against it or to accelerate a death benefit.

Tip. While insurance proceeds are exempt, if your insurance is payable to your estate as beneficiary, creditors can go after this money in your estate after your death.

State laws vary greatly and must be reviewed if applicable.

Debts that remain despite chapter 7 bankruptcy.
- Court-ordered child support and alimony.
- Most state, local, and federal taxes.
- Student loans, although these loans are dischargeable in some circumstances.
- Any debts for fraud, embezzlement, or larceny.
- Any debts for willful and malicious injury to another.
- Any debts that the bankrupt person specifically decides not to include in the bankruptcy.

The process.
- After you've filed the appropriate forms and paid the $120 fee, your creditors are prohibited from engaging in any further collection activity, including enforcing any legal remedies.
- The trustee arranges to collect and sell your nonexempt property and to distribute the proceeds among your creditors.
- Once your nonexempt property is sold and creditors are paid, your bankruptcy proceeding is closed and your debts are eliminated. Thereafter, only creditors with debts that are not dischargeable may continue to pursue you.

3.2 Chapter 13

Chapter 13, which is used less frequently than Chapter 7, is for people who are employed or who otherwise have a steady income. Under Chapter 13, a court approves a plan under which the debtor repays all or a portion of the debt in installments over time.

3.3 Comparing Chapters 7 and 13

- Because future creditors view those who have been through bankruptcy—whether Chapter 7 or Chapter 13—with similar disfavor, many debtors choose to proceed through Chapter 7 unless there is a reason to choose Chapter 13, such as nonexempt property that they want to keep.

- If you have cosigners who do not file bankruptcy along with you, under Chapter 7 your creditors can proceed against them for payment right away. Under Chapter 13, your creditors must wait until the payment schedule is completed before seeking payment from a cosigner. Under either proceeding, your cosigners are not protected unless they file bankruptcy as well.

- Under either chapter, once the bankruptcy case ends, most borrowers are no longer liable for most debts incurred prior to filing the petition.

3.4 Considerations Prior to Pursuing Bankruptcy

- If you are thinking about bankruptcy, plan ahead. The court can look at property and cash transfers made within the twelve months prior to filing and, in certain circumstances, pull that property back into your bankruptcy estate for the benefit of your creditors. Prior to the one-year period, you can convert your nonexempt property into exempt property such as placing extra money in your pension fund or relocating to Florida and purchasing a home.

- If you anticipate incurring large bills such as for medical care, postpone filing for bankruptcy until the debts are incurred.

- Inheritances or proceeds from the sale of a life insurance policy received within a certain time after discharge of bankruptcy may also be available to your creditors.

- You may want to try to figure out how to make sure that payments are made to your health providers. Like other debts, these debts can be reaffirmed at your choice.

- If you have cosigners for certain debts, you may want to consider reaffirming the debt so they are not held responsible.

- Try to keep a credit card or two free of debt. If there is no balance on an account when you file for bankruptcy, there is no reason to contact the credit card company. The account may not be closed since the creditor either may not be aware of the bankruptcy or may not care since it was not involved.

- For those who have little money, no property, and no joint debts, bankruptcy may not be worth the effort. Creditors may think of you as judgment proof in the sense that they will not bother going after you for payment because they don't think they will get any money.

- **Exercise caution.** Bankruptcy is not a step to be taken without careful consideration. While you do get to start over with a clean financial slate, the record of the bankruptcy stays on your credit report for at least seven years, which will most likely prevent your obtaining credit during that time. There may also be a stigma in your social setting or even at work.

- **Consult a skilled bankruptcy attorney.** While filing for bankruptcy is quite simple and you can do it yourself without hiring an attorney, understanding the consequences of filing and the appropriate time to file may not be so simple. Once you get advice about bankruptcy, if your situation presents no unusual circumstances, you may prefer to do it yourself.

Chapter 18

Tax

Money saved is money earned.
—Benjamin Franklin

This chapter is about earning money through tax savings. It provides a practical overview of the credits, deductions, and dependents you may be able to claim as a person living with a challenging condition, as well as deductions other people may be able to take if they assist with your medical and/or living expenses. It does not cover the entire tax code, and no issue is treated exhaustively. If you think a deduction or credit may apply to you, confirm the details from a reliable source.

Tip. Even if you rely entirely on a professional to prepare your tax return, skim this chapter to identify the issues you should address with your preparer to minimize your taxes.

This discussion follows the order of the standard IRS tax form 1040 for individuals.

Section 1. Biographical Data

1.1 Filing Status

Each year, calculate tax liability in all the different "filing status" situations for which you might qual-

ify to determine which is the most advantageous for you.

Married couples should calculate liability jointly and separately. Separate returns may result in a lower tax bill if both spouses have income and one spouse has the majority of deductible expenses. For example, if Willard has an Adjusted Gross Income (AGI) of $40,000 and has medical expenses of $5,000, and his wife, Lillian, has an AGI of $60,000, and they have the average amount of itemized deductions for their income bracket, there will be no medical deduction allowed if they file a joint return because medical expenses must equal 7.5 percent of AGI before they are deductible ($5,000 is only 5 percent of $100,000). However, if Willard and Lillian file separate returns, Willard will be able to claim some medical deduction because the $5,000 is applied against a lower AGI, having a net effect of lowering their combined tax liability.

A widower with a dependent can continue to file as married for two years after the death of a spouse.

On the other hand, **if two people live together** and one person has large medical expenses and little income, and other conditions are met:

- It may be worthwhile to get married to take advantage of the medical deduction.
- Even without getting married, it may be possible to file as head of household or to apportion deductions and credits that either person could take separately. The person to take them is the one to reap the greatest benefit. For example, if the couple owns real estate together, calculate which person would do better to take the interest deduction.
- One person may qualify as a dependent of the other for the purpose of assigning medical expenses to take advantage of the deduction.

1.2. Dependents

Claiming people as dependents is important because each dependent gains the taxpayer a deduction of $2,650 from AGI. In addition, claiming a person as a dependent may allow the taxpayer to claim credits for the medical and other expenses paid by the taxpayer for the dependent.

Dependents can be

- children.
- parents receiving over 50 percent of their support from the taxpayer.
- any person living with the taxpayer, including a friend, as long as
  - the two lived together for the whole year;
  - the taxpayer paid more than half of the person's support; and
  - the person had a gross income of less than $2,650. The person who can be claimed as a dependent does not have the option of claiming herself as a personal exemption if she files her own 1040.

Tip. Four very different definitions of *dependent* are contained in the Tax Code. Be careful to check the definition that relates to the relevant issue.

Section 2. Income

2.1 Taxable Income

Individual disability income policies. There is no tax on disability income paid by an insurance company if premiums for individual disability policies were paid with after-tax dollars.

Employer-sponsored disability income plans. The income is taxable if premium payments are made directly by the employer or if payments are attributable to employer contributions to a funded plan. Income benefits are not taxable if the employee pays the premiums with after-tax dollars. (For a further discussion, including a tip for a tax break, see chapter 8, section 2.)

Sickness and disability benefits. Sickness and disability benefits under employer-financed plans in which an employer rather than an insurance company pays health expenses or disability income are taxable income because they usually represent a substitute for taxable wages.

Indemnity payments. Money paid under an insurance contract for nonmedical services (such as indemnity for loss of income or for loss of life, limb, or sight) is taxable income.

Reimbursement for expenses. If you claim a deduction on your taxes for medical expenses and receive a reimbursement for those expenses from an insurance company in a subsequent year, that money received is taxable income in the year that you receive it.

Capital gains. You can have short- and long-term capital gains on investments, including your home. Short-term capital gains are always taxed as income. Long-term capital gains enjoy special treatment in that the maximum tax rate for these gains is 20 percent if the property has been held for more than eighteen months at the time of sale.

Gains tax on sales of collectibles and of property held for more than one year but not more than eighteen months is 28 percent. If a taxpayer's capital losses exceed capital gains for a year, the maximum amount of capital gains losses that can be claimed against other income is $3,000. If capital loss exceeds $3,000, you can carry over the unused part to later years until it is completely used up.

When a loss is carried over, it remains long-term or short-term. A long-term capital loss carried over to the next tax year will reduce that year's long-term capital gains before it reduces that year's short-term capital gains. *Unfortunately a capital loss sustained by a decedent during his or her last tax year can only be deducted on the final income tax return filed for the decedent.* It cannot be deducted by the decedent's estate.

Sale of a home. See chapter 22, section 3.

2.2 Nontaxable Income

The following is a brief discussion of certain nontaxable forms of income, including employer benefits.

Health-related payments by an insurance company, Medicare, and Medicaid. Payments made to a third party by an insurance company, Medicare, or Medicaid are not taxable income to you.

Social Security Disability insurance (SSD). SSD payments are not subject to federal or state income taxes until you receive or earn a certain amount of other taxable income in the tax year. See chapter 8, section 8.1. For lump-sum retroactive payments, see the same section.

Supplemental Security Income (SSI). This is not taxable regardless of any other taxable income you earn or receive during the year.

State Social Security payments. Taxation varies by state.

Accelerated death benefit/Viatical settlement. Effective January 1, 1997, accelerated death benefits received from life insurance contracts on behalf of a "terminally" or "chronically ill" insured are exempt from income tax. In certain circumstances, amounts received on the sale to a qualified purchaser of a life insurance policy by an insured with a life-challenging condition are also tax free. See chapter 19, section 3 for details.

Sale of a life insurance policy does not affect taxability of SSD or SSI.

Workers' compensation. Workers' compensation payments are not taxable. If medical expenses were deducted in a prior year for an injury for which the employee receives workers' compensation in subsequent years, an amount equal to the deduction is taxable.

Death benefit payments. A beneficiary of a life insurance policy is not taxed on the proceeds *if* the money is

- received under a life insurance contract, *and*
- paid, whether in a single sum or otherwise, by reason of the death of the insured.

It makes no difference who pays the premiums on the policy. A business as beneficiary of the life insurance policy may be an exception to this rule. Proceeds from a life insurance policy may be subject to tax in the insured owner's estate.

Death benefit payments under workers' compensation insurance contracts, endowment contracts, or accident and health insurance contracts are generally considered life insurance proceeds payable by reason of death for income tax purposes and are nontaxable.

Gift or inheritance. Cash or the value of property acquired by gift or inheritance is excluded from the gross income of all taxpayers. Gifts are subject to the unified tax payable by the person who makes the gift (see chapter 33, section 4). However, if a bequest actually constitutes payment for a taxpayer's services prior to the taxpayer's death, the bequest is included in the gross income of the recipient.

Employer-sponsored life insurance. Employees may exclude from taxable income the cost of group-term life insurance provided directly by their employers, only if the coverage is less than $50,000. The cost of group-term life insurance for purposes of this exclusion is not based on the employer's actual cost of providing such coverage, but is determined under the uniform premium table method. The cost of any coverage that exceeds $50,000 is taxable income to the employee.

Nontaxable interest income. For purposes of both state and federal taxes, certain interest income is nontaxable.

Long-term care. Payments received from a long-term-care policy are tax-exempt up to $175 per day. See chapter 14, section 11.

2.3 Flexible Spending Accounts and Individual Spending Accounts

Flexible spending accounts (FSA) and **individual spending accounts** are benefit programs offered by employers that give an employee the opportunity to convert a portion of salary to a tax-free FSA that may be used to pay for eligible child- or dependent-care expenses, including medical expenses. FSA spending accounts are generally thought of as arrangements solely designed to benefit the two-earner nuclear family with small children. However, these arrangements are also available to married couples and sole wage earners who have dependents as defined for purposes of FSA, such as an ailing parent or even people who are not related. In certain cases, FSAs may work for an unmarried couple where one-half of the couple is ill and not a wage earner.

Under an FSA, a taxpayer may exclude up to $5,000 in income from taxation to provide reimbursement of health care expenses for the taxpayer and the taxpayer's dependents, and expenses incurred to care for her qualifying dependents while she and her spouse are at work.

Because the taxpayer's and dependent's medical expenses, paid pretax through an FSA, are not statutorily subject to a medical expense limit, such accounts almost always generate greater tax benefits than deducting medical expenses since the taxpayer can only deduct those expenses if the total exceeds 7.5 percent of adjusted gross income.

Similarly, most middle-income taxpayers prefer to pay dependent-care expenses pretax through a dependent-care account, which has a $5,000 limit, than claim a dependent-care credit (discussed below).

Care of a friend. If a friend lives and maintains a home with the taxpayer throughout the year, receives over half of her support from the taxpayer, and is otherwise the taxpayer's dependent under the rules described below, the taxpayer may pay the friend's medical expenses through the taxpayer's FSA. Similarly, if the taxpayer must pay for the provision of nursing care in the home for the dependent sick friend to enable the taxpayer to continue working, such care should qualify for reimbursement under an FSA.

Relationship/household member test. For purposes of applying the health-care or dependent-care FSA rules, a dependent must meet a "relationship" or "member of the household" test *and* must also meet a "support" test.

To be treated as a dependent of the taxpayer under the FSA rules, an individual must have a specified blood or legal relationship with the taxpayer and receive over half of her support from the taxpayer for the calendar year in which the taxable year of the taxpayer begins. An unrelated individual who was not the taxpayer's spouse at any time during the taxable year may nonetheless be treated as a dependent if the individual's principal place of abode was the taxpayer's home and the individual was a member of the household. There is no limitation on the amount of the dependent's gross income. Related or not, the term *dependent* does not include any individual who is not a U.S. citizen or national, unless such individual is a resident of the United States or of a country contiguous to the United States.

Support. The term *support* includes food, shelter, clothing, medical and dental care, education, and the like. It also includes such items as theater tickets, holiday presents, recreational expenses, transportation costs, and church contributions.

Death of the dependent. If the dependent dies during the year, the taxpayer is entitled to the deduction if the dependent lived in the household for the entire part of the year preceding death.

2.4 Medical Savings Accounts

Self-employed individuals and individuals employed by "small employers" who are covered under a high-deductible health plan are able to deduct contributions to a **medical savings account (MSA)** to fund uninsured medical expenses for themselves and their dependents. Income earned in an MSA is tax free, as are distributions to pay for medical expenses.

MSAs are like IRAs, except they are created to defray unreimbursed health care expenses. (If you are not familiar with an IRA, see chapter 12, section 7.) Contributions to the account by an individual are deductible when calculating gross income, and contributions made by an individual's employer are excluded from gross income except if made through a **cafeteria plan.** A cafeteria plan is a separate benefit plan that an employer maintains under which all participants are employees and each participant has the opportunity to select among two or more benefits. These benefits are

excludable from the income of the participant to the extent that qualified benefits are chosen.

Contributions may be made for a tax year at any time up until the due date of the return for that year without extensions (April 15 in most cases). Employer contributions must be reported on the employee's W-2.

Distributions. At the time of distribution the similarity to an IRA ceases. Distributions for qualified medical expenses (unreimbursed expenses that would be eligible for the medical expense deduction) incurred for the benefit of the individual, a spouse, or dependents are generally excluded from income. Health insurance may not be purchased with distributions from the account (except for COBRA continuation coverage required by federal law, qualified long-term-care insurance, or a health plan purchased while the individual is receiving unemployment compensation). No exclusion is available if the medical care is rendered for an individual who, during the month the expense is incurred, is not eligible to participate in an MSA and whose contributions have been made to the MSA for that tax year.

Additional coverage. With an MSA, you cannot have two health coverages, unless the additional coverage is for accidents, disability, dental care, vision care, long-term care, medical supplemental insurance, liability insurance (including workers' compensation), coverage for a specific disease or illness, or fixed per diem coverage for hospital stays.

Tip. If you have an MSA, keep a copy of your insurance policy, proof of your contributions to your account, and canceled checks or receipts for medical expenses.

Medicare. As of January 1, 1998, MSAs may be used as a Medicare+Choice. See chapter 15, section 1.4.

Section 3. Adjustments to Gross Income

3.1 Self-Employed Insurance Premiums

A significant adjustment to gross income for the self-employed is the deduction for health insurance premiums. In addition, self-employed people do not have to meet the 7.5 percent threshold normally required before medical expenses can be deducted. For tax years 1998 through 2002, self-employed persons are entitled to deduct 45 percent of the amounts paid for health insurance for themselves, their spouses, and their dependents when calculating their adjusted gross income. The deduction increases by 10 percent each year beginning in 2003, with the maximum percentage being 80 percent for the tax years beginning in 2006 and thereafter.

3.2 Medical Payments as Alimony

Medical expenses paid to a third party, such as to doctors or hospitals, on behalf of the spouse or former spouse at his or her request qualify as deductible alimony, assuming all other requirements are met.

Tip. If you pay medical expenses for your separated spouse under a separation agreement or for your former spouse, you should deduct the payment as alimony, not as medical expenses. Alimony is fully deductible from your adjusted gross income (whether or not you itemize your deductions), whereas only the portion of your medical expenses that exceeds 7.5 percent of your adjusted gross income will be deductible.

3.3 Dependency

An important discussion for some taxpayers is dependency. Dependency is important because

- you can claim your dependent's personal exemption of $2,650.
- you can combine your itemized deductions, including medical expenses, to increase your overall itemized expenses. Otherwise, if the person does not have to file a return, her medical expenses are not used.
- you can claim a dependent-care credit if you are paying for her care while you are at work.
- you can take advantage of any tax-free benefits for dependent care your employer may offer.
- if you establish a Flexible Spending Account with your employer, you will be able to include the expenses of your dependents as reimbursable expenses.

3.4 Itemization of Deductions

Allowable itemized deductions include medical expenses, mortgage interest payments, real estate and state taxes, charitable contributions, and unreimbursed business expenses, to name a few. If you itemize your deductions and they do not exceed your standard deduction as listed on the 1040, then take the standard deduction. Your filing status will determine your standard deduction.

Tip. The IRS has prepared manuals for use of its auditors to help find abuse in different professions. If you are a member of one of the professions, these manuals can be helpful in preparing your tax return. You can obtain a free copy by writing to the IRS Office of Disclosures, P.O. Box 795, Ben Franklin Station, Washington, DC 20044.

Average deductions. Each year the IRS publishes the average amount of deductions claimed by taxpayers in different Adjusted Gross Income ranges. While the information is free, you cannot obtain it just by calling the IRS. It is listed on the IRS's Internet site at www.irs.ustreas.gov/prod/tax_stats. It is also available from various information services such as Commerce Clearinghouse (CCH) at 800-

TELL-CCH. Taxpayers who claim itemized deductions cannot rely on averages by declaring a number within the averages without having made the expenditures. You must be prepared to substantiate your deductions if audited.

Tip. If your claimed deductions exceed the average amounts, the deductions may act as a flag for an audit. A statement from a doctor suggesting you purchase the item or incur the medical expense you want to deduct should be attached to your return to help forestall an audit.

3.5 Medical Deductions

Threshold. *Medical expenses are deductible only if the total of all your medical expenses is at least equal to 7.5 percent of your Adjusted Gross Income.* For example, if your Adjusted Gross Income is $60,000, your medical expenses must equal $4,500 or more before any of the expenses can be deducted. The more income you have, the higher your medical expenses have to be before any of them can be deducted.

You and dependents. Medical expenses include your medical and dental expenses *and* those of your spouse *and* all your dependents. You can include the medical expenses of any person who is your dependent even if you cannot claim an exemption for him or her on your return because the dependent received $2,650 or more of gross income or filed a joint return. If you paid for more than 50 percent of a person's expenses for the year and that person lived with you for the whole year, then you are allowed to claim that person as a dependent and can treat their medical expenses as your own.

You cannot deduct medical expenses you paid for somebody else unless you can properly claim that person as a dependent.

What can be deducted—medical care. The medical expense deduction is specifically limited to amounts spent for medical care. *Medical care* is broadly defined to include amounts paid for the diagnosis, cure, mitigation, treatment, or prevention of disease, or for the purpose of affecting any structure or function of the body, including amounts paid for accident or health insurance and certain travel expenses. *An expenditure that is merely beneficial to general well-being or health is not an expenditure for medical care.* Also, the term *medical care* does not include

- unnecessary cosmetic surgery.
- operations or treatments that are not legal whether rendered by licensed or unlicensed practitioners.

Tip. Avoid wasting medical expenses that could be deductions by accelerating or postponing paying them into a year when your expenses will at least equal 7.5 percent of your Adjusted Gross Income. If your income varies, shift expenses into the year in which you'll make less money so you will exceed the 7.5 percent ceiling. Payments must be mailed by December 31 of the qualifying year.

What is "medical care" depends on the nature of the services rendered, not on the experience, qualifications, or title of the person rendering them. In general, medical care includes services of psychiatrists, psychologists, surgeons, dentists, ophthalmologists, optometrists, chiropractors, chiropodists, anesthesiologists, gynecologists, neurologists, obstetricians, dermatologists, pediatricians, podiatrists, osteopaths, and Christian Science practitioners. Payments made to a holistic healing center that prescribed only a change of diet would not be deductible as medical expenses.

Deductible medical expenses include wages and other amounts you pay for nursing services. Services need not be performed by a nurse as long as the services are of a kind generally performed by a nurse. This includes services connected with caring for a patient's condition, such as giving medication or changing dressings, as well as bathing and grooming the patient. Only the amount spent for nursing services is a medical expense. If the attendant also provides personal and household services, these amounts must be separated.

Hospital fees, doctor bills, and other expenses reimbursed directly by insurance companies are not expenses that can be included as itemized deductions.

Tip. People tend to think, "If it is not reimbursable from an insurance company, it is not deductible." As you see in this text, this is not necessarily the case.

Examples of medical deductions.
- Fees for medical services.
- Fees for hospital services.
- Insurance premiums you pay for medical and dental care.
- Long-term-care costs.
- Medicare Part B payments.
- If a taxpayer only qualifies for Medicare Part A because of age and therefore has to pay premiums for Part A, the premiums are deductible.
- Insurance on contact lenses for a person who requires them.
- Meals and lodging provided by a hospital during medical treatment.
- Special equipment, such as a motorized wheelchair, hospital beds, and other medical equipment for use in the home.
- Special items, including false teeth, artificial limbs, eyeglasses, hearing aids, crutches, and the like.
- Prescription drugs and insulin are the only medications that are considered medical expenses. *Prescription drugs* include those prescribed by a doctor and purchased and used in a location where the sale and use are legal— even if the sale is not legal in the United States. Over-the-counter drugs and medical remedies are not deductible, even if prescribed by a physician.
- Acupuncture, even though the state medical association does not recognize acupuncture as a form of medicine.

- The portion of a housekeeper's salary that goes toward the medical care of a sick resident.
- Social Security taxes on the wages paid to a private nurse.
- Whiskey prescribed by a physician to relieve pain (but not marijuana under any circumstances, even though its use for medical purposes is legal in some states).
- The full cost of a wig prescribed by a physician for a patient who has had hair loss due to chemotherapy (because it is "essential to mental health").
- Extra cost for salt-free or other special food *prescribed* by a doctor.
- A stereo for a person confined to the house by multiple sclerosis.
- Hand controls for the care of a handicapped person.
- A guide dog for a blind person.
- A car telephone for a person who may require instantaneous medical help.
- Treatment of alcohol and drug abuse.
- Lipreading instructions for a person who is hard of hearing.
- The extra cost of braille editions of books for the blind.
- A reader to assist a blind person at the job (this could also be considered a deductible job-related expense).
- The cost of electricity to operate medically necessary equipment such as whirlpools or central air-conditioning.

Transportation. Medical expenses include payments for transportation "primarily for and essential to medical care." Taxicab fares and other local transportation expenses such as automobile or train incurred in traveling to and from a doctor's, a psychologist's, or a dentist's office or a hospital are deductible, if substantiated as being primarily for receiving medical services.

Transportation costs incurred in attending meetings of an Alcoholics Anonymous group are deductible if your attendance is pursuant to medical advice that membership is necessary for the treatment of a disease involving the excessive use of alcohol. In addition, transportation expenses to attend support groups or other meetings on the advice of medical authorities are deductible.

Medical expenses do not include expenses that are, in fact, commuting expenses, even in the case of a disabled person.

Tip. If you use your car to travel for medical purposes, keep a record of the mileage in a diary in your glove compartment that shows where you went and how far you traveled, plus receipts for parking and tolls. You can deduct either actual expenses or ten cents a mile for the use of your car for medical reasons. Under either method, you can add parking and tolls to the amount you claim.

You cannot deduct transportation expenses if, for nonmedical reasons only, you travel to another city or country for an operation or other medical care prescribed by your doctor.

If a person is employed as a traveling companion for one who is too ill to travel alone. If the trip is for the *sole* purpose of alleviating a specific chronic ailment, the travel expenses of the companion qualify as a deductible medical expense as long as that person can give injections, medications, or other treatment "required by the patient who is traveling to get medical care and is unable to travel alone."

Lodging. Amounts incurred for lodging, but not meals, while away from home on trips that are "primarily for and essential to medical care provided by a physician in a hospital or similar facility" are deductible as medical expenses. Lodging expenses are not deductible if there is "any significant element of personal pleasure, recreation, or vacation in the travel away from home." The lodging cannot be lavish or extravagant—the IRS will allow no more than $50 per night per individual as a deductible medical expense.

Health insurance. Amounts paid as premiums for health insurance are deductible as medical expenses. Amounts paid entitling the taxpayer to receive medical care from a managed care company are also deductible. A taxpayer who is over age sixty-five and not entitled to Social Security benefits may deduct premiums voluntarily paid for basic (Part A) Medicare coverage. These payments are made solely at the option of the taxpayer and thus are similar to premiums paid for supplementary (Part B) medical insurance benefits, which are also deductible. Premiums paid for MediGap coverage are included in amounts paid for medical care, but amounts withheld from wages (or paid on self-employment income) for health insurance under the Social Security program are not deductible as medical expenses.

Long-term-care insurance. Premiums paid for long-term-care insurance are considered to be medical expenses for tax purposes. The federal law includes stringent standards for policies to qualify for deduction, and these standards are tougher than some state rules. Policies sold before 1997 remain eligible. Any plan after that should be checked to be sure it meets federal and state standards.

Household help. The expense for household help is not a deductible medical expense. However, a taxpayer may deduct household help expenses if the help is employed partly for the well-being and protection of a qualifying dependent person. This is achieved by filing a form 2441 for a dependent-care credit. Household services are ordinary and usual services done in and around the home that are necessary to run the home. They include the services of a housekeeper, maid, or cook. However, deductible services do not include the services of a chauffeur, bartender, or gardener.

Capital improvements. If you make a change in your home to accommodate your medical condition, your spouse's, or a resident dependent's, the extent to which the value of your property was *not* increased by the expenditure is the only amount that is deductible. When Gary B. paid over $10,000 to have the doorways in his house widened to accommodate his wheelchair, he could deduct all of the expenditure because it did not increase the value of his home at all. However, $75,000 of the $175,000 Jon N. spent to install an elevator in his town house was not deductible because the value of his house was increased to that extent.

Tip. Since the IRS tends to closely examine returns with medical deductions for capital improvements, obtain an appraisal of your home from a real estate appraiser or a valuation expert before and after the improvements as proof of the change in the value of the property due to the improvement. Keep the bills for the improvement and all canceled checks and the appraisals with your other tax data.

Examples of deductible residence expenses are

- construction of entrance ramps to the residence.
- widening doorways at entrances to the residence.
- widening or otherwise modifying hallways and interior doorways.
- adding handrails or grab bars whether or not in bathrooms.
- lowering or making other modifications to kitchen cabinets and equipment.
- altering the location or otherwise modifying electrical outlets and fixtures.
- installing porch lifts and other forms of lifts (not generally including elevators, as they may add to the fair market value of the residence and any deduction would have to be decreased to that extent).
- modifying fire alarms, smoke detectors, and other warning systems.
- modifying stairs.
- modifying hardware on doors.

- modifying areas in entrance doorways.
- grading of grounds to provide access to the residence.

Weight control, smoking programs, etc. While the IRS will deny any deduction designed to improve your general health, it may approve a weight control program or other treatment that is related to a specific ailment such as high blood pressure. Your argument for specific treatment is improved if a doctor will put the recommended treatment in writing, in which case you should attach a copy with your tax return.

If, as a condition of employment, you need to treat a physical condition such as smoking or obesity, the expense is deductible because you need the treatment to *keep your job.*

"Medical expenses" that are not deductible. The following expenses that we may think of as medical expenses are *not* deductible:

- Bottled water or water filter systems, unless you have a documented medical need for treated water.
- Expenses to improve or sustain your general health such as health club dues or programs to stop smoking.
- Premiums for life insurance or income protection policies.
- Payroll withholding for FICA (although it is the equivalent of a premium for SSD and Medicare).
- Medicine or drugs you bought without a prescription.
- Funeral, burial, and cremation expenses (these expenses are deductible for estate tax purposes).
- Expenses for medical operations or treatments that are illegal in the United States. The transportation expenses associated with those treatments are also not deductible regardless of the source of the treatment or operation.
- Expenses of going outside the country for treatment that is locally available.

For a complete explanation of medical expenses from the IRS, ask for publication no. 502. Call 800-829-1040.

3.6 Charitable Contributions

Generally, you can deduct contributions of money or property that you make to a qualified charitable organization. A gift or contribution is also deductible if it is "for the use of" a qualified organization, such as when the donation is made by means of a legally enforceable trust or similar legal arrangement for the qualified organization.

Verifying tax status. If you're uncertain whether a charity is qualified for tax purposes
- ask the organization for a copy of the IRS letter confirming the organization's tax status.
- if you have access to the Internet, check at www.irs.ustreas.gov.
- call the IRS, Customer Service Division, at 800-829-1040.

Your deduction for charitable contributions. The deduction for charitable contributions is equal to the fair market value of the property at the time of the contribution, generally to a limit of 50 percent of your adjusted gross income. In some instances much lower limits apply, so check with a tax adviser if you are considering contributing more than $5,000 to any charity.

While you cannot deduct the value of the time you volunteer to a charity, you can deduct the costs related to volunteer work including
- actual travel and transportation costs going to and from meetings and events, or fourteen cents a mile.
- materials you supply in the normal course of volunteering such as stamps, postage, or refreshments.
- 50 percent of the cost of meals necessary to your volunteer work.

What you cannot deduct.
- Baby-sitting costs while volunteering.
- Rent-free use of your property by a charitable group.
- Raffle tickets you purchased or money spent at a charity bingo.

- The value of what you receive. For example, if you pay $75 to attend a charity banquet and the dinner is worth $30, you can only deduct $45 (the difference between what you paid and the value of what you received).
- Contributions to specific individuals, including
  - contributions to fraternal societies made to pay medical or burial expenses of deceased members.
  - contributions to individuals who are needy or worthy. This includes contributions to a qualified organization if you indicate that your contribution is for a specific person. *But* you can deduct a contribution that you give to a qualified organization that in turn helps needy or worthy individuals if you do not indicate that your contribution is for a specific person.
  - payments to a member of the clergy that can be spent as he or she wishes, such as for personal expenses.
  - expenses you paid for another person who provided services to a qualified organization.

Tip. If you purchase a ticket to a banquet or other event and cannot attend, tell the charity to give it to someone else. This way you can deduct the entire cost of the ticket, not just the amount in excess of the value of what you would have received if you had attended the dinner. Be sure to obtain a letter from the charity describing this gift.

Carryovers. You can carry over excess contributions that you are not able to deduct in the current year. You can deduct the excess in each of the five succeeding years until it is used up, but not beyond that time. Your total contributions deduction for the year to which you carry your contributions cannot exceed 50 percent of your adjusted gross income for that year.

Tip. If you have a life expectancy of less than one year, be aware that charitable contributions (as well as operating losses, capital loss carryovers, and suspended passive loss carryovers) terminate at death. Accelerate income into the current year to utilize these tax deductions. Otherwise, the income will be included on the following year's fiduciary tax return with no offset for these items.

3.7 Interest Deduction

Loans are a nontaxable source of income, and in some cases the interest payments on loans are tax deductible. The general categories of deductible loan interest are:

- **Home mortgage interest:** Qualified residence interest is deductible by individuals as an itemized deduction as long as the mortgage debt does not exceed specified dollar limits. See chapter 22, section 2.2.

- **Investment interest:** Interest expenses on debts that can be properly allocated to property held for investment are generally deductible by individuals as an itemized deduction to the extent of net investment income. *Note that a taxpayer can borrow money to put in an IRA and deduct the interest on the money borrowed.*

- **Trade or business interest:** Interest expenses on debts incurred in a trade or business in which the taxpayer materially participates (other than a rental business) are generally deductible in full.

Personal interest is not tax deductible. Interest on credit cards, car loans, personal bank loans, and school loans is not tax deductible. Home loans, on the other hand, are usually the lowest-interest-rate loans an individual can get, and the interest is deductible.

Tip. For homeowners who need to borrow cash, the best borrowing vehicle is either refinancing an existing mortgage or taking a second mortgage.

3.8 Handicapped Expenses in the Workplace

Expenses incurred adapting your workplace to compensate for a disability or to enable a "disabled" person to do her job are deductible as "impairment-related work expenses" and are not subject to the 7.5 percent medical expense threshold or the 2 percent limit that applies to employee expenses and miscellaneous deductions. Attendant care at the place of employment is also deductible.

Section 4. Credits

For people who are disabled and for those who pay dependent care, two important credits are available. Credits are a direct reduction of tax and should be taken advantage of whenever possible.

4.1 Dependent-Care Credit

Working taxpayers who pay for dependent care in order to work are allowed a tax credit for these expenses. For lower-income taxpayers the highest dependent care credit is at most 30 percent of $2,400 of qualifying dependent care expenses (or $4,800 if there is more than one qualifying dependent). For middle-income taxpayers it is often as low as 20 percent of such expenses. The dollar limits are reduced by any amount an employer pays for such dependent care to the extent that amount is excludable from the taxpayer's gross income for child and dependent care. (See below, section 4.3.)

Expenses for dependent care may also qualify as deductible medical expenses. In such a case, that part of the amount for which the dependent-care credit is allowed will not be taken into account as an expense when computing the allowable medical deduction. Similarly, when an amount is taken into account for purposes of the medical expense deduction, it cannot be included for purposes of the dependent-care credit.

4.2 Disability Credit

Qualified individuals under age sixty-five who have retired with a permanent and total disability, and who have taxable disability income from a public or private employer, may claim a credit against taxes equal to 15 percent to a maximum of $7,500 a year, depending on the amount of Social Security and disability income received during the year. The table below outlines eligibility for the credit per filing category. Individuals must be a citizen or resident of the United States or a nonresident alien (except for certain nonresident aliens who are married to U.S. citizens where both spouses elect to be treated as U.S. citizens and to be taxed on worldwide income for the year).

For purposes of the credit, an individual is permanently and totally disabled if he or she is unable to engage in any substantial gainful activity by reason of a medically determinable physical or mental impairment that can be expected to result in death or that has lasted or that can be expected to last for a continuous period of at least twelve months. If the taxpayer is under age sixty-five, a doctor or the Veterans Administration must certify that the taxpayer is totally and permanently disabled. Gainful activity is considered to be the performance of significant duties over a reasonable time for pay or profit. This does not include work the taxpayer does to take care of herself or her home.

4.3 Employer-Provided Dependent-Care Credit

An employer can provide tax-free dependent care to an employee.

- The value of dependent care provided under an employer's nondiscriminatory plan generally is not includible in an employee's gross income.
- The amount excludable from gross income cannot exceed $5,000 ($2,500 in the case of a separate return by a married individual).
- An employee who excludes the value of child- or dependent-care services from income may not claim any income tax deduction or credit with respect to the amounts.
- There is an earned income limitation on the

Income Limits for Credit for the Disabled or the Elderly

If You Are	You Generally Cannot Take the Credit If
Single, head of household, or qualifying widow(er)	your AGI is $17,500 or more, or you received $5,000 or more of nontaxable Social Security or other nontaxable pensions
Married, filing a joint return, and only one spouse is eligible for the credit	your AGI is $20,000 or more, or you received $5,000 or more of nontaxable Social Security or other nontaxable pensions
Married, filing a joint return, and both spouses are eligible for the credit	your AGI is $25,000 or more, or you received $7,500 or more of nontaxable Social Security or other nontaxable pensions.
Married, filing a separate return, and you lived apart from your spouse for all of 1997	your AGI is $12,500 or more, or you received $3,750 or more of nontaxable Social Security or other nontaxable pensions

amount that may be excluded. For an unmarried employee, the amount excluded cannot exceed the employee's earned income for the tax year involved. In the case of married employees, the exclusion cannot exceed the earned income of the lower-earning spouse for the tax year.

• A spouse who is incapacitated or who is a student is deemed to have received monthly earned income of $200 if there is one child or dependent, or $400 if there are two or more children or dependents.

Section 5. Retirement Plans

5.1 Early Withdrawal of Retirement Funds

Any funds withdrawn prematurely from a retirement account have to be included as income. There is also a 10 percent penalty tax for the early withdrawal, but this may not apply—for example, when a taxpayer is disabled. See chapter 12.

5.2 Employee Stock Ownership Plans

To discourage taxpayers from using an Employee Stock Ownership Plan (ESOP) as a tax-free savings account for purposes other than retirement, Congress has imposed a special 10 percent tax on early distributions paid to a participant who is not yet 59½. The tax does not apply to distributions that are made to a beneficiary (or to the estate of the plan owner or participant) after the death of the owner or participant. Distributions made to a participant because he or she is totally and permanently disabled are not subject to the tax either.

Section 6. Strategic Recognition of Income and Deductions

Not all income and deductions are created equal. In some cases you can accelerate or defer income and deductions across tax years to maximize the benefits of deductions or minimize your tax bracket. Ideally, income should be claimed in years when it will be subject to a lower tax rate, and expenses should be claimed in years when they will offset income subject to a higher tax rate. Even small changes can prove beneficial, especially if you are close to the bracket thresholds.

Most people keep their finances on a **cash basis,** which means income and expenses are recognized when you actually receive or pay them. Prepaying an expense in December or delaying payment to January can help to minimize taxes, as can a similar manipulation of when you receive income.

Income. A basic tenet of tax planning is to defer as much income as possible to a later tax year. While this is not always the best approach, it is a good place to begin your year-end strategy. Keep in mind that income received on December 31, 1998, is includable on your April 15, 1999, return, while income received on January 1, 1999, is not includable until the April 15, 2000, return.

If next year's tax bracket will be lower than this year's, defer your income—provided a deferral will not jeopardize the actual collection of the income.

Some techniques to consider:

• As the end of the year draws closer, delay year-end billings until late December. This will ensure that payments will not be received until the next year. Bear in mind, however, that if you are an **accrual-method taxpayer,** rather than a cash-method taxpayer, income must be accounted for in the year in which the legal obligation to make payment is incurred.

• Bonuses given at the end of the year do not have to be paid out at year's end. Try to arrange to receive your bonus in January. Employers will not lose their deduction for the current year by delaying the payment, as long as the obligation is fixed before the end of the tax year and is paid within two and a half months of the close of the employer's tax year.

• Make sure that you are contributing the maximum allowable amount to your pension plan.

• If you must sell property this year, you can delay receipt of part of the proceeds by having the payments made in installments.

On the other hand, it may be beneficial to accelerate income into the current year, such as when you anticipate a change in filing status or income level that places you in a higher tax bracket next year. Some of the strategies for acceleration are the opposite of those used for deferring income. For example, you can bill early in December rather than January and try to collect as many receivables as possible before the end of the year.

Deductions. When planning on what year to take deductions, keep in mind that

• some deductions may be reduced if your AGI is too high. For example, itemized deductions and personal exemptions are phased out based on the excess of AGI over established threshold levels.

• any increase of AGI results in a corresponding decrease to AGI-sensitive deductions.

• certain deductions may be claimed only if they exceed a certain percentage of AGI—2 percent for miscellaneous itemized deductions, 7.5 percent for medical expenses, and 10 percent for casualty losses. Therefore, an acceleration of income into the current year may also operate to lower your allowable deductions.

Tip. Every year, individuals are forced to pass up either legitimate itemized deductions or the standard deduction amount. If your deductions exceed the standard deduction, you will itemize, but if they do not, if you claim the standard deduction, you lose the itemized deductions.

A technique called **bunching** can help resolve this dilemma. The concept of bunching is to carefully plan your expenses so that in one year you have a large amount of itemized deductions and in the next you have a low amount but claim the standard deduction. The two-year total of high itemized deductions plus the standard deduction should exceed the two-year total of deductions that are not bunched and/or standard deductions. For example, a single individual with $4,500 of itemized deductions each year may be able to bunch the expenses so that $2,500 are paid in 1995 and $6,500 in 1996. The same amount is paid over the two years ($9,000), but combining the 1995 standard deduction of $3,900 with the $6,500 of expenses in 1996 results in a two-year total of $10,400 of deductions.

Practical adjustments you can make:

• Prepay January mortgages or property taxes in December of every other year.

• Stagger medical and dental checkups so that more are in one year than the next (for example, January, June, and December of one year and June of the following year).

• Plan to give larger charitable gifts every other year.

Section 7. Audits

7.1 Avoiding an Audit

The best audit is no audit.

To lower chances of an audit, deductions should not exceed the guidelines of average deductions (see section 3.4 above). The research of Amir Aczel of Waltham, Massachusetts, a Bentley College statistics professor who published a study in 1995, indicates that 90 percent of audits are determined by the size of your deductions relative to your income level. If your deductions or claims exceed the averages, it is advisable to provide details and supporting evidence, such as an attending physician's statement or other amplifying information to make your health position as clear as possible. The IRS doesn't ask for additional information—but you may avoid questions if you include it.

The IRS computers also look for inconsistencies such as when it records that you have received income, but you don't report it, or that your calculations are not correct. While these issues may be easy to respond to and correct, anything that requires an IRS agent to give a return extra attention increases the risk that the agent will look for other irregularities or items that seem worth investigating. To minimize the risk of an audit, you want the return to be processed as smoothly as possible.

To minimize chances of an IRS inquiry:

- **Professional tax preparers:** If you use a tax preparer, avoid all preparers who do not seem reliable. The IRS keeps track of preparers and may call into question all returns submitted by certain ones.
- **All questions:** Complete all questions on the tax return, even if they don't seem to apply to you.
- **Math:** Double-check your math to be sure the numbers add up. If you have medical expenses that are deductible, consider attaching a letter from your primary physician describing your condition. The worse she makes it sound, the better. If your return does come under scrutiny, the reviewer will have a reason to pass it through.
- **Old returns:** Compare this year's proposed tax return to last year's. If the numbers are very different, double-check to make sure you didn't make a mistake.
- **Form 1099:** If you receive a 1099, be sure to report it on your return, even if it is a tax-free event. The IRS has a computer that matches 1099s to returns. Check the 1099 to be sure it is correct. If the 1099 is issued in error or is incorrect, try to have the issuer correct it or attach an explanation with the form when filing your return. Make sure you have all the 1099s you're supposed to have by comparing the 1099s you received this year against last year's batch. List the amount shown on each 1099 separately.
- **Forms:** File all required forms.
- **Dependents:** If you declare dependents, include their Social Security numbers.
- **Charity:** Attach to your return receipts from each charity acknowledging all contributions over $250.
- **Household employees:** If you have household employees, find out if you have to pay employment taxes. If so, you'll need to include an employer identification number on your tax return. You can request an employer identification number from the IRS on form SS-4. While this takes four to six weeks, the IRS does have a procedure by which you can obtain an employer ID number instantly by calling a specific number at the location where you file your tax return and then faxing the appropriate form to the person with whom you speak. Call the IRS for the phone number in your area.
- **Refunds:** Avoid claiming large refunds. A return requesting a large refund draws attention. Adjust wage withholding and estimated tax payments to balance out your final tax liability for the year, so you don't owe a large tax or receive a large refund.
- **Rollovers of retirement fund proceeds:** Report rollovers. If you received a form 1099-R concerning a rollover of retirement-plan proceeds into an IRA, you have to report the amount shown on your tax return even though the rollover is tax free.
- **Amended returns:** If you have to file an amended return, attach detailed proof of items that prompted the amendment.

Tip. Be sure to make a copy of your return and all attachments before forwarding it to the IRS. Store the return and supporting evidence as discussed in chapter 5. Keeping the documentation together will save you Life Units if you are audited and will be critical to your personal representative and/or heirs if you become incapacitated or die.

7.2 Delaying an Audit

Delaying an audit can be an effective means of saving you money. Agents are given time limits to close cases. The longer a case is open, the more likely the auditor will want to reach an agreement. The time delay will also give you time to ask your team members, including people in your support group, whether they have encountered questions about similar matters, and if so, how they handled the situation.

On the downside, keep in mind that if you lose the audit, you have to pay interest on all money due. So while delays may be an effective tactic, they could cost you more money in the long run. Also, if you delay when your life expectancy is short, your heirs will have lost the best witness against the IRS, namely you.

Tips for delay:

- Respond to all inquiries within the time limit, but do not rush into it.
- Ask for as much time as you can to prepare for the audit because auditors can lose interest or focus.
- A day or two before the audit, ask to reschedule it.
- Ask for clarification and amplification on issues. Generating paperwork and responses delays the audit.

7.3 Other Tips to Survive an Audit

Representation. Consider being represented by your tax preparer or other professional. If you are not looking well, it may pay to muster the energy, if possible, to be with your professional at the audit. Auditors are human and have a great deal of discretion.

Handling the audit yourself. If you do handle the audit yourself

- get professional help *before* you go in for the audit or respond to inquiries. Know the full extent of your possible tax liability and penalties before you argue your case, as well as the plausibility of

your arguments. It is a lot harder to backtrack than it is to take the right course from the start.
- prepare for it by assembling all information you have on your income, deductions, and credits. Try to anticipate questions and be ready with answers, but don't lead the interview.
- don't volunteer anything. What you say to help in one area may hurt you in another unexpected area. The only exception is that it may be in your interest to tell the IRS auditor about your physical condition, even if the audit is for a period before your diagnosis. Theoretically at least, IRS auditors are human beings too.

Section 8. Other Matters

8.1 Getting Help with the Tax Code

There is plenty of expert opinion available to help you plan your tax position.

The Internal Revenue Service. The quickest source of information with respect to the Tax Code is to call the IRS at 800-829-1040. Advice from a person at the IRS is no defense if the information is incorrect. However, it will at least help you avoid penalties if at the time of the call you make a note of

- the name of the person with whom you speak;
- the date; and
- the substance of the conversation, including a notation of the source of their information (such as the title and date of a tax ruling).

You can also E-mail specific tax questions to the IRS at www.ustreas.gov. You should have a response within forty-eight hours. As with oral advice, the IRS must eliminate any penalties that result from inaccurate advice the IRS gives you in writing.

You can obtain user-friendly tax guides from your local IRS office, at the public library, or by calling the above 800 number. There are more than ninety free IRS publications on particular subjects. A good general guide is publication 17, "Your Federal Income Tax," which is an in-depth discussion of most tax topics of interest to the general public. If you have a computer, you can also access any IRS publication on the IRS Web site: www.ustreas.gov.

Other assistance. For a different slant on taxes:

- Talk to a tax preparer, a CPA, an enrolled agent, an accountant, or a tax lawyer.
- An excellent and inexpensive source of assistance is one of the popular tax-software programs such as TurboTax (800-446-8848) or TaxCut (800-235-4060). The programs give tutorials and guide you through the tax process, highlighting all the options you may have for saving on your taxes. Both programs also offer audit alerts, which indicate whether any of your itemized deductions exceed the average. Turbo-Tax Deluxe even includes more than thirty IRS tax publications.
- Another source that signals when deductions exceed the norm is on the Internet at www.securetax.com. SecureTax prepares your return on-screen at no charge. You can then copy the information onto your own paper forms. If you decide to print a copy from the site or use other services, there is a charge.

Tips on using a tax preparer. If you use a tax preparer

- select a professional with expertise in your thorniest tax areas. Ask friends and colleagues whose finances are similar to yours for references and talk to several preparers before choosing one. Find out how the person keeps up with the tax law. Also discuss your "tax temperament." You may want to push the envelope to its limits or you may feel more secure only with safe returns.
- Ask for a letter with your completed return ex-

plaining any judgment calls that were made in gray areas of the tax law.
- Be sure to review your completed return carefully. Ask any questions you have. You're the person who will bear the ultimate responsibility for what is on your return.

8.2 General Considerations

State and local taxes. Almost all state income tax systems allow an exemption or credit to people who are "disabled" when determining an individual's tax liability. If you are on disability, be sure the state law is checked before filing your income tax return.

A number of states and localities reduce home property taxes for people who are "disabled." If you own a residence, check with your local real estate tax department.

Filing returns and paying taxes. If you don't file returns when they are due, the IRS can impose a penalty equal to 5 percent of the amount of the tax due *per month,* to a maximum of 25 percent of the tax due.

There is also a penalty if you file your tax return on time but do not pay the money when due. This penalty is one-half of 1 percent per month. Over twelve months, the total penalty is 6 percent. Once the IRS notifies you about the payment due, the penalty increases to 1 percent a month.

Any money owed the government, including accumulating fines and penalties, incurs interest at the rate of 3 percent above the federal short-term interest rate, compounded daily. During 1997, that meant that money owed the IRS accumulated interest at the rate of 9.42 percent annually.

Before you get creative with your tax liability, you should know that failure to pay taxes is a misdemeanor and can cost up to $25,000 and a year in jail. Attempting to evade or defeat a tax liability is a felony and can cost up to $100,000 and five years in jail. Filing a false return with the intent to evade taxes is a misdemeanor and can cost up to $10,000 and a year in jail.

Tip. Tax time is a good time to review many of your financial arrangements and be sure they are up-to-date. For example, check

- the beneficiaries on your retirement plans, life insurance policies, and the like.
- your will and advance directives. Has there been a substantial change in the value of your estate? A change in assets you specifically listed in the will? A change in the people you want to receive your assets?
- your financial plan. Consider changes since the last time you visited the plan.
- your List of Instructions. Are things still stored where you listed? Are there other changes?
- your various property and casualty policies to be sure they reflect current assets and values.

8.3 Cheating

The penalties for tax fraud are stiff, whether you're sick or not. Your estate will be liable for any taxes, interest, or penalties for which you would have been liable. If fraud is involved, there is no statute of limitations so the government has all the time in the world to learn about the situation and take action against you, your estate, and/or your heirs if the assets were distributed.

Bottom line. Tax avoidance is legal. Tax evasion is not. Do everything you can to avoid and thus minimize your taxes.

Part V

››››››››››››››

New Uses of Assets

Chapter 19

Life Insurance, a Liquid Asset

The success of Ken W.'s small company depended on his personal effort. When Ken suffered a series of health-related setbacks, his business went under. In addition to owing $25,000 in medical bills, he had a mortgage and a hefty life insurance premium to pay. He was considering selling his house with all its memories. He wasn't aware that his life insurance policy provided an answer.

Traditionally, life insurance has been viewed as an income-replacement vehicle for dependents of a deceased insured or as a fund to cover estate taxes and/or burial expenses. In some instances, it has also been used as a savings and/or investment vehicle. This chapter is about how you can obtain cash from a life insurance policy *due to your condition*—and how *in spite of your condition* you can still purchase life insurance!

Loans against your life insurance policy, accelerated benefits from the life insurance company, and viatical settlements are methods of turning life insurance into a liquid asset. Before you use any of these alternatives

- keep in mind that any of these actions will decrease the amount of life insurance proceeds available for your beneficiaries. Balance your current and future needs against those of your beneficiaries.
- consider the new uses of other assets described in chapters 20–23 to determine which of the various courses of action is best for you.

Section 1. Loans Against Your Life Insurance Policy

Even if your credit is not good, or you don't have sufficient income to qualify for a commercial loan, you may be able to obtain a loan using your life insurance coverage as **collateral** (security for repayment of the loan).

1.1 Loans from the Life Insurance Company—Cash Value

The two basic types of life insurance policies are **term** and **permanent**. In a term policy, each penny of premium purchases only life insurance. With a permanent policy, part of the premium purchases pure life insurance, and the other part goes into a savings or investment plan. To illustrate, if $100 purchases a $10,000 term policy, all that the insured has is a death benefit of $10,000. However, if the insured purchases a basic permanent policy, the same $100 is divided between pure insurance and a savings feature that grows each year. While the death benefit stays at $10,000, the insured can borrow money against the savings account feature, which is called **cash value.**

Cash value provisions allow you to borrow money from the life insurance company without having to qualify as a borrower and without delays. The contract states the amount that can be borrowed each year and the terms under which the money may be borrowed. The interest rates are usually reasonable, especially if it is an older policy. Cash value provisions are more likely to be in individual rather than **group policies**—policies issued through a group such as an employer, union, or association.

Tip. If it is not immediately clear whether your life insurance coverage has a cash value provision, call your life insurance company or agent. While you're at it, find out how much you can borrow, as well as the interest rates and other terms. This kind of question is common and will not raise any flags about your health unless you decide to inform the company about your physical condition.

1.2 Loans from Private Individuals Secured by Your Life Insurance

If a loan from your life insurance company isn't available, or if the interest charge is too steep, consider asking a friend or family member to make you a loan using the policy as collateral to secure repayment.

Consider every person or company you know as a potential loan source. Don't forget your current or former employer. Since your beneficiary has the most to lose by a sale, perhaps he or she would make the loan. People don't like to make money off their friends, particularly when in need, but a loan with a fair rate of interest may be different.

If this approach is appealing to you, consult a local attorney about the best way to set up the loan. Ideally, the loan documents should contain the following provisions:

- No repayment or interest on the loan during your lifetime (so you will not be burdened with making payments at a time when your income has probably decreased).
- The loan should be **nonrecourse,** which means that the lender can only look to the life insurance policy for repayment and not to your estate.

Tip. If willing friends or relatives do not have the cash available to make a loan, but do have equity in a house, they might raise the funds using their equity as collateral for a loan. Ultimately, the proceeds from your life insurance policy can be used to pay off the loan plus interest. The difference between the debt and the death benefit can then either go to the person who lent you the money or to any other beneficiary you desire.

1.3 Loans from Commercial Lenders Secured by Your Life Insurance

If a "friendly" loan is not available, consider obtaining a "commercial" loan from a bank or other institution. As of this writing, no banks offer loans secured by life insurance policies, but since this is likely to change, it is worth checking in case there are such banks by the time you need the money.

Several nonbanking companies make loans against life insurance policies. These companies are not currently regulated or supervised by any governmental authority. If you are thinking about a loan from one of these companies, consider:

- Even though repayment of the loan is secured by the life insurance policy, these companies usually charge interest at least equal to what most people pay on unsecured loans such as credit cards.
- The costs of initiating the loan are often high compared to a loan from a bank.
- While the intent is to repay the money on death and not while the insured is alive, the contract may provide the lender with the right to call the

loan at any time, which means that you may have to repay the loan while you're alive, even though you spent the money.

• Generally, loan contracts require transfer of ownership of the policy to the lender. This means you will have fewer rights than if you keep ownership yourself.

• What happens if the lender goes out of business or assigns your contract? If the loan is set up in a manner that permits you to borrow more money from the lender over time, as most do, you have no guarantee that the lender will be in business when you are ready to draw down additional funds under the loan.

• Can your beneficiary's interest in the policy be wiped out by the lender's actions?

• Does your beneficiary have the right to request an accounting of money due?

1.4 Advantages and Disadvantages of a Loan

Advantages of a loan.

• Loan proceeds are generally considered to be free of federal and state income tax.

• A loan can be structured so it does not *have* to be paid back during your lifetime, yet you can retain the option to pay off the loan if you so desire.

• The death benefit of the life insurance policy pays off any part of the loan that had not previously been repaid, together with any accumulated interest. The difference between that amount and the death benefit is payable to your beneficiary. To illustrate: Jean C. borrowed $50,000 against her $100,000 policy. No payments were made during her lifetime. When she died, an additional $12,000 was owed to the lender for interest. At her demise, the policy paid $62,000 to the lender and the other $38,000 to her beneficiary.

Disadvantages of a loan.

• You have to continue to pay premiums on the entire insurance policy for life.

• If you live longer than anticipated, the debt plus interest could exceed the death benefit and your estate could be liable to pay the lender the difference. This problem can be eliminated by specifying in the loan document that the loan is nonrecourse, as described in Section 1.2.

Effect on government benefits. Money received from a loan affects the asset requirements of means-based entitlement programs such as Supplemental Security Income (SSI). The receipt of this money does *not* affect Social Security Disability income (SSD).

Tip. It is critical to be represented by an attorney before entering into any loan agreement secured by your life insurance.

Section 2. Accelerated Death Benefits

Even if your policy doesn't contain a cash value provision, it may contain a **living** or **accelerated benefit.** This feature permits an advance from the insurance company of part of the death benefit while the insured is alive, provided a specified triggering event occurs. Triggering events differ depending on the policy and the insurance company, but they can include

• diagnosis of specified illnesses.

• a life expectancy of a specified period, such as twelve months or less.

• a need for long-term care based on an inability to perform the normal activities of daily living.

• a debilitating illness or permanent confinement to a nursing home.

Some companies have automatically added these provisions to their policies for free—even for policies already in existence. For others, the provision is optional and the company specifies what must be done by the insured to add the provision.

Whether the coverage is automatic or optional, no medical questions are asked before a company adds an accelerated death benefit. In fact, at least one large life insurance company allows insureds to add the provision and accelerate the death benefit at the same time.

Tip. Unless you can prove you did not know about your condition until after your first diagnosis, be certain that your policy (and every other life insurance policy you have with the same insurance company) is past the **contestable period** (if any) before checking with your life insurance carrier or broker to determine whether your policy may contain an accelerated benefit provision. A contestable period permits the life insurance company to contest the existence of the policy for a limited time after the effective date of coverage. When a policy lapses and is reinstated, the reinstatement date becomes the new effective date for purposes of contestability. The contestable period is usually two years.

Terms. The terms of an accelerated benefit vary from company to company.

- Eligibility is usually limited to insureds with a life expectancy of twelve months or less (sometimes even nine or six months). Federal employees with FEGLI coverage are permitted to accelerate the death benefit of their *basic* coverage if they have a life expectancy of nine months or less.
- The advance amounts, and charges, vary from company to company. Advances range from 25 percent to 95 percent of the death benefit, and many insurance companies place a dollar limit on the amount they will advance. If less than the entire death benefit is accelerated, the remainder (perhaps minus a small fee) is paid to the named beneficiary upon the death of the insured.
- Some insurance companies place a minimum on the death benefit to which the provision applies and some place a maximum.

- Some companies limit the manner in which distributed money may be spent (e.g., to reimburse medical expenses).

Effect on government benefits. The mere potential to accelerate a death benefit does not affect SSD, SSI, or Medicaid in any way, including eligibility. However, once these funds are received, they affect both the income and asset requirements of means-based entitlement programs such as SSI. The receipt of this money does *not* affect SSD.

Tax. Accelerated benefits for people with a life expectancy of twenty-four months or less are free of federal income tax and are specifically exempt from state income tax in several states such as California and New York. There is also no state income tax due for residents of those states that have no state income tax at all or for those that follow the federal lead in determining taxable income.

Tip. If there is a tax due, when feasible, accelerate in a year in which income is reduced or in which expenses are particularly high.

Acceleration plus a sale of the remainder. If your policy contains an accelerated benefit provision, you may be able to accelerate and then sell the remainder (as described in the following section), realizing a greater amount of money through a combination of the two than through either an acceleration or straight sale alone. However, some insurance companies do not permit a subsequent sale after acceleration.

Section 3. Viatical Settlements

A **viatical settlement** is a sale of a life insurance policy in which you, the owner, transfer all rights and obligations under the policy, including the right to choose the beneficiary and the obligation to pay premiums. In return, you receive an amount of money equal to a percentage of the full death benefit. Generally, the transaction carries no restrictions on how you (the seller or **viator**) can spend the proceeds of the sale.

3.1 Salability

Necessary medical condition. Anyone who has been medically diagnosed with a shortened life expectancy may qualify for a viatical settlement. A combination of unrelated conditions may combine to create a shortened life expectancy. While some companies will purchase policies from people with a life expectancy of five years or more, the bulk of the viatical settlement companies only purchase policies from people with a life expectancy of twenty-four months or less.

Types of policies that are salable. In general, while there are always exceptions, such as credit life insurance, any life insurance policy is salable. It does not matter if it is group or individual. It also doesn't matter whether the policy is term or permanent. Savings Bank Life Insurance (SBLI) policies are generally salable, as are Federal Employees' Group Life Insurance policies (FEGLI). Servicemembers' Group Life Insurance (SGLI) and Veterans Group Life Insurance (VGLI) coverages are salable by converting to an individual policy with an insurance company.

Tip. If you convert group coverage to individual coverage with the thought of selling it, select the method of premium payment that requires the least outlay of your dollars. Premium payments between the time of conversion and sale generally won't be reimbursed.

Individual policies. Unless your policy is an individual policy resulting from a conversion of group coverage, it is difficult to sell while it is subject to a contestable period or while a **suicide exclusion** is in effect. The suicide exclusion is the period during which the life insurance company will return premiums paid instead of the death benefit in the event of death by suicide. The contestable and suicide exclusion periods usually run simultaneously from the effective date of the coverage or its reinstatement in the event of a lapse. As with an accelerated benefit, by attempting to sell a policy during the contestable period you run the risk that, once alerted to your health situation, the insurance company may contest the very existence of the coverage.

Other factors may prevent the sale of a policy:
- An issuing life insurance company that does not have at least an A- rating by the rating services such as A. M. Best Company (908-439-2200).
- A binding agreement concerning ownership of the policy or payment of the proceeds, such as a policy that was issued as part of an arrangement between business partners.
- A prohibition in a policy against a change in ownership and/or designation of a new beneficiary. While you would think that a policy with a beneficiary that has been designated "irrevocably" cannot be sold because the beneficiary cannot be changed, there can still be a change if the irrevocable beneficiary signs a consent to the change.
- Limitations on how a policy may be assigned (e.g., as a gift only) or limitations on to whom it may be assigned (e.g., a policy may limit the class of people to whom the policy may be assigned or who may be listed as beneficiary).

Tip. It is sometimes possible to have restricting provisions removed from a particular policy or for the insurance company to make exceptions. In some states, by statute, if a policy permits any type of assignment, it is also deemed to permit assignment for value.

Group policies. Group policies have the same limiting factors as individual policies. They cannot be sold if the insurance company does not have a good enough rating, if change of ownership or designation of a new beneficiary is prohibited, or if how a policy may be assigned is limited.

In addition, a group policy is probably not salable *while you are actively working* because the coverage could be terminated by the group (usually an employer) or by the insurance company, and the purchaser's interest would also be terminated. The exception to this generalization is for those group policies that permit conversion to an individual policy if the coverage is voluntarily terminated by the insurance company, the employer, or the insured (such as when the insured quits). The amount of conversion coverage permitted is the maximum amount that would be salable. For example, if the insurance coverage is $100,000, and the employee is permitted to convert up to $10,000 upon termination, then the employee could sell $10,000 in coverage while still working.

Many group policies contain a provision known as **disability waiver of premium.** Under this provision, when the insured employee leaves work on disability, the premium payments are waived and the insurance continues for the full amount even if the group policy is terminated. The full amount of the group coverage is then salable.

Conversion from group to individual coverage. When group coverage is converted to individual coverage, such as when an employee goes on disability or otherwise leaves the employer, life insurance companies often impose new contestable clauses and suicide exclusions for the traditional two-year period on the individual life insurance policy. Although a few purchasers will purchase a converted policy subject to these provisions, there would be more purchasers (and thus, the likelihood of a higher price to you) if these provisions were removed. If this is your situation, be sure to check the insurance law of the state in which you reside. Certain states limit the additional period for which these clauses may be imposed, no matter what the converted individual policy provides.

Even if state law does not prohibit reimposition of the clauses, many insurance carriers agree to waive them on request. You should negotiate this before you convert or, if your employer knows about your diagnosis, ask the employer to use its clout to have these provisions waived.

Tip. Under New York law, upon conversion, the life insurance company may only impose a premium for a term-type policy during the first year, rather than a more expensive permanent-type premium. If you convert, check the law of your state to see if this protection has been extended to your conversion as well.

Tip. If your group coverage is not salable, it may be worthwhile to ask your employer to change the features. Most of the features that prevent a policy from being salable can be changed without costing the employer any money. It is just a question of negotiating with the insurance company.

3.2 Consequences of a Sale

A number of consequences of selling a policy should be evaluated before completing a sale.

Income tax. The Tax Code permits tax-free treatment of viatical settlements *in certain circumstances.* In general, the law provides that money received by "terminally ill" or "chronically ill" individuals from a "viatical settlement provider" for the sale or assignment of a death benefit under a life insurance contract is considered "an amount paid under the life insurance contract by reason of the death of such insured" and thus, tax-free income.

The law only applies to a "terminally ill" or "chronically ill" individual. A **terminally ill individual** is "an individual who has been certified by a physician as having an illness or physical condition which can reasonably be expected to result in death in twenty-four months or less after the date of certification." A **chronically ill individual** is one who has been certified within the previous twelve months by a licensed health care practitioner as basically requiring nursing home care. The law requires that the individual either

- be unable to perform, without substantial assistance, at least two activities of daily living for at least ninety days due to a loss of function (activities of daily living for this purpose are eating, toileting, transferring, bathing, dressing, and continence);
- have a similar level of disability as determined by the secretary of the treasury in conjunction with the secretary of health and human services; or
- needs substantial supervision to protect against threats to health and safety due to severe cognitive impairment.

There is no restriction on the use of money by a terminally ill taxpayer. Moneys paid to a chronically ill person, however, are only tax free if they are used for "costs incurred by the payee (not compensated for by insurance or otherwise) for qualified long-term care services provided for the insured for each period." This is generally thought to mean nursing home care, but other care may be included. There are also provisions in the Tax Code concerning proceeds paid periodically.

A **viatical settlement provider** is a company "regularly engaged" in purchasing policies *and* must either be licensed under the viatical settlement law in your state, if there is one, or if there is no such law, must comply with the standards in the Model Act and Regulations adopted by the National Association of Insurance Commissioners (NAIC). Since the burden will be on you to prove the tax-free status of a transaction, it is not safe to rely on what any purchaser may tell you. You will have to do your own homework. Your insurance commission can tell you if viatical settlements are regulated in your state and, if so, whether a particular company is authorized to purchase policies under the law. If there is no such law, you have

more work to do. To qualify as a "provider" the purchaser must satisfy sections 8 and 9 of the NAIC's Model Act, as well as the standards contained in section 4 of the NAIC's regulations.

If your state has a law governing viatical settlements, skip to page 240. If not, and you want to make a sale, you will need to understand the provisions of the NAIC Model Act and Regulations that follow. Also ask the purchaser for certification in writing that the offer, the disclosures, and the agreement satisfy the requirements of sections 8 and 9 of the Model Act and section 4 of the Regulations of the NAIC concerning viatical settlements.

The NAIC Model Act and Regulations. Section 8 of the act relates to disclosure. The purchasing company must disclose to you no later than the date you sign the contract the information discussed in this text about the alternatives to, and the consequences of, a sale. The purchasing company must also give you the right to cancel the deal within thirty days after signing the contract or fifteen days after you receive the money, whichever is less, and tell you the date on which you will receive your money and from whom.

Section 9 adds more rules to protect you. Before entering into a contract with you, the company must obtain (1) a written statement from your doctor that you are of sound mind and not under any constraint or undue influence, and (2) a document in which you consent to the contract, acknowledge that you have a "catastrophic or life-threatening disease," that you understand the contract and the benefits available under your policy, that you release your medical records, and that you are entering the transaction freely and voluntarily. The company must keep your medical records confidential in accordance with the law of your state. Upon receipt of your contract, the purchaser must place the proceeds due you into an independent **escrow** account. (An escrow is when an item is held by a third party and is not to be released until defined conditions are satisfied.) When confirmation of the transfer of title is received, the funds must be released to you immediately. If you don't get your money when due, you can declare the contract null and void.

Section 4 of the Regulations sets minimum pricing standards according to the insured's life expectancy, as follows:

➤ ➤

Life Expectancy	% of Death Benefit
Less than 6 months	80
At least 6 but less than 12 months	70
At least 12 but less than 18 months	65
At least 18 but less than 24 months	60
24 months or more	50

If your sale is subject to an income tax. The tax is calculated on the difference between the net proceeds and an amount equal to premiums you paid less amounts you previously received under the contract, such as dividends and policy loans, less the cost of insurance protection provided through the date of sale. The current position of the Internal Revenue Service is that the income is treated as ordinary income, not capital gains. This tax law has not yet been tested in court, and no regulations have been issued under it.

Try to limit the tax by considering the following:

• Transfer ownership of the policy prior to a sale to someone in a lower tax bracket. Keep in mind the potential of a gift and/or estate tax. If you expect to use any of this money, you have to totally trust the person who will receive it.

• Split the coverage into smaller policies and sell one of the smaller policies each year, possibly in a year when you have matching deductible medical expenses. Each policy should be given the effective date of the original policy so there is no effect on salability. If the life insurance company won't split the policy for you, consider selling a partial interest in your policy each year. See section 3.6 below.

• If there is cash value in a policy, but not enough to meet your needs without a sale, take a loan against the cash value to the maximum available. Sell the difference. The amount received as a loan is clearly not taxable. The loan won't affect the sale since the purchaser will merely deduct the amount of the loan when determining the purchase price.

State income tax. The state tax status for a sale is the same as for accelerated benefits, described in section 2.

Estate tax. Death proceeds of a life insurance policy are included in your estate if you own the policy at death or if you transfer ownership of the policy by gift within three years prior to death. If the policy is sold for value, only the proceeds from the sale that remain at death will be taxed in your estate, not the death proceeds.

Effect on disability and health insurance. The sale of life insurance coverage will not affect your disability and health insurance coverages.

Federal or state assistance programs. Benefits you have paid for (such as Social Security Disability Income Retirement, or Veterans' benefits) remain unaffected by a sale. However, if the program is based on income level or assets, the benefits will probably be affected and may even be terminated until the money from a sale is spent or divested. You will fail the income test during the month of receipt and will fail the asset test for any month in which you still have the proceeds. Benefit experts indicate that this can generally be avoided by transferring the policy before sale to a trusted friend or relative or contributing it to a special needs trust (see chapter 15, section 2.3). Another alternative is to "spend down" proceeds once you have them through a bona fide transfer of the money to third parties, including trusts, relatives, or friends.

Tip. To avoid affecting benefits, get assistance with structuring the transaction *before* you viaticate.

Your employer. If you sell a group policy you have through work, be aware that a purchasing company's verification of the existence and terms of your coverage may alert your employer to your health situation. Even if there is no official contact, it is also possible that someone at the life insurance company will gossip with someone at your company.

Outliving estimated life expectancy. The risk of your outliving estimated longevity is solely the purchaser's.

Creditors. Proceeds of a sale may be subject to the claims of your creditors. If you are considering, have commenced, or *even if you were recently discharged* from bankruptcy, seek the advice of your attorney before selling your policy.

Premium payments. Generally, after a sale your rights and responsibilities in the policy cease and the purchaser will pay the premiums. FEGLI and a limited number of group policies are exceptions to the general rule because the premiums are only payable by the employee and only as a deduction from payroll (or from continuing benefits if no longer employed).

If premiums are waived under a disability waiver of premium provision, no one will have to pay continuing premiums, although even after a sale you may still be required to periodically supply information to show that you continue to be disabled.

Accidental death benefit or double indemnity provision. In general, an **accidental death** bene-fit, also known as a **double indemnity** provision, increases the death benefit by 100 percent if death is caused by an accident. Since a sale is a transfer of all your rights to the policy, unless the sale contract specifically permits you to retain the right to these benefits, any money payable by reason of these clauses would belong to the purchaser. Be sure the viatical contract specifies that you retain the right to name the beneficiary for this and any other portion of coverage you don't sell.

Future increases in the death benefit. Some life insurance policies guarantee you the right to purchase additional insurance in fixed amounts at fixed dates. When you sell your policy, you sell the right to these increases as well unless the contract specifies to the contrary. You should either retain the right to the increases, as well as the right to designate the beneficiary for those amounts, or negotiate how a fair price will be determined and paid to you when increases are available.

Before you sell a policy. Before you complete the sale of a policy, I suggest you consult with your tax adviser and your attorney. You should also consult with an expert concerning minimizing the effect of a sale on any means-based entitlements you are receiving or expect to receive. If you have a group policy and are selling it as a group policy or converting to individual coverage to permit a sale, check to determine whether your other employer benefits would be affected by the sale or conversion of your life insurance coverage.

3.3 Federal and State Regulation

Federal regulation. There is no federal regulation of viatical settlements except the tax law and regulations concerning insurance coverage for federal employees. A federal district court ruling has held that a normal sale by an insured is not subject to the federal securities laws.

State regulation. A number of states have adopted laws concerning viatical settlements. To find out if your state has a viatical settlement law, call your state's department of insurance (see resources section).

3.4 Timing

When to begin a sale is a matter of balancing your need for money against the likelihood that you could obtain more money if you waited and became less healthy. On the other hand, if new drugs or treatments in the pipeline look as if they will extend your life, it may be worthwhile selling now rather than obtaining less money, if any, later. There is no right or wrong time.

Tip. If your policy is past the contestable period, consider testing to see whether your policy is salable and what price you can obtain. You never have to say yes to an offer, but knowing these facts can help in your financial planning. The only possible disadvantage is that if you have a group policy and your employer does not know about your condition, the information may unintentionally be conveyed.

3.5 Factors That Determine Price

Factors generally used in determining price are

- your statistical life expectancy. Purchasers will pay less to someone who has a life expectancy of thirty-six months than to a person with six months.
- the rating of the life insurance company.
- the amount of premiums (if not waived).
- the purchaser's costs, including overhead and the cost of available funds.

Tip. While the primary consideration in determining price is statistical life expectancy, I'm not recommending that you ask your doctor for an estimate. Instead, let your lawyer or a viatical settlement broker assess longevity and argue to the viatical settlement purchasing company that you

are much sicker than you appear. If you choose to negotiate, ask your doctor about factors related to your health condition that you can argue might decrease your life expectancy, but do not focus on any particular longevity.

3.6 Sale of Part of a Policy

One way to maximize your return on your life insurance is sell the policy in parts. For example, Tom W. has a $200,000 life insurance policy, a two-year life expectancy, and needs money to cover a projected shortfall in income each year. He could sell half the policy now for approximately 60 percent of the death benefit. Sixty percent of one-half of the policy is $60,000. In theory, in another year Tom will have a one-year life expectancy, which would warrant a purchase price more like 70 percent of the remaining death benefit or $70,000. Tom would make 17 percent on his money by holding off on selling the second part of his policy. If the sale is subject to tax, he would also minimize his tax by spreading the income over two years.

How to sell part of your policy.
- If you have an individual policy, ask the life insurance company to divide the policy for you, and sell one of the substitute policies. There is no need to disclose to the company your health condition or the reason why you want the policy divided. Be sure to confirm that the issue dates of the new policies are the same as the issue date of your existing policy.
- If the insurance company won't divide your policy, or if you have group coverage, consider selling part of an undivided policy. It is possible to sell remaining pieces of the policy to the same company (or, theoretically, to another purchaser or purchasers) as time goes by. If your medical condition worsens, the percentage you receive for each additional portion should be higher than the percentage you received for the original portion.

- If you eventually want to sell all or part of the undivided remainder of the policy, you will have to deal with the viatical settlement purchasing company to which you sold the first part of the policy. Deal only with a reputable company that has sufficient assets to make it likely the company will stay in business. Many companies today contract with you, but intend for your policy to be purchased by an individual purchaser. If you are only selling part of your policy, I strongly recommend against selling to an individual investor you don't know.

- **Caution:** If you sell part of a policy, you can't go directly to the life insurance company when you want to change your beneficiary on the part you retain since only owners can make changes, and the purchasing company becomes the owner. You will have to rely on the purchasing company to request the change. Be sure to get confirmation from the life insurance company that any change in beneficiary is made according to your wishes.

3.7 Beneficiaries, Payment, and Monitoring

The role of the beneficiary. You can expect that every purchasing company will require that each primary beneficiary sign a release waiving any claims to the policy. If you do not want your beneficiary contacted about your policy, consider changing your beneficiary to someone you would not mind asking to sign a release. Before you choose that person, remember that if you die before the sale is completed, that person will actually receive the proceeds of your policy. An alternative is to name your own estate as the beneficiary. You could then sign the release on behalf of your estate. If you die in the interim, the money will pass through your will.

Tip. Do not designate a beneficiary "irrevocably," unless there is a good reason. It makes it more difficult to sell a policy because you cannot make a substitution for an irrevocable beneficiary without the irrevocable beneficiary's written consent.

Payment of the proceeds of a sale. Generally, purchasing companies will pay the proceeds to whomever and however the seller designates. Insist that payment be by certified check, bank check, or by wire transfer directly into a bank account of your choice.

Tip. Be sure to insist on a lump-sum payment. Do not accept any type of installment payment unless it is legal in your state *and* the purchaser legally segregates the funds to pay the future installments or fully funds an annuity policy. The last thing you need is to lose later payments because the purchaser goes out of business.

Monitoring. Since purchasers are not paid until the insured dies, the purchaser must have a system of keeping track of each insured. There is no standard monitoring method in the industry. Some companies actually call insureds monthly to "see how you are." At the other extreme are companies that attempt to have as little contact with the insured as possible, checking credit card reports to monitor use (on the assumption that if the card is used, the person is still here), or checking with the attending physician's office.

Tip. If you don't want a telephone call from the purchaser, follow the monitoring procedure established by it precisely. At the slightest noncompliance the purchaser will usually attempt to contact you to confirm your status.

3.8 The Best Way to Sell a Policy

In theory, the sale of a life insurance policy is simple. However, since the primary factor that determines price, life expectancy of a particular individual, is more of a guesstimate than a science, offers between different purchasing companies can vary greatly. Even if a company offers higher prices than any other for a schedule of life expectancies, determination of life expectancy is so subjective that no company can guarantee the best price. Further, if you start the process, you don't want to find a month or two later that the purchasing company won't purchase the policy because of a glitch they see that either could have been corrected or is not a glitch to another company.

You have two alternatives to success. One is to go directly to at least three purchasing companies, apply to each of them with the awareness that your doctor and insurance company will be contacted by each, negotiate any price they offer (including arguing that you are going to die sooner than they anticipate), and then oversee the closing with the company of your choice.

If you choose this route, be sure to determine the net amount of the offer (some companies deduct money to pay future premiums; some deduct money to be held back for notification purposes, etc.) and to verify that sufficient funding is available to be placed in an escrow account for payment. Don't let anyone intimidate you into accepting an offer by saying it will be withdrawn unless you act immediately.

The alternative is to engage a broker who will do all the work for you. Since I founded and am still head of a national brokerage firm, I am prejudiced in favor of brokers. Here's why. A broker

- helps apply the general principles to your particular situation and gives you advice. (I am as likely to suggest people not sell as to assist in a sale.)
- provides critical expertise, particularly with respect to targeting high-paying purchasers.
- gathers the information one time from your physician and insurance company and then copies it for as many purchasers as are warranted.
- has strong negotiating skills and increased bargaining power.
- advises you and oversees the closing if there is to be one.

- works to reduce your immune-reducing stress.
- can assist in obtaining the facts necessary for your tax adviser to determine the tax status of a particular transaction.
- should work for you at no cost, being paid from the purchaser's share of the money, rather than from your share.
- *does all the negotiation, so you don't have to argue with a purchaser, or even worse, a group of purchasers, about how sick you are and how short a time you have.*

The disadvantage to working with a broker is that the purchaser may reduce the offer for your policy to take into account the commission the purchaser will have to pay the broker. In my experience this is rare. A good broker earns a commission by doing much of the work a purchaser would otherwise have to do at its own expense. Furthermore, a broker's reputation rests on its ability to obtain the highest price for the sellers he represents, thereby increasing the business he is able to bring to a purchaser. All of these factors work to keep the prices offered as high as the market will bear, which is to your advantage.

If you decide to sell a policy on your own, consider using a broker as one of the entities to which you apply.

Caution if you are selling more than one policy. Just because a viatical settlement purchasing company offers the best deal in a particular situation does not mean it will offer the best deal all the time. Check around before you sell another policy, even if there has been no change in your health.

Choosing the right purchasing company for you. There are different types of purchasing companies, but generally they fall under the heading of "self-funded" or "nonfunded."

Self-funded companies have their own money or available lines of credit with which to purchase policies. Self-funded companies purchase policies in their own name, although a group of policies may eventually be resold by a self-funded company to another company or even to individuals. This means that the ultimate owner of your policy may be an entity or person other than the company to which you originally sold it. If you are concerned about this possibility, have your lawyer look over the closing papers for the transaction to be sure there is a satisfactory provision in the contract on this issue.

Nonfunded companies purchase policies for ultimate ownership by an individual investor in the "secondary market." These companies are sometimes called brokers, but this is different from a broker that works solely on behalf of the seller. The description of the policy and the insured's medical condition may be broadcast widely to potential individual purchasers, although theoretically the insured's identity is kept confidential.

Considerations in selecting a purchasing company.

- Only deal with a company that is looking for an individual with your medical status and a policy like yours. Working with any other company is a waste of your time.
- Only deal with a company that places an amount equal to the purchase price into an independently controlled escrow account immediately upon receipt of a signed contract.
- If confidentiality is important to you, learn about the company's procedures with respect to confidentiality. If the company insists on permitting a resale of the policy, be sure confidentiality requirements extend to any and all purchasers—and that the purchaser doesn't broadcast your identifying information to a large number of potential purchasers.
- If tax is of concern to you and your state requires viatical settlement purchasing companies to register, find out whether the company is registered and in good standing. If there is no such

law, has the company complied with the minimum requirements in the National Association of Insurance Commissioners' statutes and regulations?
- What are the company's monitoring procedures?
- Some sellers only want to sell to a company that pays a good price and cares about people similarly situated. To determine the soul of the purchasing company, ask whether the company gives to any GuardianOrg; if so, how much and to which ones? Do its employees help people with serious illnesses? Be sure to verify the information.

Tip. Instead of accepting a lower price from a company that gives to a charity you care about, go for the highest price and make the donation yourself.

- Many purchasing companies add "bonuses" to their offers such as programs offering discounted drugs or other items, medical or financial advice, and the like. I have yet to see any "benefit" offered by a purchaser that you cannot get on your own or possibly through membership in an organization that you are already likely to belong to or that you could join for a minimal payment. Still, if the price is right, the "bonuses" may be of interest to you.
- The company's honesty. You don't want to work your way through the process only to find the "initial" offer is suddenly greatly reduced after six weeks of waiting for the money. Your GuardianOrg may have information on this.

Tip. Do not spend money from a viatical settlement until it is in your account. Until then any number of unforeseeable problems may prevent or delay the transaction. And do not deal with any company just because they sound "nice." Likewise, do not be lulled into thinking the company is not trying to maximize its return.

Section 4. Terminating Coverage

4.1 Individual Policies—Cash Surrender

If all other means of accessing cash from your policy fail, and if you really don't want to maintain coverage under any circumstances, as a last resort you can exercise the **cash surrender** option and terminate your policy. Under this provision, included in most individual life insurance polices, you receive a designated amount of money when the policy is terminated (in insurance parlance, the policy is "surrendered"). When this happens, neither you nor the beneficiary have any further rights to the policy. This alternative usually yields you the least amount of money of all the alternatives.

Tip. Talk with the life insurance company about decreasing the premium to an amount that works for you. The company can tell you how much the death benefit will be reduced to reflect the lowered premium. Also talk with your beneficiary or other family member or friend and see if he or she will pay all or part of the premiums.

4.2 Group Insurance—Leaving Your Job

We have already covered leaving your job to go on disability. Sometimes the employer continues to pay the insurance premiums, sometimes the employee has to pay the premiums, and sometimes the premiums are waived and no one has to pay them so long as the disability continues. If there are no rights to continue, you should at least have the right to convert to an individual policy. In any event, since the life insurance company wants relief from any situation that may lead to a claim, follow the contractual provisions precisely so the company doesn't have an excuse to terminate or even reinstate the coverage.

If you leave your job for any reason other than disability, many group policies let you convert your coverage to individual insurance without evidence of insurability. Even if you obtain additional coverage through another employer, it is generally worthwhile for you to convert as much insurance as you can afford.

If you can't afford to keep the coverage, consider borrowing the money to pay the initial premiums with a view to selling it immediately. If a friend won't lend you the money, a viatical settlement broker or company probably will.

Tip. Do not rely on your employer or anyone else to inform you of your rights to continue your life insurance coverage. At times when a client wasn't informed of a right to convert, I have argued the case with the insurance company. In each instance the company luckily agreed to "do the right thing" and issue the individual coverage as of the date of termination of work, but don't rely on the goodwill of the carrier or your employer's benefits department.

Section 5. How to Obtain Life Insurance (Even with a Diagnosis of a Life-Challenging Condition)

It may not sound possible, but even someone who has been diagnosed with a life-challenging condition may be able to purchase life insurance. Credit life insurance is discussed in chapter 21, section 1. The next sections provide advice about how to locate individual and group coverages.

Tip. Check the rating of the life insurance company, particularly if you intend to sell the life insurance coverage.

5.1 Individual Life Insurance

If you are looking to purchase individual life insurance, please read through this entire section before contacting a broker or a life insurance company.

Increases in current individual coverage. Your insurance policy may give you the right to purchase additional insurance at different periods without a medical examination or even any medical questions. It is worth checking your policies. This right must be exercised during the period specified in the policy or it expires. There is usually a new suicide period that attaches to the increase. If so, the increase cannot be sold during the suicide period, but the underlying policy still can. (Think of it as a sale of a part of your coverage—see section 3.6 above.)

The traditional approach. Depending on the nature of the condition with which you have been diagnosed, and your current health, it may be possible to obtain a regular life insurance policy that contains a **rated premium** (an extra premium) to take account of the extra risk the insurance company is assuming—just as airline pilots are "rated." The probability is good that the life insurance carrier that sells you an individual policy will insist that you purchase permanent, rather than term, life insurance. Permanent coverage of course carries a higher premium.

Tip. If you want to find out if your situation permits you to obtain coverage, for safety, contact a life insurance broker whom you do *not* know under an assumed name to find out the type of policy that would be issued, the maximum death benefit, and the premium that would be charged for someone at your age with a condition like yours. Be sure to give an accurate account of your medical history and current condition as well as your desires. Understand the information you receive is probably only an indication and not a binding price since before the policy will be issued the life insurance company will probably have to do **underwriting** (a review of your health condition to determine whether the company will issue a policy and, if so, at what price and with what restrictions).

Do not complete an application with your real name based solely on the information supplied by one broker: he may just be trying to get you to complete an application hoping to earn a commission if it works. Too many brokers don't care whether you'll be rejected. You should, since your name and the rejection will probably be reported to the Medical Information Bureau (MIB), which could jeopardize your chances of ever getting any life coverage.

Tip. If you can't find this kind of life insurance coverage in your state, call brokers in nearby states or states to which you can easily travel. You only have to be in the state in which the policy is issued at the time you sign the application for it. You do not have to be a resident of that state. If you do travel out of state to obtain this kind of coverage, retain proof of travel (such as restaurant, hotel, car rental, plane ticket, and/or gas receipts) with your copy of the policy in case the insurance company ever tries to contest the coverage on the basis that you were not in the state when you signed the application.

Tip. If you can't find a traditional policy with full death benefits, consider a policy with limited benefits, known as a **graded** policy, in which the death benefit starts small and increases incrementally over two years until the full amount is reached at the end of the second year.

Note. When applying for individual insurance, assume that the insurance company will learn everything about your health that is in your MIB file, with the exception of information learned due to a disability insurance claim. Prior to applying for an individual policy, find out what the MIB has on file about you (see chapter 3, section 6).

Simplified issue. For policies with death benefit amounts under $50,000 or perhaps even $100,000, many insurance companies employ simplified underwriting procedures, requiring only completion of questions on an application, without blood tests or physical exams. You can ask your broker for the maximum amount of coverage he can obtain without a blood test or physical exam. This is not a tip-off—many totally healthy people don't want to take a physical.

Review the applications to see if you can answer the questions truthfully. Some people have been known to lie on an application in the hope that they will survive the two-year contestable period. However, even though the policy may only contain a standard two-year contestable clause, in a great number of states, the life insurance company can deny coverage at *any* time, giving your heirs back the premiums together with interest if "fraud" is proven.

The larger the policy, the more underwriting you can expect the insurance company to do. With certain small policies, the broker may actually have the authority to issue the policy on the spot.

Some clients have expressed the fear that life insurance companies share information about people who are diagnosed with a life-challenging condition just as they often share information obtained through applications for life insurance. The American Council of Life Insurance and the MIB have both stated that such information is not shared, and that to do so may be against state law.

Tip. If you can't find simplified coverage in your state, review the tip on page 247.

Simplified issue—mortgage life insurance. In many states it is possible to purchase life insurance to cover a mortgage debt (often up to $200,000) with only a few simple health questions. It may even be possible to obtain this coverage without any health questions. While, as you will see elsewhere, I do not generally recommend that you purchase a house, if you are considering making such a purchase, obtaining this much life insurance may be a deciding consideration for you.

Since mortgage life insurance is a form of credit life insurance (the amount of the death benefit decreases as the balance of your outstanding mortgage decreases), the coverage is generally not salable and does not have any accelerated benefit feature. If you die, the coverage pays off the balance of your mortgage or the covered portion of it.

Guaranteed issue. A **guaranteed issue** policy is guaranteed to be issued no matter what your medical condition may be when you apply for the coverage. No medical questions are asked on the application. The policies are generally for smaller amounts, the premiums are comparatively high.

Guaranteed issue policies generally provide a safety valve for the insurance company if the insured dies within the first two years of the policy's existence. Generally, during that time the beneficiary only receives a return of the premiums paid plus interest (which can be as much as 8–12 percent a year). A variation is a graded policy with coverage starting low and building to the full amount at the end of the two years. Some policies decrease the death benefit after a given age, such as sixty-five.

Many companies limit guaranteed issue coverage to people over a given age, such as forty-five or fifty, or a class such as veterans.

Credit life insurance is a form of guaranteed issue coverage in the sense that no medical questions are asked. However, as with mortgage life insurance, credit life insurance cannot generally be sold, and there is no accelerated benefit feature. The main value of this coverage is that it pays the balance on your relevant credit cards upon death.

Tip. If you do research and stay alert to the situation, you may find multiple sources of guaranteed issue life insurance. Multiples of $5,000 or $10,000 add up quickly.

Tip. If you can't find guaranteed issue coverage in your state, review the tip on page 247.

5.2 Group Life Insurance

An insurer relies for its underwriting of group policies mainly on the fact that a person joins or is a member of a particular group for reasons other than to obtain life insurance. Consequently, it may be possible to purchase some types of group life insurance without providing any medical information or taking a medical exam. Opportunity for enrollment in such coverage is usually limited to specific time periods (**open enrollments**) and/or events (upon commencing a new job or joining a professional association).

Note: Since there are no medical questions with such group life insurance policies, the information that the MIB may have about your health is not relevant.

Various alternatives for obtaining group coverage are as follows:

A new employer. Many employers offer life insurance benefits to employees. As a general rule, the larger the employer, the more likely it will offer life insurance coverage.

The federal government offers life insurance to all new employees equal to a multiple of your annual salary. The salary may not be impressive working for the government, but the benefits are.

If you have a choice, and if you pay any part of the premiums, look for an employer with a younger population—it will probably have lower premiums.

Tip. It is possible to move from company to company, obtaining life insurance with each new job and converting it on leaving to an individual policy that cannot be terminated so long as the premiums are paid. Arnie K. accumulated $350,000 in life insurance this way. Do not join a group or an employer just to obtain life insurance coverage until you verify that the coverage offered is salable. Also, do not lose sight of your medical coverage, which is critical to your financial health unless you are wealthy.

Your current employer. Take advantage of any open enrollment periods.

If your employer does not have group life insurance, but does have health insurance, it may be possible to convince your employer to move the coverage to a company that offers guaranteed issue life insurance along with health insurance coverage.

Tip. Check your group health plan. It may include the right to purchase nonmedically underwritten life insurance.

Spouse. If you are legally married, or if your significant other works for an employer that recognizes nontraditional relationships, review its coverage to determine if you qualify for life insurance under his or her group policy.

Your own business. If you own your own business, consider buying insurance for the entire firm. Depending on applicable state law, you may be able to limit the availability and/or amount of coverage to certain classes of employees. Crunch the numbers. To obtain coverage for yourself, it may be worthwhile to pay 100 percent of the premiums for the employees the law would require you to cover.

Tip. Be sure any business policy you purchase permits an unlimited right of assignment. Ideally it should also have a disability waiver of premium and an accelerated death benefit provision.

Employee leasing company. If you are an employee and your employer does not offer group life insurance coverage for which you qualify, consider asking your employer to lease you from an **employee leasing company** that has group life insurance and health insurance benefits. An employee leasing company is a company that "leases" its employees to work for another company.

If your current employer won't "rent" you, perhaps another employer will.

Association. In general, the higher the dues and requirements for membership in an association or other group, the easier it is for a life insurance company to offer nonmedically underwritten coverage. The assumption is that a person does not become an attorney, for instance, just to join a bar association to obtain group life insurance.

Contact any association for which you may qualify (including reading groups, chess clubs, fraternal organizations, and political groups) to determine if they offer life insurance coverage and how to qualify. It may even be worth going to school to learn about a given area if that allows you to join an association with substantial life insurance. Remember, for you, life insurance may become a liquid asset.

School insurance. Given the average age, health, and life expectancy of students, it is understandable that these inexpensive group policies are issued without medical underwriting. If you're a student or willing to become one, this is worth checking out, but do not be surprised if full-time attendance is required.

Deferred variable annuities. If you are considering purchasing an annuity, look at deferred variable annuities. This product provides life insurance as part of an annuity policy. The amount of the death benefit under the policy is tied to the securities purchased. The death benefit varies according to the predetermined market value of the purchased securities at the time of death. The coverage provides a guarantee that if at the time of the insured's death the market value of the securities is below the amount of the death benefit, the difference is made up through life insurance coverage.

Tip. Keep in mind that the beneficiary named in your life insurance policy will receive the death benefits, not the people named in your will. If you don't want people involved with your life insurance to know the identity of your beneficiary, name your estate as the beneficiary and provide for the people you care about in your will.

Chapter 20

Options for Converting Retirement Assets into Income

Cessation of work is not accompanied by cessation of expenses.
—Cato the Elder

Retirement assets are typically considered "long-term, low-liquidity" investments—since mandatory distributions do not begin until age 70½, and voluntary distributions generally cannot be made before age 59½. Even then, voluntary distributions are subject to income tax, penalty, and excise tax. However, several options exist for converting your retirement assets into immediate cash.

Caution: Tapping into retirement funds is not something that should be done without careful consideration. Using these funds now means that asset growth will not be tax deferred. It also means the funds may not be available to you at retirement, and the money will no longer be protected from creditors, including the IRS. Consider the other new uses of assets discussed in chapters 19, 21, 22, and 23, and speak with an accountant or attorney before accessing these funds.

Section 1. Loans

Many retirement plans permit loans

- for any purpose;
- up to the amounts you have contributed (but not more than $50,000);

- subject to interest payments to the retirement plan, which in certain cases may be tax deductible (e.g., if you use the loan to purchase a home);
- that must be repaid quarterly within five years (unless the loan is used to purchase a home, in which case there is no legal limit on the repayment period);
- that are not subject to current tax unless you stop making repayments.

Loans versus withdrawals. Loans are more flexible than withdrawals because generally you do not have to demonstrate a purpose for a loan, whereas withdrawals are typically made for special purposes, such as hardship. Loans are also cheaper than withdrawals, since loans are subject to interest but not tax (if repaid on time), whereas withdrawals are subject to tax and tax penalties.

Loan options under employer-sponsored plans. Loan provisions vary among employer retirement plans, so check the specific terms of your plan regarding loan qualification, purpose, amount, and repayment. Your employer determines whether you qualify for a loan, typically by requiring you to demonstrate either that you have exhausted your personal financial resources or that alternate resources are not available to you. If you qualify for a loan from your retirement plan, you will be able to borrow an amount up to one-half of your vested account balance (typically up to $50,000).

If you have an outstanding loan balance against your employer retirement plan and are about to change jobs, you must repay the balance or you may be able to roll over the balance to your new employer's plan. If you do not repay the balance, it will be treated as a withdrawal subject to income tax and the 10 percent tax penalty for early withdrawals.

Loans from ESOP plans are not permitted.

Loan options under individual-sponsored plans.
- Loans from qualified retirement plans such as pension, profit-sharing, and 401(k) plans are permitted unless you are a sole proprietor, partner, or shareholder of an S corporation.
- Loans from IRAs and SEP-IRAs are permitted, but with heavy penalties if the loan is outstanding for more than sixty days.
- Loans from annuities are not permitted.

Tip. If you are considering a loan for more than sixty days and have more than one retirement plan, borrow from your IRA last because of the possible taxes and penalties.

Section 2. Withdrawals

Withdrawals, also known as **distributions,** can be made from your pretax or after-tax contributions. Withdrawals from after-tax contributions can be made at any time, for any purpose, and only the tax-deferred earnings on these contributions are subject to tax. Withdrawals from pre-tax contributions can only be made in certain circumstances and are otherwise subject to income tax plus a 10 percent tax penalty for early withdrawals before age 59½. However, you may be eligible for special provisions that permit early distributions, sometimes on a tax-reduced basis.

Depending on the wording in the plan, anyone who is disabled within the Social Security definition can usually withdraw funds without penalty. Disability does not change the tax status of the money withdrawn.

Throughout the rest of this section, *withdrawals* refers to withdrawals of pretax contributions.

2.1 In General

Qualified plans. Withdrawals made from all qualified plans in the event of your disability, although subject to income tax, are exempt from the 10 percent tax penalty for early withdrawals. *Disabled* is defined under Tax Code section 72(m) as "unable to engage in any substantial gainful activity by reason of any medically determinable physical or mental impairment which can be expected to result in death or to be of long, continued and indefinite duration."

Employer retirement plan and your IRA. Withdrawals made before age 59½ from your employer retirement plan or IRA, in "substantially equal payments over your life expectancy, or the joint life expectancy of you and your spouse/named beneficiary," are exempt from the 10 percent tax penalty for early withdrawals.

Pension and profit-sharing plans. Withdrawals from a pension or profit-sharing plan may also be available without a 10 percent tax penalty if the plan has an early-retirement provision of age fifty-five.

Tax-favored retirement accounts. Withdrawals from tax-favored retirement accounts are exempt from the 15 percent excise tax on annual withdrawals exceeding $155,000, for a three-year trial period beginning in 1997. People with serious health problems or critical financial needs should consider taking advantage of this three-year tax break, despite the prevailing 10 percent tax penalty for premature withdrawals.

Forward averaging. Withdrawals made at any age in the event of "total and permanent disability" are eligible for reduced income tax treatment under **forward averaging** rules. Using forward averaging rules, a lump-sum withdrawal will be treated for tax purposes as if it were made over five to ten years, resulting in a reduced rate of taxation. Note, you can only use forward averaging rules once. You cannot use forward averaging rules for IRA or SEP-IRA withdrawals. Five-year averaging will be phased out in 1999.

2.2 Options Under Employer-Sponsored Plans

Withdrawals from employer retirement plans can only be made for special purposes: to fund medical expenses, tuition costs, or a home purchase. These "hardship withdrawals" are generally subject to income tax and often a 10 percent tax penalty for early withdrawals. Your employer (using IRS guidelines) determines if you qualify for hardship withdrawals, which may include:

• Withdrawals to fund medical expenses exceeding 7.5 percent of your adjusted gross income are subject to income tax but exempt from the 10 percent tax penalty for early withdrawals (unlike other hardship withdrawals).

Tip. Your medical expenses must exceed 7.5 percent of your adjusted gross income for you to qualify for income tax deductions as well as penalty-free withdrawals from your retirement plan. The catch is that withdrawals from your retirement plan raise your adjusted gross income, in turn raising the threshold for allowable deductions. Therefore, try to consolidate your deductible medical expenses by accelerating or deferring expenses to years when you can exceed the 7.5 percent threshold.

• Withdrawals to fund college expenses for you, your spouse, or your children.

• Withdrawals to fund the downpayment for a home or to prevent a threatened mortgage foreclosure.

• Withdrawals of dividends earned in an ESOP are exempt from the 10 percent tax penalty for early withdrawals.

• If you are age fifty-five or older and about to leave your job, you can make a withdrawal from your employer retirement plan just before you roll over your retirement account to an IRA, and the withdrawal will be exempt from the 10 percent penalty for early withdrawals.

• Withdrawal of employer stock from your employer retirement plan: There are certain tax advantages associated with the employer stock in your plan, which you can apply when you withdraw the stock from your plan as you change jobs or retire. The three options for withdrawing the employer stock in your plan are to cash out, to take stock certificates, or to roll over to an IRA. Each option has different tax consequences. If your plan contains a considerable portion of employer stock that is significantly appreciable, taking stock certificates will maximize tax advantages, both for you and your heirs.

Information. You can obtain information about your plan from your employer or your union. You are legally entitled to this information.

2.3 Options Under Individual-Sponsored Plans

Withdrawals from IRAs can be made for any purpose (unlike withdrawals from employer retirement plans).

Three types of IRA withdrawals are eligible for tax exemptions:

• Withdrawals to fund medical expenses exceeding 7.5 percent of your adjusted gross income are exempt from the 10 percent tax penalty for early withdrawals.

- Temporary withdrawals made for sixty days are not subject to income tax or the 10 percent tax penalty for early withdrawals (unless the withdrawal is not reinvested within sixty days).
- Periodic withdrawals using the **life expectancy** method are exempt from the 10 percent tax penalty for early withdrawals. Allowable annual withdrawals are determined by dividing your IRA account balance by your life expectancy or the joint life expectancy of you and your spouse/beneficiary (as provided in IRS life expectancy schedules). You can begin this withdrawal method at any age, but must then make withdrawals annually thereafter.

Tip. By combining a home equity loan with the IRA life expectancy withdrawal method, you may be able to create a "tax-free" income stream to meet your contingency needs. For example, you could take out a home equity loan and use your IRA withdrawals to make the mortgage interest payments on your loan. Although your IRA withdrawals are subject to income tax, your mortgage interest payments are tax deductible, thereby creating a tax offset. Depending on your tax bracket and prevailing interest rates, the net result could be a "tax-free" source of emergency funding that might not otherwise be available to you.

Withdrawals from annuities are subject to income tax, plus the 10 percent tax penalty for early withdrawals, plus surrender charges (up to a 7 percent withdrawal penalty imposed by the plan sponsor). Generally, it is more expensive and difficult to make withdrawals from annuities than from other types of retirement plans—so if you think you might need to access your retirement funds early, don't invest in an annuity.

Section 3. Transfers

The funds in your retirement plan are "portable" investments, meaning that typically you have the flexibility (within IRS and plan guidelines) either to transfer these funds among different investment options under your plan, or to roll them over to different plans. Transfers and rollovers are generally not subject to tax, but they may be subject to certain fees, such as commissions or penalties, depending on the type of plan you have.

3.1 Options Under Employer-Sponsored Plans

If you change jobs or retire early, you can roll over your vested retirement funds either to your new employer's plan or to an IRA. *When rolling over your retirement funds, make sure not to take possession of the funds, or you will be subject to income tax.* There is also a refundable 20 percent employer withholding tax and a potential 10 percent tax penalty for early withdrawals. There is one exception: if your employer retirement plan contains a considerable portion of employer stock that is significantly appreciable, you will forfeit certain tax advantages for yourself and your heirs if you roll over employer stock to an IRA.

Note that only pretax contributions are eligible for rollover, while after-tax contributions must be distributed subject to income tax on tax-deferred earnings.

3.2 Options Under Individual-Sponsored Plans

IRAs permit transfers among different investment options offered under the same plan, and rollovers among different plans. Transfers under the same plan may be made periodically (as per plan rules) and are not subject to tax or fees. Rollovers among different plans typically are permitted once per year and are not subject to taxes, but may be subject to certain fees.

Tip. When you open an IRA, make sure that the agreement you sign does not permit the trustee to automatically renew your IRA upon maturity without your prior approval.

Chapter 21

Rethinking Credit

When Howard S. realized that he would probably never leave the hospital, he wrote a check for $10,000 on his credit card. His wife Linda cashed the check and, using his previously executed durable power of attorney, purchased a car in Howard's name. She took credit life insurance on the balance due on the car. When Howard died a few weeks later, credit life insurance paid off both debts. Linda inherited the car free and clear.

If you already have credit, protect it—and get more. If you don't have it—get it now. Get as much as you can, whenever you have the opportunity. Now, more than ever, credit is your friend. You want to be able to access credit when you need it. For example:

- Credit can be helpful in case you have to stop working and your disability income doesn't start for a time.
- Credit can help you deal with an immediate extraordinary expense.
- Credit card bonuses provide free travel, gifts, and discounts—or give you a cash rebate.
- Credit can be used to increase your life insurance—so you leave more money for your heirs—by paying off debts that would otherwise have to be paid from the assets of your estate.
- Credit disability insurance can help keep your bills current and relieve the financial strain if you become disabled.

As with many things in life, credit is available when you don't need it, and almost impossible to get when you do need it. *If you have a verifiable income, whether you are working or not, this is the time* *to get all the credit you can. Remember, however, that having credit and using it are two different things. Credit must be used judiciously. You want it for when you need it.*

Ideally, only people with a statistical life expectancy of less than two years and credit life insurance on the accounts should carry credit card debt. For everyone else, this section includes a discussion about various strategies for reducing credit card debt.

This is a good time to review the discussion in chapter 3 about checking the information maintained about you in national credit bureaus. It is essential that this information is correct to insure that the credit you want is available. If you haven't contacted the bureaus, now is the time to do it.

Section 1. Credit Life Insurance

Credit life insurance pays off the amount of outstanding debt owed a particular creditor at the insured's demise. The amount of the coverage fluctuates up or down according to the amount of the outstanding debt. Credit life insurance is sold with *no* medical questions and no physical examination of any kind. Premiums for credit life insurance are determined on a monthly basis by the amount of debt outstanding on that credit card that month.

There is no required minimum time between the application for credit life insurance and the beginning of uncontestable coverage. However, as a practical matter, some time is required to permit the insurance company to issue the policy, so it can be effective before death occurs.

Tip. Standard advice about credit life insurance is that it is a "rip-off." However, for a person with a challenging condition, conventional advice is switched on its head: credit life insurance is an easy means of purchasing life insurance at a time when it is difficult to obtain.

Consumer Purchases. Credit life insurance is available for many consumer purchases that are typically made on credit, such as furniture and automobiles. In these cases, the insurance is usually offered at the time the contract of sale is executed. Rather than fluctuate up and down, the amount of insurance decreases over time to keep pace with the continual decrease in the debt as payments are made. Premiums can usually be financed along with the principal amount of the loan.

Credit cards. Typically credit life insurance is sold by credit card companies. When you apply for a new card, if the company offers this type of insurance, you are generally informed about it when you first open the account. You may also be able to add it after opening the account by contacting the credit card company at the toll-free number listed on your credit card.

You may even be able to obtain check-writing privileges with your credit card account. Like debt that is incurred to make a purchase, debt incurred to cover the check is also paid off at death by credit life insurance.

The ideal use of credit. In an ideal world, all credit card accounts would have credit life insurance on them, and the credit card balance would be paid off every month until just before death, when the balance due would increase to equal the account limit. At death, the credit card company pays off the debt in full. With the check-writing privileges available on most accounts, that could even mean accessing cash. Ellen N. obtained $12,500 worth of cash advances just before she went into the hospital, believing that because of other physical conditions, she would not survive the operation to remove her cancerous lung. When she survived, she paid off the debt. If she hadn't survived, her heirs would have been $12,500 richer.

Use your credit carefully. Fred B. thought that he had less than two years left to live based on his understanding of his illness. He "maxed out" the balance on twelve of his fifteen credit cards (all with credit life insurance) for a total debt of almost $100,000—thinking that on his death the insurance would pay any outstanding balance. Fred is now doing well on new medication, and his "shortened" life expectancy is not so short. However, he is now contemplating bankruptcy because he is having difficulty servicing his credit card debt. Luckily, he always paid his American Express balance and has three more credit cards with no outstanding balances. If he does decide to go through bankruptcy, he may still have credit on those cards.

Fred's experience points out several important facts:
• There is always the "risk" that you will outlive your life expectancy.
• It is possible to go through bankruptcy and still have credit and charge accounts. So long as there are no outstanding balances on the accounts, the creditor has no reason to be notified of the bankruptcy and no reason to close the account. There could be closure if the credit company finds out about the bankruptcy.

• Always keep at least one card with credit life insurance free of any debt. Ideally this would be a line of credit that has check-writing privileges. Give a couple of undated, signed checks to a trusted friend. If you go into the hospital or are near death, the friend can then deposit the checks. Should you survive, the cash can be used to pay off the outstanding debt. If the account does not have check-writing privileges, you can accomplish almost the same thing by giving a trusted friend authority to make charges on your account. If the charge is used while you are alive for your medical and hospital bills and/or your other ongoing expenses, if you survive, you are in no worse shape than if you had paid the expenses out of pocket.

• A cash contingency fund is helpful for sunny days as well.

Tip. If you are considering purchasing any big-ticket items and have a statistical life expectancy of less than three years, it is a good idea to conserve your cash and finance the purchase *provided* that you obtain credit life insurance on the outstanding balance. As discussed in the investment chapter, "cash is king!" Keep your credit in shape by paying the minimum monthly payment.

Section 2. Credit Disability Insurance

Credit disability insurance is good to have, even though it would be considered expensive for people with no health concerns. It pays the monthly minimum due on a credit account for each month during which the cardholder is disabled. This insurance is available from credit card companies *without* a medical exam or any medical questions and is sold either with credit life insurance or on its own. The coverage usually has a maximum amount it will pay per month (such as $500) and a limited time, such as up to two years.

It provides breathing space by paying your monthly debt at a stressful time.

The insurance does not cover charges made *after* the commencement of disability. Review the insurance contract to determine if there is any waiting period for benefits to begin, particularly with respect to conditions that exist when the insurance is purchased. Generally there is a six-month waiting period—the insured has to work for at least six months before being able to take advantage of the coverage.

Caution. Do not rely on credit disability insurance to pay off your bills. While credit disability insurance will pay minimum balances each month, when you consider the amount of interest and the continuing monthly premium charge for credit life and disability insurance, the outstanding balance will continue to grow.

Section 3. Protect Your Credit

Pay bills on time. Paying bills on time is probably the most important factor in establishing a good credit profile. It can also mean saving money because you don't have to pay exorbitant interest charges and late-payment fees.

Tip. If you are slapped with a penalty or your interest rate is increased, try to negotiate it away by threatening to take your business elsewhere. It often works—and there is no downside to asking.

To insure that your bills are paid on time, even when you are not at home to pay them:

• Set up a bill-paying system, such as the one described in chapter 5, section 2. Explain the system to a trusted friend or a family member and staple an index card to the folder with instructions outlining the system. If you have to go into the hospital or are away for some other reason, he or she can keep the system going.

• So they will be available in an emergency, sign

checks payable to your creditors leaving the dollar amounts blank.

- Arrange for a system of simple transfers from savings accounts to your checking accounts to provide easy access to money when you need it.
- Participate in a bank program that automatically pays bills. Contact your bank to see if such a program would work for you. Balance the costs against the risks, as well as the Life Units you save each month by not having to write the checks yourself.

Protect yourself against credit fraud. Many credit card users have found themselves in credit card hell after a wallet containing credit cards and their Social Security card has been lost or stolen. Only carry the credit cards you need and do not carry them with your Social Security card. In fact, leave your Social Security card at home if you do not need to carry it.

Stability. Moving often and changing jobs frequently is not viewed favorably by creditors. Consider ways of maintaining a stable address. For example, you could use a parent's address or a family vacation home. Do not use a post office box since it is seen as a negative on credit scoring. When Ronnie R. sold his house and moved into temporary quarters, he asked the people at his old post office to hold his mail for him, which he picked up once a week until he finally found and moved into a new house. There was only one change of address instead of the four that actually occurred while waiting to locate, fix, and finally move into the new house.

Reducing credit card debt. If statistically you have longer than two years to live, the more money you spend on servicing your debt, the less money you have for your investment goals. So do your best to reduce your credit card debt, while keeping all accounts active.

Some suggestions for lowering outstanding balances:

- Cut back on your discretionary spending so that you can redirect money to paying off debt.
- Consolidate the debt that you have under the lowest interest rate possible.
- Consider obtaining a home equity line of credit to consolidate your credit card debt. The interest on credit card debt is not deductible, while the interest payable on a home equity loan is. Be careful—you have to make the commitment to keep up with your debt. A home equity line of credit is secured by your home, so you don't want to risk foreclosure and possibly lose your home by not paying.

If you have a statistical projection of less than two years to live, don't worry about reducing the debt on those accounts with credit life insurance. Just keep the outstanding balance below the maximum amount of the credit life insurance, and pay the minimum balances required to keep the account from going into default.

Tip. Determine a realistic period of time, in months, by which you want to get out of debt. Divide the amount of outstanding debt by the number of months. Pay off at least that amount of debt each month. If you miss a month or two, don't worry. Do as well as you can.

Dealing with creditors. If you are having problems with creditors, try not to panic—there are ways out. See chapter 17.

Cancellations. Simply because you have credit now doesn't mean that you will have it forever. Sometimes credit card issuers will cancel cards if there is no activity in the account, so move your charges among your accounts over the year.

Even for cardholders who have always paid their bills on time, creditors have closed accounts because the cardholder was delinquent on other accounts listed in their credit reports, or because the card issuer used credit-bureau scoring and concluded that the cardholder was not a good credit risk.

Sometimes credit cards will be canceled for no obvious reason.

Tip. If you have a problem with a credit card issuer, complain to the regulators of the bank that issued it. Banks tend to listen to the regulators, particularly about complaints.

Section 4. Getting More and Better Credit

4.1 If You Have Credit

Do not throw away those applications you regularly receive in the mail. Fill them out and get more credit. Consider two issues in this quest for more credit:

• Do not apply for several cards in a short time. When you apply for a bank credit card, the issuer reviews your national credit bureau report, and that review is noted on your credit report as an "inquiry." Too many inquiries on your report can mean that you may be denied additional credit regardless of other qualifications.
• If it appears that you will not qualify for a particular line of credit, do not apply for it. The rejection will probably show up on your credit report.

Tip. An easily overlooked source of credit is overdraft protection on your checking account. If you can get it for free from your bank, take it and save it for emergencies.

As you review credit card applications. Look at
• the interest rate. Of course you're looking for the lowest interest rate. Note that often companies offer low introductory rates that go up after a period of time. Once you pass the introductory rate, simply go shopping again for a better rate.
• whether there is an annual fee. Check the fine

print: many cards are being offered without a fee, but the no-fee offer is only for a time, such as a year.
• whether the cards offer credit life and disability coverage. If they don't, then pass them by.

Sources for information about the interest rates and fees that are being offered by various credit cards are listed in the resources section.

Tip. If you receive an offer for "preapproved" credit, don't believe it. These issuers don't have to accept you, and if you get turned down, the rejection will show up in your credit report.

Transfers to a new account. One way of obtaining more credit and lowering interest costs is to contact a bank offering a credit card and tell them that you are interested in transferring an outstanding balance to a new account if you can find a card that has an interest rate better than your existing card and that does not require an annual fee. They will often make a deal to pick up the account.

When you do transfer balances from a credit card, whether into another credit card account or a home equity loan, do not close the old account. This way you increase your available credit and decrease the amount of interest you have to pay on any outstanding balance. Once you have the new account, you can also consider contacting your old bank and trying to negotiate a lower interest rate, advising that you can get a better rate elsewhere. This can also be done at the end of a low-rate period.

The only time to close old accounts is when they are preventing you from obtaining new accounts or there are substantial annual fees. If you have an account at bank Y with 18 percent interest, and bank A offers 15 percent, you will want to move your balance to bank A. However, the combined credit available between your accounts at bank Y and bank A may be more than A believes you should have outstanding. In that case, close the account at bank Y. The objective is to have the maximum amount of credit you can qualify for, with the lowest interest rate available.

4.2 If You Don't Have Credit— Secured Credit Cards

If you do not have credit because of a poor credit history or no credit history at all, a secured credit card might be the answer to obtaining credit.

With a secured credit card, you are required to open and maintain a savings account as security for your line of credit. The amount of credit is a percentage of your deposit, typically 50 percent to 100 percent, but sometimes even more. For example, if you deposit $1,000 in a bank account, you can charge up to $1,000 on the secured credit card. While you're not receiving credit to help pay for that transaction, by paying the bank the appropriate amount every month on the "credit card," and not touching the amount being held on deposit, you're creating a credit record that you can use to help obtain regular credit accounts. You may even be able to obtain credit life insurance on this account.

Look for a card that pays you interest on the money you deposit, that requires no annual fee, has the lowest interest charge, and does not report the account to the credit bureaus as a secured account. The credit limit should be at least as high as your deposit and preferably higher. To find available cards, see the resources section.

Use the secured card frequently and pay off the balance on time every month for twelve to fourteen months. This will build a healthy credit profile, which you can rely on to help obtain an unsecured card in the future.

Only use a bank for this type of card. There are plenty of disreputable operations that prey on those desperate for credit. They would like to issue you a card with a secured line of credit—and then disappear with your money. Lists are available of reputable banks offering secured cards and the terms. See the resources section.

Once you have obtained an unsecured card. Close your secured account or negotiate with the bank to convert the card to an unsecured line of credit. Once you have an unsecured card, there is no reason to have your money locked into a low-interest or no-interest account.

4.3 If You Don't Have Credit— Other Methods

Local stores or lending institutions. If you don't have credit, consider applying for a charge card or a small loan at a local store or lending institution. Ask if the creditor reports transactions to a credit bureau. If they do—and if you pay back your debts regularly—you will build a good credit history.

Cosigner. If you cannot obtain credit alone, you may be able to obtain it if someone who has a good credit history cosigns a loan for you (which means the cosigner is obligated to pay if you do not).

Chapter 22

Real Property

If a man owns land, the land owns him. Now let him leave home, if he dare.
—Ralph Waldo Emerson

Real property can be converted into a liquid asset through a variety of means. Before you use any of the suggestions in this chapter to obtain money, explore all the alternatives in chapters 19, 20, 21, and 23 to determine which is best for you.

Section 1. Purchasing Real Property

Purchasing real property is not generally recommended for people who have been diagnosed with a life-challenging condition. Real property is not liquid and it is not flexible. A house requires a great deal of maintenance that you must either do yourself (including on those days when you only want to stay in bed or are perhaps in the hospital) or have someone else do it.

Still, it may be worthwhile if there are overriding factors such as a chance to obtain a large amount of credit life insurance or if the purchase of real property is what would make you content. Ed G.'s day job was with the federal government, but his passion was carpentry, plumbing, and electrical work. When he became "disabled," he used his retirement funds to buy a fixer-upper. Even on

days when anyone else would have been in bed, barely able to move, Ed would hook his IV to an overhead beam, load himself with painkillers, and set to work lifting, hammering, and soldering. His face and body were so thin there was barely flesh left—but there was joy.

1.1 Advantages of Owning a Residence

Alternative source of income—rental income. Renting out all or a portion of your home can provide a steady source of income (see section 2.6 below).

Debt leverage and inflation hedge. Given that a home is typically purchased with a relatively small down payment with the remainder financed by borrowing, buyers *may* benefit from the eventual appreciation in an investment that has not yet been fully paid for. The investment may also serve as a hedge against inflation, since real estate has historically appreciated faster than the cost of living. However, depending on your life expectancy, inflation may not be critical in your planning.

Equity buildup. Instead of going to a landlord, each monthly payment builds equity in your house.

Tax advantages of home ownership.
- Deduction for mortgage interest and interest on home equity financing.
- Deduction for property tax payments.
- You can exclude up to $250,000 of gain ($500,000 for married couples filing a joint return) each time you sell a principal residence. See section 3 below.
- If your real estate is worth more at your death than when you purchased it, your heirs receive a "stepped-up" basis, which means their basis becomes the value of the property as it is included in your estate. No tax is due on the difference between what you paid for the property and the new higher valuation.

Mortgage life insurance. Home ownership may also make financial sense if it allows access to non–medically underwritten life insurance.

Bankruptcy. Residences are protected to a degree in bankruptcy (see chapter 17, section 3). In some states, such as Florida, a home is exempt from your creditors' reach no matter how valuable it is.

Medicaid. A home is not counted as one of your assets in determining eligibility for Medicaid.

1.2 Disadvantages of Owning a Residence

Liquidity and risk. Real estate is essentially a low-liquidity, high-risk investment. You may not be able to sell it when you want to or at fair market value.

Stress. With home ownership, there is no landlord to call when things go awry. It's your job to maintain the house and to fix any problems. Some problems cannot wait just because you may not be feeling well at the time.

Expense. A lot of unpredictable expenses accompany ownership. They can wreak havoc with a fixed income.

Estate planning. If the house is to be sold after your demise, your heirs may typically expect to receive only 75 percent to 80 percent of the fair market value, as personal representatives may be motivated to close your estate as quickly as possible rather than on the best terms possible.

1.3 If You Decide to Purchase a Residence

There are many good sources to guide you through the purchase of a home. While the desire to purchase may be emotional, the actual purchase should be governed by reason. A house is a substantial purchase, the largest that most of us will ever make.

A few tips to keep in mind:

- Under the federal Fair Housing Act, you cannot be discriminated against when applying for a mortgage loan because of your health condition.
- When shopping for a mortgage, contact at least three lenders. Only file applications with the ones with the most reasonable rates. Keep in mind that interest rates and points are usually negotiable. Nothing is set in stone.
- Consider hiring a mortgage broker. Mortgage brokers are paid by the lending bank, and commissions may vary from bank to bank. To assure you are not steered to the bank that pays the broker the highest commission instead of to the bank that gives you the best overall deal, do your own homework before hiring the broker to obtain an idea of what bank deals are available in your area.
- The rule of thumb is that it doesn't pay to be the most expensive house on the block. Any money you spend over and above what you can receive

on a sale of the house is an expense, not an investment.

Section 2. Home Equity Conversion Plans

Home equity conversion plans provide a mechanism for accessing money from a residence while retaining varying degrees of ownership and continued possession of the property. Alternatives include mortgage refinancing, home equity loans, sale leaseback arrangements, sales subject to a life estate, reverse mortgages, and renting your residence.

As you consider these alternatives

- bear in mind that while these plans turn the equity in your home into cash for your use now, you and your heirs will have less later.
- assess the costs involved in each conversion plan, such as interest charges, application fees, sales commissions, closing and other legal costs, and possibly loss of future appreciation in the value of your residence.
- think about the risks involved with each alternative.
- consider the effect of equity conversion proceeds on any government-sponsored benefits to which you may be entitled. None of the alternatives will affect Social Security Disability Income or Medicare. Since all of the alternatives provide cash, they will affect means-based entitlements such as Supplemental Security Income and Medicaid.
- select the plan and features that meet your individual needs, including your tax situation. As a general matter
  - proceeds from any of the alternatives that involve a loan are not subject to tax.
  - any of the alternatives that involve a sale are subject to tax, which is most likely a capital gains tax, with the breaks that go along with the sale of real estate (see section 3 below).

- rental income is subject to ordinary income tax.
- discuss your options with your accountant and/or attorney.

Tip. If a loan works best for you, when considering which type of loan best suits your needs, look at the costs under each alternative, including the annual percentage rate (APR) and other charges. When comparing the APR for a traditional mortgage loan and a home equity line, be aware that the APRs are figured differently. According to the board of governors of the Federal Reserve System, the APR for a traditional mortgage takes into account the interest rate charged plus points and other finance charges. The APR for a home equity line is based on the periodic interest rate alone. It does not include points or other charges.

Tip. If you are seriously considering a home equity conversion, obtain a free copy of *Home-Made Money, A Consumer's Guide to Home Equity Conversion,* published by AARP. Ask for publication no. D12894. You don't need to be a member or over fifty to order (202-434-2277).

2.1 Mortgage Refinancing

You can refinance your house and replace your current mortgage with a brand-new one.

You must qualify for a mortgage just as if you were purchasing the home again. Don't be concerned about your health condition: *the bank cannot consider your health condition and/or life expectancy.* The source of your income (such as Social Security payments) can be considered, but only as it relates to the ability to repay the loan.

To decide if refinancing makes sense for you. Conventional wisdom is that the expense of refinancing is worthwhile if you will recoup the outlays in less than three or four years, and you plan to stay in the house for at least another year beyond that. If your statistical life expectancy is less than that, use the expectancy.

To determine recoupment:

- Calculate the amount you will save each month by making lower payments than you do now.
- Add up the costs of refinancing, including points, closing costs to cover processing your application, a credit check, an appraisal, title insurance, taxes, the bank's legal fees, fees for your own lawyer, and any other similar items. Make sure you consider the amount, if any, of the **prepayment fee** on your current mortgage (the charge if you prepay an existing mortgage).
- Calculate your break-even point—the length of time it will take to recoup any expenses incurred in obtaining the refinancing by comparing them to the amount you'll save in monthly payments. To illustrate, if you will save $250 a month, and the costs of refinancing are $5,000, it will take you twenty months to break even.
- If you are trading a mortgage with a fixed rate for one with an adjustable rate, look at the index, payment cap, lifetime cap, adjustment frequency and period, whether the loan is convertible to a fixed rate, and if there is a fee for converting.

Tip. Whether to pay for the stability of a fixed rate or go with a variable rate depends on how long you plan to keep the mortgage. The longer the period, the more attractive the fixed rate may be, particularly if interest rates are low. An adjustable mortgage is probably not a good idea unless you plan to pay it off in the next few years or have the money to cover payments at the maximum rate to which it is adjustable.

Tip. Ask if you can obtain a life insurance policy to cover the new mortgage. If you can, even if the costs are higher than your current mortgage, it may be worth refinancing, particularly if you don't have insurance on your current mortgage.

Shop aggressively. If you decide to refinance, shop aggressively and check out at least three lenders, not just the one that holds your existing mortgage even though that one may be able to offer you the best deal since it can agree to waive a new appraisal and new title insurance. You can access comparative rates on the Internet at www.bankrate.com/.

Tip. Under the law, if you request it in writing, the lender must show you the property appraisal it relies on in reviewing your mortgage application. If your application is rejected, you could use a mistakenly low appraisal as a reason to ask for a review.

2.2 Home Equity Loans and Credit Lines

You may be able to obtain a home equity loan or an ongoing line of credit, particularly if your home has appreciated in value. The loan is collateralized by the difference between your debt on the property (your mortgage) and the fair market value, so your existing mortgage remains unaffected.

A new breed of loan, known as a **high loan-to-value** (HLTV) or **negative equity mortgage,** allows you to borrow as much as 25 percent more than your home is worth. These loans have a higher interest rate and closing costs than the traditional home equity loan, but do provide more money in case you need it. If you sell your house, you may not obtain enough money to pay off your debt.

As with a mortgage, the bank

- will look at your income stream as part of its assessment of your ability to repay the loan, as well as the value of the property and your credit.
- cannot consider your health condition and/or life expectancy.
- can consider the source of your income (such as Social Security payments), but only as it relates to the ability to repay the loan.

Tip. A home equity loan may enable you to consolidate your outstanding debts with high credit-card-type interest rates and reduce your rate to a lower secured-rate loan, with the bonus of converting from payments that are not deductible (such as for credit card or auto loans) to those that are. Interest on home equity loans to as much as $100,000 is tax deductible. If the money is used for home improvements, the limit rises to $1 million in total mortgage debt.

If you are considering a home equity loan.

- Find out if you can obtain mortgage life insurance on the debt. If you can, it may be worth taking out the loan just for the life insurance. If keeping up the total payments would be a burden, save a part of the loan proceeds to cover them.

- Decide whether you would prefer to take the cash now as a loan or have it available as a line of credit. Once you open a line of credit, you can tap it whenever you need cash simply by writing a check. Usually the check-writing period (the **access period**) extends for five to ten years. The borrower then has another five to fifteen years to pay it back, with interest of course. Credit lines are better if you have recurring expenses such as a child's college tuition or if you don't need all the money now.

- Be sure you can afford the interest charges at the maximum if your credit line comes with a variable rate of interest. If no maximum is specified, assume the monthly payments could double. This is being very cautious, but your home is at risk.

- Try to find a loan that doesn't charge closing costs and other up-front fees when you're looking primarily only for a standby credit line to tap in an emergency. Avoid lenders who impose annual maintenance fees. Although "no fee" lines don't usually carry the lowest rates, they can be competitive.

- Look for a line with no fees and a low initial rate if you plan to repay the loan quickly.

- With longer-term loans, focus more on the lowest rate you can get for as long as you have the loan.

- Look at all the same factors you would consider when borrowing to purchase a house: e.g., up-front costs including application fees, appraisals (yes, you'll need a new appraisal), closing costs, points, and interest rates. A few Life Units spent in research can save thousands of dollars.

- **To find the best deal,** call at least three lenders. Create a chart that tracks the various costs, interest for a period such as three years, and closing costs, including the bank's attorneys' fees and points. Some lenders also charge continuing fees, such as transaction fees each time you borrow money.

- Under the federal Truth in Lending Act, you will have three business days to reconsider whether you want to give the money back and undo the transaction.

Tip. If you have limited income and are having trouble obtaining this type of loan from a bank, consider national mortgage lenders such as Prudential Savings Bank (800-992-2265), Merrill Lynch (800-854-7154), and GE Capital Mortgage (800-257-7818). If that doesn't work, see if you can obtain a loan from a local nonprofit or government agency on housing or community development. Ask your social worker, GuardianOrg, or your church for advice.

2.3 Sale Leaseback

Under a "sale leaseback" arrangement, you locate a buyer willing to pay for the property and to lease it back to you. This permits you to stay in your residence while providing you cash near the full market value of the property. Since it involves a sale, the buyer assumes responsibility for taxes, insurance, maintenance, and repairs. On the downside, you give up the rights an owner would have and instead end up with the rights of a renter.

The purchase price can be paid to you as a lump sum or as a cash down payment with monthly purchase payments to you from the buyer.

For potential investors. Start with your friends and family. They receive a tax-advantaged investment by helping you. Another good source is investors who expect a substantial future appreciation in the value of your property. There may also be people who want to live in your house and see this as a good device to ultimately make that happen.

Tax. The tax advantage of a sale leaseback arrangement is only available if it meets the test of a business transaction entered on a for-profit basis.

2.4 Life Estate

Another means of freeing up cash from real estate is to sell the property subject to your keeping a "life estate," the right to remain in the house for the rest of your life. As with a sale leaseback, there is an actual transfer of title to the purchaser. While the sales terms are negotiable, the seller is no longer responsible for the obligations that go along with ownership of real property.

It is difficult to find investors for this type of arrangement beyond family and friends. A nonprofit organization may be interested in this arrangement, but these plans generally include some type of charitable donation rather than a full payment for the **remainder interest,** the value of the property when the buyer finally obtains it free and clear, discounted to today's date.

Tax. As compared to a sale, including a sale leaseback, a seller who retains a life estate cannot take the onetime capital gains exclusion, and the buyer cannot take deductions for expenses and depreciation.

2.5 Reverse Mortgages

A reverse mortgage is only currently an option if you are at least sixty-two years old and you own your residence. If you are younger than sixty-two and interested in a reverse mortgage, it is worth checking when you read this text to see if this situation has changed.

Like any mortgage, a **reverse mortgage** is a loan secured by your residence. You have the right to remain in the home, but you also have the obligation to maintain it to preserve the property value, and to pay taxes and property insurance premiums. Instead of there being a monthly payment to the lender as is the case with a traditional mortgage, with a reverse mortgage the lender pays money to the borrower as an income stream, a line of credit, a lump sum, or a combination of these methods. The lender does not expect to be repaid until a named event occurs, such as a sale of the residence or your death. A reverse mortgage is possible even if there is a small mortgage or home equity loan against the premises.

Unlike a traditional mortgage.
- The loan balance grows larger as long as it is outstanding.
- *The borrower does not need a salary or other income to qualify* since the lender only looks to the value of the residence, not the ability of the borrower to repay.
- There is no need to make monthly payments.
- The borrower's age becomes a factor in determining the amount the lender will loan.

Like a traditional mortgage.
- Maximum loan amounts are limited by the value of the home, the loan's interest rates, and the lender's policies.
- The money can be used for any purpose.
- If the loan is not paid when due, or there is a default such as when property taxes are not paid, the lender has the right to foreclose and force the borrower to leave the house.

Other facts about a reverse mortgage.
- The stream of income can be **open-ended,** with monthly advances for an open period of time until a specified event occurs, or for a **fixed-term,** in which monthly advances are paid for a

fixed number of years. The fixed-term approach can provide larger advances than open-ended reverse mortgages. Because mortgage interest rates are generally variable, a fall in interest rates could reduce the monthly income you receive.

• Generally, the legal obligation to pay back the loan is limited by the value of the home. This feature, called **nonrecourse** in legalese, means the lender can only look to the house for repayment of the loan, and not to the borrower, the borrower's other assets, or the borrower's heirs. The heirs are only responsible for repayment if they wish to keep the home, in which case the reverse mortgage can usually be satisfied with a new conventional first mortgage obtained by the heirs.

• The accrued interest that is paid when the home is sold is tax deductible in the year of the sale.

• There are reverse mortgages guaranteed by the Federal Housing Administration (FHA). The FHA guarantees against a default by the *lender,* which occurs when lenders fail to make loan advances as required by the loan papers. FHA mortgages generally have a fixed term so the loan is due and payable on a specified date, or earlier if you die, move, or sell the property.

Disadvantages of a reverse mortgage.

• Depending on how the loan is structured, the homeowner may outlive the loan value of the home, and end up with no more loan money and no home.

• If the lender ultimately takes title to the house, the lender, not the borrower, takes advantage of the home's appreciation.

• A reverse mortgage requires that the homeowner use the home as a principal residence during the term of a loan. An unexpected need to move, such as due to illness, would require the homeowner to repay the loan. Typically this means the borrower must sell the house or the lender takes possession.

Other factors to consider when contemplating a reverse mortgage.

• When considering the cost of the loan, look at:
  • What is the cost of repairs to your home required by the lender as a condition of the loan, if any?
  • How much money will be used to pay off existing liens?
  • How much are the points, closing costs, and other costs? Truth in Lending Act rules require lenders to disclose all costs and fees.

• How often does the interest rate adjust and what index is used to calculate adjustments? What is the limit on how far the rate can rise or fall? The higher the rate, the faster the equity will be used up.

• What are you required to pay on an ongoing basis?

• If the payout is monthly, what conditions must be met each month before payments will be made?

• If you want a line of credit, does the lender increase the unused portion of the line of credit annually as the value of your home increases?

• Does the lender share in the equity of the home when it is sold, in addition to repayment of the debt?

• If the program is not FHA insured, and you are to receive future payments, what is the lender's financial status? Is the lender's obligation to pay the borrower continuing payments at least funded (even in part) by an annuity policy from a top-rated life insurance company?

Tip. As with any mortgage, search for a program that has mortgage life insurance. Although an insured mortgage costs more, the debt will be paid off in full on your demise.

If you are interested in a reverse mortgage. Contact your local bank and/or a mortgage broker. Consider purchasing Ken Scholen's book listed in the resources section. It is full of detailed information including advice concerning comparison of costs and of different popular programs.

2.6 Renting Your Residence in Whole or Part

Another way of accessing the cash value of your home is to consider renting all or part of it.

Explore the alternatives, such as:

- Rent to a roommate or a boarder. You may also get the added benefit of sharing food and utility bills, which means less cost for each of you. You may even obtain a caretaker in the bargain.

Tip. Consider renting to people who are receiving government assistance to pay for their housing. For example, under "Section 8" housing subsidies, the tenant pays a percentage of his or her income as rent and the government pays the rest. You receive market rates with payment that is close to guaranteed. You retain control so you can choose tenants who will be compatible.

- Use an extra bedroom as a bed-and-breakfast. Sign up with one of the B-and-B services popping up all over the country and on the Internet. You can rent the room when it suits you rather than permanently.
- If you rent out an apartment in your house, reverse the situation—you can live in the apartment and rent out the larger part of the house.
- Build an apartment in the garage, basement, or attic for your own use and rent the house.
- Think about renting out the entire residence and moving into a smaller space, using your rental income to offset the mortgage payments or rental expense of your new residence.

A reputable real estate agent should be able to give you a reasonable estimate of how much you could receive with any of these suggestions.

An ancillary benefit of renting is that you may be able to generate tax deductions for depreciation, certain expenses, and write-offs if you treat the property as an investment for tax purposes.

Tip. If you do rent part of your property, be sure

- to inform your property insurance carrier of the arrangement (or a claim may be denied in the event of a loss).
- that you are protected for liability purposes, through liability insurance or possibly a limited liability entity.

Tip. Assisted living: If you need nonmedical assistance at home, consider turning your residence into an assisted living home. You can enter into an arrangement with a GuardianOrg in which you give, rent, or sell your premises. The GuardianOrg will provide the assisted living services you need and help you become certified by the state. You can retain control as to what services you will receive and who else lives with you. Rent or payment will be assured by the GuardianOrg.

Section 3. Selling Your House

Selling a house takes time. According to *Smart Money* magazine: "Studies show that the average single-family home spends ten weeks on the market. For 40 percent of sellers, the wait is even longer at twelve weeks. . . . An unfortunate 8 percent never find a buyer at all."

Capital gains tax. When you sell your residence, your profits, known as capital gains, are determined as follows: capital gains = sales price minus your **basis** minus **sales costs.** "Basis" is the original purchase price of your residence plus any capital improvements you've made that can be documented less any depreciation you may have taken on your tax returns. "Sales costs" include commissions, fees, and any other legitimate costs associated with selling your residence. Capital gains are subject to a capital gains tax to a maximum of 20 percent if the property has been held for more than eighteen months at the time of sale.

Taxpayers are allowed to exclude up to $250,000 of gain ($500,000 for married couples filing a joint return) each time a taxpayer sells or exchanges a principal residence, although the exclusion generally may not be claimed more frequently than once every two years. Unlike previously, there is no requirement to reinvest the sales proceeds. To be eligible, the residence must have been owned and used as the taxpayer's principal residence for a combined period of at least two out of the last five years prior to the sale.

While not avoiding the capital gains tax, you can extend the taxable gain from the sale of the house over a period of years with the use of an **installment sale** (a sale in which you receive the price in installments, rather than all at once). Under installment sales, capital gains tax can be deferred to future years when installments are received. Installment sale rules apply only to assets sold at a profit.

An installment sale of a house usually involves a **wraparound mortgage,** an agreement in which the buyer gives to the seller an installment obligation in an amount reflecting the outstanding mortgage(s) on the purchased property. The buyer does not receive title to the property in the year of sale, and the seller continues to make payments on the current mortgage, ordinarily using the installment payments made by the buyer. Since the buyer does not assume, or take the property subject to, the original mortgage, the wrapped debt is not considered received in the year of sale. Thus, the gain is recognized pro rata as payments are received. There is no bunching of the gain in the year of sale.

Tip. If the real estate market in your area is hot, consider selling your house yourself and saving the broker commission. If not, real estate experts indicate that homeowners have a better chance of selling more quickly and getting a deal closer to their asking price if they use more than one broker.

Chapter 23

Other Assets

I got a lot of stuff from people I loved. When I used to pass the blue glass bowl, on some level I was reconnected with my grandmother's living room, and to the way her hair smelled. At my tag sale, it wasn't easy watching people look at my things so coldly. I even found myself wondering what kind of homes things like the bowl were going to live in. But you know, I got through it—and the people I care about are still with me, inside. I mean, it's only things, you know?

—Clara T.

Short of a sale, personal assets such as term bank accounts, stocks and bonds, and personal property such as antiques, art, and jewelry are not generally considered a source of cash. However, there are other alternatives to accessing cash based on these assets. Even if you decide to sell a personal item, preparing ahead can maximize the amount you receive.

Section 1. Certificates of Deposit and Other Term Bank Accounts as Collateral for a Loan

Any certificates of deposit and other bank accounts that include a penalty for withdrawing funds before a certain date may be used prior to maturity as collateral for a low-interest loan. These loans are available, generally without fees, from commercial lenders—particularly from the bank that issued the certificate of deposit or holds the bank account.

Section 2. Stocks and Bonds as Collateral for a Loan

The use of stocks and bonds as security for loans from commercial lenders such as banks or securities brokerage firms is regulated by the federal government. The regulations concern the amount that can be loaned, as well as the permitted type of security.

The stocks and bonds must be freely salable and unrestricted. If the stocks are listed on the New York or American Stock Exchanges, they must have a market value of $5 or more per share. If they are over-the-counter stocks, the market value must be $10 or more per share. The terms for the loan, such as interest rates, fees, and other matters, are determined by the lender.

The guidelines for the maximum that can be advanced are listed on page 271.

For any other stocks and bonds, or to secure a loan in a greater amount than permitted by commercial lenders, you will need to locate a friend or relative willing to make the loan.

❯ ❯

Collateral	Maximum Advance (% of collateral)
U.S. government bonds	
Maturing in 1 year or less	95
Maturing in over 1 year	90
Agency securities, all maturities	90
Municipal bonds	
Rated Aaa, Aa	90
Rated A1, A	75
Rated Baa1, Baa	50
Rated Ba or lower	0
Corporate bonds: nonconvertible	
Rated A or better	80
Rated Baa or better	50
Rated below Baa	0
Corporate bonds: convertible	
Rated Baa or better	50
Below Baa	0
Stocks: preferred*	
Market price over $10 per share	75
Market price $5 to $10 per share	50
Market price under $5 per share	0
Stocks: common*	
Market price over $10 per share	70
Market price $5 to $10 per share	50
Market price under $5 per share	0
Stocks: over-the-counter**	
Market price $10 and over per share	50
Market price under $10 per share	0

*Stocks listed on the New York Stock Exchange or
American Stock Exchange
**NASDAQ stocks

Section 3. Personal Property as Collateral for a Loan

Banks and other commercial lenders. If you have personal property with substantial value, such as important artwork, jewelry, or silver, a commercial lender may allow their use as collateral for a loan. Do not be surprised if the lender insists on taking possession of the property until the loan is paid off.

Tip. If you own a house, it is sometimes possible to add personal property to the value of the house when obtaining a loan against real estate. This permits an increase in the size of the loan, and the deductible interest.

Auction houses. Some auction companies have programs that will lend money against the collateral of personal assets. In these instances, the borrower is usually permitted to retain possession of the art, antiques, furniture, or jewelry. There is a catch: the auction houses usually insist that you agree to sell the assets through the auction house after your demise.

Pawnbrokers, also known as collateral loan brokers. While they seem to be rapidly disappearing from our landscape, pawnbrokers can be useful if your need for cash is short-term. Pawnbrokers generally loan money collateralized by personal property for a short time, such as three to six months, subject to high interest rates.

Generally under strict state licensing requirements, the pawnbroker takes possession of your items and gives you the money and a memorandum, note, or ticket that contains the substance of the arrangement. Unlike other collateralized loans, the holder of the memorandum or note is presumed to be the person entitled to redeem the articles pledged as collateral, so the ticket has to be carefully guarded.

If after the time specified the articles have not been reclaimed by repayment of the loan plus interest, the pawnbroker has the right to sell the pawned items. If the sale results in a profit to the pawnbroker over and above the principal plus interest and fees, the borrower generally has a period of time in which to claim this profit. The ticketholder may generally redeem the pledged articles at any time prior to the sale.

Tip. Don't be surprised if a pawnbroker asks to fingerprint you. To prevent pawnbrokers from being used as an outlet for stolen goods, many states require fingerprinting.

Personal loans. There are generally no restrictions or rules concerning use of personal property for loans by friends or relatives, except that the interest rate agreed upon may not exceed the state's usury laws.

Section 4. Selling Personal Property

4.1 Prepare Well in Advance

If you decide to sell, do not wait until matters reach the emergency stage when immediate need reduces bargaining power.

If selling your own items is too difficult, ask a friend or relative to handle it for you, for a fee if necessary.

Be sure to know the value of any items you decide to sell. You can take photos of the items or take the items themselves to expert dealers for their opinion. Auction houses will also give you an idea of value.

If you want a valuation, but don't know an appraiser, you can locate one through the American Society of Appraisers (703-620-3838), the Antique Appraisal Association of America (714-530-7090), or the International Society of Appraisers (708-882-0706). Of course, because of the conflict of interest, do not rely on a dealer's opinion of value when you are considering selling the item to the dealer.

Tip. Do not feel that you have to sell your items locally. If you live in a rural area, it may be worth taking or shipping your items to an urban area where the demand and the prices are likely to be greater.

4.2 Alternative Places to Consider for Selling Personal Property

Auction houses. An auction house conducts a public sale at which items are sold to the highest bidder. Sellers are allowed to set a minimum (a **reserve**). If there are no bids above the minimum, the goods are returned to the seller. The auctioneer's fee is usually a percentage of the sale price—ranging from 5 to 25 percent.

Consider

• the reputation of the auction house.
• if the items are appropriate for the auctioneer's expertise as well as the type of buyers who generally attend the auctions. For example, you would not want to auction world-class art at a small-town auction house. The auction house should specialize in the type of items you want to sell.
• what other items will be included in the auction. You do not want to be part of a sale in which your items are likely to be the most expensive or incompatible with the rest. Be in a sale that attracts bidders interested in the type of items you are selling.
• whether and how the auction house will advertise the sale and whether a catalog will be printed.
• whether the auction house picks up the items or you must deliver them.

Tip. Check to be sure the auctioneer carries appropriate insurance on the property while in its possession—or that you do.

Consignment. Consignment is when you give your property to a professional (usually a shopkeeper) to sell for you for a fee. The two of you together set the offering price and the minimum you will accept. The shop owner retains a percentage of the sale price, generally 20 percent, but it can range as high as 60 percent. If a sale doesn't occur within the time you and the dealer set, the items are returned to you.

Tip. Generally when goods are in a shop on consignment, the owner is obligated to keep them insured. Verify that the dealer has this coverage.

Selling items yourself. There are many alternatives for selling personal items yourself including a garage or yard sale, a tag sale in your house, setting up a table at a flea market, renting a booth in a co-op collectibles store, setting up a table at a collectibles show, or through the Internet.

If you're going to conduct a yard or garage sale, find out if any local regulations govern such sales, and check that your liability insurance covers potential purchasers coming onto your premises.

If you so desire, professionals will conduct a tag sale for you.

An excellent resource for tips in maximizing the effectiveness of a sale is *Flea* by Sheila Zubrod and David Stern (HarperCollins Publishers, 1997).

Sell to dealers. The fastest way to sell personal items is to dealers—whether you take the items to their stores or ask them to visit your premises. You can expect a low price for the items since the dealers will be looking to purchase at the equivalent of wholesale so they can make a profit when they sell at retail.

Tip. Before selling any item, take into consideration the taxable gain or deductible loss.

Section 5. Charitable Donations

Another alternative to consider is giving personal property as a gift to charity and thereby freeing up money by reducing income or estate taxes.

Gifts can be made outright or through the use of different types of trusts, such as a "charitable remainder trust," in which the person who sets up the trust has the right to keep and use the assets for life, and the assets automatically pass to the charity on the person's demise. If this is of interest, speak with your tax adviser. Perhaps the charity of your choice has the ability to advise you. If so, check its advice with your tax adviser.

Part VI

Health Matters

Chapter 24

Doctors

Each patient carries his own doctor inside him. We are at our best when we
give the doctor who resides within each patient a chance to go to work.

—Dr. Albert Schweitzer

This chapter highlights the considerations that go into choosing and maximizing your relationship with a doctor. Even if you already have a doctor with whom you are comfortable, and you may not be looking for another physician right now, I suggest you review the following discussion.

Section 1. Choosing a Doctor

When choosing medical professionals, keep in mind three general considerations:

1. You are the captain and the final decision maker. No matter how educated or experienced a doctor may be, doctors are your advisers and are there to support you.

2. Look for a doctor who fits your needs. At a minimum, you will probably need a general practitioner for your overall health and a specialist in the area of your diagnosis, although it is possible that one doctor can fill both needs. It is generally accepted that "the use of a specialist is a major advantage" for people with a life-challenging condition. For example, a study reported in the

New England Journal of Medicine found a lower death rate in patients with HIV if they had an HIV-experienced doctor.

3. After doing the amount of research with which you feel comfortable, trust your instincts when choosing a doctor.

Tip. If you live in a rural area and have a condition that is not normally treated in that area, consider moving to, or at least visiting, a large city to get proper care. You have to weigh the extra Life Units for travel against the possibility of a better quality and quantity of life.

Referrals to a specialist. If you are referred to a specialist because of a particular problem, request a list of all the likely medical causes of your condition so you can assess whether you want a specialist, and if so, what kind. If the recommendation is to see specialists in different areas, prioritize your options according to which specialist is most likely to have the answer. If your doctor can't prioritize the specialists in this manner, prioritize by the cost to you in money and time. See chapter 25, section 11.2, if you are considering surgery.

1.1 Two Routes to Choosing a Doctor

The "seat of your pants" approach. In this method of finding a doctor, you accept the recommendation of a friend, family member, or another doctor. The underlying assumption is that if "it worked for them, it will work for me." Choosing a doctor just because she is nearby is another example of this method. While these methods frequently work, it can be a very hit-or-miss proposition.

Brigitte D.'s mother chose her doctor because the friend that recommended him said he was "nice." She had a seemingly manageable situation for which she was taking twelve different pills a day, yet she was still unable to get out of bed for more than three months. Brigitte got involved and researched the available doctors' education, experience, knowledge, communication skills, and level of care. The doctor Brigitte recommended was not as nice, but quickly realized that some of the pills were canceling each other out and changed drug regimens. Brigitte's mother healed in a matter of weeks.

The ordered approach. The more reasoned approach is to do a bit of research before bringing anybody on board.

1.2 What to Look For

In addition to the general considerations listed in chapter 36, section 1, before meeting a potential candidate, consider the following issues:

Training and certification.
- At the minimum, the person must have an M.D. and a state license. While the M.D. is required for a doctor to practice in U.S. hospitals (**hospital privileges**), the degree only means the person graduated from medical school. Furthermore, a state license is not necessarily indicative of a doctor's quality (some states only require a degree plus one year of internship to obtain a license).

- Look at the country in which the doctor went to school, the name of the school, and where she did her **residency training** (post-medical-school training). The more developed the country and the better the school, the better the doctor is likely to be—although there are good doctors from all countries and all schools.
- Doctors who continue their studies in depth in their chosen field often choose to pass a demanding test administered by specialty boards composed of their fellow doctors to become **board certified.** Board certification is an indicator of additional education. It does not test experience. Some boards require doctors to keep current by requiring periodic recertification. To check whether a doctor is board certified, call the American Board of Medical Specialties (800-776-2378), call the county medical society, or look in the medical directory in your library.

Insurance and payment.
- Will the doctor accept your insurance coverage? Will she file your claims for you?
- If you're covered by Medicare, does the doctor accept assignment of Medicare payments? Does the doctor charge an amount greater than the Medicare reimbursement? If you're covered by Medicaid, does the doctor accept Medicaid payments? Your local office of the Social Security Administration keeps lists of primary care doctors and specialists who accept Medicare and Medicaid. If you belong to a Medicare health maintenance organization, it will supply you with a list of doctors.

Teaching, hospital privileges, and lab services.
- Does the doctor have teaching responsibilities at a hospital? A teaching position reflects respect from colleagues and assures that the doctor is exposed to new developments.
- At which hospital or hospitals does she have admitting privileges, and would you want to be admitted there, both from the point of view of convenience and your idea of comfort? (See the

discussion about hospitals in chapter 29.) If the doctor admits patients to more than one hospital, how does she choose who goes where?

- Does the doctor offer lab services in the office, and if so, what kind? In-office labs may save repeated trips to an outside lab, and money if the doctor charges less than outside labs for uninsured tests. On the downside, doctors can overuse their own labs for their profit.

Availability.

- Is the doctor accepting new patients?
- Are the doctor's location and hours convenient for you?
- When it comes to booking an office visit, how many people are given the same time slot?
- What is the average waiting time for scheduling an appointment?
- Does the doctor give advice over the phone to regular patients? Is there a charge for such advice?
- Is there a covering doctor twenty-four hours a day when the doctor is unavailable, or at least an answering service that acts as an intermediary in off-hours?

Tip. To learn a particular doctor's biographical information, contact the American Medical Association free at www.ama-assn.org or send $60 to 515 N. State St., Chicago, IL 60610 (312-464-5199). You can check board certification by calling the American Board of Medical Specialties (800-776-CERT). You can order a compilation, by state, of doctors who have been disciplined by state medical boards or federal agencies, and why. Call the National Practitioner Data Bank (202-588-1000) and ask for "Questionable Doctors" for the state or states in which you are interested ($15 for each individual state plus $3.50 shipping and handling).

1.3 The Informational Interview

An "informational interview" will help determine whether a particular doctor is right for you. This interview may feel awkward at first, but it can save you Life Units.

Inform the person with whom you make the appointment of the purpose of the visit, and repeat it when you meet the professional. *Confirm that the interview is at no cost to you.* Otherwise the candidate may think of the meeting as a "first visit" for which you should pay.

To get the most out of the meeting, since time with the doctor will be limited, be prepared to discuss your top three health concerns. Take with you whatever documentation you believe the doctor will want to see (such as lab tests or journals you may have about your symptoms).

Be honest about the kind of doctor-patient relationship you're looking for. Areas to think about and discuss include:

Your relationship.

- Does the doctor understand and support whatever role you want to play in your health care, including the amount of knowledge you want about drugs and treatments and/or your health condition, and which of the two of you is the final decision maker? Trying to adjust to a doctor's personality is not a good idea. Sarah McS., a breast cancer survivor, smoked marijuana occasionally to alleviate the symptoms from her chemotherapy, an idea that her doctor not only didn't sanction, but was dead set against because it wasn't legal in their state. She dreaded going to the doctor and constantly postponed and often canceled appointments rather than face his judgment. Instead of helping her heal, her visits added to her stress. She finally switched to a doctor who treated her physical condition and didn't judge her choices.
- Is the doctor willing to function as part of your team?
- If you want to consider alternative or experimental treatments, will the doctor give you an opinion about those options?
- Does the doctor have the kind of bedside manner with which you are comfortable?

Tip. Two decades of research have shown that you're likely to do better medically if you have a doctor you can communicate with—one who makes it easier for you to be actively involved in your health care. Trust your gut.

The doctor.
- Does the doctor work at disease prevention and health promotion or just take care of immediate problems?
- Does the doctor approach a patient's health conservatively, trying all procedures that are not invasive and safer drugs first?
- Does the doctor support your current feelings about end-of-life matters such as "do not resuscitate" orders, health care proxies, and living wills? (See chapter 32.)
- What is the doctor's relationship with other specialists in case your doctor doesn't have expertise that may be needed?
- Does the doctor project common sense?
- Does the doctor devote full attention to you or do other activities distract her?
- Do you feel rushed? Does the doctor take the time to listen to you and explain things until you understand them?
- When you need other medical services, does the doctor make recommendations or are you left to find them on your own (e.g., home care companies)?
- Let the doctor know about any other person (such as spouse, significant other, or friend) you want to have access to your medical information. Is the doctor willing to speak with that person?
- Is the doctor willing to send you copies of all correspondence she sends to anyone else about you, including to Social Security and your employer?

The surroundings—support staff and office.
- You'll be looking to the doctor's support staff for such matters as appointments, getting the doctor's attention when she's busy, billing, and often just the sympathetic ear the doctor doesn't have time for. Are the manager, receptionists, secretaries, and nurses trained in your condition? Are they professional? Sympathetic?
- Does the office appear to be professionally run, organized, and busy?
- Is your appointment kept on time?
- Does it appear that all your needs for X rays or simple lab tests will be met in the office, or will you have to go to another location?

1.4 Managed Care Doctors

Regardless of the type of managed care company you use, take care when selecting your **gatekeeper** and your specialist. The primary care physician is the doctor who acts as your gatekeeper and who decides which specialists you will be allowed to see and when. The managed care company will usually give you the information you need about the education and licensure of each doctor. Don't worry about whether the doctor will file claims for you: with a managed care system there are no claims to file. Questions about referrals to other doctors and choices of hospitals are also different, as noted below.

Specialist as primary care physician. Since most of your needs will require a specialist, ideally your specialist should be your primary care physician. There are plans today that permit this. For a more detailed discussion, see chapter 14, section 3.

Informational interview. Regardless of whether the plan allows a get-acquainted visit with the doctors in the plan, or you have to ask the questions on your first visit, find out the following facts, each of which will be helpful in deciding whether you want to work with the interviewed person:
- What the primary care physician thinks about
  - the managed care organization (MCO);
  - the MCO's doctor-compensation system; and
  - whether the doctor is considering leaving the

plan. You don't want a doctor who resents caring for patients in your plan or who will soon be unavailable to you.

- referring patients with your condition to a specialist, and which specialists she uses.
- matters listed in section 1.3 above under the headings "Your relationship" and "The doctor."

Also ask the doctor the following questions, which will be useful in knowing how assertive you may have to be to obtain the care you need, and how to assess the doctor's recommendations:

- How is the managed care doctor paid? If the fee to the doctor is "capitated" and she is paid a set amount per year per patient, the more she sees you, the less money she makes. The doctor may also lose money or possibly even her contract with the MCO if she suggests too many treatments or refers patients to too many specialists.
- Is the doctor bound by any "gag rules"? Many managed care companies prohibit their doctors from discussing certain subjects with patients, for example certain expensive treatment strategies. Federal regulation prevents gagging doctors in Medicare MCOs, and so do some state laws.

Changing doctors. Determine the MCO's procedure for changing doctors in the event you are not pleased with the doctor you choose.

If a managed care plan doesn't satisfy your needs. If you have a choice, change plans. However, if you work for an employer that only offers one plan, either pay for your health needs by purchasing your own coverage, or go outside the plan. As a last resort, consider changing employers. Your health coverage is that important to you (see chapter 14).

1.5 Alternative Care Practitioners

Alternative care practitioners use therapies and practices that are founded on philosophies different from those of traditional Western medicine. If you are interested in using an alternative practitioner, whether as a sole source of care or in addition to your traditional doctor, read up on the field of alternative medicine that interests you. Be leery of unrealistic claims such as "guaranteed cures." Reputable alternative practitioners usually don't make such claims.

The process of finding an alternative practitioner is substantially the same as in looking for a traditional doctor. In addition, ask the alternative practitioner whether she refers to other caregivers, including M.D.'s, if your medical problem is beyond her skills. If she doesn't, keep looking.

Do not automatically assume the accuracy of what your insurance summary says about covering a visit to an alternative practitioner and/or prescribed herbs or other treatments. Managed care companies and health insurance companies are now examining this area closely, and some are adding coverage for alternative treatments. Also check with your local hospital to find out if alternative doctors have privileges and if any limitations are imposed.

Section 2. What Do You Want to Know About Your Health and Treatment?

Some people want to know everything that is happening with their health and treatments, and others don't want to know at all. To exercise control over health-care decisions you need information about the state of your health and the alternatives. However, if you prefer to let the doctor make the decisions for you, that is totally your choice. There is no right or wrong. Whatever works for you is right. The key is to consider these matters before making a decision.

Whatever your decision, communicate your wishes about this subject to your doctor so they can be noted in your permanent health record. Also ask the doctor to let any doctors to whom you may be referred know your preferences as well. If you are referred to another doctor, confirm that the doctor is aware of your wishes concerning this matter. And of course communicate your wishes to any family members or trusted friends who may be involved in your care or have access to your medical records.

Section 3. The Doctor/Patient Relationship

Your emotional state can affect the course of an illness. A key factor in your emotional state is the kind of relationship that develops between you and your doctor. Don't expect a satisfying, comfortable relationship with a doctor to bloom at your first meeting. Establishing any relationship takes time. But if the relationship doesn't ultimately work for you, then consider changing doctors immediately.

Good doctor/patient communication is important. In addition to all the physical symptoms and facts that seem to be pertinent to your condition, openly and frankly discuss *all* relevant concerns, stresses, or psychological pressures with your doctor. She cannot read your mind and won't know about them unless you tell her.

Feel free to discuss any and all therapies you hear about that you think may be helpful. There is no such thing as a stupid question when it comes to your health.

Also, let the doctor know if you're not getting the time you need or feel like a number instead of a person, or that the doctor is not putting your best interests first.

Tip. Insist on privacy during important discussions. Ideally discussions between the two of you should be conducted in a private room with the door closed. If you feel intimidated because the doctor sits behind a desk, ask her to move to a place where the two of you can sit together. Do not have important discussions in a busy hallway.

If a problem in communication develops between you and your doctor. Look at whether you may be part of the problem. Get advice from other patients who have handled similar problems and/or from your team members. If you are friendly with the doctor's nurse, talk to her. Once you're prepared, speak with the doctor about it. If you don't want to say it, write a note and deliver it to her. If all else fails, consider changing doctors.

Assertive versus obnoxious. Keep in mind that, of all your team members, doctors are the ones particularly used to being the captain of the team. Thus, you may have to be particularly assertive with your doctor. This can be a good thing. According to researchers at the New England Medical Center, assertive patients stay healthier than similar patients who are not assertive.

If you find you've crossed the line into being obnoxious—and if you stay alert, you'll know when you have crossed the line—it can't hurt to apologize, remind the doctor that it is *your* health at issue, and ask for her understanding. You are entitled to any information you request.

Section 4. Visits with Your Doctor

It is easy to become nervous or upset when discussing something as important as your health. Prepare for your appointment by writing down the details of your symptoms, as well as whatever questions and concerns you may have. If a particular question is embarrassing or difficult to ask, consider asking it first.

Tip. If you don't note them in a journal, it may be helpful to keep a running list on which to note your symptoms, questions, or concerns as they come up. If you follow this tip, your list will be prepared continuously and be completely up-to-date.

Tip. Tell your doctor how your condition affects your activities including your ability to work. Be specific. For example, instead of just "diarrhea exhausts me," add that you are unable to stand or sit for any length of time and have to be near a bathroom. Ask the doctor to include this information in your medical records. It may be helpful for Social Security and other purposes.

Be sure to understand your diagnosis, treatment, and the purpose of any tests. If you're not sure whether you understand what the doctor is telling you, rephrase your question or ask the doctor to repeat what was said in a different way. It may help to visualize what is being explained to you. If you need her to show you something instead of telling you about it, ask for an illustration—preferably one you can take home with you. Another approach is to repeat to the doctor what you thought was said. If your understanding is not correct, the doctor will have an opportunity to clarify it.

To remember what is said

- take a notepad to write down the answer. Don't worry if at first you're uncomfortable asking questions and taking notes. If you were looking to buy a house or a car, you'd jot down notes naturally.
- take a friend. In addition to helping you remember the doctor's responses, the friend may even help formulate questions. Choose a friend who thinks objectively, with the capacity to listen and remember accurately. Ideally, this friend can also give you emotional support. Be sure you can discuss all embarrassing details in front of the friend.
- consider taking a tape recorder. You can also play it for friends or family later. Be sure the doctor allows taping before you turn on the recorder.

Tip. Ask your most important questions first in case you run out of time. If you do run out of time, ask when you can speak with the doctor again. This future time (and it can even be a phone call) is for discussing the rest of your questions, asking about information you were told that you don't understand, or asking follow-up questions after

you have digested the information discussed during your visit.

A case study—the Patrick O'Dowd method of doctor visits. Patrick, a person living with a life-challenging condition, uses the following system to maximize his doctor visits. Even if his method doesn't work for you, it provides some interesting ideas for your consideration.

- With Patrick's condition, as with most life-challenging conditions, doctors use certain markers to determine the progress of the illness or the effectiveness of the treatments. Patrick keeps his own running chart of the progress of the markers, which he takes with him to each visit. This saves the doctor the time required to otherwise flip through extensive medical records. Patrick's chart also indicates when different drugs or treatments started, so it is easy to track interventions and results.
- Patrick also makes a point of scheduling an appointment to have the test for the marker done in sufficient time *before* his doctor's appointment so there will be new results at which to look. This provides information with which to make decisions. He also makes a point of asking the doctor at each appointment to write another request for the test for the next period of time, as well as to set the date when the test should be taken.
- He keeps a running list that includes all his medications, starting with medications that are to treat his condition, then preventives (drugs to prevent infections from occurring), over-the-counter drugs, vitamins and herbs, and finally painkillers. Then Patrick lists side effects from any of the drugs. Last, but not least, he keeps track of the progress of his "old" symptoms, as well as notations of any new ones. He gives a photocopy of this list to the doctor at each visit, saving additional time.
- Next Patrick writes his questions and concerns in large letters (usually taking two lines) in Magic Marker so the doctor can see the list, its length, and that Patrick is organized. His exper-

imentation has shown that a typed list does not have the same effect of involving the doctor. He also uses different colors or underlining to emphasize matters that are really important to him.

- Patrick takes charge of the actual meeting with the doctor by insisting that his questions and concerns be dealt with *prior* to the physical exam. Since doctors always seem to find the time for an appropriate physical, Patrick has found if he asks his questions first, the answers are not rushed. Patrick's agenda in his question-and-answer period (unless there is a reason to follow the doctor's lead at any particular session) is:
  (1) Questions and concerns.
  (2) Review lab work.
  (3) Review prescriptions (what needs to be added, decreased, or eliminated).
  (4) Discuss paperwork that Patrick needs the doctor to complete (e.g., Social Security papers).
  (5) Patrick then asks, "Can you tell me anything I don't know enough to ask?" This question has been known to open discussion about treatments Patrick didn't know about or that had not yet been discussed.
  (6) Open forum for any other matters that may come up. Patrick uses this time to bring up a subject he has learned is of interest to the doctor, such as the latest movies or the local ball team. He finds it helps the personal relationship.

For Patrick's system to work, both parties have to stick to the agenda and not go off on a tangent.

Section 5. Pain

The doctor needs to know if you are experiencing pain. In your journal or in a separate file, keep a log that includes

- the day the pain occurs.
- when it hurts (including the time of day if applicable).
- the exact location of the pain in your body.
- a description of the pain (such as dull, sharp, pins and needles, shooting).
- the severity (such as on a scale of 1 to 10 with 10 being the most painful).
- how the pain affects your everyday life, such as keeping you awake at night or leaving you unable to move, walk, work, enjoy food, or exercise.
- if you are taking pain medication or doing anything else to control your pain. Note how helpful those measures are. Use the 10-point scale and compare your pain level before you administer treatments or drugs to the level approximately one hour afterward.

Take the chart to the doctor with each visit.

Tip. When discussing pain, be sure to tell the doctor what, if anything, you have found helps relieve the pain, and what doesn't. For example, tell your doctor if lying down with your feet up helps but lying down with your feet on the bed hurts, or if a heating pad helps but ice doesn't.

Tip. The pain log will also be important should you decide to file for Social Security Disability benefits.

Section 6. Second Opinions

A **second opinion** is a consultation about a specific matter from a qualified professional other than the one recommending a particular treatment. No hard and fast rules determine when to obtain a second opinion about a proposed treatment. If a second opinion seems called for, try to get the opinion from a doctor who is not affiliated with the first doctor, and preferably not in the same institution either.

Tip. If the news is significant, consider obtaining a second opinion *even* when you obtain good news.

Damien was told his tumor had dramatically decreased in size and the chemotherapy that had previously been strenuously recommended was not necessary. A second opinion revealed that the tumor had actually grown. Chemotherapy was immediately instituted to great success.

If surgery or another radical procedure is suggested, get an opinion from a person with a different background. Surgeons tend to see answers to problems in terms of surgery, while those with other backgrounds may have a different point of view. If you're still not satisfied after two opinions, go for a third one.

Many health coverages require a second opinion. Most plans that don't require it will still pay for it. If you are eligible, Medicare will pay for a second opinion.

If you think a second opinion is warranted, the odds are you should obtain one even if it is not covered by insurance.

Section 7. Medical Records

It's important to periodically inspect and/or copy your medical records.

- The information permits you to be in more control of your health care if you want to be.
- You can be sure the information is correct. This is particularly important
  - for health care decisions down the line (particularly by people who have not treated you before who may not know of the error).
  - when applying for insurance, government benefits such as Social Security Disability, or selling your life insurance policy.
  - possibly even for insurance costs.
- If your doctor retires or changes location or type of practice, records can become misplaced or lost or important medical records may be destroyed after a time.
- Continuity of care will be better since you will

be able to take a copy of your medical records with you to a new doctor or when you travel or move, or in the event of an emergency.

Most doctors and hospitals will give you a copy of your medical records when asked. However, if your request is refused, you should examine your state's law to determine your rights. Most states provide the patient a right of access to medical records held by doctors and/or hospitals. Federal regulations govern the records of long-term-care facilities that accept Medicare or Medicaid payments. Federal employees have a right to obtain medical records maintained by the government. If there is no statute, common law may give you a right to a copy of your records.

Don't be surprised if you are charged a fee for copying. Some states have a statutory maximum charge per page ranging from $.10 to $1.

When you review your record, make notes of your questions. The next time you see your doctor, bring your questions. If your doctor is too busy, perhaps the doctor's nurse will have the answers. If not, she can find out when the doctor is not busy seeing patients.

An excellent source of information about state medical records laws, as well as explanations of the entries you are likely to find in your records, is *Medical Records—Getting Yours,* a publication of Ralph Nader's Public Citizens Health Research Group (available for $10 by calling 202-588-1000 or writing Public Citizen, 2000 P Street NW, Suite 605, Washington, DC 20036).

If you have been denied access to your records, you may want to ask a patients' rights advocate in your area for help.

Tip. Rather than rely on the legal process, if your request for your records is refused, consider asking a friendly doctor to request them. The rules of professional conduct of the American Medical Association obligate a doctor to transfer records to another doctor when the patient requests it.

Chapter 25

Drugs and Treatments

A wonder drug is a medicine that makes you wonder if you can afford it.
—Sheila Z.

Being diagnosed with a life-challenging condition heightens the awareness of how everything we do affects our health and well-being. This chapter considers drugs and treatments in that context.

Section 1. Your Rights

It is your basic, constitutional right to determine your own treatment. You have the right

- to receive complete information about your health and what the future might bring.
- to be informed about the benefits and risks of any recommended drugs or treatments and available alternatives so you can make an informed decision.
- to make and change decisions about your health, including any proposed treatments.
- to refuse treatment.

There is even a federal law, the Patient Self-Determination Act, that requires all medical care facilities receiving Medicare and Medicaid payments (including hospitals, skilled nursing facilities, home health agencies, hospice organizations, and health maintenance organizations) to inform patients of their rights and their choices about the type and extent of medical care.

It is also your right to share or withhold information about your health from family members, friends, your employer, coworkers, and anyone else. I am not suggesting that you exercise that right, merely that you be aware of it.

Section 2. When Your Decision Is Required ↑↑↑

Consider the following when evaluating a treatment or drug. These tips are based in part on the advice of Charles Inlander, president of the People's Medical Society. Rather than trying to remember them all, feel free to photocopy these pages and take them to appointments.

Make sure your caregiver knows:
- What is most important to you about your medicines or treatment. Are you more concerned with

- the effect on your work?
- on your daily life?
- the fewest side effects or perhaps to avoid a particular side effect?
- taking the fewest number of pills or the shortest length of the treatment?
- cost factors?
- About any allergies.
- About unwanted side effects you've previously experienced from a drug or treatment.
- If you are or might become pregnant, or if you are nursing a baby.
- About any medicines you are taking, particularly those prescribed by another doctor or over-the-counter medicines you have started since your last visit.
- About any alternative treatments you may be using.

Make sure you know:

- The exact diagnosis and the cause of the problem you are experiencing.
- What the doctor is proposing, in terms that you understand.
- If any written information and published studies are available.
- Why you need the drug or treatment, the expected benefits, and their duration.
- What risks or side effects are involved. If there are possible side effects, what should you look for and what should you do if they occur?
- How the drug or treatment will interact with your other drugs or treatments.
- About your alternatives, including
  - the benefits and risks of those alternatives.
  - why the proposal under consideration is preferred.
- How much it will cost. If it is a treatment, does that include follow-up visits?
- If your insurance covers it. Will the doctor's office find out for you?
- How to monitor progress and to read or interpret tests.
- The extent of your doctor's experience with the

drug or treatment. If you're dealing with a specialist and not comfortable asking this question, ask your primary care physician to find out for you.

- If the doctor has a financial interest in your decision, one way or another.

If a lifestyle change is recommended, find out:

- How any suggested changes—such as in smoking, drinking alcohol, exercise, weight, diet, and the like—will improve your condition.
- How much change is needed to make a difference.
- The easiest way to implement the recommended changes.

Tip.

- Always ask a catchall question such as "Is there anything else you would ask if you were me, or that I should be aware of?"
- If there are several alternatives to choose from, ask your doctor, "If you had a child of your own in my situation, what would you suggest he or she do?" and of course, "Why?" Asking what the doctor would recommend to his child allows the doctor to express his opinions hypothetically, which may alleviate fears about liability that would normally prevent him from giving an opinion.
- Delete (and initial the deletion of) any provisions of a consent document with which you don't agree. Always get a copy of any consent documents you sign.

Section 3. Where to Find Information About Drugs, Treatments, and Your Condition

If you want to know more about your condition, a treatment, and/or drugs, this section guides you to sources of information.

Your doctor. As may be expected, one of the best sources of information is your doctor. If you're not sure about what you are being told, repeat it back to the doctor and ask if your understanding is correct. In addition to what he knows, he may have free literature for you in his office and should be able to direct you to additional resources.

Your pharmacist. Your pharmacist can answer any questions about drugs. He may even have literature about the drug.

Guardian Organization. Get all the information you can from your national and local Guardian-Orgs. Subscribe to newsletters that talk about the latest developments.

Support group. A support group is a good place to find information. A number of doctors have told me that people in a support group often know more about the course of a condition and the results of various treatments than they do.

Government. Several federal agencies offer free, comprehensive treatment guidelines about a variety of illnesses:
- National Health Information Center in Washington, D.C. (800-336-4797), refers callers to over a thousand organizations that provide medical information.
- National Institutes of Health (800-644-6627).
- Public Health Service's Agency for Health Care Policy and Research (800-358-9295).

Libraries. Look for articles about your condition in medical journals and other publications. If your library doesn't have the journals you need, locate a medical library open to the public by calling the National Network of Libraries of Medicine at 800-338-7657. In many libraries, the research librarians will do a computer search of medical databases for your condition or direct you to appropriate journals. In some libraries they will even print out the articles for a fee.

Tip. Medical journal articles may be difficult to wade through. If the words seem too technical,

make photocopies and take the copies to your doctor for an explanation. Check out the reliability of the journal before relying on the findings described in the article.

Internet. The Internet is a new source of information. You can search medical literature or access journal articles and medical textbooks. If you don't have your own access to the Internet, ask a friend who does. Many public libraries now provide Internet access.

Tip. Look in the resources section under "Treatment Information: The Internet" for a good place to start your search. Information is organized by category and is searchable by key words. The more specific you are, the more useless or irrelevant information you can filter out. Good general guides are *HealthNet* by Jeanne C. Ryer (John Wiley & Sons), $16.95, or *Health Online* by Tom Ferguson (Addison-Wesley), $17.

Tip. Check the date of the last revision each time you receive information from any particular site. If you really want to be sure to keep up-to-date, programs are available that will continually access the sites you choose and E-mail you updates.

Hired assistance. You can hire a medical researcher for a fee such as Planetree Library (415-923-3680), Health Resources (800-949-0090 or E-mail to moreinfo@thehealthresource.com), or Best Doctors (800-675-1199 or E-mail to www.bestdoctors.com). CanHelp (206-437-2291) is a resource service for people with cancer, directed by medical writer Patrick McGrady, that provides information on both conventional and alternative therapies.

Caution. *Be skeptical of any information you receive anywhere, but particularly from the Internet. Track down the source and evaluate it for yourself, or have someone with medical knowledge of your condition help you assess it. Always consider the source, including any possible biases.*

Tip. When you find information about research or treatment that seems pertinent, bring it to the attention of your doctor.

Section 4. Refusal of Treatment ↑↑↑

If you decide to exercise your right to refuse treatment altogether or to discontinue it, you can still receive pain medication and treatments to reduce the symptoms of your disease. (See chapter 30 for a discussion about hospice care.)

Your doctors will, almost certainly, offer information and advice about your decision to refuse a particular treatment or to stop treatment entirely. You may also want to consult your family and loved ones, and perhaps your religious group.

If the medical professionals or facility aides refuse to comply with your wishes

- be insistent, or be sure someone is insistent on your behalf.
- make notes, or have someone make notes, of the conversations you have about your wishes, including with whom you speak and what you both say.
- contact an attorney if all else fails.

Section 5. Prescription Drugs

5.1 If a New Drug Is Recommended

Review the considerations described in section 2 above.

On a separate piece of paper from the prescription, ask your doctor to write the exact name of the drug, the doses you are to take, and the number of times you should take it. Also ask what the drug looks like. You can then compare the information to the prescription bottle when you get it.

The National Council on Patient Information and Education recommends that you also learn

- the minimum and maximum effective dosages.
- the minimum and maximum cost for the drug

and its generic counterparts. (A **generic drug** is an unbranded drug whose active ingredients duplicate those of a brand-name product.)

- how frequently the drug's effectiveness must be monitored.
- what to do if you miss a dose.
- what food, drinks, other medicines, or activities you should or should not avoid.
- if and how often you can get a refill.
- how to store the drug.
- how to obtain any written information about the drug or its effects.

Tip. Keep a list of what medicines you take and modify the list as it changes. Keep a copy of the list in your wallet, particularly when you travel. If you have to tell anyone about the drugs you are taking, you can give them the list, or they will have it if you are unable to speak at the time.

5.2 Follow the Orders

While you are taking a drug

- take doses on time.
- don't take **drug holidays** (a period during which you stop taking the drug without professional advice). If you misplace or lose your drugs, contact your physician immediately. Wherever you are, he can probably arrange an emergency supply of drugs for you.
- don't take a larger or a smaller dosage than the doctor prescribes.
- never stop taking it without speaking with your physician first, no matter how good you feel!
- don't borrow medication.
- keep it stored as directed. Don't store drugs in the glove compartment of your car; the temperature varies too much.
- check expiration dates periodically and throw away expired medications.
- if you are on a complex drug regimen, ask for a written schedule showing the proper dosage and timing for each medication, as well as

whether it should be taken with or without food, and any other instructions.

Tip. If you suffer an adverse reaction to a prescription drug, call your health care professional immediately, then report your experience to the FDA's MedWatch program at 800-332-1088. The program monitors patients' adverse reactions to drugs.

5.3 Monitor Your Progress on the Drug

- Pay close attention to any changes in your body, particularly when you start taking a new prescription or stop taking an old one. Seek help immediately to solve any problems that arise.
- Study and evaluate test results.
- Describe to your doctor any changes in your symptoms (good or bad) since commencing the prescribed medicine or any problems you may be having taking it.
- Inform your doctor if you are not following prescription specifications.
- Do a medicine checkup every six months to spot hidden problems. Schedule a time with your pharmacist or doctor to examine all of your medications (prescription, over-the-counter, herbs, etc.). They can check for duplicate, contradictory, or outdated medication and proper doses. This is a good time to ask your doctor if you can now discontinue using any drugs. An easy drug checkup method is to put all your drugs into a bag and take it to your doctor or pharmacist.

Tip. If your blood is tested regularly to monitor a particular medication, don't switch between different versions of the drug without informing the person who administers the test.

5.4 Compliance Aids

If you are taking a batch of drugs and having trouble keeping track of them, **compliance aids** can help remind you to take your doses on time and keep track of the doses you have taken. Ask your pharmacist or doctor for what is available, or look in the catalogs listed in the resources section under "Daily Living."

Tip. A multisection screw box, which you can find in your local hardware store, is an inexpensive compliance aid. Group your pills according to day, time, and dosage. This way you only have to sort your pills every few days. Also, you can easily monitor whether you have taken the pills or not.

If timing is important, there are pillboxes with timers built in that will fit in your pocket or purse. There are also watches with timers that you can reset as needed throughout the day.

Tip. If you're having trouble taking a pill that sticks to your throat, try taking it with something that is carbonated. The carbonation seems to cushion the pill, making it easier to swallow. If the pill is the kind that starts to melt in your mouth and tastes awful, purchase empty gel capsules from your pharmacy and place the pill in the capsule before swallowing.

Section 6. Purchasing Drugs

6.1 Choosing a Pharmacist

Choose a pharmacist with the same care and consideration that you use in choosing a physician: he is another member of the medical part of your team, helping you achieve the best results from your medications. The pharmacist may know more about the benefits and risks of the drugs you are taking than your doctor does. To maximize the use of your pharmacist, think of him as an educator about drugs. The pharmacist can help select prescription and nonprescription medications effectively, inexpensively, and safely.

When considering a pharmacist

- look (or ask) for a certificate indicating that the pharmacist is licensed.

- look at the pharmacist's education. Make sure your pharmacist has at least a bachelor of science degree and is not just a pharmacy technician. Few pharmacists with a doctor of pharmacy degree work in a pharmacy. According to the People's Medical Society, the additional degree is not critical to good care.
- look at whether the pharmacist has a computer program that can create a printout about each drug, including its effects, side effects, and interactions.
- are you comfortable speaking with the person?

6.2 Choosing a Pharmacy

When evaluating available choices, consider

- if the pharmacy's prices are competitive.
- convenience of location and/or delivery.
- emergency access—how do you obtain necessary drugs when the pharmacy is closed or the druggist is not there?
- if the pharmacy stocks the drugs you need. Does it have the refill policy you want? Can you get refills at other locations? Will the pharmacist call your doctor for you?
- if an area is set aside for you to speak privately with the pharmacist if you want to.
- if the pharmacy accepts your drug insurance plan or government drug assistance program.
- if you travel for work or recreation, can your pharmacy cooperate with out-of-state or foreign drug dispensers without hassles or extra fees?
- Does the pharmacy stock generic drugs? Once a patent expires, a drug often becomes available from more than one source and the price falls. Generic drugs are usually sold at substantially lower prices than their brand-name equivalent. If your doctor prescribes a brand name, ask your pharmacist if there is a generic equivalent that is less expensive. There is a small risk that variations in the fillers or other inactive ingredients in the generic drug may alter the way the

active ingredients work in your body. Consult with your pharmacist about this. If a question remains, call your doctor.

Make sure to inform your pharmacist of any over-the-counter medications you may take from time to time, since interactions with your prescriptions are possible. For example, if you are on ibuprofen and your doctor prescribes steroids, the interaction could lead to ulcers. If the pharmacist has a decent computer program, it will alert you to inappropriate combinations.

Periodically compare the total cost for your drugs with other pharmacies to see if the price you are paying is still competitive. A few minutes of calling can save many Life Units.

Tip. If more than one doctor prescribes drugs for you, work with one pharmacy to fill prescriptions, even if the cost is a few dollars more for some items. With one pharmacist monitoring your complete medication record, it is more likely that allergic reactions and dangerous interactions can be prevented.

Tip. To save money, when filling a new prescription, consider asking for an initial one- or two-day supply to check for side effects. You're only charged for the few pills instead of filling the entire prescription. If there is no adverse reaction, you can pick up the remainder of the prescription in a day or two.

Tip. If you belong to an MCO, are under the care of a hospital-based doctor, or are being treated at a hospital clinic, you may be able to purchase drugs from the MCO or the hospital pharmacy at a discount.

Tip. If the prescription is a refill and the drug looks different from the ones you took before, ask for an explanation. It may be another manufacturer's version of the same drug, or it may be a mistake.

6.3 Mail Order Drugs

A growing alternative to purchasing drugs from a local pharmacy is ordering them through the mail. In addition to convenience, people are using these services when they want to assure confidentiality about their condition. Prescriptions by mail may be, but are not always, cheaper than a local pharmacy. Some of the mail order companies have the safeguard of computerized medication profiles that protect against drug abuse and potentially serious drug interaction. If you are considering using a mail order pharmacy, find out

- the prices of the various drugs you need.
- what to do until the medicine arrives in the mail.
- what to do if the medicine doesn't arrive.
- what to do if your supplies run out.
- what happens if the pharmacy's supply of the drug runs out.
- if the mail order pharmacy accepts your insurance.
- if confidentiality is an issue, what the packaging looks like in which drugs would be delivered.
- if a pharmacist or other expert is available to monitor the drugs you are taking, to check for improper combinations, and to answer your questions.
- if the pharmacy has computerized medication profiles to protect against potentially serious drug interactions.

You can locate a mail order pharmacy through your physician or your GuardianOrg. There are many reputable companies in the field. Large national companies include: AARP Pharmacy Service (800-456-2277), and you don't have to be a member of American Association of Retired Persons to access the pharmacy; Community Prescription Service (800-842-0502); Stadtlanders Pharmacy (800-238-7828); and STAT Script Pharmacy (800-869-6593).The Veterans Administration has a mail order pharmacy for veterans. If your insurance

coverage requires you to make a copayment or pay a percentage, ask whether the pharmacy will waive the requirement.

6.4 Buyers' Clubs

Buyers' clubs provide access to experimental drugs, foreign drugs, or alternative therapies. Some buyers' clubs provide access to marijuana. Buyers' clubs can also be an unbiased source of opinion about various drugs and treatments. Your doctor, support group, or GuardianOrg can point you in the right direction if such a club exists for your condition.

6.5 Drugs from Foreign Countries

Medicines in Mexico can be one-quarter of the cost of the same drugs in the United States. However, drugs made outside the United States are not subject to the Food and Drug Administration's rigorous standards. Some drugs may be the same as those made here, but it is not a sure thing. If you do decide to purchase drugs from abroad, be careful about what you buy and from whom.

6.6 Insurance

Check your insurance coverage to determine whether prescription drugs are covered. If they are, there may be a deductible and/or a copayment. If drugs are not sufficiently covered, look for a health plan that is better for you. If you cannot realistically switch, this is a good time to start setting money aside to cover the cost of essential drugs.

6.7 Medicare/Medicaid

Medicare does not cover drugs, but supplemental "MediGap" policies are available to cover this expense. Medicare+Choice plans also cover drugs. Medicaid does cover prescription drugs.

6.8 If You Can't Afford a Drug

- Talk with your doctor and social worker. They may have ideas for you.
- Explore patient-assistance programs run by drug companies by calling them directly. Call for a free copy of *The Patients Assistance Directory,* which lists asset requirements and free drugs available from various manufacturers (800-762-4636). The Pharmaceutical Manufacturers' Association (202-835-3400) and the Senate Aging Committee (202-224-5364) have lists of free drug programs. For a list of free HIV drug programs, contact the Treatment Data Network (800-734-7104).
- Look for state or local programs that will pay or health clinics that will provide the drugs. Call your state health department or your local GuardianOrg. Veterans without negative discharges are eligible for drugs at a cost of $2 per prescription when prescribed by VA doctors.

6.9 Taxes

Prescription drugs are deductible as "medical expenses" for income tax purposes if the appropriate threshold amount is satisfied (see chapter 18).

6.10 Take Care

Drugs may have serious effects on your activities. If you fall asleep and cause an auto accident, the fact that the drugs were prescribed will not shield you from financial liability. Drugs and exercise can also be a hazardous combination. For example, aspirin and tranquilizers mask pain that should warn you when to stop. Elizabeth R. tore a ligament because she didn't feel pain's warning signals.

If you generally practice safe sex, be particularly careful when having sex while taking drugs that may loosen your inhibitions, such as painkillers or tranquilizers.

Consult with your doctor about the drugs you are taking, including over-the-counter drugs, and how they may impact your lifestyle.

Section 7. Over-the-Counter Drugs

There is a growing trend to convert drugs from prescription-only to over-the-counter sales. While direct access to these drugs may lower your costs and increase your ability to manage your health, it also increases the risk of misuse. Just because a drug is available without a prescription doesn't mean it is harmless, or that it won't adversely interact with other drugs you are taking.

Any self-prescribed drug inherently has risks to consider:

- You may have misdiagnosed yourself.
- Certain side effects may be dangerous for you.
- Adverse interactions with prescriptions or chemotherapy.
- Developing a harmful dependence.

Before taking any over-the-counter drugs, check with your health care provider, and do your own research as described earlier in this chapter as if the drug were a prescription drug. At the least, check with the pharmacist when you purchase any over-the-counter drug you haven't used before.

Tip. Don't rely solely on the labels or inserts that accompany over-the-counter drugs. They don't tell you everything you need to know about using these drugs. You do not save money by purchasing unnecessary, ineffective, or possibly detrimental over-the-counter drugs.

Tip. It is often advisable to purchase single-ingredient over-the-counter drugs. Compare the cost of the single-ingredient drugs against the multi-ingredient drug.

Taxes. Over-the-counter drugs are not currently considered tax deductible.

Section 8. Experimental Drugs— Clinical Trials

8.1 In General

If you are not satisfied with the current drugs on the market, or they are not working for you, you may want to consider experimental drugs produced by reputable manufacturers conducting studies known as **clinical trials.** The National Cancer Institute defines a clinical trial as "an organized study conducted in people with [a health condition] to answer specific questions about a new treatment or a new way of using an old treatment." Each study is designed to find new and better ways to help patients.

Anyone who wants to access unproven drugs should do so through controlled clinical trials overseen by the federal Food and Drug Administration. Before a new drug or treatment is tried with patients, it is carefully studied in the laboratory. Nevertheless, this research cannot predict exactly how a new treatment will work with patients.

Eligibility for studies in different phases depends on the type and stage of your condition, and what therapy, if any, you have already had.

Clinical trials are divided into three basic groups.

In *Phase I,* the earliest stage of a drug's development, the safety and dosage level are tested in a small number of people. Phase I trials do not occur until enough laboratory evidence indicates that the drug will be safe for use by people. There may still be significant risk. Admission is generally offered only to patients whose condition cannot be helped by other known treatments. If the drug appears to be safe, it moves to Phase II.

Phase II is designed to find out if the treatment actually controls the condition in people. The trial monitors treatment response as well as side effects. If the drug is effective, it moves into a Phase III trial.

Phase III is conducted with a larger number of patients. It reveals the percentage of patients in which the drug is effective and further illuminates side effects. This phase compares the standard treatments with treatments that appeared to be effective in the Phase II studies.

If a clinical trial shows that one trial treatment is superior to another trial treatment, the trial is stopped and patients in each group are given the preferred treatment.

In a clinical trial, results observed in patients getting the treatment are compared with the results in similar patients receiving a different treatment or a **placebo** (inactive) treatment. Generally, if a patient in a trial does not receive the new treatment, he or she at least receives the standard treatment. *No one is given a placebo without being informed prior to entering the study that it is a possibility.*

Generally, neither the patient nor the researchers know who is receiving the therapy under study as opposed to the placebo. Since, by its nature, a clinical trial is a study of a new drug, it is not a proven therapy and it doesn't necessarily work. Only a small fraction of new drugs tested are proven safe and effective. With any new treatment there may be risks, some unknown, and some that may be permanent and serious, even life-threatening. In each case, the unavoidable risks of your condition should be weighed against the potential risks and benefits of a new research treatment.

The ethical and legal codes that govern medical practice apply to clinical trials. In addition, most clinical research is federally regulated or federally funded (at least in part), with built-in safeguards for patients. For example, federally funded and regulated clinical trials must first be approved by an **institutional review board** at the institution or group where the study is to take place. These boards protect patients. They review the study to see that it is well designed with safeguards for patients, and that the risks are reasonable in relation to the potential benefits.

Participants in a clinical trial must be volunteers. People may participate with the hope for a cure for their condition, a longer time to live, a way to feel better, or to contribute to a research effort that may help others. All patients in a clinical trial are carefully monitored during a trial and followed up afterward.

Each trial must be judged on its own merits. Some trials may not be in your best interest because they require that you stop taking other medications that are helping your condition. If there is more than one trial for a drug of interest to you, look at each one for **protocol design,** the ground rules for that trial. You may prefer the methodology of one over the other.

8.2 Costs

Usually, participating in a clinical trial costs nothing, although you may pay for blood or other ongoing tests. If there are costs, check your insurance policy to determine if it has a specific exclusion for "experimental treatment." If it's not clear, ask your insurer. Many companies handle new treatments case by case, rather than having a blanket policy.

If participation requires hospitalization that is not covered by the study, request hospital precertification from your insurance carrier as soon as possible. Ask the trial or hospital to set a target date for the procedure and give it to the insurer so the insurer has a deadline for making a decision.

Talk to your doctor about the paperwork to be submitted to your insurer. Often the way the doctor describes a treatment can help or hurt your chances of insurance coverage. Have your doctor and the hospital send an information package to the insurer that includes studies supporting the procedure's safety, benefits, and acceptance by the medical community.

If you need financial aid to participate, contact your GuardianOrg. Also let the people conducting the trial know; they may know of funding sources for their trial or cover the expenses themselves.

8.3 Before Joining Clinical Trials

Read everything you can about the drug and the trial, and discuss the drug and protocol design with your physician, preferably your specialist. Also ask the sponsors of the trial

- whether you are eligible to join.
- the purpose of the study.
- what kind of tests and treatments the study involves and how they are done.
- what is likely to happen in your case with, or without, this new treatment.
- what are the other choices and their advantages and disadvantages.
- how the study could affect your daily life.
- what side effects you can expect from the study.
- how long the study will last.
- if you will have to be hospitalized. If so, how often and for how long? Is it clear that you will not be charged for the hospitalization?
- if you will have any costs.
- if you are harmed as a result of the research, what treatment would you be entitled to and in what setting.
- what type of long-term follow-up care is part of the study.

Tip. Before agreeing to participate in a clinical trial, consider that you may receive a placebo. If joining the trial requires discontinuing current medication, or not starting other proven medication, what could happen to your condition in the meantime?

8.4 Informed Consent

If you agree to take part in a clinical trial, you will be asked to sign an **informed consent form.** This form verifies that you have received all of the information necessary to make your decision, including the trial's potential benefits and risks. Before you sign, understand what risks you face. Ask the doctor or nurse to explain any parts of the form or the trial that are not clear. *Even if you sign the form, you are free to leave the trial at any time* and can receive other available medical care.

If you join a trial, be aware that informed consent is ongoing. You should continue to receive any new information about the treatment that may affect your willingness to stay in the trial.

8.5 Locating Clinical Trials

Consult

- your doctor or a doctor who knows your case.
- your GuardianOrg.
- other people with your condition.
- publications aimed at people with your condition or that just list clinical trials relating to your condition (see the resources section).
- the drug companies directly. Their phone numbers are in the *Physicians' Desk Reference,* available in most libraries.
- the Internet.

Cancer trials. Cancer patients can determine eligibility for a clinical trial by contacting the Cancer Information Service at 800-4-CANCER or www.icic.nci.nih.gov., a comprehensive information service sponsored by the National Cancer Institute that helps patients search for appropriate clinical trials. Currently, more than fifteen hundred clinical trials are in this database.

HIV/AIDS Trials. People with HIV/AIDS can call the AIDS Clinical Trial Information Service at 800-874-2572 or www.actis.org. The service has a video, *HIV/AIDS Clinical Trials: Knowing Your Options,* for $15. Another source of HIV/AIDS information is the CDC National AIDS Clearinghouse at 800-458-5231, which has several free brochures on clinical trials.

8.6 Obtaining a New Drug Other Than Through a Clinical Trial.

Drug companies sometimes make experimental drugs available to individuals outside of a clinical trial. One means of accessing these drugs is through **compassionate use,** an exception made for individuals case by case, when, for example, a person has no further treatment options. Another alternative is through **expanded access** programs, which give an experimental drug to individuals who fit a certain medical profile. As with clinical trials, there is usually no charge for drugs obtained in this manner.

Section 9. Alternative Medicine and Treatments

9.1 In General

Alternative medicine and treatments include any medical practice or intervention that lacks sufficient governmentally recognized proof of safety and/or effectiveness against a specific disease or condition. The administration of these drugs or treatments is not generally taught in U.S. medical schools and not generally covered by health insurance providers.

According to a study in the *New England Journal of Medicine,* in 1990 one in three patients used alternative therapies, many of which were developed in the East—such as acupuncture, stress reduction techniques, and yoga—and natural products such as green algae and special diets.

Alternative or complementary treatments can be an expensive drain on your budget and must be approached with caution since there are so many frauds who just want to make money from people in your situation.

If you want to use an alternative treatment, it is best to do so through a clinical trial. As discussed above, clinical trials are regulated by the FDA and provide safeguards for patients.

If a clinical trial is not available, before getting involved in any alternative therapy, the NIH Office of Alternative Medicine recommends the following:

- Obtain objective information about the therapy. Talk with people who have gone through the treatment recently, and those treated in the past. Ask about the risks, side effects, results, and over what time span results can be expected.
- Inquire about the training and expertise of the person administering the treatment.
- Consider the costs (in both Life Units and money).
- Discuss the idea with your primary care provider. The doctor will probably have information for you, even if he does not like the idea of alternative treatments. If nothing else, the doctor needs to know what you are doing to have a complete picture of your treatment plan.

In addition, when deciding whether to try an alternative medicine or treatment, tailor the questions in section 2 to the medicine or treatment under consideration. Your GuardianOrg may also have valuable information for you.

Caution. While most alternative medicines and treatments appear to be harmless
- be sure to watch for negative reactions.
- if you postpone proven medicines and/or treatments while you take the alternatives, be sure to understand whether there is any risk, and if so, what it might be. For example, while a cancer patient rejects proven therapies in favor of unproved ones, a condition can advance beyond the point where proven therapies can help.

Tip. If you have cancer, an admirable analysis of alternative treatments is contained in *Choices in Healing* by Michael Lerner (Cambridge: MIT Press, 1994).

Insurance. While most insurance and managed care contracts do not cover alternative treatments, as of this writing more companies are beginning to cover them. If you want to explore any drug or treatment, contact your insurance carrier or your managed care company to find out if they cover complementary or alternative treatments, and if so, which ones and to what extent.

9.2 Herbs

Centuries of anecdotal evidence and a number of recent formal studies indicate that certain herbs *may* be beneficial to health. On the other hand, the U.S. Food and Drug Administration has identified a number of herbs that can cause serious harm.

There are no standardized sources of information. If herbs are of interest to you, you will have to assess the available information as best you can.

Knowing what an herb is supposed to do is just the beginning. The odds are you will not have access to the herb in its natural state and will have to purchase it, generally in pill form. Herbs are classified as "dietary supplements" and as such are *not* regulated by the Food and Drug Administration. Because of the lack of regulation, there is no guarantee that herbal pills are what they say they are.

Products go to market with no testing for efficacy. There is no way of knowing if a plant's active ingredients, whatever they are, have ended up in the herbal pills you purchase, what else is in the pills, whether they are safe, or whether the dosage is correct in general, much less correct for you. Since there are no quality controls or standard manufacturing requirements, you can't even be sure that the pills are the same within a bottle, or from bottle to bottle.

Before taking herbs.
- Consider changes to your diet or lifestyle that might accomplish your goals without taking the herbs.
- Determine what the herb is supposed to do.
- Do your own research to determine minimum and maximum dosages and possible risks.
- Check with your doctor before taking any herbs. A supplement may interact negatively with a

drug you take or pose a serious side effect. For example, when you receive chemotherapy and suppress your immune system, herbs can kill you because they may contain fungi and bacteria that are hard to isolate and treat. The doctor may know of a conventional treatment that you should try first.

- Do not rely on the printing on the package or in pamphlets. Supplements are prohibited from claiming to cure or prevent a disease, but the label is permitted to detail how a supplement affects the body's "structure of function" as long as claims are "truthful and not misleading." Label statements may not have a lot of evidence backing them up. FDA approval is not needed for package or marketing claims.
- A **naturopathic physician** (a physician who has studied natural remedies) can put you in touch with the herbs and other natural treatments that are the most reliable.

Consumer Reports did a study in this area and also recommends:

- Pregnant and nursing women should not take herbal supplements unless their doctor gives the green light.
- Check the warnings on packages and related material. Start with small doses.
- Buy herbs that at least claim to be "standardized."
- Stick to single-herb products, not combinations whose actions are difficult to sort out.
- Be alert to the herb's effects, both positive and negative.
- Stop immediately if there is a problem, and call your doctor.

Tip. More expensive is not necessarily better—and this applies particularly to herbs.

Section 10. Health Supplements

Many people fight **wasting** (rapid weight loss caused by their health condition) and other life-challenging conditions by using food supplements to build up lean-body mass. Before starting to take any of these supplements, or continuing them:

- Check with your doctor to see what he thinks of the supplement you are considering, and whether it impacts negatively on your situation or any drugs you may be taking.
- Supplements should not and cannot replace a balanced diet.
- Read labels to see if the items have been tested in a double-blind placebo control trial. If that information is not on the label, call the manufacturer and ask for detailed references and abstracts that back up the claims. Also look at the proportion of sugar to protein to ensure that the product is not all fizz and no substance.

Section 11. Treatments

11.1 Decisions

See the discussion in section 2 for considerations to think about before deciding to undergo *any* treatment.

11.2 Surgery ↑↑↑

Questions to ask *before* you agree to have surgery. To ensure that surgery is necessary and/or to maximize chances of success, ask the following questions of your physician or the proposed surgeon:

The operation
- Where will the operation be done? If in a hospital, what has their track record been with this type of operation? Can it be done on an outpatient basis? If so, what would be involved?
- What kind of anesthesia will be needed, and what are the qualifications of the person who will be giving it? Will any of the drugs you are taking, or your allergies, affect your response to the anesthesia?

- In general, what is the success rate for this operation?
- What are the likelihood and nature of complications, if any?

After surgery

- Are there likely to be residual effects from the operation?
- What is the estimated duration of the postoperative hospitalization?
- How long will it take to recover? When can you go back to work? Resume normal exercise? What kind of scar will be left after healing?
- What kind of supplies, equipment, and other help will be needed when you get home?

Choosing a surgeon. If you agree to surgery, choose your surgeon just as you would any other physician (see chapter 24). A good sign of a surgeon's competence is certification by a surgical board that is approved by the American Board of Medical Specialties. It also helps to find out how many surgeries of the type under consideration the surgeon has performed in the past year. If possible, speak with a friend or acquaintance who works in the hospital where the surgeon operates to learn what the insiders in the hospital think of the surgeon. Hospital disciplinary actions are not made public, but people in the hospital usually have the facts.

Tip. When you sign consent papers for the surgeon, be sure the consent requires that the surgeon be present at, if not actually perform, the surgery. If the papers say "doctor Y *or* his associates *or* assistants," you may end up with the associates or assistants in the operating room, rather than doctor Y. If the doctor wants other doctors to help, the consent should read, "Dr. X *and* associates" or "*and* assistants." The *and* assures the doctor will be present at the surgery.

Preparing for surgery. Studies show that knowing what to expect before, during, and after surgery reduces anxiety and fear about an operation and even improves overall recovery. Learn about what happens during the operation, what to expect while you are recuperating in the hospital, and what to expect when you return home.

- You will be asked to sign consent forms prior to the procedure. Ask to see the form at least a week ahead of time so you can review it and discuss any problems you may have with it. Before signing, make and initial any changes you want.
- Be sure your advance directives are up-to-date.
- Prepare your home. For example, if the operation will temporarily impair your balance, move throw rugs and otherwise clear paths.

Tip. If you schedule surgery for first thing in the morning, you'll sleep through the hours you can't eat.

Limit preoperative tests. Surgery patients are often subjected to a variety of "standard" preoperative tests, many of which may be unnecessary for any particular operation. Ask your doctor to review the suggested tests and limit them to the essential ones. Remind him of any recent tests that were taken before entering the hospital. If blood has to be drawn, make sure they use one sample for all tests that require blood.

11.3 Chemotherapy ↑↑↑

Chemotherapy is the use of drugs to treat a disease, particularly cancer. Because some drugs work better together than alone, chemotherapy may often consist of more than one drug (**combination chemotherapy**).

You may get chemotherapy at home, in your doctor's office, in a clinic, in your hospital's outpatient department, or in a hospital. The choice of where you get chemotherapy depends on which drug or drugs you are getting, your hospital's policies, and your doctor's preferences. When you first start chemotherapy, you may need to stay at the hospital for a short time so that your doctor can watch the medicine's effects closely and make adjustments.

As with any other therapy, you do not have to agree to undergo chemotherapy. However, if you do agree, understand the various drugs that could be used, and their potential side effects.

A comprehensive booklet on the subject is "Chemotherapy and You, a Guide to Self-Help During Treatment," published by the National Cancer Institute, which covers coping with side effects, eating well during chemotherapy, talking with your doctor and nurse, chemotherapy and your emotions, how to make your daily life easier, and paying for chemotherapy. A free copy can be obtained by calling the National Cancer Institute at 301-496-4000, or write to the National Cancer Institute, 31 Center Drive, MCS 2580, Bethesda, MD 20892-2580 (publication no. 96-1136).

Once you have agreed on a given course, be sure the drug you are receiving is the correct drug. For example, several of the drugs share the letters *platin,* but the difference in effect can be substantial. Also be sure to follow the prescribed course.

Tip. If possible, schedule your treatments right before the weekend so they interfere with work as little as possible.

11.4 Radiation Therapy

Radiation is a special kind of energy carried by waves or a stream of particles. It can come from special machines or from radioactive substances. Many years ago doctors learned how to use this energy to see inside the body and find disease. A chest X ray or X-ray pictures of your teeth or your bones are examples of the use of radiation. At high doses (many times those used for X-ray exams), radiation can be used to treat cancer and other illnesses. Special equipment is used to aim the radiation at tumors or areas of the body where there is disease. The use of high-energy rays or particles to treat disease is called **radiation therapy** (also known as **X-ray therapy, cobalt therapy, electron beam therapy,** or **irradiation.**)

Radiation therapy is an effective way to treat many kinds of cancer or other disease in almost any part of the body. It is given alone or in combination with surgery, chemotherapy, or biological therapy. A doctor who has had special training in using radiation to treat disease will prescribe the type and amount of treatment that best suits the patient's needs.

Treatment with radiation can be costly. It requires complex equipment and the services of many health care professionals. Most health insurance policies, including Part B of Medicare, cover charges for radiation therapy. In some states, the Medicaid program may pay for treatments. Financial aid referrals may be available from the hospital (contact the social service office), the Cancer Information Service (800-422-6237), or the local office of the American Cancer Society.

An excellent guide is "Radiation Therapy and You" (publication no. 95-2227), a free booklet available from the National Cancer Institute (see section 11.3). It covers what radiation therapy is, how it works, the risks, what to expect with external or internal radiation therapy, managing side effects, and follow-up care.

11.5 Unproven Treatments

If FDA-approved drugs or treatments are not working, many people with chronic or life-challenging conditions will turn to nonapproved drugs that are often touted as "cures." The FDA-approved system is not all-seeing and all-knowing, and some drugs not approved in this country may be safe and effective against a specific disease or condition. Or the so-called drugs may just be good old-fashioned rip-offs in new clothing.

Before considering an unproven medical treatment. The FDA notes some red flags to watch out for:

- Claims that the product works by a secret formula.
- Publicity only in the back pages of magazines, over the phone, by direct mail, in newspaper ads in the format of news stories, or infomer-

cials in talk show format (especially with no citation to studies published in credible medical journals).

- Claims that the product is an amazing or miraculous breakthrough.
- Promises of a quick, painless, guaranteed cure.
- Testimonials from satisfied customers.

Additional tips.

- Be careful of what source you use to assess a drug or treatment. Newspaper reports about a new breakthrough may be blown out of proportion. The articles are usually based on a press release from a person or company that has a financial or other interest in the product and on a limited test on a small number of people (such as twenty-five) and/or conducted over a short time. These reports can be used as progress and research markers but not as facts on which to base decisions.
- If you have to go abroad, or if an inpatient stay is required to protect the secrecy of the treatment, be skeptical.
- If they don't tell you the downside or the unsuccessful-treatment rate, something is wrong.
- If you ask questions of the promoters and don't understand the answers, have your medical expert talk with them on your behalf.

- If a drug or treatment is experimental, and yet you are being asked to pay for the drug, stay away. Just after the breakup of Russia, I was approached to help enroll clients in a "study" of an electromagnetic device supposedly developed for the Russian military that would "zap" a deadly virus in a person's body. The data supplied included letters from a doctor in Switzerland and testimonials from satisfied patients. While it was supposed to be a study, participants were to fly to Europe for the test at their own expense and pay "only" $10,000 to participate.
- Contact your GuardianOrg to determine what they know about the drug or treatment.

Insurance. It is unlikely that any unapproved drug or treatment will be paid for by your health insurance. Still, if you want to try such a drug, review your insurance coverage.

Tip. When you look at data regarding an unproved drug or treatment, remember that use of an unconventional treatment may simply coincide with remission or a lessening of symptoms due to completely different factors. The only way to trust results is with a controlled trial that includes enough people over a long enough time. *If it sounds too good to be true—it probably is.*

Chapter 26

Nutrition and Exercise

Our lives are not in the lap of the gods, but in the lap of our cooks.
—Lin Yutang, "On Food and Medicine"

Good nutrition and exercise are even more important to your health than to people without any health concerns.

Section 1. Nutrition

Good daily nutrition helps to decrease your medical costs, increases your income by allowing you to work longer, and contributes to the quality and quantity of your life. On the other hand, if you don't eat well, your natural defenses against illness are weaker. Poor nutrition also prolongs recovery from illnesses and so tends to increase the costs and incidence of hospitalization.

Tip. Think of nutrition as a therapy—one as important as the drugs you may be taking or the treatments you may be undergoing.

Cost. Good nutrition *may* cost you more money than your current eating patterns. The extra expense is not tax deductible as a medical expense if it is merely to improve your general health. However, if your doctor prescribes certain foods for specific conditions, the cost may be deductible.

If you can't prepare your own meals. Organizations across the nation deliver meals to homebound people who need assistance. To identify your local choices, call your GuardianOrg, your church, or the Eldercare Locator Service (800-677-6116). Also see chapter 27, section 3.6.

Food stamps. Individuals living in households that meet income eligibility criteria are permitted to participate in the federally financed, state-run food stamp program, which provides a free coupon allotment, the amount of which varies according to household size and net income. The coupons may be used in participating retail stores to buy food or to have meals delivered by authorized delivery services.

Nutrition that works for you. What nutrition works for you depends on your health condition, your lifestyle, and your exercise. Sources of information are

• your primary care physician, although historically there has not been much emphasis on nutrition in medical schools and your doctor may have only general knowledge on the subject.

- a registered nutritionist, who can tell you about the best diet for you as well as how to use foods to address symptoms that may accompany your condition, treatment, or drug regimen, such as loss of appetite, changed sense of taste or smell, nausea, vomiting, diarrhea, constipation, weight gain, weight loss, and dry mouth.
- your GuardianOrg.
- computer programs and the Internet. Software programs are available to help you analyze your food intake and create an optimal program. There are also sites on the Internet that provide a simple nutritional analysis of different foods. I hope by the time you read this text there will also be sophisticated sites to provide individualized nutritional information.
- the USDA. For free information call 800-535-4555.
- the free book noted below from the National Institutes of Health that is targeted at people with cancer, but the principles apply across the board.

Water. If you want to have your water analyzed, use a state-approved testing laboratory. To find out where you can get a list of such labs, call the Environmental Protection Agency's Safe Drinking Water Hotline at 800-426-4791. For a report on the different treatment systems available for your home and what each protects against, call the National Association of People With AIDS at 202-898-0414 for a free copy of "Should You Be Concerned about Your Drinking Water?"

For cancer. *Eating Hints for Cancer Patients* from the National Institutes of Health, National Cancer Institute, Bethesda, MD. Telephone 800-422-6237 for a free copy.

For HIV/AIDS. *Living with HIV: A Nutrition Guide, Eating Tips for HIV Disease,* published by God's Love We Deliver. Telephone 212-865-6500. Free. *Nutrition and HIV: Your Choices Make a Difference* by Peggy A. Wickwire, M.S.,R.D., available free

from the Division of Nutrition and Supplemental Food Programs, Tennessee Department of Health and Environment, C2-233 Cordell Hull Building, Nashville, TN 37219.

For MS. *Food for Thought: MS and Nutrition,* free from the National Multiple Sclerosis Society at 800-344-4867.

Section 2. Safe Food Handling

Safe food handling is as critical to your health as your food intake. Just because you didn't get sick before doesn't mean you are not at risk now. Each of the following informative publications is free:

- *A Quick Consumer Guide to Safe Food Handling,* U.S. Department of Agriculture, Food Safety and Inspection Service. Call 800-535-4555, 10–4 ET.
- An excellent guide for food storage and handling (as well as how to choose food) is *Eating Hints for Cancer Patients,* described in section 1, which works for everyone, not just people with cancer.
- *Eating Defensively: Food Safety Advice for Persons With AIDS,* U.S. Department of Health and Human Services, DHH publication no. (FDA) 92-2232. Call 202-619-0257.

Section 3. Exercise

Along with good nutrition, regular exercise is important to your health and, of course, your Life Units. It acts as a natural immune booster, helping the body keep infections at bay. Additionally, regular exercise can help reduce stress, anxiety, fatigue, and depression as well as improve sleep patterns and even bowel function. It can also increase appetite.

Any regular physical activity is good, from brisk walking to weight lifting. Participating in a sport is another good way to keep in shape. Common sense is the key.

Ideally, *now* is when exercise should be started. It can be adapted if changing health dictates. Don't overdo exercise. Your body is the best gauge to let you know when you've done too much.

Caution. Speak with your doctor before starting any vigorous exercise program—or restarting after a long period of rest. Then start slowly and work up to an appropriate intensity and frequency. Adjust your exercise program if you begin to lose weight.

Gyms. While not a problem for healthy people, bacteria and fungi at gyms can be a health threat to people with compromised immune systems. If you have a compromised immune system

- stay out of the steam room. It breeds bacteria and promotes dehydration.
- from the moment you start exercise until you wash your hands thoroughly with an antibacterial soap, don't touch your hands to your nose, mouth, ears, or eyes. If you want to be extra safe, wear exercise gloves, or take a box of alcohol or other antibacterial wipes with you. If you can, wipe off the areas you are going to be touching, if not, immediately after use wipe your hands or other exposed skin that has come in contact with equipment.
- never use bar soap from the gym. Bacteria actually breeds in the hot, wet surface of the soap. Take a bottle of antibacterial soap to use at the gym.

Drugs. Drugs and exercise can be a hazardous combination. Consult with your doctor about the drugs you are taking, including over-the-counter drugs, and learn about the risks.

Tip. Especially if you are taking a heavy daily dose of prescription drugs, avoid dehydration by drinking water before, during, and after workouts,

Cost. You don't have to belong to a gym to exercise. You can do plenty of things at home for free. The costs of joining a gym or hiring a personal trainer are not tax deductible or generally covered by insurance. The odds are a free or low-cost public gym and/or pool is nearby.

Tip. Check with your health insurance company for possible arrangements that provide gym-membership-fee discounts, or premium refunds for attending.

Tip. If you are going to join a gym or your membership is up for renewal, find out their policy in case you become ill for a time or are permanently disabled. You should at least be able to put your membership on hold for the duration of a flare-up in your condition. Also, do not renew multiyear memberships without comparing the benefits of banking the money in excess of a one-year membership against the potential future savings.

Chapter 27

Home

The ache for home lives in all of us, the safe place where we can go as we are and not be questioned.

—Maya Angelou

There are legal protections concerning the sale or rental of dwellings and apartments and many resources available to help you live at home.

Section 1. Housing Discrimination

1.1 Federal Protection: The Fair Housing Act

Sales and rentals. The federal Fair Housing Act (FHA) prohibits discrimination against "persons with handicaps" in the sale or rental of housing, or the provision of services or facilities related to housing. Just as with the Americans with Disabilities Act (ADA), courts have ruled that the diagnosis of a life-challenging condition is a "handicap" within the meaning of the law. You do not need to be physically disabled to be protected. Coverage extends not only to a buyer or renter who may be handicapped, but also to any handicapped person intending to reside in the dwelling as well as to any person associated with the buyer or renter who is handicapped.

Again like the ADA, the regulations also prohibit an owner or manager from asking about whether a prospective tenant or purchaser has a handicap or inquiring about the nature or severity of the handicap.

Rental under the FHA covers obtaining and living in a residence under a lease, evictions, and renewals. Typically the discrimination is not outright with people saying, "I'm not going to rent to you because of your diagnosis." Instead, it usually involves techniques that make the protected person feel unwelcome. The list of delaying tactics or procedures includes requiring special down payments or providing false information to keep you from buying or renting. The FHA protects individuals against this type of discrimination.

Covered sales and rentals. The FHA covers the sale of most single-family homes since most sales involve a broker, agent, salesperson, or other individual engaged in the business of renting or selling dwellings. The FHA, however, does not cover either the sale or rental of a single-family home if no such person is involved, the seller owns three or fewer single-family houses at any one time, and the seller does not use any discriminatory advertising or notices.

Sales and rentals of apartments are covered except for owner-occupied rental housing occupied by no more than four families living independently of one another. Other exclusions are

- housing owned by religious organizations.
- private clubs for their members' use.
- certain housing for elderly people.

Steering. One of the actions specifically prohibited is **steering** or attempting to steer. Steering is defined in the statute as a method aimed at directing members of a group into buildings occupied primarily by other members of the same group.

Reasonable accommodation. As with the ADA, reasonable accommodations are required both at the time of entering into a lease and during a tenancy. As a tenant:

- You must be permitted, at your expense, to make reasonable modifications to the leased premises that are necessary to permit you to have full enjoyment of the dwelling. For example, a protected reasonable modification can be a grab bar in the bathroom, widening a doorway, or even lowering kitchen cabinets. The landlord may require the premises be restored back to their original condition, but only if the requirement is reasonable. It would be reasonable for a landlord to require removal of a grab bar when the premises are vacated, but not to raise cabinets the tenant had lowered to accommodate a disability. It may even be reasonable for a landlord to require that money be placed in an escrow account to cover removing those changes when the lease ends.
- You can request reasonable changes in rules, policies, services, or practices when these accommodations are necessary to allow an equal opportunity to use and enjoy the housing. For example, assume an apartment building provides parking on a first-come, first-served basis. It would be a reasonable accommodation to require the landlord to change the policy to pro-

vide reserved parking spaces, close to accessible apartments, for tenants with problems getting around.
- It is not clear at this writing whether a reasonable accommodation involves modifying the common areas of the building to permit access under the Fair Housing Act. The courts have split as to whether this should be a landlord's or a tenant's expense.

Enforcement. There are two means of enforcing your rights under the Fair Housing Act, one of which is totally free.

1. The FHA includes a procedure for filing a complaint at the Fair Housing Department of Housing and Urban Development (HUD), Washington DC 20140, or one of HUD's regional offices, or by calling 800-424-8590. There are also substantially equivalent state or local agencies where rights under state laws are enforced.

Once a complaint is filed, HUD is obligated to investigate, attempt conciliation between you and the landlord/seller, and then either file a charge or dismiss the complaint. The government investigation is conducted at no cost to you, and if the case moves forward, the government supplies free attorneys. You are entitled to have your own counsel if you want. You can win an award to compensate for damages and for penalties, but the penalties are capped. There are *no* punitive damages available if you use this alternative.

2. You can pursue an action through the civil courts. If you win, you can request your attorneys' fees as well as costs, compensatory damage, and punitive damages.

Tip. If you have a claim under the Fair Housing Act, speak with an attorney who specializes in housing discrimination matters. I suggest that you consider filing a complaint with HUD and at least start a civil action at the same time. Let the government spend the money to do the investigation. Then, with the facts the government put together at no cost to you, you can determine whether to pursue a civil action or just seek compensation through the government or both. Your attorney can also advise you regarding the timing for making claims.

1.2 State Laws

State laws in many states mirror the protections of the FHA. To learn about the laws in your state, consult your attorney, your local Legal Aid Society (call the National Legal Aid and Defender Organization at 202-452-0620 if you cannot locate the local number), or your GuardianOrg.

Section 2. Staying in Your Own Home: Factors to Consider

It is generally preferable to stay in your current residence than to move just because of your health. Before deciding what is best for you, consider each of the following factors.

2.1 Accessibility of the Premises

If it is likely that changes will be required in your residence to accommodate your condition, think about making the changes now. You don't want to have to endure plaster dust when you're not feeling well. If reasonable changes cannot be made, you may have to consider moving.

Consider bringing in local experts for a consultation to determine whether reasonable changes can be made to accommodate possible future needs. Initial consultations with architects and with contractors are usually free and will give you an idea of what you face in terms of time and economics.

One excellent resource to help evaluate your premises and provide answers is a booklet that works for a broad range of conditions despite its title: "At Home with MS, Adapting Your Environment." The booklet is available free from the National MS Society by calling 800-FIGHT-MS. Your

state's or city's department of vocational rehabilitation is also likely to have an independent-living program that provides evaluation and advice.

Consider all the alternatives for making your home work. If, for example, you have a two-story house and all the bedrooms are on the second floor, consider making one of the downstairs rooms habitable before tackling access to the second floor. Use your imagination. If it is clear that no modification to your current residence will accommodate your future needs, consider moving—even though it may be emotionally and financially difficult.

2.2 Availability of Medical Treatment

Accessibility to your physician(s) and/or treatment centers is also an important factor to consider. Rural areas, for example, may not have the ability or the equipment to treat a specialized situation.

Do not limit yourself to the closest medical center. This can be the opportunity to move to the place that is best for your physical and emotional health. You may even consider moving to a country such as Canada or England that provides universal health care to everyone.

As you will see in section 3 below, many medical services are available at home through home health care.

2.3 Your Finances

Refer back to your financial picture, created in chapter 4. If you are not going to have enough money to continue living in your current residence, this is the time to start looking for a new residence. Even if you don't make the move now, examining the alternatives and establishing a game plan enables you to act quickly and smoothly, with less stress and expense, if and when the time comes.

Tip. If you can't afford housing, housing assistance programs aid low-income persons with disabilities. Speak with your local GuardianOrg, social worker, or your state or local human services agency.

Caution. Before you make a move, consider
- access to appropriate affordable health care in the candidate location.
- both the costs of health care and your new living facility.
- moving costs.
- traveling expenses for friends and family to visit you and/or for you to visit them.

Tip. A variety of **property tax deferral programs** are offered by state and local governments to provide loans to pay property taxes. These loans do not generally have to be repaid until the borrower dies, moves, or sells the residence. Generally, there is an age requirement, such as sixty-five, but they may also apply to a person with a disability. It's worth checking.

Public housing. If you anticipate that you may require government-subsidized housing, start applying as soon as possible. Before you apply, contact state or local agencies serving people with disabilities to find out if you may be entitled to a preference on any waiting list because of your condition.

Tip. It is a good idea to have the help of a case manager or housing advocate when applying for public housing.

2.4 Emotional Considerations

When contemplating a move, consider the emotional costs (or benefits) of relocating to a new place and any other matters that are personal to you. Will moving take you far from, or perhaps bring you closer to, friends and family, or a community with which you have strong ties?

Section 3. Home Health Care

We are experiencing a shift from hospital-based care to home-based health care. With advances in home health care, it is now possible for people with a great variety of medical needs to be cared for competently at home. Home care is usually less expensive than care in a hospital or nursing home (unless a patient needs a good deal of nursing care) and includes the additional comfort of being in your own surroundings. Your home is probably a more personal, tranquil, healthier environment than is found in most health care facilities, and you are likely to feel better there both psychologically and physically. Home care also provides greater continuity of care than the episodic care provided in a hospital.

Professional managers. If you need assistance in making arrangements for care at home, you may be able to locate a local care manager by calling the National Association of Professional Private Geriatric Care Managers at 520-881-8008.

3.1 Home Care Providers

Types of home care. There are three general types of home care. Only the third type has a standardized title:
- **Attendant care** (also known as **homemaker care**) provides such services as cleaning, laundry, cooking, and shopping. It can also include a caregiver in the home while a family member or partner is at work.
- **Nursing/infusion therapy** includes attendant care plus skilled nurses to the extent needed, including **infusions** (treatment delivered into the body through a vein over time), which until recently were only performed in a hospital.
- **Hospice care** is focused on comfort, rather than fighting disease.

Home-care workers. While there are also no standardized names for home-care workers, the following people provide services at home:

• **Personal care attendant or home attendant.** Bathes, grooms, prepares meals and feeds, toilets, does housework, laundry, household management, and drives for the patient. A personal care attendant is generally not covered by private insurance, although some insurance companies will pay **out of contract** (that is, pay for items not covered in the policy) for home attendant care if they understand that it will keep someone out of the much more expensive hospital.

This type of care may be covered in long-term-care insurance policies. It may be covered by Medicaid and by Medicare if medically necessary, for example, when this kind of care is necessary to avoid assisted-living or nursing homes. It may also be covered when it is provided as an extra service by the company that provides home medical care.

• **Home health aide.** Provides limited personal care, light housework, laundry, and shopping. May be covered by Medicaid, Medicare, or private insurance but rarely for **maintenance care** (routine care over a long period). The aide usually works for a home health agency.

• **Homemaker or housekeeping.** Does housework, cooking, laundry, errands, shopping, and similar chores. Homemakers seldom provide personal services. They can be hired through a home health agency, a domestic service agency, or privately and are not covered by public or private insurance.

• **Respite care.** Often provided by a home health agency, a person who provides **respite care** gives relief, also known as respite, to the primary caregiver. While many of your needs may be provided by family members or friends, even the most dedicated caregiver needs relief. Respite care may be covered by private insurance. It is not covered separately by Medicare or Medicaid.

• **Professional services.** Professionals who do nursing, physical therapy, nutrition, and the like. Usually a doctor's prescription is required. Your "physician of record" must agree that you meet the criteria for home health care. Nursing/infusion care is generally covered by health insurance, but check your policy to make sure. See the discussion on Medicare and Medicaid in chapter 15.

• **Physician.** Your primary care physician or specialist will remain in close contact with your home care team to monitor your care, but will probably not make daily or regular visits to your home as the other team members do. These services are covered by insurance and government programs.

Tip. Review your health insurance policy, long-term-care coverage, Medicare, or Medicaid to determine what care is covered and to what extent. *A good home care agency can do this for you.*

Tip. Some states have adopted home care options for elderly people with disabilities. If you are over sixty-five, you may qualify.

3.2 Attendant Care

You can either hire people yourself or engage a company that provides the personnel for you.

Hiring attendants yourself. If you hire an attendant, a home health aide, or a homemaker yourself, you can usually obtain help in locating the person you need through a **registry,** a service that matches your needs to their roster of available people. Keep in mind that staff selected from registries are generally not supervised, except by you. Whether the registry checks references and training depends on the registry, since registries are generally not subject to regulation.

Before hiring anyone to work in your home.
• Contact the Multiple Sclerosis Society at 800-FIGHT-MS, for a free copy of "Facts & Issues, Hiring Help at Home." The article provides general advice as well as guides for helping to hire the person or people right for you. It even includes a proposed employment agreement.

- You may be required to withhold taxes. For household help, an employer is required to withhold taxes for each domestic employee who is paid more than $1,000 per year. Household workers under age eighteen are exempt from withholding unless the individual's principal occupation is household service. There is no withholding if the person is working as an "independent contractor" instead of as an employee. If you believe the person falls in the independent contractor category, check with your tax adviser to be sure. The definition of an independent contractor for tax purposes is complicated, and the penalties are severe if you are wrong.
- Find out about the workers' compensation laws in your state. You may have an obligation to provide this insurance, even if the person is an independent contractor rather than an employee, and even if he is hired by another company. Contact your state department of labor.
- If a home care provider is going to move into your residence, include a provision in a written contract that the right to live in your residence is conditioned on their employment, which is terminable **at will** (a legal phrase for "able to terminate at any time").
- Look at your homeowners and other personal insurance coverage to find out whether you are covered against theft by a live-in employee and against liability if that person injures himself or someone else in a manner that may result in your being responsible. Ask your insurance broker for advice. If the live-in is an employee of a company, ask if he is **bonded** (has insurance to cover you in the event of theft). Of course, whether there is coverage or not, do not leave cash, jewelry, or other valuables accessible. They may be covered but irreplaceable.

An agency. An agency can provide and supervise the people you need to work in your home. These agencies are usually licensed or certified by the state. Their aides often have some formal training and are supervised by the agency. Sometimes these providers are related to a licensed home care provider, but are set up as separate entities so they are not necessarily subject to the same rules as their sister organizations.

Always confirm agency licensing with your state licensing bureau. Home-health-agency hot lines in each state are authorized under the nursing home reform law to gather complaints on agencies and disseminate information to the public. The Health Care Financing Administration administers the Medicare program and has an inspection program for Medicare-certified home-health agencies. Contact your state department of social services.

Locating registries or service companies. Your doctor/specialist, your insurance company, and your GuardianOrg are good places to start in locating the services you need. Other good sources are a hospital discharge planner; community social service agencies such as the United Way; religious organizations; your state's departments of health, aging, and social services; the National Association for Home Care, 228 Seventh Street SE, Washington, DC 20003 (202-547-7424 or www.nahc.org); or call the Eldercare Locator at 800-677-1116, M–F, 9 A.M. to 8 P.M. EST.

3.3 Nursing/Infusion Home Care

Choosing a company. The National Association for Home Care emphasizes the need for quality, availability of services, and expertise. The following checklist reviews issues to consider when choosing a home care company. You can decide which of the following are important to you.

Credentials and reputation.
- Check the agency's credentials for state and/or federal licensing and Medicare certification by phoning the Joint Commission on Accreditation of Health Care Organizations at 630-916-5600, the Community Health Accreditation Program at 800-847-8480, or the National HomeCaring Council at 202-547-6586.

• How long has the agency been serving the community of people with your condition?

The level of care.

• Does the agency have a written description of services?
• Will it create an individualized plan of care for you in writing? The plan should list which specific tasks are to be carried out by each caregiver.
• Is service available twenty-four hours a day, seven days a week? If you need assistance in the middle of the night, will they respond and, if so, within what amount of time?
• Can they accommodate your schedule?
• If you reside in more than one location, can the agency cover you in both places? If not, are they equipped to coordinate your care with another company that can serve the other location?
• If you decide to travel, does the company have branches in other cities?
• Does the agency supervise the quality of home care patients receive?
• Will the company monitor your home treatment and provide the educational training needed if you decide to administer some treatments yourself?
• If your condition could require periodic X rays or dialysis, is the agency equipped to do X rays or dialysis in your home?
• How does the provider assure patient confidentiality?

Personnel.

• Does the company employ licensed personnel or do they subcontract with outside agencies? You may be dealing with one company but another company supplies the service.
• Are there social workers on staff trained to address psychological issues?
• Are the agency's nurses or therapists required to evaluate the patient's home-care needs?
• How does the agency select and train its employees?

Money issues.

• What is the cost of daily and monthly treatment?
• Will your insurance/managed care company/Medicare/Medicaid cover the cost in full? If you're supposed to pay part of the costs, will the company accept partial payment from the insurer and/or government agency or require you to make coinsurance payments?
• Will the company bill the insurance company directly? If so, how do you keep track?

For a list of accrediting agencies and resources in your state, contact the National Association for Home Care, 228 Seventh Street SE, Washington, DC 20003 (202-547-7424).

Maximizing use of home nursing infusion care. Once you choose the home health care agency, it will receive instructions from and be supervised with respect to your medical care by your physician. It is up to you to instruct and supervise the agency about your other needs.

Evaluating home nursing/infusion care. *Be positive while dealing with your health care people since your care depends on their attitude toward you.* Nevertheless, stay alert for such problems as

• poor work habits (lateness or absence, leaving early, doing just enough to get by).
• indifferent or rough care.
• untrustworthy behavior.
• toilets, bedpans, or bathtubs that are not cleaned.
• inadequate patient hygiene care.

Tip. Consider asking a friend or family member to help you monitor the quality of the services and perhaps give them authority to speak with the person in charge on your behalf if a problem crops up. It may be to your advantage to have someone else play the "bad guy" should problems arise.

If there are problems. Speak directly to the person involved, then his or her supervisor, and finally, when you consider it appropriate, the complaint should be made a matter of public record with the appropriate regulatory agency, your GuardianOrg, and the local Better Business Bureau. If a case involves the delivery of Medicare home care services, contact the Office of the Inspector General Hotline at 800-HHS-TIPS.

Do not hesitate to change agencies if you are not satisfied. You have the right to be treated with dignity and respect, to participate in the planning of your care, to be notified of and consulted on any changes before they occur, to complete confidentiality, and to the highest-quality care.

3.4 Medical Equipment at Home

Anything that helps you stay at home saves you money and Life Units, including home-use medical equipment. Check your insurance coverage: perhaps purchasing or renting equipment is covered. If neither is covered, you can still negotiate with your insurance company—point out how much the company will save if you stay home, comparing the cost of the medical equipment to the cost of a covered hospitalization. If the person with whom you work declines to approve your request, ask for a supervisor.

If your insurance does not cover purchase or rental, explore the possibility of borrowing the equipment. Perhaps your GuardianOrg or another local community group can help you identify a source of equipment available for loan, frequently free of charge. Newsletters issued for various conditions often list equipment and unused medical supplies available for free.

If you cannot borrow the equipment, determine whether it is less expensive to purchase or to rent it. When considering rental:

- Look at the possibility of renting with an option to purchase that applies all rental payments against the purchase price.
- An advantage to renting over a purchase is that

with a rental there will be a knowledgeable company available to service the equipment for you. Check their servicing arrangements before agreeing to the rental, and read the other terms of the rental contract carefully (including who is liable if the equipment is damaged or even stolen). If you're not up to reading a contract, ask a friend or relative or team member to do it for you. If there are any questions, consult an attorney.

Tip. It would be helpful to have in your home at least the minimal equipment necessary to monitor your changing condition. Most of us already have a thermometer. In this day and age, you can obtain sophisticated equipment at a low price. For example, machines to measure your blood pressure cost about $100. (See the resources section under "Daily Living.")

Tip. If you require infusions, ask if your treatments can be administered through a portable pump, which makes you more mobile. Mobility will be important since some infusions take many hours. Portable pumps are more expensive than stationary pumps, so they will probably not be automatically provided.

3.5 Transportation

Transportation to and from necessary medical appointments and/or treatments can be difficult. Alternative solutions are:

- Ask family or friends for help with driving. The more specific you are about your needs, the more likely they will understand your request and be able to judge what is involved.
- Ask family members or friends to arrange transportation for you. If they can't drive you, they can at least take away the burden of making the arrangements for transportation.
- Ask a social worker, caseworker, or nurse to recommend paid drivers to you, or whether there is a government van, such as a county medical

van. These people understand the kind of help you may need and the services that are available.

- Ask your GuardianOrg or church group if they have a volunteer transportation program. These services are usually free, and the schedule is arranged to fit your needs.
- Ask local service clubs such as the Elks, Lions Club, Masons, or American Legion if they or their auxiliaries could schedule drivers to help with transportation expenses.
- Ask if the treatment center or medical clinic has its own van service.
- If money is a problem, ask your GuardianOrg if it has a program for reimbursement for gas and expenses, and if so, the eligibility requirements. For example, the Leukemia Society reimburses a portion of your mileage and your full cost of parking when you receive chemotherapy and other treatments.

3.6 Food and Chores

If you need help with meals and chores

- contact your GuardianOrg or local Agency for the Elderly for information about home-delivered meals.
- look under "meals" in your phone book and ask about home-delivered meals.
- ask about agencies that help with meal preparation. Some agencies have programs where a worker or nurse's aide comes to the home a few times a week for one to two hours. This person can shop for food and supplies, run errands, and prepare meals.
- ask a church group, friends, or neighbors to organize a small helper group. In addition to pro-

viding food, they can do such chores as yard work and window washing.

3.7 Insurance

There may be limits in your policy on the number of home care visits, the type of people who administer the care, or the total amount of expense covered. If the insurance company can be convinced that paying for home care is the only feasible alternative to expensive hospitalization, it may very well agree to waive the limitations in the policy or to extend coverage. Your physician and home care company are the best people to negotiate with the insurance company about these matters on your behalf.

If the insurance person with whom you have contact won't approve the changes you need, ask to speak with a supervisor. As Barry S. put it, "Three people have to tell me no three times before I accept it."

Tip. Home care companies reimbursed directly by your insurance carrier may deliver more supplies than are needed. You need to ensure that you do not exceed your lifetime maximum under the coverage and to keep premiums down. Refuse to accept excess supplies, or if you must accept them, return them unopened and let your insurance company know, in writing, what you returned and when. At least one home care company insists that items cannot be returned once the package is delivered inside the patient's residence. Ken C. stopped the deliveries outside the door of his residence, opened the packages, and returned unnecessary contents on the spot—before they entered his premises.

Chapter 28

Assisted Living and Nursing Homes

Ron W. fought against the idea of moving into an assisted living home. He felt he was too young to give up control of his life. He found that the residence was not only a home, but he gained more control over the things that really mattered to him by letting other people assist in the things that had become a problem.

If home care is no longer feasible, the alternatives to consider are assisted living homes and nursing homes that combine both care and a residential atmosphere.

Section 1. Assisted Living or "Board and Care" Homes

While assisted living homes are primarily for the elderly, they accept any residents who need assistance with living, short of the kind of nursing requirements provided in a nursing home. Some retirement communities offer a place to live, meals, and nursing care as needed.

Standards. Currently there are no objective standards developed to assess assisted living homes. If it is feasible, restrict your search to licensed homes. In addition to the protection of licensing, you can and should read the governing agency's inspection report.

Tip. Either you, a family member, or a close friend should visit and inspect the premises at least once, and preferably at least one other time. It would be helpful if one of the visits was not expected by the personnel at the home so you have a chance of seeing what life is really like there.

Factors to consider.
- The cost and means available for paying for it. If your insurance or a government program will pay, will the home accept the amount as payment in full?
- The physical appearance is important. Is it a residence in which you would be comfortable living?
- Where in the home would you live? Is it acceptable?
- How sanitary are the conditions?
- Learn about what life is like in the home by talking with the residents.
- If meals are provided, time the visit for at least one meal to assess the appearance and the quality of the food. Are there arrangements for special diets? Is food delivered to residents who are unable or unwilling to eat in the dining room?
- What are the rules and regulations about life in the home, including about going out and visitors?

- What is the cost and availability of transportation?
- What help is available in the facility? What are their qualifications?
- What are your rights concerning services if you need assistance or your health fails?
- What is the cost and availability of other services?
- What quality guarantees are there?
- Who makes the determination whether you need to be moved to a nursing home or hospital and how is that decision made? What is the patient's involvement in the decision?

Contracts. Read, or have an attorney read, the contract carefully. The contract should include all the matters you care about, including a move to a nursing home or hospital and your right to be consulted about these subjects.

Tip. Ideally, the facility should be linked to a nursing home just in case you need a higher level of care. Thus you would be able to move smoothly into the nursing home and back to the facility when appropriate.

Payment. Medicare generally does not pay for assisted living facilities unless certified skilled care is delivered, and most of these homes are not certified. In some states, depending on income, Medicaid may pay. Most insurance policies do not cover these facilities, but you can try to negotiate for coverage based on the argument that staying there is cheaper than going into a hospital.

Section 2. Nursing Homes

If it is likely that you will need twenty-four-hour nursing care and supervision, and neither home care nor assisted living homes work for you, consider a nursing home. Planning ahead is one of the best ways to ease the stress and is also the best method of finding a home compatible with your needs.

Tip. If an immediate need precludes a full assessment, at least assess each affordable home's medical/nursing care. Once you are a resident, the full assessment of the home and alternatives can continue. Be sure you can leave on short notice, such as one day.

2.1 Locating a Nursing Home

Preferably, find a nursing home that

- you can afford (through your insurance, your own money, or a government program).
- is located where you want to be (such as close to family members and friends so it is easy for them to visit, and/or near community resources you hope to continue to use).
- combines good "nursing" care with your concept of a homelike atmosphere.
- takes care of your wants as well as your needs.

For help in locating a nursing home, consult your primary care physician, a hospital's "discharge planner," professionals in the long-term-care field, your local GuardianOrg or state and local offices.

2.2 Assessing a Nursing Home

Reports. Once you have located homes that fit your general needs, start assessing them by obtaining a copy of the report the appropriate regulatory body may have issued about the home. Reports can be obtained from a variety of sources and include such items as infection control, safety hazards, nutrition and taste of food, staff training and credentials, medication errors, and availability of activities. They may also include complaints against the nursing home and the conclusions of the investigations into these complaints. According to a *Consumer Reports* article on nursing homes: "When you read a report, don't expect perfection. Nursing homes provide a difficult service . . . and even the best have deficiencies from time to time." Potential sources for reports are

- your state or local office for the elderly. The Health Care Financing Administration (HCFA), a government agency that certifies nursing

homes that accept payment from Medicare or Medicaid, requires that these offices undertake nursing home inspections.
- the Office of the Long-Term Care Ombudsman, which federal law requires each state agency on aging to have. While these offices are geared to older Americans, they will provide anyone with their information.
- the Joint Commission on Accreditation of Health Care Organizations, 1 Renaissance Boulevard, Oak Brook Terrace, IL 60181 (630-792-5000). If they have them, they will send you free reports on up to ten facilities of interest to you.

Telephone evaluation. Once you have reviewed a report, begin your own evaluation. If you start with a telephone call, you may eliminate the need to visit a particular home. Some of the key questions to cover on the phone:
- Is the nursing home certified for participation in the Medicare and Medicaid programs?
- Since nursing homes are known to allocate beds between people paying full market rates and those on Medicare or Medicaid, is there space available for you under your payment plan?
- What are the facility's admission requirements for residents?
- What is the typical profile of a resident?
- Does the nursing home require that a resident sign over personal property or real estate in exchange for care? If so, how much?
- Does the facility have vacancies or is there a waiting list?

Tip. If no Medicare/Medicaid beds are available, consider paying the market rate for several months and then changing to Medicare/Medicaid payment. It is difficult to move people out once they are in a nursing home.

Site visit. Once you have narrowed your search, inspect the facility with a loved one or team member to determine what life would be like living there. If you're not up to it, ask a family member or friend to do it for you. Choosing the best home for your needs is too important a decision to leave to chance.

If there isn't time to do an inspection, be sure the information you receive about each home under consideration comes from a broad base of sources. Do not rely on any one source in choosing a nursing home.

The following suggestions are based on a *Consumer Reports* article on nursing homes together with the recommendations of the New York State Department of Health. The list is extensive to help you focus on things that will be important to you if you become a resident. Add whatever matters are of particular concern to you before you visit any sites so you don't overlook them. Photocopy the list, with your additions, and take it with you, or give it to whoever will visit the site for you. Note your observations for each home visited for later comparison, or use a tape recorder.

Inspection report.
- If you haven't already received a copy of an inspection report, ask for one on-site. Federal guidelines require nursing homes to make their latest inspection report available and readily accessible to residents and the public, but you often have to be assertive to obtain one.

Visits.
- Tour on your own, rather than with a staff member (if the home won't let you tour alone after the first guided visit, take it off your list).
- Visit unannounced several times, at different times of the day and the week, to get a complete view of life in the home. One of the visits should be during the evening and/or on a weekend when there are usually fewer staff members on duty.

Physical appearance.
- Do they allow residents to personalize their rooms?
- Does each resident have at least one comfortable chair?

- Does each resident have his or her own dresser and closet space with a locked drawer or other secure compartment?
- Is there an out-of-doors area where residents can walk and sit and is it used?
- Does the equipment—wheelchairs, therapy devices—appear to be in good condition?
- Is there a lounge or other area where residents can entertain visitors privately?

Safety.
- Are the exits clearly marked and unobstructed?
- Are there accident-prevention features such as handrails in the hallways and grab bars in the bathrooms?
- Are the hallways wide enough for two wheelchairs to pass? Can they pass freely everywhere or are there obstructions?
- Look at safety hazards to people who walk unsteadily or with impaired eyesight.
- Is there good lighting?
- Are telephones and large-print notices placed so that the wheelchair-bound residents can make use of them?
- Are the inside temperatures appropriate, and are residents dressed appropriately?
- Are people assisted in walking for exercise or retraining?

Cleanliness.
- Check the kitchen for cleanliness.
- Check for smells (particularly for urine and feces).
- Look at the overall cleanliness of the public and activities areas.

Residents.
- You may be able to judge how successful a home is in caring for residents by observing them without infringing on their privacy.
- Look at the quality of the care and the concern for the residents.
- Do the residents appear to be content, enjoying the activities, interacting with each other? Are they well groomed? If most residents are passive, it may be a sign that the home has no activity program or that residents are kept on medications.
- Are any of the residents in restraints? If so, ask the staff why. Federal law states that nursing home residents have the right to be free from any restraints administered for discipline or convenience, unless required to treat medical conditions. In addition, under the law residents have the right to be free from neglect and any type of abuse—verbal, sexual, physical, and mental.
- Ask residents what they like and don't like about the home, and what they do when they need something to be different. Ask what they like about the staff. Ask visitors or volunteers the same questions.
- Are residents allowed to participate in the planning of their own treatment?
- If possible, speak with family members of the facility's residents. There may even be a voluntary council of family members with whom you can speak.
- Does the home give residents the freedom and privacy to attend to their personal needs?
- Are there arrangements for residents to go home for holidays?
- Visit the activities area when in session.
- Walk through the corridors and listen to what you hear.

Staff.
- How responsive are staff? Do staff respond to someone calling for help?
- Do staff interact with residents in a warm, friendly manner?
- Do staff address the residents by name?
- Try to get a handle on staff turnover if you can. A high rate of turnover is not good.
- Find out whom to speak with if problems arise, and meet with that person.

Food.
- Try to time a visit for mealtime and taste the food. Is food appetizing and of good quality?

- What arrangements does the home have for special diets? Is there a dietitian? What effort is made to make special diets taste good?
- Is there sufficient staff and equipment to help residents who can't easily feed themselves?
- Is sufficient time allotted for eating?
- Is food delivered to residents who are unable or unwilling to eat in the dining room?
- Are snacks available?
- Is the dining room clean and attractive?

Medical/nursing care.

- Look at the medical services, since medical and nursing care is crucial. Generally, you choose your own physician, even for emergency care. Will your attending physician be able to care for you while you are in the facility? Nursing homes also have their own physician. Find out who the physician is and how often she visits and reviews residents' medical records.
- How are medical emergencies handled?
- If you need more than routine medical care, ask if a specialist can be called in and how this is done.
- With which hospital or hospitals is the nursing home affiliated?
- What care is given by a registered nurse and what care by an aide?
- How many residents is each nurse's aide or direct care nurse assigned to care for? Are licensed nurses on duty around the clock?
- Does the same nurse or aide care for the resident during each shift?
- If you may need special therapy, look in the therapy rooms and speak with the staff person in charge. How frequently will the therapy be offered? How involved is the home's physician in the establishment and in oversight of the therapy?

Activities programs.

- Ideally, a program should be designed to fit the interests and skills of each person at a variety of times daily, including weekends.

- Are residents taken out for events in the community? How often? Where do they go?
- Do people in wheelchairs get to participate?
- How often are outside events brought in for the entertainment of residents?
- What activities are provided for bedridden residents?

Money issues.

- Find out what services the home provides and which ones cost extra.
- How much does the nursing home charge for (1) a daily semiprivate or private room if you need one, (2) the "extras," e.g., supplies such as diapers, catheter tubes, and for special services such as incontinence care. A daily rate seldom includes the extras. Be prepared to supply these yourself.

Tip. Prescriptions in nursing homes often cost double what they would at a local pharmacy. If the drug prices are gouging, demand the right to purchase drugs outside the nursing home.

Contracts. If a contract is required, show it to your attorney before signing. Ideally, you can cancel your stay on short notice and receive a refund of any advance payment. Preferably pay by the month.

Bottom line. *Form your own impressions. After you have done all of your research, your final judgment should include your gut feeling.*

2.3 Payment

Discrimination against Medicaid recipients is prohibited by federal law. However, as a practical matter, nursing homes all too often admit people who can pay with their own resources or private insurance, then those who qualify for Medicare, and then patients who are on Medicaid. If you have your own resources but are likely to run out while you are in the home, or you have little income, check with your state Medicaid agency before entering a nursing home to determine the financial eligibility requirements for Medicaid and be sure the home is Medicaid-certified.

Deposits. If you are covered by Medicare or Medicaid, nursing homes cannot ask for a security deposit or other form of advance payment. Many states also have laws banning deposits when the cost of care is covered by insurance or government programs. These laws are often breached, but you have the right to insist on their enforcement. Generally, a nursing home can request a deposit if you do not have any coverage.

Third-party guaranty. It is also illegal to require third-party guarantees if you are covered by Medicare or Medicaid.

Long-term-care insurance. See chapter 14, section 11.

Managed care. If you are enrolled in a managed care organization, ask a representative of the plan about coordination of health care services between the MCO and the nursing home (and Medicare or Medicaid if you qualify). Also ask which nursing homes the MCO works with in the area. Talk to a plan representative if you are interested in a nursing home outside the area served by the MCO. Some MCOs may also offer more medical or supportive services than those required by Medicare and Medicaid. Some do not require a hospital stay before approving a nursing home admission.

Medicare. Under some limited circumstances, Medicare Part A will pay for a fixed period of skilled nursing facility care. To qualify for Medicare payment
- the nursing home must be Medicare certified;
- you must have been in a hospital for a minimum of three days;
- you must enter the nursing home within thirty days of a hospital stay; and

- you must need skilled nursing care for the same condition that caused the hospitalization.

Medicare pays in full only for the first twenty days of skilled nursing care. The payment amount changes each calendar year after that. In any event, Medicare only pays for a maximum of one hundred days in any benefit period. A benefit period ends when a person has not been an inpatient of a hospital or a skilled nursing facility for sixty consecutive days.

Some Medicare supplementary insurance policies (MediGap) supplement this limited Medicare coverage.

Medicaid. Medicaid payments do not have a time limit, but Medicaid pays the lowest amount of any private or governmental payment plan. For this reason nursing homes try to avoid Medicaid as a source of payment.

For Medicaid to pay for nursing home care
- the nursing home must be Medicaid certified.
- you must meet income and assets tests (see chapter 15). In most states, if your income is less than the private-pay rate, you can be eligible for Medicaid. Your income (including SSD, SSI, and pension benefits) goes to the nursing home directly and Medicaid pays the difference between that income and the Medicaid rates.

If you have to move to a hospital from a nursing home, each state determines the length of time a nursing home has to hold a bed for the return of a hospitalized Medicaid resident. Days range from zero to fifteen. Even if there is no requirement to actually hold a bed, the law does require a nursing home to readmit the hospitalized resident to the next available bed.

Tip. If you anticipate that you will need nursing home care in the future, think about consulting with an attorney to discuss eligibility for Medicaid (see chapter 15).

It is illegal for a nursing home to require you to give up any rights to Medicaid or to prevent you from transferring your funds to qualify for Medicaid. It is also illegal to require payment for "extra" services that are included in the Medicaid payment, such as laundry. You can be charged for (but not required to take) real extras such as a television in your room.

2.4 Complaints

Congress has enacted federal legislation that gives residents certain enforceable rights, including the rights to dignity, choice, self-determination, and quality services and activities.

Ombudsman. If you have complaints about a nursing home, call the ombudsman. The ombudsman mediates disputes and has the clout to require action from the nursing home.

If you have trouble locating your ombudsman, call the Eldercare Locator at 800-677-1116. The Locator can give you the telephone numbers for area agencies on aging or for state and local departments of elder affairs, which in turn can give you contact information for your state's ombudsman.

Chapter 29

Hospitals

One of the most difficult things to contend with in a hospital is the assumption on the part of the staff that because you have lost your gallbladder, you have also lost your mind.

—Jean Kerr

Whether you choose a hospital and then pick a doctor who has privileges at that hospital, or choose a doctor or managed care organization and use the hospital with which they are affiliated, the hospital you use can be important to your health.

Hospitals in this country are among the best in the world. This chapter will make you an informed consumer with an awareness of the simple steps you can take to assure you get what you need and want, and to avoid *potential* pitfalls.

Think of the hospital as another of your team members—in this case a partner in the health process.

Section 1. Choosing the Right Hospital

You probably already know the hospitals in your area. However, it may still be worthwhile to obtain a list of medical centers from your local GuardianOrg because it will point you in the direction of hospitals that are best suited to care for people with your condition or to supply the treatment you need. You are less likely to suffer complications from treatments done at hospitals that perform a large number of them.

Evaluate the different hospitals. Ask for recommendations from everyone you know, especially people who work in the health care field. Ask people in your support group or others with your condition about their experiences with the different hospitals in your area. Were they treated as numbers or as individuals? Were they treated as partners in their care? Were all tests and procedures discussed ahead of time, or did doctors just show up for them? How about the cleanliness of the place? Which emergency room worked best for them? Check the books listed in the resources section.

By phoning you can also obtain and compare
- room costs. They will vary from hospital to hospital.
- whether the hospital will accept your form of payment.
- the hospital's rate of **nosocomial infections,** medical terminology for infections acquired in the hospital. To obtain this information, ask the hospital, your doctor, and/or contact your local

department of health. Every accredited hospital has an infection control committee, which generally includes physicians and nurses, and often a hospital administrator. Their reports are usually available upon request.

• report cards from various organizations to help make decisions about a hospital. If you use one, be aware that unique conditions can skew the results. For example, a hospital may have a high mortality rate because it gets the most difficult cases.

It may be worth taking a trip to the hospital yourself or ask a friend or relative to do it for you. What is your overall impression of the atmosphere, as well as cleanliness and the way people are treated?

Public hospitals. Don't take a hospital off your list just because it is a public hospital. Some public hospitals are very good. If the hospital is a teaching hospital, it is probably equipped with better doctors and equipment and is on top of the latest developments.

Section 2. Outpatient

Patients who come to a hospital, have their treatment, and leave on the same day are known as **outpatients. Inpatients** stay overnight.

As a general matter, as many procedures and tests as feasible should be done on an outpatient basis. You will save money and Life Units and minimize the risk of picking up an infection. Nevertheless, being an outpatient is not always in your best interest. As with most aspects of life, a balance is required. Neil N. needed a series of gastrointestinal tests. If he had done them as an outpatient, it would have required four trips to the hospital on as many different days, with four accompanying enemas. Instead, by checking into the hospital for two days he accomplished all four tests with only one enema.

If you have managed care coverage, the managed care company is likely to require outpatient procedures whenever possible—including in some instances when it may be better to be an inpatient.

If you believe you should be an inpatient for a treatment for which the managed care company insists on outpatient status, appeal the decision. (See chapter 14, section 6.)

Tip. If you have hospital indemnity coverage covering the cost of your hospital stay (see chapter 14, section 10), you receive money for each day you are in the hospital. Take this into account when deciding whether to have a procedure as an outpatient. Getting paid may make it a little easier to be hospitalized.

Section 3. Entering the Hospital

3.1 In General

Before the need arises, prepare a wallet-size list of your medical history, including a current list of medications and allergies or other chronic conditions, previous operations, current diagnosis, and drugs you are taking. If you have insurance, include your insurer and policy number. If you have a living will or other advance directive, mention it, as well as the contact information for your health care proxy. This way, you won't have to remember a lot of information when you are not feeling well and preassembly will speed up your admission.

If there is too much information to keep on a wallet-size sheet, keep the information in the emergency room tote bag described in the next section.

3.2 Entering the Hospital Through the Emergency Room (ER)

You have a legal right to be treated at a hospital ER if you have an urgent medical condition—regardless of your ability to pay. You must be treated until your condition is stable or the advantages to you outweigh the risk of a move and the hospital to which you are to be transferred has agreed to accept you.

Emergency rooms work on the **triage** system: people with the most immediate medical need are taken care of first. Life-threatening situations are always given priority. A broken arm may be the most pressing medical problem in a walk-in center, but not at a hospital that gets people from an area with a high rate of violence. You can usually get faster treatment if you arrive in an ambulance or the police bring you to the hospital. If you arrive in the hospital's ambulance, you are treated as if you are the hospital's patient, and hospital patients generally receive priority.

Tip. Prior to needing to use an ambulance, check your insurance coverage to find out if ambulance fees are covered and under what circumstances. If they are covered, by all means use the ambulance to get to the emergency room.

Tip. Check your insurance to determine whether it requires pre-authorization of emergency room care. If there's no time, and the need is urgent, head to the emergency room and call from there. If they don't give you the approval, you be the final judge as to whether you should go to the emergency room. You can battle with the insurance company later.

When you have to go to an emergency room.
- If there is time, inform your attending physician and ask him to meet you at the ER so there will be someone there with direct concern for your health who already knows your history. If he can't make it, perhaps he will at least call and smooth the way for you. It helps if the ER thinks someone in the hospital is looking out for you.
- If at all possible, take an advocate with you or have a friend or family member meet you there. If you don't have someone, be prepared to advocate for yourself. Perhaps the hospital has a **patient representative** (also known as a **patient advocate** or **ombudsman**) who can help

you. The patient representative is supposed to be the link between you and the hospital, helping you with any complaints or questions you may have about the hospital or staff.
- Be firm in making your needs known. Request comfort items such as food or liquid. Until assigned a room, you should be able to get attention from the staff. After that, you may be in for a long wait for attention.
- Always request a blanket. It sometimes takes so long to get one that it is better to have one just in case.

Tip. Have an emergency room tote bag packed at all times. Keep in it pajamas, toiletries, nonperishable food, bottled water, a book, copies of your health insurance information and health history, a batch of quarters and a list of people to call with their phone numbers. Attach a note to the bag reminding you to take a cellular phone and an inexpensive compact disk or cassette player with headphones if you have them. Leave the bag in a closet near your front door, or ask a loved one to bring it to you if you can't stop at home on the way to the hospital.

3.3 Elective Admission to the Hospital

If there is time before going into a hospital, you're likely to get better treatment by meeting beforehand with the hospital administrator. Tell him you're concerned about your stay and would appreciate his personal interest in your case. Look for something you can bring up that suggests it is in the hospital's interest to take good care of you. For example, you agreed to report on your experiences to your GuardianOrg. Mentioning the administrator's name in passing to your nurses can't hurt either.

Avoid admission on a weekend or holiday. It adds days to your stay. In most cases, you will receive only minimal medical care on those days.

Your rights as a patient. In addition to any rights the hospital may voluntarily provide, you have the right to make decisions about your medical care (see chapter 25, section 1). If the hospital accepts Medicare or Medicaid patients, you must be provided with written information about these rights as well as your right to execute advance directives. The covered facilities are also prohibited from placing conditions on the provision of care or discriminating against individuals in other ways.

Section 4. Staying in the Hospital— Making the Best of It

In general. There is always the risk of error, even in the best of hospitals. The best way to lower the risk is to be *alert, assertive,* and *informed.* If you aren't used to doing this for yourself, think of yourself as acting on behalf of your child or your best friend. There is a difference between being assertive and demanding: you'll know it when you see it, but if there's a question, err on the side of taking care of yourself. Do not rely on the hospital, or anyone in the hospital, to anticipate or take care of your needs. Be prepared to do that on your own. *If you are in no condition to do it, ask a friend or relative to do it for you.*

Partnership. Just as you treat the hospital and its staff as a partner, insist that they treat you as a partner as well. Ask for the same amount of information you would require from your doctor.

Intimidation. Don't be intimidated. If you feel too sick, vulnerable, or dependent to stand up for yourself, tell the staff to wait until someone who cares about you is there—and ask that person to stick up for you.

Avoid infection. Pay attention to the cleanliness of your surrounding area, of staff members, of equipment and its handling. Speak out, or have a friend or loved one speak out, if you see something wrong. If you have any fears of infection, insist that all staff members wash their hands or put on sterile gloves before coming into contact with you. If you have a catheter or other device for treatments through the skin, be sure all precautions are constantly taken.

Check the name band that is usually attached to a patient's wrist. Is it your name? Does it list any allergies you have? Be sure the nurse or other attendants check your band when giving you drugs or taking you for any tests or procedures.

Changing rooms. If you are assigned to a room with another patient, ask about that person's medical status to be sure you can deal with that person's illness. You won't be able to change rooms for any discrimination prohibited by law (such as because of a person's national origin or color). If you are immunosuppressed and the other patient is infectious, then by all means have your room changed.

Be informed. Learn what is supposed to happen with your medical care, why, and when so you can follow up. Also learn what should not happen, so you can guard against it. For example, you don't want to take unbuffered aspirin if you have or are prone to ulcers.

Understand what is happening. Just as you do with your physician in his office, ask the doctor to restate explanations in another way until you are sure you understand what is being discussed. Consider repeating to the doctor what you think is being said, in your own words. Ask the meaning of words, or signs near your bed, that you don't understand.

Tests. When you're in the hospital, it's easy to order tests, especially if they're covered by your insurance. Avoid unnecessary or duplicative tests, whether at admission or once you're in the hospital. They can easily become excessive. Ask for prior approval of each and every test and be sure it is noted in your record. If there are multiple blood tests, ask that they take one sample for all the tests.

Question
• the purpose of the test.
• what would happen if you postpone the test to see if your condition worsens.
• whether it will be covered by your insurance.

Tip. Refuse to have blood drawn for any unexpected or unexplained tests.

Drugs. Check, or have someone check for you, all drugs that the nurses administer to be sure that they are the ones you are supposed to be getting and that the dosages are correct. Although hospitals do have systems of checks to keep mistakes from ever reaching patients, mistakes can happen.

Tip. You may receive resistance from the staff to your checking up on them. This is an understandable knee-jerk reaction. Explain as you would to someone you care about and don't want to offend that this is not personal. You have heard about errors in hospitals and are being a careful consumer. If you didn't trust them, you wouldn't be in that hospital in the first place.

Tip. Take a list of your medications to the hospital, including the dosages, so that the doctors in the hospital can order those drugs for you. Ask whether there will be any charges. Add that information to your list including the name, dosage, purpose, and instructions. If possible, find out the shape and color of any new pills. Use your list to check any pills the nurse brings you.

Tip. Before undergoing a procedure
• ask the questions starting in chapter 25, section 2. Take a photocopy of the list to the hospital if it will help.
• find out how much it will cost.

Food. Hospital dietitians will generally try to meet your reasonable requests. If it's allowed by the hospital, and you're not on a special diet or having your intake measured, consider calling a restaurant that delivers, or ask friends and family to bring you food.

Doctors. If you become uncomfortable with your doctor for any reason, you can change *even if* you are in the hospital. Before changing, see the discussion in chapter 36, section 1.2.

Residents and interns. Residents and interns are in the hospital to gain practical medical experience. They also help the attending physicians by providing care for patients while the attending physician is not present. If you believe that any of them are not up to proper standards, request that they be removed from your case.

Nurses. *Work with the nurses as part of your team.* They are the people in the hospital who tend to your needs. It helps to befriend them. It can't hurt to be polite, even as you make sure they follow up on your requests and get answers to your questions.

Many facilities now use less qualified staff for many functions formerly performed by registered nurses. Since you have a right to refuse treatment by anyone, you can require that registered nurses, and not nurse's assistants, handle all procedures. If you're not comfortable with any other activities assistants handle, speak with the supervisor.

Tip. Don't be concerned that the hospital may not have enough staff to do the things you request. You have a right to expect good care, and too few staff members is not an excuse.

Complaints. If you're not happy with your care, complain in the proper order: the offending person first, then the supervisor, then the hospital administration.

Advocate. Ask a friend or family member to act as an advocate to be sure you get the service you deserve and are paying for.

Friends and family. Do not hesitate to tell friends and family what you need, whether it is a neighborhood update, bringing you your favorite foods, or taking care of matters large and small. They can't know what you need unless you tell them. The odds are they will be willing to help. Susan R.'s difficult day was transformed when her friend Susan S. brought her dog to the street outside the hospital room window for a play session that Susan R. could watch.

Hospice care. If you need in-hospital hospice care, read chapter 30. However, just because you are in hospice care does not mean that the advice for maximizing the use of the hospital, and minimizing expense, should be ignored. If you become too sick to tend to these matters, be sure a friend or family member will do it for you.

Section 5. Tips to Make Your Stay Easier

- Take framed and/or unframed photos of loved ones or places that evoke peaceful feelings.
- Either take or rent an inexpensive VCR so you can watch your favorite movies or educational tapes and ask friends to bring them. Many hospitals will even supply a VCR upon request.
- Have your mail and newspaper brought to you daily. It helps to stay in touch with your home routine.
- Take musical tapes, relaxation tapes, or a radio. Earphones should be used if you are in a semi-private room.
- Take aids for sleep and comfort, such as small pillows or favorite blankets.
- Take walking aids, such as canes or walkers.
- Take whatever you use at home to make yourself look presentable, such as turbans or head coverings.
- If a special mattress is used at home (such as an eggshell mattress), ask that the same kind be used in the hospital. If you ask ahead of time, it is more likely it will be available on admission.
- Consider purchasing an inexpensive answering machine to take to the hospital. With a machine, you can monitor your calls so you are not disturbed when you want to rest. You can also decide with whom you want to speak, and when. If a batch of people are calling you to find out how you are, you may even want to go so far as to give a daily update on the outgoing message. The machine should be inexpensive because your door has no lock and theft is regrettably all too common in hospitals.

Tip. Set up a phone tree. If a lot of people would be calling you for updates, ask a friend or relative to work out a system of calling the concerned people and letting them know, and a phone tree so each person calls another.

- No one will have a major burden, everyone will know your status, and you can get some needed rest.
- A phone tree also creates a support group for your friends and more distant relatives. Your being in the hospital will not be easy on them either.
- Keeping people in touch through a phone tree will also help them to mobilize smoothly, if and when you need them.

Section 6. Money-Saving Tips

To save money while you're in the hospital

- avoid unnecessary tests
- keep a daily log of the services and medications you receive. If you're too sick to do it, ask a friend or family member to keep track for you. Include the dates of admission and release, the

dates you are in a specialized unit such as intensive care, tests, medications received, doctors' visits (including name, specialty, and what they did), and personal items received. The log should also include every item you are provided, including every aspirin, toothbrush, and supplies used as part of a medical procedure. Because many hospitals are under financial pressures and trying to control their bottom line, they are charging for every service provided, including many that used to be free.

• refuse to be seen by any doctor you don't know. Find out who the doctor is and what he is doing in your room. After you identify who the doctor is, and what he intends to do, you can make the decision whether to allow him to proceed.

• bring your own food or have it delivered, if the hospital allows it. It'll save you money and will probably be a good deal more to your liking. Be sure it fits within the food recommended by the hospital dietitian. Tell the hospital that you have done this, then check to be sure you aren't charged for meals.

Section 7. On Discharge from the Hospital

When you are being discharged from a hospitalization, ask for a copy of the discharge summary. It provides a synopsis of what happened during your stay. It also lists your diagnoses, your home plan, and your future doctor appointments as well as medications on discharge. Get a list from your doctor of dos and don'ts to follow until your next visit with him.

Early checkout. While you can legally leave a hospital at any time against medical advice (AMA), leaving the hospital prior to receiving your physician's approval may jeopardize your insurance coverage. Hanako H. packed to leave the hospital on a day her doctor had unexpectedly left town without formally authorizing her discharge. She

was almost out the door when she was informed that if she left AMA, she, not the insurance company, would be responsible for the entire bill, which was over $10,000. (She created such an uproar that the staff managed within a few hours to track down the doctor and obtain approval for the release.)

Check your hospital bill. If you have managed care coverage and do not pay any part of your hospital bill, skip this section.

All too often people don't check their hospital bill. Even if you're covered by health insurance or Medicare, you may be required to pay a deductible and possibly even a percentage. Even without a required payment on your part, the amount of the bill can deplete your lifetime limit. This is particularly true if you end up with multiple trips to the hospital.

Hospital bills tend to be long and complex and written in unfamiliar codes. However, they are also notoriously inaccurate. For example, in a recent five-month investigation of ninety-seven hospital bills in Connecticut, state officials found errors in 31 percent of the bills.

It's worth an investment of a few Life Units to

• demand an itemized bill and review it carefully for errors.

• look for duplicate billing, which can often happen with minor items and unrequested items. Look at the names items are given—they can be given different names and then billed repeatedly.

• look for unrequested or unauthorized charges, especially if you asked for advance approval for all tests. A "thermal therapy kit" may actually be an ice bag.

• look for charges for services that were not rendered, or items that were not delivered.

• look to see if the charge is the same for all similar tests. Dyson L. was charged different amounts for each of four chest X rays.

• *watch for phantom charges.* Hospitals have a standard list of fees automatically charged for certain procedures. Often a medical treatment can involve only one or two components of a procedure. The hospital administrator may assume that you had every component.

- particularly check for charges during surgery, where a lot goes on and gets charged to the bill.
- do not pay for the doctors' failure to coordinate their work if the doctors ran duplicate tests. Redundant or shoddy testing should not be your burden.
- look at charges with general headings like "nutrition" or "anesthesiology." Any general heading warrants further inquiry.
- If the meaning of the codes isn't printed on the bill, ask for a copy of the explanations.
- If you have a large bill that is confusing to you, seek assistance.
- The National Emergency Medicine Alliance will provide you with a free booklet on hospital and medical bills. Call 800-553-0735.
- The National Association of Claims Assistance Professionals will refer you to a professional who specializes in medical-claims counseling and processing. Call 708-963-3500.
- The hospital billing-department representative can also be of assistance.

Tip. Don't pay the hospital bill as you are leaving. There is not sufficient time in which to review a detailed bill. Insist on reviewing the bill before paying it.

If you find an error in your bill. Put your concern in writing and attach specific documentation for the suggested correction. Send this information to both the hospital and, if applicable, to your insurance company and/or Medicare or Medicaid. Keep a copy with your files.

If you do not receive satisfaction, contact the hospital patient representative or patient advocate. This person will explain your rights as a patient and what alternatives you have regarding any disputes. While theoretically working for your interests, this person is paid by the hospital. If you are still not satisfied, contact your health insurance company to find out the average amounts charged for similar hospital procedures in your region. If you are not insured, obtain these amounts from any health insurance company.

If you don't receive an acceptable response, or if the charges seem exorbitant, consider sending the bill to the consumer advocate of your local television station and/or newspaper.

Chapter 30

Hospice Care

Whatever God has brought about / Is to be borne with courage.
—Sophocles, 401 B.C.

The modern concept of **hospice care** started in the early part of the twentieth century as a reaction against the intense pain and suffering people experienced dying in hospitals apart from their families. Hospice care is a concept, rather than a place. It focuses on the comfort of the patient, rather than the fight against the illness. It can be provided at home or in hospice facilities, which can be located in hospitals or nursing homes. It has more to do with life and dignity than with death and loss of hope. There are a great many misconceptions about the idea of hospice care.

Hospice care is a team approach involving experts from different backgrounds. Instead of continuing to treat a condition when a cure is virtually impossible and available treatments are not working, hospice care focuses on providing quality of life and relief from pain and other symptoms. It helps people live until the last moment, working to keep patients alert, pain-free, and as productive as they would like to be for as long as possible. The patient's comfort overrides all other concerns. For example, even in a hospital setting, visitors, including children and possibly pets, are allowed twenty-four hours a day as compared to restricted hours with no children or pets allowed. Support is also available to help family members choose the care they want for their loved ones.

There is always the right to reinstate traditional care at any time, for any reason, such as when a condition goes into remission.

The variety of services provided round the clock by a hospice care team include

- physician care provided by the patient's primary physician and the medical director of the hospice organization.
- nursing care provided by trained nurses.
- medical social services.
- spiritual support and counseling.
- home care aide and homemaker services.
- physical, occupational, and speech therapies.
- help with food planning provided by a dietitian.
- continuous care in the home.
- support services provided by trained volunteers.
- hospice inpatient care if necessary.
- for the family, respite care, counseling, and bereavement support.

To provide as much privacy as possible, hospice workers do not generally wear uniforms. While some religious groups have hospices, they do not usually require patients to follow their beliefs. Hospices respect advance directives, since they do nothing either to prolong life or to shorten it.

Hospice care is becoming increasingly more flexible, and you may negotiate which therapies you will retain and which you'll give up. Some hospice patients have even entered experimental studies or begun promising new treatments.

Under Medicare regulations, hospices without an inpatient facility must contract for beds at a hospital, nursing home, rehabilitative center, or other institution in order to provide care. In this case, the hospice rules are followed, not the institution's.

Choice. It is always your right to decide whether hospice care is appropriate and which program suits your needs. However, before entering a hospice program, a physician must certify that a patient has been diagnosed with a terminal illness and has a limited life expectancy (usually six months or less).

Section 1. Locating a Hospice Agency

Generally the best way to find hospice care is through your physician specialist. Hospices, or the personnel they employ, must be licensed in some states, usually by the state Department of Health. Having a license does not assure quality, but not having one may indicate a problem.

A certified hospice is eligible for Medicare and Medicaid payments. To become certified an agency must show that it meets basic federal and state standards for financial management and patient care. Specific standards and their enforcement vary by state.

Tip. If you are having difficulty finding a hospice program or need additional information, contact the Foundation for Hospice and Homecare (202-547-6586) or the Hospice Association of America

(202-546-4759). You can also call the Hospice Hotline at 800-658-8898 or write the National Hospice Organization, 1901 N. Moore Street, Suite 901, Arlington, VA 22209.

Section 2. Assessing a Hospice Agency

When evaluating the quality of care provided by a hospice, either you or someone on your behalf should consider the following.

Qualifications and references.
- Is the agency accredited, certified, and/or licensed for hospice care? If so, for what services and by what organization?
- What does your GuardianOrg say about the agency?
- What references can the agency provide from professionals who have used this agency? Call these references and ask these people about their experiences.
- Does the agency have malpractice and liability insurance? Are they willing to supply you with a copy of these policies or at least a certificate showing the coverages?

Plan of care.
- Will the agency provide you with a written statement outlining a plan of care for you and costs? The plan of care should list specific duties, work hours/days, and the name and telephone number of the supervisor in charge.
- Does the agency provide a plan of care that is prepared for you specifically by an experienced registered nurse or social worker, not an agency clerk? Is the determination of your needs conducted in the home instead of on the telephone? Who determines what you can do for yourself? Was your plan of care created after consultation with family physicians and/or other professionals already providing you with health and social services? With your prior authorization, were other members of your family consulted?

Services.
- Where are the services offered?
- If the agency does not provide full services, what can the agency do to obtain other home care services as needed, such as home-delivered meals?
- What role does the family physician play?
- What are the educational levels and qualifications of their professional staff?

Costs.
- What are the costs? Do you have to use the services for a minimum number of hours per day or days per week? Who pays for the employee's Social Security or other insurance? Are there additional charges for travel, supervision, home evaluation, or medical supplies? How does the agency handle payment and billing?

Other matters.
- What procedure does the agency have for emergencies? For complaints?
- Who handles paperwork for Medicare, insurance, and hospital billing?
- Will the hospice honor your advance medical directives?

Tip. Either you, a family member, or a friend should be sure that each person from the hospice agency who comes to your home sees the plan of care so everyone understands the ground rules.

Section 3. Evaluating Hospice Services

Look for the same factors as discussed in chapter 27, section 3.3, about home health care companies.

Section 4. Payment

With hospice care, a patient pays only for the services she or the family cannot provide and that are not covered by insurance. In 1995, the charges were estimated at $1,810 for a day in a hospital and $323 for a day in a skilled nursing facility. In contrast, hospice care was estimated at only $105 per day of care. A study by Mor and Kidder compared the costs of both home care and hospital-based hospice programs to those of conventional care for cancer patients. The cost of treatment for conventional care patients was nearly three times as high as that of home care hospice patients.

If hospice care is not covered under your health policy, negotiate, or have someone negotiate on your behalf, with the insurance carrier. Private insurers are concerned about the high costs of medical care and are increasingly willing to reimburse for optional services that can be demonstrated to be appropriate, cost-effective alternatives to hospitalization.

Hospice services are covered under Medicare. At least thirty-eight states currently offer hospice care as an option under their Medicaid programs.

Hospice care is also a covered benefit under most private insurance plans and managed care organizations. Military personnel and their dependents are covered for hospice care under CHAMPUS. If you choose to leave hospice care and either reinstate traditional care or dispense with care entirely, you can still return to hospice care, and Medicare, Medicaid, and most private insurance companies and MCOs will allow readmission.

If there is no coverage at all, the National Hospice Organization standards do not permit rejection based on inability to pay. Costs are paid by private donations.

Chapter 31

Bodily Changes

Here's my morning ritual. I open a sleepy eye, take one horrified look at my reflection in the mirror, and then repeat, with conviction, "I'm me and I'm beautiful, because God doesn't make junk."

—Erma Bombeck

As your condition progresses, your appearance may change. No matter how insignificant the change, it can threaten a sense of well-being, cause feelings of loss and anger, and put a strain on personal relationships. This chapter discusses the physical aspects of those changes.

Section 1. Looking Good

Your worth is based on who you are, not on what you do or on what has happened to your body. Still, the old adage "If you look better, you will feel better" is often the case. While it is important not to let the way you look interfere with your psychological well-being, a number of aids can assist with the physical changes your condition may cause.

Emphasize your best features. Whether you're a man or a woman, make the most of your features with attention to your hair, makeup, clothes, or accessories. Feel good about yourself. Find new products that help you look better. Ask your local

GuardianOrg, your social worker, and other survivors for ideas and sources of products.

Reconstructive surgery is available to replace an array of surgical removals. Your doctor can tell you what is available and how to access it.

Section 2. Hair Loss

Chemotherapy, radiation, or other drug treatments may cause hair loss, brittle hair, or a change in texture or color. While different treatments affect hair differently, and everyone's experience is individual, *these changes are usually temporary*. If hair loss is a possibility, ask what you can expect with such questions as:

- When will my hair be likely to begin to fall out?
- How much hair loss should be expected?
- When should I expect my hair to return?

Hair replacements. If you're not comfortable with the change, consider scarves, hats, turbans, caps, and/or wigs. Of course, you can always shave your head entirely and go for the "bald is hot" look.

If you would consider wearing a wig (and today's wigs can be all but impossible to detect), put away a sample of your hair color and texture, as well as photos of how your hair looks. You may even consider purchasing the wig ahead of time or before you lose a lot of hair, for an accurate match in color, texture, and style.

Tip. Think about changing the color and/or style of a wig if you want to divert attention from any other physical changes that occur.

Tip. Wearing a wig before you need it may ease the adjustment.

Wig experts recommend a blend of natural and synthetic hair because the synthetic part of the blend helps the style stay better. All natural-hair wigs are more difficult to maintain, and 100 percent synthetic wigs do not have the same natural look.

Before purchasing a wig, check with your insurance company to see if it will be covered, and if so, under what circumstances. Many companies think of the loss of hair as similar to a loss of a limb that requires a prosthesis. If they do, ask your physician to write a prescription for a "wig prosthesis." Your receipt for the wig should also refer to it as a "prosthesis." If the wig is not covered, and you have to pay for it yourself, it may be tax deductible if it alleviates the mental discomfort related to hair loss as a result of a disease.

You can buy wigs or hairpieces at a specialty shop, through a catalog, or by phone. If you need a source, call the American Cancer Society at 800-ACS-2345. You may even be able to borrow a wig or hairpiece. Check with the local chapter of the American Cancer Society or with the social work department at your hospital. Donated wigs are available free from Y-Me Wig (800-221-2141).

Tip. If you get night sweats, consider wearing an absorbent turban to avoid catching a cold.

Section 3. Skin Changes

Skin problems can result from various treatments and/or drugs, as well as an increased sensitivity to the sun. Your physician will likely advise you about any changes to expect and what to do about them. You should always let your doctor or nurse know right away if you develop severe or unforeseen skin or nail changes. Sudden or severe itching, rashes, hives, or respiratory problems may indicate an allergic reaction requiring immediate treatment.

The American Cancer Society has a free nationwide program known as "Look Good . . . Feel Better," which helps women with cancer learn specific ways of handling side effects on skin and hair of cancer treatment. The program includes one-on-one consultations, group sessions, and self-help materials including a video and brochure. For information, call 800-395-LOOK or your local American Cancer Society office. Perhaps by the time you read this text there will also be a program for men. It's worth a call to the American Cancer Society to find out.

Section 4. Dressing

If your clothes become too large due to an unwanted weight loss

- have a few necessary items tailored to fit. Ask the tailor to tack the alteration, and to be sure not to cut any fabric—so you can let the clothes out when you return to your normal weight.
- borrow clothes from a friend who is close to your new size.
- shop for a few necessary items in a secondhand or thrift shop. If the shop is run by a charity, you'll help the organization at the same time.
- if money is tight, ask your religious organization for clothes.
- if money is not a consideration, consider a

shopping spree. You can always give the clothes to a charity when you gain your weight back.

There are many products available to help you dress. (See the resources section.)

If you need help in better understanding any of these subjects, contact your GuardianOrg or ask other people with a similar condition, your social worker, or your specialist or his staff.

Section 5. Contraception and Sterility

A life-challenging condition or its treatment may affect men and women who want to have children. For women, fertility and fetal development may be affected. Men may face sterility. There are usually protective measures that can be taken to preserve fertility and potency.

If you and your specialist have not already discussed the issue, this is the time to discuss

• pregnancy.
• the effects of your condition or any treatment you are undergoing or considering on your ability to have children.

Section 6. Sex

Sex, and the intimacy that comes with it, are important to your well-being. However, trouble having sex is not uncommon for people diagnosed with a serious condition. The difficulty can be caused by the physical condition itself, certain drugs or drug combinations, or emotions. It is even possible that a little of each comes into play.

It may be that all that's necessary is a change in your drugs, or the condition may be temporary. There are also creative ways of giving and receiving pleasure.

Many doctors are reluctant to bring up the subject, so it's probably up to you. Speak to your physician or pharmacist. Other avenues for advice include your support group, your therapist, and your GuardianOrg. Your GuardianOrg may even have an ongoing workshop or lecture about this topic.

Section 7. Options for Coping with Body Changes

Ask for a referral to rehabilitation services that can help you overcome problems. For example:

• Physical therapy can help women reduce swelling in their lymph glands and increase arm strength after a mastectomy.
• Occupational therapy can help people regain strength and coordination and plan for a return to everyday activities.
• Speech therapy can help people communicate better after a laryngectomy.
• Rehabilitation counseling can help people deal with feelings and concerns about body changes.

Find out about the use of special products to overcome disability or discomfort. Mechanical aids and artificial limbs (sometimes called **prostheses**) can help you maintain many functions. Talk to your attending physician and a rehabilitation professional.

Learn from others who have the same problem. They can give you practical tips to make your new situation easier.

Get help if you need it. If the changes are so great that you need daily assistance or help to move around, ask your nurse or the social worker at your hospital about homemaker services, home health services, seminars and classes, rides to the hospital, and other community services.

Part VII

›››››››››››››

Estate Planning

Chapter 32

Providing for the Possibility of Incapacitation

It has been reported that Jacqueline Kennedy Onassis refused life-prolonging medical intervention before her death from non-Hodgkin's lymphoma, and that former president Richard Nixon insisted on receiving comfort-easing care only—not any heroic measures. They both made sure their wishes were satisfied through use of advance directives.

Section 1. An Overview of Advance Directives

Advance directives ensure that your wishes with respect to physical and financial matters will be carried out if you lose the capacity to make such decisions for yourself.

Physical matters. If you become incapacitated and don't have advance directives:

- Medical authorities can, and *may even be required by law to,* extend your life for years, no matter how meager the existence and *at your expense.*
- In an emergency, your consent to a procedure will be assumed. At other times, someone else, generally your legal next of kin, will have to make stressful decisions without your guidance. A court may appoint a person to make the decisions. The appointee may be a relative or a stranger.
- People you may want to make these decisions will not be considered, particularly if they are not your legal next of kin.

- You can expect extraordinary medical charges. According to one study (among many that reach the same conclusion), hospital charges for last hospitalizations for Medicare patients averaged more than $95,000 per patient. Yet, the average cost for patients with a type of advance directive known as a living will was only $30,000.

Financial matters. If you become incapacitated and someone doesn't tend to your financial health, it can become disastrous. Aside from the possibility of losing your residence because no one has the authority to pay the rent or mortgage, you could lose all your medical coverage and life insurance because no one is paying the premiums. Also, no one could act quickly in a financial emergency without costly and time-consuming court guardianship proceedings for authorization.

If incapacity occurs and appropriate steps have not been taken, an interested party would have to go to court with whatever documentation the court requires. Time-consuming notice would have to be given to all interested parties. If there is money involved, you can expect that relatives and creditors will come pouring out of the woodwork. Obviously, having a court sort out your finances can involve much time and expense.

Complementary. The different advance directives may seem duplicative but they actually complement each other.

State law and forms. Check the laws of your state to determine the legal requirements for advance directives; e.g., some states that recognize living wills do not allow any restrictions on food and water. *Be sure the wording of the document and your execution of it conform precisely to the state law.*

The specific forms and the execution requirements for each state can easily be obtained. For instance, the Cancer Information Service at 800-422-6237 has information on how to obtain the forms for your state. For a fee of $3.50 per set ($3.79 for New York State residents and $3.70 for residents of Washington, D.C.), appropriate state documents can also be obtained from Choice in Dying, a nonprofit organization located at 200 Varick Street, New York, NY 10014 (800-989-9455 or 212-366-5540), or they can be obtained free from Choice in Dying via the Internet at www.choices.org. Any hospital or medical care facility in your area should also be able to supply you with this information, or consult the sources listed in the resources section.

If you live in a state that does not legally recognize advance directives, or if an advance directive is improperly executed. It is still important to state your wishes in writing. Even if the directive does not have the force of law behind it, the right physician or court will be likely to abide by your wishes.

The advice of an attorney may be helpful to ensure that your documents accurately reflect your wishes and are legally effective.

Travel between states. If you split your time between states, be sure the documents meet the requirements of each state. Alternatively, create a separate document for each state in the form preferred by that state. Even though a majority of states have reciprocity agreements that honor out-of-state documents, the advantage to using multiple directives is that familiarity with the state-approved form may prevent delays in validation. A costly delay may occur while lawyers, nurses, doctors, or technicians study an unfamiliar form.

Choosing your agent. In general, any designated agent should be

- at least eighteen years old.
- someone you are confident will fight for your wishes, if necessary.
- someone who is agreeable to acting as your advocate.
- ideally, someone who knows you well enough to have a clear idea of your preferences, including any religious considerations that need to be taken into account, so he or she can make an informed decision.
- available by telephone, but he or she does not have to be related to you, living with you, or even in the same area.

Even if it is legal in your state, do not consider naming your treating doctor or an employee or operator of the treating health facility as your agent. There is too great a conflict of interest.

Tip.
- Name the same agent in each of your medical advance directives, so there is no conflict. This advice does not extend to agents for business affairs or guardians of your children.
- Name more than one agent in case the first agent is unavailable when needed or refuses to serve. Be clear in the document about your order of preference and that each agent named may act separately (the word in legal terminology is *severally*).

• In any documents dealing with health matters, insert all of your agent's telephone numbers including work, home, summer, and as many addresses as you have so they can be contacted as quickly as possible.

A discussion to have. Despite the emotional difficulties, discuss your wishes with your agents ahead of time. How can someone respect your wishes if you don't make them known? It's not necessary to drive yourself crazy thinking about every possibility, but be clear about your core beliefs, and about as many matters as are important to you.

Tip. Write a letter containing your wishes as a memory aid for your agent.

Oral directives. Since some states permit oral advance directives, it may seem that written documents are unnecessary. However, proving oral discussions is difficult (particularly if testimony is contested) and costs time and money at a time when you can't afford to waste either.

Periodic update. Reaffirm directives by re-initialing and redating them yearly and when your circumstances change (such as when a woman becomes pregnant). Dr. Julie was reluctant to follow the wishes expressed in Graham's living will because it was seven years old. Luckily, Graham's son had a copy of a new living will that Graham had executed a year before but had neglected to give his doctor.

To revoke any advance directive. Any directive can be revoked at any time by destroying it and/or executing a document revoking it and notifying any persons who have copies, including your physician.

Changing agents. You can change agents at any time by notifying them and anyone else who may have a copy of the document (custodians), prefer-

ably in writing. Give custodians a new, properly executed document naming the new agent(s).

Access to the documents. Be sure to inform your spouse, significant other, and/or close friends of the existence and whereabouts of all advance directives. Do not keep them locked away, especially not in your safe-deposit box.

Tip. Advance directives concerning your health can be photocopied to a reduced size so you can carry them when traveling.

Enforcement. For assistance in ensuring that your wishes, or those of a loved one, are honored by the health care system, contact a local attorney; Choice in Dying; or Gentle Closure, 60 Santa Susana Lane, Sedona, AZ 86336 (520-282-0170).

Section 2. Health Care Power of Attorney ↑↑↑

In general, a **power of attorney** is a document in which you, the maker (also known as the **principal**), give another person (the **agent** or **attorney-in-fact**) authority to act on your behalf, as if the agent were you. The document specifies the matters to be covered, which can be specific, such as selling your house, or broad, to do just about anything you can. You determine the time during which the power of attorney is in effect. It can be effective immediately or start at a specified time or upon the occurrence of a named event.

The **health care power of attorney,** also known as the **medical power of attorney, health care proxy,** and **durable health care power of attorney,** is a special kind of power of attorney triggered only in the event of your incapacity or incompetence. As implied in its name, this document requires hospitals, nursing homes, doctors, and other health care providers to obey the agent's decisions as if they were yours. In most states no adult, not even spouses, can make medical decisions for another person without this proxy. While as a practical matter your physician *may* listen to your spouse, why take the chance?

The document must include the word *durable*. Powers terminate in the event the principal becomes incompetent unless they include the word *durable*.

The health care power can be tailored to give your agent as little or as much authority as you choose, but generally it authorizes your agent to make all decisions regarding your health care, including

- the use or withholding of life support and other medical care.
- whether to place you in or check you out of a health facility such as a hospital.
- decisions not specifically covered by a living will.

The power of attorney can also give the agent the right

- to deal with Medicare, public benefits, and private insurance companies.
- to review your medical records.

The health care power of attorney does *not*

- give any authority with respect to financial matters, administering involuntary psychiatric care, or sterilization.
- generally cover medical treatment that would provide comfort or relieve pain, which means that a health care proxy cannot refuse pain relief on your behalf.

Tip. An unmarried partner is not considered a relative under the law and could be barred from visiting you. The health care power of attorney gives that person visitation rights. If you have chosen someone else as your proxy, make sure that you also create a document that provides your unmarried partner access to you.

Duration. The durable health care power of attorney generally only takes effect when two physicians, including the physician of record, certify that you are not capable of understanding or communicating decisions about your health. It will apply as long as this condition continues.

Copies. At least four *original* copies of a durable health care proxy should be executed: one each for the agent, your physician, your pharmacist (to permit an exchange of information without worry about invasion of your privacy), and one to take to the hospital with you should the need arise. (Consider keeping this last copy in your emergency-room bag; see chapter 29, section 3.2.) Make sure your agent knows to have the document placed in your records at the hospital in the event that you cannot present the proxy document upon admission.

Section 3. Living Wills ↑↑↑

Permitted in one form or another in all states, a **living will** is an advance directive that describes your "end-of-life" wishes concerning life-sustaining medical treatment and procedures in the event you become incompetent or unconscious. The living will describes the physical condition(s) the maker determines to trigger the document's provisions, as well as the types of treatments and/or procedures to be avoided. *It only becomes effective as the final statement of intent when the person who executed it is unable to make or express his or her own decisions concerning medical care.* Any instruction to withdraw life support may have no effect during a female patient's pregnancy.

A living will can be drafted in general terms such as to "withhold or withdraw any and all procedures that delay death," or it can be drafted to be specific about authorized and unauthorized procedures. As a general matter, nutrition or water are not withheld if death would result solely from dehydration or starvation rather than an existing illness.

Tip. Check with your doctor to ensure she will abide by your directive. If your doctor won't agree, find out why. If you can't come to an agreement with your doctor and yet don't want to change to another physician, perhaps she would agree to be superseded by a predesignated physician in the event of your incapacity. In some states, any doctor who is furnished a copy of the declaration is required to make it a part of the patient's medical record and, if the doctor is unwilling to comply with the directive, must transfer the patient to a new doctor.

Your values and beliefs. Decisions about end-of-life medical treatments are deeply personal and should be based on your values and beliefs. Because it is impossible to foresee every type of circumstance, think about the quality of life that is important to you. You should consider

- your overall attitude toward life, including the activities you enjoy and situations you fear.
- your attitude about independence and control, and how you feel about losing them.
- your religious beliefs and moral convictions, and how they affect your attitude toward serious illness.
- your attitude toward health, illness, dying, and death.
- your feelings toward doctors and other caregivers.
- the impact of your decisions on family and friends.
- talking about end-of-life decisions with your family, friends, doctor, and/or a clergyperson.

Homework. Talk with your doctor to find out what *may* happen to people with your condition, and what treatments *might* be used, including **life support** treatments. Life support temporarily replaces or supports a failing bodily function until the body can resume normal functioning. At times, the body does not regain the ability to function without life support. Thinking about these matters will not make them happen.

Be as specific as possible. Try to identify procedures as specifically as possible so that little, if any, decision needs to be made by the people trying to carry out your wishes. For instance, instead of using a general phrase like *heroic measures,* which could mean any of a number of medical procedures, list your wishes about:

- **Cardiopulmonary resuscitation:** A group of procedures performed on a person whose heart stops beating (cardiac arrest) or who stops breathing (respiratory arrest) in an attempt to restart the heart and breathing. It can include mouth-to-mouth breathing, chest compressions to mimic the heart's function and cause the blood to circulate, or drugs, electric shocks, and artificial breathing aimed at stimulating the heart and reviving a dying person.
- **Major surgery:** Your wishes could be stated in terms of "major surgery" or specific surgery could be indicated.
- **Respirator** or other **mechanical breathing:** Breathing by machine through a tube in the throat to replace the function of the lungs.
- **Dialysis:** Cleaning the blood by machine.
- **Blood transfusions.**
- **Artificial nutrition** and/or **hydration:** Nutrition and/or liquid is given through a tube in a vein or in the stomach to supplement or replace ordinary eating and drinking. If you want your agent to have the right to withhold nutrition or hydration, Choice in Dying suggests it may be best to include a general statement such as "My agent knows my wishes concerning artificial nutrition and hydration." Adding more to the general statement may unintentionally restrict your agent's authority to act in your best interest.
- **Pain medications.** These may indirectly shorten life.

You could also state a general procedural preference tied to a projected outcome. For example, in the event of lung failure, you could decide that you want to be placed on a respirator if it is likely that you will survive it, but not if the likelihood for survival and return to a quality of life that is important to you is slim. You can also state your preference in terms of medications and procedures that treat the symptoms rather than the disease (such as painkillers, blood transfusions, tube feeding, or a respirator).

Relationship to health care power of attorney. It is good to have both documents. The agent named in your durable medical power of attorney becomes involved if you become unable, even temporarily, to make a health care decision. The person named in your living will only becomes involved if you are near death and a decision needs to be made about withholding or discontinuing further medical treatment or sustenance. While it is safest to designate the same person as agent in both documents, if you don't, *be sure to include a provision in your living will to the effect that "if there is a conflict between the health care proxy and this living will, then the (name the person in the selected document) shall prevail."*

Section 4. Do Not Resuscitate Order ↑↑↑

A **DNR** (do not resuscitate order) prohibits your medical team from taking measures to revive you in the event your heart or lungs stop functioning if you are near death. Your wishes concerning resuscitation may be contained in your living will. However, if you only want to cover this one situation, you can execute a separate DNR order.

A DNR order only applies when the heart stops beating or the lungs stop breathing. A DNR order only applies to CPR. It does not mean that other treatments are not offered or given. That is where the living will comes in.

Only a few states have laws governing DNR or-

ders. Generally, DNR orders are regulated by a health care facility's policies.

Note: Some states require DNR documents to be executed prior to each hospital admission in order to remain effective. If you want to have a DNR order, for safety tell the hospital admitting personnel when you are admitted to a hospital or nursing home that you want to execute a DNR (and be sure it goes into your record).

Section 5. Guardianship

In the event of incapacitation, judges generally appoint an **evaluator** (usually an attorney who will be paid from your assets) to evaluate the situation for the court. If the allegedly incapacitated person is found to be unable to make financial and/or health decisions, the court appoints a **guardian** (also known as a **conservator**) to make the necessary decisions for a specified time.

Usually the guardian is an attorney who has no clue how you would want your life managed. The guardian most often ends up just paying bills rather than making appropriate decisions that could incur liability. In addition, the court-appointed guardian will require payment for services from your estate, adding another drain on your finances.

You can imagine how expensive the procedure, and the resulting decisions, can be to you and your estate. Even worse, the guardian may be intrusive in your life and decide totally opposite to what you would want. It also depends on the state and the court as to whether the guardian can or would transfer your assets to satisfy Medicaid eligibility requirements.

Tip. Not only is a guardianship likely to be more expensive than creating the durable power of attorney described below, appointment of a guardian also entails public disclosure of personal matters and financial information. However, if you prefer to have court supervision of the guardianship with the additional protection that brings, and full disclosure to all interested parties, then rely on a guardianship and do not execute a durable power of attorney.

Preneed designation of guardian. In some states, you can execute a **preneed designation of guardian,** which designates your desired guardian in the event of need. Only judges can determine who the guardian will be, but they will generally follow your designation.

Section 6. The Durable Power of Attorney ↑↑↑

One method of avoiding a court-appointed guardian is by use of a **durable power of attorney.** A durable power of attorney is a type of power of attorney that is used for business and other affairs. Because it contains the magic word *durable,* it does not terminate if the **principal** (the person who executes the power of attorney) becomes unable to communicate or is otherwise incapacitated. It does terminate on death of the principal.

Powers can be effective immediately or, if the law of your state allows it, can be **springing:** the power "springs" to life when an event or events described in the power occur. For example, it could be stated that the power only becomes effective if and when you, the principal, become incapacitated.

The document can give the agent or some third party the power to determine when the principal has become incapacitated. This doesn't mean your agent can just declare you incapacitated. The agent must start the process by asking your doctor to certify incapacity. An effective provision that balances the needs of the parties and timeliness would be to permit the agent to determine incapacity with the confirming advice (or agreement) of two physicians, one of whom is your attending physician. If you do not provide any instructions, a court may have to make the determination.

Tip. Provide in the power of attorney for a periodic reexamination of your capacity.

Powers can be general, or limited to matters specifically stated such as dealing with Medicaid or Medicare, signing checks or paying bills. Powers do not generally (and in some states may not) cover health, marital status, or testamentary dispositions. In a few states, a principal is allowed to delegate to the agent in the durable power of attorney various health care powers in addition to control over financial matters. In some states, such as New York, a health care power of attorney must be a separate document from a power of attorney used to manage the property and financial affairs of the principal.

To be sure the agent has all the necessary powers to take care of unforeseen matters, it is preferable to include a general list of important specific powers in addition to the ones specified in the state statute. Unless these powers are specifically mentioned, the agent's actions may be limited to only the matters described in the statute. Consider giving your agent the power to

• change your domicile to a state where Medicaid rules are more favorable.
• access safe-deposit boxes.
• renounce or disclaim an inheritance and/or insurance proceeds. This could be useful for estate and Medicaid planning unless prohibited by state law.
• sign tax returns, sign IRS powers of attorney, and settle tax disputes in case of an IRS audit.
• deal with and collect proceeds from health and/or long-term care insurance. With respect to your life insurance policy(s): to take a loan against the coverage, to accelerate any death benefit, and even to sell the coverage.
• make gifts or continue a gifting plan that can be used to systematically reduce the size of an estate and thus the estate tax or to qualify for Medicaid.
• your right to revoke or amend the power of attorney itself.

Tip. To preclude any questions about your competency, when you execute a power, attach a letter from your attending physician stating that you are competent.

A power of attorney, like all of the other documents discussed in this chapter, can be revoked at any time. It is revoked automatically when the principal returns to mental competence or dies.

Tip. In some states the appointment of a guardian or other representative terminates the power of attorney. In those states, name the agent to also act as your conservator, committee, or guardian.

Consult with a local attorney before signing any power of attorney to be sure of the correct wording and effectiveness in the state in which you reside.

Whom to choose as an agent. Unlike in matters involving your health, where timeliness is usually important, you may consider appointing two or more people to act together as your agent for your nonhealth affairs. The decisions involved in business affairs are quite different from those involved with health, and the checks and balances that two people provide may be of value.

Copies. If you execute a durable power of attorney, execute up to six duplicate originals since many companies or organizations insist on having an original for their files. Also, go to your bank, your stockbroker, and any other financial institutions you deal with and get a copy of their power of attorney form. Although each of these companies would eventually accede to your form, they are likely to give your agent a needless hassle if your power is not on their form. They can also be expected to hassle over a power executed more than a few years ago, so it is best to re-execute this document every few years.

Tip. Whether required by statute or not, include the notarized signature of your agent or agents on your power. It is the authenticity of that signature upon which the person to whom the power of attorney is presented will be relying.

Section 7. Revocable Living Trust

For purposes of this chapter, it is only important to know that another alternative to guardianship is the creation of a revocable living trust. A revocable living trust allows you to be in control, while appointing a successor to take over if you become disabled. These entities are discussed in chapter 33, section 3.6.

I do not recommend creation of a living trust solely to avoid guardianship. However, it is an ancillary benefit to be considered when exploring the uses of such a device.

Section 8. Preneed Decisions Concerning Minor Children

By being prepared, you can control the situation in the event of your incapacity or death and assure that your children are taken care of in accordance with your wishes rather than those of a court-appointed guardian.

Tip. If you use any of the alternatives mentioned in this chapter, discuss with your potential choice for guardian your views on education, moral upbringing, religion, possibly nutrition and exercise, and any other matters of importance to you. Confirm your thoughts in writing so you do not have to rely on the person's memory. Include relevant personal information about each minor—such as likes or dislikes, medical history, and school history.

8.1 Guardian for Children

One method of protecting your children is to petition the court to appoint a guardian now. This gives you the opportunity to present your version of why your candidate should be appointed. On the other hand, appointment of a guardian now means that you have to give up your legal rights to your children. While the children could live with you, and you can always ask the court to revoke the guardianship, no decisions could be made about the children unless you obtain the agreement of the guardian.

Standby guardian. In some states you can go to court now to have a person named **standby guardian**—which means the person doesn't become guardian until a specific event happens, such as your incapacitation. In addition to the advantages of a guardian just discussed, there is the added advantage that the person is in place to start acting immediately if something happens to you.

Preneed designation of guardian. Another alternative in some states is to use a variant of the preneed designation of guardian described in section 5, designating a person as a guardian for your children. It provides for the care of your children without your giving up custody now, since it does not take effect until (and only for as long as) there is a "need."

Identifying the guardian. If your children's other parent is alive and involved in their lives, that person would normally become the guardian. But if that person is abusive, estranged from the children, or is unfit, you will want to pick another caretaker.

When choosing a person to serve as guardian or substitute guardian:

• Many therapists suggest that the children be involved in identifying a guardian. In any event, this may be a good time for the children to spend more time with their potential guardian.
• Do you and the person share the same thoughts on raising children? Will that person follow your wishes?
• Does the person want to raise your children, and do they all get along?

• Does the person have the energy and resources to raise a child? Does he or she have a friend or family that can help out if necessary?
• If you are considering naming a couple as guardian, be sure to state what happens if they no longer live together. You don't want your children to be the sad object of a messy divorce.
• Keep in mind the court will probably check to see if the person has any prior complaints filed against him or her, particularly concerning child abuse.

Tip. The other parent of your children has the right to request custody of them. To avoid a hassle, try to obtain the other parent's written agreement to your chosen guardian. If that doesn't work, or if even the request would be problematic, speak with an attorney about how to handle the situation.

8.2 An Adoptive Family for Your Children

If there are no appropriate family members or friends to care for your children if you die, consider choosing a "second family" for the children. Taking such an action now relieves stress for both you and the children. Children will be reassured that they will not be left alone or abandoned if you die. There are local programs to help parents find adoptive families.

An adoption has the following advantages:

• The children, once adopted, have the same right to support and benefits from the adoptive parents as if they were born to them.
• The adoptive parents do not risk losing custody.

Disadvantages:

• You lose all of your rights to custody of the children and to make decisions for them.
• The adoption may also add more stress to the children because it could be a constant re-

minder that a parent is ill and will probably be gone one day.

Adoption generally requires the consent of both parents if they are alive and have not abandoned the children. A court must approve the adoptive parent(s) and will probably conduct an investigation to make sure the person or people are fit to be parents. Adoption is permanent, while guardianship or custody may be temporary.

8.3 Foster Care

Foster care, placing your children with adults who will be responsible for them, without adopting them, is a fail-safe alternative if you are not able to care for your children and no other care is available. If you need financial assistance to keep your children out of foster care, or if you want to explore setting up foster care now, contact your GuardianOrg, a social worker, or your local welfare agency for advice.

Section 9. Where to Store Advance Directives

Do not keep any advance directives in your safe-deposit box. They would not be accessible when needed. Preferably the documents should be kept as noted below.

Tip. Choice in Dying has an electronic living will registry. As part of the registration service, the organization will review your advance directive to verify validity. In case of a medical crisis, the registry will immediately fax a copy of your document twenty-four hours a day. The onetime registration fee is $45 for members, $55 for nonmembers.

Document	Original	Copy
Durable power of attorney	in your possession* and/or your attorney's	the agent and any alternate
Durable power of attorney for health care	in the possession of the agent and/or your attorney	your primary physician, pharmacist, nursing home, and/or hospital
Living will	duplicate originals to your doctor and the person who will make decisions for you	let close relatives know your wishes
DNR	original to your doctor	next of kin
Preneed designation	in possession of the named guardian	your attorney

*Documents in your possession should be stored in a fireproof, accessible file or drawer.

Chapter 33

Providing for the Passage of Assets to Your Heirs

I'm not really superstitious, but I am afraid if I write a will, I'm going to die.
—Ellen N.

Regardless of health or age, every adult should plan for the transfer of assets when he or she dies.

Section 1. In General

Why plan? If you don't decide who gets what and then take steps to implement those decisions, state law will make the decisions for you in ways that seldom have anything to do with your desires. Their choice of heirs is generic, not specific to any individual. Likewise, if you are involved in a relationship that is not legally recognized, your assets will pass to your blood relatives, leaving the person you care about in the cold—particularly if one of your assets is your mutual home.

What assets? Before focusing on how you will dispose of your assets, review the financial picture you created in chapter 4. To view your finances for estate planning purposes:

- All permanent, term, and group life insurance should be valued at the death benefit minus any outstanding loans or accelerated benefits received. In addition to coverage you may have through your employer, be sure to include cov-

erages through any group, union, association, and political or fraternal organization to which you may belong.
- Delete from your calculations any debt that is covered by credit life insurance since the insurance will pay the debt.
- Reduce the value of jointly held property with a right of survivorship by the amount that the surviving joint owner can prove he or she paid. The presumption for tax purposes is that the first-to-die owner of a jointly owned property paid for it all, except for the amount the survivor can prove he/she paid. If you reside in a community property state, your spouse may own one-half of your assets even if they are not listed in his or her name, so only include your half interest.
- Even though you do not own them, include in your calculations assets over which you have a power of appointment to pay to yourself, your creditors, your estate, or creditors of your estate, since they will be included in your estate for estate tax purposes.

Tip. This is a good time to review beneficiary designations in life and/or accidental death insurance policy(ies), retirement plan(s), bank accounts, trusts, and contractual arrangements that have a provision that takes effect at death. No matter what you state in your will, these designations will prevail. If any designation doesn't reflect your wishes, change it. Connie T. was horrified to find that the ex-husband she had jailed for not making his child support payments was still listed as the beneficiary on her largest life insurance policy.

Funeral arrangements. Your will is not admitted to probate until a period after your demise. Therefore, it is important to make your funeral wishes known now to those who will carry them out (see chapter 34). It is also a good idea to state your desires in your will to confirm your intent.

Title. If any of your assets are registered with another person, check the title to determine what happens when you die. For example, if you own your house with another person with a "right of survivorship," the house passes automatically to that person on your death.

A chart on the next page shows the legal consequences of various forms of ownership. The consequences noted will become clear as you read through the remainder of the chapter.

Goals. Regardless of the state of your health, ask yourself what you want to happen to your assets if you die tomorrow. Decide how to balance your desires with those of your loved ones and then take taxes into consideration.

Think about whom you want to receive your assets and when. For example, if you want to leave a substantial amount of money to a ten-year-old, you may want the child to receive only the income from the principal until age twenty-one, at twenty-one to receive a portion of the principal, and at age thirty to receive the balance—at a time when he is likely to be able to handle money.

Also, think about alternate heirs in the event that a person named in your will dies before you or before the time stated to receive an asset.

Periodic review. *Review your total estate plan annually, updating it as necessary, and perhaps letting those involved know about any changes that you feel are pertinent to them. A good time to do this is when you're compiling tax information each year.*

Section 2. Your Will

Now that you have a fix on your assets and what you want to do with them, *you need a challenge-resistant, legally valid, up-to-date will (also known as a **last will and testament**). This is necessary regardless of health, wealth, or marital status.*

Cost should not be a factor in determining whether you have a will. Wills are generally not expensive, ranging from a few hundred dollars to a few thousand for a complex will. Many GuardianOrgs have lists of lawyers who will prepare one for free.

Your desires. A will disposes of your property in virtually any way you choose. There are certain limitations however. A will cannot
- change the disposition of property subject to title or contract restrictions (such as property owned in joint name with right of survivorship, or contractually determined business interests).
- disinherit a spouse. At the very least, your spouse may be entitled to the amount that would have been received if you had died without a will. In some states, such as New York, while the spouse can make an election to receive a percentage of your assets in spite of the terms of the will, a spouse cannot elect against life insurance or even against assets in a revocable trust.
- bequeath assets to an illegal organization.
- impose on a bequest conditions that are socially undesirable and therefore generally unenforceable (such as leaving money to a daughter provided she agrees to divorce her husband).

What your will must include. Your will must include *who* will receive your assets, *what* they will

˃ ˃

Legal Consequences of Various Forms of Ownership

Form of Ownership	Subject to Probate	Subject to Federal Estate Tax	Control During Your Lifetime	Can Pass by Will	Subject to Claims of Creditors Before Death	Subject to Claims of Creditors After Death	Available to Beneficiaries
Asset solely owned	yes	all	full	yes	yes	yes	delayed
Asset owned jointly by spouses	no	one-half	divided	no[1]	yes	no[2]	immediately
Asset owned jointly by others	no[1]	all[3]	divided	no[1]	yes	no[1]	immediately[1]
Assets in bank account (Totten) trust	no	all	full	no	yes	no	immediately
Assets in custodial account for minors	no	none[4]	none	no	no	no	immediately
Life insurance owned by insured	no[6]	all	full	no[6]	no	no[6]	immediately
Life insurance owned by other than insured	no[6]	none[8]	none	no	no	no[6]	immediately

Continued on next page

Legal Consequences of Various Forms of Ownership *(cont'd)*

Form of Ownership	Subject to Probate	Subject to Federal Estate Tax	Control during Your Lifetime	Can Pass by Will	Subject to Claims of Creditors before Death	Subject to Claims of Creditors after Death	Available to Beneficiaries
Life insurance payable to deceased's estate	yes	all	full	yes	yes[7]	yes	delayed
Assets in a revocable living trust	no	all	full	no	yes	no[9]	immediately[5]
Assets in an irrevocable living trust	no	none	none	no	no	no	immediately[5]

1. Provided that the joint owner survives.
2. Unless debt was incurred by both joint owners.
3. Except to the extent your estate can prove that a surviving joint owner contributed to the acquisition or improvement of the property.
4. Unless you are a custodian as well as a donor.
5. Subject, however, to all of the terms of the trust, which may include a provision postponing distribution of the property.
6. Provided that a beneficiary designated in the insurance policy survives. Otherwise, the proceeds become a part of the probate estate.

7. Limited to the cash surrender value of the policy.
8. Unless the policy is assigned to another within three years of the date of death.
9. Some states expose revocable trust assets to creditors' claims.

The chart is from *The Executor's Handbook* by Theodore E. Hughes and David Klein, copyright © 1994 by Theodore E. Hughes and David Klein. Reprinted by permission of Facts On File, Inc.

receive, *when* they will receive them, and *how* the distribution will be administered. Each of these subjects are covered in order below.

2.1 Who Will Receive Your Assets

If you are married, in a relationship, or have children, your answer to the question of who will re-

ceive your assets may be clear. If you're single, you may need to take some time to consider who and what is important to you.

Tip. Whether as a payback for helping you or to assist others in a similar situation, consider leaving at least a part of your estate to a GuardianOrg that does research on, advocates for, or provides support to people with the condition with which you have been diagnosed. If you are considering donating a large percentage of your estate, ask a local attorney or research for yourself whether in your state of residence there is a maximum you can leave to charity without challenge by your legal heirs.

Tip. If any of your beneficiaries are having marital problems, check the local law regarding whether inheritances are treated as separate property for divorce purposes.

Minors who are beneficiaries. If any of the people you want to leave your assets to are minors, as defined by the laws of your state (usually a person under age eighteen, although twenty-one is not uncommon), the court will appoint a guardian to hold or manage any money or property left to them. As described in chapter 32, section 5, you can influence who the guardian is by a preneed declaration of guardian. As an alternative, in your will you can nominate the person or persons you would like the court to appoint as your child's guardian and an alternate. While only the court can appoint a guardian, the will can be used in court as proof of your wishes.

An alternative that can provide flexibility is to create a trust in your will to hold your child's property. The trust would start on your demise and continue until your child reaches whatever age you specify. It also allows you to give the trustee(s) instructions about how you would like the money invested and spent. This idea also works for anyone to whom you want to leave assets but isn't "good with money."

Tip. If a friend or family member is asked to be the trustee, he or she is likely to agree to serve without compensation. Trustee's fees can deplete the value of your bequests, particularly if the trust is long-term.

Tip. Whether you use a guardian and/or a trustee, in a side document, *not* in the will, you should write the guidelines that are important to you for the person who will have legal responsibility for your child.

As an alternative to a guardianship, many states have adopted the Uniform Transfers to Minors Act, which permits you to leave your property to a named custodian for the benefit of your children. Property left to the custodian will be managed and distributed in accordance with the detailed rules set out in the Tax Code. A custodian does not have any legal responsibility for the child. The property will be distributed at age twenty-one. If you retain any control over the account at your death, and the child has not reached age twenty-one, the account will be included in your estate for estate tax purposes.

Note: While I am not suggesting it, if you want to disinherit a child, your will should specifically state that fact. If your state permits disinheriting a child and you don't mention it in your will, the child may still have a claim against your assets.

2.2 What They Will Receive

When setting the amounts to be given to various beneficiaries, anticipate changes in your financial affairs. For example, it is acceptable to list specific dollar amounts that are small relative to the current size of your net estate, but don't specify dollar amounts that are large relative to your net worth. When George S. wrote his will, he was worth $250,000. He left $10,000 each to several friends and relatives, and the remainder went to Susan. Since his estate had shrunk by the time he died, Susan got little after the $10,000 gifts were distributed. This was not George's intent.

Tip. Leaving personal assets to a trusted person makes it easier to change your designated beneficiaries from time to time. Give that person a letter specifying which items go to whom. Since the letter does not have the full import of a will, it can be changed at your whim. If the will makes reference to the side letter, and the letter is found in a place where it is expected, this type of disposition is legally binding in most states. In those states where it is not legally binding, you will have to rely on the integrity of the person you choose. If any items that person is to give away exceed $10,000 in value, or $20,000 if married and his or her spouse agrees to the gift, a gift tax will have to be paid, so leave them money to cover the tax.

Tip. If you own property jointly with a right of survivorship with someone family members don't like, it is possible the family will contest the disposition. You can protect against a contest by leaving the property to the joint owner in your will.

Debts. Debts at the time of your demise that are not paid off by specific insurance must be paid before any assets can be distributed to your beneficiaries.

If an asset is subject to a debt, specify whether you want the bequest of that asset to be subject to the debt, or whether the debt is to be paid off first. For example, if there is a mortgage on your house, and you have assets that could pay off the debt, specify whether you are leaving the designated beneficiary the house subject to the mortgage or whether you want other assets used to pay off the mortgage.

2.3 When They Will Receive

Generally, a will passes assets to your beneficiaries upon your demise. But, as noted in section 5 below, your heirs will not receive the assets until sometime during or at the end of the probate period. In some states this is not a problem because procedures are so simple that the transfer to the beneficiary can occur rather quickly. In others, the nature of the required proceedings can take a good deal of time even if everything moves as quickly as possible.

2.4 How the Disposition Will Be Administered

You will need to name a person to "execute" the wishes described in the will. This person, the **personal representative,** also known in some states as the **executor,** should be someone who

- has the mental capacity to understand your wishes;
- the sense of responsibility to actually carry them out; and
- is friendly to, or at least not hostile toward, your heirs.

Responsibilities of the personal representative. The personal representative will gather all your assets and do the necessary administration, which includes
- informing the appropriate people.
- gathering your property and having it appraised.
- paying debts.
- preparing and filing requisite estate and income tax returns.
- preparing an accounting.
- distributing the assets to your heirs.

Identity of the personal representative. The personal representative does not need to know the law. An attorney can be hired by the estate as a guide.

If the personal representative is not an attorney, you can expect the estate to be charged a fee for the personal representative (usually the statutory fee, although the representative could take less or waive the fee altogether), and an additional fee for the attorney. If the personal representative gathers all the information and drafts the necessary forms, the attorney's billed hours can be relatively small. The money the personal representative receives is a tax deduction to the estate, so if there is an estate tax, the money is passed to the representative at the lower income tax rate.

If you want to choose an attorney as a personal representative, discuss whether the attorney will charge one fee or two. Although the functions of personal representative and attorney are different, in some states only one charge is allowed if an attorney fills both functions.

Before you appoint someone in any official capacity in your will, get their consent. Don't allow the appointment to be a surprise.

Successors. Be sure to provide in your will for a successor personal representative in case the first named person dies or is unable or unwilling to perform the role.

2.5 Protect Against Challenges

No matter how competent you are, and how closely you follow the requirements for the creation of a valid will, a will can always be challenged. In many states, when a will is admitted to probate, the people who would inherit under the law if you died intestate are entitled to notice and to challenge its validity. There may be other people or entities who would consider challenging a will. Whether it is true or not, it may be claimed that just because of your diagnosis, you were legally incompetent to make a will, or that one of the beneficiaries unduly influenced you.

In general, you must have **testamentary capacity** in order to execute a will, which means you must be able to show that you understand

- you are making a will;
- the nature and extent of your estate;
- the nature and extent of your dispositions; and
- the natural objects of your bounty—your legal heirs (even if you are not going to include them in the will).

To protect against possible challenges, follow precisely the requirements of your state with respect to the execution of a will. Also make sure that the witnesses

- are not relatives of yours;
- are not named in the will as primary or contingent beneficiaries; and
- do not otherwise stand to benefit from your death.

Also consider any or all of the following alternatives:

- So there can be no question about the substitution of pages, be sure all the pages are bound by something like a staple and that it has not been unstapled before you sign. Initial each page in an innocuous place such as the bottom right-hand corner. When you have the witnesses sign, ask each of them to add their initials in the same area as your initials on each page. The pages can be held in such a manner that the witnesses cannot read the substance of the will even while they are adding their initials, and then their signatures at the end of the document.
- Videotape, without interruption in the filming, the execution of the will. Ideally, the tape should start with a discussion proving to the viewer that you have necessary testamentary capacity. You should also state on camera that you either wrote the will yourself or, if someone else prepared it, that you read it over word for word and that by signing the document you know you are executing your will as your own free act. If your survivors would consider the provisions in your will unusual, explain why you are making such dispositions. Name your witnesses and get their consent to act as your witnesses on tape. The camera should then record your initialing the pages and signing the will in sight of all the witnesses and their initialing each page and signing at the end. It should be obvious throughout the tape that all witnesses are present with you during the entire proceeding. Give the tape to your attorney to hold, or store it in your safe-deposit box.

  Caution: The tape could work against you if

you do not look competent, if you look ill, or if a person who could be accused of undue influence over you is present. Some people associate looking poorly with thinking poorly or being incompetent. Don't videotape the proceedings if you speak haltingly even if that is your normal speech pattern. The person or people who will decide from the videotape about your competence do not know you and will only have the tape as a measure.

- If a videotape doesn't work for you, consider asking a court reporter to attend the execution of the will to record your exact words.
- Look for witnesses who are presentable and articulate. They should already know you so they can state, if necessary, that you appeared no different from usual.
- Ask the witnesses to sign an affidavit immediately after execution of the will stating that
  - you asked them to act as witnesses to your execution of your will.
  - they witnessed you execute your will in their presence and in the presence of each other.
  - they signed your will in your presence and in the presence of each other.
  - in their opinion you were of sound mind, memory, and understanding.
  - you could read, write, and converse in the English language.
  - you understood the nature of your assets and the identities of the people who would receive your assets if there were no will.
  - you were not suffering from any defect of sight, hearing, or speech or from any other physical or mental impairment that could affect your capacity to make a will.
  - you were not under any undue influence. Their signatures should then be notarized. It would also help if each witness made notes (to be kept with the will) about the conversations that took place that indicated your competence.
- Consider having your psychotherapist or physician as one of the witnesses, or at least ask one of them to sign an affidavit or other document

attesting to your capacity on the same day you execute your will. They should store the original of the document in their files, and place a copy with the original of the will. If all else fails, at least ask your doctor to make a notation about your legal competence in your file at a date as close as possible to the date of the will's execution.

- A clergyman would also make a good witness.
- State in your will that if any beneficiary challenges its validity, whatever would have been payable to the challenging beneficiary is payable to another named beneficiary. This only works if you are leaving the challenging beneficiary something substantial, so that the challenging beneficiary has something to lose if he contests the will. It also works if the challenge causes pain to someone the challenger cares about. For instance, when Graham C. was concerned about his brother Daniel challenging his will—which left nothing to Daniel, but a substantial sum of money to Daniel's children—Graham wrote in his will that if Daniel challenged the will, all the bequests to Daniel's children would go to Graham's friend Cheryl.
- While, as a general matter, you should only have one will, one way to protect against challenges is to intentionally write "serial" wills with a significant time (such as a few weeks) between the execution of each will. Under this method, if a later will is challenged, the earlier will stands (and presumably doesn't give the challenging party any more than under the later will).

In the hospital. If you or the person you care about is in the hospital as you are reading this, and there is no will, it's not too late to write one. If necessary, find out if your state is one of the few that permits oral wills or **holographic** wills (handwritten wills) and, if so, what the requirements are. Generally, a valid holographic will must expressly state that it is a will, must be entirely in the handwriting of the person who makes the will, and must be dated and signed. The will could be placed in the hospital's safe-deposit box until the patient's discharge from the hospital.

Even if holographic wills are permitted in your state, consider executing a traditional will. The hospital can probably provide witnesses and/or a notary, even if somewhat reluctantly. The reluctance comes from fear of liability, but it can usually be overcome by a request to the appropriate supervisory person. If necessary the hospital ombudsman or patients' rights advocate can help collect the necessary people.

I oversaw execution of Gordon M.'s will as he was literally being wheeled into surgery. His estranged wife might have challenged the will on the basis of a preoperative injection, so I had a doctor and a nurse interview him before he signed. Luckily, he survived the surgery. We executed the will again in the formal setting of my law office a few weeks later to prevent any challenge.

2.6 Writing Your Will Yourself

If your will is going to be "simple," you can write it yourself, provided you act cautiously and with knowledge. Examples of a "simple" situation:

- If your only assets of value are $10,000 in a bank account and a few antiques from your parents, and you want to leave everything to your wife, who is also to act as the administrator of your estate. Your son is to succeed her as beneficiary and administrator if she dies before you, or within sixty days after your demise.
- Your estate is well below $625,000 in value, you have no surviving spouse, and you want to leave everything equally to your adult children who are alive at the time of your death, or everything goes to the survivor if one of them predeceases you.
- Everything of real value is titled to automatically pass to the people you care about.

Consult an attorney rather than writing your own will if you

- want to disinherit a spouse or children.
- have infirm or incompetent heirs.
- own a small business.
- want to leave a gift that is conditional on some event or is in a trust.
- have mutual wills with your spouse but want to change your dispositions.
- anticipate a challenge to your will (especially if it could be argued that you were not of sound mind or were under undue influence).
- have complex ownership or business arrangements.
- have minor children.
- have a spouse who is not a citizen of the United States.
- have real property located in another state.
- have a substantial amount of assets.
- have any complication at all in either your assets or how or to whom you want your assets distributed.

Even if the situation is "simple," you should be cautious. You will not be here to correct mistakes. *Precisely* follow the requirements in the state of your residence. Call your GuardianOrg for the rules if you can't find them on your own. It is definitely better to err on the side of safety. For example, when two witnesses are required, use three. When identifying your beneficiaries, be precise by adding to their names their relationship to you (e.g., my wife, Carol Brown, or my niece Kathy Woodside) and a current address, which should be stated as "currently residing at . . ." List alternates in the event the person predeceases you, or the entity goes out of business.

If you need to research your state's law, most law libraries in county courthouses are open to the public, and the librarians there are generally helpful to nonlawyers who wish to learn how to do their own legal research. Ask them how you can locate the state's statutes concerning wills.

Do-it-yourself will kits are available from stationery stores, on numerous software programs, and in books that are easily available, several of which are listed in the resources section. However, *an invalid will is the same as not having a will at all.* A will is susceptible to challenges for a number of reasons, and when money is involved, you can expect people to act unexpectedly. The risks involved in writing and executing your will yourself are not worth the few Life Units you will save.

Tip. If you prepare your will yourself, have an attorney familiar with the laws of your state review it before execution. If you've already done it, it's not too late to get it reviewed now. A will can always be amended or rewritten entirely. Even if you cannot obtain a will for free, most attorneys charge little for preparation of a will.

2.7 Where to Keep Your Will

A "safe place" is the easy answer, but it should not be so "safe" that no one can find it. A will that is lost or destroyed by an unhappy survivor can leave you intestate. In addition, you must be sure it is accessible to those who either have a legal obligation to file it with the court or would personally want to see it filed because they stand to benefit.

While a safe-deposit box is the place that usually springs to mind, it can be a mistake in those states where the box is sealed immediately upon the death of the renter, delaying probate and incurring additional costs. In my experience, it is best to leave the original of your will with your attorney, if he is willing to accept it, and to keep a copy in a safe place that can easily be located by your beneficiary. The copy should indicate the location of the original.

List of information and instructions. To make things easier, keep the List of Instructions described in chapter 5, section 3, with the will or the duplicate. If you didn't create the list when you were assessing your situation, now is a good time to do it. It will assure that your desires are carried out, in the fastest and least expensive manner. Include any instructions you want people to have with respect to maintaining your assets, such as instructions for a continuing business. Since circumstances can change rapidly, it is best not to include these instructions in your will.

2.8 Moving from State to State

Generally, moving from one state to another will have no effect on the validity of your will. However, the will must have been valid at the time it was made. If you move permanently, even though your will should remain valid, state laws can have an impact. For example, if you move to California or Texas, the community property laws of those states will override the dispositions in your will for property acquired after the move, or for property that you specifically convert from common law property to community property. If you move, have your will reviewed by a local attorney.

2.9 Changing or Revoking Your Will

An out-of-date will can sometimes be worse than no will. If you want to change your will, you can either write a new one or change the existing one with an amendment called a **codicil**. The requirements for execution of a valid codicil are the same as the requirements for a valid will. Generally, the codicil contains a description of the changes you want to make, as well as a catchall statement that what is not changed in the will is intended to remain in effect. Have an attorney help you write your codicil since you may inadvertently affect the validity of all or part of the rest of your will. If your will is a simple one, it may be just as easy to execute a new will.

Revoke your will. You can revoke a will or a codicil by destroying the original document. If the document is to be superseded by another document, it is important to state in the later document that it revokes and supersedes all previous documents, so there is no question about your intent.

Section 3. Will Substitutes

A **will substitute** is anything that moves property from one person to another without going through a will, and thus probate. Some of the methods are

- registration of title.
- listing a beneficiary on a retirement plan.
- trusts.

Each of these various methods has its advantages and disadvantages.

Tip. As a general matter, a decedent's creditors (other than the IRS) cannot attack assets that pass through a will substitute unless the beneficiary is the estate or unless the state legislature grants that right (which some do, particularly with respect to revocable trusts).

3.1 Registration of Title

If you refer to the chart in section 1 above, you will see the effects of various means of title registration. For example, through a joint tenancy with the right of survivorship, an asset automatically passes to the other named person. The downside of such an arrangement is that the other person has a stake in the asset immediately upon the registration of title, and you can't change your mind about his ownership without his consent.

3.2 Registration of Bank Accounts in General

You can pass title immediately by registering your bank account as a "pay on death account." This type of registration lets you control the money while you are alive, but it automatically passes to your beneficiary on your demise.

3.3 Totten Trusts

Totten trusts are a form of registering savings bank accounts and certificates of deposit. The owner retains full control during his lifetime and pays taxes on the interest. On the owner's demise, the ownership of the account passes to the named beneficiary without the need for probate. Unlike the other trusts mentioned above, there can be no conditions or age restrictions on the bequest. Since usually only one beneficiary can be named per account, if more than one beneficiary is to be named, there has to be more than one account. All that is necessary to establish a Totten trust is a signature card at the bank, at no cost to the owner.

3.4 Custodial Accounts

The Uniform Gifts to Minors Act or the Uniform Transfers to Minors Act has been adopted by every state. These laws are used when assets are to be set aside for minors to be used when they become adults. If money is set aside in a regular account, the income is taxable to the person who opened the account at his high tax rates. If it is provided for in a custodial account under one of these model laws, the first $1,000 of the account's earnings are taxed at the child's rate and the balance at the account holder's rates until the child is fourteen years old. After fourteen, the entire amount earned is taxed at the child's rates, which are presumably lower than the adult's.

The money cannot be used for the account holder's needs. Funds spent on behalf of the child must be for "extras," not the basic needs parents are expected to satisfy such as food and shelter.

On reaching twenty-one, the child receives the money and has unrestricted use of it, no matter the purpose for which the account holder set it up. If the person who set up the account dies while serving as custodian before the child reaches majority, the money in the account will be counted as part of the account holder's estate for estate tax purposes.

3.5 Trusts in General

Another mechanism that bypasses probate is the use of a **trust,** particularly the use of an increasingly common instrument known as a revocable living trust, which will be discussed in the next section. A trust can be a useful tool for a lot of people—not just the rich. A trust is a legal entity like a paper bag into which you put whatever assets you want. On the bag, you put instructions for use of the contents. You can hold on to the bag or give it to someone else. Whoever holds the bag must follow the instructions.

There are **living trusts** and **testamentary trusts.** A living trust is created while the **grantor,** the person who sets up the trust, is still alive. A testamentary trust is created under the terms of a will. A living trust can either be **revocable,** which means it can be revoked or changed by the grantor, or **irrevocable,** which means that it can't be changed after it is created. If the trust is revocable, things can be taken out or put into the trust. Instructions can also be changed. If the grantor becomes disabled or dies, the trust is managed by someone else the grantor designated (i.e., the bag is handed off to someone else who will follow the instructions).

Trusts can generally do everything a will can, and sometimes they can do things a will cannot. For example, a trust can be set up to hold assets for a minor beneficiary, paying expenses that are defined by the grantor (such as education or medical expenses) until a certain age, when either the income or principal or both are passed to the beneficiary.

Tip. Although there are many self-help books on the subject, trusts are sophisticated and complex. *Please do not consider creating any type of trust arrangement without consulting an attorney.* This should not involve more than five or ten hours of an attorney's time.

3.6 Revocable Living Trusts

A **revocable living trust** is a trust that can be revised at any time during the owner's lifetime. A re-

vocable living trust is much more flexible for passing interests in property than joint ownership and should definitely be considered by anyone

- with a substantial net worth.
- with complex assets.
- with an ongoing small business.
- with out-of-state property since it prevents the need for creating an expensive and time-consuming ancillary probate in that other state.
- who anticipates a will contest.

Advantages of a revocable living trust.
- A trust is more difficult to challenge than a will. To challenge a trust, the challenger must start a lawsuit. To challenge a will, the challenger just enters the probate proceedings with little, if any, expense.
- Since the assets legally transferred to the trust are owned by the trust and not by you, they are not subject to probate—with no public disclosure of the terms. During your lifetime, the assets can be given away or sold, or new ones added, and you can have full use of any income that the assets produce.
- You can serve as trustee or as cotrustee with anyone you choose. If you prefer, a revocable living trust allows you to give management duties to someone else as trustee while you receive the income, minus the trustee's fee, if any.
- You have the chance to see how the arrangement works and continually make necessary adjustments.
- If you become incapacitated for any reason, the trust already names a successor trustee who will immediately take over and thereby eliminate the need for a guardian and any related disputes—at least with respect to the assets in the trust.
- It allows for certain controls and management of your property after death that are not available with a will (e.g., bequests to minors to take effect at a certain age).

- A trust can provide for quicker distribution of assets to beneficiaries, but it does not completely eliminate delays. The trustee still has to collect any debts owed to your trust after you die, prepare tax returns, pay bills, and distribute assets, just as the executor of a will would.

- Provision can even be made in your will that any assets not in the trust be "poured over" into the trust on your death. Likewise, the trust can be named beneficiary of a life insurance policy, retirement plan, and contractual benefits. As noted above, check state law to determine whether a revocable trust is subject to creditors' claims.

- If you want your estate administered by someone who doesn't live in your state, a living trust might be better than a will because the trustee probably won't have to meet the residency requirements some state laws impose upon personal representatives.

- If you own real estate in another state and a revocable living trust holds the title to that property, there is no need for complicated, time-consuming "ancillary probate" procedures in that other state.

- It saves probate expense, which in some states can be substantial.

Disadvantages of a revocable living trust.

- A living trust is generally more expensive to establish than a will, both in legal fees and in the costs of transferring title to property to the trust.

- Since it is a separate entity, trust assets have to be kept separate from your other assets and are subject to ongoing legal and accounting expenses. However, these expenses may be offset by savings to your estate after death.

- There are no ongoing management fees if the **grantor** (the person who creates the trust) is also the trustee or if the trustee agrees to serve without compensation. There is also no separate tax identification number if the grantor is the trustee and the trust is revocable. This doesn't change if there is a cotrustee because it is still the grantor's revocable trust and his tax number is used. When the grantor becomes disabled or dies, a new tax ID will be needed with the attendant ongoing expenses. With an irrevocable trust, a separate tax ID number is required from the outset.

- Depending on the state in which the property is located, putting your home in a revocable trust might jeopardize a **homestead exemption** (a legal concept that lets a person who goes through bankruptcy keep his residence in spite of the bankruptcy), result in a transfer fee, or cause your property to be reassessed for property tax purposes.

- Conflicts can arise between the beneficiaries and the trustee or between different classes of beneficiaries.

Tip. Don't transfer ownership of any tax-deferred retirement accounts, such as a 401(k) or an IRA, into these trusts unless you are disabled for Social Security purposes. The IRS will consider it a taxable distribution and may charge you a 10 percent penalty tax.

Creditors and taxes. Although the revocable living trust creates a separate entity that does avoid probate, it does *not* generally protect against your creditors or income and federal estate taxes. You are responsible for taxes on whatever income the trust assets produce. On death, their entire value may be subject to federal estate income tax.

If your trust is the legal owner of an insurance policy on your life and your estate is worth more than $625,000 upon your demise, the trust will have to pay estate taxes on the proceeds of the policy. The only type of trust that can own a policy on your life and yet remove the death benefit from your estate is an irrevocable trust. (Note: the limit of $625,000 gradually increases to $1 million in 2006. See section 4 below.)

You still need a will. A revocable living trust does not make a will unnecessary. You still need a will to take care of assets not included in the trust. If you have minor children, you probably need a will to suggest or nominate a guardian for them. A trust also won't affect nonprobate assets (e.g., jointly owned property).

If you want more information on revocable living trusts, several books are listed in the resources section. See also the tip on page 358.

3.7 Credit Shelter Trust/ Bypass Trust

A revocable living trust can be used to create a **credit shelter trust,** also known as a **bypass trust.** This tactic is often used for married couples with an estate over the $625,000 exemption. If an estate is worth $1.25 million, the husband places the first $625,000 in a revocable living trust. The trust can provide an income to his wife and can allow the trustee to give parts of the principal to his wife or children. The rest of his estate is left to his wife tax free because whatever you leave a surviving spouse is tax free. When the wife dies, the first $625,000 of her estate passes tax free. When she leaves that amount to the children, the effect is that all $1,250,000 passes to the children with no estate tax. Note: a credit shelter trust can also be established in a will.

Tip. Life insurance can be used as a surrogate trust. You can generally pick an alternate payout such as one that pays interest only for a time, then the **corpus** (the rest of the money) is paid to the beneficiary at a date you set.

3.8 Irrevocable Living Trust

This instrument generally only works for people of substantial means and is not used often as an estate planning tool because, as the word *irrevocable* implies, you forever relinquish ownership and control of the trust assets and income. In addition to avoiding probate, this instrument also helps reduce both current and future taxes. Contributions to this trust are considered to be a gift subject to the gift tax. As with a revocable living trust, consult an attorney before establishing this trust.

3.9 Charitable Remainder Trusts

Most charitable gifts given at any time during the owner's lifetime are tax deductible. If a gift is not to be given outright, it can be given through use of a **charitable remainder trust,** in which a beneficiary or beneficiaries are taken care of as you specify, and the remainder of the trust goes to the charity. Some charities offer donors a lifetime income in return for a large gift. Consult a tax adviser before making any of these gifts.

3.10 Incorporation

When a person dies owning a business interest in the form of a proprietorship or partnership, the personal representative is faced with the decision of whether to liquidate the business, sell it as a going concern, or pass it on intact to the beneficiaries. If the business is incorporated, the personal representative can pass on the shares to the beneficiaries, and the decision of what to do with the business is theirs alone. It is also easier to settle the probate estate. Do not incorporate without seeking appropriate legal advice.

3.11 Retirement Plans

The designation of a beneficiary to a retirement plan automatically passes the assets in the plan to the beneficiary upon your demise, no matter what a will may provide.

IRA. The distribution of an IRA at the time of death is not subject to any withdrawal penalty. The distribution is taxable income to the beneficiary unless it is to a surviving spouse, who can elect to treat the entire inherited interest as his or her own, rolling it over to another new IRA, and avoiding taxable income for the year received. This also applies if the spouse receives an eligible rollover distribution from the deceased's employer's qualified plan or tax-sheltered annuity. The receiving spouse can then roll over all or any part of it (or all or any part of a distribution of deductible employee contributions) into a new IRA. He or she *cannot* roll over a distribution into another qualified employer plan or annuity.

A spouse may receive from the IRA up to $5,000 without tax consequence, as a death benefit exclusion. A spouse cannot roll over into another IRA any part of the distribution that qualifies for the $5,000 death benefit exclusion.

Any beneficiary other than the spouse cannot claim a death benefit exclusion for any part of a distribution from a deceased's IRA. A beneficiary other than a spouse also cannot treat an inherited IRA as though he/she established it. The IRA may not be rolled over into, or receive a rollover from, another IRA. No deduction will be allowed for amounts paid into that inherited IRA, nor can deductible contributions be made to an inherited IRA.

The beneficiary of a Roth IRA receives the funds with no income tax.

Section 4. Minimizing Taxes

The process of transferring wealth can literally be a taxing one. The federal government imposes a tax when substantial amounts of property are transferred either by gift or inheritance. A married person can give a spouse, while alive or upon death, an unlimited amount of property, money, and other assets without either party being taxed. This is called the **unlimited marital deduction for spouses.**

For any other beneficiary, including children,

the law is not so magnanimous. The federal system is **unified,** which means the tax is on a combination of all assets that are transferred during lifetime *and* at death. The total amount of property that can pass without any tax (the Unified Gift-Estate Tax Amount) is as follows:

Year	Estate Tax Starts At
1998	$625,000
1999	650,000
2000	675,000
2001	675,000
2002	700,000
2003	700,000
2004	850,000
2005	950,000
2006	1,000,000

Taxes over the limit are steep, beginning at a rate of approximately 37 percent and increasing to 55 percent for amounts over $3 million. State taxes can also be substantial.

Help with the tax code. See chapter 18, section 8.1.

4.1 Gifts

Gifts can be made tax free during a person's lifetime up to $10,000 per year per recipient, or $20,000 per recipient when made jointly by a married couple. After 1998, the amount will be indexed annually to reflect inflation. There is no limit on the number of people who can receive these gifts. Gifts within these limits are not counted as part of the Unified Gift-Estate Tax Amount. Valuation of a gift can get tricky. Gifts over the limit become part of the Unified Gift-Estate Tax credit.

For estate planning, if the objective is to reduce taxes, making gifts during one's lifetime is generally better than at death. Gifts have the ancillary advantage of reducing your tax liability for income generated by the donated assets.

If there is a tax to pay, only the donor pays the tax. The beneficiary of the gift is never responsible for a tax, and the gift is not taxable income. The recipient can pay the tax, if that is a condition of the gift, but the tax paid by the recipient is considered income to the donor.

Gifts: educational and medical purposes. One exception to the $10,000 limit is that you may give tax free an unlimited amount to a beneficiary for educational or medical reasons. The gift must be to a third party such as a hospital or a university and cannot be to the beneficiary directly. *Thus, a donor may pay a second party's health expenses, or educational expenses, without limit and without being taxed for it.*

Gifts made in contemplation of death. In general, gifts that are made with strings attached so that you still have control during your lifetime are not considered to be completed gifts until your death and thus do not avoid estate taxes.

4.2 If Your Net Worth Is Close to or More Than the Unified Gift-Estate Tax Amount

If your net worth is close to or more than the Unified Gift-Estate Tax Amount, including pensions and other retirement arrangements and the death benefits of all life insurance policies you own, you should consult with your tax adviser for the best method of minimizing taxes. This is particularly true if you own a substantial interest in a family business or one owned by just a few people or if your spouse is not a U.S. citizen. The following discussion about the various means of minimizing taxes is to provide you with an idea of the issues.

Tip. If you are very ill and not married to the person to whom you want to leave your estate and your net estate is close to the Unified Gift-Estate Tax Amount, consider getting married if the person is a U.S. citizen so that the estate can pass estate-tax free due to the unlimited marital deduction.

4.3 Trusts

Taxes can be minimized through use of an irrevocable trust as described in section 3.8 above.

4.4 Retirement Plans

Retirement assets distributed to your heirs are subject to estate tax, income tax, and in some cases, excise tax.

4.5 Real Estate

Real estate with a large gain in it. For tax purposes, the value of real property at the date of your death becomes your heirs' basis. Consequently, no capital gains tax is ever payable on the difference between your basis and the value at your date of death. Because of this "step-up," it may be worthwhile to hold on to real estate with a large amount of appreciation in it to avoid the capital gains tax on the appreciation.

Real estate with a loss in it. Whatever the size of your estate, if you have a valuable property with a loss in it, you should consult a tax adviser. Under current laws, the tax basis for the property is "stepped down" (reduced) to the value at the date of death, and any potential loss deduction would be forfeited. If you have substantial income, it might pay to sell the property and deduct the losses. I say "might" because it doesn't pay to generate losses that are more than $3,000 in excess of your capital gains. Excess losses can't be deducted each year. While they can be offset against future capital gains, if there are no such gains in future years while you are still alive, the deductions will be lost. An alternative would be to sell the property at its current value to a close family member. Although your loss would not be deductible because the purchaser is a family member, any future gains the family member realizes will not be taxable to the extent of the previously disallowed loss.

4.6 Bonds

Some treasury bonds issued by the U.S. government can be purchased on the open market for substantially less than their full face value because the interest rate is below current interest rates. These bonds can then be used to pay estate taxes at the full face value of the bond. Used this way, these bonds are known as **flower bonds.**

Tip. Flower bonds should only be purchased when death is imminent. They may not be a good investment before then because they yield so little income.

4.7 Debts

Any debts owed to you that are canceled on your death are considered an asset of the estate subject to tax even though the estate never collects the money.

4.8 Liquidity

While considering taxes, you must also consider whether there will be enough cash or cash equivalent assets (assets easily converted to cash) to pay the estate taxes and administrative costs without disturbing assets you want to pass to your heirs. If there is not, then you should make plans now to provide that liquidity, possibly through purchase of life insurance with your estate named as beneficiary. (See chapter 19, section 5, about how to purchase life insurance.) Life insurance policies

payable to a beneficiary other than the estate are no help with respect to taxes and may even hurt. Although the personal representative can argue that the beneficiary should pay the estate tax on money payable directly to the beneficiary, it may be difficult to obtain any money from the beneficiary once he or she has the money from the life insurance company.

Tip. If you can't provide the necessary liquidity, let your heirs know what you suggest they do to raise the funds, including which assets to sell and in what order. How-to advice will be critical for your heirs. It should not be in your will since circumstances can change and you don't want to execute a new will unnecessarily.

Section 5. What Your Heirs Can Expect

Realistically, unless you leave all your assets in a trust, there will be a delay in passing them on to your heirs. It may take up to thirty days just to start probate, and it may take up to two years, or even longer if there are complications, to complete the transfer. The amount of time it takes doesn't necessarily relate to the size of your estate.

Automatic transfer of title. Even assets that automatically transfer to the beneficiary, such as the proceeds of life insurance or a title registered in joint name with the right of survivorship, may be held up pending court appointment of the personal representative, and the personal representative's obtaining appropriate tax waivers from the state.

Bank safe-deposit box and accounts. As soon as the bank has notice of your death, it generally seals your safe-deposit box and prevents entry by anyone, even a joint owner, until an appropriate representative of the taxing authorities is present to unseal and inventory the contents of the box.

Your bank accounts are also frozen unless, as described above, they are titled in such a way that title automatically passes on your demise to another person.

Taxes. The federal estate tax return must be filed, and the tax, if any, paid no later than nine months after the date of death. State tax due dates vary, but generally do not exceed nine months after the date of death. If an estate tax is due, your heirs can generally expect that the personal representative will not make any payments to them until the IRS and the state have signed off on the return.

If your heirs need money while the estate is being probated. If no provision has been made for partial payments, they can request advances from the personal representative. If he won't agree, they can petition the court.

Sale of assets. Unless you have specified to the contrary, bequests are usually paid in cash, which means that your assets will generally be sold to pay them.

Trusts. If you have placed your assets in a trust, as described above, your heirs will not be subjected to delays because title does not change on your demise. Title was, and will continue to be, owned by the trust.

Accounting. As a general matter, neither the estate nor any trust will be settled without the court and/or the beneficiaries reviewing a detailed accounting and approving it.

Disclaiming an interest. A beneficiary can refuse to accept (**disclaim**) any inheritance, provided the disclaimer is within the appropriate time set by state law.

A discussion with your heirs. Let your heirs know how you think assets should be handled or maintained, particularly if one of the assets is a business. Unless the value of a specific asset is volatile, it may also help to let them know not to make any decisions while emotions are strong, and to do the minimum necessary until they have a chance to make a decision with clarity. If you have specific people who can give them advice, let your beneficiaries know. At all costs, quick, emotional decisions should be avoided.

Chapter 34

Funeral Arrangements

The best way to get somebody to live is to tell him the cost of a funeral.
—Michael S.

A funeral is simply another of life's events for which *everyone*, whatever his or her physical condition, can and should plan ahead. *If this subject is too stressful for you,* leave it to your personal representative (executor) and/or your heirs to decide, but at least alert them to the information in this book.

Why plan ahead? Thinking about your funeral now will accomplish several purposes:

- It will save your estate money. Decisions will be made rationally rather than quickly at an emotional time which can lead to misguided extravagance. A survey conducted by a Houston television station (KPRC-TV) found that prices for the same "minimum" service, including the lowest-priced metal casket, varied from $1,495 to $9,910 at different Houston mortuaries. The price of a metal casket alone varied from $485 to $5,895. Will your loved ones really be in shape to shop?
- It will assure your wishes will be carried out.
- It will relieve stress on the people you care about.

Section 1. General Information to Think About

Freeing yourself. The first thing to do is to free yourself from what the funeral industry wants you to think and decide what works for you. All over the world, burial customs are different. There is no absolute standard. Even in this country, services used to be at home with an inexpensive casket. There was no embalming unless the body had to travel a distance for burial. Outside the United States embalming is still the exception rather than the rule.

The people who are in the business of handling funerals now call themselves funeral directors. If you substitute the word *salesperson,* you'll be on proper guard when dealing with them.

Federal Trade Commission "funeral rule." The Federal Trade Commission (FTC) has stepped into the arena of funerals because of the abuses that have occurred. The FTC "funeral rule" requires that all funeral charges must be itemized and, to help you comparison shop, available over the telephone. The rule also requires that as soon as face-to-face discussions start about the services the mortuary provides or about prices, you must be given a list you can take home of important legal rights and requirements regarding funeral arrangements. The information to be provided must include

- the costs of caskets (generally the most expensive part of a burial).
- the costs of embalming (not generally required in any state except in certain special cases).
- caskets for cremation (since they will be destroyed, an inexpensive casket will do).
- required purchases (you do not have to purchase unwanted goods or services or pay any fees to obtain those products and services you do want, other than one permitted fee for overhead, which includes money for the funeral director and staff).
- if any goods and services are required by state law, as well as identification of the specific law requiring the purchase.

Tip. If any funeral director says something is required because of state law, ask to see a copy of the law. Most state or local burial laws in the United States are minimal.

Once you decide what you want, the funeral provider is required to give you an itemized statement of the total cost of the funeral goods and services you select. Seeing the total provides the opportunity to reappraise your decision.

Most states also have licensing boards that regulate the funeral industry. You may contact the licensing board in your state for information or help.

Tip. Let your heirs know not to feel locked in just because a body has been delivered to a mortuary. The mortuary cannot prevent a move or charge "lots of money" for it. It may be difficult to talk about this with your loved ones now, but if you don't, they'll have an even harder time later.

Talk about it. After you've done your research and made up your mind as to what you want, talk with your loved ones about your findings and your desires. *Basically a funeral is for the benefit of the living.* Unless you add legal strings, your heirs will be free to ignore your wishes and have the funeral they choose. Reach agreement with them, and consider putting it in writing, about the subjects discussed in this chapter, as well as your wishes with respect to

- how long the period before burial or mourning period afterward should last.
- whether the casket will be open or closed.
- what clothing or covering you will be buried in.
- whether the service should be public or private, and if private, for whom.
- what will be in the service, such as music, speakers, and readings.
- the religious or other customs to follow—or not.
- whether or not there should be flowers.
- whether there should be donations to a charity, and if so, which charity?

Tip. There is no foolproof method of assuring that your wishes will be respected. Although prepayment is not usually recommended, you may consider prepaying for the arrangements you want as added incentive for your heirs to follow your wishes.

Spokesperson. Name a spokesperson who will know your wishes and, not incidentally, will be able to carry them out—or to make the decisions in case you don't want to. Don't just include this information in your will because by the time it is probated, it will be too late. If you don't decide who is in charge, state law will designate who has the right to make the decisions.

Tip. Consider marking people who should be notified of your demise in your address book—and indicating those you do *not* want notified. We all have a lot of names in our books of people who have no real involvement in our lives. Unless you take the few minutes to do this exercise, your survivors will probably notify everyone in your book. An easy method of doing this is to make a photocopy of your address book and cross out the names of people who should not be notified. If you've ever had to make these calls yourself for a friend or loved one, you will appreciate the value of this exercise.

Burial benefits. Certain entitlement and other programs and organizations provide a burial benefit that should not be overlooked. Social Security will reimburse the surviving spouse $255 provided the deceased was covered by Social Security in his or her own right. Children entitled to survivor's benefits may also be eligible for a death benefit. In addition, trade unions, fraternal organizations, the Veterans Administration, credit unions, and workers' compensation also provide burial benefits.

Infectious diseases. Special embalming charges for individuals with infectious conditions such as HIV/AIDS violate the Americans with Disabilities Act, as well as the standards of the Occupational Safety and Health Administration, which requires that every body is to be treated as if it had a blood-borne infectious disease. If your condition warrants, inform your heirs and family of this protection.

Section 2. Disposition of the Remains

Organ donation. In considering what to do with the remains, first, decide whether you want to donate various tissues and organs for transplant. The Universal Donor Law has been enacted in every state to permit individuals to authorize these donations. *Even if you authorize use of organs for transplant, your family's permission will still be sought—so be sure the family knows about and agrees with your*

desires. Removal of donated organs does not produce disfigurement and does not interfere with customary funeral or burial arrangements, which remain the responsibility of the family or estate. For more information about the "gift of life" and a universal donor card, ask your doctor or call the Living Bank at 800-528-2971.

Next, decide among the possible dispositions of the body. Least expensive options are considered first.

Donation to a teaching institution. The least expensive disposition is to donate the body to an institution for teaching or research purposes. In addition to being basically cost free, this disposition is also a generous contribution to science that allows students to learn what a body is all about. If the donation is made to eliminate burial cost, be sure the institution will dispose of the body. Also be sure your next of kin agrees to permit the donation. Then confirm the donation in your legal will.

For information on body donation, call the National Anatomical Service at 800-727-0700, twenty-four hours a day. The service will help you locate a medical school in need. If necessary, arrangements for refrigeration will be made by the service with a local funeral director until transportation is provided. The service can also provide for final disposition of the body. Be sure to discuss whether you want the expense of refrigeration, transportation, and burial borne by the recipient institution.

Cremation. The next least expensive alternative to consider is cremation. The cost ranges from $350 to $500 total, which includes transportation of the body, cremation body container, cremation fee, and all documents.

There are companies that will take care of the cremation, as well as bury the remains at sea or return the remains (known as **cremains**) to whomever you specify.

Be aware that in disposing of the cremains, local law must be taken into account. For example, it is not legal to scatter cremains in San Francisco Bay. For additional information, contact the Neptune Society, a for-profit organization that has offices nationwide, at 800-645-3722 or the Internet Cremation Society at www.cremation.org/home2.html.

When you think about cremation, do not confuse the issue by thinking, as many do, that there is either a cremation or a "funeral." There can be a funeral with the body present, and then a cremation, with the possibility of a memorial service to follow. It is even possible to have a viewing prior to a cremation in a rented casket, followed by a cremation in an inexpensive one.

Keeping the body intact. If the body remains intact, it will be buried in a casket in the ground **(interment)** or above ground in a mausoleum **(entombment)**, both of which entail expenses for your estate.

Embalming. While **embalming** (the replacement of body fluids with chemicals to slow down the body's deterioration) is prevalent today, it is usually unnecessary. It is only necessary where the body is to be transported a distance or across state lines or if death was caused by a contagious disease.

Refrigeration is the usual alternative to embalming when the body must be preserved for later disposition. If you desire to locate the law in your state, contact the Conference of Funeral Service Examining Boards, 520 E. Van Trees, P.O. Box 497, Washington, IN 47501 (812-254-7887). A summary of the pertinent laws of the various states is also contained in *Caring for Your Own Dead* by Lisa Carlson (Hinesburg, Vt.: Upper Access, 1987).

Casket. The container in which a body is buried, the **casket** (also called a **coffin**), is frequently the single most expensive item purchased in a traditional funeral. The expense can be totally avoided

because, as the FTC advises, a casket is not required for a cremation or even a burial.

If you want to use a casket, consider purchasing it from a wholesaler or company that sells caskets directly to the public—often at a savings of 50 to 75 percent off the price you would pay at a funeral home. They may even offer an additional discount for purchasing preneed (see the resources directory). A simple pine box can be purchased for as little as $200. Many of these companies, including the mail order companies, guarantee delivery within a few hours from a casket distributor near the funeral provider. *Under the funeral rule, it is illegal for funeral homes to levy any additional handling charges if you make your own or choose to purchase a casket directly from the supplier.* Some funeral homes try to get around the rule by requiring that a family member be present at the mortuary premises to accept delivery of the casket. Don't let this inconvenience put your money in their pocket unnecessarily.

Tip. The homemade boxes our forefathers were buried in cost practically nothing and can provide a handy heir or friend with a way to participate in the funeral and work through her grief.

If you do purchase a casket from a funeral home, ask to see all their caskets, including the ones they can order, not just the ones they carry or are offering to show you. Market research indicates people tend to purchase the "middle-priced" casket. What is "middle-priced" depends on what other caskets you are shown and in what price ranges. If you are shown caskets that range from $1,500 to $5,000, the tendency is to pick one in the $2,000–$3,000 range. If you are shown caskets from $200 to $5,000, you might feel comfortable picking a much less expensive casket, even though the salesperson may not be happy.

Tip. If you purchase a casket, ask the mortuary or other seller to attach a color photo of the casket to the contract so your heirs can be sure they receive what you intended.

Tip. If you prefer a metal casket, beware of "protective seals." The theoretical purpose is to prevent deterioration of the body by making the casket airtight. The reality is anaerobic bacteria, which thrive in an airless atmosphere, are sealed in, and the result is the opposite of what is intended. No caskets preserve a body indefinitely.

Containers. To prevent the ground from sinking as a casket deteriorates, many cemeteries require use of a **burial vault** or a **grave liner**. More expensive vaults may look better and may slow deterioration of the body, but they don't prevent it. Funeral directors, trying to sell an expensive burial vault, often erroneously state that copper-lined or marble vaults keep air and/or water out of the coffin.

Section 3. Ceremonies

Funeral services and memorial ceremonies. Whatever your choice as to disposition, there can be ceremonies with the body present (a **funeral**) or without (a **memorial service**). A memorial service is generally less expensive than a funeral. It can take place anywhere, such as in a home (the cheapest), in a place of worship (the next least expensive), a community center, a theater, a restaurant, or in a funeral provider's facility (the most expensive, often running from $1,500 to $3,000 for a few hours of funeral service plus attendant "professional fees," which can add $700 to $2,000 unnecessarily). A funeral service can be held with or without a viewing or a memorial service can be held after burial, or there can be both.

The funeral rule allows mortuaries to add a fee for overhead, which can be upwards of $2,000, with all other costs such as the casket and funeral service being added to that. If you do decide to use a mortuary for the body, consider using the least expensive mortuary in your area (which can reasonably be anywhere within a 50-mile radius) and having the public viewing and service at home, at a public facility such as a banquet room, outdoors, or at your house of worship.

In addition to selecting the site of the funeral and/or memorial service, you may even wish to plan the service, including who is to speak, what flowers if any, and even what music is to be played. Consider requesting donations to a specific charity such as your GuardianOrg in lieu of flowers.

Tip. Consider saving the cost of cosmetic services and embalming by having a closed-casket ceremony. On the other hand, embalming may be worthwhile to avoid a weekend or holiday burial since weekday burials are usually less expensive.

Cash advance items. These are goods and services that are paid by the funeral provider on your behalf, such as a cemetery plot, flowers, obituary notices, pallbearers, and clergy honoraria. Some funeral providers charge you their cost for these items, while others add a service fee to their cost. If a service fee is added or if the funeral provider receives a discount, refund, or rebate for these items, this fact must be disclosed to you. Before agreeing to these items, look at them carefully. Most, if not all, of the items can be fulfilled by your heirs at no cost at all. For example, someone close to you can probably write the obituary, and you may even consider writing it yourself.

Choosing a mortuary. While traditionally people choose a mortuary by how close it is to their residence or for its status, a price comparison is definitely in order. The alternatives described above are also to be considered. If the price is right, an on-site visit is recommended to meet the staff and look at the facilities.

- Are they what you expect?
- Do they schedule more than one funeral at a time, and if so, what are the logistics of the various funerals? This is particularly of concern with respect to parking, the public areas, and the soundproofing of the various rooms.

- Do they provide an appropriate separate space prior to and/or during the funeral to suit your survivors' needs and sensibilities?
- Does your gut tell you this is the right place?
- Is the mortuary a member of any association, and if so, what are the requirements for membership in that association? Generally, membership in some association is better than none at all.

If it does not work out with a particular funeral home, there is a right to switch funeral homes at any time. Although payment will have to be made for services already rendered, the funeral home may not hold the body hostage for payment.

Tip. Morticians often believe they should direct all aspects of the funeral. However, you and your family should be in charge of the funeral. The mortician's job is to fulfill your desires. Note that forty-one states let you bypass funeral homes altogether. While this may mean more paperwork, a guide to the laws of your state can be found in Lisa Carlson's *Caring for Your Own Dead* (see section 2 of this chapter).

Section 4. Choosing a Resting Place

If you or others close to you own country property, home burial may be a low-cost option in many states. If this is of interest, check your local law. If there is to be burial in a cemetery, a plot in a church cemetery or a town-owned cemetery is usually the least expensive. A lot in a national cemetery and a marker are free of charge to veterans, their spouses, and minor children.

Purchasing a burial plot now for you and your family will lock in the cost as well as eliminate decisions to be made. Plots are cheaper if they are of the "two-depth" variety, one casket on top of the other.

When choosing a cemetery, be aware that the funeral rule and the disclosures it requires only apply to mortuaries—not cemeteries. Consider the following:

- Does the cemetery and/or plot meet the requirements of your religion?
- What restrictions are placed on the types of permanent markers or monuments? Do you have to purchase them from a particular supplier? Is there a charge if the marker is purchased elsewhere? What is the charge for **setting** the marker (securely putting it in the earth)?
- What are the charges to open and close the grave during the week? On weekends? Are there any other charges such as tips to gravediggers?
- What is the charge for upkeep of a grave site or for "perpetual care" of the site? Will the cemetery let you see how much money is in its perpetual care fund, and does the amount appear to be adequate? Ideally funds for perpetual care should be placed in trust and not be part of the cemetery's general operating fund.
- Are other plots available for the burial of loved ones nearby?
- Does the cemetery require in-ground vaults around the casket to keep the ground from settling?
- Walk around. Does the cemetery look well cared for?
- Does the contract specify the specific plot or plots you are interested in purchasing? What does it provide if you move or if you pay in installments and death occurs before the full amount is paid?
- If you are concerned about relocating, does the cemetery participate in a credit-exchange program that enables you to transfer the value of your plot to another participating cemetery?

Tip. When purchasing a plot, be sure everything you care about is written into the purchase agreement.

Section 5. Payment Arrangements

Preplanning. If your estate is to be responsible for disposition of the body, you can preplan a funeral either as an individual or as a member of a funeral and memorial society. These societies are non-profit groups that started more than fifty years ago as consumer cooperatives aimed at reducing the high cost of funerals and providing their members dignified funerals at minimal cost through preplanning. For a modest membership fee, they provide information and advice on funeral arrangements at a reasonable cost. For more information about funeral and memorial societies, including one in your state, contact Funeral and Memorial Societies of America (a nonprofit organization) at P.O. Box 10, Hinesburg, VT 05461 (800-458-5563). If you prefer, there are also private for-profit advance funeral planning companies.

Prearranging/prepaying. So far the discussion has been about prearranging your funeral. While you may want to prepay a burial plot or a casket, consumer groups such as American Association of Retired Persons recommend against prepaying for funerals. Although a prepurchase may protect against inflation, if you pay in advance, you lose the use of your money during the intervening time and could lose all your money if the mortuary goes out of business or if you move and the purchased program is not transferable. It would be better to set the money aside in an interest-bearing account.

Tip. You may consider going against traditional advice and prepaying for funeral arrangements *if* you have no survivors or if you want to set aside funds to leave yourself eligible for Medicaid. You may also want to consider prepaying if you can obtain life insurance from the funeral provider to cover the costs and if the safeguards mentioned in the next paragraph are provided. Many funeral providers are given the power to issue the life insurance policy on the spot. This "guaranteed issue" coverage (see chapter 19, section 5.1, for a discussion of guaranteed issue coverage) increases the amount of life insurance you leave your beneficiaries.

If you do want to prepay the funeral. Look for the following safeguards:

- Be sure the company has a solid reputation, is appropriately licensed, has been in business for at least twenty years, and puts the money into a trust fund. Age and reputation don't guarantee anything, but if they've been in business this long, the odds are they will continue to be here for the foreseeable future.
- The money you prepay should be held as a separate fund not subject to the funeral home's creditors. Ideally, you should also be credited with any interest earned.
- If the firm goes out of business, your money is returned.
- If you change your mind about the funeral or move, you can cancel and receive a refund of all or at least most of your money.
- The price must be guaranteed despite inflation.
- Any funds left over should be refunded to your estate.

The safest means of prepayment is through a separate savings bank account registered "in trust for" or "payable on death" to the funeral provider. While interest earned each year is usually subject to income tax, you have use of the money and can even take all of it out of the account while alive. On death, the account automatically belongs to the funeral provider. An alternative is to name a family member in place of the funeral home. If there is money left over, your survivors will get to keep it.

If you may need to qualify for Medicaid in the future, set up the account as an irrevocable trust. Be sure family members know about these plans and arrangements and where copies of the contracts are kept.

Part VIII

,,,,,,,,,,,,,

Your Team and Other Matters

Chapter 35

Support Groups

I desperately needed to talk to someone who had gone through this dark and lonely forest before me—someone who knew what to expect next and how long the pain would last.

—Helena V.

Stepping into the security of such a group of people can be like coming home for those who have been too long isolated by their private, painful concerns.

—Peter C.

Because of the importance support groups can play in emotional and physical health, they have their own chapter.

Section 1. What Is a Support Group?

A **support group**, also known as a **mutual-help** or **self-help group**, provides emotional support and practical help in dealing with problems common to all members.

Support groups complement professional treatment. Such groups are generally free with the exception of those run independently by a psychiatrist or psychologist.

Section 2. Why Join a Support Group?

Studies show that participants in a support group benefit by sharing information and feelings, particularly regarding

- the practical aspects of living with a particular condition.
- treatments, health care, and medicines.
- the various specialists in the area.
- decreasing costs.
- accessing moneys and other services that may be available locally.
- a participant's emotional life and coping.
- family life and friendships.
- loneliness and isolation.

A published study on longevity indicates that support groups can also help keep participants healthier and extend their life. The study by Dr. David Spiegel at Stanford University found that, on average, women with breast cancer who participated in a support group lived twice as long as those women in a control group who did not.

Likewise, in a study involving people with AIDS, networks composed predominantly of peers were associated with greater psychological well-being than networks containing high percentages of relatives. It was also found that the degree to which the person felt he gave support to his network members was significantly correlated with psychological well-being. These findings are consistent with previous research on social support and life crises.

Section 3. How a Support Group Works

Usually facilitated by a professional social worker or therapist trained in the area, but generally effective even without a professional facilitator, support groups are made up of people with a similar diagnosis who meet regularly. If there are enough people, support groups can be divided into subgroups according to interests or stages of the condition's progression. There are even support groups for family members or caregivers.

Each group determines its own programs and meeting schedules. Some groups are limited to regular members and some are "drop-in," permitting people to attend when it works for them. Some bring in outside speakers periodically.

Either the group or the facilitator or both choose a topic or topics for discussion. All members are encouraged to participate in every session, but participation in every discussion is not necessary.

Support groups have no set duration. Many are close-ended, such as for a twelve-week period, while others go on for years and years at the discretion of the members.

Usually, everyone who participates in a support group agrees to keep all matters discussed there, as well as the identity of the other members of the group, confidential.

Section 4. Different Types of Support Groups

Support groups come in three basic varieties: line, telephone, and on-line.

Live groups, as the name states, meet face-to-face.

Telephone groups meet on the telephone.

Members do not have to leave their homes or even dress. This can be a great benefit for someone who is too ill to travel or, at the other extreme, for a person who is traveling. For many people it is easier to share their emotions while on the telephone rather than face-to-face.

If you don't want to talk, but only want to get information, you can just "listen in" on the chat sessions. Last but not least, telephone support groups can be developed and customized individually and for every ailment, no matter how uncommon.

On-line support groups work like a regular support group except that, for the most part, rather than having a live discussion, it is usually set up in a "bulletin board" format. Each time a group member logs on to the group, the member communicates by leaving a message to which other members respond. At any time a group member can reread past messages and take part in the conversation posting a message himself.

It is also possible to have real-time computer conferencing where group members log on at the same time and type messages back and forth to each other. The messages show up as they are typed. Unlike in the bulletin board message system, these conversations aren't saved for later unless you choose to print them out for yourself from your own computer.

On-line support groups have all the advantages of a telephone group, plus anonymity. You can log on with any name you choose, from any account. A friend of mine who is a celebrity in her field and is usually treated differently because of it is treated the same as all other members of the group because she logs on under a code name.

Another advantage to an on-line group is access twenty-fours hour a day, seven days a week.

Tip. If you are really concerned about your anonymity, in addition to using a code name, consider accessing an on-line support group from a friend's computer or through one of the anonymous mail-forward servers such as www.anonymizer.com. If you want a particular person to have your contact information, set up an appointment and telephone number with that person to exchange the information.

Section 5. How to Locate a Support Group

Support groups are usually sponsored by GuardianOrgs or by private therapists. Ask people with conditions similar to yours, your physician, therapist, and/or GuardianOrg. If those sources don't work, contact National Self-Help Clearinghouse, 33 W. Forty-second Street, Room 1227, New York, NY 10036 (212-840-7606). If you are looking for a group on-line, in addition to the sites for the GuardianOrgs, look at www.liszt.com.

Chapter 36

Your Support Team

Until Jerry C. was diagnosed, his life was rather simple. He had dealt with an attorney once when he bought his house. He had an accountant he saw once a year at tax time, an insurance broker he saw once, ten years ago, and of course, he had a general physician. He was startled, six months after his diagnosis, when he realized he was working with nine different experts and had just been advised to speak with one more.

Whatever your economic situation, many experts in different areas are available to assist you. This chapter covers how to decide when the various experts are necessary, how to choose them or to assess the ones you may already have on board, how to maximize your relationship with them, and how either to cover the costs or to access their services without charge.

The sequence in which various team members or matters are addressed by no means suggests their order of importance to you. The relative importance of each will vary over time.

Section 1. General Considerations

1.1 How to Choose Team Members

As you choose team members, keep these two general considerations in mind:

1. You are the captain and the final decision maker. No matter how educated or experienced they may be, these people are your advisers and are there to support you. It's your life and health so it's your decision.

2. Trust your instincts. After you do the amount of research with which you feel comfortable, trust your gut instinct when deciding who will fill an expert position.

The two routes to finding a team member.

The "seat of your pants" approach—going with the recommendation of a friend or physician. As discussed in chapter 24 with respect to choosing a physician, the "seat of your pants" method of finding a team member is to blindly accept the recommendation of a friend, family member, doctor, or even the Yellow Pages, when it comes to choosing an expert to assist you.

The ordered approach—research. The more reasoned approach is to do your research before bringing anybody on board.

With a reasoned approach, the initial step is to determine what kind of person you need (e.g., if you need a lawyer, is it a litigator, a tax expert, a contracts person, or an estate-planning expert?). Create a to-do list of the matters that you expect the person to handle to provide an idea of what services and expertise you need from the particular person. Then:

• Ask around for leads. Talk with
  • other professionals in the field whom you trust for a recommendation.
  • people with a condition similar to yours.
  • trusted friends.
  • your GuardianOrg.
  • associates.
  • family members.
• As a last resort, you can respond to ads, but be particularly wary of choosing a team member this way. The person may not really be an expert in the field, and even if she is, she may not be that good.
• If licensing is required, check the appropriate licensing authority to determine if the people you are considering really are licensed, whether they have had complaints against them, and if so, what kind. Licensing does not prove competence, but it is a good sign.
• If there are professional organizations with respect to the person's specialty, find out whether she is a member of any of them. Again, this does not prove competence, but it is a good sign.
• If peer certification is available that signifies education and experience, does the person have this certification?

Interview. Before you actually hire a prospective team member, have an "informational interview" with several candidates. Seeing several candidates gives you options, as well as bargaining power in negotiating prices for services. These interviews may feel awkward at first, but they can save you money and Life Units.

Be sure to inform the person with whom you make the appointment of the purpose of the visit, and *confirm that the interview is at no cost to you.*

Since the free visit will be short, be prepared before the meeting:

• Try to anticipate the documents or facts that the person will consider relevant to the subject you want to discuss and take those documents to the meeting. If you're not sure what documents may be needed, when you set up the appointment ask what the expert would like you to bring with you. Be prepared to lay out the facts. Let the expert define the issues. For example, if you want to speak with an attorney because you are having a problem at work, don't define it as an Americans with Disabilities Act problem. It would be better to say you are having a problem with your employment because of your physical condition.
• Prepare a written list of questions. Prioritize them in case you don't get to all of them in the interview.
• Discuss whatever ground rules are important to you. If you are dealing with an office full of people, with whom will you actually be working?
• Find out the base rate charged for services and get an estimate of the overall cost. For example, if a physical therapist charges $50 an hour, how many hours will be required? Ask what you can do to keep the costs lower and what is expected of you.
• If you believe the services should be covered by your insurance, whether it is health or property and casualty insurance, confirm with the expert that the services are covered, and to what extent. If you are expected to pay for any portion, how much will that be?
• Do you and the person share the same outlook and philosophy?
• Obtain a sample retainer agreement or letter that describes the relationship between you.
• Make written notes after the meeting to remind yourself of what you learned and your thoughts about the person. You'll need them for comparison when you meet more than one professional.

Tip. Before you sign a retainer agreement with any team member, have another team member review it. For example, the lawyer should review the accountant's retainer letter and vice versa.

While you're in the candidate's office, consider:

• Does the office appear to be professionally run, organized, and busy?

- Is your appointment kept on time?
- Does the candidate devote full attention to you or do other activities distract her?
- Do you feel rushed?
- Does the candidate project common sense?

Tip. As you select team members, consider enlisting one or two of the selected members to accompany you to other interviews to solicit their thoughts on the candidate and the proposed arrangement. Their insights can be helpful. For example, if you interview a financial adviser, take your lawyer and/or accountant. If chosen team members insist on charging you to go to the meeting and you don't want to spend the Life Units, at least get their thoughts on what they would look for and ask about. The more your team members are involved in choosing the other members, the more they will actually feel like a team.

1.2 Other Matters to Consider

Intimidation. Many people feel nervous or intimidated when meeting professionals. If you feel that way, remember that you are the one doing the hiring and your satisfaction is the most important thing.

Attitude. When dealing with team members, take a positive approach and assume that your team members actually want to help you. Be assertive, but not aggressive. There may be a fine line between the two. Assertive will get you what you need while aggressive is likely to put people on the defensive, which leaves them less likely to go the extra distance to assist you.

Second opinions. If you are uncomfortable with the advice you receive, seek a second opinion.

Changing personnel. If the professional doesn't fill your needs, find one who does. It's no sin to fire a lawyer, a doctor, or any other professional—no matter how long you have been with her or what emotional ties may exist. I'm not suggesting you change on a whim. You will be trading the known

for the unknown. The new professional will need to take the time to become acquainted with you and your history. You will spend Life Units bringing the new member up-to-date. Still, if the balance indicates a change should be made—make it!

Tip. Check with other members of your team when contemplating ending a long-standing professional relationship, particularly if you are considering changing physicians. If you're acting emotionally, they can help shed some objective light on the situation. If not, they may have suggestions for how to end the relationship without burning bridges and may even have suggestions for replacements they know from experience will likely fill your needs.

Openness. Tell your professional *all* the facts that may impact the matter under discussion, including the embarrassing ones.

Confidentiality. You can generally expect that between state laws and the ethics of the profession, your professional team members will keep your affairs confidential (except to the extent that may be required by law). Your relationships with your attorney and your physician, in particular, are protected as privileged. If confidentiality is of concern to you, caution is advised when speaking with nonlicensed members of your team. If you have a question about the confidentiality of a specific fact you want or are asked to reveal, ask your attorney whether the matter is protected by confidentiality.

Maximizing use of your team member. Have your facts in order prior to meetings. Since you are probably paying most of these people by the hour, you will spend less money if you organize the facts rather than ask the expert to do it for you. On the other hand, if putting things together overwhelms you, let the professional do it. The effect of stress on your immune system isn't worth it.

Billing. Every time you get a bill from a team member, ask yourself whether you have gotten fair value for what you and/or the insurance company are being charged. If not, talk it over with your team member.

Changing economic circumstances. If your circumstances change, speak with your team member before deciding to discontinue her services for financial reasons. If you're open about your financial situation, you'll be surprised how many people will continue to work with you. If they can't, they may have an affordable referral for you.

Refusal to treat. In addition to prohibiting discrimination in employment based on disability, the Americans with Disabilities Act also prohibits discrimination by **public accommodations.** The term *public accommodation* is broadly defined and includes the "professional office of a health care provider, hospital or other service establishment." This prohibition means that people with disabilities cannot be excluded or segregated from nondisabled people based on presumptions, fears, or stereotypes. Thus, it has been found that a dentist who refused to treat a patient solely on the basis of the patient's disease violated the law. Similarly, an emergency room admitting physician violated the law when an HIV-positive person suffering a severe allergic reaction was denied admission because of his HIV status.

If you believe you have been subjected to a violation of the Americans with Disabilities Act, discuss the matter with your GuardianOrg or an attorney for advice on how to proceed.

Section 2. *Physician* ↑↑↑

See chapter 24 for a discussion on how to select your physician.

Section 3. *Lawyer* ↑↑↑

3.1 Do You Need a Lawyer?

The first question is whether you need a lawyer at all. At the one extreme, you can hire a lawyer to act as coordinator with your team members. At the other extreme, some people are comfortable handling certain legal work themselves. Sometimes, other less expensive professionals can do the job. For example, accountants can handle routine tax matters. In California, brokers can handle real estate closings. In matters involving small claims, each state has a small-claims court geared for use without an attorney. Most local bar associations can help determine whether an attorney or another person is best for a situation.

Don't expect any one attorney or law firm to be competent for all of your legal needs. If you hire a generalist when you have specific needs, you may end up paying for that attorney's education.

Tip. Consider saving money by hiring an attorney as a "legal coach" for advice along the way.

3.2 What Type of Lawyer Is Right for You?

Do you want a large firm with all its contacts and in-house resources or a smaller one with more personalized service and generally lower fees? With a smaller firm, the attorney you hire is usually the one who works on your case. In a medium to large firm the expense, and often the quality, depends on who in the firm works on your case. You may discuss your situation with one person, but another one will do the actual work. A third choice may be a sole practitioner who has expertise in areas of concern to you.

Tip. If you need information about an attorney, the leading directory of lawyers, Martindale-Hubbell, is now on-line at www.martindale.com. For no charge, you can learn a lawyer's background. It also provides a mechanism to search for an attorney by region and specialty area.

If you don't have the money to pay legal fees, see section 3.5 below.

3.3 Communication

Discuss the ground rules that are important to you including

- how you want to be updated and how often (keeping in mind, of course, that each of these discussions takes time and will cost you money).
- whether you want to see drafts of documents and any costs for sending them to you.
- that no major strategic decisions regarding the case should be made without your permission.

3.4 Fees

Lawyers bill either at a fixed fee per hour or as a percentage of an amount. When an attorney works for the party who files a lawsuit for payment equal to a percentage of the amount awarded, if any, it is known as a **contingency fee.** If you are to be charged by the hour, in addition to learning the hourly rates of the various attorneys who may be involved, find out the minimum amount of time that will be billed each time something happens. For example, how much does the attorney charge for each telephone call? The standard charge is a minimum of six minutes per call.

If a contingency fee applies, find out whether your lawyer's expenses will be deducted before or after the award is divided. Before is preferable because it means more money to you.

In addition to fees, find out what other charges such as photocopying you can expect to incur and how are they billed. How often will you be billed?

Tip. Even a lawyer's fees and retainer agreement are negotiable. You have nothing to lose by asking. The more you shop around, the more likely you can ask the attorney of your choice to reduce her rate to equal a specific competitor's. Also, the more business you give the lawyer, the better your bargaining position when asking for a reduction in fees. It is even possible to **barter** (trade your goods or services for legal fees). If the lawyer agrees to accept barter, consult your tax adviser for the tax consequences, if any. You also have nothing to lose by trying to renegotiate a bill after you receive it. Many firms, when questioned on a bill, will at least cut it a little.

Tip. When you merely want to convey information to your attorney or ask for an update, perhaps an assistant or secretary can convey the information or give you an update at no cost to you.

3.5 Prepaid Services, Clinics, and Legal Aid

Prepaid legal services. Like health insurance, prepaid legal service plans make legal costs manageable by payment of a set sum in return for coverage in the event you need legal services. Today, many of these plans are provided by employers, unions, and associations. While all plans cover the cost of legal consultation and advice, they generally just cover basic, simple legal needs.

Different types of plans available are:

- **Referral/discount plans:** Not a true prepaid plan, these plans provide a system in which a member of the group is referred to an attorney or law firm that provides free or low-cost advice and consultation.
- **Access plans:** These plans provide unlimited legal advice and consultation and, generally, cover the review of documents sent by mail to the plan attorney, as well as preparation and review of simple legal documents such as a will. If additional legal services are needed, the member is referred to an attorney who has agreed in advance to furnish such services at a discount.
- **Comprehensive plans:** Usually only available on a group basis, these plans cover the above services plus coverage for both in-office and courtroom work in most areas of the law. As with health insurance, the member may be responsible for deductibles and/or copayments.

When evaluating a prepaid legal service plan, factors to consider are

- the amount of the premium.
- the services covered, such as writing documents, litigation, and/or court representation, as well as the restrictions placed on those services.
- the lawyers' qualifications. Also look at how the plan decides which lawyers it includes.
- the reputation of the firm. If you have a claim, how successful has the firm been in pursuing claims of your type?
- whether you have a choice concerning which attorney handles your matter.
- whether, and how, access to attorneys may be limited.
- whether the plan covers preexisting legal problems (most don't).
- if a matter is not included in the plan, who will handle it, what are their qualifications, and how much more will you have to pay?
- if you're not happy with an attorney, can you switch? If so, can you choose the new attorney or will she be assigned?
- how are complaints handled?
- is the company financially secure?
- in practice, do the attorneys return calls promptly?

Legal clinics. Legal clinics primarily process routine, uncomplicated legal matters, usually at a low cost and sometimes for free. They can be managed by attorneys (who are generally looking for new business), by law schools (to give students real-life experience), or by nonprofit groups (which advocate a cause, such as assisting women in a divorce). Some GuardianOrgs provide free legal clinics among the services provided to clients.

There are also clinic-type law firms that often advertise heavily on television and generally use standardized forms and paralegal assistants. **Paralegals** are people who are not attorneys, but who are trained in special legal matters or procedures. States differ as to what services they can perform.

Tip. For simple matters, an experienced paralegal may take care of your needs for about one-third to one-half the cost of an attorney. To find a reputable paralegal, call the National Federation of Paralegal Associations at 871-941-4000 (or log on to www.paralegals.org/ProDirectory/home.html) .

Legal aid. If money is a problem, legal aid programs throughout the country may be able to fill your legal needs. Though there is a right to a free attorney in most criminal cases, you do not have such a right in civil matters. Clinics generally have restrictions on your area of residence, size of family, and income. They can be located through your local bar association or county courthouse. The Legal Services Corporation in Washington, D.C., at 202-336-8800 can tell you how to contact your local Legal Services Corporation for housing matters and some civil actions.

Section 4. Financial Planner ↑↑↑

4.1 Do You Need a Financial Planner?

It is preferable to consult a qualified financial planner before instituting a financial plan, even if the only purpose is to review a plan you create yourself.

A good financial planner will review your total financial picture and help you hone your goals. The planner will then work with you to create a detailed plan for making your assets, insurance coverages, and government programs work for you in the best way—given your income, expenses, goals, and physical condition. The planner can also help you keep the details described throughout this book in perspective.

4.2 Choosing a Financial Planner

Be aware. There is little regulation of the financial planning industry, and in most states just about anyone can claim to be a financial planner—with or without appropriate training.

Although an overwhelming number of financial

planners are dedicated, responsible, and competent, many people who call themselves financial planners are really just insurance or securities salespeople in disguise, intent on pushing a particular financial product at the expense of your real needs. They may be licensed within subsets of financial planning, such as insurance and securities, but generally they are not regulated for their financial planning activities. If your state regulates financial planners, be sure the planner is registered.

Tip. Recognize that the background of the planner sets the tone. With a planner's tax background, you can expect a lot of focus on taxes; an insurance background tends to focus on the insurance tools available to meet needs; and a securities background focuses on the use of securities.

Beware of planners who promise quick riches or instant financial gain. Building secure finances is not accomplished overnight or with one single investment.

Tip. Your ideal financial planner should have expertise in working with people with a shortened life expectancy. As you are aware, many of the standard financial planning answers do not work for you. It is better to have a professional already knowledgeable in these issues than one you have to pay to become educated on your behalf. If you've read through this book, you may know more about the areas that are critical to your financial well-being than any financial planner who is not an expert in this area.

Certification. The major groups that represent financial planners who have taken courses, have passed exams, have a minimum number of years of experience, and have been awarded certifications are the National Association of Personal Financial Advisers (NAPFA), members of which are fee-only financial advisers (800-36-NAPFA or 847-537-7722), the Registry of Financial Planning Practitioners of the International Association for Financial Planning (IAFP) (800-945-4237 or 404-845-0011), and the Institute of Certified Financial Planners (ICFP) (800-282-7526 or 303-751-7600). Each group will give you the name of planners in your area.

Two of the better financial planning courses are given by the American College in Bryn Mawr, Pennsylvania, and the College for Financial Planning in Denver. When students pass exams and have at least three years of planning experience, they can use these initials after their names: ChFC, chartered financial consultants, for graduates of the American College, and CFP, certified financial planner, for graduates of the College for Financial Planning. Many planners also add initials from their other fields; e.g., CPA for certified public accountants or CLU for chartered life underwriters. While financial planning may be the easiest profession to join these days, at least a CFP or ChFC gives assurance of a degree of knowledge.

4.3 Compensation and Loyalty

Various compensation methods are used by financial planners.

- Most financial planners earn all or part of their living from commissions on the products they sell (either as a sales charge per investment product or as a fixed percentage of total sales), without a charge for the planner's advice or preparation of a financial plan (**commission basis**).
- A planner who works on a **fee-only basis** is compensated entirely from fees on an hourly or project basis, or as a percentage of the assets under management.
- Some planners use a **fee-offset** arrangement where commissions from the sale of financial products offset fees charged for the planning.
- Some planners work on a combination **fee plus commission** arrangement: a fee is charged for consultation, advice, and plan preparation plus a commission from recommended products.

A planner who gives you investment advice for a fee is supposed to register with the Securities and Exchange Commission. Such advisers should also disclose any conflicts of interest, tell you how they are compensated, their educational backgrounds, and what their experience has been in financial planning.

Tip. While it is the planner rather than the means of compensation that usually determines whether your needs will be met, you might want to pay for a fee-only planner so you know the advice is more likely to be objective.

4.4 The Interview

Before your first meeting with a financial planner, go through the exercises in chapter 4 so you have your papers organized and an understanding of your income and expenses, as well as your net worth. Think about your long-term financial goals and discuss them with your spouse or partner.

In addition to the questions discussed in section 1.1, consider:

- Is the planner an expert in planning for people with a shortened life expectancy? If you have a specific financial planning concern, does the planner have expertise in that area?
- How long has the person been a financial planner? What education has she had as a financial planner? Does she take continuing education courses, and if so, in what area(s)? What did she do before becoming a financial planner?
- What professional affiliations does the person maintain?
- What is the planner's business philosophy?
- Will the planner give you a written financial plan as described below?
- Is the person registered with the Securities and Exchange Commission to advise about investments? If so, ask for parts one and two of the form the SEC requires them to complete, which will give you information about their background.

- How is the planner going to determine your unique needs?
- How many companies does the planner represent? If the answer is "just one," the odds are the planner is really just a salesperson for that company.
- How does the person keep up with the latest financial developments and research recommended products?
- Do you get along personally?
- How does the person plan to work with you in the future? A plan isn't just made once, but is a living thing that needs to be revisited periodically to be sure you're on track and to make changes to reflect changing times and your changing circumstances. Clarify the extent of written advice, numbers of meetings, availability for special counseling, and whether you will be expected to purchase investments or other financial products through the planner.
- Ask for references from clients whose situations are similar to your own. Then check those references.

4.5 A Good Financial Plan

A good plan is based on your needs, your views, and your goals. It should be easy to understand and should state the facts as well as make specific recommendations. A good plan should

- be in writing.
- be short so it can easily be digested.
- be molded to your needs.
- list any assumptions made.
- identify trouble spots.
- include a picture of your current finances, including a cash flow analysis and net worth statement.
- review your current insurance and make recommended changes with possible savings in premiums.
- recap your investment portfolio with recommendations.

- touch on retirement planning.
- recommend the estate planning tools mentioned elsewhere in this book.
- include a tax analysis and otherwise list financial areas where you need assistance.
- give you alternatives when it makes recommendations as well as an idea of how to implement and pay for the various ideas suggested. Even better, it should list priorities.

4.6 Maximizing Use of a Financial Planner

It is up to you to keep on top of your finances. No one has as much stake as you do regarding your finances—not even your financial planner.

Once you have a plan, review it with your planner at least once a year, and review it again every time your circumstances change, no matter how often that may be.

The power to buy and sell. Do not give any planner the power to buy or sell assets for you without doing *very* extensive homework about the person and insisting that you receive a copy of the insurance bond covering the planner in the event of dishonesty or other malfeasance.

Section 5. Accountant ↑↑↑

5.1 Do You Need an Accountant?

If your tax situation is simple and you file a short form, you probably don't need an accountant. Otherwise, it would be a good idea to at least describe your general situation to one. In addition, a discussion concerning any and all medical expenses you may have and whether you are deferring income or expense to your advantage would be to your benefit. Without an accountant, you may not be minimizing your taxes.

5.2 Choosing an Accountant

Like attorneys, accountants are licensed by the state after taking exams. You can check with your state board to confirm licensing and find out whether your current or potential accountant has had any disciplinary action taken against her. The board will not generally inform you of any pending disciplinary action. An accountant with CPA (certified public accountant) after her name has met additional educational experience requirements.

It helps if an accountant is a member of the American Institute of Certified Public Accountants (AICPA). Members of AICPA's Division of Firms submit their records for a regular review by other Division of Firms members.

Look for an accountant with whom you share the same philosophy. You may want to be conservative in your taxes, or you may want to push the envelope to maximize tax savings with the attendant greater risk of an audit. Find out if the accountant has expertise in medical questions.

Tip. Get your attorney's input on prospective accountants. The two of them will probably be working closely together.

Section 6. Insurance Broker ↑↑↑

You can purchase property, casualty, and even life insurance directly from the insurance company, or through various other impersonal mechanisms such as the Internet. However, unless you are sure of the exact coverages you need, including the limits and deductibles that are right for you, you would probably be better off using an insurance professional who is legally bound to work solely in your interest.

State licensing is certainly critical, but it is only a first step. Since insurance brokers typically work for a commission, the more time the person has invested in becoming an accredited expert, the more likely she will work for you and your needs rather than the almighty commission. Thus, if you are considering purchasing life insurance, look for someone who has the initials CLU (chartered life underwriter) after her name. If the question is property and/or casualty insurance, look for someone with a CPCU (chartered property casualty underwriter) after her name.

Tip. To assure coverage, let the broker know immediately when you acquire any assets or make any professional moves, such as starting a new business. Also let the broker know when you dispose of any assets so your coverage, and premium, can be reduced.

Section 7. Stockbroker ↑↑↑

If you want professional assistance in managing your portfolio, it is important to work with a broker who understands your situation. As you have seen in chapter 13, "Investments," your health conditions should be factored into your investment decisions.

Keep in mind that while a stockbroker may provide expertise and research analysis, her payment is from the sale of financial products. While that is not to say that all brokers will put their commission ahead of your interest, bear that possibility in mind when dealing with a broker. Also, keep in mind that professional portfolio management is no guarantee that your investments will grow or even keep pace with inflation.

Full-service or discount brokers. If you do want to use a broker, there are two distinct types to consider. A **full-service broker** (the traditional broker) makes investment recommendations, offers advice on asset allocation, and will manage your portfolio. Standard commissions are about two and a half times more than those of a discount broker, although active investors can usually negoti-

ate a rate lower than standard. **Discount brokers,** on the other hand, just execute buy and sell orders according to your instructions. Some also offer a few basic services. The commission varies based on the number of shares traded and the price per share.

Locating a broker. Check with satisfied people who have the same objectives you do. Also check with family members, friends, colleagues, your attorney, and your accountant. Avoid people who invite you to a seminar or cold-call you.

Do your homework about the broker. Find out
• the broker's track record. Did the professional advice result in above average returns for her clients over the years since 1986? The year 1986 is picked so you can evaluate how well the broker did through the crash of 1987 as well as during the bullish times. You can ask for a certified history of the firm's and the broker's own research recommendations, as well as client references.
• the broker's education and work background.
• whether the broker's fees for professional advice are tied to the performance of your investment portfolio and, if so, in what manner.

Verify licensing and whether there have been any complaints about the broker. The best place to start is the Central Registration Depository (CRD), a database run by the National Association of Securities Dealers (NASD). There may be unproved charges in the report, so review it with a grain of skepticism.

You can access this information a number of ways:
• You can obtain a CRD report by calling your state securities agency.
• Call the National Association of Securities Dealers' Public Disclosure hot line at 800-289-9999.
• The NASD has a Web site (www.nasdr.com) that, in addition to providing investor-protection in-

formation, allows consumers to request a free CRD report on both a broker and her brokerage firm.

Be sure the broker is a member of the National Association of Securities Dealers. Look at the financial condition of the firm. Look at the number of floor brokers it has at the various stock exchanges so you can assess if your orders are executed promptly. It also helps if the firm has insurance provided by the Securities Investors Protection Corp., which covers losses up to $500,000 caused by the firm's bankruptcy, but not losses from bad advice, broker misdeeds, or market downturns. For broker misdeeds, ask for confirmation that the broker and/or firm has errors-and-omissions coverage in the event of mistakes and sufficient dishonesty coverage to protect your investment against theft and similar loss. Check out commission schedules and services.

The interview. Discuss your assets, investment objectives, and risk-tolerance decisions. Be sure you can relate to the broker. Look at whether you will be given the time you need and whether the suggestions you get fit your goals. Let the broker know up front that you are aware the firm often has incentives to move certain securities. Let the broker know if she recommends any such securities to you, you want to be informed about the incentives so you can make a qualified decision.

How to work with a broker. Play an active role in your portfolio management even if you work with a full-service broker. While I'm not suggesting you become paranoid about the subject, prudence suggests you pay close attention to what is happening: we all know how tempting money can be. Periodically revisit the issues you raised in the initial interview and change brokers if you feel the need. Also keep an eye out for "churning" or "switching" (frequent purchases and sales), trading you didn't authorize, unsuitable investments, misrepresentation, or theft.

If you think you have been mistreated by the broker. Investors who lose money in the market through the negligence, misrepresentation, or manipulation of a broker have a good chance of recouping those funds. Carefully check confirmation slips as soon as you receive them and reconcile them with your monthly statement. If you see that something is wrong, immediately notify your broker's branch manager of your complaint in writing, with copies to the broker and the firm's compliance department. If you first notify your broker directly, it puts her on notice to cover mistakes. If the firm doesn't make good, you can proceed to arbitration covered under your contract with the brokerage house.

Section 8. Claims Assistance ↑↑↑

If you have indemnity-type health insurance or a managed care plan with the right to go outside the system, keeping track of and filing claims or appeals can become a nightmare. This is especially true when you are not feeling well and most likely to be incurring the most claims. (See chapter 14, section 5, for an easy-to-use system for keeping track of claims.)

If you need help and do not have a friend or family available, consider a claims assistance professional. To locate one in your area, you can contact the National Association of Claims Assistance Professionals at 708-963-3500. Membership is open to anyone with an interest in health insurance, so it is not a membership that you can count on. Your GuardianOrg may be able to refer you to claims assistance. As a last resort, look for ads in the phone book under medical claims assistance.

Section 9. Home Care Team ↑↑↑

More and more people want to remain and be treated at home. Home care often requires the services of visiting nurses, attendants, certified home health care agencies, and occasionally a doctor's visit. Most cities have visiting nurses and home care companies that can perform a large variety of services at the patient's home, including

- delivery of oral and intravenous drugs.
- postsurgical treatment and wound care.
- infusions of antibiotics and fluids.
- dialysis.
- blood transfusions in some states.
- some X rays with portable X-ray machines.
- occupational or physical therapy.
- nurses to evaluate the need for these therapies as well as the need for a homemaker (cook), a home attendant (to help with bed-to-chair or eating or toileting), or other services. Nurses also have a vital function in teaching self-management to the patient and/or care partner and can alert the partner to when to call the doctor.

See chapter 27, section 3, for a discussion on how to choose the people or company to fill these needs.

Section 10. Pharmacist ↑↑↑

Although we tend to choose a pharmacy on the basis of convenience and price, the pharmacist is important. Generally the pharmacist is the most readily accessible health-care professional most of us have—and no appointment is needed. Also, prescription errors are made more often than we would think. A conscientious pharmacist is needed to add a layer of protection and catch any errors.

Pharmacist and pharmacy. Since the subjects are so interrelated, see chapter 25, section 6, for a discussion about choosing and maximizing the use of a pharmacist and pharmacy as well as minimizing the cost of your drugs.

Section 11. Dentist ↑↑↑

With respect to a dentist, it is important

- that the dentist understand your condition and what drugs and/or treatments you may be taking.
- that the dentist practice proper hygiene, particularly when your immune system may be lower than normal.

Locating a dentist. Pick your dentist according to your needs. Recognize there are general practitioners and specialists. Specialists may be "board certified," just like surgeons. Certification is not necessarily an indicator of higher skill, merely of additional education.

Dentists either use DDS (doctor of dental surgery) or DMD (doctor of medical dentistry) after their names. According to the American Dental Association, there is no practical difference between the two degrees.

If you have a dental insurance plan, find out whether the dentist accepts it and to what degree before you go to her. Since you will probably have to pay most, if not all, the cost, price is critically important. Find out what the price is before you consent to a procedure. Donald L. gave his new dentist the go-ahead to put in a filling. From past experience, he assumed it would cost about $100. The bill was $450.

Tip. Some dental schools have free or low-cost dental clinics staffed by dental students. Contact any dental schools in your area to see if they have such clinics. The National Foundation of Dentistry for the Handicapped, 1600 Stout Street, Denver, CO 80202 (303-573-0264), may be able to guide you to free care from a participating dentist.

The interview. Since infectious diseases can easily be spread in a dental office, and you may be vulnerable to infection, review the dentist's infection control methods. The following questions are based on recommendations of the People's Medical Society.

- What day-to-day infection control procedures are used in the office, and do the dentist and anyone else who may have contact with your mouth wear gloves, masks, and eyeglasses? If not, stop there and go on to the next candidate.
- How are dental equipment and materials disinfected? Are all instruments and items that can withstand exposure to heat sterilized? Are sterilized instruments wrapped in sterilized wrapping for storage? Are disposable items used wherever possible?
- Are all sterilization units checked periodically to verify that they are sterilizing properly?
- Is the hand piece (the device at the end of a tube that holds the attached drill or polisher) flushed regularly before and between each patient?
- Does the dentist wash her hands with antiseptic before each appointment?

How does the dentist use **dental X rays** (X rays of your teeth for diagnostic purposes)? They are necessary for proper dental care, but can be hazardous and should be limited to as seldom as possible and given only with appropriate protection against scattered radiation. It's not a good sign if the dentist has a rigid schedule for taking dental X rays or if the equipment is out-of-date with scattered instead of directed X rays.

Dental hygienist. Most dental offices include a number of people who perform specialized tasks. The hygienist is the person of most concern to you because she cleans your teeth. Dental hygienists must complete an educational program and pass regional and state board licensing examinations. If you insist that the dentist clean your teeth, mention this when you interview the dentist or set up your appointment and find out the difference in cost.

Dental clinic. One way to save money is to search out a clinic associated with a dental school. The advantage of these practices is generally their low cost. They are also usually conveniently located with a "no appointment necessary" policy.

The same research you have done about a dentist in general is necessary before you choose a dental clinic. The quality of dentists in clinics may be lower than that of private practitioners, but not necessarily. The pace may be too fast for you to feel comfortable, or you may need follow-up or personalized care that is not available in most dental clinics.

You may have to wait all day at the clinic during your first appointment. In addition, many of these clinics are teaching facilities where you receive care from a student whose work must constantly be evaluated. All of this takes more time than does a regular dentist. Do a Life Units evaluation here to determine which is more valuable to you: the time you will save by going to a regular dentist or the money you will save at a dental school clinic.

Be wary of dental clinics not associated with a dental school.

Denturists. Some states permit denturism—a system under which technicians are trained and licensed to take impressions, construct, and fit dentures. They are usually much less expensive for dentures than dentists, perhaps charging from $200 to $300 versus $500 to $2,000 for the same work by a dentist.

Section 12. Nutritionist ↑↑↑

Good nutrition is important to your health. If you decide to use a nutritionist to help maximize the positive effects of your food and minimize the negative effects, bear in mind that in most states just about anyone can call herself a nutritionist: there is no licensing or other qualification required.

Qualifications to look for. Look for certification. The designation RD (registered dietitian) is issued by the American Dietetic Association. To qualify, a person must have a bachelor's degree in food and nutrition or dietetics, complete a work study program or internship for practical experience, pass a national qualifying examination, and maintain the RD status through continuing education courses. You can obtain a list of registered dietitians by sending a self-addressed, stamped envelope and $1 to the American Dietetic Association, 430 N. Michigan Avenue, Chicago, IL 60611.

If your doctor, GuardianOrg, or your friends don't have a nutritionist to recommend, you can get a list of nutrition consultants in your area with advanced degrees in nutrition from reputable schools from the American Nutritionists Association, P.O. Box 34030, Bethesda, MD 20817. For this list, send a self-addressed, stamped envelope with $1 and a letter explaining what you want.

The interview.

- How long has the person been in the business of nutrition counseling?
- Has she ever worked with people with your condition before? How many people? What approach does she use for your condition, and with what results?
- Are her techniques and advice based on research? If so, what research?
- How many people have tried this way of living and to what result? Look for careful, controlled, scientific studies. Ask for the names of people who have tried this approach and speak with them.
- Is the advice based on information the individual will not disclose?

Tip. If the nutritionist recommends a product that is only available from the nutritionist and/or contains secret ingredients, the inherent conflict of interest could reasonably lead you to avoid the products.

Section 13. Social Worker ↑↑↑

Unlike your other team members, a social worker will usually be assigned or be available to you either from a hospital or a GuardianOrg. Social workers are professionals who are familiar with government and nonprofit programs and services that may be available to you. They are paid by the organization for which they work.

Social workers can have a variety of educational and professional backgrounds. Ask about the background of your social worker in order to properly evaluate her advice. Because of her background, a social worker may, for example, steer you toward means-based entitlements and suggest you transfer your assets to qualify. If this occurs, review this advice independently to be sure it's best for you.

In addition to informing you about the programs that may be available, social workers can help you qualify for them and even complete the paperwork if necessary.

Section 14. Mental Health Provider (Psychiatrist/Psychologist) ↑↑↑

Emotional reactions to a diagnosis are likely to include disbelief, fear or apprehension, anger, and depression. Issues of self-esteem may well rise to the surface. You may feel guilt at "letting down" family and friends, not being able to accomplish all your usual tasks, or at somehow being responsible for developing the condition. Your emotions may reasonably be expected to fluctuate up and down with the ups and downs of your health. Grief over losing the illusion of immortality is not uncommon.

Emotional distress may not always require professional help. But when problems threaten to become overwhelming or interfere with everyday life, or you feel as if you are stuck on the downside of a normal emotional roller coaster, there's no need to feel defeated. Sadness, dark moods, bad days, and depression are part of life for everyone, but negative emotions that should be dealt with are as different from sadness as an upset stomach is from an ulcer. You can deal with these issues alone or you can add a therapist to your support team.

From a purely financial point of view, a therapist may be critical to your timing as to when you want to leave work on "disability." If it is questionable whether your physical condition meets the definition of disability for your work, private insurance, and/or Social Security purposes, a recommendation from a qualified mental health professional that you go on disability can make the difference. It is not a simple task to dispute a mental health provider's finding of "debilitating depression" or other psychological reason why disability status is warranted.

Tip. Your whole family lives with you and your diagnosis. Studies have indicated that a life-challenging condition that leads to depression affects not only the stricken person, but also the spouse/partner and children, as well as the functioning of the family. Since everyone is affected, some kind of counseling should be considered to help the whole family adjust. This is especially true if children live with you. Many GuardianOrgs offer family-oriented programs that you should consider. Contact your local chapter for information or for referral to a counselor.

Choosing a therapist. According to a survey by *Consumer Reports* in 1995, "people were just as satisfied and reported similar progress whether they saw a social worker, psychologist, or psychiatrist." However, for purposes of determining whether a person is disabled for insurance and Social Security, there is an order of preference of which you should be aware (see chapter 9, section 2). Also keep in mind that a psychiatrist is a trained medical doctor and can prescribe medications. A psychologist is not a trained M.D. and cannot prescribe medications. If you see a psychologist and drugs such as mood regulators are indicated, there will be a referral to a psychiatrist.

When you look for a therapist, competence and personal chemistry should be your priorities. You must share your most intimate thoughts, feelings, and experiences with your therapist. According to the *Consumer Reports* survey, the more diligently a person "shopped for a therapist—consulting with several candidates, checking their experience and qualifications, and speaking to previous clients—the more they ultimately improved."

Maximizing use of a therapist. The same survey also found that once in treatment, those who formed a real partnership with their therapist—by being open, even about painful subjects, and by working on issues between sessions—were more likely to progress.

Referral sources. If you decide to work with a therapist, ask your doctor for a referral. Other good referral sources are national professional associations or their local or state chapters. For information or referrals you can call the American Psychiatric Association at 202-682-6220, the American Psychological Association at 202-336-5800, or the National Association of Social Workers at 800-638-8799, ext. 291. Also, contact your GuardianOrg, local universities, hospitals, and psychotherapy and psychoanalytic training institutes. Family and friends may also know of reputable therapists.

Section 15. Caregivers

Your caregivers, the people who provide your emotional and physical care, as well as the rest of your family and friends, are important to your well-being.

As with any other relationship, whom you want to act as your caregiver(s) is your choice. Generally, caregivers gradually emerge from among your circle of close family and friends. Sometimes the wrong person responds. If that happens, change caregivers. If you are unhappy with a caregiver who emerges, communicate that—but with kindness and consideration. Perhaps there is a way to make that person feel helpful without monopolizing your time and attention. Suggesting such an alternative will help to let the person down easy.

If no caregiver emerges independently, the choice will be up to you. Past success is the greatest predictor of future success. Someone you've been close to before when times were rough, or who handled rough times well, would probably be a good caregiver. The person should have a strong empathetic sense and be capable of speaking, listening, and acting from the heart—without his or her own agenda.

Tip. To assist in making your caregiver choices, make a list of family members and friends with whom you are comfortable and in order of caregiver preference.

If you don't have eligible candidates among friends or family members, speak with your GuardianOrg, social worker, or spiritual adviser. I'm constantly surprised at the number of good-hearted people who volunteer to be caregivers for people they don't know. The depth of the relationships I've seen evolve has been immense for both parties.

Burnout. Watch for caregiver burnout. Before it occurs, be sure there are arrangements for respite: for someone to give your caregiver(s) a break.

Tip. Review your insurance coverage to see if respite care is covered. This is a common feature of long-term-care policies.

Consider pointing your caregivers toward taking care of *their* emotional needs by joining a support group for caregivers. In addition to taking care of themselves, they may learn information that is helpful to you.

Tip. A good source for caregiver advice is *Sometimes My Heart Goes Numb* by Charles Garfield,

Ph.D. (Jossey-Bass Publishers, 1995). While the book concerns AIDS caregivers, the advice applies to all caregiving. Regardless of the condition, the human need is the same.

The best advice for caregivers: they, and you, should do what comes naturally.

Section 16. Family and Friends

One way to lessen feelings of isolation and anxiety is to live as normally as possible. Let your family and friends know that as much as possible you want to continue with life as it was before.

Independence can mean using help when you need it. Letting family and friends know what you would like them to do and that you need their support will help them—and you. Don't hesitate to ask friends and relatives to visit if you are feeling up to it. Let them know what they can do for you and what you can do for yourself. They will be grateful for specific suggestions.

You can set the tone for those around you. They will look to you for guidance. You can make them feel comfortable. For your benefit and theirs, don't let the conversations continually center on your condition.

Tip. You don't have to be noble and heroic if you don't feel that way.

Don't be surprised if closeness with friends ebbs and flows. Ironically, the fear of loss may cause a friend to withdraw. Remember that if friends disappoint you, fear, not lack of caring, is probably the reason.

Those who are close to you need understanding just as you do. They need time to adjust to your illness and to their feelings of confusion, shock, helplessness, and even anger, all stemming from the possibility they may lose you. It may be helpful to try to imagine how they feel and to realistically assess what they can and can't do.

If you need assistance in relating to your family and friends, speak with your social worker, your clergyperson, or your therapist. It is also a topic for discussion at a support group.

For additional information, whatever your condition, obtain a copy of "Taking Time, Support for People With Cancer and the People Who Care About Them," published by the National Cancer Institute, free (800-422-6237).

Children. If you have minor children, see the discussion in chapter 2, section 13. Also see the resources section.

Section 17. Clergy People/Spiritual Adviser

Your relationship to the universe and to the spirit is totally personal. A clergyperson and/or spiritual adviser can be helpful in all kinds of situations such as determining who and when to tell of your condition, monitoring and bolstering relationships with family and loved ones, and helping you keep a positive outlook with the strength of a spiritual underpinning. Even with nonbelievers, a clergyperson or other spiritual adviser can be of great help.

Section 18. Malpractice/Errors and Omissions

All your professional team members must conduct themselves in a manner that is reasonable according to the standards in the particular professional community. If they don't, and you are damaged, you are entitled to compensation.

If you think one of your professionals has not acted properly

- act immediately. **Statutes of limitation** (laws defining the time by which you must sue or lose your right to sue) vary and can be limited.
- start making detailed notes of the situation.
- if there is physical damage, take photographs.
- speak with two or three attorneys in your community who specialize in malpractice actions. If you have a good case, you will find an attorney who will take the case on a contingency basis. If no attorney agrees to work for you for a contingency fee, it probably means your case is not that strong and is not worth your spending the Life Units or money to pursue. The amount of the contingency fee is negotiable.
- in choosing this type of attorney, look at the quality of the experts whom the attorney uses. Experts are critical to any malpractice case— malpractice actions are typically won or lost based on the quality of the experts testifying on your behalf. Ask whether the attorney will advance the money for the requisite experts. This is negotiable. It is also negotiable whether the fees for the experts are paid out of your share of the ultimate award or the attorney's share. Generally, these fees are paid from your share.

Chapter 37

Travel

Whether we're sick or healthy, walking around or confined in a wheelchair, we can choose to wait for death, or we can choose to live until we die. Knowing that death may be in the near future is no reason to give up on life. I love to travel, and the rest of it be damned.

—Lewis L.

Section 1. In General

The key to traveling with a life-challenging condition is to anticipate possible complications ahead of time. While the following advice may appear daunting, if you follow it, you should be able to travel and have a good time. In 1991, I traveled literally around the world with a person living with AIDS. We followed the tips you will read about. When a health problem cropped up in Sydney, we were prepared. Travel was not as spontaneous as it could have been, but it was definitely worth it for both of us.

Of course, before embarking on any journey you should consult your doctor regarding whether you should go. If you are in a weakened condition, give serious consideration to traveling with someone, preferably healthier than you are. It will help to have someone you can count on to step in and assist you in the event that something happens, no matter how unlikely that may seem.

Section 2. Choosing Your Destination

In general.
- Match your destination to your physical capabilities.

- Consider whether there will be doctors available trained in treating occurrences associated with your condition. If you include a destination with a high risk of infectious disease or a lack of reasonable access to physicians or medical facilities, be aware of the closest facility and how long it would take to get there in an emergency.
- If you want to head to a warm climate, find out whether any of your drugs would react negatively with the sun. Your eyes may also be more sensitive to sunlight and its damaging effects.

If you're considering traveling outside North America.
- Does the country prohibit entry to people with your condition?
- Ask your doctor whether the required inoculations, if any, may be harmful to you.
- To ensure that you are aware of the possible threats to your health in a potential destination, ask your doctor, the Centers for Disease Control and Prevention's International Traveler's Hotline at 404-332-4559 (www. cdc.gov/travel/travel.html) or call the Public Health Service at 404-639-3311. The Public Health Service provides a person-to-person consultation with a travel adviser.

• If applicable, does the country have resources to adequately screen blood or provide sterile needles? Your local Red Cross office can advise you about safe sources of blood overseas.

Tip. Consider joining the International Association for Medical Assistance to Travelers (IAMAT), which guarantees treatment by English-speaking doctors should the need for medical care arise during your trip. IAMAT operates in 125 countries, and its doctors are trained in the West. IAMAT is at 317 Center Street, Lewiston, NY 14092 (716-754-4883).

Section 3. Making Travel Plans

Making arrangements.

• **Rest:** Rest will be required. Be sure to include plenty of rest time in your itinerary or your body will force you to rest at what may be an inopportune time.

• **Cancellation:** When booking any arrangements, check the cancellation policy for the means of travel and the hotel.

• **Special requests:** If you will need the use of special equipment on your trip, from a wheelchair at the airport to an IV pole or a refrigerator for medications, be sure to make those requests in advance with the travel conveyance and/or the hotels. The same goes for any special dietary needs. The Americans with Disabilities Act prevents public accommodations from discriminating against you because of a disability. It also requires reasonable adjustments on your behalf.

• **Syringes and needles:** If you are traveling abroad, you should bring a signed letter from your doctor explaining why you are carrying needles and syringes.

• **Travel agent:** Travel agents can help to alleviate the stress. It doesn't cost you to use one because they are paid by the airline, hotel, and the like. An agent with a Travel Career Development Diploma issued by the Institute of Certified Travel Agents has completed a course in how to get more information beyond that listed in the airline data banks.

• **Train:** Information on accessibility of trains and stations and assistance available to passengers who are disabled may be obtained from an authorized travel agent or by calling Amtrak at 800-USA-RAIL. Travelers with disabilities who have a card or a physician's letter showing disability are allowed a 25 percent discount on round-trip travel by Amtrak with the exception of certain holidays.

• **Hotels abroad:** Unless you are fluent in the local language, consider staying in a hotel with an English-speaking staff (not necessarily part of a U.S. hotel chain). They are more likely to be able to steer you to medical assistance than the staff at a hotel where no one understands your language. The nonprofit Society for the Advancement of Travel for the Handicapped (SATH) (212-447-SATH) provides information as to whether particular hotels are handicapped accessible as well as other travel tips for people who are physically disabled.

Section 4. Preparing for Your Trip

Once you know where you're going, it's time to start preparing for your trip.

• **Health issues:** One of the most important ways to make sure that you stay healthy on a trip is to leave home healthy. A pretrip medical checkup is always a good idea. If you're going abroad, schedule your visit to the doctor at least eight weeks before your departure in case of negative reactions or the need for several visits.

• **Obtain a summary of your medical records:** Carry this in your wallet or with your passport. The summary should include an update on your condition, medications being taken, allergies, list of drugs that cause adverse reactions, and your blood type. Also take a copy of your eye-glass prescription.

- **Time zones:** If you are going to cross time zones, ask your doctor about how to adjust your medication schedule and write it out in advance so you won't have to figure it out on your trip.

- **Possible symptoms:** Discuss symptoms that you might experience while away and be prepared with the appropriate medication as well as early warning signs about your condition that indicate you should seek help.

- **Doctors:** Ask your doctor for a list of doctors specializing in your condition as well as hospitals and facilities you can use on your trip should the need arise. It would be helpful if he would write a letter of introduction (even if it is addressed "To whom it may concern" or "Dear doctor") to help you get the services you might need.

- **Health insurance:** Check your coverage carefully to determine whether you are going to be covered in the places you will visit and to be aware of what you must do to be reimbursed. If your coverage is through a managed care organization, consult the carrier before your departure on the required procedures in the event of an emergency or illness during your trip. With Medicare and Medicaid, there is no coverage outside the United States, except in limited circumstances near the U.S. borders.

Tip: Medical evacuation can be critical, especially when you are traveling abroad. If your health policy doesn't cover this risk, consider obtaining the coverage through a trip-cancellation policy—provided it doesn't exclude preexisting conditions.

- **Advance directives:** Check your living will and health care proxy to be sure they are up-to-date. While these documents may not be binding in another state or country, they can be helpful.

Tip. Carry these documents with you on lengthy trips. Include contact telephone numbers. Let your

traveling companion or tour guide know where they are packed. If you don't want to carry these documents, be sure your traveling companion or, if you are traveling alone, the hotel knows the contact information for your decision maker(s). Also consider filing your advance directives with an entity from which they can be retrieved no matter where you are, such as DocuDial (see chapter 32, section 9).

- **Travel insurance:** Travel insurance (which is generally purchased through a travel agent) covers cancellation or interruption of your trip, emergency medical care while you're traveling, lost or stolen baggage, and other similar problems. The following discussion examines the risks to consider as well as alternative means to cover them.

  - **Health coverage:** If your health insurance doesn't cover where you will be traveling, or if it doesn't cover medical evacuation, you should definitely obtain travel insurance.

  - **Trip cancellation or interruption:** Look at the fine print of the travel arrangements. For example, your plane ticket, which is often the biggest cost of the trip, may be refundable in the event of cancellation for health reasons—or permit you to use the credit for a future plane trip. If you can't cancel, consider purchasing a travel policy with cancellation coverage.

  - **Travel accident:** Many major credit cards include travel accident insurance when you use them to buy airline, rail, boat, or bus tickets.

  - **Your belongings:** Your homeowners policy probably covers your luggage.

  - **Bankruptcy of tour operator:** United States Tour Operators Association (USTOA) guarantees travelers against bankruptcy of its members. Several states protect travelers against insolvency of travel agents. Cruise lines leaving U.S. ports are also covered. If you pay by credit card and the tour operator goes bankrupt, you may be able to stop payment through the credit card company.

Tip. If you desire travel insurance, *only* purchase a policy that has no preexisting-condition exclusion. If your travel agent doesn't have such a policy, call Travel Guard International (800-826-1300), which will waive the exclusion if the policy is purchased within six days after making your initial deposit for the trip. If all else fails, call a travel agency that works with many people with a life-challenging condition.

Section 5. Packing for Your Trip

In general.
- Always have your doctor's name, telephone number, and fax number in your wallet, clearly marked.
- If you use any medical equipment such as a wheelchair, take spare parts.

Medications. Assume that you won't be able to get anything you may need for your health at your destination or while traveling to and from there. Take all of the necessary medication for the time you expect to be away *plus* a few extra days in case some unforeseen problem develops. To avoid confusion, medications should be kept in their original labeled containers and not mixed together in one vial. This is particularly important for customs agents if you cross international borders.

Tip. If you don't want to carry all your medication, consider sending some ahead to your destination(s) by traceable overnight mail and advising the hotel how to store them until your arrival. Confirm their receipt before you leave.

Pack in your carry-on luggage
- at least a few days' supply of medications.
- medications for diarrhea, which can be set off by a change in eating habits or the tap water (even in the United States).
- pain relievers.
- a thermometer.
- unmedicated petroleum jelly and deconges-

tant nasal sprays, which are helpful for long plane rides (see section 6 below).
- your favorite cold remedy.
- sleep aids if you are changing time zones.
- any medications for conditions that are quiet at the moment, in case they flare up.
- high-potency sunscreen, sunglasses, and a hat if you are going to be in the sun, particularly if your medications make you more sensitive.
- a phrase book in the language at your destination if you're not sure about your fluency. The book should include medical phrases so that in an emergency you can accurately describe symptoms to a non-English-speaking doctor.
- if your immune system is compromised, commercial iodine or chlorine tablets and/or a small immersion heater with an international converter or adapter to boil water to make tap water drinkable in an emergency.
- insect repellent, long sleeves, and high-potency cortisone creams if you are traveling in an area with insects.

Section 6. Planes and Trains

If you have a compromised immune system. Plan your trip to avoid crowds and poor air circulation. Consider:
- Travel at nonpeak hours.
- Try to avoid crowded waiting rooms. Sit in more remote areas of the terminal, away from the congestion, or join your favorite airline's passengers' club where they have a private lounge. Amtrak also has private lounges.
- Pack surgical masks for high-traffic areas. Although it is somewhat unusual in our country, in other countries such as Japan people concerned about airborne diseases commonly wear surgical masks.

When flying:

• Travel directly when possible.

• Book a seat in the front. Most planes circulate air from the front to the back. Air in the front should be fresher, and you won't have to walk past as many other passengers.

• If your seats are preassigned, boarding the plane last will also delay your exposure to a crowded space until the last possible minute.

• Let the airline know as far ahead as possible about your needs.

Tip. Passengers with disabilities have priority on shipping assistive devices or on taking them into the cabin. These rights are described in "New Horizons for the Air Traveler with a Disability," available free from the U.S. Department of Transportation at 719-948-3334.

Reducing health risks while on board a plane.

• Avoid dehydration by drinking lots of fluids (four to five ounces every couple of hours). Avoid alcohol and drinks that contain caffeine since these will further dehydrate you.

• Bottled water, ginger ale, Sprite, or canned fruit juices are the best liquids to drink since undistilled water may contain potentially harmful bacteria. Always wipe the outside of the can or bottle before you drink or pour.

• Avoid ice that may have been made from tap water.

• On long flights, to help repel cold and flu viruses, keep the mucous membranes moist by dabbing unmedicated petroleum jelly in each nostril. Nasal decongestants and nasal saline sprays are also good remedies for counteracting the discomfort of abrupt pressure changes and dry flight air.

• Avoid sitting next to anyone with a cold or cough.

• Airline pillows are freshened once a day at most, which means that several other people may have used the pillow before you get it. Bring your own covering for the airline pillow or bring your own inflatable pillow.

• Particularly when traveling internationally, your efforts to avoid stomach problems should begin on the plane. Avoid eating fresh fruit and vegetable salads. Seafood should also be avoided as well as undercooked eggs and meats. Ask for extra bread and cheese packets if necessary. Consider packing your own food in a thermal box if you know your system is sensitive. Also keep in mind that University of Texas studies show that Pepto-Bismol taken "just in case" during trips may be an effective protection against diarrhea.

Section 7. At Your Destination

Medications. Keep to your medication schedule. If you've crossed time zones, adjust your schedule to the one you discussed with your physician.

Food. Infections that can cause traveler's diarrhea can cause much greater harm if you have a weakened immune system. *When it comes to food in areas with less than sanitary conditions, a good rule of thumb is boil it, cook it, peel it, or forget it.*

Tip. Due to the possibility of an incapacitating emergency, carry with you at all times ID and the name, address, and phone number of where you are staying.

Section 8. Water

If you have a compromised immune system. *As a general rule, while traveling (even within the United States) avoid ingesting tap water or using ice in drinks.* Alcoholic beverages will not kill the disease-causing organisms in tap-water ice.

• Drink only from bottles or cans and wipe the lip before you drink or pour.

• Use bottled water when brushing teeth, and make sure water does not enter your mouth when taking showers. Do not put contact lenses or teeth in anything but distilled water.

• Bottled carbonated water is safe, but noncarbonated bottled water is safe only if the original seal is intact, and sometimes not even then.

• *If you plan to swim, be aware of pollution problems.* The safest bet is a properly chlorinated pool.

Section 9. If You Become Ill While Away

• **Physicians:** If your doctor didn't give you a recommendation, ask the manager of the hotel whom he would use. If you are overseas and require a doctor's attention, ask for a "western-style" doctor and hospital to receive the kind of care with which you will be most familiar. You can locate one through the U.S. embassy or consulate, the airline, or English-speaking employees of multinational corporations in the area.

• **Hospitals:** If you require hospitalization, hospitals associated with a university usually have English-speaking doctors as well as qualified specialists.

• **Drugs:** All drugs throughout the United States are the same. If you travel abroad, obtain the generic or trade name of all drugs you receive for your home doctor or in case you develop an allergic reaction. Many drugs have a different name outside the United States.

• **Sterilization:** If injections are required, make sure the syringes come straight from a sterilized package or have been sterilized prior to use. When in doubt, ask to see how the equipment is sterilized (this is where a traveling companion might step in and be of help). If necessary, buy your own sterile needles and syringes.

• **Blood transfusion:** If you are injured, postpone any blood transfusion unless it is absolutely necessary. According to the Centers for Disease Control and Prevention, a possible alternative to consider before a transfusion is plasma expanders. If you do need blood and you are outside the United States, try to ensure that it is properly screened, or better still, get one of your blood-compatible traveling companions to donate it for you.

• **Payment for health needs:** Most foreign doctors, hospitals, or clinics require payment in cash unless you have a direct-payment travel policy. In a major crisis seek help first and then worry about payment. Your health is more important than whether your carrier or plan will pay. If you must call an MCO for approval and advice about treatment (MCOs usually have health care professionals available twenty-four hours a day), call home and ask someone there to make the time-consuming calls for you. You may also ask the airline you are using to make the calls for you as a special service.

• **On leaving a hospital:** Be sure to get copies of all bills and if possible a copy of your chart, as well as letters from attending physicians explaining why you needed treatment. *If you can't obtain these documents, ask that they be mailed to you at the earliest opportunity so you will have all the documentation you need for reimbursement and for your medical file at home.* Get telephone and fax numbers, and a contact name, to follow up if necessary.

Chapter 38

And . . .

Many people allow illness to disfigure their lives more than it should. . . .
There is always a margin within which life can be lived with meaning and
even with a certain measure of joy.

—Norman Cousins, *Anatomy of an Illness*

This chapter addresses important matters that do not readily fit into other chapters.

Section 1. Medical Identification

If you have an allergy that may be life threatening or if you just want to convey information about your condition in the event of an emergency that renders you unable to communicate, there are several alternatives to consider:

- Medic Alert Foundation, 2323 Colorado Avenue, Turlock, CA 95380 (800-432-5378), provides wearable necklaces and bracelets with tags that are engraved with your most critical medical conditions and personal ID number, along with a phone number for their emergency response center. The tag alerts an emergency team to call to access your medical record. Medic Alert can even provide the caller with the name and phone number of a family member to contact. Cost is $35 plus $15 a year.
- Save-a-Life, 382 Boston Turnpike, Suite 202, Shrewsbury, MA (800-755-6648 or 508-845-

1396), provides business-size medical cards that include a microfilmed medical history. The card is viewed by the physician through a machine or low-powered microscope. In case facilities to read the information aren't available, Save-a-Life will fax the attending physician's report. The cost is $21 for two years.

Section 2. Lying

Some people who have been diagnosed with a life-challenging condition adopt the attitude "I can cheat or lie as I please. I won't be here when they catch it." As a practical matter, I strongly caution against this attitude. The odds are you will end up spending a great deal of money and precious Life Units fixing things. Even worse, in some situations such as applications for health or life insurance, if you complete the application dishonestly, you may find that the insurance company contests the existence of the policy just when you need it.

As Jacques Chambers, a nationally known expert on benefits for people with life-challenging conditions says, "I neither condone nor recommend deception to my clients. My job is to reduce stress, and if someone lies on an application, I don't think their stress has been reduced very much."

Section 3. Student Loans

Student loans are forgiven when you leave work and go on disability.

Caution. If you change the terms of the loan, such as the amount of your periodic payments, it is considered a new loan and not forgiven if you were disabled at the time the change was made.

Section 4. Pets

Pets can be good for your emotional/physical health. However, they can pose a risk of infection to people with a lowered immune system, whether the lowered level of immunity is temporary such as during chemotherapy or more permanent as with HIV disease.

Anyone with a compromised immune system should

- avoid contact with animals that have diarrhea.
- avoid contact with pets' feces.
- be sure that litter boxes are emptied (not just sifted) daily.
- wash hands with soap and water after handling pets, especially after cleaning their litter boxes or living areas and before eating.
- have pet birds checked by a veterinarian for psittacosis.
- have any sick pet checked promptly by a veterinarian. Neither sick pets nor their excretions should be handled by a person with a reduced immune system.
- avoid contact with reptiles such as snakes, lizards, and turtles.

If you need help with pets, and friends or family can't take over the necessary chores, there are organizations around the country that assist with dog walking, changing litter, providing foster care for the animal in case the owner goes into the hospital, and even planning for the animal's welfare in case the owner dies. Since the groups are local, their services and client bases vary. If a group exists in your area, it can be located through your local Humane Society, or perhaps you can find assistance through your GuardianOrg or support group.

Section 5. Transportation to and from Physicians or Treatment Centers

If transportation is a problem, there are services that provide transportation to and from your medical appointments. Contact your local GuardianOrg or social worker. You can also call the Eldercare Locator at 800-677-6116. Perhaps your physician and/or the facility in which you will be treated also provide transportation.

Section 6. Parking Spots for the Disabled

Parking spots are not just for people with a visible handicap or who have lost the ability to walk. They are also for people who may not be able to walk long distances. In most areas, you do not need to be a driver or a registered owner of a vehicle to get a permit.

Contact your state Department of Motor Vehicles to determine

- eligibility requirements.
- what you need to verify eligibility.
- how often you have to prove eligibility or otherwise renew the permit.
- the cost of the permit.

Tip. If you do not appear to be physically handicapped, prepare an answer in case an obnoxious person questions why you park in a reserved parking place. Your response, if any, should be whatever is comfortable for you.

Section 7. Other Legal Rights

7.1 Public Accommodations

Under the ADA, protection against discrimination in public accommodations extends to "the goods, services, facilities, privileges, advantages, and accommodations of any place of public accommodation." The term *public accommodation* is broadly defined to include

- professional offices of health care providers, hospitals, or other service establishments.
- places of lodging.
- restaurants, bars, or other establishments serving food or drink.
- places of exhibition or entertainment such as movie houses and theaters.
- any place of public gathering.
- stores.
- museums or other places of public display or collection.
- places or recreation.
- gymnasiums, health spas, golf courses, or other places of exercise.

Private clubs and places run by religious organizations are not considered places of public accommodation.

Businesses must make reasonable modifications to their policies, practices, or procedures if it would rectify discrimination. For example, if a hotel does not allow pets, it would be reasonable to request a Seeing Eye dog exception for a person who has lost her vision.

Questions or complaints should be directed to the Office on the Americans with Disabilities Act, Civil Rights Division, U.S. Department of Justice,

P.O. Box 66118, Washington, DC 20035-6118 (202-514-0301).

7.2 Communications

The ADA requires telephone companies that offer services to the general public to provide telephone relay services for people with hearing or speech impairments. Similar requirements are imposed by the Federal Communications Commission (the FCC). If you have a problem, contact the Federal Communications Commission, 1919 M Street NW, Washington, DC 20554 (202-632-7260).

7.3 Federally Assisted Programs and Activities

Another federal law, the Rehabilitation Act of 1973, affords individuals with disabilities protection against discrimination in *all* federally assisted programs and activities. This law has been interpreted broadly so that, for example, an entire university or corporation is barred from engaging in discriminatory practices if any of its departments or units receive federal funds. The act also protects against employment discrimination by federal agencies or federal contractors.

7.4 New Construction and Alterations

New construction and alterations of buildings open to the public are supposed to permit access to people who are disabled. If you have a question about whether a building complies, contact the Architectural and Transportation Barriers Compliance Board, 1331 F Street NW, Suite 1000, Washington, DC 20004 (800-USA-ABLE).

The Job Accommodation Network (JAN) provides free "public access" information to businesses and services that must comply with the accessibility requirements of the ADA. Call 800-232-9675.

7.5 Transportation

Public. Individuals with disabilities must be given special public transportation services comparable to those provided to the general public. Hours and days of service, service areas, response time, and fares are also covered. Contact the Department of Transportation, 400 Seventh Street SW, Washington, DC 20590 (202-366-9305).

Private. The provisions of the ADA apply to businesses whose primary business is transporting people. The ADA Private Transportation Hotline at 800-605-6605 (9 A.M. to 3 P.M. central time, M–F) answers questions, makes referrals to experts, and has free publications concerning the ADA regulations on private transportation providers. Ask for a free copy of "The ADA Private Transportation Handbook."

Afterword

In my life I have had to face the pain of many personal challenges. As the years go by, I have begun to see how meeting these challenges has always provided me with an opportunity to grow or to perceive life from an enriched perspective. This is the perspective that convinced me I should write this book, to pass on the practical knowledge I have gained with the hope of saving time, money, and emotional distress for other people facing personal challenges.

Researching and writing *Be Prepared* has reinforced the version of reality I've come to through living with, and caring for, people with a life-challenging condition. It has been particularly gratifying for me to work and exchange knowledge and experiences with the courageous survivors, experts, friends, and family mentioned under the pseudonyms and in the acknowledgments of the book.

Please share your comments and suggestions to help make *Be Prepared* as practical as possible for future readers. If I did the job I set out to do, this will only be the first of many editions. In the meantime, I will be posting suggestions, updates, and "Tips," as well as other information of interest, on the Internet at www.be-prepared.com. Please E-mail me or write to me care of St. Martin's Press.

David S. Landay
New York City
April 1998

Resources

As a supplement to the resources and information sources specified in the text, the following list covers areas of broader interest. If you don't see the resource you need with respect to a specific topic, you can access information in the text through the table of contents and the index.

Advance Directives

- Choice in Dying, 200 Varick Street, New York, NY 10014 (212-366-5540 or 800-989-9455). State-specific advance directives with instructions.
- Gentle Closure, Inc., 60 Santa Susanna Lane, Sedona, AZ 86336 (520-282-0170). Forms and advice for a fee.
- Stationery stores usually stock forms with instructions for execution, including such publications as *Living Wills and More* by Terry J. Barnett and the *Living Will Kit* published by Rediform.

Alternative Treatments

- *AMA Reader's Guide to Alternative Health Methods* by S. Barrett and W. Jarvis.
- *Fundamentals of Complementary and Alternative Medicine* by M. Micozzi, foreword by C. Everett Koop (Churchill Livingstone, 1996).
- OAM Information Center, Office of Alternative Medicine, National Institutes of Health, 6120 Executive Boulevard, EPS Suite 450, Rockville, MD 20892-9904. Telephone 888-644-6226 or 301-496-4000 to speak with a specialist, 8:30 A.M. to 5 P.M. EST, M–F. Fax back system at 301-402-2466. A federal government office to investigate and share information with the public about the effectiveness of various forms of alternative medical care. The agency also provides a directory of alternative health care associations.

Children

- *Facing the Future: A Legal Handbook for Parents with HIV Disease.* A primer for any parent with a life-challenging condition, by Brooklyn Legal Services Corp. and Gay Men's Health Crisis. Telephone Brooklyn Legal Services Corp. at 718-237-5546 or GMHC at 212-807-6664.
- *How to Help Children through a Parent's Serious Illness* by Kathleen McCue, MA, CCLS, with Ron Bonn (New York: St. Martin's Griffin, 1994).
- Kidscope, 3400 Peachtree Road, Suite 703, Atlanta, GA 30326 (404-233-0001), a nonprofit organization, publishes educational material for children of a parent living with cancer. Even if you aren't living with cancer, the ideas may be helpful.

Credit

- Cardtrak, at 800-344-7714 or 301-695-4660 or www.cardtrak.com. Cardtrak provides credit card information including a survey of banks or savings institutions with low interest rates; a no-annual-fee survey; a survey of which cards provide which bonuses (e.g., airline miles and for which airline) and rebates; and a survey of which financial institutions offer secured cards with details. A monthly newsletter of listings is $15.
- Consumer Action. Publishes "Rebuilding Good Credit" as well as separate surveys of secured and unsecured credit cards. Available free by sending a stamped, self-addressed envelope to Consumer Action, 717 Market Street, Suite 310, San Francisco, CA 94103 (415-777-9648). Annual memberships including updates to the surveys are $25.

Daily Living

- *Adaptive Resources: A Guide to Products and Services.* Published by the National Stroke Association at 800-787-6537. A free catalog of suppliers of equipment, clothing and dressing aids, services, and miscellaneous resources.
- *American Medical Association Catalog of Products for Family Health.* P.O. Box 7104, Dover, DE 19903-7104 (800-864-5050 or www.ama-assn.org). Health, exercise, and safety products.
- Backsaver Products Co., 53 Jeffrey Avenue, Holliston, MA 01746 (800-251-2225) has a mail order catalog of products to help relieve back pain.
- *Easy Street Catalogue.* Easy Street, 8 Equality Park West, Newport, RI 02840-2603 (800-959-EASY). A free catalog of helpful products such as a digital blood pressure monitor, inexpensive medication organizers, a pill splitter, and easy-grip knobs.
- The Mature Mart, 145 Fifteenth Street, Suite 1031, Atlanta, GA 30309 (800-720-6278 or 404-881-9816 or www.maturemart.com). The company carries products that are "disability friendly," such as easy-to-grip kitchen tools, bathroom aids, and medication aids, including a pillbox geared to multiple prescriptions that must be taken on different schedules.
- National Association for Continence, P.O. Box 8310, Spartanburg, SC 29305-8310 (800-BLADDER). Has a resource guide to incontinence products ($10 plus $3 s/h).
- Project Link, State University of New York at Buffalo, 515 Kimball Tower, Buffalo, NY 14214 (800-628-2281). A nonprofit, national direct-mail information service that takes information from manufacturers of products that assist daily living and distributes it to individuals. Specify your ailment or the type of assistance you desire. Project Link also has information on possible sources of paying for devices.

Funerals

Caskets

- Carpenter plans may be ordered from Richard Johnstone, P.O. Box 1062, Pioneer, CA 95666, $19.50.
- Consumer Casket USA, Erie, PA, at 800-611-8778, a wholesale casket supplier.
- Direct Casket, Costa Mesa, CA, at 800-772-2753, a wholesale casket supplier.
- www.xroad.com/~funerals/, an Internet site that lists a variety of wholesale casket companies as well as price comparisons.
- Funeral and Memorial Societies of America (a nonprofit organization), P.O. Box 10, Hinesburg, VT 05461 (800-458-5563 or www.funerals.org/famsa). Information on wholesale caskets, cardboard caskets, rental caskets, and cremation.

Federal Rules

- FTC Public Reference, 600 Pennsylvania Avenue NW, Room 130, Washington, DC 20580 (202-326-2222 or www.ftx.gov). Free publications include "Funerals: A Consumer Guide" and "Caskets and Burial Vaults," a brochure about the use and protective claims of caskets and burial vaults, as well as funeral planning.

Preplanning

- National Funeral Directors Association, 11121 W. Oklahoma Avenue, Milwaukee, WI 53227-4096 (800-228-6332).
- Funeral Service Consumer Assistance Program, P.O. Box 27641, Milwaukee, WI 53227 (800-662-7666).

Gifts (the proceeds of which go to charity)

General

- *Gifts That Make a Difference.* Describes gifts sold through nonprofits, by Ellen Berry (Foxglove Publishing [1992], 598 David Parkway, Dayton, OH 45429).

Cancer

- American Cancer Society, Washington Division, Inc., at 800-729-1151. Holiday greeting cards and cookbook.
- Jacqueline Green at 814-371-4331 sells items with a cancer-survivor logo such as caps, lapels, key chains, T-shirts, and sweatshirts. All net profits go to Adult Getaway, a nonprofit that provides vacations for people with cancer.

HIV/AIDS

- Broadway Cares/Equity Fights AIDS, 165 W. Forty-sixth Street, Suite 1300, New York, NY 10036 (212-840-0770, ext. 250, twenty-four hours a day), has a catalog of gift items.
- The Names Project Foundation (the AIDS Memorial Quilt), 3310 Townsend Street, Suite 310, San Francisco, CA 94107-1639 (800-872-6263). Gift items.
- The National AIDS Awareness Catalog at 800-669-1078. Items from different HIV/AIDS GuardianOrgs.

Government Benefits

- *The AIDS Benefits Handbook* by Thomas P. McCormack (Yale University Press, 1990). While this book is written for people living with AIDS, it is an excellent resource for anyone who wants to access or has questions about government programs, including SSD, SSI, Medicare, and Medicaid.
- *ProBenefit$ Handbook* by the Benefits and Insurance Department of AIDS Project Los Angeles (213-993-1409). A professional guide to public benefits and private insurance for people with HIV but applicable to everyone applying for government disability benefits. Includes suggestions for completing appropriate Social Security forms, copies of which are included.

Guardian Organizations: National

(For local organizations, either call the national organization and ask for local resources or look in the yellow pages under the name of the pertinent condition.)

ALS (Lou Gehrig's Disease)

- Amyotrophic Lateral Sclerosis (ALS) Association, 21021 Ventura Boulevard, Suite 321, Woodland Hills, CA 91364 (800-782-4747 or 818-340-7500). Provides local referrals for counseling, training, and support.

Alzheimer's Disease

- Alzheimer's Association, 919 N. Michigan Avenue, Suite 100, Chicago, IL 60611 (800-872-3900 or 312-335-8700). Research and advocacy. Provides support and assistance to affected patients and their families.

Cancer

- Alliance for Lung Cancer Advocacy, Support and Education (ALCASE), 1601 Lincoln Avenue, Vancouver, WA 98660 (800-298-2436 or 360-696-2436). Information (including customized information), support, and advocacy.

- American Brain Tumor Association, 2720 River Road, Suite 146, Des Plaines, IL 60018 (800-886-2282 or 847-827-9910). Condition and treatment information; access to support groups.
- American Cancer Society, 1599 Clifton Road NE, Atlanta, GA 30329 (800-ACS-2345 or www.cancer.org). Publications and information; referrals, research, education, and advocacy. Programs include "Man to Man," a program for men with prostate cancer, and "Look Good . . . Feel Better" for women.
- American Foundation for Urologic Disease, 330 W. Pratt Street, Suite 401, Baltimore, MD 21201 (800-828-7866). Condition and treatment information concerning prostate cancer and other urologic disorders.
- Cancer Care, Inc., 1180 Avenue of the Americas, New York, NY 10026 (800-813-HOPE or 212-302-2400 or www.cancercareinc.org). Free professional counseling, support groups, education, condition and treatment information, referrals.
- Corporate Angel Network, Westchester County Airport Building 1, White Plains, NY 10604 (914-328-1313). Arranges travel on corporate planes for cancer patients undergoing treatments in specified centers.
- Cure for Lymphoma Foundation, 215 Lexington Avenue, New York, NY 10016 (212-319-5857). Research; support and information.
- Gilda's Club, 195 W. Houston Street, New York, NY 10014 (212-647-9700). Support and counseling.
- International Center for Post-Laryngectomees Voice Restoration, 7440 N. Shadeland Avenue, Suite 100, Indianapolis, IN 46250 (800-823-1056). Condition and treatment information, support for people with cancer-related voice loss.
- Leukemia Society of America, 600 Third Avenue, New York, NY 10016 (800-955-4572 or 212-573-8484). Concerns leukemia, lymphomas, and multiple myeloma. Counseling, financial assistance, speaker bureau, research, referrals, and information.
- Lymphoma Research Foundation of America, Inc., 8800 Venice Boulevard, Suite 207, Los Angeles, CA 90034 (310-204-7040). Research, treatment, and condition information.
- National Alliance of Breast Cancer Organizations, 9 E. Thirty-seventh Street, Tenth Floor, New York, NY 10016 (800-719-9154 or www. nabcoinfo.aol.com). Information source and advocate. Physician referrals.
- National Brain Tumor Foundation, 785 Market Street, Suite 1600, San Francisco, CA 94103 (800-934-2873 or 415-284-0208). Research, counseling, support. Publishes *Brain Tumors: The Resource Guide,* free.
- National Breast Cancer Coalition, 1707 L Street NW, Suite 1060, Washington, DC 20036 (202-296-7477). Grassroots advocacy to eliminate breast cancer.
- National Coalition for Cancer Survivorship, 1010 Wayne Avenue, Silver Spring, MD 20910 (301-650-8868). A resource network linking cancer survivors nationwide to the support resources in their communities. Publishes *National Directory of Cancer Support Services* ($10).
- National Kidney Cancer Association, 1234 Sherman Avenue, #203, Evanston, IL 60202 (847-332-1051). Research, information, publications, and advocacy. Publishes *We Have Kidney Cancer,* a fifty-six-page book for patients.
- Share (Self-Help for Women with Breast or Ovarian Cancer), 1501 Broadway, Suite 1720, New York, NY 10036 (212-719-0364). Condition and treatment information, support groups of and for women with breast and ovarian cancer.
- Susan G. Komen Breast Cancer Foundation, 5005 LBJ Freeway, Suite 370, Dallas, TX 75244 (800-462-9273). Research, education, help line.
- Wellness Community, 2716 Ocean Park Boulevard, Suite 1040, Santa Monica, CA 90405-5211

(310-314-2555). Psychological and emotional support for survivors and families.

• Y-Me National Organization for Breast Cancer Information and Support, 212 W. Van Buren, Fourth Floor, Chicago, IL 60607-3908 (800-221-2141 or 312-986-8338 or www.y.me.org). Peer support. Manual for starting support groups. Prosthesis bank for women with financial need.

Cerebral Palsy

• United Cerebral Palsy, 1660 L Street NW, Suite 700, Washington, DC 20036 (800-872-5827 or 202-776-0406 or www.ucpa.org). Information and referral source. Direct services—including therapy, family support, recreation programs, and employment assistance.

Cystic Fibrosis

• Cystic Fibrosis Foundation, 6931 Arlington Road, Bethesda, MD 20814 (800-344-4823 or 301-951-4422 or www.cff.org). Research, care centers, and clinical trials.

Diabetes

• American Diabetes Association, 1660 Duke Street, Alexandria, VA 22314 (800-232-3472 or 703-549-1500 or www.diabetes.org/custom. asp). Research, information, and advocacy. Referrals through 800-DIABETES.

HIV/AIDS

• National AIDS Fund, 1400 I Street, Washington, DC 20005-2208 (202-408-4848). Grants to community organizations.

• National Association of People with AIDS, Inc., 1413 K Street, Washington, DC 20005 (202-898-0414 or www.napwa.org.). Advocacy, public education, treatment information.

• National Minority AIDS Council, 1931 Thirteenth Street, Washington, DC 20009 (202-483-6622). Training programs and public education.

• Women Organized to Respond to Life-Threatening Diseases, P.O. Box 11535, Oakland, CA 94611 (510-658-6930). Support for women with HIV.

Huntington's Disease

• Huntington's Disease Society of America, 140 W. Twenty-second Street, Sixth Floor, New York, NY 10011-2420 (800-345-HDSA or http://hdsa.mgh.harvard.edu). Services, education, and research.

Kidney

• American Kidney Fund, 6110 Executive Boulevard, Suite 1010, Rockville, MD 20852 (800-638-8299 or 301-881-3052 or www.arbon. com/kidney). Education, financial assistance, information.

• The National Kidney Cancer Association, 1234 Sherman Avenue, Evanston, IL 60202 (708-332-1051). A computer bulletin board system for survivors and physicians: 708-332-1052.

Leukemia

• Leukemia Society of America, 600 Third Avenue, New York, NY 10016 (800-955-4LSA or 212-573-8484 or www.leukemia.org/). Research, education, advocacy, and support.

Liver Disease

• American Liver Foundation, 1425 Pompton Avenue, Cedar Grove, NJ 07009 (800-223-0179, 800-465-4837, or 201-256-2550 or sadieo.uscf.edu/alf/alffinal/homepagealf.html). Research and assistance in locating doctors and medical services.

Lung Disease

• American Lung Association, 432 Park Avenue South, Eighth Floor, New York, NY 10016 (800-LUNG-USA or 212-889-3370). Information and speakers' bureau.

Lupus

- Lupus Foundation of America, Inc., 1300 Piccard Drive, Suite 200, Rockville, MD 20850-4303 (800-558-0121 or internet-plaza.net/lupus/). Services and support. Newsletter.

Multiple Sclerosis

- Multiple Sclerosis Foundation, Inc., 6350 N. Andrews Avenue, Fort Lauderdale, FL 33309 (800-441-7055). Conventional and alternative treatment information. Referral services.
- National Multiple Sclerosis Society, 733 Third Avenue, New York, NY 10017 (800-344-4867). Referrals, counseling, family support, independent-living and employment programs.

Myasthenia Gravis

- Myasthenia Gravis Foundation of America, 222 S. Riverside Plaza, Suite 1540, Chicago, IL 60606 (800-541-5454). Support groups, research, treatment information.

Parkinson's Disease

- National Parkinson Foundation, Inc., 1501 N.W. Ninth Avenue/Bob Hope Road, Miami, FL 33136 (800-327-4545 or www.parkinson.org/). Information and support group referrals.

Sickle Cell

- Sickle Cell Disease Association of America, 200 Corporate Pointe, Suite 495, Culver City, CA 90230-7633 (800-421-8453 or 310-216-6363 or www.icfs.org/bluebook/bb000291.htm). Public awareness and educational materials. Referrals for treatment information.
- Sickle Cell Information Center, P.O. Box 109, Grady Memorial Hospital, 80 Butler Street, Atlanta, GA 30335 (404-616-3572; fax: 404-616-5998).

Spina Bifida Hotline

- Spina Bifida Association of America, 4590 MacArthur Boulevard NW, Suite 250, Washington, DC 20007 (800-621-3141 or 202-944-3285 or www.sbaa.org). Information and referrals, newsletter.

Other National GuardianOrgs of Interest

- American Council of the Blind, 1155 Fifteenth Street NW, Suite 720, Washington, DC 20005 (800-424-8666 or 202-467-5081 or www.acb.org). Referrals on all aspects of blindness, scholarship assistance, braille magazine.
- American Pain Society, 4700 West Lake Avenue, Glenview, IL 60025 (847-375-4700). Information on pain treatment centers around the country.
- The Humor Project, 110 Spring Street, Saratoga Springs, NY 12866 (518-587-8770). Catalog of humorous material for coping with a challenging condition.
- National Stroke Association, 96 Inverness Drive East, Suite 1, Englewood, CO 80112-5112 (800-STROKES or 303-649-9299 or www.stroke.org). Treatment, rehabilitation research, and support services.
- United Ostomy Association, 1111 Wilshire Boulevard, Los Angles, CA 90017 (800-826-0826 or 714-660-8624). Ostomy information and peer support.

Hospice

- Hospice Education Institute, 5 Essex Square, P.O. Box 713, Essex, CT 06426 (203-767-1620). Referrals to a regularly updated directory of hospice and palliative care programs nationwide, plus general information on hospice care and on bereavement issues and services.
- *National Homecare and Hospice Directory.* Published annually by the National Association for Home Care, 228 Seventh Street SE, Washington, DC 20003-4306 (202-547-7424). $135. A directory containing information on more than 18,500 home care, hospice, and home care aide providers, including, in many cases, the services they provide plus the geographic area served.

• National Hospice Organization, 1901 N. Moore Street, Suite 901, Arlington, VA 22209 (800-658-8898 or 703-243-5900). National organization for hospice care and hospice providers. Helps locate a hospice organization in your area.

Hospitals

• *How to Find the Best Doctors, Hospitals and HMOs for You and Your Family,* Castle Connolly Medical Ltd. (1995).

• *The Savvy Patient* by David R. Stutz, M.D., and Bernard Feder, Ph.D. (Consumers Union of the U.S., 1990).

• *Take This Book with You to the Hospital* by Charles B. Inlander and Ed Weiner (Peoples Medical Society, 1993).

• *America's Best Hospitals, U.S. News and World Report,* published by John Wylie & Sons. Rates hospitals state by state by specialty.

Insurance Commissions

Alabama: Commissioner of Insurance, 135 South Union Street, #181, Montgomery, AL 36104 (334-269-3550).

Alaska: Director of Insurance, P.O. Box 110805, Juneau, AK 99811-0805 (907-465-2515).

Arizona: Director of Insurance, 2910 N. Forty-fourth Street, Suite 210, Phoenix, AZ 85018 (602-912-8400).

Arkansas: Insurance Commissioner, 1200 West Third Street, Little Rock, AR 72201-1904 (501-371-2600).

California: Commissioner of Insurance, 300 S. Spring Street, Los Angeles, CA 90013 (from Los Angeles: 213-897-8921; rest of state: 800-927-4357).

Colorado: Commissioner of Insurance, 1560 Broadway, Suite 850, Denver, CO 80202 (303-894-7499).

Connecticut: Insurance Commissioner, P.O. Box 816, Hartford, CT 06142-0816 (860-297-3800).

Delaware: Insurance Commissioner, 841 Silver Lake Boulevard, P.O. Box 7007, Dover, DE 19903 (302-739-4251).

District of Columbia: Superintendent of Insurance, 441 Fourth Street NW, Suite 870 North, Washington, DC 20001 (202-727-8000).

Florida: Insurance Commissioner, State Capitol Plaza, Level 11, Tallahassee, FL 32399 (904-922-3100).

Georgia: Insurance Commissioner, 2 Martin Luther King, Jr. Drive, 704 West Tower, Atlanta, GA 30334 (404-656-2056).

Hawaii: Insurance Commissioner, P.O. Box 3614, Honolulu, HI 96811 (808-586-2790).

Idaho: Director of Insurance, 700 West State Street, Third Floor, Boise, ID 83702 (208-334-2250).

Illinois: Director of Insurance, 320 West Washington Street, Fourth Floor, Springfield, IL 62767 (217-782-4515).

Indiana: Commissioner of Insurance, 311 West Washington Street, Suite 300, Indianapolis, IN 46204 (317-232-2385).

Iowa: Commissioner of Insurance, Lucas State Office Building, Sixth Floor, Des Moines, IA 50319 (515-281-5705).

Kansas: Commissioner of Insurance, 420 S.W. Ninth Street, Topeka, KS 66612 (913-296-7801).

Kentucky: Insurance Commissioner, 215 W. Main Street, P.O. Box 517, Frankfort, KY 40602 (502-564-3630).

Louisiana: Commissioner of Insurance, P.O. Box 94214, Baton Rouge, LA 70804-9214 (504-342-5900).

Maine: Superintendent of Insurance, State Office Building, State House, Station 34, Augusta, ME 04333 (207-624-8475).

Maryland: Insurance Commissioner, 525 St. Paul Place, Baltimore, MD 21202 (410-468-2000).

Massachusetts: Commissioner of Insurance, 470 Atlantic Avenue, Boston, MA 02210 (617-521-7794).

Michigan: Insurance Commissioner, P.O. Box 30220, Lansing, MI 48909-7720 (517-373-9273).

Minnesota: Commissioner of Commerce, 133 E. Seventh Street, St. Paul, MN 55101 (612-296-4026).

Mississippi: Commissioner of Insurance, 1804 Walter Sillers Building, P.O. Box 79, Jackson, MS 39205 (601-359-3569).

Missouri: Director of Insurance, 301 West High Street, Suite 630, Jefferson City, MO 65102 (573-751-5107).

Montana: Commissioner of Insurance, 126 N. Sanders, Mitchell Building, Room 270, Helena, MT 59620 or P.O. Box 4009, Helena, MT 59604 (406-444-2040).

Nebraska: Director of Insurance, 941 O Street, Suite 400, Lincoln, NE 68508 (402-471-2201).

Nevada: Commissioner of Insurance, 1665 Hot Springs Road, Suite 152, Carson City, NV 89701 (702-687-4270).

New Hampshire: Insurance Commissioner, 169 Manchester Street, P.O. Box 2005, Concord, NH 03301 (603-271-2261).

New Jersey: Commissioner of Insurance, 20 W. State Street, Trenton, NJ 08625 (609-292-5363).

New Mexico: Superintendent of Insurance, P.O. Drawer 1269, Santa Fe, NM 87504 (505-827-4500).

New York: Superintendent of Insurance, Insurance Department, Empire State Plaza, Building #1, Albany, NY 12257 (800-342-3736 or 518-474-4550).

North Carolina: Commissioner of Insurance, P.O. Box 26387, Raleigh, NC 27611 (919-733-7343 or 800-662-7777).

North Dakota: Commissioner of Insurance, Capitol Building, Fifth Floor, Bismarck, ND 58505 (701-328-2440).

Ohio: Director of Insurance, 2100 Stella Court, Columbus, OH 43215-1067 (614-644-2658).

Oklahoma: Insurance Commissioner, P.O. Box 53408-3408, Oklahoma City, OK 73152 (405-521-2828).

Oregon: Insurance Commissioner, 350 Winter Street NE, Room 440, Salem, OR 97310 (503-378-4271).

Pennsylvania: Insurance Commissioner, 1326 Strawberry Square, Harrisburg, PA 17120 (717-787-5173).

Puerto Rico: Commissioner of Insurance, Martinez Juncos Station, Box 8330, Santurce, PR 00910 (809-722-8686).

Rhode Island: Insurance Commissioner, 233 Richmond Street, Suite 233, Providence, RI 02903 (401-277-2246).

South Carolina: Insurance Commissioner, 1612 Marion Street, P.O. Box 100105, Columbia, SC 29202 (803-737-6160).

South Dakota: Insurance Commissioner, Insurance Building, 910 E. Sioux, Pierre, SD 57501 (605-773-3563).

Tennessee: Commissioner of Insurance. 500 James Robertson Parkway, Fifth Floor, Nashville, TN 37243 (615-741-2241).

Texas: Commissioner of Insurance, P.O. Box 149104, Austin, TX 78714 (512-475-3726 or 800-252-3439).

Utah: Commissioner of Insurance, State Office Building, Room 3110, Salt Lake City, UT 84114 (801-538-3800).

Vermont: Commissioner of Insurance, 89 Main Street, Drawer 20, Montpelier, VT 05620 (802-828-3301).

Virginia: Commissioner of Insurance, 1300 E. Main Street, P.O. Box 1157, Richmond, VA 23218 (804-371-9694).

Virgin Islands: Commissioner of Insurance, Kongens Gade 18, St. Thomas, VI 00802 (809-774-2991).

Washington: Insurance Commissioner, P.O. Box 40255, Olympia, WA 98504-0255 (360-753-7301).

West Virginia: Insurance Commissioner, P.O. Box 50540, 1124 Smith Street, Charleston, WV 25305-0540 (304-558-3394).

Wisconsin: Commissioner of Insurance, P.O. Box 7873, Madison, WI 53707 (608-266-0102).

Wyoming: Insurance Commissioner, Herschler Building, Room 3E, 122 W. Twenty-fifth Street, Cheyenne, WY 82002 (307-777-7401).

Guaranteed Issue Life Insurance— Sources

- Central United Life Insurance Co. (ages 21–80), 800-669-9030.
- Gerber Guaranteed Life Plus (ages 40–80), 914-761-4404.
- IntraAmerica Life Ins. Co. (ages 50–75), 800-323-4542.

Hospital Indemnity (Income) Insurance Policies—Sources

- American Association of Retired Persons, 601 E. Street NW, Washington, DC 20049 (800-523-5800).
- Citicorp Insurance, P.O. Box 7055, Dover, DE 19903 (800-237-4365). For people with Citicorp credit cards or checking accounts.
- Gerber Lifetime Hospitalcare Plan, 204 W. Main Street, Fremont, MI 49412-1179 (800-253-3074).
- Physician's Mutual Insurance Co., 2600 Dodge Street, Omaha, NE 68131 (800-325-6300).

Legal Representation

- American Prepaid Legal Services Institute, 541 N. Fairbanks Court, Chicago, IL 60611 (312-988-5751). A nonprofit organization that provides names of prepaid services throughout the United States. Or look in your yellow pages under "legal services."
- Legal Services Corporation, 750 First Street NE, Eleventh Floor, Washington, DC 20002-4250 (202-336-8800). A nonprofit corporation established by Congress "to seek to assure equal access to justice under the law for all Americans" with limited financial means. The Legal Services Corporation publishes a free program directory listing all affiliated legal aid organizations throughout the country.
- *Representing Yourself—What You Can Do Without a Lawyer* by Kenneth Lasson and the Public Citizen Litigation Group (Penguin, USA, 1995) (202-588-1000). A practical guide to representing yourself.

Magazines—Special Interest (in addition to newsletters published by GuardianOrgs)

Cancer

- *Coping,* P.O. Box 682268, Franklin, TN 37068 (615-790-2400 or www.copingmag@aol.com). Nationally distributed consumer magazine for people with cancer and their families.
- *MAMM,* 349 W. Twelfth Street, New York, NY 10014 (212-242-2163 and subscription @mamm.com). Nationally distributed consumer magazine for women with breast cancer and their families.

Caregivers

- *Today's Caregiver,* P.O. Box 800616, Miami, FL 33180-8616 (954-962-2734; outside southern Florida: 800-829-2734 or www.caregiver.com).

HIV/AIDS

- *Art & Understanding,* 25 Monroe Street, Suite 205, Albany, NY 12210-2743 (518-426-9010 or www.aumag.org). Artistic, literary, creative, and cultural responses to the HIV/AIDS crisis. Monthly.
- *Body Positive,* Body Positive, 2095 Broadway, Suite 306, New York, NY 10023 (212-566-7333 or www.thebody.com). Practical information source. Monthly.
- *Positively Aware,* Test Positive Aware Network, 1258 W. Belmont Avenue, Chicago, IL 60657-3292 (773-404-8726 or www.tpan.com). Medical and social issues.
- *POZ,* 349 W. Twelfth Street, New York, NY 10014 (212-242-2163 and subscription @poz.com). Articles about living with HIV/AIDS. Monthly. Available in Spanish.

Hospice

- *Crossroads of Life,* 12125 Woodcrest Executive Drive, St. Louis, MO 63141 (314-453-9993). Articles for caregivers and patients.

Medicaid

- *The Medicaid Planning Handbook* by Alexander A. Bove Jr. (New York: Little, Brown and Co., 1992).
- *Avoiding the Medicaid Trap* by Armond D. Budish (New York: Avon Books, 1995).

Medicare

- Medicare Hotline, Health Care Financing Administration, Office of Public Affairs, U.S. Department of Health and Human Services, 800-638-6833, 8 A.M. to 8 P.M. EST, M–F; or call the Social Security Administration at 800-772-1213.
- *Your Medicare Handbook,* Health Care Financing Administration, Office of Beneficiary Relations N-1005, 7500 Security Boulevard,

Baltimore, MD 21244-1850 (www.hhcfa.go). An excellent detailed description of Medicare coverage (including MediGap insurance).

Organ Transplant

- Organ Transplant Fund, Inc., 1102 Brookfield, Memphis, TN 38119 (800-489-3863). A nonprofit organization; information and financial assistance; candidates.

Pain Management

- American Chronic Pain Association, P.O. Box 850, Rocklin, CA 95677 (916-632-0922). Offers a support system for those suffering chronic pain, guidelines for selecting a pain management unit, and referrals to six hundred chapters internationally.
- National Chronic Pain Outreach Association, 7979 Old Georgetown Road, Suite 100, Bethesda, MD 20814 (540-997-5004). Information clearinghouse about chronic pain and its management; publications; and referrals to pain management specialists, pain clinics, and pain support groups.

Physicians' Fees

- *Physicians' Fee Reference: A Compendium of Physicians' Fees Providing Health Care Professionals with 50th, 75th and 90th Percentiles in U.S. Dollars,* Wasserman Medical Publishers Ltd., P.O. Box 27365, West Allis, WI 53227 (800-669-3337), $129 plus $5 s/h. Provides the usual, customary, and reasonable fees for a given procedure in your area.

Real Estate: Reverse Mortgages

- *Home Equity Conversion Information Kit,* D15601, AARP Home Equity Information Center EE0756, 601 E Street NW, Washington, DC 20049. A free publication that includes an extensive state-by-state "Reverse Mortgage Lenders List." You can obtain the names of lenders making reverse mortgages in your area by downloading AARP's list at www.aarp.org.

- *Your New Retirement Nest Egg: a Consumer Guide to the New Reverse Mortgages,* including a reverse mortgage locator, by Ken Scholen, published by National Center for Home Equity Conversion (1996), 7373 147th Street W., Suite 1115, Apple Valley, MN 55124 (800-247-6553).

Revocable Living Trusts

- *The New Book of Trusts* by Leimberg Associates, $49.95 (self-published, 1997) (610-527-5216).
- *Understanding Living Trusts* by Vickie and Jim Schumacher, $24.95 (Schumacher Publishing, 1998) (800-728-2665).

Transplants—Bone Marrow

- *The BMT Newsletter* has a list of attorneys who handle bone marrow transplant cases when an insurer refuses to pay (708-831-1913). The newsletter will either recommend an experienced attorney in your area or will suggest attorneys who will consult with your attorney.

Travel

- *Access Travel—Airports,* published by Airports Council International–North America, Consumer Information Center, P.O. Box 100, Pueblo, CO 81002. Specify publication 580Y. Free plus $1 s/h.
- Cancer Care, Inc., at 800-813-HOPE or 212-221-3300, has a list of organizations worldwide that provide information with respect to cancer.
- Moss Rehab Travel Info Service, a service of Moss Rehab (a rehabilitation hospital). Provides travel information tailored to your specific needs. Telephone 215-456-9600.
- National Patient Air Transport Hotline (NPATH) at 800-296-1217 is a clearinghouse for patients who need but cannot afford full-cost travel for medical care. Some resources are free based on patient status.
- *Travelin' Talk,* 130 Hillcrest Plaza, Suite 102, Clarksville, TN 37043-3534 (931-552-6670). Contains listings of an international network of

people willing to share their knowledge of their hometowns with travelers with disabilities visiting or passing through their location. It also lists discounts for the disabled. The editor is in a wheelchair himself. $35.

Treatment Information
All Conditions

- Centers for Disease Control and Prevention, 1600 Clifton Road, Atlanta, GA 30333 (404-639-3534 or www.cdc.gov/). Information on treatments, research, and community resources.
- See chapter 25, section 3, for research assistance.

Cancer

- Breast Implant Information Network, 800-887-6828. Provides medical and legal information for women with or considering breast implants.
- Guardian Organizations: See the organizations for cancer under "Guardian Organizations: National" above. Most have newsletters. Cancer Care, Inc. publishes "A Helping Hand: The Resource Guide for People With Cancer," which lists national and regional resources.
- Cancer Information Service, National Cancer Institute, Office of Cancer Communications, Building 31, Room 10A16, 31 Center Drive, MSC 2580, Bethesda, MD 20892-2580 (800-422-6237, M–F, 9–4:30, EST). A U.S. government agency that provides information on all types of cancer, treatment options, and medical resources. Answers questions about cancer; makes referrals to local support groups and other resources. Also has information on pain management.
- Patient Advocates for Advanced Cancer Treatments, 1143 Parmelee NW, Grand Rapids, MI 49504 (616-453-1477). Information on treatments of prostate cancer.

HIV/AIDS

- *AIDS Treatment News.* Biweekly; developments in research, experimental therapies and treatments. John James, P.O. Box 411256, San Francisco, CA 94141 (800-873-2812 or www.immunet.org/-immunet/atn.nsf/homepage).
- AMFAR, 212-682-7440. Publishes *AIDS/HIV Treatment Directory.* Updated quarterly; $55 a year.
- *Positive Living,* published by Aids Project Los Angeles, 1313 N. Vine Street, Los Angeles, CA 90028 (213-993-1362 or www.digitopia.com/-apla).
- *Treatment Issues,* published by Gay Men's Health Crisis, 129 W. Twentieth Street, New York, NY 10011 (212-337-3695). Newsletter of latest therapies.
- National AIDS Clearinghouse, a service of the Centers for Disease Control, 800-458-5231. Classifies and distributes information and educational materials.

Treatment Information: The Internet

The Internet provides information on the latest medical developments (see page 288).

General

- www.achoo.com. Internet health care directory.
- GuardianOrgs provide information on their sites: e.g., the American Cancer Society at www.cancer.org.
- healthatoz.com, a search engine for health and medicine.
- Healthfinder (www.healthfinder.gov), a government-sponsored search engine that is user-friendly. It includes links to health information and resources.
- Health-related lists will E-mail you with newly posted information on the topic of your choice if you are a subscriber. E.g., www.liszt.com.
- Hospitals have created sites with information about treatments. See the Department of Neurology's link at the Massachusetts General Hospital site for a good list of hospital-affiliated Web sites.
- Medaccess at www.medaccess.com. A variety of health-related information, including information about health care newsletters and links.

- Medscape at www.medscape.com has articles from such sources as the National Institutes of Health and the Centers for Disease Control and Prevention.
- National Library of Medicine, 800-638-8480. Internet access at Medline is www.nlm.nih.gov.
- *New England Journal of Medicine* is on-line at www.nejm.org and at medscape.com
- Newsgroups. For anecdotal evidence about a treatment, consider posting a question on a newsgroup targeted to a specific interest such as DejaNews at dejanews.com.

Cancer

- American Cancer Society, www.cancer.org, contains information about specific cancers, including alternative treatments.
- ASCO On-Line. An organization that represents over ten thousand cancer professionals. See the "patient page" plus a "search index."
- Cancer Care, Inc., www.cancercareinc.org, contains links to Web sites for information by cancer diagnosis.
- CancerNet. A quick and easy way to obtain, through electronic mail, cancer information from the National Cancer Institute (NCI). You can request information from the NCI's Physician Data Query (PDQ) database and fact sheets on various cancer topics. E-mail address: cancernet@ici.cc.nci.nih.gov. Or access treatment information at the CancerNet Web site: www. nci.nih.gov.
- Cancer Research Institute site, www.cancerresearch.org, includes information about treatments and clinical trials and a resource directory.
- Cansearch, a site that provides access to cancer information sites, www.cansearch.org or type www.access.digex.net.
- *The Journal of the National Cancer Institute.* Information and articles geared to the professional, cancernet.nci.nih.gov/jnci/jncihome.htm.
- Oncolink, a project of the University of Pennsylvania Cancer Center. Excellent research tool for information concerning cancer, research, and treatment at www.oncolink.upen.edu/.

HIV/AIDS

- AIDS Resource List, www.teleport.com/~celinec/aids.shtml/. Comprehensive listing.
- The Body, www.thebody.com/. Multimedia information resource.
- *Bulletin of Experimental Treatment for Aids,* www.infoweb.org/treatment/index.html. Links to different HIV/AIDS newsletters.
- HIV Infoweb Searchable Library, www.infoweb.org. On-line library.
- *John James Newsletter* (concerning treatments), www.jri.org.
- National AIDS Clearinghouse, www.cdcnac.org. Part of the CDC. Continuously updated treatment and resource information.

Water

- *The Drinking Water Book: A Complete Guide to Safe Drinking Water* by Colin Ingram (Berkeley, Calif.: Ten Speed Press, 510-527-1563). $11.95 plus $2.50 s/h.
- "What's On Tap, Cryptosporidium in U.S. Public Drinking Water," published by National Association of People With AIDS, 202-898-0414. Free.

Will Preparation

- *The American Bar Association Guide to Wills and Estates* (Times Books, 1995) (800-793-2665).
- *The Complete Will Kit* by Jens C. Appel III and F. Bruce Gentry (John Wiley & Sons, 1990).
- *Keys to Preparing a Will* by James John Jurinski, JD, CPA (Barron's, 1991).
- *Nolo's Simple Will Book* by Denis Clifford, Esq. (Nolo Press, 1989) (800-992-6656).
- *Willmaker 6,* Nolo Press (800-992-6656). A computer program that includes simple wills with the legal requirements for execution of a will in each state. $49.95.

Bibliography

Abrams, Donald, ed. *AIDS/HIV Treatment Directory*. New York: AMFAR, 1996.

Appel, Jens C., and F. Bruce Gentry. *The Complete Will Kit*. New York: John Wiley & Sons, 1990.

Appelgarth, Ginger. *The Money Diet*. New York: Viking, 1995.

Balch, James F., and Phyllis A. Balch, CNC. *Prescription for Nutritional Healing*. New York: Avery Publishing Group, 1991.

Barnett, Terry J. *Living Wills and More*. New York: John Wiley & Sons, 1992.

Bartlett, John G., and Ann K. Finkbeiner. *The Guide to Living With HIV Infection*. Baltimore: Johns Hopkins University Press, 1993.

Bausell, R. Barker, Michael A. Rooney, and Charles B. Inlander. *How to Evaluate and Select a Nursing Home*. Massachusetts: Addison-Wesley Publishing Company, 1988.

Beam, Burton T., Jr. *Group Benefits: Basic Concepts and Alternatives*. Pennsylvania: American College, 1991.

Belth, Joseph M. *Life Insurance*. Indiana: Indiana University Press, 1985.

Bolles, Richard Nelson. *Job Hunting Tips for the So-Called Handicapped or People Who Have Disabilities*. California: 10 Speed Press, 1991.

———. *What Color Is Your Parachute?* California: 10 Speed Press, 1992.

Brenner, Lynn. *Building Your Nest Egg With Your 401(k)*. Connecticut: Investors Press, 1995.

Bridge, William. *Transitions, Making Sense of Life's Changes*. Massachusetts: Addison-Wesley Publishing Company, 1980.

Buckingham, Robert W. *Among Friends, Hospice Care for the Person With AIDS*. New York: Prometheus Books, 1992.

Burkett, Larry. *The Financial Planning Workbook*. Chicago: Moody Press, 1990.

Burris, Scott, Harlon L. Dalton, and Judith Leonie Miller, eds. *AIDS Law Today: A New Guide for the Public*. Connecticut: Yale University Press, 1993.

Carlson, Lisa. *Caring for Your Own Dead*. Vermont: Upper Access, 1987.

Castle Connolly. *How to Find the Best Doctors, Hospitals and HMO's for You and Your Family*. New York: Castle Connolly, 1995.

Center for the Study of Services. *Consumers' Checkbook*. Washington, D.C.: Center for the Study of Services, 1996.

Christianson, Stephen G. *How to Administer an Estate*. New York: Citadel Press, 1995.

Clifford, Denis. *Nolo's Simple Will Book.* California: Nolo Press, 1989.

Collins, Evan R., Jr., with Doron Weber. *The Complete Guide to Living Wills.* New York: Bantam Books, 1991.

Communicating for Agriculture. *Comprehensive Health Insurance for High Risk Individuals.* 9th ed. Minnesota: Communicating for Agriculture, 1995.

Cousins, Norman. *Anatomy of an Illness As Perceived by a Patient.* New York: Bantam Books, 1979.

Crockett, Paul Hampton. *HIV Law.* New York: Three Rivers Press, 1997.

Davidson, Cynthia. *The Over 50 Insurance Survival Guide.* California: Merritt Publishing, 1994.

De Solla Price, Mark. *Living Positively in a World with HIV/AIDS.* New York: Avon Books, 1995.

Dolan, Daria, and Ken Dolan. *Smart Money: How to Be Your Own Financial Manager.* New York: Berkley Books, 1990.

Dominguez, Joe, and Vicki Robin. *Your Money or Your Life.* New York: Penguin Books, 1992.

Dresner, Susan. *Managing Your Business Image.* New York: Successful Ways and Means, 1993.

Edelston, Martin, and Ken Glickman. *Bottom Line Personal Book of Bests.* New York: St. Martin's Griffin, 1997.

Eidson, Ted, ed. *The Aids Caregiver's Handbook.* New York: St. Martin's Press, 1988.

Elias, Stephen, Albin Renauer, and Robin Leonard. *How to File for Bankruptcy.* California: Nolo Press, 1996.

Elias, Stephen, and Susan Levinkind. *Legal Research: How to Find and Understand the Law.* California: Nolo Press, 1995.

Ferri, Janice. *There Is Hope: Learning to Live with HIV.* 2nd ed. Illinois: HIV Coalition, 1994.

Francis, Walton. *Checkbook's Guide to Health Insurance Plans for Federal Employees.* 1997 ed. Washington: Center for the Study of Services, 1996.

Garfield, Charles. *Sometimes My Heart Goes Numb.* San Francisco: Jossey-Bass Publishers, 1995.

Garner, Robert J., Robert B. Coplan, Barbara J. Raasch, and Charles L. Ratner. *Ernst & Young's Personal Financial Planning Guide.* 2nd ed. New York: John Wiley & Sons, 1996.

Gaudio, Peter E., and Virginia S. Nicols. *Your Retirement Benefits.* New York: John Wiley & Sons, 1992.

Givens, Charles J. *Financial Self-Defense.* New York: Pocket Books, 1995.

————. *Wealth Without Risk.* New York: Pocket Books, 1995.

Gordis, Philip. *Property and Casualty Insurance.* New York: Rough Notes, 1984.

Green, Mark. *The Consumer Bible.* New York: Workman Publishing, 1995.

Hallman, G. Victor, and Jerry S. Rosenbloom. *Personal Financial Planning.* 5th ed. New York: McGraw-Hill, Inc., 1993.

Herzog, Richard B. *Bankruptcy: A Concise Guide for Creditors and Debtors.* New York: Arco Publishing, 1993.

Hoffman, Barbara, ed. *A Cancer Survivor's Almanac.* Washington, D.C.: Chronimed Publishing, 1996.

Houts, Peter, ed. *ACP Home Care Guide for Cancer.* Washington, D.C., 1994.

Huber, Jeffrey T., ed. *How to Find Information About AIDS.* 2nd ed. New York: Harrington Park Press, 1992.

IDG Books Worldwide, Inc. *Personal Finance for Dummies.* California: IDG Books Worldwide, 1994.

Inlander, Charles B. *The Consumer's Medical Desk Reference.* New York: Hyperion Books, 1995.

Inlander, Charles B., and Karla Morales. *Getting the Most for Your Medical Dollar.* New York: Pantheon Books, 1991.

Inlander, Charles B., and Cynthia K. Moran. *77 Ways to Beat Colds and Flu.* New York: Walker and Company, 1994.

Inlander, Charles B., and Ed Weiner. *Take This Book With You to the Hospital.* Pennsylvania: People's Medical Society, 1993.

Janik, Carolyn, and Ruth Rejnis. *The Complete Idiot's Guide to a Great Retirement.* New York: Alpha Books, 1995.

Jurinski, James John. *Keys to Preparing a Will.* New York: Barron's, 1991.

Karpel, Craig S. *The Retirement Myth.* New York: HarperCollins Publishers, 1995.

Kehrer, Daniel. *12 Steps to a Worry-Free Retirement.* Washington, D.C.: Kiplinger Times Business, 1995.

Krughoff, Robert. *Consumers' Checkbook.* Washington, D.C.: Center for the Study of Services, 1996.

Lavine, Alan. *Your Life Insurance Options.* New York: John Wiley & Sons, 1993.

Levinson, Daniel J. *The Seasons of a Man's Life.* New York: Ballantine Books, 1978.

Magee, David S. *Everything Your Heirs Need to Know.* Chicago: Dearborn Financial Publishing, 1995.

Martelli, Leonard, Fran D. Peltz, William Messina, and Steven Petrow. *When Someone You Know Has AIDS, a Practical Guide.* New York: Crown Trade Paperbacks, 1993.

McCall, Dr. Timothy B. *Examining Your Doctor.* New Jersey: Citadel Press, 1996.

McCormack, Thomas P. *The AIDS Benefits Handbook.* Connecticut: Yale University Press, 1990.

Monaghan, Kelly. *Part Time Travel Agent.* New York: Intrepid Traveler, 1994.

Morris, Kenneth M., and Alan Siegel. *The Wall Street Journal Guide to Understanding Personal Finance.* New York: Lightbulb Press, 1992.

Morris, Kenneth M., Alan M. Siegel, and Virginia B. Morris. *The Wall Street Journal Guide to Planning Your Financial Future.* New York: Lightbulb Press, 1995.

Naeve, Pamel Priest, and Isabel Walker. *Estates: Planning Ahead.* California: Northern California Cancer Center, 1994.

National Association of People With AIDS. *Caring Commitment and Choices.* Washington, D.C.; NAPWA, 1994.

New York State Bar Association. *Consumer Bankruptcy: A Primer for the General Practitioner.* New York: NYSBA, 1981.

Ostberg, Kay. *Using a Lawyer . . . And What to Do If Things Go Wrong.* New York: Random House, 1985.

People's Medical Society. *Your Complete Medical Record.* Pennsylvania: People's Medical Society, 1993.

Perritt, Henry H., Jr. *Americans With Disabilities Handbook.* 2 vols. New York: John Wiley & Sons, 1996.

Petrillo, Madeline, R.N., M.Ed., and Singay Sanger, M.D. *Emotional Care of Hospitalized Children, an Environmental Approach.* 2nd ed. Philadelphia: J. B. Lippincott Company, 1980.

Pilot, Kevin. *Credit Approved.* Massachusetts: Adams Media Corporation, 1992.

Pond, Jonathan D. *The ABC's of Managing Your Money.* Washington, D.C.: National Endowment for Financial Education, 1993.

———. *The New Century Family Money Book.* New York: Dell Trade Paperback, 1993.

Price Waterhouse, LLP. *Secure Your Future.* Illinois: Irwin Professional Publishing, 1996.

Rabkin, Judith G., Robert H. Remien, and Christopher R. Wilson. *Good Doctors, Good Patients: Partners in HIV Treatment.* New York: NCM Publishers, 1994.

Romeyn, Mary. *Nutrition and HIV.* San Francisco: Jossey-Bass Publishers, 1995.

Rosenfeld, Isadore. *Dr. Rosenfeld's Guide to Alternative Medicine.* New York: Random House, 1996.

Runde, Robert H., and J. Barry Zischang. *The Commonsense Guide to Estate Planning.* Illinois: Irwin Professional Publishing, 1994.

Ryer, Jeanne C. *HealthNet.* New York: John Wiley & Sons, 1997.

Saint James, Elaine. *Living the Simple Life.* New York: Hyperion, 1996.

Schmedel, Scott R., Kenneth M. Morris, and Alan M. Siegel. *The Wall Street Journal Guide to Under-*

standing Your Taxes. New York: Lightbulb Press, 1994.

Schneider, Ira S., and Ezra Huber. *Financial Planning for Long-Term Care.* New York: Insight Books, 1989.

Scholen, Ken. *Your Retirement Nest Egg.* 2nd ed. Minnesota: NCHEC Press, 1996.

Schumacher, Vickie, and Jim Schumacher. *Understanding Living Trusts.* 4th ed. California: Schumacher Publishing, 1996.

Sestina, John E. *Fee-Only Financial Planning.* New York: Dearborn Financial Publishing, 1992.

Shelby, R. Dennis. *People With HIV and Those Who Help Them.* New York: Harrington Park Press, 1995.

Siano, Nick. *No Time to Wait.* New York: Bantam Books, 1993.

Simpson, Carol. *At the Heart of Alzheimer's.* Maryland: Manor Healthcare Corp., 1996.

Sinetar, Marsha. *Do What You Love, the Money Will Follow.* New York: Dell Trade, 1987.

Spears, Dee Ella, ed. *Living With AIDS.* 3rd ed. New York: Gay Men's Health Crisis, 1993.

Stern, Ken. *The Comprehensive Guide to Social Security and Medicare.* New Jersey: Career Press, 1995.

Thomas, William, III, ed. *Social Security Manual.* 1996 ed. Ohio: National Underwriter Company, 1996.

Times Books. *The American Bar Association Family Legal Guide.* New York: Random House, 1994.

United Seniors Health Cooperative, *Long-term Care Planning,* A Dollars and Sense Guide, 1998.

United States Department of Education. *Summary of Existing Legislation Affecting People with Disabilities.* Washington, D.C.: United States Department of Education, 1992.

United States Office of Consumer Affairs. *Consumer's Resource Handbook 1994.* Colorado: United States Office of Consumer Affairs, 1994.

Weltman, Barbara. *Your Parents' Financial Security.* New York: John Wiley & Sons, 1992.

White, Barbara J., and Edward Madara. *The Self Help Sourcebook.* 5th ed. New Jersey: American SelfHelp Clearinghouse, 1996.

Zubrod, Sheila, and David Stern. *Flea.* New York: HarperCollins, 1997.

Index

Note: Books and pamphlets are listed under "books/handouts." Hotlines are listed under "hotlines." Internet addresses are listed under "Internet." Organizations are listed under "organizations/services."